A BETTING ON CHRISTMAS ROMANCE SERIES BOX SET COLLECTION

BOOKS 1-3: THE BILLIONAIRE'S CHRISTMAS MIRACLE, THE BILLIONAIRE'S SECOND CHANCE CHRISTMAS, FINDING CHRISTMAS WITH THE BILLIONAIRE

CHELSEA HALE

Copyright © 2021 by Chelsea Hale

Published by Crescendo Ink

All rights reserved. This book is a work of fiction. Names, characters, places, and incidents are either a product of the author's imagination or are used fictitiously. Any resemblance to actual events, locales, or persons, living or dead, is entirely coincidental. No part of this book may be reproduced in any form or by any electronic or mechanical means, including information storage and retrieval systems, without the express written permission of the author.

978-1-953155-08-5

202106152

A BETTING ON CHRISTMAS ROMANCE SERIES BOX SET COLLECTION

OTHER BOOKS BY CHELSEA HALE

A Sundaes for Breakfast Romance Series
Mr. Write
Camera Wars
The Companion
Legally Yours

A Falling for You Billionaire Romance Series
The Undercover Resort Billionaire
Secrets, Fireworks, and her Billionaire Boyfriend
Her Fake Christmas Eve Billionaire Boyfriend
Snowed in with the Movie Star Billionaire
Matched with the Cowboy Billionaire
Her British Billionaire Best Friend
Her Italian Billionaire Fake Fiancé
Hart to Heart with the Billionaire

A Betting on Christmas Romance Series
The Billionaire's Christmas Miracle
The Billionaire's Second Chance Christmas
Finding Christmas with the Billionaire

Others
Perfect Catch

THE BILLIONAIRE'S CHRISTMAS MIRACLE

A BETTING ON CHRISTMAS ROMANCE - BOOK ONE

CHELSEA HALE

For those who keep Christmas all-year,
not just in December.

"Blessed is the season which
engages the whole world in
a conspiracy of love."
—Hamilton Wright Mabie

PROLOGUE

HOW THE BET BEGAN - (PLEASE NOTE EACH PROLOGUE IS SIMILAR)

The salty air whipped around Troy on the top deck of Hunter's yacht. He'd spent the last three days catching up with his three college roommates, enjoying the Mediterranean breeze. Getting out of New York City always did him a world of good.

"This has been a great trip," Scott said. "I'm sorry to see it over so soon. Are you sure you can't stay another week, Kyle?"

Kyle Montgomery laughed. He was the only one of the group that was married, having married his high school crush after college. "You guys are welcome to stay, but my team won't be happy if I miss Saturday's game. We're up against the rivals. Just missing practice this week might get me in trouble."

"We can't stay without you," Hunter said. "It wouldn't be the same without the four of us."

They lounged on the top, watching the land in the distance. Europe was beautiful this time of year.

"Just like old times," Troy said.

"Old times?" Kyle repeated. "I suppose, but not really like old times. I haven't been a bachelor in a long time. I have kids now. It's not the same for me."

"How's your charity going?" Scott asked Kyle.

"Every year it does more good in the world," Kyle said vaguely. "Happy Moments is dedicated to just that. Bringing happy moments to others. It's rewarding. It's too big for us to manage on our own any more, but Kandice and I still play an active role in it."

"I think I'd like to do that," Troy said. They were all billionaires; all of the friends had reached success and recognition in their own way. But something felt missing, and Troy had a feeling it had more to do with charity work than anything else. Kyle seemed to have it all. Maybe it was the NFL fame he wore so casually, or maybe it was that he spent his time when he wasn't on the field, helping others.

"Having a charity foundation and being involved in the work are two completely separate things," Kyle said. He leaned forward, resting his elbows on his knees. "But I could help you, if you're interested in getting involved or starting your own charity."

"I'd like that," Troy said.

Scott laughed, tilting his sunglasses down. "I bet you a million you couldn't do it."

"I'll take that bet," Troy said.

"A million for what?" Hunter asked. "I'm in for a million."

Scott rolled his eyes. "You don't even know what the bet is."

Hunter shrugged. "It's only a million. Chump change."

"Betting for charity seems to defeat the point," Kyle said.

Troy nodded. "Fair enough. How about when I win your money goes to the charity of my choice?" Troy looked at Scott.

Scott shrugged. "You can do whatever you want with money you win. But you're not going to win, so it's a non-issue."

"I'll win," Troy said confidently. "Just give me the stakes." He always won. It was what made him successful.

"You have to start a charity," Scott said.

"Or, we could open up the entire bet to everyone," Kyle said.

"It wouldn't be fair to include you," Scott said to Kyle. "You already own a charity."

Kyle leaned back in his chair. "I'll be the moderator then. The judge."

"What are the rules?" Troy repeated.

"How about you need to start a charity by Christmas?" Scott suggested.

Hunter shook his head. "It's mid-October. If you want to make an impact by Christmas you need to scale it back."

"What if you have to help a charity that's already up and running?" Kyle suggested. "*That* could be done before Christmas."

Scott tilted his head. "How would we determine the winner then?"

Troy sat quietly, trying to think of an answer to the question Scott posed. He'd win, so it was just a matter of what the rules would be. Waves against the side of the boat pulled his attention to the water, and he watched the sun gleam on the ripples.

Kyle snapped his fingers. "I've got it. You need to be personally involved with helping a charity succeed. I like the deadline of Christmas, and it would be nice to pick a winner before the New Year. Entrance fee is one million dollars. The winner gets the three million dollars to donate to the charity of his choosing—most likely the one that you choose to help, but I'm open to negotiation on that point. The person who donates the most will win."

Hunter laughed. "I can donate the most. I can write a check tomorrow. Easy enough."

Kyle shook his head. "Not monetarily. I'd say you need to cap your own personal or business donations to $10,000."

Scott scoffed. "How do we determine a winner if we're only allowed to give such a small amount? We'll all just give that amount and then we'll be tied."

"You have to make a difference in the charity. No assistants can help, and you can't just assign it to a team of people from your companies. You have to *personally* be involved with it. Help with your time." Kyle shrugged. "Be creative. You're all brilliant—you can all figure out a way to do something."

"And we only have from now until Christmas?" Scott confirmed.

Kyle nodded. "What if we make the deadline December 23rd, and the winner could be announced on December 24th."

"And you're the judge?" Troy asked.

Kyle scrunched his face. "No. I don't want to be accused of being partial to anyone. I'll have Kandice be the judge. Maybe we'll have a weekly check-in phone call and she can hear all of your progress and what you've been up to. She can be the one to make the final decision. Whatever she decides, stands."

Hunter, Scott and Troy all nodded.

"Sounds fair," Troy said. "I'm in, if everyone else is." It was easy to take on this challenge. He would have this bet in the bag, no problem.

Scott shrugged. "Why not? My company is a well-oiled machine right now. I have some extra time. Hunter, what about you?"

Hunter sighed. "This eats into my plans to spend the next month on my yacht, but yeah, I'm in. When do we start?"

"As soon as it works for everyone," Kyle said.

"I have a few things to wrap up at work before I can take the time off," Scott said.

Kyle nodded. "How about we start in two weeks? Maybe that will give you time to research which charity to help."

"And we need to spend the full eight weeks helping the charity of our choice?"

Kyle nodded. "Eight weeks of helping. No assistants helping you with the charity. And don't try and get past the rules. Kandice will find out."

All of them laughed. They shook hands on it and within an hour they'd wired money to Kyle for the bet.

The Billionaires' Christmas Gifts Bet was officially underway.

ONE WEEK LATER TROY WALKED INTO HIS NEW YORK OFFICE IN Midtown Manhattan. The humidity here was more unbearable than it had been in the Mediterranean on Hunter's yacht, but that might have also been the fact that he was now in a suit. "Cara, I need a list of charities that I can help between now and Christmas. Probably something local. See what you can find." He headed into his office, without waiting for her to respond.

Cara was only a step behind him. "Mr. Rasmussen, you know I can't help you on this project. I received a call from Mrs. Montgomery yesterday. She emailed me all of the rules. I don't want to hurt your chances of winning by helping you."

Troy looked at her. "Research is considered helping?" He blew out a breath. He supposed he could search the internet for opportunities—how long could that really take?

"According to the official rules, I'm not allowed to help at all," she said the words hesitantly.

Troy nodded. "I'm not trying to get around the rules," he assured her. "I'll start searching for it after my morning meeting."

Troy spent every spare minute he wasn't in meetings researching for a charity to help with. The possibilities were endless and that was just locally. His vision blurred as he bookmarked a few more webpages with possibilities.

A knock sounded at his door. "Come in," he said.

Cara poked her head in. "How is the research going?" she asked.

He looked up from the monitor where he'd spent the better part of the entire day trying to find the right fit. He sighed. "I don't think I tell you enough how much I appreciate all the work you do on the back-end of everything. I assume things are easy to look up and information is just there, but you make it seem so seamless."

"Web surfing isn't working?"

"I'm still looking."

"Have I ever told you about one of my favorite Christmas traditions?" she asked.

He tilted his head, not sure where she was going with this. "The tree lighting at the Rockefeller Center?"

"That one is up there," she said. "But I mean from my childhood. There's this small town in upstate New York, and every winter my family would go there for Thanksgiving and then for the Christmas Forest Festival. It was an amazing *charity* event." Cara's eyes sparkled as she emphasized the word "charity."

Troy nodded. "That's an interesting idea, Cara."

She nodded. "The rules specifically state you can't work with a charity or foundation that you've helped with before, so maybe you look outside New York City."

"That could be a great opportunity. Where is it?" Troy asked.

"Upstate a couple of hours from here, in a town called Red Oaks."

"Thanks for the idea," Troy said.

"I didn't give you an idea. I just told you what I like." She gave him a grin and left the office.

Troy spent the next hour online reading all of the testimonials on the Forest Festival. The fundraiser helped those in need of a Christmas have a Christmas. It worked with the local children's hospital in finding temporary housing while parents stayed close to the hospital during their children's treatments. The entire project looked like the kind of thing Kyle had described on the yacht. He copied the foundation's address onto his calendar. This weekend he was going to drive upstate and figure out a way to help. Finding an opportunity like this so quickly would give him an advantage.

THE RULES

OF THE BILLIONAIRES' CHRISTMAS GIFTS BET

- *Find a charity of your choice*
- *$1,000,000 Entry fee*
- *8 weeks of helping a charity of your choice – You must be personally involved*
- *No assistants*
- *No delegation to teams at work*
- *No talking to participants about the bet*
- *$10,000 max you can donate to the project*
- *Check-in with Kandice (and Kyle)*
- ***Deadline:** December 23rd; Winner announced on December 24th.*
- ***Winner receives:** $3,000,000 to donate to the charity of their choice.*

CHAPTER 1

Hailey's heart almost burst when she saw her aunt's name, "Helena Waters," light up on her phone. It was a passing excitement. "Hello?" she said, knowing that there was no way that the person on the other end was actually her aunt. Not unless she went back in time to May, before her aunt passed away.

"Is this a Ms. H. Waters?" a woman's voice asked.

Hailey sucked in a breath, glancing at the large calendar on her wall. October. Not May. For a moment, she wished time travel was real. She mustered a voice that wouldn't crack. But seeing Aunt Helena's name on her screen—the woman who'd felt like a second mom to her—had thrown her for a loop.

"This is Hailey Waters," she finally choked the short sentence out.

"Ms. Waters, my name is Edna. I was a friend of Helena at the foundation. I'm so sorry to be the bearer of bad news, but The Red Oaks Foundation is looking to expand its building and try a few new things this year. Plans have moved faster than we anticipated and the wrecking ball will be here by next week. There's a closet, well a couple of closets, that are full of items that specifically belonged to Helena. We wanted to make sure you were able to look at the items first before they were donated."

Helena had been an amazing decorator, and Hailey could only imagine the treasures she'd find in such big closets, but everything that she'd wanted from her aunt's house she'd taken with her in the summer after the funeral. How much more could there be? She drew in a slow breath. She'd already made peace with this. She'd already said goodbye to the town this past summer. Hailey closed her eyes, hoping the words would come easier. "I'm okay if anything that was stored at the foundation stays at the foundation. After all, the Forest Festival will only be enhanced by the beauty of what my aunt picked out."

The pause that filled the space on the phone felt like the distance between where she was in Seattle, to where her aunt had lived in upstate New York. "Ms. Waters, as a foundation, we've decided to dispense with the Forest Festival this year." Hesitancy laced Edna's voice.

"What? Why?" This was her aunt's legacy in the small town of Red Oaks. They'd put on the Forest Festival every year for thirty-seven years. How could it just stop? Her aunt had been involved in it since it began. It was what she'd spent all of her free time doing. Helena had practically adopted the whole town through the event, though she'd never had children of her own.

"I'm sorry, Ms. Waters. I know it must come as a shock, but without your aunt, it just won't be the same. She was the reason the Forest Festival tradition lasted as long as it did. She knew exactly what to do and how to do it so that the Festival ran like clockwork."

The idea that Helena was the lifeblood of the Forest Festival came as no surprise to Hailey. Memories from so many Christmases spent with her aunt and attending the Forest Festival hit her like a tide breaking against the shoreline rocks. Hailey pushed away the wave of grief that threatened to knock her over. "You need me to come and clean out a closet?"

"I think it's best if you are here in person. I heard that you were already out here in the summer for the funeral. I'm sorry to make you come back again, but I'm sure your aunt would want you to go through her things before the building is torn down."

With the building being the priority, Hailey wanted to clarify. Maybe it was just balancing the new building that was too much to do with the Forest Festival. They'd most likely sponsor it again when the foundation moved to their new building. The tradition wouldn't just end. It couldn't. "So will the Forest Festival take place again next year? You're just taking a break from it this year?" She couldn't even imagine winter in Red Oaks without the Forest Festival. It seemed wrong somehow. Another wave of sadness hit her. She wouldn't be visiting in the winter again—wouldn't be going to her aunt's house for Christmas or for any of the days before when the Forest Festival was in full swing. The house had been left to her in the will, but back in June, when she was given the deed, she couldn't think straight enough to make a decision about what to do with it, but now ...

Edna's voice cut through her thoughts. "Ms. Waters, I don't

think we will continue this tradition. It had a good run, but it's time for us to try new things. The foundation is moving in a new direction."

A new direction? What did that mean? She drew in a small, shallow breath. Maybe it was time to sell her aunt's house too. And move on. She could keep everything in her memory, but without the Forest Festival, Christmas in Red Oaks would be bleak. "When would you like it cleared out again?" she asked.

"The wrecking ball comes on Monday morning."

Monday morning? It was already Wednesday. If she wrapped up a few things here in Seattle, she'd be able to delegate her weekend parties to her assistant, and she could start on Friday afternoon. Would that give her enough time to go through the closets? She could figure out what to do with her aunt's property and with the contents of the closets later. With any luck she could be back to Seattle before Monday morning. Then she wouldn't have to witness the destruction of the foundation building where her aunt had built a legacy that would die the same year she did. It was all too much.

"I can be there this weekend," she finally mustered.

"That's wonderful. The rest of the building will be emptied, but I will come and unlock the building for you," Edna promised.

"Thank you," Hailey said.

"And if there's anything else you need …" Edna's voice trailed off.

"The name of a good moving company to load up everything I'm taking away." Hailey's event planner mode dialed into the supplies she'd need, but if there were large trees to move or heavy decorations, hiring a moving company would help her get things done faster. She didn't want to stay in the past for very long. She only wanted to clear the space.

"I can help you more than that. I will make sure that a moving company is already ready to go for this weekend. We have a large moving truck that we use for delivering all of our trees after the Forest Festival. They'll be able to help you."

"Thank you," Hailey said.

"There's also a small trust from your aunt in connection with the Forest Festival. She left it as part of her donations, but now that we aren't doing the Festival, the money can be turned over to whichever charity you'd like," she said. "I can show you the paperwork."

"Is the money enough to cover the cost of the Festival?" Hailey asked hopefully. Maybe there was a still a chance …

"No. Unfortunately it won't cover it. But the main reason for cancelling has to do with the labor-intensive nature of the event. The Red Oaks Foundation feels it's time to try something less … time consuming. Streamlining our process on how we raise money will help us be more efficient with our resources."

Less time consuming? Streamlining? The words felt like a change from the small town way of raising money to a cold, sterile machine. "I understand," Hailey said, though she really didn't. She was one of the most highly efficient and sought after event coordinators on the West Coast, but time was something that was crucial to every event. Every project. It was the time that ultimately came through and made her events recognizable in the media. Once she hung up with Edna, she called the realtor in Red Oaks. It was time to list Helena's house and get it sold.

Hailey waited in front of the old Red Oaks Foundation building on Friday morning. The office space looked like it was only barely held together. It made sense that the headquarters would be torn down. Hailey's heart squeezed, missing her aunt more as she stared at the building that would be reduced to rubble in less than a week. A car drove around the cones used as barricades to keep people from parking in the parking lot, pulling up next to Hailey's rental.

A woman in her early fifties stepped out of the car, coming around to where Hailey stood on the sidewalk. "I'm Edna," the woman said, then gave Hailey a quick hug. "I worked with your aunt for the last six years. She was a wonderful woman." Edna pulled a ring of keys out of her coat pocket.

Hailey's throat constricted, but she managed to respond with, "She was."

Edna looked at her with kind eyes. "I'll show you where her stuff was kept. I'd hate to see it demolished without family looking at the contents first."

Hailey wasn't the closest relative, but she was the one that was stipulated in the will, and she'd honor her aunt's last wishes.

Edna unlocked the building, and they both stepped inside. Edna hadn't been exaggerating when she had said the place would be empty. The building wasn't big, but the entryway felt cavernous without any furniture. Dim bulbs lit the way down the hall towards several doors. The hallways had cork boards and nail holes where pictures and announcements used to hang.

"Here we are," Edna said. "Now, anything you don't want

can be loaded with the movers too. Just let them know, and they will drop it off for donations or take whatever you don't need. The rest of it is up to you."

"And the hospital won't use any of this?" Hailey asked, wondering if some of the trees could be repurposed.

"The hospital has its own stock of decorations. Nothing is needed. Most of this stuff was your aunt's personal property. Now that we aren't doing the Forest Festival anymore, we don't need any of it."

"And there's no chance that you'll do the Forest Festival again next year, when you have more time to prepare?"

Edna shook her head. "Like I said on the phone, this was your aunt's project. She was the force behind it. When your aunt started getting sick at the beginning of the year, we didn't have the time or resources to aid her. She kept a list, but now ... well now it seems too much without her. It wouldn't be the same. We're looking for an easier approach to receiving donations."

"What about all the good it did for the hospital?" Hailey asked, knowing that would have been her aunt's top concern.

Edna blew out a breath. "They are sad to lose the support, but they have other ways to raise money throughout the year."

Hailey swallowed, not wanting to pry further. There was nothing she could do about it, but make peace with it. Helena Waters was gone. The Forest Festival wasn't happening again. And the sooner Hailey finished up in Red Oaks, the sooner she could get back to Seattle and mourn all of the changes by herself. "Thanks for letting me in."

Edna nodded, putting the keys in her hand. "This is your aunt's set of keys. Keep them until you're finished. You have my number if you need anything else while you're in town, right?"

Hailey nodded. "What time is the moving truck supposed to be here?" She glanced at her watch. It was still before noon. If she could make a dent in this today, she could spend most of tomorrow with the realtor.

"Three," Edna said.

That was close to five hours of working time. That was probably plenty. "Thanks," she said.

After Edna left, Hailey went to work. The closet, as Edna had called it, was more the size of a large conference room. When Hailey went to what she thought was the end, it went back further. Red and green boxes lined the wall on one side. The other side held various Christmas trees, some put together and wrapped with plastic, and still others were in their boxes. At least everything was organized. A back shelf held miscellaneous decorations. A thin layer of dust covered everything.

Hailey circled around the shelf in the middle of the room, working her way toward the front of the room again. She turned on her favorite playlist and blasted the music from her phone speaker.

Pulling down the very first box on the shelf, she set it in the middle of the floor. Inside the box were several ornaments. If Edna had had her come all the way from Seattle just to see if Hailey had wanted to keep a few gold and silver ornaments, Edna was wrong.

As Hailey dug further into the shelves, she found boxes full of keepsake sentimental ornaments, and others full of Helena's personal stuff. Hailey wiped her forehead. It would take a lot more work than she'd planned to get through this closet.

It was 4:30 PM before Hailey looked at her clock. The movers still hadn't shown up. She left a quick message with Edna about it. Hailey had categorized enough of the boxes to know what she was keeping and what she was leaving on the first wall. The contents were well labeled.

She hadn't realized how much her aunt had used paper instead of electronics to keep her records. Receipts and invoices were all stapled and filed in a complicated system. Toward the back was a row of green and red banker's boxes. Hailey lifted the lid, expecting to find more color-coordinated ornaments in each box.

She coughed as the disturbed dust floated through the air and tingled her nose. No ornaments, just another set of file folders. She closed the lid, trying the next box. Again, it was more files. She opened three more boxes before a pile on top of the files made her stop. A bundle of envelopes, sitting on top of the files, were bound with coarse twine. A sticky note on the stack simply said, "Read and file."

Hailey pulled at the twine and the bow immediately untied. The letter was addressed to Helena and there was a Christmas stamp in the corner. Hailey was sucked into the cursive handwriting on the Christmas notecard.

"Dear Helena,

This year has been hard for me. Attending the Forest Festival was the highlight of the winter. I was feeling low, and the Forest Festival brought me through. Thank you for all of your hard work. I shudder to think what I would have done without it this year.

With love, Charlotte"

Hailey returned the card to its envelope, then pulled out the next one.

"Dear Helena,

Thank you for your encouragement to donate a tree for the Festival this year. I've wanted to help decorate a tree for a number of years, but your invitation was what I needed. My family and I had so much fun as we decorated our themed tree. I will never look at a Christmas tree quite the same way again. Thank you for believing in me.

Your friend, Patricia"

Hailey touched the outside of the card, where a raised Christmas tree had glitter sprinkled on it. She returned it to the envelope, then glanced at the sticky note. "Read and file."

Hailey bit her lip, then looked back in the box at the first file. The file was full, but not with receipts and invoices like the first several boxes had been. This one was full of letters. She moved to the next file and the next. All of the files in this banker's box were full of letters, cards, and pictures. A file in the back held several sheets of white computer paper. Each page had a crayon drawing on it. Hailey pulled out the first picture, then flipped it over. A date, a name, and the hospital were on the back in her aunt's handwriting. Hailey pulled out the next and the next. The pattern was the same. She pulled the whole box off the shelf and moved it to the floor. She crouched next to it, craving to see everything her aunt had saved.

The filing system seemed complicated. She couldn't quite tell how they'd been filed. She took out another green and red banker's box, and found the same thing. The entire box was heavy with letters, drawings, and cards. Ribbon and paperclips kept letters and envelopes together.

Hailey read more, getting lost in the praise and the gratitude until her head swam with the emotion from it. The Forest Festival meant so much to so many, not just to her, not just to her aunt—but to the town. The surrounding communities supported this beautiful tradition. The hospital administration had written Helena a note every year expressing their gratitude for her work with the hospital and with the Forest Festival. Hailey teared up as she read the tender stories of the miracles and the moments in peoples' lives that surrounded the Forest Festival.

A gold file folder caught her eye, and she read through more letters. Occasionally there was a sticky note on one of the letters, in her aunt's handwriting with details about the person, or a reminder to write a note back.

Hailey shifted from her crouched position to a kneeling one in front of the open box. She pulled out another letter. She wasn't sure what she would do with the eight boxes that had sentimental objects and thank you letters, but she didn't want them destroyed with the building.

"Hi," a man said.

Hailey startled and dropped the letters onto the pile. She turned to face a tall, handsome man wearing jeans. His brown hair fell in a gentle wave over his forehead. Hailey scrambled to her feet, blinking her emotions back.

"Hi. I was beginning to wonder if you'd come at all tonight," Hailey said to the man who was obviously the mover. Her breath caught as his muscles rippled, bulging against his white polo.

The man tilted his head. "I didn't know I was expected." His chocolate brown eyes held surprise.

"You were expected, and you're late." Hailey dusted off her hands on her jeans, trying to play off her notice of him. "But no matter, you're here now. All of the boxes in this pile are headed to my aunt's house. Well probably all of it will go there, until I figure out where to donate the rest." She looked around the room, before settling her gaze back on the man in front of her. "I'm Hailey."

"Troy," he said, putting his hand forward and shaking hers. "Looks like you're doing some remodeling."

She almost laughed at the statement. Remodeling or completely decimating the area. But that wasn't her concern. She'd get out her aunt's stuff.

"So this is what you use for the Forest Festival?" he asked.

Emotions threatened to surface. She blamed it on all the letters she'd read through. Her aunt should have filed Kleenex in those banker's boxes. Every letter had pulled at her heart, making her wish the Festival could still be a reality. "This is what has been used in the past." Of course that wasn't going to happen this year.

"I'm here to volunteer, so however I can help." The sincerity in his eyes captured her. Maybe that was the power of the Forest Festival.

"I'm clearing out this whole room. Did you bring a crew or anything?"

He looked confused. "It's just me, but I will help with whatever you need."

"These boxes can be loaded." It wasn't much but it was a start. She pointed to another stack. "I'll take these ones with me and sort them at my aunt's house."

Hailey went through a few more boxes while Troy took boxes out. She carried a banker's box full of letters, all filed by year. Her aunt had made a difference in the community, and it was evident from the weight of the cards and letters in the box. She walked to the front of the building, and then stopped when she saw the stack of boxes next to the front door. "Shouldn't we start loading these in the truck?" she asked.

He tilted his head. "Truck?"

She looked out at the shiny sports car that was parked next to her rental. The rest of the parking lot was empty. "Unless you have some serious trunk space in the back of that car, you brought the wrong vehicle."

"What are you talking about?"

"Aren't you part of the moving crew Edna hired?"

He shook his head. "I'm here to help volunteer for the Forest Festival. I came to the headquarters assuming they'd have information for me on how I can get involved. Your website wasn't very detailed. It didn't even have a phone number."

Hailey blew out a breath. "That's because there won't be a Forest Festival this year. It's been ... cancelled." Permanently. But she couldn't bear to say the words aloud. It felt so final.

The man looked so stunned, it was almost comical. "That can't be. I-I was told that this was a tradition. I came all the way up from New York City to help."

Hailey tilted her head. "I'm sorry you drove all this way." She bit her lip. She'd come even further and the whole situation felt cold and hollow. "The foundation is going in a *new direction*, trying to make more money without doing much work." She muttered about the cold and sterile way they were changing the feel of this beautiful tradition.

"You sound happy about this," he said dryly.

He'd caught her sarcasm. "Obviously." She rolled her eyes.

"There must be something we can do," he said. "I need this to happen. Maybe we can talk to Ms. Waters. My assistant said she is the person to talk to."

Tears sprang to Hailey's eyes, and her throat strangled as she mustered composure to keep her voice steady while blinking her tears away. "She would be the person to talk to, but my aunt passed away a few months ago."

A crease formed along his forehead. "I'm so sorry," he said. "I didn't know."

Hailey shook her head. "It's okay. The Forest Festival was her pet project. I didn't realize how much she wanted to do the whole project herself, but she was essentially the glue in every single decision, and the whole thing ran like clockwork. I was called in to clean out the closet since there was some personal items mixed in with the decorations."

She showed him the small stack of letters she'd carefully retied with the twine. She'd figure out how to file them later, but in the meantime, she'd secured them back together. She pulled out her favorite from the stack. A shaky hand had written the message of gratitude on a card with a house blanketed in snow, a Christmas tree in the window.

He took the card, scanning through it quickly, then his gaze jumped back to the top, moving slower through the message. He handed the card back to Hailey. "This seems like a special tradition your aunt was a part of."

Hailey smiled. "All of these boxes are full of similar letters," she said. Her heart squeezed at the realization that she'd spent the last couple of hours reading the stories of people who had been touched by the Forest Festival. She couldn't let this tradition just disappear. She could be at peace letting go of Red Oaks—she had a life in Seattle. But would Red Oaks really be okay without the Forest Festival? The thought weighed on her, pushing her with energy.

He nodded, but didn't say anything. He took the box from her and loaded it into the trunk of her small rental car. He brought out the rest of the boxes she wanted to go through in more detail, and they maneuvered the smaller trees together.

"So a moving company is supposed to come and take this stuff somewhere?" he asked, looking at the growing pile in the front entryway.

"That was the plan, though unless it gets donated, I'm not sure what I'm going to do with all of it," she said.

CHAPTER 2

Troy loaded another one of the colorful banker's boxes into Hailey's car. They'd packed them in the trunk, the backseat, and the passenger seat, and it still wasn't enough room. His mind was on overload as he tried to think of something to do or say. Her grief over her aunt was palpable.

He'd pushed aside his disappointment at not being able to be involved in the first foundation that he'd chosen. He could find another opportunity—he still had two more days to figure out his idea and let Kyle know about it. It was plenty of time.

She shoved against the car door. "I can come back for the last couple of boxes," she said. "I have until Monday morning to clear everything out of the building." A piece of hair fell into her face, and she wiped her brow and moved the strand of hair out of her light blue eyes.

"When will the moving company come?" he asked her. The draw to this passionate woman who cared about this service project was too great to leave just yet.

"Hopefully tonight. I don't want to miss them. Maybe I'll wait around for a little longer."

Curiosity struck him. "They just took everything else out of the building and moved, leaving you to do the rest by yourself?"

She shrugged, her shoulder lifting against her dark, curly hair. "I have a feeling they're all just as heartbroken about not putting on the Forest Festival. My aunt did a lot of good with it, but I can't tell if they really couldn't pull it off in the time frame or if without my aunt, they're really unsure what to do. At any rate, they're going in a different direction. The wrecking ball comes Monday."

He glanced back at the building. The structure was old, but not old enough to be considered classic or historical. It was an outdated structure. He held a box in his arms. "I can put this in my car and follow you home."

"I know we've had a good time loading up these boxes, but I'm not about to take you home with me." Her eyes sparkled.

Troy's jaw slacked. That was not what he'd meant. "I'm just trying to be helpful," he said. What he wanted to do was win a bet, that's why he'd come.

She tilted her head at him. "Aren't you a little old to be a Boy Scout?"

He smiled, enjoying the banter. He could play along. "There is no age limit. I'll be working on my knot tying and bird house building merit badges next week."

She grinned. "Impressive."

"What can I say? I'm an impressive guy."

She rolled her eyes. "Cocky much?"

"Not usually. It must be the cold air; I forgot my coat."

"Some Boy Scout," she smirked.

"Ha! Touché!"

The wind picked up, bringing a chill in the air as the sun sank toward the horizon.

"If the movers come today, I can always have them bring the extra boxes to my aunt's house." She looked around the stacks surrounding them at the front of the building, though they were still not finished emptying the storage room. "Now I feel bad that I thought you were the moving company."

He waved a hand in the air. "Don't feel bad. Boy scout, remember? Happy to help." He wasn't in his suit. It was fine to be mistaken for normal. Actually, it was quite refreshing.

She laughed at the joke. "I'll call Edna again and see if I can get a time on the movers," she said.

He nodded, watching as she paced on the leaf-covered sidewalk, twisting a lock of brown hair as she left a message. It gave him a brief moment to collect his thoughts. Hailey was intriguing and beautiful. The way her eyes lit up during their banter and when she'd showed him the letters, had captured him. There was a spark there. The wind picked up and she hugged her arms around her when she walked back to where he'd been standing.

"We could wait inside while they come," he said, his pulse racing more as her blue eyes gazed at him. Her eyes were a light, captivating blue.

"You don't have to wait. You've already done plenty," she said.

He weighed his plans for the evening. Originally he thought he'd spend most of the evening brainstorming about how to help and be involved with the charity event, but now, it was either stay and get to know Hailey, or head to his hotel that was down the street, and search for another opportunity.

"I don't have anything pressing," he said. "Why don't we move a few more boxes and you can tell me about your aunt and the Forest Festival."

He opened the door for her, and they headed back to the storage room for another box of ornaments.

She nodded. "My aunt started it before I was born. Her nephew was really sick at the time. He'd been in and out of hospitals for months. Each time they were moved to a new city to run more tests, his parents would stay at hotels or with friends if they knew someone close. It was a lot of strain on them financially. When they came to Red Oaks, they stayed with my aunt Helena, but their costs had been so high that my aunt wanted to raise money for them and others like them that had drained their bank accounts while their kids were in hospitals." She paused.

Troy watched as her features scrunched together and smoothed out, like she was trying to think of the right words. Normally he would have asked a question, or made a comment, but he felt more than anything that silence would be the best thing in the moment. They balanced a large box between them. The box didn't weigh much, but the size and shape made it awkward to carry alone.

Once they put the box down, they moved back to the storage room for the next box. Hailey cleared her throat. "It was nearing Christmas, and my aunt decided to work with the Children's Hospital here to see if she could raise awareness and money at the same time. They agreed to help. She went from business to business asking for donations. She didn't have a place to hold the charity event, but she knew the owner of the tree farm. They held it just after Thanksgiving that first year, at the tree farm lot. To make it a little more festive, my aunt brought a bunch of decorations for the trees. During the event they ended up auctioning off the trees as a last-minute idea. After that first year they moved the event indoors, but they kept the tradition of auctioning off decorated Christmas trees ever since." She inhaled a deep breath, like what she'd said had removed all of the oxygen from her.

Troy walked next to her, trying to read the look on her profile. "It sounds like a worthy cause—an amazing event." Was this how Kyle felt when he worked with his charity, Happy Moments? His heart tugged at the idea. Something like the Forest Festival would create Christmas in a whole new way.

"It really was. I rarely missed a year of coming to the festival." She moved toward a box, grabbing one end, and he quickly took the other. "The aroma from the cinnamon rolls is the first thing to hit you as you walk through the doors. The combination of the cinnamon and the fresh pine trees smell like Christmas. In one corner, groups of carolers take turns singing for the patrons. Some come dressed up in old-fashioned coats, scarves, and top hats, like they're straight out of a Dickens' novel."

They put the box down, repeating the process of walking back to the storage room. "Tell me more," he said.

"Rows and rows of Christmas trees through the entire events center makes the room feel like a forest—like wandering through the wonder of Narnia. Every tree is unique, but the entire thing works together. I'd always pick out the tree that I would bid on if I had the money, and I would always guess which one would go for the highest bid. Santa is in the North Pole, greeting children. Performers dance and sing. It's noisy and crowded with people, and it's one of the best moments walking through the aisles amid the bustle."

Her eyes lit up as she talked about her memories. Troy had seen the boxes of letters from the town, the volunteers, and others who had come to the festival, but this festival mattered to Hailey in a deeply, personal way.

"I wish I could see it," he said. The way she'd described it, it was beautiful.

"I suppose there's always new traditions to make. I just wish ..." She shook her head, looking away from him.

They moved in silence down the hall, but Troy couldn't resist breaking the silence this time. He had to know what her wish would be. He didn't know why it was important, but he knew it was. "What do you wish?" he asked softly.

"I wish I could talk the foundation into one more year of the Forest Festival. Just one more time ..."

"Why not try?" he asked.

She shook her head. "It's October. The event is held the second week in December. That's why Edna let me go through the closet, and take out anything I found sentimental from my aunt. Without my aunt, this doesn't run."

"But what if it could work?" he asked.

She bit her lip. "It would take a miracle."

"Isn't that what Christmas is all about?" he asked.

She smiled, a gesture that lit up her entire face again. He could practically hear the wheels turning in her head.

❄

THE MORE TROY HEARD OF THE FOREST FESTIVAL, THE MORE HE was convinced that he wanted to do this, more than any other charitable work he'd researched for this Christmas. Kyle and his buddies may have interested him with winning a bet, and he was determined to make the most of what he could do.

But the idea of this project excited him. The dream of him helping was quickly slipping away. Would other communities do the same thing? And would it be the same without the passion Hailey described the Forest Festival with?

A car drove up. The headlights peered through the large glass doors they sat in front of. It was definitely not a moving truck.

"Edna's back," Hailey said. "She was one of my aunt's friends."

Edna came through the door, looked at Troy with some surprise, and then turned back to Hailey. "I'm so sorry, I just got your message and was close enough in the area I thought I'd come over and see how things are going. Still no sign of the moving company?"

Hailey smiled, though Troy noticed it wasn't the vibrant smile she'd given him earlier. "Just about done. I'll have the moving crew bring out the rest of the trees, but I don't have any place to move them to."

"I hope it was still worth it for you to come here," Edna said, looking at their mounds of boxes.

Hailey nodded, a spark in her eye. "I'm not going to lie, I'm really going to miss the Forest Festival."

Edna patted her arm. "We all are, dear. But as I said before, we're moving in a different direction."

Hailey bounced on her toes. "You've got to let me do this."

"Do what?" Edna asked.

Hailey's gaze didn't leave Edna. "I want to put on the Forest Festival this year."

Edna looked at her, eyes wide. "There's too much to do to get everything ready. Helena would spend almost the entire year getting ready for the event."

Hailey pursed her lips. "My whole life is event planning. I work on tight deadlines."

Edna shook her head. "Event planning is one thing, but there is a whole list of things to do. The foundation can't—"

"I'm not asking for the foundation resources. Surely my aunt already started making preparations for this year's Christmas Forest Festival, before she passed away, right?"

Edna gave a small nod. "She did. She had her list of repeat donors, so I suppose some of it was routine."

Hailey's eyes widened. "So that's a start."

Edna sniffed. "That's barely a start. All donations have yet to be confirmed."

"I have a little money to get started. My aunt's donation. I want to use it for this."

"All of our resources are being used elsewhere."

Hailey blinked, and Troy could see the determination in her eyes. Hailey wasn't backing down. "Like I said, I do this for a living, I can handle this."

Edna narrowed her eyes. "Our volunteer staff alone takes over a hundred people to run this event on the day of, and that doesn't include the weeks leading up to it. It would be more than a full-time job from now until mid-December to make it work."

"I can work from Red Oaks full-time for the next eight

weeks to make this happen," Hailey said, confidence in her voice.

"By yourself?" Edna asked, her voice concerned.

"I'll help her," Troy said. Both women turned to him, one pair of eyes looked full of hope and the other seemed to be filled with incredulity.

Hailey's eyes widened. "You're going to help me?"

Troy nodded.

Hailey turned to Edna. "He's going to help me. If I worked on this full-time from Red Oaks, could I ask for help and resources from the other volunteers, without putting the foundation out?"

Edna raised one thinly penciled eyebrow, then blew out a breath. "I can't guarantee anything."

"We'll figure the volunteer piece out," Troy said.

"You'll let me try?" Hailey asked, excitement bubbling up in the question.

Edna glanced around the empty building, dimly lit with mismatched lightbulbs. The place had seen better days. "I know you're still grieving your aunt. We all are. But trying to bring back this dream won't bring her back."

"I know that," Hailey whispered. "But it's all I can do right now."

Edna nodded, then turned to Troy. "What are your qualifications? Have you ever been involved in putting on a charitable event of this size?"

Troy knew he couldn't reveal who he was, it was part of the bet. The charities that he and his friends chose to help shouldn't know that they were billionaires with limitless resources. That wasn't the point. Throwing around their money wasn't the goal of this. Kyle wanted them to help in ways that couldn't be measured with the bottom line. Troy still wasn't exactly sure that that meant he was qualified to help. Without his assistant, without his money, except for the $10,000 he was allowed to use, he felt as naked as the undecorated Christmas trees they'd dragged out of storage.

His internal thoughts must have taken too long because Edna continued, as if his silence had been all the answer she'd expected. She turned to Hailey. "We all miss your aunt. And in some ways maybe that's the real reason for letting this tradition go. It's not the same without her here running every aspect. Like I mentioned before, your aunt was talented in almost every aspect of her life and she did a lot of good with this event, but that doesn't mean that we will keep this tradition long term."

Hailey nodded. "I understand, but I have to try. One more year."

Troy didn't know Hailey more than talking with her the last couple of hours, but he knew Hailey wasn't the type to give up easily. Something inside of him sparked. His $10,000 might not get them as far as they needed, but it was certainly a start. He couldn't have his assistant do work for him, but he could certainly pick her brain for ideas, right?

He liked being at the office, because he liked seeing business run, but if he took off for a few weeks, his empire would still run smoothly. He had people in place to do that. He had the ability to delegate and let others run the show. He was content to hire the people it took to make his business successful. Maybe that ability and the way he'd helped streamline his own business over the last couple of years would be skills he could offer in this situation.

Edna turned to the front door. "If the moving crew doesn't show up in thirty minutes, you'll likely have to come back tomorrow and finish the rest then."

Hailey nodded. "Thanks for all of your help, Edna. I'm grateful for all the letters that were sent to my aunt. Thanks for letting me go through everything before the wrecking ball came. So I have your blessing to put on the Forest Festival?"

"I don't know," Edna said slowly.

"Give us a week," Troy said, before he could think the better of it.

Both sets of eyes looked at him again. "A week for what?" Edna asked.

Enthusiasm bubbled from Hailey. "I'll show you the traction I can make in one week," she said.

Edna pursed her lips. "You realize that normally we hold the Forest Festival mid-December. It starts off the Twelve Days before Christmas. That's barely eight weeks away."

Eight weeks was exactly the schedule he needed to keep to. "If a significant amount gets done in a week, maybe there's still a chance that we can put this on," he said, looking to Hailey for support.

Edna looked at both of them appraisingly. "I'm intrigued. I'll evaluate what you've done after a week. If there is enough progress, and sponsors are still on board for this Festival, then you'll have my backing for putting it on."

Hailey's eyes widened. "Thank you so much!"

Edna nodded. "But you're running this. Our resources are spread thin as it is."

"That works for me. What information can you give me that will help? And what about advertising?"

Edna seemed ponderous. "I have photos from the last several years. They're on the website. There's also a list of donors from the previous years, though, like I said, I haven't contacted any of them this year. Your aunt's files on the Forest Festival are all in the boxes. She never kept anything electronic."

"So, just to clarify, if I spend the next week working on this, you'll agree to host it again?"

"I want to see your progress on this first, and see where we get to. If you're serious, I'd have to see a lot of movement in the next week to be able to start advertising."

Hope shone in Hailey's light blue eyes, and Troy was captivated by them. Edna said goodnight, and exited the building.

Once Edna had driven away, Hailey spun in a circle. "Eek!" she squealed and then jumped into Troy's arms, giving him a huge bear hug. "We've got this! Thank you!"

Troy hugged her back, feeling the loss of her touch when she pulled away.

She breathed deeply. "I'm so happy."

He nodded, enjoying the moment with her. The same enthusiasm that had filled her was taking hold of him too. "Okay, where do we start?"

"*We?*"

"Yes, *we*. I said I was going to help you," he said.

"Do you even live here?"

"No, but I was serious when I said I came here to help. It wasn't an idle offer."

"You really were serious about getting that Service Merit Badge, weren't you?"

He raised an eyebrow. "I would never joke about that."

She rolled her eyes. "Seriously, though, where are you from?"

He shrugged. "I'm from the City."

"New York City is a long commute," she said.

He waved his hand in the air. If there was a chance that the Forest Festival could still work for this year, he would be there to help it. "I don't mind staying. I have … some time off I can take."

"You're nice, and you were helpful with Edna, but why would you take time off for this? You've never helped in the Forest Festival before, and you're not local." Suspicion seemed to lace her words.

Troy knew he couldn't lie to her. He also knew that the full truth was something that he couldn't share either. He focused on what he could honestly share. "Can't I just want to help?" he asked. "I like the badges."

She arched an eyebrow at him. "Do you need service hours? Are you out on parole?"

Troy laughed. He thought about the conversations he'd had with his college roommates recently. "No. I've saved a lot of time off. I'm here because I needed a different pace in my life, to really get into the Christmas season this year. The city was stifling, and I just needed to breathe a little. A coworker of mine mentioned that this town was great for that, and that the Forest Festival was one of her most favorite childhood memories. Listening to you talk about your aunt and reading the letters …

I realized that this might be the exact opportunity I was looking for."

"You picked a great time of year to come. There's something about the change in the seasons here. The red leaves still hanging on to the trees. And then with the Forest Festival on, everything is beautiful when it's covered in snow." Tension seemed to lift from her shoulders. "I would appreciate the help. Normally I'd fly a few people from my company out to help, but I already know what's on their list for this week."

Troy nodded. "When do we start?"

Hailey looked around at the boxes they'd been sitting on, waiting for the movers to come. "Right now." She pulled out a notebook and a hand carved wooden pen. When her pen hit the paper a list appeared almost out of nowhere.

"You really know what you're doing," Troy said, impressed.

"It'd be faster on my computer with my event planning templates, but this will have to do for now." She drew boxes and columns on the paper. "The first thing we're going to need is the sponsor's names and the donation list. I'm sure that's what Edna was hinting at finding among the files. She wants to know that putting on the benefit event will be worth it."

"What kind of donations?" he asked. He knew that he could spend up to $10,000 of his own money, but that wouldn't get them very far. But he needed to do something with the money —pay for a service, hire a crew. Something. He couldn't simply donate it.

"We'll have a better idea when we see the list. Sponsors for the trees. Sponsors for the event. It's going to cost more than a pretty penny to put it on. I would have assumed they'd have a fund from last year to get this one started, but Edna and her team have gone a different direction with their foundation since my aunt passed away. But I can use the money my aunt donated. That's mine to figure out what to do with, so it's a start."

Excitement flowed through him as he thought about working with Hailey for the week. "So you'll find the list, or can I help going through boxes tonight?"

"I'll find the list. Does tomorrow work for you? What time will you be here in the morning?" she asked.

"I'm staying at a hotel not too far from here. I can meet you any time."

"How about over breakfast?" she asked.

He nodded. "Where?"

"You've never been to Red Oaks before?"

He shook his head. "Never."

She smiled. "Then The Pancake Tower it is."

"Do they have good pancakes?" he asked jokingly.

She laughed. "You haven't lived until you've had their Buffalo Tower."

"I assume there's only one in town?"

She nodded. "Yes. It's a great little place. We could go over plans and see what is feasible in a week." She stood up from the boxes. "I'm going to assume that the moving crew will be here in the morning, and maybe Edna will call me when they're available. We should probably go."

He agreed and held the door open for her. She locked up the building, then unlocked her car with the push of a button.

He opened the car door for her. "Drive safe," he said.

She paused by her door before getting in, looking directly into his eyes for a long heartbeat. "Thanks. You too."

He helped her into the car and watched as she drove out of the parking lot. He wondered if his brain was more aware that he might be able to help with the Forest Festival in a significant way, or how smooth Hailey's hands were when he'd helped her into her car.

When her taillights disappeared down the winding road, he wished he'd gotten her number. Maybe they could have grabbed dinner tonight together too. At any rate, breakfast tomorrow couldn't come soon enough.

CHAPTER 3

Hailey brought the last of the boxes into her aunt's house from her rental car. She set them in the living room. Thanks to Troy from New York City, she'd been given a week to prove herself. If this Forest Festival was meant to be this year, he'd be the one to help her.

A thrill ran through her. He'd been helpful and attentive. He didn't have to help. There was no obligation for him, and he didn't have the personal tie that she did, and yet, he'd said he would help her this week. She looked around the front room, needing a quilt to wrap up with. She turned on the fireplace, and headed upstairs to get the desired blanket.

The wooden stairs groaned in a few places, and she ran her fingers along the chair rail. The dust lifted easily onto her fingers. It would definitely need a cleaning before she listed. She peeked her head into the first room. It wasn't where her favorite blanket was stored, but she paused in the doorway. Hailey bit her lip. If she was going to stay at her aunt's house for the next week while she worked on the Forest Festival, she'd have to reacquaint herself with the house, without her aunt here.

She inspected room after room, memories flooding into her mind with each flicker of the lamps that burst to life when she flipped the light switches. She remembered playing hide and seek in some of the rooms, crouching behind the nightstands or under the beds.

Her aunt had always let Hailey pick which room she wanted to stay in. Sometimes she picked a different room, but her favorite one had pale blue walls, and a large window overlooking the backyard. Three more squeaky footsteps on the hardwood floor had her to the last closed door on the left.

Her heart squeezed as she flipped on the next light. The pale blue walls seemed darker than she'd remembered in the summer, or maybe it was just the lack of daylight brightening up the space. The butterfly quilt she loved was folded perfectly on the foot of the bed. Happy memories of reading in the corner rocking chair and pretending she was a princess in this room raced through her mind.

It had taken her until now to really explore the place again. She'd been through the main floor rooms, but she hadn't wanted to disturb the upstairs. She ran her hand across the smooth wood of the nightstand table and picked up the picture displayed there. It was her and her aunt in the backyard on a picnic blanket. Hailey couldn't have been more than nine or ten in the picture. "Miss you," she said softly to the picture, when she replaced it on the nightstand.

She pulled the butterfly quilt off the end of the bed and hugged it. The heartache at missing her aunt expanded in her chest. It was too much to process right now. She closed the door of her favorite room and headed back downstairs.

Once she was settled on the couch, she dug through the paperwork until she found a list of donors and donations. Sponsors from previous years were also paper clipped together. Thankfully it hadn't taken her too long to find them. After a light dinner, she made some hot chocolate.

She opened one of the boxes that held letters to her aunt, the box that she'd only skimmed through. She pulled out a folder from five years ago and wrapped the butterfly blanket snuggly around her shoulders. After an hour of reading the letters, she was convinced that trying to keep this tradition going was worth it. And without Troy she wouldn't have even had a chance.

HAILEY BREATHED IN DEEPLY AS AROMAS OF HOT MAPLE SYRUP and crispy bacon wafted toward her when she walked toward the entrance of The Pancake Tower the next morning. She looked around the bustling restaurant crowded with people, and even more memories, but didn't see Troy.

Framed photographs of the latest winners of the Pancake Tower Challenge proudly displayed smiling men and women next to large stacks of pancakes. The popular diner looked the same as it had every time she'd come with her aunt. The blue sparkly vinyl still covered the booths, and the pads of the chairs. Had they been well taken care of or just recovered over the years? Either way the place held its value.

Hailey didn't have to wait too long for a booth to empty and be cleared before she was seated. She looked around again for Troy, her mind swimming at the memory of him yesterday—how he'd helped her, how he'd volunteered to assist her, how they'd just looked at each other, his chocolate brown eyes making her melt when he helped her into her car. Maybe they should have exchanged numbers yesterday—that would probably be a good thing for this coming week as they worked together.

His shiny dark car, more gray than black, pulled up in front of the restaurant. Her heart thudded against her chest when he got out of his car. She'd noticed how good looking he was last night, but now as he walked into the restaurant, she took in all of his features with a heightened sense of appreciation. He'd lifted the boxes with ease yesterday, his muscles strong and defined. With a leather jacket covering them up, she focused on his neatly trimmed beard that showcased his chiseled jaw. His smile drew her in. When he came toward her booth she blinked, not wanting to be caught staring.

"Good morning," he said. His greeting felt like sunshine on the brisk October morning.

She smiled widely, hoping he hadn't noticed her staring. "I thought you'd ditched me, not that I'd blame you," she said playfully.

He tilted his head at her. When she couldn't handle his gaze anymore she glanced down at her menu. She knew exactly what she wanted to order, but there was no reason for him to know that, and the menu provided a buffer from that smile and his chocolate eyes.

He pulled her menu down gently, his eyes connecting with hers, making her feel warm inside, like she'd already polished off the pumpkin hot chocolate that she had yet to order. "I took a wrong turn."

She shook her head, holding in her laugh. "Some Boy Scout you are." She glanced out the window. In less than a month the whole town would be enveloped in snow, the town always feeling like a Winter Wonderland. "I hope you'll come back for the Forest Festival. It really is something amazing."

"I wouldn't miss it. It will be the best Forest Festival Red Oaks can remember."

Hailey nodded. Troy's enthusiasm caught her, seeming to sweep her up in a hot air balloon of hope.

"I like the way you think," she said.

He smiled, showing his teeth like she'd given him a huge compliment. "In my humble opinion, it's the only way to do business." He opened his menu and asked Hailey for recommendations. Troy ordered, and so did Hailey.

They talked through Hailey's process for tackling this next week. It was focused on sponsors, and on looking at the venue, and asking previous businesses that had been used, for support. Tackling this felt like the most important event planning account she'd ever been handed. More than anything she wanted it to measure up to the high standards her aunt had set for the event and the town. Hailey knew she had the skills to do it, and with the way Troy was diving head first into this project, she wasn't concerned about the tight deadline or the outcome. Troy exuded confidence and strength, and last month she'd thrown a birthday party with eighty children invited on a tight schedule. She had this Forest Festival, no problem.

"We have a lot of donations to sort through. Many businesses donate trees and donate various other things in kind. I can't quite tell what all the donations are. My aunt must have had a system for remembering it," Hailey said, glancing through some of the paperwork she'd brought from her aunt's files. "At any rate, the businesses are where we should start, to see if this list is still accurate for this year. The events center looks like it has been booked for the Forest Festival, but I'm not sure if Edna has cancelled that booking or not. So that's another thing to check."

"You're certainly organized," Troy said.

Hailey smiled. "I have to be in my line of work. It's all about getting everything in a row. I can better analyze and execute an event when everything is in order."

Troy grinned. "Any other goals for the week?"

"I think if we can at least get twenty trees and decorations donated this week, along with a few other businesses for sponsors, that should be enough traction to convince Edna to help us out with the advertising. I also think we should talk to the hospital and see what their needs and goals are this year for Christmas. Maybe they have some ideas."

Troy nodded. "Where were you going to have the moving crew move the Christmas trees and decorations?"

Hailey hoped there would be room at the foundation's new headquarters, but she doubted she could arrange that on a Saturday. "In my aunt's garage, at least for the time being."

"And those would be used as decorations at the festival?"

She nodded. "Everything will be donated."

"What about talking to the guy who owns the tree farm?" Troy asked, looking down at one of the papers from the file.

"Good idea," Hailey said. "We can drive by the lot and talk to him."

Their food came out, and Hailey laughed at how wide Troy's eyes became when he saw the Buffalo Tower he'd ordered. "You didn't tell me it was enough to feed an army," he said.

"Like I said, you haven't really lived or visited Red Oaks until you've tried it."

The tower was covered in whipped cream. He took a bite. "Wow, this really is amazing," he said.

Hailey smiled. "I'm glad you like it. My aunt and I would split a short buffalo stack when I would come and visit her."

He moved the plate toward her. "There's more than enough to share."

She laughed, gesturing to her much smaller stack. "I have more than enough here," she said.

They talked more about the coordination for the day, deciding to follow the leads for the hospital and the tree farm today, and then work on sponsorships on Monday when more local businesses would be open.

Troy polished off half of the Buffalo stack, before he gave up on eating the rest. He paid for their meal, and walked toward the exit. Troy stopped at the wall of framed pictures. "Are those the Buffalo Tower eaters?"

Hailey shook her head. "These are the Pancake Tower winners. Each of them ate all of those pancakes in less than an hour."

Troy's eyes widened. "Local town tradition?"

Hailey nodded. "Free Tower pancakes for a month if you can do it." She pointed to a wall with a much smaller group of pictures. "Those are the Buffalo Tower winners. You have to eat all of it in less than forty-five minutes to get your picture up there."

"It can't be done," Troy said.

Hailey laughed. "Well those five did it. Free meals for a year if you do it though."

"Not worth it," Troy said, patting his stomach. "I'm so full from just half of it."

Hailey smiled. "You have to admit it's the best thing on the menu though."

"I can't admit that until I try other things on the menu," he said. "Looks like we'll have to come back."

"Looks like we will," Hailey said, looking into his eyes.

He opened the door for her and they stepped outside. Hailey wrapped her scarf around her neck against the chill in the air, though the sun was shining.

"Should we ride together?" Troy asked. "I'm happy to drive."

She nodded. It would be much easier to coordinate if they were together. "Sounds good," she said.

He opened the door for her, and she settled into the luxury sports car, *Italia Midnight*. They headed over to the old foundation building, where the movers were finishing moving the last of the trees into the moving truck. Once everything was loaded Hailey locked the door, wondering why she bothered when it was going to be torn down in two days.

Hailey gave her aunt's address to the movers. When the moving crew finished unloading the Christmas decorations, the two car garage resembled a discount Christmas store after the holiday. It was only a temporary home, since all of this decor would be used to help create the Forest Festival.

Hailey gave Troy directions to the tree lot. They arrived at the barren area. Hailey directed him where to park, and they both got out of the car.

"Where are we?" Troy asked, looking around.

Hailey spread her arms out wide, turning almost in a complete circle. "This is the Red Oaks Tree Farm, or at least it will be." She gestured to the open space between the tall, skinny buildings that seemed to be smashed together on Main Street. "I know it doesn't look like much, but this area holds the festivities in the town. In the summer it's the home of traveling carnivals and where the 4th of July parade starts. There's enough room here to house all of the floats as they wait their turn. In the winter it's the Tree Farm."

"This looks like a great location," Troy said, looking up and down the street. "Should we start talking to local businesses while we're here, and save the hospital visit until Monday?"

"Let's find Lester and see what he thinks about either donating trees for decorations or for the ones that would be auctioned off. He works over there, in Lester's Wood Shop."

Troy nodded. "I'm following your lead."

They went into the wood shop. A man behind the counter, old enough to be her grandpa looked up when they entered the store. "Do my eyes deceive me, or is that really little miss Hailey Waters?"

Lester had always called her that since before she could see above the counter. "It's really me." She beamed up at him.

He came around the counter and gave her a hug. "It's been too long since I've seen you. I was traveling when your aunt passed away, but I heard her funeral was beautiful." His eyes reflected the sadness she'd felt over the last couple of months, and it was magnified with her being in Red Oaks without her aunt.

Nothing felt the same. Every corner, every street, every

store had memories of her with her aunt attached to them. "It was a beautiful funeral," she finally managed to say.

"What brings you back ...?" he asked, letting the end of the question dangle, as if he didn't want to fill in the words.

She'd always come to spend time with her aunt. Without her here, Hailey had also wondered if and when she'd be back. But now she was here, and it was where she was supposed to be. "I came to clean out the storage closet aunt Helena had at the foundation. It's going to be knocked down next week."

"I heard that was happening. I suppose that's the way of things sometimes," he said, looking around the wood shop that probably hadn't changed much in the last twenty-five years either.

"Edna has gone a different direction with the foundation, but she's given me and my ... friend ... a week to prove that we can pull the Forest Festival off this year."

Lester whistled. "You're just like your aunt—always thinking much bigger than anyone else."

"You think it's too big?"

He shook his head. "Not for you." He picked up the wood he'd been working on. Thin and thick parts balanced out the piece, likely the beginnings of a Christmas candlestick. "What can I help you with?" he asked.

"We're here to figure out the donation side of things this year," Hailey said.

Lester smiled at Troy, shaking his hand and introducing himself. "I'll tell you the same thing I told Helena the first year she asked me and my Pop to donate. We're always happy to donate to worthy causes. Our trees are reasonably priced, and some will be straight up donations. The other ones I always gave her a discount on and she'd sell them for much higher when they were all decorated. I'm happy to do that for any of the volunteers who choose to donate a decorated live tree. I'm happy to get them a tree at my own cost."

"That's very generous of you," Hailey said.

"I was sad to hear that the Forest Festival wouldn't be held this year, so this is a pleasant surprise to find out that it's still going to happen."

"That's what I'm here for," Hailey said, glancing at Troy. "Our aim is to make it the most memorable Forest Festival Red Oaks has ever seen."

Lester smiled widely. "You're cut from the same cloth as your aunt, so I have no doubt you'll be able to pull this off."

"Thanks for your confidence. You're the first person we've talked to. So far we're doing really well."

He laughed. "Your aunt has done several different things over the years, but I'm happy to help with the sound for any of the performances," he said.

"That would be great. Thanks, Lester."

He nodded. "Best of luck to you. If you're around next week, I'll have my famous caramel apples out."

"I wouldn't miss them. They're my absolute favorite caramel apples," she said.

CHAPTER 4

On Tuesday afternoon, Troy and Hailey split up talking to businesses. They'd stuck together all of yesterday and this morning as they'd talked to businesses and the hospital together. So far they'd received all of the pledges, and confirmed the donations from each of the businesses, but now they needed to move faster. The small town seemed generous for what it could give, but Troy knew it wasn't nearly enough to put on something like they were planning to tackle in such a short amount of time.

They wanted to make the most of their time, and splitting up had made sense when they made the decision, but Troy found himself missing Hailey's company. The way she talked about life and memories of this small town, made him wish he could have grown up in a small town. Everyone seemed friendly and helpful. The time had flown by fast as they'd walked from one business to the next together.

Since lunch, the task hadn't been nearly as fun. He missed

hearing Hailey laugh. Two businesses ago, they'd both walked out of the businesses at the same time, directly across the street from each other. She'd waved and given him a thumbs up. He'd done the same, and then they'd both disappeared into the next business on their respective sides of the street.

Troy glanced up from the desk where a woman scribbled on a small piece of paper. Rows of chocolate boxes and pictures of candies filled the entire space of the back wall. "Mr. Rasmussen, this is what the Red Oaks Sweets can donate."

He looked at the paper, expecting it to be a dollar figure. He was wrong. It was a list of candies and chocolates, with amounts, weights, and packaging. It looked very generous, but donations in-kind weren't going to fund this project. This would come in handy, but would it be enough to convince Edna to help them with the advertising? He'd talked to seven businesses so far today, and all of them were in-kind donations.

Troy smiled, hoping he conveyed his gratitude for the offer. "Thank you," he said. "I know this will mean a lot."

She nodded, beaming back at him. "It's my pleasure. We've loved this tradition, and this is the most we've ever been able to donate, so we're happy to help."

Troy shook her hand before leaving the woman's office. When he was back in the front of the store, he noticed a display with special caramel apples. The bright tag on the cellophane read, "Lester's World-Famous Caramel Apples." Troy smiled, wondering which kind Hailey would like. She'd mentioned these were her favorite caramel apples, and here they were ready to be purchased. There were four different kinds. Troy didn't know which one to pick, so he bought one of each.

Troy and Hailey met halfway down Main Street, outside of

the Red Oaks Library. Businesses were closing for the evening. He crossed the street toward her.

Hailey began laughing. "I think I just got the most random donation yet," she said.

"More random than the forty-inch Styrofoam balls from yesterday?" he asked as they walked toward where his car had been parked since lunch.

Hailey could barely contain her giggles. "Brace yourself. We are now the proud caretakers of 144 origami swans."

Troy joined in the laughter. "Swans?"

Hailey sucked in both of her lips, trying to hold in her laughter, but it didn't work. "Yes. The woman in the small paper shop was absolutely serious that this was her donation this year."

"I wonder how long those take to fold?"

"No idea," Hailey said. "I also have no idea what we're supposed to do with them."

"I'm sure you'll think of something—put them on a lake or something." He grinned at her.

She bumped into his arm. "Ha ha. I don't think this has ever been donated before. What would my aunt do with this kind of donation?"

"Maybe it's a representation of one of the days of Christmas —Seven swans a swimming," Troy suggested.

Hailey nodded. "But that still doesn't give us a clue as to what to do with them. Some things won't be ready until the end of November for pick-up, but a lot of them are ready whenever we want to take possession of them."

Troy nodded. "From the sounds of it, most people expect pick-up relatively soon, so that's exciting."

"Maybe we could decorate a tree with them," Hailey said.

"I like that." They were almost to his car when Troy said, "So, would you like to go out for dinner?"

She tilted her head at him, but before she could respond, he added, "To continue talking about the festival, of course."

She smiled. "Sure, that sounds good. We have a lot to discuss."

He opened her door, giving himself the extra moment as he walked back to the driver's side door to compose himself, wishing he would have just asked her out on a date. Would that have been too forward? He didn't want to make their time working together awkward. He swallowed, then got in the car, and started the ignition. Less than a mile away was a small cafe he'd looked up. The place had great reviews. "What about this place?" he asked her.

She smiled. "It's one of the favorites in the town. Good choice."

They were seated quickly, and Hailey ordered without looking at the menu. The waitress wrote down her order, then turned to Troy. Hailey knew everything about the town and ordered the complicated specials just the way she wanted them. He ordered his food, and then they both took turns sharing what each business planned to donate. Troy produced the Red Oaks Sweets paper with the delineated donation on it. Pick-up for that would be a day before the event, to ensure the freshest chocolates and candies.

"You won on the most interesting donation with the origami swans," Troy conceded.

"Thank you," Hailey said. "That's exactly what I was going for. I definitely wanted to win today." She laughed.

"However, I got the sweetest deal today, with the candy company," he said.

She rolled her eyes. "Next time, I'm taking the side of the street with the sweets. Did they give you samples?"

He nodded. "She wouldn't let me out of the store without trying a couple."

"Figures," she said. "You get edible donations, and I get paper." She laughed. Then her eyes widened. "Wait, was that whole bag you were carrying all samples? You have to share."

Troy grinned. "They gave me a few samples for you. But the rest is for dessert tonight. I bought some of Lester's Caramel Apples for us."

"For us? Thanks. You won't be disappointed. They're so good."

"That's what you said when Lester was talking about it."

She smiled. "You remembered."

He nodded. "I didn't know what kind you wanted, so I bought one of each."

"They're the most delicious caramel apples I've ever had," she said.

Hailey looked at the list they'd compiled in her small notebook. "This is a great start, it really is, but there is still a lot more work ahead. It's doable, of course, just a lot of work."

"Should we scale the festival back this year? I'm sure the town would understand. Maybe Edna would like the change."

She looked at him as if he were crazy, then shook her head. "That's exactly what we can't do." She looked at the pieces of paper in front of them—a representation of everyone who'd helped. "My aunt was the glue to this entire project. But Edna was wrong. The Forest Festival can live on, even in my aunt isn't here." Her eyes glistened momentarily but after a blink it was gone. "The town cares about this. The letters are proof of that. So are these donations."

Their food came and they began eating. The small cafe was crowded. The red shaded light hanging directly over their table seemed to make the small cafe cozier. Troy's heart swelled for this woman that he'd only come to know over the last couple of days. She was passionate about the Forest Festival, and perhaps it was exactly what she needed. He wanted to figure out a way to raise some capital, and quickly. "Maybe I should go into the City and talk to some people there. I know some investors, and they might be able to help."

Hope gleamed in her eyes. "I'm sure going into the City isn't necessary. You've already done a lot to help this. Unless you need to head into the City for work?"

He tipped his head, wondering if she was trying to figure something out about him with her comment. "I have a lot of vacation stored up. In fact, if needed, I could take the rest of the year off and still have more vacation than I know what to do with."

"How nice that you can take off from work so easily," she said.

He nodded, wanting to change the subject away from his work. He looked out the window of the small cafe, his gaze settling on a family. A small boy rode on the dad's shoulders, and the mom pushed a stroller with two more children. Another taller boy walked next to them. Rarely was that a picture he'd see in the City. He looked back at the beautiful brunette in front of him. "What about you? You took off quickly from what I can tell. Won't work miss you?"

"I own my own company," she said proudly. "I will have to fly back to Seattle in about two weeks to take care of a few events, but other than that, I have great assistants and employees that do an amazing job. I doubt I'll be missed too much."

He covered her hand that rested on the table with his own. "You might be missed at work, but Red Oaks is happy you're here." And he was happy she was here too.

TROY HADN'T THOUGHT ABOUT THE LOGISTICS OF EATING caramel apples when he'd bought them, not really. He'd imagined that they could be eaten straight from the stick, but Hailey had vetoed that idea. Instead they went back to her aunt's house to enjoy their dessert. Troy cut the apples away from the stick that went through the core, while Hailey made hot chocolate on the stove.

"Hot chocolate is my favorite drink to go with caramel apples," Hailey said. "It sounds like a sweetness overload, but I use a darker chocolate, and the flavors balance out nicely." She poured hot chocolate into matching Santa Claus mugs and handed him one. He carried the plate of caramel apples and followed Hailey to where she sat on the couch in front of the picture window.

"Drinking hot chocolate reminds me of sledding as a kid. My dad always brought a thermos full of hot chocolate. He'd leave it in the car, and we'd come back after being on the hill and warm up. That's when it always tasted the best," Troy said.

"Where did you grow up?" she asked.

"Colorado," he said.

Hailey smiled. "I'd always pick a Christmas book and sit as close as I could to the fireplace. Sometimes the hot chocolate would get cold before I remembered to drink it when I was in the middle of a good book."

They drank their hot chocolate swapping memories of Christmas and holiday traditions. When they were finished with their mugs, Hailey took them into the kitchen and rinsed them out. "Would you like a tour of the house?" she asked.

He nodded, following her around the Victorian mansion. She told stories about each room, relating childhood memories, and sharing about the renovations the house had seen. She touched every surface and chair rail with such care and love. Everything seemed to mean more to her, and the way she talked about playing in the different rooms held something tangible that he couldn't quite articulate. It was like she understood the house and its structure, but also its place in history. "You love this place, don't you?" he asked.

She nodded. "It holds a lot of memories for me. Memories that I don't quite remember until a smell reminds me of a room, or the floorboard squeaks just like it did when I was hiding during a game of hide and seek."

"Is it … hard … to be back?"

"I suppose in some ways it is. I'm trying to gain the closure I need. It's good to have the Festival to focus on."

The more time he spent with Hailey, the more he agreed. It was nice to work together with her on the Festival. This week had gone by so fast, and he was looking forward to getting to know her better.

CHAPTER 5

On Friday morning, Hailey sat next to Troy in Edna's new office. The small building on Center Street was clean and bright. Windows graced almost every wall, which gave a view to both the outside and the inside of the building. Hailey tried not to think how much money was used to create the building—money that could have gone to the Forest Festival or another charitable event. Hailey shook the ungenerous thought away. The old building the foundation was in before did not meet the standard building code, and a leak in the roof had revealed just how much chemicals had been stored in the walls. It was a health hazard, so wrecking the old building and creating a new one made sense.

Hailey had typed up the list of all the donations she and Troy had managed to secure over the last week. It was three pages long.

Edna finished on her phone call and then looked up to both of them. "How did the week go?" she asked.

Hailey forced her fingers to loosen the grip on the papers so that they wouldn't wrinkle. "It went really well," she said, placing the list on Edna's desk, hoping she sounded confident, but not over-confident. "I can't tell you how excited we are to put on the Forest Festival this year," Hailey added.

"We?" Edna asked. "The two of you then?"

Hailey looked to Troy. Perhaps she shouldn't have used the word "we" to Edna. She should have asked him first. There was a part of her that hoped he'd stay involved in this project. This past week had been … fun with him. But another piece of her knew that if he didn't stay, she could do this herself. Her aunt had done it, so she could do it. She just needed Edna's stamp of approval, and a promise that the foundation would take care of their usual advertising for the event.

"I'll be here," Troy said, not breaking eye contact with Edna.

Hailey released the breath she didn't know she'd been holding. Things were falling into place. Troy didn't have to stay, and yet he chose to. This was her dream she wanted to fulfill, but Troy was offering to help. Giddiness ran through her. She hadn't realized just how much she'd hoped he would stay until this moment. The thought of not having his company during the rest of the preparations had weighed on her more than she wanted to admit. They'd grown close over the last week.

"This is a good start," Edna said slowly. "Unfortunately, it's not enough." She slid the paper back toward Hailey.

"We've only been working on this for a week," Hailey said.

Edna nodded. "But the Festival is now in seven weeks. I know this is something you've put your heart into, but most of these are places that donate regardless. There's nothing new that's substantial enough to get this running. I'm sorry. We're finally in the black as a foundation, and we need to keep it that way to close out our fiscal year, or we lose our endowments that have been granted to us."

Hailey felt like she'd been punched in the gut, the wind knocked out of her. They'd worked hard, spending every business hour soliciting all of the local businesses, trying to make this work. Troy had been a good sport about it, but this was his vacation time he'd used, and for what? All for nothing. Her heart sank. She closed her eyes, wishing there was some way she could get a Christmas miracle right about now.

Was that even possible in a month that wasn't December? She opened her mouth to speak, but no words came out. Suddenly, warmth filled her. She looked down at where her left hand had gripped the armrest of the chair so hard it was turning white. She could barely see the whiteness underneath Troy's hand that covered hers. She relaxed her grip on the armrest, and Troy kept his hand firmly on hers. She was about to thank Edna for her time when Troy spoke up first.

"It's obvious that this foundation is in the best of hands with you as the President." He gave Edna a smile that practically sparkled. "You're able to make tough decisions when it comes to time and resources, and that's no small thing."

Hailey blinked. What was Troy up to?

The beginnings of a smile started at the corners of Edna's mouth. "Well, thank you," Edna said, her voice breathier than before. Was that a blush under her makeup?

Troy continued to smile. "Of course, you understand that this is only our local *in-kind donations*," he said. His voice was authoritative, commanding the room like there were hundreds of people there, even though there was just the three of them. "So far we've raised $10,000 in cash."

Edna's eyes widened at the dollar amount Troy had thrown around and so did Hailey's. No business had given them money, and none of the single donations were anywhere close to that figure.

Edna put a hand to her heart, playing with her necklace. "$10,000 is certainly a lot for this event," she said. "It won't get you everything. The building fee alone—"

"What if the foundation could get the events center venue donated?" Troy asked. "Would that be possible? I'm sure it would help publicity for you." Another winning smile from Troy, his eyes practically dancing.

Edna smoothed down her hair, smiling widely. "I must say I'm impressed with you—with both of you. $10,000 is enough for me to approve this project, though I expect you'll have more donations coming?"

Troy nodded. "You can count on that, as long as the Forest Festival is on the calendar and advertising can start right away."

Hailey felt like she was watching a ping pong match the way her gaze bounced from Troy to Edna's as they discussed the particulars.

"Advertising will start next week. The foundation will cover the venue and the publicity. And you're welcome to use any of the foundation's Christmas decorations. They are in the back storage."

Hailey tilted her head, surprised by Edna's sudden generosity. "I thought I already went through all of the Christmas decorations the foundation owns."

Edna shook her head. "You went through everything that

was personally owned by your aunt. In good conscience I couldn't absorb her stuff without you seeing it first."

Hailey nodded. That seemed fair. "So there's more decorations?"

"Much more," Edna assured her. "I can't offer you much help in the way of resources on staff for the actual night, but you're welcome to ask individuals and see if they're willing to volunteer."

"Thank you so much for your help, Edna. It's clear that this foundation wouldn't be the same without you," Troy said. "We're looking forward to making sure that this year's Forest Festival is the most memorable you've ever had."

Edna raised both eyebrows, then smoothed her hair down again. "That's a tall order, but either way, I'm sure it will be a wonderful event."

"Thank you," Hailey said to Edna.

"If you're available tonight for the Red Oaks Carnival, it might be a good time to announce to the public that the Forest Festival is happening."

Hailey looked at Troy, wondering if he'd planned on going back to the City for the weekend. Either way, she'd be here. "I'll be here."

"Me too," Troy said.

"I'll let John know that you'd like a few minutes to share the announcement."

"Thanks," Hailey said, and then they were dismissed. She wasn't sure how it happened but she and Troy left Edna's office and her hand was still attached to his. She savored the touch of her hand in his for a moment before she pulled away, reality of what he'd done setting into her. "How could you—" She couldn't get the right words out. He'd promised Edna they'd raised $10,000 with more to come. That wasn't even possible. Not this weekend, not next. They'd gone to almost every single business in just under a week, and none of them made monetary contributions in that size.

Troy looked at her for a moment, awkwardness crossing his features. "Uh, sorry. I didn't mean to hold your hand—I just wanted to let you know I was here for you." He shook his head.

Heat raced into Hailey's face. "Not that. That was actually sweet of you." Hailey shook her head as they walked out the front doors. They didn't have $10,000, not anywhere close to that figure.

He raised an eyebrow. "Now I'm confused."

He opened the car door for her. She sat in the passenger seat, moving the dials for her seat heater.

Troy came around to the driver's side and slid into the car. He seemed completely unaffected by the lie.

"$10,000. Troy. Edna only agreed because of the $10,000 and you turning Mr. Charming on her!"

Troy's features relaxed, grinning. "You think I'm charming?"

"What? No! You're missing the point!"

He faced her, that charming smile filling his whole face and making her melt inside. "No, I'm paying very close attention."

"Stop! Be serious! I'm not going to lie to put on the Forest Festival. I can't do it. We need to go and tell Edna that our paper list is accurate. That has to be enough to get us the approval and support, or we can't do it." She unbuckled her seatbelt, wanting to go and solve this problem right now.

A smile tugged at the corner of his mouth as he moved the

car into reverse and headed out of the parking lot. "We won't tell Edna any such thing. I have the money."

Hailey wasn't sure what to think. When he'd brought up the idea of going back to the City to get sponsors, she'd assumed that they'd be able to get what they needed from the town, and so a trip into the City seemed like a long drive for something that wasn't needed. How had he raised that much money?

"When did you have time to get that much for a donation?" Her mind reeled. They'd spent their days talking to businesses. They'd spent their evenings strategizing and flirting a little. It was a pleasant surprise that he'd secured such a big donation, but she was still confused by the timing.

He stopped at the traffic light when it turned red and looked at her. His eyes seemed to be searching hers, before he finally said, "I didn't find any time for it. It's my personal donation to the Forest Festival."

"It's yours?" She blinked, her heart speeding up by the revelation. She'd thought to donate to the Forest Festival, but all of her liquid cash had been tied up in expanding her own business. She thought through some of her investments. She'd already given her aunt's money to the cause. Maybe once the expansion took off, she'd be in a place to pull extra money out. "I can pay you back."

Pain flashed across his face, but he smoothed it out. "If you did that, it wouldn't be a donation. I don't want you to pay me back. I want to help."

"But that's so much—"

He cut her off, not allowing her to finish the sentence. "It's the least I can do." He winced, looking at her with piercing eyes that took her breath away. "I wish I could do more. I want to do more … I just can't." He ran a hand across his face, looking like he'd say more.

"It's enough though," she said quietly. She put a hand on his shoulder, gratitude swelling inside of her at his generous donation. It felt like he'd personally given her a Christmas miracle. Like this whole event would be possible because of him. Solely because of him. "Thank you," she said, wishing she could properly explain her feelings that those two words couldn't quite convey.

He nodded. Multiple car horns honked, and Troy looked in the rear-view mirror. "And that means we have a green light," he said, laughing when he drove through the intersection.

A green light. Exactly. That's what this moment felt like. "You don't have to stay though," she said. "I mean, you've already done so much, taking a full week off of work, and now donating more than all of the other donations we've been able to get."

He pulled into the cafe's parking lot and parked the car. "Are you kidding, I'm not going anywhere. You admitted you think I'm charming and now I must know what else you think in that beautiful mind of yours."

"Beautiful?"

He nodded. "Beautiful."

"But using up all of your vacation—"

"Don't worry about my vacation time. I use it when I want to, and how I want to. And you're not going to convince me that this is a waste of my vacation time."

"Now who's telling secrets." Her heart still erratic from his compliment.

He smiled at her.

"Are you sure?" She didn't want him to feel obligated.

He took her hand in both of his. "I'm 10,000 dollars sure."

She nodded, realizing that even with Edna's close friendship with her aunt, there was no way that Hailey would have received the green light to proceed on this event without him. "I'd really like your help on this project," she admitted. "I couldn't have gotten this far without you."

He smiled. "I have a feeling you would have figured out a way."

She shook her head. "Nope, you're the person I can't live without right now." Heat raced through her cheeks as she replayed the sentence in her head.

Troy laughed. "Then I'm doubly glad to be here," he said. He got out of the car, opened her door for her, and extended a hand to help her out. Her hand stayed in his as they walked into the cafe for lunch.

Once they ordered their food, Troy sat back in the booth. "Tell me about this carnival tonight. What's it like?"

"What's it like?" Hailey repeated his question. Hailey thought of the times growing up where she'd attended. Every tradition in Red Oaks brought back a flood of memories. "It's the official start to winter. It's the last outdoor event the town puts on before it snows. It's cozy and builds the community. The whole town comes out for it, even in the bitter cold. It's just … magical."

"It sounds magical," he said.

"When I was younger, I went with my family. We lived several hours away, but we always made the weekend trips in for aunt Helena. As I got older, I mostly hung out with friends or a boyfriend during the events." Her aunt, in addition to running the Forest Festival, had been on several committees and volunteered in multiple ways for the different events. It was one of the reasons Hailey had become an event planner. It had always looked so glamorous in her mind. Now with a thriving event planning business, she knew it wasn't all glamor, but it was still what she was passionate about. "It's a great evening and makes for a great family event or even a great date night."

"It sounds like I need one then," he said.

She tilted her head, confused. "Need what?"

"A date."

"Oh." A wash of giddiness spread over her. "You'd think a Boy Scout would be more prepared than that." She grinned at him.

"Will you be my date for the evening?" he asked.

She lifted one shoulder around. "Sure, I could show you around."

He smiled. "That's not quite what I meant."

Thoughts fumbled inside her head. "Okay."

"Okay, you'll be my date?"

She nodded. "I'd love to."

CHAPTER 6

Troy picked Hailey up, and they headed to the Red Oaks Carnival on Main Street. For the town being small, the entire area was packed. They weaved through the crowds, working their way to the center where apple bobbing and pie eating contests were already in full swing.

"This is the Carnival," she said.

"It's a happening place," he said. They bought food and walked around. He kept hold of her hand as they navigated through the crowds, not letting go when the crowd dispersed.

A man in a white and orange striped barbershop suit with a matching straw hat called to them. "Take your turn at the darts and win a prize."

"Friendly competition?" Hailey asked.

"You're on," Troy said, giving a few of their brightly colored tickets to the man. They were each given three darts.

Hailey threw the first one and it popped a green balloon. The man took the paper from where the popped balloon had been and handed it to Hailey. "You can redeem this at the prize counter," he said, smiling at her.

Troy's first dart bounced off a balloon.

Hailey smiled, leaning against the counter next to Troy. "Looks like I'm winning so far in our friendly competition."

Troy laughed, knowing it was just a game, but still wanting to do his best. "Round one goes to you," he conceded. "Your turn."

Hailey's next two darts hit their mark, and only one of Troy's popped a balloon. Troy shook his head. "Darts are apparently not my thing today," he said.

"You're a good sport about it," Hailey said, doing a victory dance. "I could give you a few pointers." She pointed to the sharp part of the dart, laughing at her own joke.

Troy gave another set of tickets, and they were each handed three more darts. "Okay, I'm ready for my lesson, oh wise teacher."

Hailey laughed. "I do know the secret." She stepped aside. "You can go first."

"So your pointers?"

Hailey smiled. "The pointy end goes into the balloon. They pop better that way." She bumped into his shoulder, and he nudged her back.

Troy chuckled and shook his head. "You're so helpful," he said, and threw a dart harder than he had the last round. A yellow balloon popped and the man in the striped suit handed him a paper with his prize code on it.

"Look at that. I'm an excellent teacher." She wiped a pretend tear from her eye. "I'm so proud." She gave him an exaggerated hug, and his arms instinctively wrapped around her. The moment didn't last long, but everything about the hug felt electrified.

She threw her dart, popping another balloon. She stepped away with a smug smile on her lips.

Troy popped two more balloons. "I really can't believe that your strategy made a difference." Or that he'd been able to focus on throwing darts when his brain was still wrapped up replaying the simple hug.

"Aiming. It's essential in carnival games," Hailey said.

They cashed in their prize codes for little stuffed animals and a plastic snake. "Want to do something even more fun?" she asked.

Troy nodded. "What did you have in mind? Don't tell me you're a ring toss expert too."

"Let's find some kids to give these prizes to," she said. She walked up to a picnic table where a family was eating dinner. She gave one toy to each of the three children sitting there, after asking their parents' permission.

Troy followed suit, heading to the next table.

They met back on the other end of the tables, his hand finding hers again, now that they'd distributed their prizes. "You're right, that was a lot of fun." He was struck by Hailey's generosity and observation of others around her. She was thoughtful and sweet.

John came up to them. "Are you ready to make your announcement, Hailey? Red Oaks will be so excited to hear that the Forest Festival will be held this year."

Hailey nodded. "I'll be right back."

Troy nodded, and then looked at his phone when it rang. "It's work," he said. "I better take this."

"I'll meet you after my announcement."

He picked it up, wondering what the after-hours emergency was. "Hi Cara. What fire can I help you put out tonight?"

She laughed. "That's actually my line. And no, nothing is urgent, but Kyle left a message for you. I'm not sure why it didn't go to your cell phone first though."

"Patch him through next time. I bet he wants you to know that I'm supposed to report every week."

"Will do, boss. How are things in Red Oaks?" Cara asked.

Troy thought of all the time that he'd spent with Hailey. They'd laughed together and worked hard over the last week. "It's been refreshing."

"The cool clear air will do that to you. You can breathe deeper outside of the City," Cara said wistfully.

Troy had definitely not been thinking of the air quality. Hailey was more the breath of fresh air. He'd never known anyone quite like her. Her passion and determination to see her aunt's legacy live on in the small town was endearing. "Cara, I'm going to spend the next little while out here," he said.

"Can you define 'the next little while' for me with something that I can pinpoint on a calendar?"

"I plan to stay here until the Forest Festival is completed." Maybe longer, he thought, though he didn't voice it. It was a passing thought, especially since it was silly. After all, Hailey wouldn't be here after the Forest Festival was finished either.

"I'll make sure everything you need will be accessible by email, and I'll reschedule the meetings you have next week with the Board of Directors."

"Thanks, Cara. You're the best."

"Enjoy Red Oaks, Troy."

Troy hung up with his assistant, and then called Kyle, ready for his weekly report. Earlier today he'd assumed he was going to have to bail on the whole idea entirely, and start from scratch, but with his last-minute decision to let Hailey know he was going to donate, it felt like everything was on track.

"Troy. You're the first one to call in this week. How did it go?" Kyle asked.

"It went really well," Troy said, thinking through all of the moments he'd had with Hailey from the first day he met her until now when they'd worked so hard to get the donations together. It had been an exhausting but fulfilling week.

"That's good to hear. I want more details, but let me grab Kandice and get her on the phone too. She's going to judge this little contest, so I want her to be up on all of the details so she hears everything first-hand. Is that okay with you?"

"Sounds good," Troy said, suddenly feeling like he was in the hot seat and that he should have something grandiose to announce. A moment later, Kyle's wife, Kandice, said, "I'm here. Hi Troy."

"Hi Kandice," he said, walking away from the crowds to be able to hear them better. He wandered toward the parking lot.

"Okay, let's get started," Kyle said.

"Tell us about your week," Kandice said. "Have you picked a charity to work with?"

"I did," Troy said, then proceeded to tell them all about the Forest Festival event, and meeting Hailey. He gave details about their plans, and how they'd spent the week gathering donations to prove to Edna they were serious. It was a lot to download to Kyle and Kandice. When he finished there was a pause.

Finally, Kandice asked, "Have you told Hailey about why you're doing this? Was she curious?"

"She asked me about it, especially because she was concerned about my vacation time. I didn't tell her about the contest."

"It's for the best," Kyle said. "Your assistant knows, so you can have help balancing work. Don't feel like you have to delegate all of your regular work from now until mid-December. It's not required. If you need to commute or go in for meetings, that's fine."

He understood Kyle's words, but he wasn't sure how that would work. He wanted to be involved with this project and see it finished. "Like we said on the yacht, we all have plenty of vacation. I'll make sure I'm not neglecting my business, but right now I'm okay on that front."

"Have you spent any of your own money yet for the Forest Festival?" Kandice asked. "I'm going to keep track."

Troy cleared his throat. "None of it has been spent, but I told Edna that there was a $10,000 donation made to the Forest Festival. Hailey pressed me on it, because nobody around here gave that kind of cash donation, and I told her I was donating it. But we haven't done anything with it yet."

"I see," Kyle said. "What do you think, Kandice?"

"It sounds like it's within the limits of the rules. Remember it can't just be donated to the cause, it needs to be used for something," Kandice said.

"I understand," Troy said.

"Tell us more about the donations you've received," Kyle said.

Troy told them about the in-kind donations, mentioning a

few that stood out to him as the most unique. "While you're keeping track of the giving and donating side, I'll send you a copy of the donations we've received so far. Roughly half of what was donated was from my efforts, but they were on a list from previous donors, so I wouldn't say they count toward what I've helped with. We were just making sure that the list we had was accurate."

"I look forward to seeing the list," Kandice said. "Nice work this week. It seems like you're well on your way with this challenge."

"Thanks," Troy said, feeling like her praise meant something to him. He wanted to do well. He wanted to win, and so far he was on the right track.

"Check in again next week and let us know how things are going," Kyle said. "The Forest Festival is lucky to have you helping them."

"That's what Hailey said. She's convinced that the festival wouldn't be happening without my pledge of a donation. Edna had all but turned us down before I mentioned the money."

"Really?" Kandice said. "That's an interesting point. I'm glad for her sake and the festival's that you brought it up. Just be careful with throwing money around."

Troy wanted to say that it was only ten thousand, but as fellow billionaires, they understood that. "Not throwing around money might be the hardest thing of this whole situation. They could really use it, and I have it. I could really make a difference."

"You're already making a difference," Kyle said. "Stick with the rules."

"I'm doing my best," Troy said.

“That’s all we expect,” Kandice said. “Good luck this week.”

“Thanks,” Troy said, and then they said their goodbyes. Troy wondered how Hunter and Scott were doing on their first week. He wanted to know if each of them had found what they wanted to work on. He knew he could call them up at any hour of the day or night, but for the next seven weeks they weren’t supposed to talk about their individual projects. Troy wasn’t sure if that made the competition feel easier or harder. He wanted to compare himself to their progress, but that was probably the exact reason the rule was in place.

Troy headed back to the stage where he found Hailey. “It’s time to try the ring toss,” she said, laughing.

Troy nodded. “You’re in charge,” he said.

CHAPTER 7

Hailey looked around the shared office Edna had given her and Troy to work at during the duration of their time in Red Oaks. Saturday morning around the foundation was a quieter day. Hailey wasn't sure how much time they'd use the office, but it was nice to know they had a place to work if they needed.

Edna had suggested they look through the Christmas decoration storage to see what they could repurpose, and know what they wanted to use, before the foundation building started decorating with it. It was the second weekend in a row of going through Christmas decorations, but somehow with Troy by her side it didn't feel as daunting. It also wouldn't hold the specific personal triggers that going through her aunt's things had caused her.

A calendar reminder of today's event that her company, Perfectly Planned Parties and Events, was in charge of popped up on her phone. It was Mr. Tingey's retirement party. She called her assistant, wanting to make sure that everything was set for the day.

"Hi, Hailey." Janelle's voice was perky, even with the time difference.

"Hi, Janelle. How are things going today?"

Her assistant laughed. "They're going well. I'm sure you're wondering about the retirement party today, and not about my amazing date last night, so hold on because I have a lot to download before I need to get back to my post in ten minutes."

Hailey sat down. "I'm ready for the details."

"Okay. There were two fires yesterday. One was an actual fire in the kitchen."

"Oh no," Hailey said. "Is everyone okay?"

"Yeah. The whole building was evacuated, but as it turned out it was a water leak from the floor above. Water filled the heated stove through the overhead vent and that caused the steam to set off the alarm. It was kind of nuts. Anyway, everything is fine now, except that the oven is out of commission. I'm pretty sure we'll have a replacement in the next hour, so we should be good there. Decorations arrived in plenty of time that we weren't scrambling, and …" She continued talking and Hailey took notes, realizing just how capable her assistant was. It was so nice to be able to delegate things and know that everything was being handled—even the fires.

Troy knocked on the door while Janelle talked about the cake fillings and the last-minute change from mint to cherry. Hailey pointed to the phone, and gave a shrug of her shoulder, mouthing the word "sorry" to Troy. He nodded, and pointed down the hallway. He'd start going through things without her. She nodded, mouthing "thank you," and continued listening.

As Troy headed toward the storage closet Hailey almost told Janelle that she'd catch up with her later.

She wanted to talk with Troy. Their impromptu date last night at the Carnival had been a lot of fun. Tingles spread through her fingers from when he'd held her hand. Maybe it was just a necessity to navigate the crowd, but then they'd ended up holding hands for the better part of the evening, and she hadn't minded.

Hailey ended the phone call, after Janelle assured her that things were running smoothly. Janelle promised to call again if there was anything more to report about the day. Hailey was grateful for such a competent employee. It made being away from her job a little easier.

She straightened the few folders on the desk and then headed out of the office to find Troy. A smile held onto her lips as she practically skipped toward the main hallway where Troy had gone only a few minutes earlier.

A woman sat at the reception desk, talking to a man. The receptionist pointed toward Hailey, and the man turned around, looking in Hailey's direction. Her smile immediately fell. What was Paul doing here?

Paul smiled at her, walking fast toward her and giving her a huge hug. Hailey stiffened as his arms wrapped around her. Troy wrapping his arms around her last night immediately filled her mind. Where Troy's had been tender, Paul's hug felt crushing. "I've missed you, Hai," he said, reverting to the pet name he'd used when they'd dated years ago.

She cleared her throat, awkwardly stepping away from his hug.

He let go of her but reluctance was written on his face.

She kept her face and her tone neutral. "What are you doing here? I thought you lived up in Silverwood now." Him living next to the ski resort was precisely why she'd avoided the area over the last couple of winters when she'd been in Red Oaks. Chance encounters were not her thing.

His wide smile grew, if that were possible. "You remembered. Yeah, I've been up there for the last couple of years. With my money from my inheritance I bought a chateau that overlooks the ski resort. It's amazing. You'll have to come and see it."

She ignored the invitation, and went back to her original question. "So what brings you into Red Oaks?" There was no way that this was a coincidence. He was happy to leave his small-town roots, and made that very clear. Hailey, too, had never planned on living here, but it wasn't because she didn't love the town. She still loved the charm and the close-knit feel of the place. It had always been great for a visit with her aunt. But Paul had never embraced Red Oaks.

"You do, of course." His eyes searched hers. "I knew you coming back was a sign. A buddy of mine attended that little shindig the town put on last night and said you were up on the stage making an announcement."

"I'm helping with the Forest Festival this year," Hailey said, knowing that if he'd been filled in on the announcement then he already knew as much, especially if he was trying to track her down at the foundation.

He gave her a lopsided grin. "I remember kissing you next to several of the trees during one of the Forest Festivals."

She rolled her eyes. "That was a long time ago. We broke up. I'm still not sure why you're here."

He stepped closer to her and she took another step back. "I want to rekindle things with you. We'd be great together."

"I'm not interested," she said flatly.

"You will be when you know how much my inheritance was." He smiled like that mattered to her. It didn't.

She pursed her lips. "Paul, I'm not—"

Paul interrupted, running over her words. "My buddy says you guys are hurting for donations. I have my inheritance you know. It's five million. My investors say with their expertise I won't have to work ever again. They're taking care of the details. I just spend money when I want to spend money. I could donate to your Forest Festival, if you wanted me to."

She sighed. "Of course you're welcome to donate. We're grateful for all of the help we can get."

"How about $2,000?"

"That's nice of you, Paul. Thank you."

Paul shrugged. "I'm not going to donate without getting something for it. That makes no sense. I want to spend time with you."

"You're trying to bribe me to go out with you? No." She couldn't believe what she was hearing. He sounded like the same Paul she'd grown up with. The same one she'd dumped years ago. Nothing had changed, except that he thought he could buy his way into people's lives and hearts. She wouldn't fall for that. Not again.

He lifted one shoulder. "Think of it as an exchange. Come

have dinner with me at my chateau, and I'll donate $2,000 to your cause."

Hailey blanched at the idea. She couldn't help comparing Paul and Troy again. She didn't know Troy well, but Troy had been willing to donate for the Forest Festival because he'd believed in the cause, not because he was trying to get something out of it. And he hadn't made any stipulations on giving the money. It had never felt like an exchange or a bribe. "No. Paul, I'm sorry, but—"

He pushed a finger to her lips, stopping her sentence. She backed up again, running out of room to keep her personal space personal. "Don't answer now. The offer is still on the table. I want to date you, Hailey. I know you're probably not in town too long, but I'd like to make the most of the time we have together."

Before Hailey could answer, Troy came down the hallway. "Hailey, look what I found. Do you think we can use it?" He laughed, then stopped, looking between Paul and Hailey.

Hailey's eyes stayed connected with Troy. "What did you find?" Her voice felt wobbly.

Troy held up a huge mistletoe, and Hailey found her opening, she just hoped Troy would forgive her for it.

CHAPTER 8

Troy looked between Hailey and the guy she'd been talking to. He'd seen them talking together as he'd walked down the long corridor. They obviously knew each other.

Hailey turned toward him, and mouthed the word, "help," a few seconds before he reached them. "You found a mistletoe?!" Her words sounded unnaturally loud and high. She started laughing and then looped her arm through his, snuggling close to his side. "Oh, Troy, that's going to be perfect." She pulled him forward toward the man she'd been talking to.

"Who's this?" the guy asked, his features darkening.

"Paul, this is Troy. Troy, Paul. Paul is my ex-boyfriend. We grew up together."

"I don't live here anymore though," Paul said, a smug look on his face. "I live in Silverwood, by the ski resort in a custom-built chateau. I'm Paul Jones the Third."

Troy bit the inside of his cheek to hold in his laugh. This guy was definitely putting on airs. "How nice for you," Troy responded.

"And who are you?" Paul asked holding out his hand.

"Troy Rasmussen," Troy said automatically, as he shook Paul's hand more firmly. Paul tried to tighten his grip, but Troy squeezed first, keeping eye contact with the guy.

"And …" Paul said.

"Oh, you want a title. Right. I'm the man Hailey can't live without." Troy released the handshake, satisfied when Paul shook out his hand once it was down at his side.

"Is that right?" Paul asked.

Hailey moved closer to Troy, and Troy put his arm around her shoulders. She leaned into him. "That's right," she answered. She took the mistletoe from Troy's hand. "Nice work on finding this, honey. I'm sure we can put it to good use, even if we don't use it as a decoration for the Festival."

She looked him in the eye, trying to communicate something, but Troy wasn't exactly sure what. All he knew was she'd asked for his help when she'd walked toward him, and he wasn't going to let her down. He liked her too much for that.

He took her hand with the mistletoe in it and lifted them both in the air, then gave her a quick kiss. The touch was almost too light for him to enjoy, but he knew that she was trying to get rid of this guy, so it was the least he could do. But when their lips collided, he wished he was kissing her for real, and not just to get rid of her ex. He'd thought of kissing her all week long. They'd spent the better part of every day together, planning and laughing and talking.

This was not how he'd seen their first kiss going, at all. He savored the few seconds he could and forced himself to pretend that it was the most natural thing in the world to steal a kiss from the woman who couldn't live without him. If they were really dating, really in love, not just trying to get rid of an old ex, a little peck wouldn't have phased him. But his head was spinning. She opened her eyes slowly, a smile never leaving those beautifully kissable lips. Finally he said, "Agreed. This decoration definitely works."

Paul rolled his eyes and turned to go. Then he stopped, pivoting around. "I'm confused. Why didn't you say you were seeing someone earlier?"

Troy looked between the two of them, knowing that there was no way he could answer Paul's question.

Hailey's grip on Troy's arm tightened just slightly. "I told you I wasn't interested, Paul. You're the one who made your donation conditional on me going out with you. I never agreed to that."

"Hmph. Maybe next time I'll offer $3,000. I bet you would have had dinner with me for $3,000."

Hailey made a noise in the back of her throat.

Could Hailey be so easily bought? Warning bells went off in Troy's head.

"You're wrong," Hailey said. "I don't want your money. I don't need your money. We've already had very generous donations by people." She looked directly at Troy, and Troy hoped with everything in him that she didn't bring up the dollar amount he'd given. He didn't want the attention, especially not for this project. She looked back to Paul. "Some people choose to give because they have good hearts, and because they care about the cause without an ulterior motive."

A pit formed in Troy's stomach. He wanted the words Hailey spoke to be true. But the truth was, he never would have found this cause had he not been on the yacht when the competition was decided. He was trying to raise the most money he could for this cause. He did care about the cause, and Hailey, but that wasn't the end-all of his motivations. He mentally smacked himself.

"I just offered you $2,000, and you snub my gift." Paul pointed a finger at Troy. "How much did Troy Rasmussen give to this cause?"

Troy blinked, not wanting to get into this. "Donations are not public knowledge," he said.

At the same time, Hailey said, "Troy gave $10,000 to the Forest Festival. And it was a gift with no strings attached. It had nothing to do with whether or not I'd go out with him."

Troy's eyes widened. The proverbial cat was out of the bag, and likely climbing up the walls leaving scratch marks. Could this get any more awkward?

"So $2,000 isn't good enough for you? I'm a millionaire, but I don't throw around $10,000 for just one thing. But if I did, would that prove something to you? Would it prove I think we should give us another chance?"

Hailey looked between Troy and Paul, and Troy knew that she was trying to reconcile all of it. He couldn't give her the go-ahead with this guy that she obviously had no current feelings for, but the truth was, they weren't together either. Maybe if he hadn't been around, maybe she would have taken the offer.

"It's not about the money, Paul. It's never been about the money." She blew out her breath.

"How about I donate $10,000 if you let me be Santa this year then. That's the least you can do."

Hailey's answer came faster and stronger this time. "No. You're missing the whole point of the Forest Festival, Paul. You can't buy your position. That position is a tradition. It's not something that can be bought."

"I'm already helping her with the role of Santa," Troy said, hoping that was helpful.

Hailey's eyes widened, but she didn't say anything. He couldn't tell if that was a good thing or not.

Paul glowered. "You're going to have an Outsider be Santa? Someone who doesn't even understand the importance of it. I grew up here. I should have the right to be Santa."

"Paul, you should go now. I've already made up my mind on who will play the part of Santa. We've got a lot to get ready for the Forest Festival. If you'd like to volunteer during the Festival, you're welcome to, but you won't be getting any special treatment."

"I'm rich enough I don't have to donate time anymore," he said, then stormed out of the building.

When Paul was gone, Hailey exhaled, leaning closer into Troy. "I'm so sorry," she said.

"It's okay," he said. "That guy has some nerve."

She looked after where Paul had stormed out. "He wasn't always like that. It's the wealth." She shook her head. "Wealth changes people and usually not for the better."

Troy didn't completely agree with the statement. Not everyone who had money changed for the worse. But that was

Hailey's experience with her ex. She wasn't impressed by her ex's money. In a way it was a positive thing.

Their hands still held onto the mistletoe. "This was exactly what I needed." She blushed. "Thanks for saving me."

"Anytime," he said. And he meant it.

CHAPTER 9

Hailey couldn't stop thinking about Troy's quick kiss for the rest of the day. It was quick thinking on his part to make the whole situation look real. Troy had never said that he was her boyfriend, only repeated the line she'd given him earlier about not being able to live without him. Paul was the one who had inferred that that meant they were more serious.

Yes, they were seeing each other every day, but not in a romantic way. At least not until that kiss. It had been brief. She'd barely been able to enjoy it before the moment had ended. She wanted to repeat it again. She'd felt the sparks between them, the chemistry. It had been fun talking with him all week, but now there was something different. A connection on a deeper level that she wanted to explore.

She took easily twice as long as she needed to in sorting and categorizing all of the Christmas decorations. After they'd seen all of the decorations they'd go to see the events center venue on Monday. It was a natural choice, though Edna had given them the ability to change the venue if they wanted to. As an event planner, Hailey could see the pros and cons to sticking with the same venue, but before changing the location she wanted to know what Troy thought.

"Does that ornament hold a memory?" Troy asked Hailey, breaking her out of her own thoughts.

She looked down at the non-descript snowflake. There was nothing particularly special about it. "No. It's just a snowflake." She put it down in the box, and pulled out something else. "Why do you ask?"

"You were staring at it for about five minutes. I didn't want to interrupt your moment or your memory if it was something special."

"My thoughts were elsewhere," she said, wishing she could tell him what was on her mind.

He only nodded, not pushing her for more information. That wasn't like him. He'd been chatty all week long. Every time they'd been together he'd asked her questions, wanting to know more about Red Oaks and the Forest Festival. Realization that she'd monopolized the conversation all week hit her.

"Tell me more about you," she started, keeping her eyes on the ornaments. All of these boxes could be used. It was just a matter of seeing the events center and creating the decorating plan.

He shrugged. "What do you want to know?"

"What do your holiday traditions look like? I feel like we've mostly just talked about me and the town's traditions."

"I've loved learning about this town, and the Forest Festival, and how many memories you have here. It's … refreshing."

"Do you go home for Christmas?"

He nodded. "Most of the time. Sometimes we celebrate Christmas by going on a family vacation, but typically I go home for Christmas."

"And where is home?" Did he squirm at her question? She wondered about that.

"My parents live in Colorado. That's where I'm originally from."

"That's quite the change from New York City."

He nodded. "Just like Seattle is a different place from Red Oaks."

"Do you like city life?" she asked.

"I do. I like the pace and the bustle. What about you? Do you miss the small-town life?"

"I didn't grow up here, only visited a lot. I'm from Pennsylvania. When I'm here, I always enjoy being here. Seattle doesn't move at the same pace as New York City, but it has its own cadence, and I like it. I've worked for some amazing people. I love the area. I love throwing extravagant events."

"How extravagant?"

Hailey shrugged. "Sometimes when I ask for a budget, I'm told that the sky is the limit and to spare no expense."

"Millionaires?"

Millionaires, like Paul? No way. "More like billionaires."

Troy straightened. "How do you know they're billionaires?"

Hailey tilted her head. "Reputation, mostly. I mean, they typically don't go about bragging about their status or anything."

"Not like Paul?" he asked, his eyes held interest.

Hailey laughed at that. "Paul is only a millionaire, and barely one at that."

"A completely different viewpoint between the two groups then?"

Hailey shrugged. "I guess I haven't thought about it." But yes, there was a huge difference.

"So these lavish parties you coordinate, you like being in that circle?"

Hailey paused, wondering about his sudden interest in her high-end clients. After Paul's childish remarks the way he threw around his money, she did not want to be lumped into a group like that. It didn't matter to her how much money her clients made, she just never thought about it in that way. "My clients are nothing like Paul. I like what I do, and the people that I meet when I'm working. My company focuses on bigger events. Word of mouth travels quickly in small circles, so I make sure that all of my clients have an excellent experience, but it's not like I'm traveling in those circles unless I'm in charge of the event."

"That makes sense." He kept his face neutral, and Hailey wondered what that meant.

She pulled out another decoration. A mistletoe ornament. She laughed, and Troy looked up from the box of wreaths he was going through. "What's so funny?"

"You were earlier." She held up the small mistletoe. "It was really quick thinking of you." She resisted the urge to put her fingers to her warming face at the memory of his kiss. If she tried, she could make it last longer in her head than it lasted in reality.

He gave a single nod. "It looked like you wanted help getting rid of him. With any luck it did the trick."

Hailey twirled the ornament around in her hand. Was it bad to hope that if it didn't work the first time that maybe she'd be able to steal another kiss? "If not, we could always try again," she said playfully.

Troy grinned. "I can have him come back."

"Or not," Hailey said. They could absolutely just try the mistletoe out without her ex watching.

He smiled, but it didn't quite reach his eyes.

This would take all day if they went through each box one by one. Maybe it was just best to say they'd use everything they could, and see what Edna said about that. "Maybe we should call it a day," she said. "All of this stuff is usable. We'll just take anything that Edna is willing to let us use, and we really should look at the venue before we decide how to use everything."

"I'm here to help," he said.

Hailey wondered if there might be a reason for the distance between them since their pretend kiss in front of her ex. She bit her lip as they walked through the storage room door together. She leaned back into the room to turn off the light. "I know you said you had a lot of vacation time, but are you here for the weekends too? I mean, don't you have a girlfriend or someone that you want to go visit?"

It was a shameless way to fish out the information, but she didn't care. She had to know. Paul had jumped to conclusions with the way Troy had talked to him, and the way Troy had kissed her, but without reassurance, she wasn't sure what to think. They'd grown close over the last week, but it seemed like a chill separated them shortly after their kiss, and she couldn't put a finger on why.

Maybe he really had just wanted to help her get out of her awkward moment with Paul. But if Troy had a girlfriend, he could have just as easily put his arm around her to make a similar impression. Why jump to a kiss so soon? And why was her stomach still feeling like it was in a bounce house from the experience? It wasn't even a long kiss. It was just a sweet, tender kiss. And there went her stomach again, bouncing around like it would never stop. Did he feel the sparks between them the way she did? Or did he even notice? She couldn't tell.

He stopped walking, looking at her. "You think I'm the kind of guy who would kiss someone if I already had a girlfriend?"

"No, I just … I'm not sure what to think," she rushed to say the words, not sure that her admission made anything better. But from his question, he also hadn't denied having a girlfriend either.

"I don't have a girlfriend," he said.

"That's good. I mean, that's a relief." She shook her head, willing her stomach to stop bouncing around so she could think straight. "I mean, it's nice to know that you're available to … help with the Forest Festival." She started walking again, this time more quickly toward the outside doors. Anything to get away from this very awkward conversation.

He matched her speed. "I may take a weekend or two and go back to the City. There are a few things I need to get set, for work."

"That makes sense," she said, mentally doing a happy dance that he wasn't attached.

"What about you?" he asked.

"Seattle is much too far away to commute home on the weekends. Besides my assistant is handling things, and she's doing a great job."

"I meant do you have a boyfriend?"

"No."

"I find that hard to believe," he said.

She shrugged. "Believe it or not, being an event planner interferes with my social life."

He raised an eyebrow. "How so?"

"The events I plan, especially for my high-end clients, are all on their time schedule. Holidays, weekends, long weekends. When I'm really busy I have events back to back almost every night during the week too. It can be a lot."

"You work holidays?"

She nodded. "It's my busiest time. It makes sense when you think about it. People want to throw parties on holidays. So I'm always available for every holiday. I open my bookings a year in advance, and I'm already full on all holidays for the next year."

"That's a lot," he said. "Would you hire more staff to help you with that?"

"I have a decent sized staff, and they covered the Halloween parties that were planned for the last two weeks. My assistant took over my November events already, and I should be back for at least half of my December events. I could hire more, but my clients have come to expect me to personally attend their events, to make sure everything runs smoothly. I will bring help when the party size requires it, but, small circles and word of mouth means I'm asked for by name. Clients don't want me to pass their event off to someone with less experience. It's flattering, in a way."

"It sounds exhausting to plan others' parties and then not enjoy a holiday because you're working," he said.

She shrugged. "I don't look at it that way. It's been a great business, and I'm grateful for the success. This year's 4th of July party I coordinated for Brooks Morgan made National News. National! It was exhilarating. Since then, the company has been even more busy, though for everyone without a direct referral to me, I've passed to my assistants and event directors."

"I heard about Brooks' party," Troy said, impressed. "That was you?"

She beamed and nodded. "That type of recognition doesn't just come by throwing a party on July 3rd or July 5th. I was there. I was still able to enjoy the setting."

He opened her door for her, and it wasn't lost on Hailey that he was still a gentleman around her, even if things between them had gotten a little weird after their kiss.

"Where are we off to? Should we go look at the venue? Or should we have some lunch?"

"We haven't eaten at the Red Oaks Pizza Parlor yet since you've been in town. Would you like to try it? It's just off of Main Street, but it's really good."

"It sounds good," he said.

Hailey noticed how much hadn't changed since she was a teenager. The door still squeaked the same. The pictures were still the same. The place had been frozen in time. They were seated in a booth and after ordering, their conversation seemed like yesterday's, devoid of the awkward, weird vibe that had hung in the air since their kiss. They ate quickly, talking mostly about the morning, though avoiding any more conversation about the mistletoe and their kiss.

When they finished eating and started walking towards Troy's car, Hailey stopped. The air was crisp, but the sun was shining in a beautiful blue sky almost devoid of clouds. "The events center is less than a mile away. Want to brave the walk?"

He smiled, and her breath caught. "I can handle the walk," he said.

The sidewalk was narrow, requiring them to walk closely to each other. Their hands brushed each other as their strides matched, and she found her arm looped through his when they pushed closer together as someone passed them. She was about to regain her arm, but it stayed there, locked in his.

Troy cleared his throat. "I need to know what you honestly think."

She nodded. If it was whether or not she liked kissing him, the answer was yes, but it would help to have a few more data points. She pushed the thought aside, not wanting to jump to conclusions. The cold air nipped at her cheeks. She was sure that was why they felt the need to heat up right now. "I've only given you my honest opinions so far."

"That's good to know. So about this Santa thing. You gave me a look when I was trying to help you with the conversation earlier."

"I did." She remembered the moment well. He'd offered something that she didn't know how to accept. It was really too much on the time of this man she'd met a week ago. Yes, he was helping her. Yes, she was grateful. But he had no idea what he'd just volunteered for.

"Was it a happy, 'I'm glad you volunteered' sort of look, or was it something else?" His gaze was so direct, so focused.

She could melt under that type of focus. She smiled and

shook her head, still wondering her luck at his willingness to help her recreate this tradition for the town. She wanted to give it new life, so it would continue on for years, even if she wasn't in charge of it every year. That's why she was doing this. And he was here to help. It warmed her. "You're so helpful. But you basically volunteered yourself for the most intensive job of the whole Forest Festival. I don't want to put that kind of pressure on you. I'm grateful you volunteered. I'm not sure Paul would be right for the job anyway, but, maybe you'll want to know more about it before you decide if this is really the job you want to take on."

He stopped on the sidewalk, turning to face her straight on. "Before you tell me about it, is it something I could do?" he asked.

She thought about the responsibility, the weight of Santa who would deliver all of the trees and presents personally to each family. He would be at the Festival, interacting with the children, posing for pictures, and giving each of them a small, velvet bag of chocolates with a candy cane attached to the outside. She remembered years of attending the Forest Festival as a little girl, always excited to see Santa after she passed the rows of decorated Christmas trees.

One year, she recognized her aunt's neighbor as the one who played Santa, but it hadn't lessened her enjoyment of the experience. She studied Troy. He'd been selfless through the whole last week, working in stride with her to get this entire thing off the ground enough to have approval to keep going.

She poked him in the abs, and smiled. "This isn't exactly a bowl full of jelly, but I think you'd be perfect for the job."

"Then I'll do it," he said.

"You don't know what you're signing up for," she said.

"I'm helping you. That's what's important."

Her breath caught, and she was unable to form the words she wanted to express her gratitude. Maybe things had been weird between them an hour ago, but now, there was none of that. He was just back to helping her, and she knew she needed the help. "Thank you, Troy. You've really been such a ... good friend."

"The Forest Festival is important. I'm here to help make it as good as I can."

"That means a lot," she said.

"So what do I need to know about being Santa?"

"First things first, we need to find you a Santa suit that fits as soon as possible."

His eyes widened. "You mean an actual Santa suit?"

She nodded. "Last year's suit went missing. I guess I didn't think about it until now. Maybe if we reserve it now we can get it here in plenty of time. I bet we could find one online."

"This would be the popular season," he said.

She pulled out her phone, doing a few quick searches. "The first two websites are a bust. I bet I could find one though."

"Maybe I'll look in New York City when I'm there next."

"Probably a good idea, then you'll know what fits you. Looks like some of these online sites won't ship for another ten weeks. That's definitely longer than we have."

"I'll find a suit," he said confidently. "So, besides the suit, what else do I have to do?"

"You basically get to do everything. You'd open up the entire weekend of the Festival, pose for pictures, regular Santa stuff, of course."

"Of course."

"Then my favorite part of the whole Festival is that after the silent auction is over, Santa delivers all of the gifts himself."

Troy's eyes widened. "Really?"

Hailey nodded. "I told you it was a big job. Smaller things that are bought can easily be handed to each person, but the trees and their accompanying gifts all get wrapped up by volunteers, and then Santa helps deliver everything, with the help of his elves, of course."

"People will be in elf costumes for this?"

Hailey shrugged. "A few people will, especially if they already own their costumes, but mostly it will be people in elf hats. The delivery process can take anywhere from one to four days, just depending on how many donations we have and how far out they are. Of course, we can always make the deliveries, or have someone else dress up as Santa too, to help the process move along. I remember one year my aunt used five Santas to get all of the work done. It was pretty incredible."

"This sounds doable," he said.

"If you're sure?"

"Count me in. I just need to find a suit."

CHAPTER 10

Troy dropped Hailey off at her aunt's house and headed toward his hotel. They'd spent the afternoon walking around the town. They'd seen the events center, and while Hailey had asked for his opinion, he was sure that she'd already made up her mind. He wasn't sure how large this Festival would be, but from the sound of it, it would be well-attended.

The events center looked like a big, red barn from the outside, but on the inside, everything was furnished and heated. The main room seemed to have plenty of space to hold enough trees. Several other smaller rooms branched off, giving enough space for storage. The second level had a walkway around the entire perimeter of the lower floor, allowing patrons to see the trees from a bird's eye view.

He phoned his assistant, Cara, hoping she'd forgive him for calling on a Saturday evening.

"Good evening, Mr. Rasmussen," she said. "How can I help you?"

"You're on a date, aren't you?" he asked. She rarely called him by his last name unless she was being social with friends. He felt bad for interrupting. There were a few muffled words and then static. Dropped call? "Cara, are you there?"

"I'm here, just moving out into the lobby. One moment." Her voice came out a little clearer, though it was very quiet.

"I'm sorry to interrupt your evening. You know you can always let it go to voicemail," he said, wishing he'd just sent her an email about the Santa suit instead of calling to tell her about it.

She laughed. "If I let it go to voicemail, how would I be able to get out of this awful evening? This date is not going well. Your timing was impeccable. Now what can I do for you? Please tell me it's something urgent that I need to rush out and solve right now, because I really don't want to finish this evening."

"Is it really that bad?" Troy asked.

"I'm downplaying it right now, it's worse. I need something urgent. Give me your hardest task first. I'm ready for it."

"I need a Santa suit," Troy said.

Cara laughed, then abruptly stopped. "Wait. You're serious?"

"Serious."

She sighed. "Well that won't do."

"Why not?"

"First, it's not urgent enough. Second, you're probably calling because it's something you need for your charity competition, and I can't help with that." She groaned.

Troy's mind raced. "No, we can make this work. And it is urgent. Hailey has entrusted me to be the Santa of the whole Forest Festival."

"Really?" Cara sounded astonished. "That's a huge compliment to you. I remember that being one of the best parts of the whole event. Wow. She must really like you."

"That's the next problem I need to solve. Let's not get ahead of ourselves."

"Ooh, I want the details on that too. But back to your Santa suit, I don't think I can help."

Troy needed Cara's help. There had to be a way. "What if I wanted to purchase the Santa suit for me personally, instead of just renting it for the Forest Festival?"

"I might question your sanity."

"Here me out. I've already given the $10,000 I can donate, and hopefully next week we're going to earmark it for what they need. I don't want to pull from my donation to rent a suit for me."

"What if you are Santa at our company Christmas party this year? Is that something you'd be up for?"

Troy squirmed. "I suppose I could," he said.

"That's good because I don't want to stretch the rules. But technically, if you already owned a suit, you could use it to help with your volunteering efforts without it being a problem."

"So I'm basically buying the suit to be the Santa at our company Christmas party?" he asked.

"Exactly. I'll make sure I can get it to you in time for the Forest Festival."

"You're a genius, Cara," he said.

"Thank you for the compliment, but this hair-brained plan of lunacy is all yours."

"You'll help me find a Santa suit?"

"I'm sure I can make the arrangements for that. Now help me, and tell me that you need me to work on this tonight as soon as possible, so I can get out of the rest of my date."

Troy obliged. "Drop everything you're doing. I need you to work on this now so I can get the suit as soon as possible."

Cara sighed loudly. "Thank you, Troy. I owe you one."

"You can always use me as an excuse if your date is really going that bad. There's always something urgent I need checked on."

"You're the best," she said, her voice sounding brighter.

"Thanks. I better let you go and cancel your date."

"Not so fast. You can't insinuate you like someone and then say there's a problem, and expect me to forget that detail, just because you hide it behind a Christmas outfit question."

Troy ran a hand across his face. "I'm not sure there's really anything to even say at this point. Hailey Waters is great to work with, and I love spending time with her. The Forest Festival project wouldn't be nearly as fun without her ..."

"So far, I'm getting the idea of why you like her, and I'm not seeing where there's a problem."

"Her ex is rich."

"How rich?"

"Millionaire status—maybe multi-millionaire. From the way he puffs it up, you'd think he owned everything he looked at."

"New money, then?" she clarified.

"New enough, I suppose. But I don't hold when people earn their money against them."

"Fair enough. So, her ex didn't have money before, but now he does, so now she's interested in him?" she guessed.

"No. She's definitely not interested in him. She looked panicked when she was talking to him. I kissed her because I had a mistletoe decoration in my hand. It seemed like the right thing to do at the time, but, she made comments afterward about wealth. She doesn't like it. She works for billionaires, and so I don't know what to do with the information. She doesn't know who I am, and I think as long as that's the case, things could be great between us."

"Eventually you'd want her to know who you really are, more than just some random person who's come to save the annual Christmas charity event."

"Hence the problem. The moment she finds out, I'll be in the same position as her ex."

Cara blew out another breath. "I see. That is difficult. What did you say her name was again?"

"Hailey Waters. She owns an event business in the Seattle area."

"I'll see what I can find out, and let you know."

"There's nothing to find out. There's definitely chemistry between us, but the moment she knows who I am—"

"Maybe she'll see past the wealth. You don't know if that's the only reason why things didn't work out with her ex."

"Fair point."

"Looks like I have two urgent tasks. I better let my date know it's going to be a long night of work ahead for me."

Troy shook his head, wondering if she was really playing up how bad her evening was going just so he wouldn't feel bad about interrupting it. "It's urgent, but get to it when it makes sense to you. If you decide that you'd like to cancel on your date, you can always put in an order on the company card."

She laughed. "You know I will. Thanks for calling, Troy."

"Thanks for always helping me solve my problems."

"That's my job," she said, and then hung up.

CHAPTER 11

Hailey's mind blurred through the entire day. Troy had dropped her off an hour ago at her aunt's house. He'd been sweet, saving her in front of her ex, and volunteering to be Santa. He'd been the perfect gentleman. And he'd promised he'd help with the Forest Festival preparation. The task was more than enjoyable with him helping.

Butterflies swarmed in her stomach as she remembered their mistletoe kiss from earlier. She shook her head. He'd barely brushed his lips across hers. It was hardly enough of a kiss to be swooning over.

She went through her aunt's house, switching gears. She needed something to take her mind off of Troy. Thinking about him in any way besides a friend who was helping her out was pointless. The large Victorian home had been cleaned out of much of the excess furniture and sold in an estate sale back in June when she'd been here for the funeral. It was now sparsely furnished, almost ready for showings with a realtor. She bit her lip.

They'd saved the tradition of the Forest Festival, thanks to Troy again. Committing to such a big project when she lived on the opposite end of the country felt like lunacy, but there was a piece of her that couldn't just leave the project to someone else, no. She'd see it through. But what to do about the house? Now would be a much better time to try and sell than in December, but it was nice to have a place that she could stay while she was working on the Forest Festival. She'd figure out when to list it another day.

She willed herself to focus on something else, anything else. Nothing came. She got ready for bed, but the monotonous tasks of brushing her teeth and washing her face did nothing to help her focus. She still couldn't think straight. She needed a plan—she was an expert when it came to planning, but as she curled up in bed, no inspiration came to her. Her thoughts still mulled around Troy.

When she tried to focus on the Forest Festival, Troy was the first thing that popped into her head. She pushed the pillows beneath her head, readjusting her position, hoping that would somehow help her focus on the event. She knew how to push past the distracting pieces in a situation so she could focus on the purpose and needs of the event. She'd built an incredibly successful business doing just that.

Maybe it was because she was too close to the … project. Maybe the legacy of this tradition was what was weighing on her, and so the mental discipline was something she'd have to really focus on. Perhaps that was why she was getting distracted, because this was so big and so personal. Thoughts of

Troy persisted. She rationalized that that was natural considering he was working with her so closely.

She tried to think of the Forest Festival like she would any other big event, separated from the people—person—who was helping her. But as her mind drifted toward sleep the only thought that came through the swirls of information was how much she'd wished they'd kissed for real. And for longer.

HAILEY WOKE UP TO HER PHONE BUZZING. IT WAS NOT HER alarm. She swiped at the screen, trying to send the call to voicemail, but gasped when she saw the caller on the phone. "Hi Troy," she said, hoping she didn't sound as tired as she felt.

"Hailey, I'm sorry to wake you, I just received great news."

She yawned. "It's okay. I was getting up soon." She pulled the phone away from her ear for a moment to look at the time. It was not even 6:00 AM. Mornings felt like she was still on Seattle time. She blinked, trying to focus as he spoke rapidly.

"I just secured another sponsor for the Festival," he said.

"That's great," she said.

He gave her the figure and the details, but it all seemed to blur together. Once he'd finished telling her all about it so rapidly that her head felt like it was spinning he said, "I'm going to let you get back to sleep. I'm sorry I woke you. I couldn't wait to share the good news."

"Thank you, Troy. It means a lot to me that you're doing so much." In the back of her brain she still wondered why he was helping. He had no connections to Red Oaks, other than a coworker who'd come to the Forest Festival—something like that. Her brain was too fuzzy to remember the details.

"I'm happy to help," he said.

"Why do you want to help again?" she asked. Maybe in a few hours she'd have the ability to filter such questions, but right now curiosity took over.

There was a longer pause, and her eyes felt heavy as she waited for the answer. Finally he said, "Service merit badge, remember?"

"Oh, right. You must really want that badge, Boy Scout."

"I do, and it was either this or knitting scarves for the homeless shelter. Trust me I tried, but they didn't like the scarves I was making. The stitches were uneven."

"Wow." She stifled another yawn, not wanting to miss the banter, but feeling sleep pushing at her eyelids.

"I think this is more fun," he said.

"We are all about fun here." She rubbed her forehead. "Seriously though, why?"

"At first, I only wanted to help in the Festival, but now it's more ... I care about you, and this Festival and seeing that this special town has one more chance to feel the magic of this event makes it even more important."

Her eyes flew open as butterflies filled her stomach, seeming to eat away at where heartache had been only the night before. She wished she could see his face right now, to read the sincerity in his eyes. He admitted he'd cared about her. "You do?"

"Of course I do."

Hailey wasn't quite sure what to say. Questions from yesterday and his acting weird seemed to fall into place. The awkwardness of a kiss that maybe could have been more on both sides, not just hers, if it had lasted longer came into her mental view.

Troy cleared his throat. "Hailey? Are you still there?"

She wanted to answer. Sleep and tiredness had all but fled from her, but she was tongue-tied. She opened her mouth to say something, but no words came out.

"I wish I could tell you everything about how I feel," he said. "Sweet dreams, Hailey."

The call ended, and giddiness ran through her. Troy's last admission when he thought she'd fallen back asleep rang through her as she stared at the ceiling for the next hour before she got out of bed.

HAILEY MET TROY FOR BREAKFAST AT THE PANCAKE TOWER. SHE never ate out this much when she was at home in Seattle. Maybe it was time to do some grocery shopping, though she wasn't sure if she wanted to stock up with food if she was going to list her aunt's house soon. That was still a decision she needed to make. It was convenient to be there, but if the price was right, wouldn't it be better to sell it now?

She and Troy chatted about the food, and the weather. Snow was forecasted for later in the week. They avoided the conversation they'd had over the phone this morning, and she was sure he hadn't meant for her to actually hear the last sentence he'd said.

A squeal came through the small diner and Hailey looked up to see an old friend. "EEE. Hailey Waters? Someone said you were back in town, but I didn't believe them." The woman practically pulled Hailey up out of her seat to give her a hug.

"Hi, Emily," Hailey said, when she was finally able to breathe again. "How are you?"

"The better question is, how are you doing, honey? I didn't think we'd see you back here so soon, after, well, you know."

Hailey nodded, her throat constricting. "I'm here to sell the house," she said automatically. She'd been thinking about it since yesterday in between all of the thoughts that were filled with Troy. She scrunched her forehead. "And I'm working on the Forest Festival."

Emily kept eye contact. "I did hear that you had something to do with the Festival even happening this year, but I didn't know you were still here working on it."

Hailey nodded. "I'll be here until it's finished."

Emily's eyes widened. "Really? Then we need to get together." She finally turned to Troy. "I'm Emily. Hailey and I have known each other since we were seven years old and I moved next door to her aunt. Hailey was my favorite friend when she'd come and stay with her aunt in the summers."

"Where are my manners? Emily, this is Troy. Troy is … helping me with the Forest Festival." Hailey blinked at the handshake between Emily and Troy.

"It's nice to meet you, Emily," he said. "Any friend of Hailey's …" He let the sentence dangle.

Emily gave her a sideways glance, like she couldn't believe that was the only connection between the two of them, but she smiled broadly and said, "Nice to meet you."

"We should catch up," Hailey said, when there was a lull. "I'd love to get together for dinner or something while I'm here, and you can fill me in on what you've been up to. I'm afraid I wasn't in the mood to be social when I was here in the summer."

Emily gave her a sympathetic nod. "It was understandable. Truthfully, I didn't expect to see you again so soon. We all miss your aunt. Especially at the hospital. She really made a difference."

"Thank you," Hailey said, choking out her gratitude. She gave Emily her phone number.

"We should totally double," Emily said. "I've been seeing a guy from work."

Hailey's mouth dropped open as she made eye contact with Troy. "Uh, I don't think—"

"We'd love to," Troy said.

Emily smiled. "Great. There's this place in Silverwood by the ski resort, with a perfect view of the snow-covered mountains. You're going to love it."

Hailey forced a smile. "That sounds great."

Emily glanced at her watch. "I better get to work. It's a long shift today. I'm off tomorrow night, if that works for you guys?" She looked between them.

Troy nodded. "Tomorrow night sounds great," he said.

Hailey agreed, grateful that Troy was taking the idea in stride. It was just dinner, and they'd been going out to eat for over a week together. Having other people join their table and discussion didn't need to be a weird thing. They could go as friends, it was fine.

Emily beamed. "I can't wait. Oh, and don't let me forget, I'd love to help you out with the volunteering side of the Forest Festival."

Hailey smiled. "Thanks, Emily. That's kind of you. I'll add you to the list."

After Emily said her goodbyes, Troy turned to Hailey. "She seems really nice."

Hailey nodded. "She is really nice. She's a nurse at the Children's Hospital."

"And she's willing to volunteer for the Forest Festival, so that's one more person on our growing list," he said.

"Every little bit helps," she said.

They finished up their meal, and then Troy asked, "What's on the schedule today, boss?"

Hailey laughed. "I'm definitely not your boss."

"You're in charge of this whole operation."

"I was thinking we could do our research on how many trees we want for donations." She looked at her notebook to confirm her numbers. "We already have eighteen, and that's a great start, but I don't think it's anywhere close to enough. This event brings in people from outside of the town too, so there's potential for a lot more donations. We could start asking in other towns."

"If we had more cash donations, could we use that money for trees and decorations?"

Hailey nodded. "Sure, we could do that, but then we're the ones who are doing the tree set-up and planning. We could do a few trees ourselves, but part of the beauty of this event is that it gets the entire community involved. Everyone decorates the trees in such different styles, that it's nice to have the variety. We still have time to get more donations."

Troy nodded his head. "That makes sense."

They spent the day planning out their strategy for talking to businesses in two other neighboring towns, dividing up the businesses, and researching which companies had been solicited in the past. They made flyers asking for tree donations, then printed them. They'd distribute them over the next week.

At every question, Troy had sound advice on the approach for each of the small businesses. He researched each company and had looked up the owners online.

After a few hours at the foundation offices, they went to Hailey's aunt's house and worked in the living room. Hailey made them some hot chocolate, and they drank it while she scribbled plans down her book.

Hailey looked up from her notebook, where she'd been wrapped up on one side of the couch. She watched Troy's hands fly across the keyboard, like he was doing the easiest task in the world. "You're really good at this," she said.

Troy flashed her a boyish grin at the praise. "Thanks. Just trying to earn my keep," he said, and he went back to typing.

"What is it you do again?"

His hands stilled, hovering over the keyboard. "I work in data collection mostly. This kind of stuff is second nature."

"I don't even know what that means," Hailey said.

Troy shifted on the couch, turning toward her. "It means I get paid money to figure out things for my clients. Mostly it has to do with data mining. Truthfully I don't always understand it myself." He shook his head, a grin on his face. "Thankfully I work with people who are much smarter than I am."

"Do you like what you do?" she asked.

He nodded. "I really do. It's exciting and fast-paced. It feels like I'm finding buried treasure when I get a nugget of information that is helpful, especially in relation to this type of work."

"What do you mean?"

He turned his computer screen toward her. "Take this business, for example. On the surface, a cabinetry shop might not seem like a great fit for a business to go and solicit. But if we look deeper at this page ..." He clicked onto the bio sheet of the owner. "... We get a good idea about what the owner values. Hard work is one of them, but he's also worked with the Happy Moments charity in some of their international projects. He's taken his skills and blessed others with them. That says something about his character."

"We're still trying to go to every single business. Regardless of whether or not their business appeals to the Forest Festival, they still might have a desire to help," Hailey suggested.

"Exactly. But now we have something to connect about," he said. "We know that he's the kind of person who will get behind a worthy cause, so it would be good for us to remember that when we're talking to him, because while he is giving, he does seem to be very busy, especially this time of year."

Hailey thought about it for a moment. Troy was able to connect with people. It seemed like he had that gift. "Looks like you're going to be the one talking to him. I don't know much about Happy Moments."

Troy nodded. "I'd be happy to talk to him."

CHAPTER 12

Troy couldn't believe his good luck. He was finding out so much about the different businesses, and each of them had a story that he felt like he could relate to. Even without his name or title as a CEO and billionaire, he was able to affect change, and connect with people. It was an odd sensation to realize that maybe his title or his name had held him back in some ways.

Without the stress and pressure of his title, without people knowing that he was a billionaire, they seemed to focus on the immediate goals of helping the Forest Festival, instead of trying to impress Troy Rasmussen. Things were going his way, and he didn't have to try harder to get the results he wanted.

The reality was people wanted to donate and be part of something larger than themselves, especially at this time of year. It was encouraging, and Troy was grateful that he'd decided to get behind a cause this holiday season too. There was still several weeks until the actual weekend of the Forest

Festival. They'd made great progress, but they had their work cut out for them.

"You mentioned to Emily you're going to sell your aunt's house?"

Hailey nodded, her beautiful curls bouncing on her shoulders with the gesture. "It was originally the main reason to come here, in addition to clearing out the closet at the foundation. I still need to go through a few more boxes of my aunt's stuff. I'm not sure how much of it I'll want to ship back to Seattle with me, but if there are a few things, I'd like to take them on this trip." The light in her eyes seemed to dim. "My aunt would be so sad to see it go. She'd always talked about turning it into a place where families could come to be close to their kids."

The idea caught hold of Troy. He could see her carrying on her aunt's dream. It sounded amazing. "Why don't you do that?"

She hesitated, a mixture of emotions on her face. Finally she said, "My life isn't here. I wouldn't know the first thing about it."

"It'd be a beautiful place for it."

"Agreed," she said, glancing around the main living space. "I'm donating everything I make on the house to the Children's Hospital, so in that small way, it's hopefully staying true to my aunt's idea."

Troy wasn't sure what to say. He could tell Hailey was hurting, but wasn't sure if it was from grief or from selling the house. "Would you ever consider keeping the house?" he asked, trying to gauge where her strongest feelings came from.

Hailey shrugged. "I'm not really sure what I would do with it." She bit her lip, and Troy could see the internal struggle that manifested itself as two vertical lines between her eyebrows. "It is part of me, but I … I just don't think I would do the maintenance on it, you know. Red Oaks is a long way from Seattle."

It was the reminder he needed too. She was only here until the Festival was over. He was only here until the Festival was over too. This wasn't their town. They weren't really living here. She was staying in a home that would be up on the market soon. He was living out of a suitcase in a hotel.

"You could rent it out," he suggested.

Hailey nodded. "I thought of that, but in all reality, after this Festival, how many more years will I come back to visit in a town that my aunt doesn't live in anymore? Dealing with a rental property company feels like a pain. My family doesn't live here. I'd be coming back for the memories—the nostalgia." She shook her head. "It's a long plane ride when that's my reason."

"So you'll list it soon?" he asked.

"I haven't figured the timing out. My plan was to list it last week, but that was before the Forest Festival became a reality. Now I don't know how to really do that when I'm still living there while I'm in town. If it sells too soon, then, what do I do? I can't afford to stay at a hotel every night." She laughed lightly, then narrowed her eyes. "I feel bad you're spending so much money there."

He shrugged it off. "After the first week, I extended for the rest of my time, and the hotel cut me a deal for staying so long. It was actually more reasonable than you might think." He didn't want her worried about his financial situation, especially because he didn't want to deceive her more than he had to. Kyle hadn't made lodging part of the $10,000 he could donate, so he was fine to stay at the hotel on his own dime. He hadn't even blinked at the idea of paying for his entire stay upfront, regardless of the discount. He just knew it was something he didn't need to be bothered with.

"They really cut you a deal?" she asked.

He nodded, wanting to alleviate her concerns. "I tried to find a local Bed and Breakfast, but the two that were closest would have had me switching rooms every few nights to accommodate their booking schedule." He'd liked the idea of a B&B because it wouldn't have drawn a lot of attention, like a hotel would, but he didn't want to move rooms that much. They were also farther outside of town. He liked being close to the foundation, to the center of the action, and closer to Hailey.

"There used to be a B&B on the corner of Main Street, but it caught fire a few years ago. It was quaint, not even as big as my aunt's house, but it was warm and cozy. My aunt and I stayed there for a few days when she was getting some remodeling done."

TROY AND HAILEY SPENT THE FOLLOWING DAY PUTTING UP FLYERS advertising both the Forest Festival and asking for tree donors. They also solicited businesses for donations, and volunteers in Blue Pines. Troy had been right about the man who owned the cabinetry shop. He gave a generous cash donation and also offered custom-made nativity pieces for the silent auction. Hailey looked like she was going to cry from the generosity, and Troy was happy that he'd kept the conversation light, and hadn't had to name drop Kyle Montgomery—the founder of Happy Moments—to connect with the man.

They drove back from Blue Pines to Red Oaks together.

Hailey fidgeted with her purse strap in her lap. "So, about tonight ..." she began.

Troy nodded. He'd been anticipating their double date. Not because they were going out with friends but because he could actually put a label on one of their outings that it was an official date. "Did Emily get back to you with the details?" He couldn't wait to spend time with her outside of the stress of the Forest Festival.

"She did, but ..." She twisted in her seat, facing toward him as they drove the final mile back to her aunt's house. "Are you sure you want to go? It's just a fancy restaurant. We've been eating out a lot." She studied him.

Did fancy restaurants bother her? She threw amazingly incredible parties for rich and famous people—fancy seemed to be second nature in that atmosphere. Was she worried about the cost of food? Or was she simply tired of eating out?

He kept his eyes on the road, staying well within the speed limit, and kept his voice calm. "What's really bothering you, Hailey?" When she didn't answer he glanced at her from the corner of his eyes. "You can tell me."

She shook her head. "I don't want you to feel like you're roped into a double date. It was Emily's idea. I can always catch up with her another time."

Troy cared for Hailey. He liked her more than he could admit, and he wasn't going to let the fact that it was someone else's idea to go on a double date stop him from having an enjoyable night. He stopped at the red light and looked at

Hailey. "I don't want you thinking that somehow just because I didn't come up with the idea that I'm not all for the idea."

"What are you saying?"

"Hailey, will you go on a date with me?"

Her mouth fell open but no words came immediately out. She blinked, her intense blue eyes studying him. "You really want to go on a date with me? Not just appease my friend for an evening out?"

"Obviously."

She sucked in a breath, her words coming out breathy. "Okay."

He covered her hand with his, and she released the purse strap. The light turned green, and Troy went through the small intersection. A real date with Hailey. He couldn't wait.

CHAPTER 13

Hailey raced to her room when Troy dropped her off. He'd be back in less than an hour, but now that he'd asked her out, not just agreed to her friend's ideas to double, the date felt more real. Stress over what to wear ran through her mind, which was silly. She'd just spent the whole day with him. He knew how she looked, and she'd had dinner with him multiple times. He'd been sweet with her, but at the moment the officialness of tonight had her holding up all of the clothes she'd brought with her to Red Oaks, wishing she had more options.

She ignored the shivers that ran down her spine when she thought of her hand brushing against his over the past few days. It was silly, but the words he'd said when he thought she was asleep repeated in her mind.

For some strange reason she'd brought up her hesitation about the double date because for all intents and purposes he'd been roped into it. And the moment that she'd brought up hesitations, he'd immediately assuaged her fears and asked her out on the date. Now that this date with Troy felt real, her insides betrayed her feelings. She cared that he wanted to ask her out.

When the doorbell rang, Hailey smoothed down the red dress she wore. The dress had been a last minute add to her suitcase. She'd only planned to be in town less than a week, but she was glad she always packed at least one dressier outfit. She paired it with a sparkly black purse and matching heels.

She opened the door, and the expression on Troy's face was complete shock. He wore slacks, a button down without a tie and a sports coat. "You look nice," she said.

Troy cleared his throat, then said, "I hope it's dressy enough. I didn't bring many options." He looked down as if he was genuinely concerned about it.

"You're perfect."

"You look amazing," he said.

She blushed. "Thank you," she said, reminding herself that he was a gentleman and would have said she looked amazing regardless because he was nice like that.

He took her arm, and walked her to the car.

Time sped by as they made their way to the mountain ski resort lodge. Hailey tried to ask more questions about the Festival, talking strategy and numbers, just like Troy had been doing all day today, but at each question, Troy answered it and then asked personal questions.

Emily had made an early dinner reservation. It was almost too early to be considered dinner, but as they drove up the winding canyon to the lodge, Hailey realized why. The trees were covered in thick blankets of snow. The sun sparkled on it, turning the entire drive into a winter wonderland.

Troy parked the car in the lodge's parking lot and helped her out of the car.

Hailey hugged her coat around her when the mountain breeze blew around them. "It's beautiful up here," she said.

Troy nodded, pulling her close, looping her arm through his. "I couldn't agree more," he said.

The air between them felt electrifying. Hailey pointed to a lookout point adjacent to the lodge. "We got here fast," she said, knowing that Emily wouldn't be here until the reservation time in twenty minutes. "Want to go look at the view?"

Troy smiled. "Do you think you'll be warm enough?"

She controlled her chattering teeth as another gust of wind blew snow from the barren trees and the top of the lodge. "It will just be a few minutes."

"Sounds good." They walked to the lookout point, not far from where they'd started. "I don't often get to the mountains," he said.

"I imagine not in the middle of New York City."

"I travel outside the city," he said. "I just don't always make it to the mountains. It's beautiful up here."

She agreed, drawing in a deep breath of the fresh, cool air. "Mountains in Seattle aren't very close, but I've gone to Mount Rainier several times. It's a steep hike in some places. Even in the middle of July there are still places in the shade that have a significant amount of snow. Poles line some of the steep areas, so it makes the climbing easier."

They watched a few birds soaring through the air. A squirrel jumped from one tree to another breaking their focus on the birds.

"There's something about winter that makes me want to sit by a fireplace and drink hot chocolate."

"We used to watch Christmas movies that way," he said.

She laughed. "I like that. It doesn't quite feel like the Christmas season to me without a tree full of lights and ornaments." She paused. "Maybe that's what I've been missing at my aunt's house. I should bring in a Christmas tree from the garage."

He smiled. "I could help you with that. Once upon a time I moved a lot of Christmas trees and boxes of ornaments. I'm practically an expert."

She laughed, looking out at the mountain view, the snow covering up all of the dead and dormant trees with something beautiful. She gestured to the landscape. "I love this, everything frosty and white. Christmas time is my favorite time of the year." She laughed at herself. "That sounds cliché, doesn't it?"

He squeezed her arm that was looped through his. "Not at all. I think it's a great time of year." His eyes held sincerity, and interest, like her thoughts really mattered to him.

She cleared her throat. "We should probably get in to dinner," Hailey said. "I wouldn't want Emily to think we didn't show up. I have an idea about the Forest Festival I want to run by you—" She moved to walk back the way they'd come, but Troy stopped, their entwined arms preventing her from moving forward, so instead she looked at him, a question on her face.

"I don't want to talk business tonight," he said, his eyes seeming to read every movement in her face.

Tingles shot through her fingertips where he was gently holding them, all the way to her neck. "You don't?"

"I think we've had our fair share of business meetings over the last several days."

"That's true." Her head swam, her senses more keenly aware of the way his thumb brushed over her knuckles.

A thought wormed its way to her consciousness. Emily thought that they were a couple, which is why Emily had suggested a double date. But she didn't want to pretend that they were together for Emily's sake. Getting rid of her ex had been one thing, but there was no need to fool Emily, a friend that she'd only had minor contact with since college. "I don't want to pretend—"

"I don't want to pretend either," he said.

"I can't keep up the appearance of anything while we're working on the Festival. It wouldn't be—"

He lowered his head, not allowing her to finish her thought when his lips touched hers. The thought fled from her memory and she couldn't recall it back. She responded to his kiss, getting lost in the moment. He pulled her closer, his heat warming her as he circled his arms around her. The concerns she'd had earlier melted away. The kiss was gentle and sweet. Her fingers ran along the collar of his sports coat as she settled them around his neck, pulling him closer for an extra heartbeat. She pulled back from his kiss, their eyes locked on each other.

Her mind was muddled, mixing thoughts and feelings and emotions together into something she couldn't explain or articulate. She couldn't think of anything. Finally, she said, "That kiss certainly beats the first one." Her words came out breathy and light. She bit her lip, unsure of her admission.

He laughed, and she joined in with him. "I agree," he said. "Last time it was for show."

"And this time?" she asked, working to regulate her breathing. Both the mistletoe kiss and this kiss had caught her off guard.

He brushed his lips along hers again, leaving heat as it radiated through her, before he pulled away slowly. He kept his forehead close to hers, their eyes too close to focus properly. "This time there is no one around. This time it's real." He lifted her chin slightly and kissed her one more time.

She wrapped her mind around the last thing his lips had audibly said to her. *This time it's real.* His lips continued to weave beautiful words to her senses as they kissed. The moment felt magical in the midst of the winter wonderland. Her heart raced, but she barely had time to enjoy the contact when she heard her friend calling her name. They broke the kiss as Emily came toward them on the wooden walkway.

"There you two are," Emily said. "We've been looking all over. Our reservation was just called."

Hailey pressed her lips together, her pulse erratic, but matching Troy's. Troy looked at her with wide eyes. Had he felt the same way about their kiss that she did? Her heart flipped. She was glad she'd been holding onto Troy so tightly, the kiss had knocked her off balance, and she was in very real danger of falling, and not just because she was in heels on a slippery path.

Emily introduced them to her date, and they all headed

toward the lodge for dinner. Troy kept his hands threaded through Hailey's, and they followed the other couple inside. She squeezed his hand. She and Troy would talk soon enough, but in the meantime, she couldn't do anything but smile. She'd just experienced the best kiss of her life.

CHAPTER 14

Troy watched as Hailey caught up with her old friend. They chatted about what life had been like for each of them over the last five years, and Troy learned much more about Hailey than he would have otherwise. They laughed together at inside jokes, and Troy found Hailey's laugh infectious.

"So when did you guys get together?" Emily asked, including Troy in the conversation for the first time since they'd decided which appetizers to split.

Troy wasn't sure how to answer, so he continued chewing the shrimp cocktail slower than he had before, hoping Hailey would fill in the information she wanted to share with her friend.

Hailey smiled. "This is more of a recent thing," she said.

"And in all the time we spend together, it never seems to be enough," Troy said, hoping it didn't come out too forward. He liked Hailey. He wanted to spend more time with her, but he'd take any time he could with her. Right now their focus was on the Forest Festival, and that was okay. Every day they spent on the event made a difference.

Emily nodded. "Well you two are sure cute together. Devon and I just got together over the summer. I guess it's been a few months now, but with our alternating schedules at the hospital, it makes it a little more difficult. I feel like we spend every free minute we have together, and it's nowhere close to enough."

"Rotations will be better in a few weeks," Devon said. "Hopefully our schedules will match up a little better."

Emily smiled at Devon. "I hope so," she said, giving him a kiss. When the kiss lingered longer than just a peck, Troy averted his eyes, focusing on Hailey and smiling. She smiled back at him, holding his hand underneath the table.

With the distance from their own kiss, Troy wondered about his own choice in kissing Hailey without it being for show around her ex. The concerns he'd had about why she'd broken up with her ex surfaced again. She'd had a problem with her ex's wealth. So how would that be different for him? He had more wealth than her ex. Would it really keep them apart? He decided he'd ask her about it another time, when they weren't in the middle of a double date.

They chatted through dinner, and Troy found he got along great with Emily and Devon.

"Thanks, Em, for volunteering for the Festival. It really means a lot to me that you want to help," Hailey said. "In trying to get an idea of staffing, we're pretty open at the moment. Is there something specific you want to help with? You've pretty much got all of the options open."

Emily smiled. "Do you have a lot of volunteers yet?"

Hailey looked toward Troy, then back to Emily. "Our numbers are small at the moment, but they're growing. We've only been at this for a little bit."

Emily nodded. "How did you get Edna to approve the Forest Festival this year then? She's usually such a stickler on having volunteers lined up before she'll say yes to an idea, even if it's been a tradition."

Hailey tilted her head toward Troy, and finally responded with, "I think she was impressed with the capital that we raised in such a short time, and she was hoping that we could repeat it." Hailey sighed. "Truthfully, I'm not sure that we can repeat such a generous offer from any other donor to the project, but the amount was enough to get Edna interested in it."

Emily looked at Devon. They smiled at each other. "I have good news for you. Last year I was in charge of all the hospital volunteers. I know a lot of them will want to come and help with the Forest Festival, as soon as I tell them about it."

Hailey stared at her friend. "Really? That would be great."

"I'm happy to help. The Forest Festival is such a huge part of not just our community, but what we do all year long at the Children's Hospital. In fact, let me take care of all the volunteers. There's no reason you guys should do it all by yourselves."

Hailey smiled, gratitude evident from her friend's kind offer. "Thanks, Em."

Emily nodded. "Just give me the contacts of the people who have already committed to volunteer, and I can help with the rest. I'm assuming Edna has a record of who volunteered last year and how many shifts were needed."

"Yes," Hailey said. "I think that is one of the few pieces of information that she tracked separately from my aunt. My aunt seemed to have a system down that included keeping most of the details in her head."

TROY DROPPED HAILEY OFF AT THE BEAUTIFUL VICTORIAN mansion. "This was fun," he said.

She nodded. "Thanks for a great date."

"It was just dinner."

"It was still great," she said.

"We'll have to do it again sometime," he said.

She laughed. "We've been having dinner together every night."

He leaned toward her as they stood on the wraparound porch outside the front door. Sure they'd had dinner together before now, and practically every other meal together since they'd met, but the kissing was new. "Then I guess we should keep that tradition going," he said.

She stepped closer to him, her hands resting on his chest. "I'd like that," she said.

He bent lower, his eyes never leaving hers. She didn't move away, only lowered her lashes for a fraction of a second before his lips found hers. He cupped her cheeks with his hands, caressing her jaw and cheeks. He moved to pull back, and was surprised when she held on tighter to his jacket, not letting him leave yet. She broke the kiss, and he caught his breath. "Good night, Hailey," he said, his breath visible between them in the cold night air.

"Good night, Troy."

TROY'S HEAD WAS STILL SPINNING FROM HIS DATE LAST NIGHT. Kissing Hailey in the mountains and again on the doorstep was still engrained in his memory. He wanted to kiss her again. Thoughts of forgetting the entire Forest Festival to court her had crossed his mind, but he doubted that would go over well. He'd be patient, and in the meantime they could go on a few more dates and get to know each other outside of the Forest Festival preparations.

He took the stairs down to the first floor, almost laughing at the idea of using the elevator for four stories. He preferred the exercise, even when he was on the thirty-eighth floor in New York City, he still preferred the stairs when he had time.

He passed by the main desk and walked through the lobby. He was almost to the exit when he heard someone call his name from behind him. "Mr. Rasmussen?"

He turned to see the morning staff at the front desk. "Yes?"

"I have a delivery here for you, sir. It came early this morning, with instructions that it was to be delivered to you personally."

Troy smiled. "Thanks. I can get it when I get back."

The man, whose name tag said George shook his head. "The orders were specific—to you personally, as soon as you are seen."

Troy nodded. "I'll take it now then. Thanks." He held out his hands expecting a small package.

George lifted a large white cardboard box with red writing on it, from under the counter. "Here you go, Mr. Rasmussen."

Troy took the box. "Thanks, George," he said.

George waved back. "Looks like a fun early Christmas present," he commented.

"Something like that," Troy said, and made his way back to the elevator. The box wasn't overly heavy but it was an awkward size to carry. Troy set it on the floor of the elevator as he went back to the fourth floor.

Once inside his room, he opened the box and pulled out a brand-new Santa suit. It was the best replica of a real Santa suit that he'd ever seen. He put the coat and the pants on his bed.

There was also a hat, gloves, red and white striped socks that looked like candy canes, and black leather boots with gold buckles. Inside a small red glasses case were gold half spectacles. Another small package revealed a moleskin book with age-worn distressed paper. On the front was stamped the words: "The List."

He unwrapped the next bundle in the box, putting the white tissue paper in a pile as he pulled out a present sack. His suit was a brilliant red, but the sack was a dark red that almost had hints of purple in it. A gold cord tied around the mouth of the velvet sack. A thick black belt with a gold buckle that matched the boots was next. A white cotton bag held a wig and a curly white beard. A string of large sleigh bells hung on a wide leather strap. He shook them tentatively, then with a little more force. It sounded like Christmas, and snow, and holiday memories all wrapped into one.

A small booklet gave instructions on how to "get into character," with his new costume. It had phrases for talking with children, the proper way to create a jolly, "Ho ho ho!" that didn't sound like a cough, and the trick to inflating the velvet sack with air to make the bag look full without adding extra weight to the bag. The coat came with a belly stuffer to add extra realness to the costume.

The entire thing was genius. He had to hand it to Cara. She'd gone above and beyond in finding such high quality so quickly.

He glanced at his watch. He might be a little late to meet Hailey at the foundation this morning, but maybe he could catch her before she left for the foundation and have her meet him for breakfast at the hotel. He called Hailey. With any luck, this would be a fun surprise.

"Good morning," Hailey said.

"Good morning," he said, not realizing how much he'd missed her voice until he heard it again right now. "I was wondering if you'd like to live on the wild side and come have breakfast with me at the hotel. Meet you in the lobby in thirty minutes?"

"Okay."

"I'll be waiting by the fireplace," he said.

"I'll be there."

As soon as he hung up with her, he dressed in the Santa suit. Everything was self-explanatory, though putting on the fake gray and white eyebrows was more of a challenge than he'd anticipated. The curly white beard caught in his own short beard. He'd need to remember to shave before wearing it again, but other than that, everything seemed to be good. When he had his entire costume on he stood in front of the full-length mirror to inspect.

It didn't look a thing like him. He looked like the real Santa. He'd inflated the present sack as suggested, and threw it over his shoulder. It bounced a little. He practiced swinging it over his shoulder, giving it just the right amount of force that it stayed next to his shoulders instead of bouncing away like an inflatable toy. He held "The List" book in one hand, and shook the bells in his other hand that held the present sack rope.

With the transformation complete, he called Cara.

She answered on the second ring. "Good morning, Mr. Rasmussen," her perky voice came through the phone.

"You've really outdone yourself this time," he said.

"So it fits perfectly?" she asked.

"Down to the boots and gloves. How do you do that?" he asked, genuinely curious.

"I know how to order clothes and ship them. There's this new fancy thing called the Internet. Not sure if you've ever heard of it, but you can order just about anything from the comfort of your home. It's pretty amazing."

He laughed. "I know how the internet works. But how did you know my size?" He'd meant to give her all of the information, but he'd been preoccupied with the Forest Festival and with Hailey, that getting back to Cara about the size for his Santa suit had slipped his mind.

"I used your tux measurements."

"And my shoe size?"

"You keep an extra pair in your office closet. I just gave them the brand and the size and they went to work on the rest."

"Well, you're amazing and resourceful. Thank you."

"I'm just doing my job. If I had to wait until you gave me the information, it would be St. Patrick's Day before you got a red suit, and how would that be helpful?" She laughed.

"You're right, that wouldn't be helpful at all."

"So you like the suit? Be honest, but know that I bought the highest quality upgraded everything, and it's all custom to you. And it's non-refundable. So if it doesn't work for you long-term, I suppose you could always donate it to a charitable foundation that needs a Santa suit or something."

He laughed. "This is better than what I had in mind. It's perfect."

"I'm glad," she said. "Take a picture. I want to see how it turned out."

"I'll do that," he said.

"Is there anything else I can do for you this morning?"

"Nothing else at the moment. Just keep everything running as smoothly as you can this week."

"Check your messages sometime today or tomorrow. I'm only sending you ones that I can't delegate or solve myself. You don't have much, but there are a few messages you'll want."

"Thanks, Cara."

"No problem, boss."

CHAPTER 15

Troy made it downstairs and surveyed the lobby. Some people glanced his way, but after a few strange looks they went back to what they'd been doing before he'd arrived in the room. A few people mingled, others drank coffee in solitude while reading the local paper set on each table. Hailey was nowhere in sight. That was good.

Two high wing-backed chairs sat on one side of the gas fireplace. It created more ambiance than actual heat, but Troy already felt warm. Next time he'd wear cooler clothes underneath his suit—shorts and a t-shirt. We wished he'd told Hailey to meet at a table far from the fireplace, but it completed the Santa look, so he settled into the wing-back chair next to the blaze, anticipating her first impression of him as Santa.

Troy pulled the spectacles down farther on the bridge of his nose, thankful that the glasses didn't actually have a prescription. He opened "The List" book halfway, pretending to be engrossed in the blank pages, just like he would with a novel.

He fanned them again, noting the last several pages had instructions regarding Santa's Famous List.

Guidelines included asking questions without judgment on whether or not someone had been naughty or nice. It focused on the positive, allowing for children to want the attention of saying that they'd been bad or deserved coal. Between this and the booklet he'd skimmed over quickly upstairs, the Santa Claus persona felt like an in-depth perspective on a whole different life.

He saw movement out of the corner of his eye. He looked up expecting it to be Hailey. It wasn't. A girl with dark ringlets and hazel eyes stared at him. She couldn't have been more than four. He looked up to see her parents at a nearby table.

The dad spoke first. "I'm sorry to bother you, uh, Santa, but she wanted to come and tell you what she wanted for Christmas. Is that okay?" The dad looked at him hesitantly.

Troy looked between the dad and the mom. The mom looked earnestly at him.

Troy nodded, but his mind went blank. He wasn't really Santa. He'd had no training for this. Five minutes with a how-to manual was not training for how to talk to kids about what they wanted for Christmas. Sure he looked the part, but he had literally no clue what he was doing. He pulled from everything he'd just read. It had to be enough. It had to be what he needed.

He smiled at the little girl, keeping his voice quiet, realizing just how conspicuous he was in the middle of the hotel lobby. "Ho, ho, ho," he said. "And what's your name?"

She moved forward, immediately grabbing his gloved hands. "I'm Kenzie," she said. "Are you Santa?" The girl's hazel eyes seemed to pierce right through him.

He looked toward the front desk where George seemed to be watching the scene with interest. Kenzie's parents too, seemed to be holding their breath, waiting for his answer.

He gave Kenzie the biggest smile he could, wondering if it could even be seen under his white beard. "That's what people call me. But I have lots of names. Sometimes I go by Santa, and sometimes I go by Kris Kringle. And in other parts of the world I have other names."

He could almost catch Kenzie's parents releasing their breath, relieved at his answer.

Kenzie's eyes widened. "I have more than one name too!" She said it loudly, with excitement. "My real name is McKenzie, but almost everyone calls me Kenzie. And sometimes my dad just calls me squirt. I don't really know why he calls me that, but he does. I think it's because maybe one time I squirted him with a water gun at the swimming pool."

The girl was delightful and Troy found his laugh coming out in another jolly, "Ho, ho, ho."

"Kenzie, I have a very important question to ask you."

"Okay." Her eyes grew large, expectantly awaiting every word he spoke.

"Have you been a good girl this year?"

She nodded solemnly, like she was taking the question to heart.

"And what are you hoping for, for Christmas?"

Her eyes searched his. She leaned an elbow on one of his knees, propping her chin in her hand. "Can I ask you for anything?"

How could he answer that question? He looked to her parents, who seemed just as interested in her answer. He smiled, wondering how much of his smile was actually seen through the snowy white curls that fell across his cheeks, mouth, and chin. At least it did a good job of covering up his own beard. He resisted the urge to pull the white hairs out of his mouth, not wanting to mess up his appearance, or give away the secret that he wasn't the real Santa.

"You can ask for anything," he said, knowing that asking for something and actually getting it were mutually exclusive.

She looked back at her parents, then turned to Troy. She curled one finger repeatedly, until he'd bent his ear low enough for her to whisper to him. "What I really want most of all for Christmas is a baby brother." From the expressions on her parents' faces it was evident that they'd heard her answer.

Troy couldn't read Kenzie's parents' expressions, but he stroked his beard, trying to appear ponderous as the wheels inside his head spun into overdrive. Nothing in his perusal of the Santa Booklet gave him any idea on how to answer her. He took a deep breath, hoping her parents would be okay with what he said. "Baby brothers or sisters are not something that I can bring in my sleigh."

"But I really want one," she said.

He nodded. "I'll write it down on the list. Is there another thing you might want?"

"You mean I can ask for two things?" The child's wide eyes shimmered, as if she'd never considered asking for something else.

He nodded again.

"After a baby brother, I want my very own playhouse, with a bed for each of my stuffed animals."

"I'll let my elves know," he said, looking toward her parents. They nodded, smiles on their faces.

As the mom walked hand in hand with Kenzie toward the front doors of the hotel, the dad stayed behind.

Troy stood, and the man shook his hand. "I can't thank you enough," the dad said.

"You're welcome," Troy said, confused by the dad's gratitude.

"She's been on a little brother kick for the whole year. Every time we ask her what she wants to do on the weekend or who she wants to play with, she only says she wants to play with her baby brother. When we asked her what else she'd like for Christmas, she has replied with the same thing—a baby brother. Thanks to you we have at least one other thing to think about getting her this year."

Troy nodded. "I'm glad I could be helpful."

"You're the best Santa I've seen in a long time," the dad said.

Troy nodded at the compliment and the dad hurried to catch up with his family. He blew out a breath, sitting back in the chair, his hands gripping the chair arms. That had been harder than he'd planned. He hoped it would get easier, thinking on his feet about what to say, knowing that in all reality there was no way for him to promise anything that children asked for. It was a very difficult situation.

"Still, the best Santa he's seen in a long time is saying something," he muttered to himself in the quietest, jolliest voice he could manage.

"I agree," a familiar female voice said.

Troy looked up to see Hailey. She seemed to appear out of nowhere.

He coughed. "I didn't know I had an audience," he said a little sheepishly.

She shrugged. "I've been waiting for someone. He should be here any minute, but in the meantime I had to take the moment and watch you with that little girl. She was adorable."

Troy nodded. "She really was."

"Mind if I have a seat while I wait for my friend?" she asked.

Troy wanted to laugh. Was she pulling his leg, or did she really not recognize him? He gestured to the seat next to him. "It's all yours," he said. "I was saving it for you."

She laughed, taking the seat next to him. "How long have you been doing the Santa gig?"

He coughed. She really didn't recognize him. Did his voice sound that different muffled under the beard? "It's a relatively new thing," he said. Should he tell her it was him? He wondered how long she'd take to figure it out. Likely not long.

"Well, you're a natural. I run events for people and trust me, I've worked with a lot of Santas and not many of them have been as convincing as you."

"Thanks," he said. "But I think it's the suit."

She scrutinized the fur on his wrists and looked at his boots, and finally his velvet present sack. "It's definitely a nice suit, but that's not the reason why you're so good at it."

He wasn't sure what to say, so he kept quiet.

"What did she ask you for?" Hailey asked. "The little girl, I mean. What did she want for Christmas?"

Troy wondered if there was some sort of code against telling other people's Christmas wishes. He'd better play it safe. It was one thing for Kenzie's parents to know, and quite another to tell someone else. Besides, if Hailey had recognized Troy, maybe she was testing him. He'd better err on the cautious side. "Santa can't tell what other people want." He winked at her.

"An excellent answer," she said. She drummed her fingers on the chair arms and looked at her watch. Now would be a good time to tell her that he was here, and she didn't have to wait for him anymore. Surely, she recognized him, right?

"Can I ask you a question, Santa?" she asked.

"You want to ask for something for Christmas?" he asked, wondering if Hailey would actually tell him something personal, especially if she thought he was a stranger.

She shook her head. "I'm a little older than your typical demographic to be interviewed on whether I've been naughty or nice."

"One is never too old to ask for something from Santa," he said, lifting the fake bushy white and gray eyebrows that were attached to his own.

"Fair enough," she said. "I'm curious about your timing. Isn't November a little early to start dressing up?"

Troy smiled. "Maybe this was my Halloween costume?"

She laughed. "That was last month. What brought you here?"

He scratched the side of his cap. "A car? Reindeer sleighs aren't the fastest at delivery 364 days of the year. They save their speed for Christmas Eve."

She laughed again. "Did you come up with that on the spot, or is that from a 'Santa Joke Book' or something?"

His eyes widened. "Is there such a thing as a Santa Joke Book?"

She shrugged. "I have no idea. Do you teach lessons on how to be Santa?"

Was that a thing? As an event planner, maybe she'd know. Santa lessons might come in very handy, though he supposed if she hadn't figured out who he was yet, maybe he was playing the part convincingly enough. He looked around the room, wondering how many people heard their conversation, but it seemed like no one was paying much attention. He lowered his voice anyway. "I'm making this up as I go along. Are there actual places Santas can go to take lessons?"

She bit her lip. "I've never heard of a place, I was just curious if you teach it. I have a … friend … who's never done this before. Maybe you could give him some pointers?"

He tilted his head. "Is this the same 'friend' you're waiting for now?"

She blushed. "Yes. He should have been here by now." She looked down at her phone, but made no attempt to text him. Thankfully Troy had put his phone on silent before dressing up in his Santa suit. He didn't know much, but he felt like it might kill the Santa Claus picture if his phone suddenly rang. "So, you're dressed up in November just to spread Christmas cheer early?"

It was time to let her know who he was. "I was actually trying on the new suit. I heard there might be a need for a Santa for a fundraiser around these parts." He cringed. Did he just say 'these parts'? It sounded much more Western than Santa.

Her face actually fell at his reason. That was not the response he'd expected. "You're an amazing Santa," she said. "You really are. And what a coincidence that I'm running into you here, of all places. I'm actually the one who's in charge of the Forest Festival. Well, me and my friend." She twirled her hair between her fingers, a gesture that he hadn't seen from her since the first day they met. Was the Santa persona really able to break through people on such a subconscious level?

"I don't believe in coincidences," he said.

Another twirl of her hair. "I don't usually either." She glanced around the room, probably looking for him again.

"So about the Forest Festival?" he asked.

She shook her head. "I'm sorry. If Santa were an auditioned role, you would have the part, no question. But that position of Santa has already been filled. I can't go back on my word. I think he … probably needs it more."

Troy nodded. An itch from the beard penetrated through his skin on his left cheek. He was in danger of ripping the entire thing off to show Hailey it was him. But something stopped him. Maybe it was the few other guests in the lobby, but he felt instinctively that he couldn't burst the Santa bubble that he'd created. It was better to leave this moment how it was.

"Maybe another time," Troy said.

"If something comes up, I'd love to use you as a backup, or book you for another Christmas party," she said, her words came in a rush. "Do you have a Santa card? I suppose it's too much to hope that you travel for this gig?"

Troy patted his Santa coat, as if he were feeling around for a card. He would never need to have a Santa card. This wasn't going to be something he actually did on a regular basis, but he'd play Santa for Hailey if she needed him for a backup at a party. "I don't have a card … with me."

She nodded. "Do you travel?"

"When the reindeer are free I can make it down from the North Pole."

"You're already getting booked up for the holidays, I bet." It wasn't a question.

He nodded. "I have several days already booked." It wasn't an exaggeration. The Forest Festival was almost a solid week, plus the deliveries and then his assistant had thankfully already blocked off his calendar for the night of his company Christmas party. He'd originally assumed that everyone would recognize him, but Hailey still seemed to be oblivious. Maybe that's how he should run his own Christmas party too. Just show up with the Santa persona, and not be the CEO for an evening.

"Is there a good way to get a hold of you?" She held out her phone.

He blinked. She really was serious and she had no clue who he was. He turned over his gloved hands. He wouldn't be able to put in a number on her smart phone. She understood and punched in the numbers as he gave her the digits. He'd send her directly to Cara's number, on the off chance that she'd call before he told her it was him.

She looked at the number. "New York?" she asked.

He shrugged. "Santa has to have a home base. Reception in the North Pole is dicey."

She laughed. "This is your number?"

"My elf will answer the phone. Her name is Cara. She'll get you in touch with me."

"And I ask for ...?" She held the screen toward him. The name on the contact was currently blank.

He cleared his throat. Did he sound different? "Ask for Santa."

She put in Santa on the name line and saved the contact.

Then she stood. "I'd better go see what happened to my friend. He's never been this late before."

"Is he more than just a friend?" Troy couldn't help but ask the question. The way she used the word throughout their whole conversation. Was she trying to convince Santa or herself?

She blushed. "Maybe more than just a friend. I don't know what we are actually. He's something. We're ... something, maybe—maybe that's my Christmas wish."

Troy wanted to react to her statement by telling her who he was, but he kept himself in character. She'd basically told Santa her feelings for Troy. He touched the side of his nose, hoping it seemed like a "Santa" thing to do. "I thought so."

Hailey bounced on her toes. "Can you keep a secret, Santa?"

He nodded. "Of course," he said.

"I more than like him. I'm definitely falling for him." She covered her mouth like she'd revealed an earth-shattering secret.

He smiled at her, wanting to tell her it was him, and knowing that if before was bad timing, now was even worse. He said something along the lines of congratulations to her, all the while his head spun at the vocal revelation. He was falling for her too. He wanted to say just that, but she interrupted his thoughts.

"Thanks again for the amazing performance this morning. It's been a long time since I've been impressed by a Santa, and I've hired a lot of them." She shook Troy's hand.

"Thank you. I wasn't trying to create the performance, it just happened."

"That's always the case when you wear the Red Suit. We'll be in touch."

Troy nodded. Hailey looked at her phone and then held it to her ear as she headed out through the lobby doors. Troy made a bee-line for the elevators, pulling out his own cell phone from his present sack as soon as it started vibrating. He pushed the elevator button up, and swiped the phone on. When the elevator door opened and there was no one inside, he pulled down the beard. "Hello?"

"Where have you been?" she asked. "I thought we were going to meet for breakfast."

"Sorry, I got … held up in a conversation, for work." He was grateful for the reception in the elevator that hadn't dropped the call. He headed straight for his room. He would breathe easier once he took off the suit. She'd find out soon enough who her favorite Santa really was, but until then, maybe he'd keep it as a happy surprise.

She blew out a breath, her tone changing. "Oh, sorry about that." She gave a nervous laugh. "I forget sometimes that you have a real job that isn't just helping with all of my whims for the Festival."

"I don't mind your whims," he said. "Besides I'm having a lot of fun with my role in helping you." In fact there was nothing else he'd rather be doing in his life than helping Hailey succeed, and spending time with her.

CHAPTER 16

"Thanks, Troy," Hailey said into her phone as she sat outside the hotel. For a few minutes she'd actually thought Troy had forgotten about breakfast. Her stomach rumbled, and she hoped it didn't come through on the call. Until this moment, she'd glossed over the fact that Troy's work might require him to check in while he used vacation time for a couple of months. She felt insensitive for not thinking about it.

It'd been so helpful to have someone to bounce ideas off of, and he was so good at commanding the attention of everyone when they'd gone to the different businesses. He was a natural. But it was more that she couldn't imagine any of this without him. Her heart was wrapped up in him. Giddiness sprinkled itself over her at the thought.

She bit her lip, the words that she'd spoken to Santa racing around in her mind. Maybe he could be more than just a friend. It was a delightful thought, and one that she wanted to explore with Troy. Their kiss in the mountains last night had made her weak in the knees for the rest of the evening. She'd tried to remember anything that she and Emily had talked about over dinner last night, but all of it had gone in one ear and out the other when her thoughts centered on Troy. She hadn't wanted to let go of their doorstep kiss either. She'd laid awake thinking about kissing Troy for a long time last night.

"So, is it too late for breakfast?" he asked. "Or should we call it brunch?"

"I'm still in the mood for breakfast," she said, her stomach rumbling again at the mention of eating food.

"Are you close by?"

"Waiting for you," she said.

"I like the sound of that."

"Ha. So the hotel breakfast?"

"I'm waiting in the lobby," he said. "Where are you?"

"You're not. I was just in the lobby five minutes ago," she said.

"I'm here by the fireplace, right where I said I'd meet you."

"I-I'll be right there," she said, hanging up the phone and standing up from the bench. She walked back inside, her nerves firing on all cylinders. She'd had a stomach full of butterflies when she'd walked in earlier, but they'd all calmed down as soon as she'd focused her attention on the mysterious Santa. He'd been sweet with the little girl. She'd watched from the lobby, standing next to a pillar. Santa had had the posture, the look, the gestures. From her vantage point earlier, she hadn't been able to hear the little girl's request, but she'd watched the whole scene like a silent movie, filling in the motives and the emotions when it was appropriate. The entire thing was perfect.

As she glanced to the chair Santa had been in, she saw Troy sitting there, reading the local newspaper, as if he'd been there the whole time.

"Where were you before?" she asked.

He blinked at her, a neutral look on his face when he said, "What are you talking about? I've been in this chair all morning." He straightened out the newspaper, engrossing himself in the black and white newsprint.

She shoved his shoulder. "No you weren't. Santa was just here. Where were you before you were here?"

"In my hotel room?"

She rolled her eyes. "You're impossible. Is this seat taken?" She pointed to the wing-backed chair that she'd sat in before when she'd been talking with Santa earlier.

"I've been saving it for you," he said. "It might be hard to eat our breakfast in these chairs."

She moved the chair back, revealing the small round table, and pulled the table forward between the two chairs. "There. This should work."

A server came over to them, offering them menus. Troy folded the newspaper, laying it on the hearth.

"I ran into someone this morning," she began, after looking through the menu.

Troy tilted his menu down. "You ran into someone? Did that hurt?" His eyes held a gleam in them.

She shook her head, covering up a laugh with a cough. "Not like that. I mean, I met someone this morning."

Troy looked at her thoughtfully. "Should I be jealous?" He seemed to hold another sparkle of a laugh in his gaze.

She giggled. "I don't know, should you be jealous?" She bit her lip, loving the banter between them.

Troy rubbed the bottom of his chin. "Maybe I should. I mean, we only kissed yesterday and I'm still in a fragile state about what that really means for … us. Telling me you met someone this morning doesn't really bolster my confidence in the relationship area." He smirked at her.

"Ha ha," she said, pushing his shoulder. "Not like I *met someone*, met someone. I met Santa."

Troy laughed.

She tilted her head. "What's so funny?"

"You really met Santa?" His eyes were curious.

"I did."

"I'm definitely not jealous," he said.

She laughed. "I didn't think you would be."

He paused for a heartbeat, then said, "Would you rather he be your Santa Claus for the Forest Festival?"

"Didn't you already order your Santa suit?"

"Not the question," he said, his eyebrows drawing together.

She shook her head. "I think you'll do a great job as Santa, besides, it's something really fun. If I could pull off being Santa for it, I would. Just the opportunity to connect with everyone on a different level is amazing."

"I agree," he said, with such conviction in his eyes it took her by surprise. "I think there must be something to it. I can see why it would be a coveted position. Would you ever be Mrs. Claus?"

Her eyes widened. "No. I'm definitely not old enough to fill that role," she said, touching her hair. "There's no way I'd be believable."

He frowned at her. "Aren't we close to the same age? And you think I can pull off Santa Claus."

"That's different," she said, realizing she'd painted herself into a corner. "Besides. I already have a cute elf costume. I'll be the one helping the kids to smile while they get their pictures taken."

"I don't think there's any difference," Troy said. "If I can pull off Santa Claus, then you could definitely pull off Mrs. Claus."

Hailey could feel her cheeks heating. "They've never really had a Mrs. Claus here before."

Troy nodded. "I think you'd be amazing at it," he said sincerely.

Hailey looked around as they ate their food. "Speaking of amazing, you really should have seen this Santa Claus. The entire costume looked custom. I've never seen such a well-dressed Santa before. He was pretty modest about it, but with a suit like that, I have a feeling he's been doing this for easily ten years."

Troy smirked. "Ten years, huh? Is that what he told you?"

"Just a guess. Maybe it's been longer, who knows. He was a pro at the part too."

"It sounds like you should hire him for the job. I might be a disappointment after a seasoned Santa appearance."

Hailey shook her head. "I'm not bringing it up to compare, not really. I guess I'm still in awe at seeing a Santa so early in the season. That's all. I wish you would have seen the way he talked with the little girl who came up to him. It was magical."

"Magical?" He leaned back in his seat, looking at her for a long moment. "I wish I could have seen what you saw."

Clouds had gathered in the morning, whispering the arrival of snow, but not falling until their breakfast was almost over. Hailey put a hand to her heart, the little flurries outside the window next to their chairs bringing her mind straight back to their kiss from last night. She could feel the warmth settling on her cheeks. She probably looked like a giddy little school girl. She finished her bite of food, about to announce the change in the weather, when Troy interrupted her thoughts.

"Look, it's the first snow of the year."

Her heart pounded at his excitement, and at the memory in Silverwood. "Soon we'll be walking in a winter wonderland."

"I think that's an excellent idea," he said, watching the growing flakes fall and stick to the trees and sidewalk.

"The antique shop said that their donation is ready, and they want us to come and see it. It's not far from here, if you want to brave the weather," Hailey said, smiling. They finished their breakfast, and she wrapped her scarf around her neck as they headed outside.

Troy's gloved hand found hers as they walked down the snow dusted sidewalk. Their footprints melted the snow, leaving a meandering path behind them. Christmas wreaths with large crimson bows hung from each of the lamp posts down Main Street, but now with a little dusting of snow it felt more like Christmas. Hailey savored the moment.

They approached the small antique store with the bright orange door squashed between a row of windows displaying newer and older items. Brass shone from decorations, while other items looked like they'd been purposefully weathered to attain their antique status.

A bell rang as they walked through the door. Cinnamon and the smell of oranges filled her senses inside. Light Christmas music hummed in the background. Every inch of the store held something to see, an old-fashioned type of charm that filled the space. They looked at the Christmas display area, not seeing anyone working in the store.

"Is this your kind of store?" Troy asked.

"What do you mean?"

Troy shrugged. "You decorate for events, pulling from a range of stores, but if you were to pick something for you, where would you go?"

Hailey looked around the store, tilting her head. "There are definitely some treasures here," she said, taking an ornament with a large velvet ribbon off the tree. The crystal star distorted the light behind it, almost seeming to glow in her hand. "This is my style." It was more than her style. She loved it. "This would be something I would hang on my own tree."

"It's beautiful," Troy said.

The shop owner came through a doorway in the corner, ushering them to see what he'd created for the Forest Festival. Hailey reluctantly returned the star ornament to the tree bough, determined to buy it as soon as she saw the owner's donation. She followed the owner quickly.

After admiring the tree and asking about delivery, Hailey and Troy returned to the front of the shop. She picked up a few old-fashioned wreaths to use as decorations for the Forest Festival, but when she came back to the tree, the star ornament was gone.

She asked the woman at the cash register about it, as Troy hung back, looking at a few more of the decorations. "Did anyone buy the star ornament that was on that tree?"

The woman looked around the shop, her eyes wide. "I'm sorry, miss. Christmas decorations tend to move quickly through our store."

They'd barely been in the back room ten minutes. She sighed. "Well, it was a beautiful ornament," she said, wishing she'd held onto it instead of placing it on the tree.

CHAPTER 17

Don't be mad," Troy said to Cara. He paced in his hotel room, knowing he probably should have alerted Cara sooner, but he had spent the entire day with Hailey enjoying the first snow.

"See, when you start out a phone call like that, I assume I'm supposed to be mad." She laughed. "What did you do this time?"

"I may have panicked and given out your personal number to someone," he said.

"Am I pretending to be your girlfriend to let someone down not so gently? Because I do feel like I've become an expert in that," she said.

"Would you be mad about that?"

"Of course not. It's actually kind of fun!"

"That's good to know for the future, but that's not why."

"I'm waiting," Cara said. "Who did you give my number to? A single guy who needs a date to the Forest Festival?"

"Hailey."

"The girl you've been working with? Doesn't she have your direct line already? Why shuffle her through me?"

"Well, I couldn't give her my number when she asked Santa for his contact information, could I?"

"Why didn't you just tell her it was you?"

Troy ran a hand through his hair. "I thought she knew it was me. After she opened up to me as Santa, and then asked for how to contact Santa, I realized she didn't know that it was me. I'd just asked her about her friend, thinking she knew the whole time that it was me, and it would have been so awkward to tell her right at that moment. So I panicked and gave her your number."

"So, I'm supposed to answer every possible unknown call on my personal phone with some sort of greeting about the North Pole?"

"I'm texting you her number, and if she ever calls, you can pretend to be an elf for Santa."

"An elf? Really?"

"I warned you not to be mad."

She laughed. "I'm not mad, I just think you're going to a lot of trouble for this woman."

"I really like her, Cara."

"Then you should just tell her the truth."

"I will. I'm going to. But I wasn't going to admit that after she'd confided in someone she thought was a perfect stranger. This is only if she calls in the next couple of weeks, before the Forest Festival. If she calls after that, well, she'll already know by then. I'm going to be the same Santa at the Forest Festival."

"Did you give your elf a name?"

"I just used your name. I figured that was easiest."

"So, let me get this straight. Say she calls me and asks for Santa's availability. What am I supposed to say? Do you want me to book you an event?"

Troy scratched the back of his neck. He and Hailey needed to at least talk about their relationship openly together before he revealed that he was Santa. After that it would be a non-issue. He could explain to her that he wasn't really available to do any Christmas party for her. She would understand. He supposed that if she was really in a pinch, he'd come and help her for an event anyway, though playing Santa at a ritzy party he could have been invited to, felt a little odd. But if Hailey was planning ahead and wanted to book something between now and the time he could talk to her about it, what would he do? "Check my calendar and see if it's something that I can feasibly do. If it is, sure you can put it on my calendar."

"And if she asks you to travel for it?"

Troy sighed. There were so many possibilities. But Hailey was completely mesmerized by him being Santa. He'd seen it in her eyes. "I'll travel for Hailey, as long as she's in attendance at the event."

"I'm writing all of this down," Cara said. "So, she's an event coordinator. She's going to book multiple events at a time. So what's your limit on how many you'll do for her?"

"I can't imagine you finding much room in my calendar to begin with," he said.

"Humor me. You're the one who got yourself into this mess. I'll be thorough so I don't have to call Santa in the middle of the phone call to get this figured out."

"Fair enough. Two is probably the max," he said, though even as he said it he knew he'd be willing to do more. He'd throw out his whole winter schedule if it meant spending more time with Hailey after the Forest Festival. Warmth spread through him at the thought. He wanted to see her after the Forest Festival. He'd jumped into this competition with the idea of winning, but right now that didn't matter. The competition had brought them together. He'd focus on that, whatever it looked like after she went back to Seattle and he went back to New York City. Right now, he was keeping his options open.

"Got it," Cara said. "Anything else I can do for you, boss?"

"Yes, one more thing. Hailey is going to put her aunt's house up for sale. Have my realtor look into this property and see what he thinks."

"I'll have him pull the value and all the specs to see if it's a good investment," Cara said.

Good investment? That hadn't been in his thoughts at all. It didn't matter if it was a good investment. It wasn't for him. It was for the dream that Hailey had shared with him about the house. "I don't need the specs. I've seen the house. I just want to know what the realtor thinks, then put an offer in." He'd surprise Hailey with the house once he turned it into a place where families could stay close to the hospital. His Christmas present to her. A wave of excitement shot through him as he imagined how she'd respond to the gift.

"You've got it. Put an offer in on a house, regardless of the property value, and book up to two events as Santa if Hailey calls."

"That's right," he said.

"You're going to a lot of trouble for her," Cara said.

"I know. She's worth it."

AT THE END OF THE WEEK TROY CHECKED IN WITH KYLE AND Kandice. Kandice especially found the whole interchange with Hailey in the Santa suit interesting.

"It was like I was a different person," he said. It had been really fun. He'd been able to give the young girl more than just a promise of a gift, but hope. He hadn't realized at the time just how deeply it had affected him.

"And you paid for the suit using some of your donation to the foundation?"

"Not exactly," Troy said. "I've decided that I'm going to play Santa at my company's Christmas party, so I bought the suit for the company, not for thc foundation."

Kyle coughed. "That's fudging the rules," he said.

"I'm not sure it is," Kandice said. "If the primary purpose for him getting the outfit was for his party, or say he already had a Santa suit, we wouldn't dock that against him."

"His work party wasn't the primary reason, only the excuse," Kyle countered.

"Let's hear it from Troy," Kandice said. "How does this fit in?"

Troy blew out a breath, wondering if the entire challenge was blown because he'd bought an expensive Santa suit. "I probably wouldn't have wanted to dress up for my Christmas party without the push of the foundation. Money is tight for them. They could hire another Santa who already had a suit, or they could reimburse me for the cost of the suit, but when it comes right down to it, after interacting with Kenzie, I don't know. I want to be Santa at my Christmas party. Yes, the foundation was the push for it, but you should have seen this little girl and her parents. The way Hailey talked about it after ... well, let's just say I'm excited to play Santa and help."

"You're not out of the competition over this, but make sure that your choices for this stay within that $10,000. Buying a suit that you'll wear again is probably not a big deal for our purposes," Kandice said.

"You're too easy on him," Kyle said.

"Maybe, but after the praise of his performance his first time as Santa, I'm hoping I can get him to come to Texas for Christmas, so we can see him in person."

Troy laughed. "I'm sure the praise was exaggerated."

Kyle laughed. "Sounds like you guys are doing well on your project. Is there anything Kandice or I can help you with?"

Troy tried to think of anything, but he couldn't, and soon they said their goodbyes. He was excited for another week ahead of him, and for how well everything was going.

"How is the Forest Festival going?" Cara asked. "I'm really excited to see it."

"It's coming along," Troy said. "We're still working on getting enough trees, but we're getting there." He'd had the thought to ask Hailey about the extra trees they'd cleaned out of the storage closet that had belonged to her aunt. He wondered if those would be possibilities, or if she had other ideas for how to use them. "But I think I might have stumbled onto an idea for a few more trees," he said.

"You're really enjoying this, aren't you?" she asked.

"More than I'd expected to," he admitted.

"That's great," she said.

Speaking of trees, he wondered about their company trees and the status of each of them. "How do our trees look for the office?" he asked.

She laughed. "Are you looking for more donations?"

"We could always use a few more trees."

"Come to think of it, I was planning to replace the trees in our front lobby. There's four of them, maybe you could donate those somewhere?" Cara's voice was excited.

"Yes, that's good," Troy said.

"No. No, Troy. That's not good. That's outside the scope."

"You came up with the idea, I was just agreeing with you," he said.

She laughed. "I think you're missing the point of helping here. It's more about the service I think, than it is about the donations."

"I don't think I'm missing the point. I think for the first time I'm finally getting the point."

"If you donate more than your $10,000, you'll be at risk of losing your million, and then you won't earn the three million for the competition. You'll be able to help them out much better by winning the competition," she reminded him.

He knew that everything she said was logical. It didn't make sense to throw away the three million and lose the million he'd put in just because he wanted to help right now. But helping now felt more important than helping later. "I don't care about the competition anymore."

Cara made a choking sound. "I'm sorry, what was that? I think our connection went bad for a minute. It sounded like you said that you don't care about the competition. You always care about winning."

Troy ran his hand through his hair. What was he saying? What was he thinking? "I care about helping Hailey and about the Forest Festival. That's more important than winning the bet."

"But three million dollars—it's worth that?"

"So I lose the bet? It's only three million dollars."

"Don't do it."

Troy sighed. "You're right, I won't."

"I do have a donation for you," Cara said.

"Okay, what is it?"

"I'm bringing a tree."

"Cara, we just went over this. I can't have others help me."

"I'm not doing it for you. I'm doing it for Red Oaks, and I want to see this Hailey that you're crushing on."

"You're really going to donate a tree?"

"If that's okay with you," she said quietly.

"I think that sounds like a great idea. Thanks, Cara."

"I just need permission to take a few days off work. Do you think you could help me with that part? I'd like to come and volunteer during the Forest Festival too. And no, I won't let anyone know you're my boss."

He laughed. "Fair enough. I know Hailey will be more than happy to have the extra help."

"Would you like me to label the tree from you as well, or are you doing your own tree?"

It hadn't crossed Troy's mind that names would label the trees, but it made sense. "Not from me. It's your tree, not mine. I'm not trying to take the spotlight here." If anything, he wanted to hang in the background, helping Hailey without needing the praise. He wasn't actually undercover. He'd used his real name, but he didn't make it a point to flaunt his donations. After seeing the way her ex threw around money and boasted about it, he didn't want to be anywhere in the realm of that.

CHAPTER 18

Hailey had balanced her time between work on the Forest Festival with Troy, and just spending time with Troy for the last four weeks. They'd spent the last two days picking up all of the donations and transporting them to the events center. The 150 pounds of chocolates and candy canes, both to sell and give away, was the final pick up last night. Everything was going well.

Christmas music played as volunteers set up trees, turning the events center into a literal forest of decorated evergreens.

Hailey watched in awe as Emily walked around the room with a clipboard. Emily had received Edna's approval to take over the volunteer schedule for all of the volunteers from the foundation and from Red Oaks. It was remarkable. Hailey had to admit that she appreciated having that task delegated, though she was used to doing it with her business. It was nice to see that Emily was capable of keeping everyone on task.

Where was Troy? They were going to set up her aunt's trees together and decorate them.

Paul came up to her. "Hi," he said.

Hailey looked around, wishing Troy was close by. "Paul. What are you doing here?"

Paul pursed his lips. "Emily reached out to me and asked about volunteering, so here I am."

"I thought you weren't happy about volunteering if you couldn't be Santa," she countered.

Paul shrugged, not giving away any emotions. "It's for the kids, right? So, of course I'll help."

Hailey nodded. "Thanks."

"Anything for the kids," he said.

She quirked an eyebrow at him, wondering if he was really just doing it for her, or if he cared about the kids. It didn't matter. Emily had organized the volunteers, and so she could step away from having to work directly with him. "Emily is really the person you'll want to see for your assignment."

"I'm still willing to donate," he said.

She shook her head. "I'm seeing someone, and he doesn't donate with strings attached."

He snorted. "Just because you don't see the strings, doesn't mean there aren't any. Why would a billionaire work on this project anyway? It makes no sense." A challenge flashed in his eyes.

Hailey tilted her head. "What are you talking about?"

He studied her. "You think it's hard to figure out? A simple Google search led me right to the info. If you want to pretend you don't care about the money, that's fine with me. But don't act like there's not a reason your boyfriend is giving to this foundation. His $10,000 is hardly a drop in the bucket to the billions he has."

Hailey shifted. Was Troy a billionaire? And what did it matter? "We don't spend our time together talking about bank accounts," she said, trying to sound confident.

"You didn't even know? Wow, Hailey." He shook his head. "Maybe you don't know him as well as you thought you did."

Hailey rolled her eyes. "If you're going to help volunteer here, then go get an assignment from Emily. If all you're going to do is put people down, you can leave."

He backed away, palms in the air. "Just something to think about. Why is a billionaire trying so hard to get others' business for this small-town charity, when he could easily fund the whole thing himself?"

Hailey walked away from Paul, unwilling to answer. Thoughts ran around her as she walked toward the far end of the room, as far as she could get away from Paul. She headed toward the large present decorations—empty moving boxes that had been painted or wrapped with colorful butcher paper. In the back of her mind Paul's accusation of Troy ate at her.

Troy came around the corner, a stack of empty boxes wrapped as presents in his arms. He looked like the little mouse in her favorite princess movie, carrying cheese, trying to keep all of them stacked together.

"Here, let me help," she said.

"Thanks," Troy said. He placed a few of the boxes around the large evergreen tree, and stood back. He frowned. "I'm not really good at placing these presents."

Hailey waved a hand in the air. "That's okay." She began stacking them, varying the color and sizes. She tipped one on its side, and angled another one, propping it up on one corner artistically. She stepped back next to Troy to take a look at the full picture.

"How do you do that?" he asked. "It looks like what Christmas morning feels like."

She smiled. "We all have our talents—and our secrets."

He tilted his head.

She continued, wondering if she could ask him about what Paul had said. "My talent is arranging displays to make them look good."

"And what about your secret?" He grinned at her.

"I guess the secret is I learned it in high school, when I was in charge of window displays at the small department store. I had to be very creative in small spaces—give things a 3-D effect in a very narrow space. I don't even think about it now. It just comes naturally. I feel that the look is right, more than I know why I actually place things where they go."

"That's quite amazing," he said, admiration shining in his eyes. "So in all of this decorating my talent is—what? Moving large boxes that look heavy?"

She shrugged. "That's a needed talent."

"I don't have a story that goes along with moving boxes. So I guess I don't have a secret," he said confidently.

"I'm sure you have lots of secrets," she said, biting the inside of her bottom lip to keep her from saying more. She needed to think more about Paul's conversation before she accused Troy of anything … What would she even say? If he was a billionaire, and he was doing something nice to help the Forest Festival, why was it any of her concern? It shouldn't change anything between them, right? But the thought that he was keeping it a secret from her wormed its way into her consciousness. She'd thought that they'd been open with each other through all of the weeks that they'd worked on the Festival together.

"Maybe." He snapped his fingers. "I did have a surprise to tell you about though," he said. "A delivery truck should be here tomorrow, from New York City. Seven trees with decorations will be set up for the silent auction. That's almost how many we wanted to fill our quota."

She hugged him. "That's great news. Wow. Another donation from New York City. You're well connected," she observed. She watched him closely, wondering if he would share any insights.

He shrugged. "It is where I live and work, so maybe it's just easier for me to connect with people there," he said.

"I don't know about that. You seem to connect with everyone you meet on a personal level."

"Maybe it's just a skill."

"Or a talent."

He nodded. "Sure. One of those. I do a lot of ... business ... with people and networking is part of the job. Probably not unlike what you do in your business, relying on word of mouth, and other people helping you network to your next event."

She conceded that that was true. She wanted to pull up her phone and run an internet search on his name. What would pop up? "With my aunt's trees from the foundation closet, we're only a tree or two short of what I was hoping for. Did you still want to go and pick out trees to donate together? You mentioned there was that beautiful shop in the City that had unique handcrafted ornaments we could use to accent with." Would the timing work? They were in a rush to get ready for the Forest Festival, and yet she wanted to take a road trip for the final details. They were tight on time, but she wanted to see the City with him, through his eyes.

He nodded, but the look in his eyes betrayed him. Something was wrong. He closed his eyes, and when he opened them again, his features were pinched.

"I really want to. But the thing is, I'm out of money." He cringed as he said the words. "I was hoping there would be some of the $10,000 left after we paid for the equipment and the trucks for delivery, but I looked at the books this morning. The reality is, we might be a little short on our donations. We're trying to keep as much as we can so that all of the proceeds go directly to the hospital. We could try charging a delivery fee for each tree bought, but I thought we'd decided against that."

"That was what we decided," she said, not wanting to add the extra charge when people would already be paying a lot of money for the trees.

"I can try and get more sponsors. Last week I got another $500 donation." He blew out a breath, rubbing the back of his neck. "Next year all of this will be so much easier."

Paul's words about Troy rang through Hailey's ears. She couldn't wait until she looked him up on the internet. She had to know now. "Can I ask you something?"

His reply was immediate. "Anything."

She straightened one of the presents, moving it a quarter of an inch on top of a larger present, then looked him in the eye. "Why are you excited about a $500 donation?"

"Every little bit helps," he said.

She took the plunge. "Paul googled you. I guess I have a lot of questions."

"Okay," he said, his voice staying level, but his jaw muscle flexed.

"You're more than doing well in your business." She kept her eyes on him, waiting for the slightest hint of something.

He nodded. "I am. Does that make a difference?"

"I don't know. That's a lot to process. I mean, I knew you were rich, from the car, and staying in the hotel for weeks, but …" She drew in a long breath. "Paul said you were a billionaire." She emphasized the last word.

He looked around the room, then led her through the nearest exit. They walked along a small hallway, before they went through a door that led outside. He looked at her in the eyes. "I am," he admitted.

"But you've run out of money for the Forest Festival? You've spent all of your time getting sponsors, and yet, you could have just funded everything without the work."

He winced. "It's complicated. On so many levels."

She nodded like she understood, though she didn't. Then she shook her head. "I feel like I should have known this about you," she said quietly.

"Things with Paul made me unsure how you would feel about my money." He stuffed his hands into his jeans' pockets.

"My issue was with Paul and how he acted, not the fact that he has money."

"When you were vocal about his wealth, I was interested in you. I still am." His eyes searched her. "I wanted you to get to know me for me, and not lump me into the same category as your ex."

"I would never have thought of you as the same type of person as Paul. My issue wasn't with Paul's wealth. It was how that wealth changed him as a person. It was the putting on airs, and thinking he could do whatever he wanted because he was rich and all of a sudden a big shot about it. He threw money around to impress people."

Troy's brows sunk towards his eyes. "Who's to say that isn't me too? You don't really know what I act like when people know I have money. My bank account and holdings far exceed his. Maybe I do the same—"

Hailey shook her head. "You don't. I know you don't."

"I guess I'm going to miss you being blissfully ignorant of how much I make," he said.

"Why? My respect for you has gone up in some ways, not down."

"Only some ways?" he asked.

How could she explain the thoughts and feelings that were encircling her, wrapping her up like a present. "The jury's still out," she said coyly.

He chuckled and touched her arm, his fingers sliding down her coat, until they reached her hands. "So my money isn't a problem for you?"

"No," she said. "Honesty then between us?"

"No more hidden secrets, so I have something to confess," he said, a glint in his eyes.

She raised an eyebrow.

He took a step closer to her. "I have to be honest, the swan tree is coming home with me."

He looked into her eyes, then his gaze dropped to her lips. She savored the kiss, wrapping her arms around his waist. The kiss felt like an explanation that let her worries melt away. Paul had brought Troy's billionaire status up, likely in hopes of severing the bond that they'd created. What Paul hadn't known was that that piece of information, talked through, had actually brought them closer together, not farther apart. Troy's cologne mixed with the cold winter air, and when he finally pulled away from their kiss, she brought him back for another one.

They could both see the puffs of their breathing in the air, and for the first time Hailey felt the cold from outside. She rubbed her hands together. They either needed to return into the warmth of the building or continue kissing if they stayed outside.

"I need you to trust me," he said, blinking hard like he was trying to choose his words carefully. "I'll get more donations if we need so we can have more trees available, but my $10,000 is all I can do right now. I want to do more, believe me, I do, but I just … can't."

She smiled. "I trust you." They walked back inside arm in arm.

CHAPTER 19

Troy went to get another ornament box he'd stored in one of the storage rooms for the tree that he and Hailey were decorating. He was glad they'd been able to talk about his money outside. Somehow that cleared the air between them, allowing them to focus on the final preparations for the Forest Festival. It was going to be a long night to get everything ready, but so far things were moving relatively on schedule.

Cara had arrived last night, but with all of the Forest Festival responsibilities, he hadn't had time to touch base with her. He spotted her and went down the aisle where she meticulously worked on one of the seven trees she'd been entrusted with. They weren't the largest trees in the group, but each tree had a different theme. They'd all come from different business donations in New York City in addition to the tree that Cara had personally donated. She was working on her third tree. He wouldn't have to count them as part of his personal donation with Kyle and Kandice, and the Children's Hospital would get a benefit from it.

"These look great," Troy said to Cara, admiring her handiwork.

"Thanks," she said. "This Festival is really coming together this year."

Troy nodded. "It really has. For a little while, I was concerned that we wouldn't be able to pull it off."

"That's because you're used to solving everything with money."

"You probably think that it's silly that it's hard," Troy said.

"You had something riding on this besides just the money," Cara said. "It's not like you to back down from a challenge."

"Soon the bet will be over, and I'll be able to leave all the stress of it behind." He much preferred to solve problems with money. This had been a stretch for him.

"I bet you'll be glad to get back to the City," she said.

He nodded. "I miss it." Though he didn't miss it as much as he was going to miss Hailey, but he didn't need to mention that to his assistant. He didn't want to think about leaving right now.

"That's the spirit," Cara said, adding more ornaments to the tree. "The realtor got back to you. The email is in your inbox." She showed him her phone with a message on it. "Do you think you'll win the bet?" Cara asked.

Troy nodded. "Without the Forest Festival in the position it was, I probably wouldn't have stood a chance, but yeah, I'm in a good position to win. And I'm going to buy the house."

"What about the bet?"

"What about it?"

"You can't donate more than what you've already done or you'll break the rules."

"I already have that covered, but Hailey doesn't know about it. She can't know about it." He already had an offer into the realtor. Hailey had planned to use the money to donate to the Children's Hospital through giving a fund that would cover the Forest Festival every year. It would be brilliant if she could get the money that way. His offer had been more than the asking price for the Victorian mansion, but she was worth it.

"You know this isn't going to help you win the bet," Cara said, pointing to the email on her phone. "In fact, it might look like you're trying to win the bet with more money."

And this was why he ran his own company. And why he didn't give control away. He didn't like not being able to make the decisions he wanted to, to help the way he wanted to, all to win a bet. He didn't need the bet for money, it had more to do with winning than any monetary value. But not being able to make his own decisions didn't feel like winning.

"Maybe I don't care about the bet anymore."

"You're not going to forfeit the three million dollars, are you? Not when you're this close."

Troy didn't know what to say. He saw his assistant's point of view, but Hailey meant more to him than the three million. So he'd lose a million to one of his friends. So what? He wanted to say those very words aloud, but then stopped himself. He couldn't wish that he'd never been involved with the competition. It was the only way he would have ever met Hailey. And in that sense, it had done its job. He didn't need to win. He'd already won. But Cara didn't need to know all of the details. "You're right. I'm here to win." At least that was true on one account. Now he was going to forget about winning against his friends, and focus on winning Hailey over.

"You get the girl, the house and win the bet in one fell swoop. It sounds like a very Merry Christmas," Cara said. "The only thing left to decide is what you'll do with the three million."

Troy nodded. "Hailey can't know anything about it."

She nodded. "Understood."

CHAPTER 20

Hailey sucked in a breath at the admission Troy made. This whole time everything had been a charade. Troy had been pretending that the Forest Festival mattered, that *she* mattered. All for some stupid bet involving millions of dollars. It was likely more than they would raise for their entire event. She closed her eyes tightly. She didn't want to see the truth. What she thought was real … hadn't been real. Her insides twisted, pulling and turning, like a messy ribbon discarded from the present, no longer useful, just a tangled ball ready to be disposed of.

She moved quietly, back the way she'd come through the rows of trees, not wanting to be detected by Troy and the woman he'd been talking to. Her thoughts replayed Troy's words over and over. The confidence he'd exuded in winning the bet—getting the girl, the house, and the money. She swallowed hard. This was not happening. She knew she couldn't hear anymore. It was too much. It was all too much.

She flew through the doors, finding herself in the hallway. She grabbed the first thing she saw, a long-handled push broom that had seen better days, and began sweeping the hallway clear of the Christmas debris.

Volunteers and those donating trees were still bringing in their trees to setup. No doubt the hallway would be full again before the end of the night, but right now, with the amount of adrenaline coursing through her veins, she needed to clean something.

The stiff blue bristles of the broom made a whooshing sound against the concrete floors as she moved pine needles and silver and gold glitter into a large pile before getting the dustpan and finishing the job. One hallway done. Still more to go. She'd planned to spend this time with Troy, but she couldn't. She'd been part of a bet. Good for him that he was going to win, whatever that meant. But she'd lose. She swept with more vigor, completing the next long hallway in half the time.

"There you are," Troy said. "I've been looking all over for you." He looked at his watch, tapping the screen playfully. "You want to catch dinner with me, before we're up until who knows how long to get this whole place ready for tomorrow afternoon?" He cupped one hand next to his mouth, like he was about to whisper a very important secret. "Santa is coming tomorrow."

Anger flared through her. She still hadn't seen his costume, and she'd looked forward to seeing him as Santa since she'd given him the position, but not anymore. He didn't care about her. He only cared about his bet.

"You go without me. I have work to finish." She didn't look at him, just continued pushing the broom down the hallway.

It took him a few seconds to catch up to her. "Wait a minute." He stepped in front of the broom. She tried to go around him, but he held his hands up. "What's going on?"

She shrugged. "I actually thought I knew. But I don't. Maybe you can fill me in."

He lifted her chin until she made eye contact with him. "Hailey, what's wrong?"

It was that look in his eyes. The look of complete bafflement. And she wouldn't be fooled by it. She used to think that look was endearing. But not now. She crossed her arms, the broom handle awkwardly stuck between her arms and her chest, almost hitting her in the nose. She narrowed her eyes. "You tell me. You said no more secrets. And then you hide more from me." She shook her head. The chemistry between them was so strong, it had felt like a life-time of time spent together instead of only a couple of months.

Understanding flashed in his eyes, and then something else —pain, maybe? His forehead creased with a line of worry. "I can explain," he said, his tone much slower and softer than he'd just used with her. The former excitement in his voice when he'd mentioned going out to dinner just moments ago had left.

"Then explain," she said. For a brief second her heart melted —like snow brought in from a winter's day. Maybe he had a reason. A solid reason for keeping it from her. She mentally prayed for that. She could let go of the anger if he could explain it. She leaned forward, hungry for the words he'd say.

"I wanted it to be a surprise," he started, running his hand through his hair in his characteristic way he always did, that Hailey recognized happened when he seemed to be thinking through a problem he needed to solve.

"A surprise?" He'd had a bet to be a surprise? She didn't understand it, but she kept that to herself. She watched him, seeing the internal struggle as it moved across his face.

"My realtor is still working with your realtor. Nothing is finalized until after the Forest Festival. I wanted it to be a surprise."

Now he wasn't making sense at all. "You're buying my aunt's house?"

"I couldn't let your aunt's dream die."

He took a step closer to her, lightly tugging on the broom handle that she'd folded against herself. The effect brought her closer to him and made her arms unfold. The idea that he'd put an offer on her aunt's house swelled inside of her. Thoughtful. Sensitive. Attentive. A billionaire who cared about preserving history, or at least her history. The whole thing felt beautiful. "My aunt's dream?"

He pursed his lips. "To make it a place where families could stay while their children were in the hospital."

Her eyes widened. "That's why you're buying the property?"

He nodded. "I think it's worth it." His eyes held tenderness.

"You don't have to buy it," she said, wondering where she was going with that thought. Would she actually turn the property over to him without selling it? So many conflicting emotions ran through her head.

"That's why I wasn't going to tell you about any of it," he said.

She laughed, loving this moment, wishing she hadn't spent

so much of her last hour sweeping the floor trying to work out her stress and anger at something that was so easily fixed up. Then a question popped into her mind. "You weren't going to tell me about it, but I would have found out about it eventually. Is that what the bet was about?"

Troy's smile faded instantly. "The bet?" he repeated, the words sounding strangled in his throat. His eyes searched hers. "What do you know about the bet?"

Confusion struck her. "Only what you've just said about the house and the realtor."

He shook his head. "I'm sorry, Hailey. I can't … tell you anything. Not right now."

She nodded, her chin lifting higher as she pressed her lips together. "You have more secrets than just the realty deal?"

"That wasn't really a secret, it was a surprise."

"So what's the bet?"

"I … can't," he stopped, closing his eyes tight. When he opened them, they were pleading with her. "I can explain—" he said slowly.

"Go ahead," she said, waiting for the explanation.

"I just can't explain right now." He cringed as he said the words.

He'd just told her all about the realty deal that he was going to surprise her with. But he couldn't tell her about a bet? There was something going on, but why wouldn't he tell her? They weren't any further in their relationship. She repeated her earlier line. "You said no more secrets. I said I need honesty." The words felt dry and crackly as she said them.

"I need time and trust. I will explain, I just can't right now."

"If you want trust, you need to give it too. Trust me with it.

Explain now." She pushed away memories from long ago. She pushed away comparisons to her ex. She pushed all of it away from her brain.

"Hailey, I just can't."

"Trust comes after people are honest, not before." Her mind raced through all of the possibilities. She could come up with nothing, no reason that he couldn't tell her something. Unless ... "The bet is about me?"

He glanced sideways, then lowered her voice. "I can give you a full explanation, I just need you to give me time. I can't tell you yet."

"Because I'm part of the bet. My knowing will mean you lose your bet?"

"It's not what you think." He rubbed his hands up and down her arms but she shook his touch away and stepped back.

He didn't deny her guess. If she knew about it, he would lose his bet. The bet was more important to him than she was. She didn't even care what the bet was. It didn't matter. It didn't hurt as much as the fact that someone she was falling for couldn't trust her with something important.

"I don't need you to explain," she said. He could win. That was what he wanted. It was what always had mattered to him. In fact, if she looked back at their time together, she could see that. He was on fire about getting donations, about helping people see the need to make this work in their lives. Troy was the person who had to win. And it was probably what made him a successful businessman. A billionaire. A very single successful billionaire.

His features softened, as if she'd given him the perfect

answer. He thought he'd won here. "Thank you, Hailey." He looked at her thoughtfully for a moment. "Dinner?"

She shook her head. He'd misunderstood her. He might still win, but she'd definitely lost. In more ways than one. "You don't need to explain, because we're done. I can't be with someone who doesn't trust me, and can't confide in me. I can't discover surprises or secrets and always wonder what is more important."

"Hailey, wait. I want to explain—"

"But you can't, or you won't. Not yet. Not until it's okay with your timing and winning your bet. Am I right?"

He opened his mouth to say something and then quickly shut it, shaking his head.

Hailey blinked rapidly. This was not how she'd envisioned starting the Forest Festival—the beginning of the Twelve Days of Christmas. "I need some space," she said.

He nodded like he understood. "I'll be here when—"

She shook her head furiously. "No. You won't be here."

He tilted his head, a question knit between his eyebrows. "I'm helping with Santa tomorrow and for the rest of the week. We can talk about this when the Forest Festival is over."

He couldn't be Santa. She couldn't have him have ties to her life here. That meant the Forest Festival. And her aunt's house. This was her last time in Red Oaks, and she wasn't going to have her last few days spoiled by the memory of him. Cutting ties now was her option. The only way to get through this mess of wrapping paper and wadded up tape that her life was becoming under the current situation.

"I want you to take back your offer on my house," she said,

her back as straight as she could hold it. If she didn't keep her composure she was going to crumble.

"What? I don't understand," he said slowly. "Hailey, I know we're not exactly seeing eye to eye right now, but give me a few days, and it will all make sense."

She shook her head. "I can't, Troy. It's not going to work. Please take back the offer."

"And if I don't?" The challenge was in his eyes.

She reminded herself that those who always won could be stubborn when they were playing to win. But he wasn't going to win, not on this. "I'll let my realtor know that all offers currently on the table are unacceptable."

The look in his eyes changed. "You're making a mistake."

She shook her head, not trusting herself to speak. She knew what she was doing. "I'm not. I'm going to auction it off at the Forest Festival." The words spilled out and sounded ridiculous.

"You won't get the kind of offer on it that you already have," he said.

She wanted to admit that he was probably right, but that was beside the point. "It doesn't matter. What I need is trust. And honesty. And both of those things can't be bought off like it's no big deal."

It was a long moment between them. Sounds of the volunteers on the other side of the wall from them finally hit Hailey through the blood that had been pounding in her ears. She needed the broom back, only to see that Troy had set it on the floor. His eyes bored into hers, willing her to take back what she'd just said, but she couldn't. She started walking toward the door. The hallway was too full of emotion, too full of Troy. Her hand was on the door, about to push through it, when he finally spoke.

"Wait," he said.

She turned back to him, her hand still on the metal bar to let her through the door.

He exhaled. "I'm sorry," he said. "For everything."

She nodded, knowing if she spoke it wouldn't come out coherent or steady.

He ran a hand through his hair. The hair that she'd once loved to run her hands through. She shook the thought away, knowing that she would never touch his hair again. "I'm guessing you'd prefer I don't play Santa this week."

Her eyes widened, but then she nodded. He'd heard the speech she'd given at the beginning about what that position had meant to her. At least it sounded like he'd internalized it. Her voice came out hoarse. "I suppose that would be best."

He nodded, his shoulders slumping, a defeated look on his face. "If you can't find someone before tomorrow, I will still do it. I don't want to let you down ... more ... than I already have."

"I have two other Santas I can call before I resort to asking my ex," she said, the words were spoken before she could recall them back. She could feel their stinging even as they left her mouth.

He winced. "I wish our time together didn't end this way."

Wishing wouldn't change things. He could have actually changed things. But his bet was more important to him. And he didn't trust her enough to explain. The whole realization felt like a bad piece of fruit cake in her mouth she needed to spit out. "Me too," she whispered, so quietly she wondered if he even heard her before she pushed through the door to see the progress on the trees being set up.

The door shut loudly behind her, reverberating in her ears. She shot a text off to her realtor, explaining her change of plans for the house. She pocketed her phone and tried to lose herself in the idea of letting her last Forest Festival be amazing, regardless of her feelings about Troy.

CHAPTER 21

Troy stood alone in the hallway. All the oxygen seemed to be sucked out when Hailey left. He wanted to follow her. He wanted to explain, but he stopped himself. She'd already given him multiple chances to explain and he'd messed every single one of them up. He couldn't do anything until he could explain the bet. He rolled his eyes.

The stupid bet. He'd wanted to see her face when he presented her with the check for three million dollars to donate to the charity of his choice—correction, the charity of *her* choice. But that hadn't been worth it.

He was willing to spend half that for her aunt's house for a half-baked crazy hair-brained idea that he'd had, that he'd wanted to talk over with her after the Forest Festival.

Stupid timing.

Stupid bet.

Stupid him for choosing the timing and the bet over her.

He cringed. He'd set things right—somehow. But first he

had to follow through on his promises. At least the ones he could still keep.

He called his realtor, then hers. He cancelled the deal, confirming multiple times that it wasn't a prank, and that while his offer had been genuine, that Hailey had asked him to pull out so he was going to respect her wishes.

She was making a mistake, he could feel it.

He headed out to his car and texted Cara to meet him in his hotel lobby when she was done with the setup of the Forest Festival. He didn't want to stress Hailey out by going back into the events center, when it was clear that he wasn't wanted around. He was smart enough to at least know when to quit.

TROY LOOKED UP FROM HIS CHAIR BY THE FIREPLACE IN THE hotel lobby when Cara walked toward him. He smiled. A face that wasn't angry with him right now. It was just about the best thing he could imagine at the moment.

Cara took the seat that Hailey had occupied the last time they'd sat there together. He pushed the image of Hailey out of his mind.

His assistant tilted her head. "Okay, tell me why my phone has been lighting up like a Christmas tree for the last hour while I was trying to finish decorating?"

"Hello to you too," he said, trying to keep things normal. He kept his voice low, though he doubted the couple snuggling on the far couch at the opposite end of the room was paying any attention to the business meeting he and Cara were having.

She raised her eyebrows, waiting for an answer.

"It was three text messages. Okay, four if you count the gif." He really was pathetic.

She shook her head. "I'm not talking about *yours*. Four *is* pretty light when I'm on a business trip away from the office." She pulled her phone out of her purse, revealing the evidence on the screen. "Your realtor. Hailey's realtor. Then there was Hailey calling, and then—"

"Wait. Hailey called you?"

"Twice."

He opened his mouth, not sure what to say. "Why does she have your number?"

She waved a hand in front of his face. "Troy? Are you okay?" She arched an eyebrow at him but then continued, "You gave her my number, remember?"

His brain felt muddled, before it cleared, settling on the information Cara had just given him. His eyes widened. "She called you to book my first Santa job?" he asked. This would also come to bite him. He'd never admitted to being the Santa she'd met before. He'd had some elaborate idea that kissing her as Santa under the mistletoe would be an excellent way to tell her, but now he was glad that she didn't have that ammo of secrecy to hold over his head too.

She tilted her head. "You've got two jobs in Seattle right before Christmas. She booked you for two days in a row."

His heart pounded. "My schedule was free for that?"

Cara rolled her eyes. "I wouldn't have booked you if you'd been unavailable. Besides, I thought that you'd like an excuse to visit her anyway. I booked those two weeks ago." She waved a hand in the air dismissing the off-topic conversation. "This time she actually called and asked if you were available for this week too. I told her no, of course, since you're doing the Forest Festival already, but I thought you'd like to know that she must be talking you up to a lot of people that she's booking for her events."

His heart slammed against his chest. "Hailey wants to book Santa this week? For how long?"

His assistant shrugged. "I didn't get the details because you weren't available. She did sound like she was in a panic though. Sounds like her Santa quit on her."

Troy nodded, but he needed to know for sure before he got his hopes up. Hailey had multiple events and parties booked every single night in December except for Christmas Day. She had assistants running all of them while she was away, but maybe she was calling Santa, er, him, for one of those events on the West Coast. "Call her back," he said quickly.

"You're booked already," she said slowly.

"I want to know where she wants Santa, and if she's already found someone." And he wanted to know if he was the first or second choice before she tried her ex who she'd deliberately not given the position of Santa too originally. Ugh. How low had he fallen in her esteem if she was willing to give her ex, the whole reason he'd gotten the Santa job in the first place as Troy, the role of Santa now? He only had himself to blame.

Cara nodded. "I'm on it. What else can I do for you?" She didn't make a move to call Hailey during their meeting. Normally he appreciated how well she stayed focused during their meetings, but today, he needed the information.

He shook his head. "I want to listen in. Let her know that Santa wanted more information about the job. Once she gives you the answer, put her on mute, and tell me the details."

She smiled at him, and he could tell that she wanted to ask him what was really going on. Instead of asking questions, she found Hailey's number in her recent calls list and tapped the screen.

Troy drummed his fingers on the table as Cara began talking to Hailey.

"Hello, Miss Waters?" his assistant confirmed. "This is Cara the Elf, from Santa's Workshop." Cara rolled her eyes when Troy smiled at her title.

She paused, listening to Hailey, then Cara spoke again. "Santa just got back to the North Pole and was interested in learning more about the emergency that you've run into for this week and weekend. Can you tell me where you were hoping he could be?" She listened to the response, then made eye contact with Troy. "Oh, in upstate New York … close to the hotel you met Santa in." She stared at Troy, but all he could do was cringe.

Troy listened as Cara repeated some of the crucial details. His heart thudded loudly. He flexed his fingers, wishing he was patched into the call so he could hear everything first-hand.

Cara nodded several more times, then shook her head, all the while she only said, "Hmm," or "Mmm." His assistant listened a lot longer, and then finally said, "I'm going to see if I can catch Santa before he … goes to check on the reindeer." Cara ran a hand over the bridge of her nose. "Would you mind if I put you on hold for a quick minute while I see if I can talk to him?"

She waited for confirmation and then pushed the mute button on her phone.

Troy forced a smile. "Quick thinking on the reindeer comment," he said.

Cara didn't look amused. "What's going on?" She lowered her voice. "The realtors say the deal is off the table, and now Hailey is giving me this huge sob story about what happened between the two of you. I assume she's making it up so that she can get some sympathy points with "Santa," but still."

"Whatever she said is accurate."

His assistant's eyes widened. "Don't you even want to know what she said?"

He shook his head.

She waved a hand in the air. "Fine if it doesn't matter. What matters is she needs a Santa, and she's willing to pay a LOT for one, on such short notice if you're available for the entire time. She can't have multiple Santas around. She has to have the same one for continuity."

He hadn't thought about that. "I did say that if she couldn't find a Santa, that I'd fill in, as Troy."

"Yeah, well, hope that you don't make that mistake right now, because after what I just heard, you'd better hope that she doesn't discover that you're Santa this week. So are you going to do it? Are you going to be the "Santa" she doesn't know is actually you?"

His heart rate sped up. He'd be around for the entirety of the Forest Festival, and she wouldn't know it was him. She'd see him, but not see him. But if she found out, she'd be more livid, making the entire Festival worse for her. He didn't want to hide behind the suit and the wig. He didn't want to pretend around her. He wanted her to see that he'd been genuine the whole time. Protecting the secret of the bet wasn't to hurt her, it was to help her. He could explain all of that next week. He cringed. Technically he couldn't explain it until he got the call on Christmas Eve. "She has other options," Troy said.

Cara rolled her eyes. "Not after what I just heard. I mean, sure, send her into the arms of her ex. She hates him maybe slightly less than she hates you right now, so maybe they'll be a good fit." She huffed out the words.

"You know what I mean," Troy said.

"Why did you even have me call her back? You knew that this was for this week. Why make her tell a complete stranger her story about it, and then not want to do it? You obviously care for her. Act like it."

"How?" Frustration rose inside him. "She doesn't want to be around me."

"She won't be around you, she'll be around *Santa*. You want to fix this, so fix it."

"I can't fix it as Santa," he said. "I have to tell her it's me. She has to know who she's asking or everything will blow up in my face."

"When she finds out that the Santa she wanted so badly to play the part at the Forest Festival is actually the same person she just kicked out of the Forest Festival, she's going to feel more betrayed, not less. So you'll have to pick your battle. Make her more mad at you, or do your best to solve her current problem right now. You can tell her it was you after."

He huffed out a breath. "You're right. I can't tell her I'm Santa until I can talk to her as Troy, and get this whole thing cleared up."

"That's logical in an irrational sort of way, but you don't have a lot of time to fix this before Santa has to make a decision. You don't have to let her ex play Santa. You know you really don't want that."

He cringed. "You're right. Tell her I'll do the entire Forest Festival."

Cara beamed at him. "Finally you're making some sense." She said something about a brooding billionaire under her breath, but before he could respond, she unmuted the phone and told Hailey the good news. She'd have the Santa she'd always wanted for the Forest Festival.

His assistant took a few more minutes on the phone call, glanced up at Troy several times, and finally laughed, before saying goodbye to Hailey.

"What?" Troy asked, wanting to be filled in on the rest of the conversation.

"I'm surprised you let her go so easily. She sounds like a good match for you."

"I have to make things right before I can think about that," Troy said cautiously. He'd thought they were a good match too, but if she flew off the handle at everything she didn't know, maybe he'd have to regroup and think about it first.

His assistant straightened in her chair. "How can I help?"

He had to set things right. For starters, he needed to get out of the bet, completely. And he needed to figure out a really great apology gift for Hailey. "Place a call to Kyle Montgomery. Let him know that I'm bowing out of the bet."

His assistant's eyes widened. "Surely a few more days—"

Troy shook his head. "No. Tell him I'm out."

She cleared her throat. "And if he asks for a reason?"

"Tell him I'm done playing by other people's rules. I'll donate how I want to. I won't be stuck with arbitrary rules."

She nodded slowly. "Okay. Anything else I can do for you?"

"Stay close to the Forest Festival tomorrow. Santa won't have a lot of breaks, but I'll need help this week if I'm going to figure things out. Keep me posted on what Kyle says."

TROY WALKED INTO THE FOREST FESTIVAL, DECKED OUT IN HIS Santa suit. He had his large sack slung over his back and shook the bells. It was still early in the day. The Festival didn't officially open for three more hours, but he couldn't wait any longer to come.

Volunteers were setting up the ticket table. Finishing touches of wreaths and fresh holly were being hung. Christmas music filled the air. Troy recognized a few of the volunteers as people from local businesses that had made donations. "Ho, ho, ho," he said, then turned to the man who ran the Tree Farm. "Thanks for coming, Lester. It means a lot to have your support."

The guy looked at him. "How do you know my name?"

Troy realized his mistake, mentally berating himself. He thought quick on his feet. "I'm Santa Claus," he laughed what he hoped sounded like a jolly laugh. "I know everything."

The man was obviously perplexed, looking around him. Troy was about to tell him who he really was when the man spotted his ID card that was strung around his neck with a lanyard. The older gentleman laughed heartily. "For a moment there, I wondered if you were the real thing," he said. "That was a good one." He went back to hanging up the wreath.

Troy blew out his breath slowly, careful not to inhale too

quickly and catch white hair between his lips. That was a close one. Too close. He'd have to be more careful as Santa. He needed to ask people their names first. Or just not be so personable. He dismissed the thought almost as quickly as he thought it. It was in him to be personal—to make connections. That was what had drawn him to be the way he had been with the little girl in the hotel. And that had been the whole reason that Hailey had liked his version of Santa in the first place. Hailey would expect that. But he'd be more careful. He didn't want to give himself away.

A door pushed open from the Forest Festival room. "Santa?" Hailey came through the door. The same door she'd left through, leaving him in the deserted hallway last night.

He stood in roughly the same spot as when he'd seen her last. He wanted to run to her, to apologize. To explain everything. He was done with the bet, but he wouldn't tell her that over the phone. He needed to do it in person, when he was Troy. "Hailey," he said, breathing out her name. Her scent was in the air.

She came quickly toward him. "Hi Santa," She beamed at him. She tilted her head. "How did you know my name?"

The air rushed out of him. To her, he was only Santa right now. It wasn't Troy that she was smiling at like she'd just gotten what she wanted for Christmas. He was currently Santa, the person who'd saved her Forest Festival after Troy had realized that playing Santa for her would add additional stress to her over the week. He couldn't do that to her.

She blinked and waited for his answer.

He cleared his throat. He'd better keep his Santa voice all day if he was going to keep her from being stressed and feeling like she'd been lied to. Again. "My elf passes on all of my messages." He moved his hands against his side, only then realizing that he still held the bells in his hand. He stuffed them inside his large coat pocket.

She smiled her kissable lips at him. "It's so good to see you again. I'm so relieved you're here. Let me show you around."

Heat ran through him as she led him through the doors. Being next to her, but not being able to tell her anything, or apologize was acute torture.

"Welcome to the Forest Festival," she said, her tone hushed.

Troy looked around. He'd left before everything was finished last night. The wonder and the transformation felt like stepping into Narnia. It was completely amazing. Rows of trees stretched the entire length of the room. Each sparkled with lights, and ornaments caught that light, creating a dazzling spectacle that was hard to completely take in.

He'd imagined this moment—the first time he and Hailey would see the completed Forest Festival, the way it would come together regardless of the naysayers that had tried to convince her otherwise. She'd had in her head the vision of what it could be, and he hadn't fully grasped onto the final display until this moment. Sure, he'd helped, but it had been Hailey's passion for her aunt's legacy that had pushed her. It was beautiful. "Wow," he said, barely getting the word out as he tried to soak in all of the details.

She beamed at him. "It's something, isn't it?"

He nodded. "You've obviously done a lot of work, pulling this off."

Her expression clouded. "I had help, and besides, it's not a success yet. We'll know tonight if all the work was worth it.

The first day is usually the best attended." She ducked her head.

He smiled under his curly beard, but he wondered how well she could see it. Would his lips look remotely familiar to her? Likely not. That was the Santa magic. People saw what they wanted to see. And what she wanted to see was a seasoned professional Santa who knew how to make the Christmas season magical for others. He wouldn't let her down. Not when he could do this. He looked into her eyes. "You don't need the numbers or the donations or the attendance to be a success." He gestured to the room. "This is what success and hard work and perseverance looks like."

Her eyes glistened, and she sniffed. "Thanks, Santa."

He closed his eyes. He was Santa. He had to remember that. "You're welcome, Hailey."

She blinked rapidly. "Let me show you around, and tell you a little more about what you'll be doing."

"Lead the way," he said, happy that she gave him the tour and told him everything he'd be doing. It was almost like they were still a team working on the Forest Festival again like they had for the last several weeks. Acute. Torture.

CHAPTER 22

Anticipation ran through Troy as he waited for the Forest Festival to officially begin. He was in an overstuffed wing-backed chair with candy canes on either side of him. His present sack had been filled with mini candy canes to give out to the children when they came to see him, as well as small velvet sacks of chocolates. He wiggled his toes in the black leather boots. He'd already been in costume for a couple of hours.

Hailey stood next to the microphone on the main stage. He was diagonally behind her. She tapped the microphone, checking to see if it worked. "Welcome to the Forest Festival," she announced. The crowd cheered, and she proceeded to explain the day's events. The first day was bound to be more crowded, as those who wanted to bid on trees and other Christmas decorations wanted a chance to look at the trees available. The bidding didn't open until the evening. She explained the procedures and how to mark a bid.

Troy smiled as he watched her take ownership of the room. When she'd finished her announcements and explained the refreshments stand, she stepped away from the microphone and Christmas music immediately began playing.

She made a face like she'd sucked on a lemon, blushing and looking down when she realized Santa had caught her making a face.

She walked toward him and for a split-second Troy wondered if she could see him through the costume. But she only said, "Um, ignore my face."

"I don't think it's possible to ignore a face as beautiful as yours." He coughed, wondering if that was an appropriate thing for Santa to say to her.

She blushed again. "I meant the face I pulled. I-I wasn't planning on being the one to announce it. I was going to have my … other Santa announce everything."

He tilted his head. "You're a natural in front of a crowd."

"I have to be. It's basically my job. But I prefer a smaller crowd. I don't always get them, but then, I don't usually have to make announcements up on a stage, with a microphone. I do it, but, it's just one of the parts of my job I don't love as much." She shivered.

Troy nodded, feeling bad that even though he was Santa and could have made those announcements, she hadn't given him that task. "Well, if I can help in any way while I'm here, let me know. Santa is always happy to make an announcement for you." He smiled, wishing he could hold her. Instead he gripped the armrests tighter.

Hailey nodded. "Thanks, Santa. You've already helped more than you'll ever know." She bit her lip.

He wanted to ask her more about that. He wanted to hear what she'd told Cara, and now he wished he wouldn't have dismissed all of those details so easily yesterday. But before he could ask what she meant, she started speaking again.

"The line for the kids will be starting in about five minutes. Is there anything I can get for you? Bottled water?"

He shook his head. "I'm good at the moment."

"I'll be around if you need something. And I'll have two volunteers who will be here with you. One of them will always have a radio, so keep us posted."

"I will. Thank you, Hailey."

Hailey disappeared into the Forest Festival, and Troy had little time to think about Hailey over the next hour as he greeted children, posed for pictures, and gave out candy canes. Volunteers rotated through the North Pole, helping take the pictures and also making sure that he was stocked with candy canes.

There was a lag between children in the line, with a sleepy little boy who didn't seem like he was in the mood to see Santa, whether he was given a treat for it or not. As the mom wrestled with the small toddler, Troy picked up on a conversation behind the mounds of cardboard snow decorations making the North Pole look like the North Pole.

"I heard her announce it. She's going to auction off her aunt's house at the Forest Festival," a woman said.

"I've had my eye on that property for years," a man's voice said. "I talked to Hailey's aunt multiple times about selling, but she never would. I made offer after offer on it." There was a pause. "It really would be the best place to put condominiums. We could capitalize on the location. The land is big enough.

Nobody here wants that property as much as I do. We could get a huge discount on it, and the wrecking ball could be there by New Year's. When did she say it would be auctioned off?"

The woman spoke lower, and Troy strained his ears to hear more.

Out of nowhere a toddler came bounding toward him, and between the loud toddler's voice calling, "Santa" and his squeaky bubble shoes, he couldn't hear the rest of the conversation. When the toddler's turn was over, he stood up from his chair, hoping to look like he was stretching. He couldn't see the people who'd been talking, but the voice had sounded familiar to him.

An hour later when his volunteers rotated, he heard the voice again, and confirmed the guy's identity. Paul, Hailey's ex, was the one who had a dream to build condominiums. In all reality, perhaps it would bring some business to the sleepy town, but Troy was going to fight it. Hailey had asked him to rescind his offer on the house, and he'd kept that promise, but maybe as Santa he could at least raise the price enough that her ex or anyone bidding for it would have to pay a fair price for it. He hated the idea of it being knocked down though. He had to at least tell Hailey. She had to know. But would Santa be able to convince her it was a bad idea to auction it off at the Forest Festival?

CHAPTER 23

Hailey looked around the Forest Festival. The first day was more than halfway finished and already it felt like a smashing success. Bids were starting to pour in for the trees. Volunteers had regularly reported how busy their rows were. They'd helped patrons record their bid for each tree they'd been interested in, and many of them had been going between trees non-stop during their volunteer shift.

Between the bustle of kids and adults chatting through the aisles, the clinking of glasses and forks against plates in their dining area, she could barely hear the underlying Christmas music anymore. Every half hour the place became more filled. Very few people were leaving. She'd already given a few statements to both the local news reporter and journalist, who were covering the Forest Festival. The online edition of the article would post later tonight and hopefully draw in a larger crowd for the rest of the week. With any luck the footage would air on the evening news.

A twinge of sadness filled her as she watched Santa for probably the tenth time in the last hour. He was so good with the kids. She imagined that he'd spent most of the last ten years perfecting his ability to talk with children the way he did. It was endearing and at the same time the sadness hit her again. How she'd wanted to see Troy in that role. She laughed at the silliness of that thought now.

Troy was so personable with all of the businesses they'd gone to. He seemed to bring a natural energy into each encounter with people, and she'd wanted to see if he could translate that into the Santa role. Was Troy good with children? Did he have nieces or nephews in his life? They hadn't spent much of their time talking about extended family, except for her aunt, but then she realized that was mostly because she'd talked so much about her aunt.

Hailey shook her head again. "I'm not thinking about him," she muttered to herself, though she was. She looked at Santa one more time, wishing Troy had never offered to get out of the position. This Santa was amazing, the best she'd ever seen, but each time she looked his way, or heard the jingling of bells, she missed Troy. She held a hand to her forehead.

What was wrong with her? Troy hadn't been honest with her. She couldn't pine for him anymore. She *wouldn't* pine for him anymore. He'd made his choice, and he hadn't chosen her. She inhaled deeply through her nose, determined to let this Santa know how grateful she was that he'd come.

She looked toward the North Pole, where Santa had been sitting each time she'd looked up toward the stage. A rope blocked the chair and Christmas tree off from access to the patrons. He'd probably gone to get dinner. Santa's "Elf" that she'd been in contact with had made it clear that Santa needed his own private dressing room and place to eat. His anonymity was very important to the work he did, and she understood that. To be as good as he was, he probably had to protect himself a little. She busied herself for the next half an hour, smiling at patrons and admiring rows of trees that she'd already seen a dozen times.

A red-headed volunteer heading toward the North Pole carried a large bag of candy canes. Hailey headed her off before she reached the doors that would allow her access to the stage from the main room. "I can take these," Hailey said.

The volunteer nodded. "I was going to stay and help Santa," she said.

"You can go and get dinner now if you haven't already. I can take a shift helping Santa," Hailey offered.

The redhead beamed. "Thanks. I've been wanting to try one of those freshly made cinnamon rolls."

Hailey nodded. "Ask them for the North Pole Special, and you'll end up with a dusted layer of candy canes on top of it with no extra charge. It's delicious with the hot chocolate."

"Thank you," she said, practically skipping away in the opposite direction.

Hailey pushed her way through the door and onto the stage. The striped clock showed Santa would be back at any minute. She spread the candy canes out on the gold tray that was next to Santa's chair. He'd put several into his present sack, but it had been an awkward thing to reach from, so they'd found the charger tray to put on the table next to him. She arranged them into a spiral, letting all of the canes point the same way. The design swirled beautifully.

"In about two minutes all of your hard work will be messed up," a voice said behind her.

She turned around and smiled. "Hi Santa," she said.

"Hello Hailey." His deep voice was rich with vibrato.

"It's my turn to volunteer in the North Pole." She smiled brightly.

He looked at the ornamented list that was propped next to a book. "What happened to Sally?"

Hailey smiled. "She heard about the North Pole cinnamon rolls, and I told her I'd take her shift. You're stuck with me for the next half hour, if that's okay."

He nodded, his beard moving as he smiled. "You're the boss, so I suppose you can take whatever position you want to."

"I actually wanted to thank you," she began.

"For what?" He sat down in his chair, holding his arms open toward the first child in the line.

Hailey stepped back, only now realizing that trying to tell him thank you for helping her make this day what it needed to be was going to be difficult. As the little girl took her candy cane from Santa and hopped off his knee, she took the little girl to her mother, giving them directions for how to exit the North Pole and return to the Forest Festival. With her as the sole volunteer next to Santa, she kept the line going as fast as she could, only then realizing how ill equipped she was to help him.

At the end of the thirty minutes, she swapped with the volunteer at the beginning of the line, and watched Santa as he listened to one child after another tell their hopes and dreams. From this side she wasn't able to hear what they were saying, but she was able to get a front view of his smile and his entire suit. He really made the best Santa she'd ever seen. He smiled in her direction after each child, and it took her way too long to catch onto the fact that he was smiling at the next child in line, and not her.

"I THOUGHT YOU WERE SELLING YOUR HOUSE TODAY," SANTA SAID casually, when the Forest Festival was finished for the evening. He slung his present sack over his shoulder, and took out the bells that were in his pocket.

"They made an announcement that the house would be ready for auction on the last night. You might have missed the announcement when you were eating. I couldn't get everything lined up like I wanted to for tonight," Hailey said. The realtor was still working out the details on the way to make the sale work so that someone couldn't bid $1 and buy it. It had to be a reasonable bid, and it was causing her realtor a slight panic attack.

Santa's words cut through her thoughts. "That's nice of you to donate the proceeds of the house. It's a very generous offer."

"It will be if there are any bites on it," she said, not sure what else to say. There was no way that she'd get as much as the offer she'd turned down from Troy. Her realtor had repeatedly told her as much after informing her how much Troy had been willing to buy the house for, and the stupidity of that move finally sunk in. She should have just taken his offer. She didn't need the house. She wasn't coming back. But she couldn't bear the thought that Troy would own her aunt's house, and she'd never have the option to see it again, especially not the way they'd left things.

"How much is the house worth?" he asked her.

She studied Santa, and told him the price. "I should be able to get $750,000 for it." Perhaps it was a little optimistic, and it was still less than what Troy had offered on the house, but she needed the power that came from thinking positively.

Santa nodded. "That's a generous donation. I'm sure the Children's Hospital will appreciate it."

Hailey nodded. "I hope so. And speaking of that, I wanted to thank you for jumping in at the last minute." She looked around the darkening room as row by row the power was shut off to the Christmas trees. "I don't know what I would have done without you."

Santa paused next to the chair and smiled. "You would have managed, I'm sure."

She shook her head. "For all of the beauty of the trees, and the donations, it's Santa that draws the crowd."

"There were many more people among the trees than in Santa's line," he said, as they headed through the candy cane rope entryway out of the North Pole.

"Maybe that's true the first day, but that won't be the case for the next couple of days," she said.

"Are you trying to scare me off?" he asked, giving a jolly laugh that sounded a little forced.

She shook her head. "No, just trying to tell you how grateful I am for you. I-I wasn't sure it would work into your schedule, and I'm grateful it did."

He nodded. "I'm happy to be here. I've heard great things about the previous Forest Festivals."

"I hope it lives up to those expectations."

"It has so far," he said.

"That's good to know, Santa." She paused, tilting her head at him. "Does it ever get old that people call you Santa?"

"It hasn't so far."

"You've been doing this for a while?"

"Longer than I ever planned to," he said.

They walked toward the doors and Hailey did a quick check that everything was shut down before she locked up for the night.

"Thank you for trusting me enough to let me come to the Forest Festival. It was a great day," he said.

She looked around the now deserted parking lot, except for her rental car. "Did you need a ride?" she asked.

He shook his head. "I have an Uber that should be here any moment," he said.

Headlights drove toward them, stopping in front of where they stood. She waved. "I'll see you tomorrow then," she said. "Goodnight, Santa."

OVER THE NEXT FEW DAYS, HAILEY KEPT BUSY DURING THE Forest Festival. Each time she drove past the hotel, she noticed Troy's car. But every morning and evening it was in the same spot. It hadn't moved. She wondered if he was just able to get the same spot every day or if he was just not leaving the hotel.

Pain stabbed through her at the thought that she'd asked him to stay away. And he'd listened. She wished he would come and see the Forest Festival, at least to see what they'd created. He'd been instrumental in putting it on this year.

The line for Santa dwindled for the last time on Saturday evening. The final bids for the rest of the trees not already bought swarmed in. Santa looked around. "Well, it looks like I'm done here," he said. "I better get on my way."

"You can stay for the festivities," Hailey said. "And you haven't tried a North Pole cinnamon roll yet."

Santa patted his white beard against his chest. "It's a little too messy to eat with the beard on," he said.

She nodded, sticking out her hand to shake his. "I'm sorry we can't have you stay longer. We're going to be finishing the auction with the last largest trees to be bid on."

"And your house? Or did you change your mind?"

"It's technically not my house, it's my aunt's," she said, though she realized that it now actually was hers through the inheritance. She just didn't think of it as hers.

"But you're selling it?" he asked.

She nodded. "It will go to the highest bidder, as long as it's a fair price for the house."

Santa nodded. "Merry Christmas, Hailey. Thank you for letting me be part of this." He looked around. "I sincerely wish I could help you deliver all of these trees. I've heard from the other volunteers, it's usually Santa who helps with that."

Hailey nodded. "It's okay. The volunteers can wear Santa's hat and be Santa's helpers for the few days of deliveries. I heard from your Elf that you're a very busy Santa Claus."

He laughed—that jolly Christmasy laugh. "She keeps me and the reindeer on track for where we need to be."

She shook his hand.

"Can I ask you a question?" he asked.

Hailey moved the small table off the stage so it could be ready for the auctioneer. The larger trees were featured toward the front of the room, and would soon have spotlights on them. "Sure," she said.

"What happened with the other Santa—I believe you called him your friend the first time we met."

"You have a good memory," she said.

"Have to be in this profession. I have a lot of names, and favorite toys to keep track of." He paused. "So this friend, did he have an emergency come up or something?"

Hailey shook her head. "You know, I wish you really were Santa and I wouldn't have to explain it."

He nodded, but didn't say anything.

She sighed. "We kind of had a falling out."

Santa stroked his beard. "A long-time friend?"

She shook her head. "I felt like I'd known him forever, but no, it's just been a few months. I really liked him, but …" She let the sentence trail off.

"More than just a friend then?"

She nodded. "A lot more than just a friend. But he wasn't being honest with me, and I can't deal with that. It reminds me too much of …" She paused, and looked in Santa's eyes. "Never mind. It doesn't really matter. The past is in the past, and that's that. I suppose Santas don't have to worry about that sort of thing."

"I suppose the real one doesn't," he said.

He helped move the chair he'd been sitting in, and soon the stage was completely clear of any of the North Pole decorations.

"I'd better get ready to introduce the auctioneer," she said.

"I'm going to go and see the trees I haven't looked at yet."

She brushed the frosty snow that stuck to her hands after moving the North Pole decorations and headed back on the stage.

CHAPTER 24

Troy used the back stairs to enter into the hallway, heading straight for his private dressing room. He dialed Cara. She picked up after the first ring.

"Hey boss," she said. "Nice job, Santa."

"Thanks, it's surprisingly been a lot of fun," he said.

"Things seem to be going well between you and Hailey," Cara said in her perky voice.

Troy rubbed his hand across the white beard, pulling it down from his mouth and scratching his face for the first time in hours. "Only because she hasn't recognized me." He touched the deepened grooves that crinkled like real skin when he smiled. "You were right, the stage makeup up close for Santa did the trick."

"You're still going to tell her who you are?" she asked.

"Yes. Did you talk to Kyle?" he asked. He'd been waiting to hear back from Kyle since the beginning of the Forest Festival.

"I did a few hours ago. Apparently, he was out of reception

for a few days, whatever that means. Maybe he was in the mountains where there was no reception?"

"It means he doesn't want to be bothered for a few days."

"Huh. You should try that sometime."

"Sure. I'll try it next year. Put it on my list of things to do."

She laughed. "He had a message for you he wanted me to say exactly before he would discuss your options with you."

Troy held a fist to his forehead, careful to not smear the age spot makeup on his skin. "What's the message?"

"The entire message is, "Why play?" I'm not sure what it means. I can call him back and ask," Cara said.

Troy sighed. Of all the things that Kyle could have said, this was probably the only one that had Troy changing his mind. "You don't need to call him back. I know what it means."

"What does it mean?" Cara asked.

Troy sighed, looking at himself dressed as Santa, in the dressing room mirror. "It means I won't quit. That's what it means."

"So, you're going to lose on purpose? Break the rules?" Cara clarified.

He felt defeated. He may stay in the competition, but he'd already lost Hailey. "No, Cara. It means I'm going to finish what I've started."

"Okay boss, explain, please."

"It's a quote we had in our dorm room in college. Kyle was a football star, even during his Freshman year. He had those two words next to his desk. Underneath them were all the reasons to play. And all the reasons why when you choose to play, that's your choice. Once you've made the decision to play, you don't quit, you don't cheat, you don't lose. You play and you win. And you win when you stick with the plan."

"Huh. Such power in two words."

Troy nodded, though his assistant couldn't see the gesture through the phone. "Probably the most powerful thing he could have said," Troy conceded. Such a small phrase, but so much meaning that stretched toward him from years ago. He'd seen those words in action all throughout college, especially with Kyle. They were powerful words after a victory, and they were even more meaningful after a defeat. He'd learned from Kyle that being defeated was not the same as losing. Victories could be achieved and recorded with a simple glance of a scoreboard, but losing was simply a state of mind. Winning could always occur if you answered the question, 'Why play?' correctly and followed through.

"One more thing," Cara said.

"Go for it."

"They're on the second tree for bidding. And people are bidding high on these ones. It's a "bid to be seen" kind of place."

"Do you have my bid number?"

"In my hand. I'm near the front on the right-hand side as you face the stage."

"And you registered the name as—" This had to be right or everything would go so wrong.

"Santa Claus."

"And the LLC?"

"It was set up as soon as you bought the suit and said you wanted to be Santa at the company Christmas party."

"I can't have this tied back to me. Not yet."

"It won't be, but you won't want me holding your number

when the bidding starts. Hailey probably saw us talking together the other day when …" She didn't finish the sentence, but Troy had it clearly in his mind which day she referred to. The day Hailey had broken up with him.

He adjusted the beard over his mouth again, smoothing it until it was perfectly in place. "I'm headed toward you right now," he said. Turning out the light in the personal dressing room, he made his way into the hall and pocketed his phone.

Bidding on the third tree had begun when Troy entered the Forest Festival as Santa. It felt like a wonderland in here, and he wished for the hundredth time that he'd been able to walk hand in hand with Hailey through the entire thing. He wanted to know her opinions on the different ornaments, and see what sparked a Christmas memory for her.

Cara slipped by him, discreetly handing him a number attached to a wooden stick. The bid on the last tree continued higher and higher. His assistant was right. There were high rollers among the group. When the gavel banged against the wooden podium, the winner came up and said a few words. Apparently that was a tradition when one of the auctioned items were bought. As soon as the woman sat down, the auctioneer drew everyone's attention.

On the wall behind the auctioneer flashed a picture of Hailey's aunt's house. The Victorian mansion seemed to come to life through the still image. *Stay calm.* Originally he'd hoped to be able to mend things with Hailey before she'd been able to sell it publicly at the auction, but since that didn't happen his next best strategy was to drive the price as high as he could without being too obvious about it. He didn't want to be too eager in his bidding—being Santa would draw enough attention as it was.

Paul's bid was the first one up. Troy watched the crowd as more bids were added. Paul's smile seemed smug as the bid approached $400,000 and competing bids slowed down. Troy didn't turn completely around, but he sensed that the remaining bidders fell away. The auctioneer held the gavel up, ready to strike the wooden block, as his mouth moved a mile a second.

"$400,000, going once …" The auctioneer started the countdown for Paul's bid, but he didn't get far.

"$425,000," Troy said. He couldn't let Hailey's house go for that cheap. It was worth so much more.

The auctioneer continued to raise the price as Troy, dressed in his Santa suit, continued to bid each time Paul did. Troy was determined to let Hailey get a fair price for it. The price jumped $25,000 on each successive bid. Troy kept his hand raised high with his number, but watched Hailey, as the auctioneer continued. She looked between the bidders, surprised. Troy wasn't bidding to win, only bidding so that Hailey didn't lose. She'd had an amazing offer from him on the Victorian mansion, and she deserved to at least have that again.

Silence filled the room as the auctioneer said, "Do I hear one million?" He smiled at the remaining two bidders.

Troy kept his gloved Santa hand high. He glanced toward Paul, who seemed to be turning red in the face. Troy wondered how much of his profit was being eaten away for the condominium idea. The auctioneer jumped higher in number, going up by $100,000. Troy didn't mind, he would force the price higher, and if Paul didn't want to pay it that was fine with him.

Gasps rolled across the crowd when the bidding passed two million. Was Paul only staying in it to prove something? Surely the idea of owning the property at over four times the cost had to seem less lucrative, but Paul was not backing down. Troy smiled under his Santa beard, enjoying the game of it all.

Hailey's eyes bounced between him and Paul through the process.

"Do I hear three million dollars?" the auctioneer asked.

Troy kept his hand raised.

"Folks we may be close to the finish. Three million going once … Three million going twice …"

Troy held his breath.

"Sold, to … Santa." The auctioneer looked down at this paper, likely matching the number Troy held with the list of bidder names he had in front of him. "Yes. Sold to Santa. Congratulations."

The crowd cheered, and Hailey visibly relaxed.

Out of the corner of his eye, he noticed Paul's disappointment, but he couldn't worry about that. Hailey would be happy, both to have a better deal than he originally offered and because it wouldn't be wrecked to the ground. He'd remembered when they first met at the Foundation's old building, and while it was a health hazard, she'd been affected by the idea of taking a wrecking ball to the history of the building.

"Santa, would you like to come up and say a few words," the auctioneer beamed at him, stepping away from the microphone.

Troy's eyes widened, as he felt the crowd push around him, ushering him to make a quick speech, like all the other winners had done. He hadn't thought about it before because he'd only planned to drive up the price.

He made his way to the microphone and took a deep breath. Hailey was on the opposite side of the stage from where he entered, and he kept his eyes trained on the audience in front of him, though he could feel her stare on him.

"Christmas is about giving," he started. "That's why I'm here. This donation is for a good cause. Everyone in this room has been generous with their time, their donations, and their money. Christmas is a time when we can focus on making life better for others. I have it on good authority that this Forest Festival wouldn't have happened this year without one person in this room. Congratulations, Hailey Waters, for a successful Forest Festival." He looked at her directly for the first time since taking the stage to make his short speech. He clapped his gloved hands loudly in her direction, and soon there was a spotlight on her as the rest of the crowd cheered.

When the clapping died down, Troy said, "Hailey, would you like to say a few words?"

Hailey walked forward to the mic. "Thank you, Santa. I don't really know what to say," she said, her eyes glistening, her voice unsteady. "From the preliminary numbers this Forest Festival looks to be the most successful one we've had in years. I know the Children's Hospital will be so thrilled by all of your generous donations. All of the proceeds tonight from your ticket, to your food purchases, and anything that you've bid on goes directly to the Children's Hospital. Countless volunteers have worked tirelessly for the last several weeks to ensure that no overhead is taken. It's all donated. I couldn't have done this alone, and I didn't. I had a lot of help from people who cared a lot about this project."

Troy couldn't help but smile, wondering if she thought of him through any of it. It didn't matter though. What mattered was it had worked. The Forest Festival was a success. Hailey's house brought in more than she'd expected, and the glow on her face made all of it worth it.

Hailey said a few more things, thanking everyone again, and letting them know that there would be a website with information about next year's Forest Festival.

The news surprised Troy. But before he could think about it, Hailey came up to him and shook his hand.

"Thank you, Santa," she said. "For everything."

He smiled. "It's been my pleasure to be here. So, you've decided to continue with the Forest Festival?"

Hailey nodded. "After this year, I'm not sure how I could do anything else." She bit her lip. "If you're available to book out this far in advance, we'd love to have you back," she said.

Troy nodded, but he couldn't commit to it without her knowing who he really was. And right now, on the stage in front of hundreds of people who were walking slowly to the exit was not the time to tell her who had really just purchased her house. "Perhaps we should let the dust settle from this year first. In a few months when you begin planning, if you really want me back, I'll be here."

She tilted her head at him. "Okay," she said. "Could I ask you another question?"

He nodded, but he felt his guard rising. "Sure."

"Why bid on the house? Don't get me wrong, I'm grateful, but I thought you weren't local."

He blew out the breath he'd been holding. It was such a complicated question, and he wasn't sure he could even explain all of the reasons himself. He cared about her happiness. He had fallen for her and … but that didn't matter. He couldn't say any of that as Santa. Finally he settled on the easiest answer. "I wanted to make sure you got the best donation you could. It was about to sell for less than the market value."

"I'm grateful, but what are you going to do with it? I'm not unaware that it's a big piece of land … in a prime location." She rubbed her hands together in front of her, a sign she was actually nervous about the answer.

He was glad that Paul hadn't won, at least the whole thing wouldn't be demolished. Condos wouldn't be part of Troy's plan. Troy knew exactly what he wanted to do with the Victorian mansion. But he couldn't tell Hailey. Yet another thing he needed to keep from her. He shook his head. When it came right down to it, Troy and Santa were still two different people in Hailey's mind.

Troy cleared his throat. "I'd need to see the property, of course, but Santa buys lots of things this time of year for those who are wishing for them. Not everything can be made at the North Pole with elves."

Hailey laughed. "You're really into this whole Santa thing, aren't you?"

Troy nodded. "It's the safest thing to do when I'm dressed up as Santa."

Hailey looked like she'd say more, but then the auctioneer came to talk to Troy about signing for the house, and the paperwork that would legally bind him to the purchase price, with conditions allowing for inspections. He took the pen and signed in several places, then the auctioneer flipped another page over and had him do the same thing again.

Hailey came over and said, "Thanks again, Santa. I'll see you in Seattle next week."

Troy nodded to her, wishing he could talk over the details with her.

The auctioneer looked at his signature. "You're signing as Santa," he said warily. "Look, if this is a joke, we just lost some very decent bidders who were serious about this property."

It was because he was signing as Santa. He nodded. "I understand your concern, but I'm keeping the purchase of this property quiet. I have a business for my Santa Claus … job. It's filed in the State of New York. My business will be buying this property." He added "LLC" after the Santa Claus name.

The auctioneer blew out his breath, checking the bidding number again. Bidders were vetted ahead of time, and thankfully his assistant had taken care of all of it. He turned the paper to get the specifics on Troy's bid number. "This is highly unusual," the auctioneer said. "But your name is listed as Santa Claus and …" His eyes widened and his voice dropped to an excited whisper. "This says you're approved for a purchase up to fifty million?!"

Santa put a finger to his lips. "That is classified information that no one else except you needs to see."

He nodded. "I don't know where Santa would get that sort of money …"

"A snow bank?"

CHAPTER 25

Troy woke up early the next morning. He'd packed his suitcase the night before, and he wanted to leave before the rest of the hotel ate breakfast. Last night at the Forest Festival had been amazing. At the front desk he turned the plastic room key card into George.

"I saw you on the morning news," George said conspiratorially. "The Forest Festival was an amazing success. Congratulations."

George had known that Troy was working with Hailey on the Festival, but hadn't been given the memo that all of that had changed this week. "You must be mistaken," Troy said, pointing to himself. "I didn't actually attend the Forest Festival."

George grinned, seeming to get a joke that Troy hadn't said. "Ah, right." He lowered his voice. "Santa made the headline news. He was incredible bidding on the prize house like that."

Troy's eyes widened. This was not good. He didn't want publicity for it. In fact that was the very last thing he wanted.

George put a tablet onto the counter, allowing Troy to watch the thirty second clip about him in between the camera panning around the entire Forest Festival. The bottom left-hand corner of the screen revealed the footage was caught by a local news station. That was fine.

More than half the town had attended on just the last night alone. They'd already seen first-hand what had happened. The interview of Hailey started, but George removed the tablet after the spot about Santa was over. Troy wanted to see the rest of the program. But with the name of the news station in his head, he'd be able to pull it up when he was in the comfort of New York City.

TROY WAS ALMOST BACK TO THE CITY WHEN A PHONE CALL CAME through. For a moment he allowed himself to believe it was Hailey, but even after leaving text messages and voicemails, he hadn't heard anything from her. He answered the call.

"You didn't report in for your last week." Kyle's voice came through the car's speakers.

"That's because I had Cara relay the message that I was done with the competition."

"Did you get my response from your assistant?" Kyle asked.

"I did, which is why I decided not to follow through with quitting," Troy conceded. "But there's nothing to report—not really." He didn't want to go into the last week. Everything was still too raw.

"I'm pretty sure you pre-spending the winning amount of

the competition is something to report," Kandice said, her voice laughing.

"I didn't … How did you …" He wasn't doing that as part of the competition.

"It's all over the news. Congratulations, *Mystery Santa*. You've created quite the stir. Everyone wants to know who you are and what you'll be buying next. Tell us about it." Kandice sounded interested.

"Mystery Santa?" he asked.

"That's what they're calling you, since you played Santa at the Historic Forest Festival. I guess people have interviewed most of the volunteers who ran the tables, including Hailey, and the auctioneer. The other bidders have put in their two cents about it too. Anyway, the whole thing has been blowing up my feed online, and we're in Dallas."

"I wasn't doing it for the attention, or for the competition," Troy said.

"I suppose it could be a coincidence that it's the exact amount for the winner," Kyle conceded.

"I was trying to make sure Hailey got a fair price for her house," Troy said, then proceeded to tell the entire story of the week. He explained about how he and his assistant had been talking, and how Hailey must have overheard enough to assume she was part of the bet. He told them about backing away from the role of Santa and Hailey agreeing to it. But then in a strange twist of fate how she'd reached out to him as the Santa she'd met when he was trying to surprise her in costume. His assistant had encouraged him to take the part of Santa. None of it had helped his relationship with Hailey. And from the talks he'd had with her as Santa, she wasn't as broken up about the relationship ending as he was.

"It sounds like you've had an … eventful week," Kandice said.

"It was definitely that," he said.

"Would you change anything if you could go back and do it over again?" Kyle asked.

"I'm so glad I *don't* have to do it over again," Troy said, remembering the acute torture of being around Hailey, but not really being able to talk to her the way he wanted. She only saw the perfect Santa Claus in front of her.

"So you'd keep everything the same?" Kandice clarified.

"I'd have to. If it wasn't for the competition I never would have met Hailey. I hated that the bet got in the way of our relationship. I still don't think it's solvable, but doing what I did as Santa at least lets me leave the situation the best that I can."

"How will you work closing on the house? You'll have to be there for it with her."

"I've thought about that," he said. "The whole reason she pulled the house deal from me was because she was mad at me. She was going to only receive thirty percent of what I'd originally offered if I hadn't helped drive the price up in the bidding. I think it's better if Santa buys the house and fades from her life. She'll get the money and she'll be happy with the donation. And it will be much better than her realizing that I've lied to her. Again."

"Did you lie to her about bidding on the house?" Kandice asked.

"She thinks Santa bought her house," Troy said slowly.

Kyle laughed. "I doubt she thinks that the *actual* Santa bought her house."

"The competition is officially over for you. We'll let you know on Christmas Eve what the results are. The other two are still finishing up their projects for the next week. You're not bound by the contract anymore. You can explain it to her."

"I'm not sure she'd listen," Troy said.

"That's tough, man," Kyle said.

"Ugh. I can't take this anymore," Kandice said. "Troy, you're going to listen very carefully because I'm not going to let the competition be held responsible for your broken heart."

Troy turned up the car volume, moving through the green light as he headed into the City. "I'm listening."

"Here's what you're going to do."

CHAPTER 26

Hailey walked into the grand ballroom at the Summers Resort in Seattle, Washington with her final checklist. She'd originally handed this party off to her assistant, until Santa's Elf, Cara, had called to let her know that Santa required Hailey to attend both parties for him to make his appearance.

It was a small price to pay for getting the Santa that had made National Headline News and had gone viral over the last week. She wondered if there would be a security detail for him. The press had been hounding her for inside information on how to locate him, and she was glad that she'd only had his assistant's phone number and no address. She was sure if the Mystery Santa wanted to be found, he'd be able to contact the press himself.

Her phone buzzed and she lifted the papers on her clipboard to see her screen, but it wasn't Troy. He hadn't called her since she'd left New York after the Forest Festival. His texts had slowed down to every other day. She'd wanted to respond. He'd said that he could explain in person. Her heart ached to know, but she hadn't had the courage to text back. Not after the way she'd uninvited him from the Forest Festival. It was all too painful.

The message was from Santa's Elf. Santa had arrived earlier that day, and had checked into the hotel. She breathed an audible sigh of relief.

Her assistant, Janelle, heard her. "You've been mopey this whole week. I can handle this weekend of parties. Go home and sulk in front of the TV."

Hailey shook her head, trying to give a genuine smile. It fell flat. "I'm sorry. I'm trying."

"I've really got this party," Janelle said.

"I know, but Santa specifically asked that I be here," Hailey said, and they finished the rest of the checklist. "I'm going to go change."

Her assistant nodded. "I'll meet you back here in fifteen minutes, and we'll confirm with the caterers about the timing for the evening."

Hailey agreed, noting how confident Janelle sounded after Hailey had been away for a couple of months. Emotions swam through her. Hailey loved that she built a business that could be sustained when she was away from it, but her heart ached at the idea that she didn't belong here anymore, that somehow she wasn't needed to run her business.

She pushed those thoughts aside, focusing on the fact that Santa had asked that she specifically attend. That was something, though it was probably just for a friendly face in the different city. She headed toward her hotel room to change into her red sequined gown for the party, so she could blend in with the company instead of stand out as she monitored the mingling. Back to back parties at the same hotel made it much more convenient to stay overnight.

When Hailey returned to the ballroom, Santa was already in the room. He stood up from the chair on the far end of the room, smiling at her.

"Here's our 'Mystery Santa,'" Hailey said when she came closer to him.

"Shh. I definitely don't want people making a big deal about it while I'm trying to help you with this party."

"It was a big deal though."

He shrugged. "It didn't need to be," he said.

"You're dressed as Santa and making a huge donation, it was bound to catch people's attention."

He looked around. "You mentioned I'm giving out presents while I'm here?"

Hailey nodded toward the stack of them. "Everyone gets a present from the company. I believe it's the same box for everyone, so it's just a matter of handing them out to everyone."

"How will I know if I've given them a present already?" he asked.

"They will give you a card with their name on it."

Santa nodded. "I can handle that. Should I put them in my sack?"

Hailey nodded. "That might be fun."

"No posing for pictures with children at this party?"

Hailey shook her head. "Tomorrow there will be children, but tonight, it's passing out the presents, and then announcing dinner."

"Do I stay in the chair during dinner? Or do I leave before that?"

"Stay until the end if that's okay. That way if you miss anyone for delivering presents, then you'll be able to catch them at the end."

"Easy enough."

Soon guests filled the ballroom. Christmas music played softly under the chatter that started. Caterers walked around with appetizer trays. Hailey watched from one corner of the room.

Santa came over to her. "Is now a good time to give out presents?" he asked.

She nodded. "It will be great. Thank you."

Santa moved around the room, handing out presents to each of the employees. The company had a nice touch using a Santa for delivering their Christmas gifts.

She connected with the caterers through her headset, giving instructions on when to make another round with the appetizers, but other than that she had very little to do. Her assistant really had pulled off her job without her there. It was encouraging to know that she could put so much trust in her, and that things would work out.

After dinner, Hailey checked on Santa. She'd offered him food, but he'd made his apologies, not wanting to eat while he was in his suit.

As the party wound down there were only a few presents that he still needed to hand out. Hailey had him stand by the door as they exited, giving the last few gifts away.

Hailey breathed in a deep breath and talked to Janelle, downloading a few last-minute things for tomorrow's party.

Janelle nodded at everything Hailey said. "You know I've taken care of everything for tomorrow," she said. "Now you need to go upstairs, find something to watch and drown your sorrows in something chocolatey from room service."

Hailey lowered her voice, not wanting to be overheard, though only Santa stood remotely close enough to hear. "I'm fine."

Janelle laughed. "You're most definitely *not* fine. And I want details. Whoever this guy was that broke your heart must have meant a lot if—"

"It's in the past. I'm fine." She turned back to see Santa reaching into his pack. "Thank you so much for coming all of this way," she said, smiling widely and trying to sound cheerful.

"It was my pleasure." Santa paused, like he wanted to say more.

Hailey raised her eyebrows, waiting for him to continue.

"You're sure you want to sell the house?" he asked.

Her eyes snapped to his. "Why would you ask that?"

"I saw the way you looked at the projection of it. It looks beautiful."

"It is beautiful."

"You also watched the bidding very closely."

Hailey nodded. "There was a provision in the auction that it had to at least make it to the fair market value. I suppose I was a little worried that it wouldn't make it that far."

"But you had an offer on the property, prior to the auction. You could have always gone back to that."

"Maybe," Hailey said, though she doubted Troy was interested in it now.

"Do you want to keep the house?" Santa's eyes looked straight into hers.

Hailey mustered up a smile. "Not as much as I want the donation for the hospital."

"I'd donate the money without the sale of the house," he said. "You can keep it."

Hailey shook her head. "I want the house to be used. It's for a good cause. I don't want to go back on the deal."

Santa handed out another present as someone handed him a slip of paper.

Curiosity took over, and before she could think the better of it, she asked Santa, "Why are you buying this house anyway?"

"Do I need a reason?" he asked.

She shrugged. "No, but I assume you have one. I'm getting a much better end of the deal—not that I'm trying to talk you out of it. It's all going to the Children's Hospital."

"I bought it for someone else," he said. "I knew that she really wanted to ... own it."

"Your wife?" she asked.

"I don't have a wife."

She nodded her head. Maybe it was for another relative. He didn't seem anxious to give her the information so she stopped prying for it.

He nodded. "We'll sign the paperwork after Christmas then?"

"I'll be out there just before the New Year, between parties."

He nodded. "I can make that work. Let me know when you solidify your plans."

"I just have to be back by the day before New Year's Eve. It's a big day for throwing parties."

Santa nodded. "I'm closer travel wise than you are. I'll be there when the realtors work it out."

She stood and shook Santa's hand. "Thank you," she said. "For buying my aunt's house and for coming all of this way to help with my parties."

"Merry Christmas, Hailey," Santa said.

"Merry Christmas, Santa."

Santa moved toward the door. "I'll see you tomorrow."

Hailey nodded. "Thanks, Santa."

Hailey and Janelle walked toward the elevators. "I'm serious. I'm ordering chocolate and you're going to spill all about this guy from Red Oaks."

"I told you, he wasn't from Red Oaks, I just met him there," Hailey said.

Janelle waved her hand in the air. "See, already more details."

The woman at the front desk stopped Hailey. "Ms. Waters, a package just arrived for you."

"For me?"

"My instructions were to give it to you personally. A special delivery."

Hailey expected to see something for the Christmas party tomorrow, but instead the woman handed her a smaller, flat box wrapped in a dark wine-colored paper with a hunter green bow. "Thank you," Hailey said, taking the present. She opened the gold notecard that was wedged between the ribbon and bow. Inside there were only two words: *For Hailey*.

"Aren't you going to open it?" Janelle asked.

Hailey nodded. She unwrapped the present and gasped. It was a crystal star ornament—the one she'd admired from the antique store—the one that had been sold in the time she and Troy had gone from the front of the store to the back.

She touched the delicate gift, then held it up by the thick, velvet ribbon. The light caught the color in the ornament, making the ornament appear brighter than when it was laying in the box. Her heart thudded. Only one person knew how much she'd admired the ornament. Troy had lingered behind, and she'd been the first to head toward the back of the store. Had he purchased it then? She moved the tissue paper out of the box and found an envelope with her name on it.

"Dear Hailey,

I'm sorry for the way things turned out between us. I want to make things better. I can explain everything now. I'm sorry I couldn't earlier. Can we talk in person when you come back to Red Oaks? - Troy"

Janelle glanced at the card, steering Hailey toward the elevators. "Yep, definitely time for some chocolate."

"SPILL IT," JANELLE SAID WHEN THEY'D GOTTEN UP TO HAILEY'S room. Room service came with hot fudge sundaes.

Hailey poured out the entire story of her time with Troy, from mistaking him as an employee of the moving company to their fake kiss under the mistletoe to their real kiss in the mountains, and all of the moments in between that had her remembering the giddy sensations she'd felt.

Then she told Janelle about their breakup in the hallway, and hiring a different Santa, and pushing Troy away from the

Forest Festival. She showed Janelle the notecard, his desire to explain everything.

Janelle took Hailey's phone off the table, shoving it into her hands. "He wants to talk, so talk to him."

Hailey shook her head. "I can't."

Janelle rolled her eyes, her spoon clattering as it dropped to the table. "Why not? From everything you've told me about him, he seems great. And he says he can explain. So let him explain."

"But it's all the things. I don't even know if his explanation will hold water when I listen to it." She bit the inside part of her lip, then shook her head.

"You said he's texting you still?"

"It's been slowing down. He's been trying to get a hold of me —to explain, but I just can't, er, haven't wanted to hear the explanation."

"Why not?" Janelle asked.

"What if the explanation is just an excuse? I don't think I could handle that."

Janelle picked up her spoon, swirling it in her ice cream. "I suppose that's a valid fear."

"That's not the biggest fear. What if his explanation is brilliantly thought through? He's had over a week to think of something really good. I can't take anymore secrets."

"And what if he just tells you the plain truth?"

Hailey wanted to be brave, wanted to hear the plain truth. But something inside of her hesitated. "That's even scarier. Because then I'd probably have to leap."

"You keep mentioning secrets, but surely you haven't told

him everything about your life? You must have some secrets, too?"

"Just because we haven't discussed every aspect of my life, doesn't mean that I'm keeping a secret from him though," she said.

"Maybe he had the same thoughts."

"But these were really big things."

Janelle nodded. "Again a valid point, but I'm going to be the voice of reason here. They were big to *you*. Perhaps they weren't a big deal to *him*. Maybe he just saw things differently."

Hailey took in a deep breath, considering Janelle's words. She opened the box, pulling out the ornament and looping the ribbon through her fingers, letting it spin. "Maybe that's one of the problems. We don't see things the same way. He's used to getting his way, and he has the net worth to make anything happen."

"That amount doesn't seem to matter to you."

"It doesn't, not really." She kept her eyes trained on the ornament, the way it caught the light.

"Why did he choose that particular ornament?" Janelle asked.

Hailey looked toward her, only to see that her gaze was fixed on the spinning crystal. "What do you mean?"

Janelle shrugged. "You mentioned his net worth, that he's a billionaire used to getting his way. You know he could shower you with gifts. Why would he choose that when the sky is the limit on what he could give you?"

"On the day of the first snow, we spent the day in Red Oaks looking through the small shops. The antique shop had all their Christmas decorations out. We originally went in to see the tree the antique shop was donating. He asked what I liked, wanting to get my opinions and figure out my Christmas style when it was just me, and not me decorating for someone else. This was the one that caught my eye in the store when we first walked in.

"I told him how much I liked it. We went into the back of the store, where the antique shop had stored their Forest Festival donations. We were back there maybe ten minutes, possibly a little longer. I was so enthralled by the entire place, but I was determined to buy that first ornament I'd seen. When I came back up to the front of the counter it was gone. He must have found another one like it, and he remembered." The memory caught hold of her.

"It sounds like he knows you." Janelle held out a hand. "May I?"

Hailey handed it over to her, and Janelle studied the ornament. "If you saw this at an antique store, he didn't just find another one of these."

Understanding dawned. "He must have bought it that day then?"

Janelle shrugged, giving the ornament back to her. "Either that or he has some amazing online shopping skills."

Hailey placed it in the box. "He could have given me anything in the world," she said softly.

"Would anything else have been as meaningful?" Janelle asked.

Hailey sighed. "That's beside the point. I know Troy and I had a connection and chemistry and all of that, but that's not what's up for debate. The fact is I just don't know if I can trust him. He kept things from me. He wouldn't explain things. That's not the way to have a relationship with someone, to build a life with someone. Honesty and trust are important to me."

"But he says he can explain now. Give him a chance."

Hailey bit her lip, not willing to commit to Janelle's suggestion yet. "How did this present even find me here? There's no address. It didn't come through the mail."

Janelle shrugged. "Who knows. Maybe Santa brought it."

Hailey snapped her fingers. "I'll ask him about that tomorrow."

"I don't see how that answers anything."

"I can get more information. Maybe Santa can tell me more so I can be prepared, when … if I talk to Troy."

Janelle rolled her eyes. "Santa is great and all, and don't get me wrong, I absolutely love his costume, but don't you find it a little incongruent that you're even going to ask Santa about it?"

Hailey tilted her head. "What do you mean?"

"I mean, Hailey. You want trust and honesty from people and I get that, but why would you assume you could trust Santa more than you could Troy? You don't even know who Santa is."

"Of course I know who Santa is. He's Santa." The words felt hollow even to her own ears.

Janelle smirked. "You know that doesn't hold water, right? Besides. Santa is keeping his identity a secret from even you. He didn't tell you who he was, before or after the publicity."

"So?"

"So, you'll allow Santa to keep the secret of his identity, but you're unwilling to let Troy actually explain himself?"

"It's not the same," Hailey countered.

"Agreed. Santa hasn't once given you anything to go off of to trust him, except to don a custom-made suit. At least with Troy you had some history. You relied on him for weeks. He had to have given you at least a few reasons to trust him during that time, right?"

A lightbulb turned on in Hailey's brain. Janelle was right. Hailey had been unhappy with the timing, but he had offered multiple times to explain things to her, even though the explanation wasn't immediate like she'd wanted. She rubbed at her forehead. "I think I've made a huge mistake."

"Lucky for you, he still wants to talk." Janelle held up the card.

He wanted to talk in person. She'd allow him that.

She texted Troy. **I think we need to talk.**

His reply came almost immediately. **I'd like that.**

In person.

Agreed.

CHAPTER 27

The bitter cold hit Hailey as soon as she left her rental car. She hurried along the freshly shoveled walk of the Red Oaks real estate office, snow piled high on both sides. She stamped her feet off at the mat and let herself inside.

She pulled out her phone, realizing that she'd never confirmed details about meeting with Troy in person, though she'd told him she was coming back to Red Oaks. If his explanation could solve this thing between them, he'd be worth the drive into the City. She texted him. **I'm in New York, in Red Oaks. When I finish closing on the house, could we meet in the City?**

His response came immediately. **I'm actually not in the City right now, but I do want to talk in person.**

Hailey's heart stuttered. She'd missed Troy. Had he gone home for Christmas? She frowned at his text that he wasn't around. It would be fine. They'd figure things out. Maybe it wouldn't be this trip after all.

"Ms. Waters," the realtor said.

We'll find another time. Hailey pressed send on her response. She looked up from her phone that she'd been staring at and smiled at her realtor. "Hi. Sorry about that."

"Not a problem. We're just about ready for you. If you want to wait in the conference room, the buyer is already there."

"I half expect Santa to be here in his suit," Hailey said, laughing.

The realtor nodded. "He was adamant about not drawing attention from the press during closing, so I think he wanted to be in Cognito."

Hailey raised an eyebrow, convinced that Santa would come as Santa. "I'll go introduce myself," she said.

"He wanted to talk to you before we finalize the details of the sale." He gestured toward the conference room. "I'll be in in a few minutes with the documents, and we can get started."

Hailey was almost ready to slide her phone into her purse when she saw a text from Troy. She clicked into it.

I hear The Pancake Tower is a great place to get breakfast food at any time of the day. We should go for lunch there sometime.

She closed her eyes, letting beautiful memories dance across her consciousness. As much as she wanted to pick up where they'd left off a few weeks ago, she needed answers before she could open her heart again. She needed to hear his explanation. **We need to talk first.**

He responded as she walked through the conference room. **Agreed.**

Dropping her phone into her purse, she closed the conference room door behind her. It was time to put Troy out of her mind for the next hour while she focused on closing on her house with Santa.

The conference room had a large table with a dozen chairs surrounding it. The blinds on the windows had been pulled up, revealing a view of the snow-capped mountains, the sun barely visible through the clouds. The room was bright with the overhead lights and the reflection of the snow from the outside.

Santa sat in the farthest chair from the door, his back to her as he looked out the window where wind blew around the snow. The only thing she could see above the executive swivel chair was his Santa hat.

"Hi Santa," Hailey said.

"Hi Hailey," Santa said, still turned away from her.

"My realtor said you wanted to talk with me before we closed," she said it confidently enough, but she hoped with everything in her that he wasn't changing his mind.

"I did," he said, still not turning around.

It felt strange to talk to the back of his head, and she moved farther into the room. "I hope there's not a problem with the deal."

"There might be."

"I don't understand," she said moving closer to him. "What's wrong, Santa?"

"You're not going to like this," he said slowly.

Fears rose up in her. Had he only pretended to want the property for so much? Would they be renegotiating right before closing? She shouldn't even be in his closing, but he'd asked her to be here. Was this why? "You don't really have three million for this deal?" she guessed.

"What? No, that's not it. The money was donated at the Forest Festival. I'd never dream of backing out."

She breathed easier. "Well it can't be that bad then," she said.

"It's worse. You may not want me to buy the property when you find out."

She stood only a few feet away from him, but still he didn't turn around. She wished she could talk to him face to face, look him in the eye, read his expression—something. "When I find out what?"

"When you find out who wants to buy the property."

"Okay. You're buying the property, I don't underst—"

Santa spun around, taking off the Santa hat that had hidden his dark hair. "I wanted to explain this before we got to closing."

Hailey blinked several times before her brain believed her eyes that she was looking at Troy and not Santa. Troy was dressed in regular clothes. "Troy? Why are you here?"

Troy blew out a breath. "I have a lot to tell you." He motioned to the chair next to his, and she sat down.

"Did you ask Santa to bid for you?" she asked, her brain trying to figure out how he would know the exact time of the closing if Santa hadn't told him. She'd been vague at best about her travel plans when she'd texted Troy.

Troy smiled. "No. I bid on the house."

She swallowed. "I don't believe this," she said. How was Troy the Mystery Santa? She was stunned. "You're … Santa? But I met Santa when I was waiting for you."

Troy rubbed the side of his jaw. "And I was waiting exactly where I said I was going to be, and you assumed that I was late."

"The whole time? You didn't just pay off the Mystery Santa to buy the house?"

He shook his head. "I wanted to tell you when you first met Santa, but I thought you'd caught on that it was me, until you walked away. I could tell how impressed you were with the Santa, and I wanted it to be a surprise when I showed up at the Forest Festival."

She gave him a half smile. "I suppose that would have been a great surprise."

"I didn't mean for it to continue on past then, but then, before the Forest Festival—I just didn't want to cause you pain, and I didn't really think that you'd call up the other Santa you had met to fill in for me."

Her brain tried to follow everything, trying to reconcile the last couple of weeks. "Then why not tell me in Seattle?" she asked.

"And ruin your parties by having you upset at Santa? I couldn't do that. You'd booked the Seattle events with my assistant earlier than the Forest Festival, so I figured before Seattle you would have known it was me, and we could have spent the weekend sightseeing or something." Troy's eyes pleaded with her. "It all kind of backfired and blew up in my face."

"And the present?" she asked.

"Santa was the only way I could think of to get it to you, and then I didn't want to jeopardize the next day's party, so I left it at the front desk," he said.

"None of this explains your bet about me and how we even got into this mess in the first place," she said, wanting to get back on topic.

Santa, er, Troy nodded. "The bet was never about you," Troy clarified. "A few months ago I was with my college roommates, and one of the guys who has a huge charity foundation gave the rest of us the challenge to try something different for our Christmas giving this year. We could only spend $10,000 to help the charity of our choice, and we needed to spend a significant amount of time working on it."

"That was the bet?" she asked.

Troy nodded. "There were lots of stipulations to go along with it. Each of the three billionaires who were challenged gave Kyle a million dollars. The winner of the challenge would get the three million to donate to their charity of choice."

"So, why not just explain that to me? I already knew you were a billionaire. The money didn't surprise me."

Troy exhaled loudly. "One of the rules of the competition was that I couldn't tell anyone about it. But after it became a sticking point, I tried to get out of the competition completely. That didn't work, so I stuck it out. I wanted to tell you, but I couldn't when you asked me."

She sucked in a breath. Relief washed over her. The bet hadn't been about her. "So where does that leave us?"

"With me madly in love with you."

"After all I put you through?"

"It doesn't change how I feel."

She nodded. "And you really want to buy this house?"

He nodded.

"You're not going to live here though?" she asked.

"Me? No, not full time. But Santa needs a place." He shrugged, putting his hat back on. "Technically, Santa is buying it. I have the company set up for it and everything."

Hailey nodded. "It won't be a secret where Santa's summer home is."

"I don't think I need secrets anymore." He stood, moving closer to her. "Can you forgive me, for everything?"

She nodded. "I already have," she said.

He kissed her, and she wanted to melt into the kiss, but the realtor's throat clearing separated them quickly.

"Looks like we have some business to take care of," Troy said, nodding toward the realtor. "Rain check?"

HAILEY KEPT HER FINGERS THREADED THROUGH TROY'S. SNOW clung to her boots as they navigated the powdery snow, circling Santa's new property. The whirlwind of paperwork was finalized in record time.

"Santa said he was buying this house for someone," Hailey said thoughtfully, still trying to reconcile all of the moments that Troy had played Santa. "I suppose that was your cover when you played Santa?"

He handed her the house deed. "It's a late present, I know."

She blinked. "You bought the house *from* me, to give back *to* me?"

He shrugged. "I thought we could create your aunt's dream together. Turn it into a place to help families with hospitalized children."

Moisture pooled in her eyes, attracting the cold, so she blinked them back. "I like that idea," she whispered.

They walked around the entire property, stopping once they reached the front porch again. "We have a lot of work to do to make that happen," she said.

"Maybe a new coat of paint?" he asked.

She nodded. "A red door."

"And a welcome sign," he said.

She could see it in her mind.

They stood in silence for a few more minutes, taking in the house covered in snow, imagining the possibilities.

"Did you ever find out who won the competition?" she asked.

He tilted his head at her, then nodded. "I did." He pulled out a bright red envelope and handed it to her.

She took it and read the enclosed letter. "Wow," she said, when she'd finished reading the letter.

"The money is ready to go."

"You're giving it to the Forest Festival?" she asked, trying to make sense of the last part of the letter.

He shook his head. "It's the first deposit into your charity. Call it what you want, but I have a few ideas on how we can partner with the hospital to help more families."

"You're doing this for me?"

"Of course it's for you. Anything you want. I love you, Hailey."

This time when the tears formed they fell. She sniffed, wiping her tears away with her glove. "I love you too," she said.

He pulled a Christmas handkerchief out of his coat pocket, handing it to her.

"Thanks," she said, dabbing at her eyes. "A handkerchief? Really?"

"I'm the man you can't live without, remember? Of course I'm always prepared." He grinned.

She rolled her eyes. "You really are a Boy Scout."

She kissed him, pouring in all of the gratitude that she felt for someone who'd completely changed her life. He wrapped her up in his arms and the moment was as perfect as she could imagine.

EPILOGUE

DECEMBER, TWO YEARS LATER

Santa led Mrs. Claus up the three stairs toward the front door of the beautifully redone Victorian mansion that stood on the corner of Main Street in Red Oaks. The sign on the dark red door said, "Welcome to Santa's."

He paused in front of the door, and she pulled his hat down on his head. "Perfect," Mrs. Claus said.

He stroked her face with his gloved hand. "You're beautiful dressed as Mrs. Claus. I can't believe this is our second Christmas together," he said.

"Technically, it's our third," she said.

He laughed, the jolly ho-ho-ho laugh that had become more natural to him after two years of playing Santa. "Yes, but I mean since we've been married. As I recall, our first Christmas we knew each other, we weren't really together."

"Fair point." She laughed. "I feel like I'm going to need a new costume, especially with our Christmas bundle on the way." She patted her rounding belly.

"We don't have to stay for the full month this time," he said. "We can make this visit shorter."

She shook her head. "Santa's house needs to have Santa visiting. Besides, it's great for the families who have children who've been on long-term treatment in the hospital. I know the brothers and sisters of those kids love the interaction." She stood closer to him and he wrapped his arms around her.

He glanced at his watch. "At any minute, we can make our entrance," he said. He opened up the ice box on the porch, next to the front door and pulled out his worn present sack. It was already full of gifts, labeled with the children who were currently staying at the house.

Santa leaned down and gave his wife a kiss. "I love you," he said.

"I love you, too," she whispered back.

All of a sudden, the Christmas lights decorating the entire porch, and all of the eve lighting, turned on. Patterns of red, white, and green lights reflected off the house and against the snow. "That's our cue," she said. He gave her another quick peck. She laughed. "Santa, they're waiting."

"Right," he said and turned the knob. He stepped onto the rug and stamped his feet. "Ho, ho, ho. Merry Christmas, everyone!"

Like the Book?

Please leave a review for The Billionaire's Christmas Miracle on Amazon.

It's the best way you can say thank you to an author!

Thank you so much!

Read Hunter's Story Next!

Read The Billionaire's Second Chance Christmas Now! It's included in this box set!

A billionaire who wants to give back to his hometown, his best friend's younger sister who is in charge of the project, and the Christmas gift that could heal the heart break of the past, and give these two a second chance at love.

Join Chelsea's VIP Reader's Club

to stay updated with new releases, get free books, access to exclusive bonus content, and more!

Join Chelsea's VIP Reader's Club.

See all of Chelsea's books.

Books in this Series included in this book:

Troy's Story: The Billionaire's Christmas Miracle
Hunter's Story: The Billionaire's Second Chance Christmas
Scott's Story: Finding Christmas with the Billionaire

THE BILLIONAIRE'S SECOND CHANCE CHRISTMAS

A BETTING ON CHRISTMAS ROMANCE - BOOK TWO

CHELSEA HALE

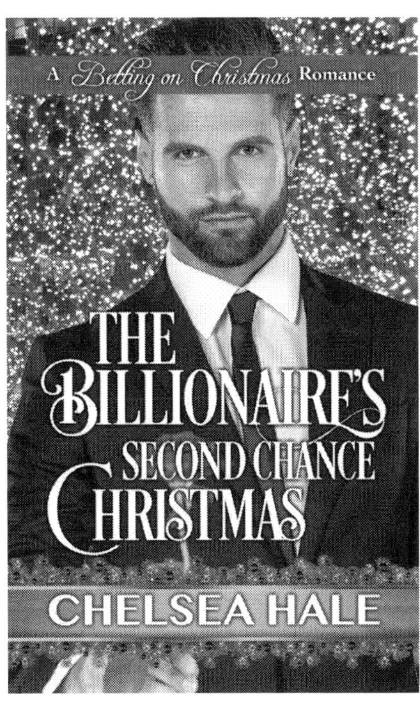

"Maybe Christmas, he thought, doesn't come from a store. Maybe Christmas ... perhaps ... means a little bit more!"
- Dr. Seuss, How The Grinch Stole Christmas

PROLOGUE

HOW THE BET BEGAN - (PLEASE NOTE EACH PROLOGUE IS SIMILAR)

Hunter lounged on the top deck of his yacht as the Mediterranean breeze whipped around him. He and his college roommates had spent the last three days catching up and enjoying the beautiful coast. Europe was beautiful this time of year.

"This has been a great trip," Scott said. "I'm sorry to see it over so soon. Are you sure you can't stay another week, Kyle?"

Kyle Montgomery laughed. He was the only one in the group that wasn't a bachelor. He had married his high school crush after college right around the time he'd signed with Dallas and began his career in the NFL. "You guys are welcome to stay, but my team won't be happy if I miss Saturday's game. We're up against the rivals. Just missing practice this week might get me in trouble."

"We can't stay without you," Hunter said. "It wouldn't be the same without all four of us."

"Just like old times," Troy said.

"Old times?" Kyle repeated. "I suppose, but not really like old times. I haven't been single for a long time. I have kids now. It's not the same for me."

"How's your charity going?" Scott asked Kyle.

"Every year it does more good in the world," Kyle said casually. "Happy Moments is dedicated to just that. Bringing happy moments to others. It's rewarding. It's too big for us to manage on our own any more, but Kandice and I still play an active role in it."

"I think I'd like to do that," Troy said.

Hunter let his thoughts drift as he grabbed a soda and some snacks, only vaguely listening to the banter between his other three buddies. All of his friends had reached success in very distinct ways. They were all billionaires, all hard workers, but he was glad they still made time to get together every year and do something. Last year it was skiing in the Alps. This year it was his yacht. Truthfully, Hunter was surprised that Kyle could take the time off during his season, but it was only four days.

Scott laughed, tilting his sunglasses down. "I bet you a million you couldn't do it."

"I'll take that bet," Troy said.

"A million for what?" Hunter asked, rejoining the conversation as he sat back down with the group. Troy and Scott were always betting. In fact, they'd had crazy bets back in college too, though back then the price tag hadn't been a million dollars. It was amusing, and he and Kyle would sometimes join in on the bets. This would complicate the terms as their involvement messed with the outcome for Scott and Troy. In fact, that might be fun right now. "I'm in for a million," Hunter said.

Scott rolled his eyes. "You don't even know what the bet is."

Hunter shrugged. "It's only a million. Chump change."

Kyle filled Hunter in on the conversation he'd missed. "Troy was asking about my charity, and I was just pointing out that having a charity foundation and being involved in the work are two completely separate things. But I offered my help if Troy or any of you want to get involved or start your own charity."

"That sounds cool," Hunter said.

Kyle turned to Troy. "Betting for charity seems to defeat the point, don't you think?"

Troy nodded. "Fair enough, Kyle." Troy looked at Scott. "How about when I win your money goes to the charity of my choice?"

Scott shrugged. "You can do whatever you want with money you win. But you're not going to win, so it's a non-issue."

"Oh, I'll win," Troy said confidently. "Just give me the stakes."

"You have to start a charity," Scott said.

Hunter watched his two friends. All of them were good at winning. All of them were competitive. It was what made them all so successful.

"Or, we could open up the bet to everyone," Kyle said.

"It wouldn't be fair to include you," Scott said to Kyle. "You already own a charity."

Kyle leaned back in his chair. "I'll be the moderator then."

"What are the rules?" Troy repeated.

"How about you need to start a charity by Christmas?" Scott suggested.

Hunter shook his head. Troy and Scott loved doing huge bets, but they both needed a reality check. "It's mid-October. If you actually want to make an impact by Christmas you need to scale it back."

"What if you have to help a charity that's already up and running?" Kyle suggested. "*That* could be done before Christmas."

Scott tilted his head. "How would we determine the winner then?"

Troy was quiet.

Hunter was amused by all of it. He'd pretend to be invested in whatever the contest was just to see Scott and Troy fight for first place. It was always entertaining to watch them go at each other. He leaned back, taking in the view. The sun gleamed on the rippling water and waves lapped against the boat.

Kyle snapped his fingers. "I've got it. You need to be personally involved with helping a charity succeed. I like the deadline of Christmas, and it would be nice to pick a winner before the New Year. Entrance fee is one million dollars. The winner gets the three million dollars to donate to the charity of his choosing—most likely the one that you choose to help, but I'm open to negotiation on that point. The person who gives the most will win."

Hunter laughed. Kyle had made this bet way too easy. "I can give the most. I'll write a check tomorrow. That's easy enough."

Kyle shook his head. "Not monetarily. I'd say you need to cap your own personal or business donations to $10,000."

Scott scoffed. "How do we determine a winner if we're only allowed to give such a small donation? We'll all just give that same amount and then we'll be tied."

"You have to make a difference in the charity. No assistants can help, and you can't just assign it to a team of people from your companies. You have to *personally* be involved with it. Donate your time." Kyle shrugged. "Be creative. You're all brilliant—you can all figure out a way to do something."

"And we only have from now until Christmas?" Scott confirmed.

Kyle nodded. "What if we make the deadline December 23rd, and the winner could be announced on December 24th?"

"And you're the judge?" Troy asked.

Kyle scrunched his face. "No. I don't want to be accused of being partial to anyone. I'll have Kandice be the judge. Maybe we'll have a weekly check-in phone call and she can hear all of your progress and what you've been up to. She can be the one to make the final decision. Whatever she decides, stands."

Hunter, Scott, and Troy all nodded.

"Sounds fair," Troy said. "I'm in, if everyone else is."

Scott shrugged. "Why not? My company is a well-oiled machine right now. I have some extra time. Hunter, what about you?"

The truth was Hunter was looking forward to the challenge. It would be great. He knew he could win, but he didn't need to let Scott or Troy know that. Hunter sighed dramatically. "This eats into my plans to spend the next month on my yacht, but yeah, I'm in. When do we start?"

"As soon as it works for everyone," Kyle said.

"I have a few things to wrap up at work before I can take the time off," Scott said.

Kyle nodded. "How about we start in two weeks? Maybe that will give you time to research which charity to help."

"And we need to spend the full eight weeks helping the charity of our choice?" Troy asked.

Kyle nodded. "Eight weeks of helping with something that's meaningful to you. Remember, no assistants helping you with the charity. And don't try and get past the rules. Kandice will find out."

All of them laughed. They shook hands on it and within an hour they wired their money to Kyle for the bet.

The Billionaires' Christmas Gifts Bet was officially underway.

THE RULES

OF THE BILLIONAIRES' CHRISTMAS GIFTS BET

- *Find a charity of your choice*
- *$1,000,000 Entry fee*
- *8 weeks of helping a charity of your choice – You must be personally involved*
- *No assistants*
- *No delegation to teams at work*
- *No talking to participants about the bet*
- *$10,000 max you can donate to the project*
- *Check-in with Kandice (and Kyle)*
- ***Deadline:** December 23rd; Winner announced on December 24th.*
- ***Winner receives:** $3,000,000 to donate to the charity of their choice.*

CHAPTER 1

Hunter drove through the middle of Texas, amazed at how much dust was caking over the new dark gray truck he'd bought at the dealership near the airport. He remembered a lot of things about Texas, but somehow the dust hadn't been part of the memory. The rain in the Portland area where he'd lived since college kept the earth from creating dust clouds like the ones that had followed him for the last 150 miles as he drove into the heart of Texas, where the land was flat and you could see for miles in every direction.

He turned up the country station, recalling his love for the music he rarely played when he was at home now. It had been nine years since he'd been back to Texas when he came to celebrate his parents' retirement from the small town of Golden Ridge. They were now living hundreds of miles north in Colorado, but them moving away wasn't the biggest reason he hadn't returned. He'd purposefully avoided Golden Ridge, unable to come back to the place where he'd been rejected, until he'd made the bet on the yacht with his college roommates.

What Kyle had said about finding something personal and meaningful in this competition had struck him. He wasn't oblivious to the fact that there was a myriad of places to serve from now until Christmas, but he sensed something further in Kyle's words, like maybe there was more to the bet than simply staying under the budget of $10,000 that he had to grasp.

It had helped that his mom had called him and told him about the Johnson's General Store, and that had solidified his decision. She'd given him all the specific details about the lightning strike and the damage. Though she hadn't been a resident of Golden Ridge for nearly a decade, she still kept up with her friends there.

He'd only been on the call with his mom for a couple of minutes when the idea struck him. Helping the Johnsons rebuild the store was exactly what he needed to do! He knew that if he had just called up old Mr. Johnson to tell him he was coming to help, Mr. Johnson would have thanked him for the offer and told him they would get along fine. That was Mr. Johnson's way. But, if he showed up unannounced ready and willing to help, there was no way Mr. Johnson could brush him off as easily.

Hunter let his mind wander back to his youth, to the many times Mr. Johnson had helped him. While working for his family's construction company, Hunter had spent his free time whittling the wood scraps, and Mr. Johnson had given him a shelf in the store where he could sell his creations. Mr. Johnson was always finding ways to help others, and now Hunter felt like it was his opportunity to return the favor.

He'd also learned from his mom that Golden Ridge's hotel was under construction. Even though his parents were retired, they still held an ownership in their construction company in Golden Ridge so the family kept tabs on the business.

Sixty miles outside of his final destination, Hunter stopped at Sunset Meadows—a town that was not much bigger than Golden Ridge. He checked into the local hotel and brought his bag to the room. With his lodgings secure, there was no way that Mr. Johnson would turn away his help. He jumped back into his truck and drove the rest of the way to his destination.

In the dimming light of the evening, Hunter could barely make out the weathered sign at the edge of the town but he doubted the once cheery *"Welcome to Golden Ridge"* would have been much clearer in the broad daylight. The town boasted 1,000 people (it was probably less now) however his thoughts went immediately to only one. Was Oakley still in Golden Ridge?

He pushed the brakes, complying with the new speed limit, and the truck responded immediately. Oakley hadn't been the reason he came back, not really. Sure, he was curious about her. He spoke with her older brother often enough. Travis was still his childhood best friend, but they'd grown up and gone their separate ways, and even though they kept in touch, Hunter rarely asked about Oakley. Sometimes Travis would voluntarily mention a tidbit about her. The last Hunter had heard she was almost engaged to someone. The thought made his throat constrict. What if she was married and still living in the town? He straightened up and gripped the steering wheel tighter, forcing himself to deal with the bumpy road. Oakley had always talked of moving—of leaving the town—especially when she got married.

He drove on Main Street, passing all the quaint shops and cozy restaurants until he reached Johnson's General Store. He sucked in a breath. The charred building was barely recognizable. Where the store front once stood, a gaping hole allowed a glimpse into what was left. The building had mostly been reduced to piles of ash and splintered wood. Hunter closed his eyes against the sight.

He'd seen natural disaster damage before when he'd worked for his dad's construction company. He did that for a number of years before trading his desire to build things physically with his love for building things electronically. Coding was now the building blocks he used to make his business successful. It helped that he understood the complexities behind large software security systems. His billion-dollar company *Secured* became the result of his dedication. But his security only went as far as the computer systems. It would have done nothing in this case. He blew out a breath. The Johnsons had a major project on their hands. He was glad he showed up when he did. He knew he could help.

After surveying the General Store, Hunter headed to a nearby coffee shop that he didn't recognize. The shop was one of the newer ones on the street, built since the last time he'd been in town. The diner would have been an obvious choice, but he wasn't really in the mood to chat it up with every person in town before he was reacquainted with Mr. Johnson. He just needed to know where the Johnsons were staying. Surely someone in the coffee shop would know that. He wasn't trying to go incognito in his hometown, but Kyle's words about finding something meaningful meant he needed to start in Texas.

Hunter waited his turn in line at the coffee shop and then ordered a sandwich and a hot chocolate. As he paid for his food, he asked the cashier, "I'm trying to find Mr. Johnson. Do you know where he's staying?"

The woman frowned. "He's not in town. His store was damaged by lightning."

"Do you know which town he is in?" Hunter tried the question again.

She shook her head. "I only know that he's not in Golden Ridge, but if you go to the meeting at Town Hall tonight, someone there might know."

"The Town Hall meeting?" He lowered his head. The last thing he needed was a meeting where the whole town would be in attendance. He just needed to find someone who knew the answer to his question so he could find Mr. Johnson and then coordinate how he could be of assistance. Helping the Johnsons rebuild their store and home wouldn't just benefit them, it would benefit the whole town.

The cashier handed him his change along with an orange flyer. It gave the details about the Town Hall meeting which was scheduled to start in an hour.

"What's this?" he asked the cashier.

"There's a group of us small businesses that are getting together to help them."

"What about their insurance?" Hunter asked.

The girl bit her lip, eyeing the other customers behind Hunter before saying, "Their fire insurance was minimal at best. It wouldn't cover damage caused by lightning."

"Thanks," he said. "I'm interested in helping." He looked down at the flyer again and took his food from the counter. He situated himself on a barstool that faced outside. From here he couldn't quite see where the Johnson's General Store was.

A man came and sat next to him by the window. "I heard you asking questions about the Johnson's store. Are you serious about helping?"

Hunter nodded, swallowing a large bite of his food. "I'd like to do what I can while I'm in town." He'd taken longer than planned to get things in order before he could start the challenge in order to be away from the office for the next several weeks. He was grateful his mom had told him about this project in a timely manner.

"You should come to the meeting tonight. There's a core group of us willing to help, but I'm afraid it's been a tough year all around for people. I hope we have enough support for this project, but …" the man shrugged. "It would be good to have as many people as we can get there tonight."

Hunter shook the man's hand and thanked him for the invitation. As he finished his food, Hunter reread the flyer. It urged everyone to rally around the Johnsons and give aid where they could as this year's Annual Golden Ridge Christmas Service Project. Hunter smiled. Winning this bet would be easier than he thought.

CHAPTER 2

Oakley Larsen looked around the practically empty Town Hall room. The room wasn't large, but with only a few people in the space, it felt cavernous. She pushed her strawberry-blonde hair over her shoulder and took a deep breath to calm her frayed nerves. It would be fine.

She'd been elected—more like forced—into running this year's Christmas Service Project. She was happy to be in charge of it, but with the recent lightning strike at the General Store, she knew she had to change her focus of this year's service into helping the Johnson family. They lived above the store so it wasn't just their livelihood, but their home that had been lost in the fire.

The large white and black clock at the back of the room seemed to grow in size with each movement of the second hand. A few more people trickled in. She focused on the papers in her hand. She'd prepared a small speech to give today, but if there were only the same people as last week, it wouldn't make sense to deliver it.

Trying to rebuild the General Store before Christmas was going to be a feat, and without enough funds to start the building process it would be almost impossible.

The minute hand clicked into its place at the top of the clock, and Oakley stepped to the podium and welcomed everyone. The seats were more than half full, roughly fifty people.

"Thanks for coming, y'all," she said into the microphone. "This is fixin' to be a very busy service project this year, and I appreciate each and every one of you who have taken the time to come and help one of our dear friends and neighbors in Golden Ridge. I know I have memories of going to the General Store when I was very young, and Mr. Johnson was always the kind man behind the counter who'd give me a piece of candy."

A gentle rumbling enveloped the crowd, and she stepped aside as others told their favorite stories from knowing the Johnsons. After a few comments, she continued, "My mom has been in contact with Mrs. Johnson. She's found out that they definitely plan on staying in town and that they intend to rebuild. My mom is quite the detective and slyly asked if they'd change anything from their original design. It sounds like they want to make a few alterations, but the store was built the way they liked it, so structurally everything will be the same as before."

"How long do we have on this project?" one woman asked.

"Good question. The goal, of course, is to finish by Christmas, but for sure by the New Year. We're hoping we can get the exterior done before the Johnsons come back into town.

They are currently staying with their daughter in Oklahoma while they work through the insurance battle. As William Rigby can attest, the insurance company will likely do little for them. Surveyors have already come out and seen the site, and we've been given the go ahead to start rebuilding. It would be great if we can show the Johnsons at least *some* progress on the building when they get back from Oklahoma, but again we don't know exactly how long they will be gone, especially if the insurers keep dragging their feet. I know we can't keep it a secret from them for long." She pulled out the wooden chart she made showing the donation number at $4,609.00. "Were there any more donations for this project?"

A man in the back raised his hand. "Half the proceeds of my week gives us another $700."

Oakley smiled, thanking the man and moving up the marker. She hoped the social pressure would help people want to donate.

"I got a deal on the wood for the framing, so I can donate the first load of it," Joe said.

"I'll pay for the second load," Max offered.

Oakley thanked everyone in turn and wrote down the donations. She wrote frantically, trying to get everyone's down, as more people added to the pile of donations.

"I've got the time to volunteer rebuilding the General Store for the duration of the project," a familiar voice called over the crowd.

Oakley's heart nearly stopped. She knew that voice as well as she knew her own, though it had been years since she had heard it. The insides of her jumped and danced and stumbled and fell all at the same time. She looked up from the paper she'd been recording everyone's donations on. Her eyes sought out his eyes, locking on the man in a dark jacket who was standing in the back.

"And I'll donate $10,000," he added.

A hush fell over the crowd. While the crowd turned to see who had spoken up, Oakley hadn't taken her eyes off him. $10,000 was more than double all of the prior donations combined! She should be thrilled, but she knew that those blue eyes were trouble. His hair had darkened since she'd seen him last, but everything else about him remained the same. That strong jaw, the rippling muscles that filled out his jacket, those captivating eyes. Hunter.

Oakley blinked, then plastered on a smile, knowing that the Johnson's General Store would benefit from his generosity, and wrote down the donation with shaking hands. She swallowed, but her throat remained dry. "Thank you, Mr. Paxton." She managed to make the words sound aloof, which caught her by surprise. Who knew that after nine years—practically a full decade—of not seeing him that he'd still look as gorgeous as ever, and she could be *cool* about it? He took her breath away even now like she was the same teenage girl crushing hard on her brother's best friend, but she could stand in front of a room of people on her heels and stay steady when she addressed him. It was progress over the last time she'd seen him. That was something at least.

The rest of the meeting went by in a blur, and Oakley could barely process it all. Hunter's donation had set a wave in motion through the room. Wallets opened wider and deeper than they ever had before. More and more folks came forward with donations and ideas. Plans to start on this project were finalized and they would be able to get started in two days with the donations in hand. Her heart swelled for their generosity, and yet there was an unspoken question on her mind. What in the world was Hunter Paxton doing in Golden Ridge?

Many people filtered out through the doors, but several stayed and talked. Oakley noted the significant crowd around Hunter. That was fine, but she wasn't going to join them. She didn't have anything to say to the boy who'd broken her heart at least twice—possibly more. She picked up the stack of papers and her wooden sign and focused on the evening's win. The donations pledged had exceeded her expectations. This was why she loved living in Golden Ridge, and why she'd come back here to run her online design business after college. Everyone was so kind and helpful, always coming to the aid of their neighbors and friends, and that was evident tonight. Though she had to admit that part of their giving spirit was stirred by the man who'd left town and never given it a backwards glance. Still, the town had come through for the Johnsons, and that was what mattered.

Oakley felt the pressure of her heels on the light wood floor more than she heard them. She walked softly on her toes, putting her heels down as lightly as possible, hoping to quickly escape without Hunter noticing. To be honest, he'd never really noticed her at all, except to incessantly tease her and make her feel like she'd had two older brothers instead of just one.

She was two steps from the exit, when he suddenly moved in front of her and blocked her way.

"Hi, Oakley," he said, his tone casual, his smile bright.

She forced a smile as she shielded herself from looking into his irresistible eyes. Whoever said Kryptonite came only in green and red had never met Hunter. Her Kryptonite was always blue –the shade of dark azure enveloped in the steely gray rings of Hunter's piercing eyes, to be exact. They reminded her of the dark blue that graced the majority of the sky during a sunset. *Kryptonite.*

"Hello, Mr. Paxton," she said, repeating his last name again. Formal. Professional. Distant. That's what she needed to keep herself standing on her heels when she started feeling weak in the knees.

He gave her a boyish grin, running his hands through his wavy hair that had darkened with age. His once caramel-colored hair would be considered chocolate now. Of course, she convinced herself that she would have noticed that detail on *anyone* that she hadn't seen in nine years, not just him. She'd seen his pictures occasionally online—anytime his security company won an award—but she'd always thought that it was either the hair products he used, the lighting of the pictures, or possibly the post-processing editing session that had made his hair appear darker.

"What?" she asked, when the boyish grin stayed on his face.

"I thought you were just being formal before, because you only call me Mr. Paxton when you're unhappy with me. What did I do wrong this time?" He said it like he didn't have a care in the world, like nothing had changed in nine years, and therein lay the problem.

"What are you doing here?" she asked.

He blinked. "A man can't visit his hometown?"

"Of course a *man* can." She gestured around the room. "But why are you *here*?"

"My mom told me about the Johnsons, and I came to help. Surely you're not gonna hold *that* against me?"

"I'm not holding it against you. It's actually really nice," she said, biting her lip as she thought about what she wanted to say next.

He spoke again. "What are *you* doing here?"

His question took her aback for a moment. "I live here."

He smiled. "You live in Town Hall? Wow."

She rolled her eyes, but she couldn't suppress her smile. She wanted to slug him playfully on the arm, but she kept herself in check, her arms not leaving her side. "You know what I mean. I live in Golden Ridge."

"You always had big plans about moving away after college," he said.

She nodded, surprised he remembered. She had had big plans once, but she always wanted her plans to match his. "Turns out I can do all of my commission artwork from anywhere thanks to this little thing called online sales," she replied sassily.

"Good for you! You always were so smart with your designs," he said, his eyes warm with the praise.

"Thanks." She couldn't look into his eyes anymore, so her gaze settled on his lips which made things worse. She pushed aside the memory of those lips, wanting to leave this conversation as fast as possible. She needed to get back to their original discussion. "I appreciate your donation. It is very generous ... but you don't have to stay."

His jaw muscle flexed.

Categorizing all of his looks when they were younger had

been a mistake. She could tell he was trying to gain control of whatever it was he was about to say.

"You want to run me out of town, is that it?" he asked, with a tone that gave no room for arguing.

"Your donation will be enough. We can even send you pictures. But I know you have a company to run in Portland, and the Johnsons will understand."

"You really *are* trying to get rid of me! Too bad you can't fire volunteers." He smiled, his eyebrows raising in an irresistible way. "I announced to the whole room that I'm here through the end of this project. I can't leave now."

She blanched. "But that could be weeks." How could he just show up and stay like that? Maybe she'd never really understood him like she'd thought.

He stepped closer to her. "I'm more than fine with that."

"There's no commitment just because you pledged your donation. We'll find the staff we need to complete this project," she said, knowing that probably sounded like she was rambling.

"And break a promise?" He looked at her. "I would never do that."

She opened her mouth to say something but no sound came through. Her brain felt disconnected from her vocal chords.

His gaze shot another Kryptonite blow. "Oaks, if there's a problem between us, let's fix it."

"Us? There was never an *us*."

He shifted his weight and looked down, breaking the hypnotic spell that had begun to weave its way between them. "Right." He coughed. "But there is a problem?"

She smiled widely. "No, no problem," she said quickly.

"Great, then it shouldn't bother you if I help."

"It doesn't bother me." She took a deep breath. "Do you still know how to use a hammer?"

He laughed. "I can prove I haven't changed."

She gulped. Perhaps he meant that to reassure her, but that was what she feared. More proof that he hadn't changed. He was still the old Hunter—the same Hunter—who had broken her heart. Her lungs squeezed. With any luck the rebuild would go faster than originally planned. The quicker she moved through this project, the quicker he'd leave … again.

OAKLEY LET THE SCREEN DOOR SLAM WHEN SHE ENTERED HER parents' large farm-style house several miles outside of town. The midnight blue sky was too dark to remind her of Hunter's eyes during the drive, but she'd thought about them anyway.

"Still the same," she muttered. She rolled her shoulders, letting the tension go. She had to admit he wasn't all bad. It really was good for the Johnson family that Hunter had spoken up when he did.

Nine years. She bit her lip. She hadn't noticed a ring on his finger. Of course, she'd only glanced at his left hand once or twice. She shouldn't want to Google him to find the information. She never purposefully tried to look online for info about him before, but social media had been plastered with stories on him for years and occasionally she'd see one and read it. In the last article she'd read, he'd gotten quite serious with a beautiful blonde. The story had alluded to a pending announcement between the couple.

"Hi, honey. How did your meeting go?" her mom called from the kitchen.

Oakley went toward the smell of freshly baked bread and something citrusy. Ellen Larsen was a beautiful older woman. Her silver hair was knotted in a bun and she was wearing her favorite apron. She sliced a large piece from the steaming loaf and put it on a plate, sliding it across the island toward where Oakley sat down on the swinging barstool. "It went really well. What are you making?"

Her mom grabbed the silver saucepan off the stove. "I'm trying a new recipe," she said, letting the saucepan cool on a wooden trivet. "This is an orange cranberry marmalade. I'm thinking of making them as Christmas gifts for the neighbors if I can get the recipe just right."

"I think I could be a good taste tester—just to make sure that it's safe for the neighbors," Oakley said, laughing.

Her mom lifted the wooden spoon from the saucepan and dribbled the marmalade onto the hot bread Oakley held. She smeared the marmalade onto her own slice and sat on the barstool next to Oakley. "Tell me all about the meeting."

As she sampled a corner of her jam-soaked bread, Oakley showed her mom the long list of donations. "Mom, this is seriously so good."

"Good enough to give away as a present?" her mom asked between bites.

"Definitely."

Her mom beamed.

Oakley spread more marmalade onto her bread. "Actually, Mom, on second thought, this is definitely *not* good enough to give away as presents. I think we're gonna be stuck eating all of it ourselves."

Her mom laughed. "If it's good enough that you don't want to share, it's nearly perfect." She pointed to the total on the donation list. "That can't be right, can it? That's a lot more than you thought you'd raise. That's wonderful, dear!" She scanned through the list. "Mr. Paxton donated? Did Ray conference call into the meeting from Colorado?"

"No, his son donated. Hunter is actually in town," Oakley clarified.

Her mom clapped her hands together like Christmas had come early. "Oh, my boy is here again!"

"He's not really your boy, mom," Oakley said.

Her mom waved away the comment like she was trying to cool steaming bread. "I know that. But it's been too long since I've seen him. Is he in town for long, do you know?"

Oakley blew out a breath. Her mom would bug her until Oakley told her all of the details. "I think he plans to stay and help with the General Store rebuild."

"Really? That's wonderful. You should invite him over for dinner."

"Mom, I don't live here anymore."

"Then extend the invitation that I'd love for him to come for dinner. He can come at his earliest convenience. I'll make his favorite on whatever day he comes."

"Who's coming for dinner?" her dad asked as he entered the kitchen.

"Hunter is in town!" her mom exclaimed.

❄

Oakley drove home after telling her parents all about the meeting and Hunter's surprising appearance there. They interrogated her with at least twenty questions about him that she had no idea how to answer and then wouldn't let her leave until she promised to invite him over for dinner. She would extend the invitation on behalf of her parents, but that didn't mean that she had to be there. The usually quick drive felt longer as she was lost down memory lane, remembering years of rearranging her schedule to make sure that she was there every time that Hunter came over for dinner. Hunter and Travis were always together and rotated between their houses for dinner every other night.

She shook her head, erasing those recollections. Things were different now. She was no longer the starry-eyed teenager who lived for every comment and conversation she had with Hunter. He might stay around and help, but that didn't mean she had to be affected by him. *Professional*. That was her word while he was in town. He may still think of her as the gangly kid sister always hanging around and wanting to play with her older brother and his friends—correction—friend, but she'd show him that she was different. She didn't need his attention anymore.

She pulled onto the long dirt drive up to her house as her mind wandered back to the first time he had broken her heart. Sadness, longing, and hurt all warred to be the dominating emotion as she recalled that agonizing day.

CHAPTER 3

OAKLEY - SOPHOMORE YEAR OF HIGH SCHOOL

Oakley ran through the house, pinching herself multiple times on her arm, delighted that she felt every single nip. Her dreams had basically come true, and it wasn't a dream at all—she had a line of red marks on her arm to prove it! Every penny she'd thrown into a fountain seemed to float to the surface. Every birthday wish since she was nine echoed together—her sixteenth birthday most recently playing through her mind.

All she wanted was to be noticed by the boy she'd crushed on for more than half of her life. Sure, Hunter Paxton noticed her. He was her older brother, Travis's, best friend so of course he knew who she was. Travis had always complained that she wanted to tag along when he hung out with his friends, though that was not quite true. She never cared to go with Travis when he was with Jay, Ed, or Charlie.

Hunter had let her come along once when she was very little, and he had been kind to her. But she was older now. She was in high school—a *sophomore*. Travis and his friends were all seniors, but for the first time she felt like she was on their same level. She wasn't just the 'annoying kid sister' anymore.

She had moved on from junior high, and through all of her birthday wishes and lucky pennies combined, Hunter had actually taken notice of her in a different way. Tingles ran up and down her arms. It couldn't have been a coincidence that he'd picked out her very favorite chocolates—chocolate turtles and the strawberry cream chocolates—from the General Store to add to the note he'd written asking her to the dance. She found it outside of her door when she came home.

As a sophomore, just being asked to the Senior Prom was a huge deal. But, to be asked by the boy she daydreamed about since being beguiled by his magical blue eyes was the most incredible feeling. Her legs felt like they were caught in quicksand as she rushed around the house trying to find Travis and Hunter. They were usually found hanging in Travis's room or snacking in the kitchen. Their backpacks were there next to the dining room table, and Hunter's car was parked out front, but there was no sign of them.

She wandered outside, heading to the back of the yard to take the short cut to her best friend Sandy's house. Oakley needed to share the good news in person. Texting wouldn't do. The rope ladder swung in the breeze and she heard voices coming from the treehouse. So *that's* where the boys were hiding. Oakley bit her lip, wondering if she'd be welcome to interrupt their treehouse time. It had always bugged Travis, although Hunter had always tried to make her feel welcome.

She grabbed the rope ladder, but ultimately decided against climbing it, and instead wandered around to the other side of the tree where there was a plastic tube that connected to the treehouse, allowing for secret messages to be shared. She'd used it a couple of times when she was younger to eavesdrop on the boys' conversations. She took a deep breath, and moved the cap away from the tube, wondering if she'd be able to hear anything. Voices floated through the pipe, allowing her to pick up their distinct voices.

"Who did you ask to the dance?" Hunter asked Travis.

"Janie Hopkins. I went to a dance with her last year."

"Do you like her?" Hunter asked.

Travis laughed. "Not like *that*, but she's a good friend. Who did *you* end up asking?"

There was a pause that felt like it could fill the whole state of Texas and then some. Oakley held her breath. "I decided to ask a sophomore this year," Hunter said.

"That's smart," Travis said. "Especially if you're tired of all the other girls in the grade. She'll make all the senior girls jealous. Who is it?"

Oakley imagined in the silence that Travis had given Hunter a fist bump.

"I actually asked Oakley."

Oakley's cheeks heated at the tender way he said her name. She breathed in the warm air that was filled with hope and possibilities. She'd come looking for Hunter to give him her answer, to tell him yes, but now she wondered if she should answer him back in a cuter way. Her mind spun with the options of a candy-bar poster or stuffing his car full of balloons or something.

"Oakley, Oakley? My sister?"

"Yeah."

"Why would you pick Oakley? I'd never pick Oakley."

Another pause. Oakley listened with baited breath. Of course Travis would never pick her. Travis was her brother. The idea would be disgusting. But even though Travis and Hunter acted like brothers, it didn't mean that Hunter had to be like a brother to her.

"Of course you'd never pick her. She's your sister."

There. At least one of them was making sense. Oakley's heart fluttered that they'd come to the same conclusion at about the same time. They thought alike. It was one more thing to add to her list of reasons why they were meant to be together. She covered her mouth to keep herself from squealing aloud.

"Fair enough. But why Oakley?"

"Well, like you said, we've already dated senior girls. The dance is only two weeks away, and all the other senior girls have already been asked."

"So, a safe date then?" Travis asked.

"Yes, exactly. A safe date." Hunter paused. "I mean she's your sister so she practically feels like ... my family too."

"That makes sense," Travis said.

"So you don't mind if I take your sister to Senior Prom?"

"Why would I mind? I mean it's not like you like her or anything."

"Right. I mean at this point, it's my poor planning and a lack of other options. She'd basically be doing me a favor." Hunter rushed his words.

"She'll probably think you're doing *her* the favor, since she'll be one of the youngest people attending the Senior Prom," Travis said.

"Right. A win-win." Hunter's voice sounded confident.

A lump formed in Oakley's throat. Her brain tried to process what she'd heard, wanting to make sense of it. Trying to figure out what to do. She blinked back the tears that wanted to settle on her lashes. She couldn't cry when she'd just applied a fresh coat of mascara, the kind that promised to make the lashes look longer and the eyes look bigger, but the caveat was that it wasn't waterproof. Hunter Paxton had ruined her dream, shredding it to pieces. Candles on a cake were just sticks of wax burning. Trusting in those flames to make her wishes come true had been juvenile.

She could hear them coming down from the treehouse, and only barely made it to the tire swing, pushing off from ground before Travis and Hunter were on the ground.

Travis headed inside the house, but Hunter hung back, his hands in his pockets. "Hi, Oakley," he said.

Oakley pushed away noticing the way his voice softened when he talked to her. She must be imagining it. No longer would she be the delusional girl, hopelessly falling for Hunter. Her voice betrayed her, coming out more breathless than she liked. "Hi, Hunter."

He looked around. "Have you been home long?"

"Long enough," she said. Long enough to hear what she wished she hadn't. Had she not been so excited to confirm the dance date with Hunter, she wouldn't have overheard the treehouse conversation. She could have gone to the dance blissfully unaware, and completely delusional. Ignorance could have been bliss. But her new knowledge dragged misery into the mix.

He scuffed his shoe in the dirt. She had categorized his features, his movements, his everything for years, and she was surprised that he looked so nervous. He rarely acted anything except confident and self-assured around her. But *she* didn't make him nervous. That would never be an emotion created from her presence.

She continued swinging, trying to ignore the boy of her dreams who stood next to the tree, his eyes never leaving her. "I left you something in front of your door. Did you get it?"

She slowed the swing, her feet dragging in the same dirt he'd been kicking at. He didn't feel the same about her, though she'd hoped for the better part of five minutes that him asking her to the dance was a sign of something more. But no. What had he called it? *Poor planning and a lack of other options.* The words sounded like nails on a chalkboard inside her head. She cringed. She wasn't stupid enough to hold onto the fantasy that had just been squashed. "I did. Thank you for the chocolates. They're my favorites." She'd share them tomorrow with all of her friends, not saving one for herself … but she could acknowledge that he paid enough attention to get her favorite kinds.

"Did you see the note with the chocolates?" he asked.

Oakley drew in a breath, allowing her feet to completely stop the swing. "I did."

His blue eyes looked around before settling on her again. His smile grew. "Good," he said. "Do you have an answer for me?"

Oakley had imagined this moment for months, years even. And here it was. Her long-time crush was *actually* asking her out. She'd be a fool to say no. But what else could she do? She wouldn't be his last-resort date. He had agreed with Travis that she should relish the opportunity just because she'd be invited to Senior Prom as a sophomore. She closed her eyes. Choosing to be a fool would be better than living through the event and making her heartbreak worse than it already was. No. It would be better not to go to the dance at all. Swaying to the music with Hunter holding her between his arms would be torturous. He didn't feel the same way. If she said yes, it would make everything so much harder.

"I do … have an answer."

Hunter beamed his smile that practically melted her.

Oakley felt her resolution wavering. She needed to speak quickly, before all rational thought left her brain. "I'm sorry. I can't."

Hunter blinked, his face a mixture of confusion and hurt. "I don't understand. It's the Senior Prom."

She mustered up a smile, gripping the chain links of the tire swing. She would keep her resolve. "It's *your* Senior Prom, not *mine*. I'll go to Senior Prom when *I'm* a Senior, not before."

Hunter's eyebrows scrunched together, and she knew that he was trying to figure out the rejection. "Plenty of sophomores and juniors go to Senior Prom."

"Then maybe one of *them* will go with you." She pulled hard on the chain links to get her feet under her. She walked away from the swing, not waiting to hear Hunter's response.

CHAPTER 4

Hunter drove the hour back to his hotel, his thoughts settling on Oakley. She'd been as mesmerizing as ever, and she was all grown up. Her once red hair was more like a strawberry-blonde now. She commanded the room, getting donations of materials and money. Her bright green eyes filled with excitement as the number of donations increased. Her smile had been bright until she saw him.

He sighed, doubting anyone else in the room could have picked up on the subtle shift in her cheek that made her dimples less prominent. Her jaw had tightened. He'd seen that look in her before—the disappointment he had caused. She'd grimaced when he said he hadn't changed. Did she not believe him? Being a billionaire and having more money hadn't affected him negatively. He'd prove that to her. He *was* still the same.

He shook his head. If they were going to work together, he

might have to cross that old bridge. He swallowed, saving the thought for another day.

He placed a call to his assistant, letting her know that he was going to be staying in Texas through Christmas, and possibly through New Year's if the project went that long. Then he called Kyle. He finally had something to report.

"I was beginning to think you were bowing out of the challenge," Kyle said after they exchanged hellos.

"It took a little longer than planned to get everything in order with my company before I could focus on the Christmas challenge."

"Fair enough. Let me grab Kandice, and we'll hear what you've got."

"Hi, Hunter," Kandice said a few moments later.

"Hi, Kandice. How are the other two doing at the challenge?"

Kandice laughed. "I'm not going to say anything about anyone else. And if you talk to them you're under strict instructions not to bring up your individual Christmas service projects. It's hard enough to judge as it is."

Hunter chuckled. "I have a solution."

"What's that?" Kyle asked.

"Simple. Declare me the winner, and we can all go our separate ways and enjoy Christmas. I'm gonna win anyway, so we might as well let the other guys down gently."

Kandice snickered. "You're funny, Hunter."

"Quit stalling. Let's hear your report. You've taken a week longer than the other two to give us a call," Kyle said.

"I'm in Texas."

"Favoritism won't be shown to you just because it's our preferred state," Kyle said.

"I know that."

"So why Texas then?" Kandice asked.

"I'm in Golden Ridge, well actually just outside of it in a slightly bigger town called Sunset Meadows."

"I thought your family moved to Colorado," Kyle said.

"They did when my dad retired but, other than my time in college, I never called Colorado home," Hunter explained. "When you mentioned that our choice should reflect something meaningful, I knew I wanted to start here."

"You didn't already have something in mind before you drove out to Golden Ridge?" Kandice asked.

"Well, kind of," Hunter said. He explained how his mom had told him about the Johnson's General Store being struck by lightning. Describing it brought back his meeting with Oakley. Though part of him had hoped to see Oakley while he was in town, their conversation didn't go as expected. She had always been so attentive to him when they were growing up, but her curt dismissal opened up old wounds, making them feel fresh again. Senior Prom came to mind. As did the last Christmas he'd seen her. He had lost his heart to her, and she'd trampled it multiple times. He cringed. He picked Golden Ridge for the competition because it was part of him, but he hadn't thought through the logistics of what would happen with Oakley—that he would still be unwanted and unwelcome with her.

"Hunter? Are you there? How did things turn out at the Town Hall meeting?" Kandice asked, pulling him back into the call.

"I pledged my $10,000 to help, along with volunteering." He told them all about the meeting and the momentum his bid seemed to give the room.

Kyle sighed. "Technically, flashing around your money isn't the best way to serve."

"It's what I could do, and it helped rally others. I'm well known in Golden Ridge; my identity isn't a secret. People know what I make and about the company I started."

"You can't tell anyone about the bet," Kandice reminded him.

"I'm following the rules," Hunter said. "I'm not just donating the money to a charity. All of it will go toward rebuilding the General Store here. It's a big deal for Golden Ridge, and I have a soft spot for old Mr. Johnson. He always gave me candy when I came in the store. He usually favored the girls, but he always gave me my favorite treat too."

"You're going to help with the construction on the store and house?" Kyle asked.

"I'm gonna help any way Oakley will let me," Hunter said.

"Oakley? Does Oakley's last name start with an L?" Kyle asked.

"Yes. It's Oakley Larsen," Hunter confirmed.

"You've known her most of your life, right?"

"You have a good memory," Hunter said. "Yeah, she was my best friend's younger sister growing up. She's in charge of the project."

"How fun to reconnect with people," Kandice said. "Sounds like a hidden benefit to the bet."

Hunter wasn't sure if it was a benefit or a detriment, but he agreed. "Yeah, it is. Her brother is back East, but once the project gets under way I'm looking forward to catching up with people." Oakley may not give him the time of day, but he could certainly look up old friends and neighbors he had when he lived in Golden Ridge. The town had always been friendly.

"Keep us posted on your progress, and we'll talk to you next week," Kyle said.

HUNTER SPENT THE NEXT FOUR DAYS WORKING ON THE SITE, clearing debris from the land and helping with the construction. He spent time measuring and cutting, and anything else John, the project foreman, needed help with. Others rotated their work before or after their regular jobs, but Hunter was able to be the one constant person volunteering there. Driving the hour back and forth from Sunset Meadows everyday allowed plenty of time for his mind to wander, but it just wouldn't stray beyond Oakley.

He expected to see everyone through his twelve-hour days, but he hadn't seen Oakley since the meeting at Town Hall. He hoped to run into her at some point, but hadn't yet. She was either really busy, or really good at avoiding him. She had said there was no problem between them. She said that they could work together, but so far that wasn't a reality. He sighed, wishing he'd kept his feelings to himself all those years ago. He'd always compared every other girl to Oakley, even in high school. He dated a lot, trying to find someone who could measure up to her—someone that was as much fun to be around—but there was just no one else he'd rather spend time with. When he got bored with the small talk on a first date, he'd imagine what Oakley would have said and quit paying attention to his actual date. This pattern led to many first dates, but never any second ones. It had been exhausting in high school.

At least in college she hadn't been close enough to pine over, and he had roommates to hang out with. He had seen her over some of his holidays home during college while she was still in high school, but once she went away to school herself, their timing never lined up. He hadn't seen her since his last winter break in college nine years ago.

He took a deep breath. The past was in the past, but he couldn't help but feel like she was avoiding him. He headed toward the edge of the property where the sidewalk adjacent to the site had been turned into a refreshment stand. Volunteers took turns replenishing the water coolers, and the restaurants and bakeries brought food and treats for those working on the project. Hunter wiped his forehead with the back of his hand and grabbed a cold drink of water.

"Slowing down?" a familiar voice teased.

He turned instantly to stare into the green eyes that matched the voice he'd know anywhere. His heart swelled. "Annie Oakley. I didn't know that you still lived around these parts," he said, subtly hinting at her absence at the site all week.

She rolled her eyes. "You know that's not my name." She studied him. "So you're still here."

"I told you I would be." An awkward silence filled the space between them. "Haven't seen you all week."

"I'm sure you're all broken up about that. I don't have to supervise this. John has everything under control."

"I always miss you when I don't see you," he said, topping off his water cup just to give himself something to do.

She brushed off his comment with a coy, "I wasn't quite sure until now, but yep, it's the same Hunter. The same exact guy who knows just what to say to mesmerize all of the ladies." She raised her chin just slightly, fixing her eyes on his, daring him to disagree with her. "Your charms don't work on me."

He already knew that. Nothing worked on her. He looked all around. "I don't see anyone else around here that I'm trying to charm."

A deep blush formed on Oakley's cheeks, the very color that used to match her hair before it had lightened. "So you're really in town until this is finished?"

Her immediate change of subject didn't go unnoticed, and he wanted her to know that he was serious about his commitment. "Unless you have a problem with that."

Her eyes widened. "Like I already said, I don't have a problem with it at all. In fact, I don't have any thoughts on the subject one way or the other."

"Then why do you seem so bothered by the fact that I'm here?"

"Don't you have a girlfriend to get back to? I mean, that's a long time to be away from someone," she said.

He laughed. "I suppose it would be a long time to be away if I had a girlfriend."

"You didn't actually answer the question. Aren't you almost engaged to someone?"

He raised an eyebrow. "You actually read the online gossips?"

She lifted a shoulder. "Sometimes it comes through on my social media feed."

"Well, that's old news. I haven't dated her in a couple of years. Things were never as serious as the media made it sound."

She nodded. "Well, how nice that you can just come and go as you please then," she said.

"And what about you?" he probed. This was the question that had been on his mind since he'd seen her again. "Do you currently have your eye on anyone?"

She choked on the water she was drinking. "Obviously not … I'm just looking at you."

"I'd be flattered if that were the case," he said, wondering if she'd ever thought of him as more than her brother's best friend. Were they really too close to being like family for a romantic relationship between them to be possible? Is that what the problem had been nine years ago? She didn't respond to him words, so he tried again. "I meant do you have a boyfriend?"

"No."

John approached and Oakley handed him a drink. "Here you go, John," Oakley said, smiling at him. The foreman thanked her for the refreshment and got back to work.

"I suppose I should start filling the cups. I'm manning this station for the next couple of hours," she said.

"Ah, and here I thought you'd just come to talk to me," Hunter said.

Oakley looked him square in the eyes. "Sure. I came *just* to talk to you." She batted her eyelashes at him, then shook her head. "You know that's not my style."

He knew lots of things about her that she probably didn't even realize, like how she used sarcasm to cover up her feelings. Or how she pretended to be brave when she saw spiders. He even recognized how she bit the inside of her cheek when she was nervous, making her dimple dance in the most irresistible way. And she also said things that she didn't mean just to get a rise out of others. In a word, she was an enigma.

All growing up, there'd be one minute when she'd wanted to play with Travis and Hunter and the next she'd want nothing to do with them. She'd be daring and say bold things, and then she'd pull back and be timid. He'd even agreed to arm wrestle her once when they were little, just because she wanted to see if she could win. When she lost, she acted like it was no big deal. Perhaps he should have let her win to gauge her reaction. Maybe then she would have been less perplexing. Now he realized that she was still the same Oakley, and she still drove him crazy.

"I wouldn't know anymore," he said. "Maybe we could get together and catch up over dinner or something." He held his breath. He was a billionaire, someone who made his money designing and implementing complex systems. He had mastered the art of taking strategic paths and calculated risks, but Oakley still had him on his toes, never knowing what to expect.

Her eyes grew wide and for a brief moment he imagined that she might actually be flattered by the invitation. He snapped back to reality as she spoke.

"Speaking of dinners, I forgot to tell you that my parents want you to come over for dinner. Mom said she'd make your favorite."

"I'll never say no to your mom's chicken pot pie," Hunter said. "My mouth is already watering."

"Mom and Dad will be happy to see you. What day works for you?" she asked.

It wasn't lost on Hunter that she didn't include herself in the *'happy to see you'* group. "I'm open. What day works for you?" He was thrilled at the idea of a home-cooked meal with people that felt like a second family, and especially spending more time with Oakley. His fare since returning to Texas consisted mostly of fast-food and room service by himself, although the lunches from the diner had been fresher and with other volunteers.

"Me?"

Hunter nodded. "I assume you're gonna be there for family dinner."

"I don't live with my parents," she stammered.

"You don't go home to eat dinner with them every now and again?"

"Of course I do, but they want to see *you*."

An idea formed in his mind, and he grinned. "Tell them I'll come on whichever day you'll join me."

Oakley bit her lip, and Hunter could practically hear the wheels turning inside her head. "How about tomorrow night?"

"Tomorrow night is perfect. And you'll be there? You're not just planning to leave me with your parents so you can go out on a date now, are you?" He kept his voice light, attempting humor to gain confirmation that she wasn't dating anyone. She could have just started seeing someone, and maybe didn't use the term boyfriend yet. He just wanted to be sure.

Her smile faltered. "Like I said before, I'm not seeing anyone."

He nodded. "Thank you for the dinner invitation. I'm looking forward to it."

"Dinner on weekends is at five o'clock. Don't be late."

He remembered all too well the strict schedule they kept, especially with her dad working the ranch. "I wouldn't dream of it."

She nodded, a smile almost gracing her perfectly kissable lips. The rest of the day her lips were all he thought about, especially the teasing way they curved when her eyes laughed at him.

HUNTER GLANCED AT THE CLOCK ON HIS DASHBOARD AS HE DROVE into Golden Ridge on Saturday night. 4:57 p.m. With any luck, the clock would be fast, and he could make it to dinner by 5:00 p.m. Oakley had been clear about the importance of punctual arrivals for dinner, and he didn't want to disappoint her.

He drove faster down the long winding road that led to Oakley's house. The Larsen Ranch had been a second home for him growing up. As he wound toward it, the longing to be here in Golden Ridge grew. There was something about this place, about the connections he had here, that weren't easily forgotten. Memories flooded his mind, happy moments, sad moments, and growing pains that had molded him into the successful person that he was.

He pulled up to the house and parked the truck. The dashboard read 5:07 p.m. before he took the keys out of the ignition. Dust settled around the truck as he got out and made his way up the path to the wraparound porch.

He stood on the steps for an extra heartbeat. He knew where the doorbell was, but he couldn't remember ever using it. He always walked right in, even when Travis wasn't home. He took a breath, wondering what the right answer was. His pointer finger found the doorbell, and he rang, noting he'd never heard the ring tone from the outside before.

Ellen's voice could be heard through the slightly opened front window. A moment later the door opened. "Hunter Paxton! Now I knew it couldn't be you, because the Hunter I know would have just walked right in. How are you?" She gave him a big hug.

"I'm doing well. How are you, Mrs. Larsen?"

"Mrs. Larsen sounds so formal. You know you can still call me Mom."

"Thanks, Mom," Hunter said, as he followed her inside. The aroma in the house was like coming home. The scent of his favorite meal enveloped him as he walked through the familiar hallway to the back of the house where the large kitchen was open and inviting. Great windows on the opposite side of the kitchen table flooded the room with natural light.

They joined Oakley and her dad, Andy, at the kitchen table.

Andy stood and shook Hunter's hand. "It's good to see you, son."

"I'm sorry I'm late. Thank you for inviting me to dinner," he said.

"You know you're always welcome whenever you're in town. But the real question is, how come we haven't seen you here sooner?" Ellen asked.

Hunter looked at Oakley before answering. "I've been keeping busy at the Johnson's."

Ellen nodded. "I understand, and it's good of you to come into town to help with it. Oakley says you're here until the project is done, is that right?"

"That's right."

"Where are you staying?"

"At the hotel up in Sunset Meadows," Hunter replied, scooping a large helping of chicken pot pie.

"That's quite out of the way," Andy said.

Hunter nodded. "It's the closest I could get with half of the Golden Ridge motel under construction. The construction crew has switched their focus to working on the Johnson property."

"Makes sense," Andy said.

"No, it does *not* make sense," Ellen disagreed with her husband. "I feel like my other son finally came home, and what does he do? He stays an hour away at a hotel. It's not right."

"Mom, Hunter can stay anywhere he wants. He's a grown man," Oakley said.

"I know that, dear. But Hunter is *family*. And family doesn't need to stay at a hotel when there are vacant rooms in our house."

"That's kind of you, Ellen, but I don't want to impose—"

"Since when have you ever imposed? In fact, have you ever rang the doorbell here before tonight? You're spending two hours a day driving. You could cut that down to six minutes each way if you stayed here. Think about that."

Hunter did. He saw the pleading in Ellen's eyes and the shock in Oakley's. He'd be much more useful to the service project if he were closer. Besides, Ellen and Andy had always been like second parents to him. He didn't want to intrude, but he also didn't want to offend them by not taking them up on their generous offer. "If I'm not putting you out, that would actually be very helpful. Thank you."

Ellen smiled at him. "You're not putting us out at all. We'd love to have you stay for as long as you're in town. You can sleep in Travis's old room."

"That's very kind of you. Thanks, Ellen," he said.

"Now that that's settled, tell us about what you've been up to," Ellen instructed. "And how are your parents are doing?"

Hunter updated them with highlights of his life since he'd been there nine years ago. It almost felt like reading his bio as he told the group about the different things he'd accomplished. He filled them in on his siblings and his parents. He answered all their questions and asked them about the ranch.

When dinner was over, and their places were cleared, Ellen spoke. "Hunter, why don't you go grab your things from the hotel, and I'll have your favorite pie ready when you get back?"

"You're spoiling me," Hunter said, laughing. "You'd better be careful or you might find yourself with a permanent house guest."

"Just like old times," Ellen said, her face bright.

Andy and Ellen both laughed but Oakley stood still. Her frown sent creases into her forehead.

"Is there anything I can pick up for you in Sunset Meadows?" Hunter asked.

"The same Hunter. Always so thoughtful," Ellen said. "Now that you mention it, we're running low on Gregor's Raspberry Honey."

"Mom, he's not an errand boy," Oakley said.

Hunter smiled. "But I offered. I really don't mind—"

"No, Oakley's right," Ellen said. "Where are my manners, making our houseguest do errands? Oakley, why don't you go with him and then you can pick it up for me."

Oakley opened her mouth, like she'd object, then shut it again. Finally she said, "I don't want to put Hunter out," she answered. "I can go into Sunset Meadows on Monday and get your whole list. That way I can stay here and help you with dessert."

"Dessert is ready to go. It's already chilling in the fridge. I'll pop it in when y'all leave Sunset Meadows, and it should be coming hot out of the oven when you walk through the door."

"You've never put me out," Hunter smiled, his gaze holding Oakley's. "I'm happy to stop at the store."

Oakley nodded, her shoulders falling. "Well, we'd better go if we're gonna make it before the store closes."

They were almost to the front door when Ellen hollered, "Oh, and pick up some syrup for breakfast. Hunter's favorite kind was always … some kind of berry."

"Boysenberry," Oakley whispered under her breath. She called back to her mom. "Got it!"

Hunter opened the front door for her and she awkwardly stepped past him. They walked in silence toward the truck. There had to be a way to win her over, or at least find a way to be civil while he was staying at her parents' house.

He helped her up into the truck and grinned at her as he climbed in.

She raised her eyebrows. "What?"

"You remembered my favorite kind of syrup was boysenberry."

She shifted. "Some things you don't forget."

It wasn't an earth-shattering moment, but it was a start. He could build on that. Hunter started the truck, reversing slowly down the long driveway, and made the turn toward Sunset Meadows.

CHAPTER 5

Oakley adjusted the heater vents in the truck as they drove, finding anything to keep her hands from fidgeting in her lap.

"As I recall, your favorite was all of the toppings." Hunter chuckled.

She rolled her eyes. "Is it really considered remembering when you state that I like all of them? It's like saying my favorite is all of the songs, or all of the colors. It's not really remembering anything specific at all."

"Is that so?" Hunter asked. He put his foot on the brake as the only light heading out of town turned red, switched the dials on his digital screen, and hit play.

The volume increased as Alvin and the Chipmunks sang a silly Christmas song. "I remember that this was one of your *most favorite* songs growing up," he teased.

Oakley couldn't hold in her laugh any longer. "Yes, you remember me *so* well."

"You used to run around the house chasing us with this song," he said. "Sounds like a favorite to me."

"I was what, seven?" she said.

"You brought it out once when we made sugar cookies. Trav and I were in junior high so you would have been at least twelve."

She bit her lip, reminiscing on all the years they had made their traditional sugar cookies together. They would deliver them to their neighbors and friends. Others would join them occasionally, but it had always been the three of them. Every year. Her mom had called them the Three Musketeers. The sweet memory quickly faded as she thought about the sugar cookies from nine years ago. Pain stabbed her, and she pushed it away. She wouldn't go there, not right now. She would choose to remember the better years. "That used to be such a fun tradition," she said, gulping past the words that she wanted to say.

"Do you still do it?" Hunter asked.

"Do what? Make sugar cookies and play the Chipmunks?"

"Yeah."

She looked out the window. "That tradition kind of died out. It was really more of a Three Musketeers thing—well more like *'Two Musketeers'* and a tag along kid sister."

"I never thought of you like that," he said quietly.

"I'm tagging along with you right now!" It was so easy for him to look back and not remember how things really were, but she wouldn't be fooled.

Hunter remained quiet, his eyes focused on the road. The headlights pierced the darkness and stars shone brightly in the expansive sky.

Oakley tilted her head back and looked out the sunroof. "So many stars."

"Remember that time we went out to Red Rock Point and watched the stars?" he asked.

She turned towards him. "I do. I felt like the coolest freshman getting to go with y'all and your other junior friends."

"Were there others with us? I thought it was just the three of us," he said.

Oakley laughed. "Yeah, there were two other guys and at least four other girls. Don't you remember, you liked that short blonde? What was her name? Started with an N … Natalie maybe?"

Hunter chuckled. "I forgot I liked her. I can't believe you remember that, but then I've always known that you had an amazing memory."

"Some things are hard to forget." She remembered all of the girls he'd gone out with. It wasn't too difficult since Hunter and Trav double dated all the time and almost always brought their dates over to meet the Larsens. Sometimes he dated the popular girls, and other times he dated the athletic girls. For all the differences in each of his dates' features and personalities, she could never get a good read on his 'type'. They were all so different. Very few of his dates had red hair, though. Perhaps that should have been her first sign all those years ago.

"And some things aren't worth remembering, I guess," he said. "I really only recall being there with you and Trav."

"Trav had his girlfriend there," she said. "I think they mostly stayed by the campfire."

"What was his girlfriend's name?" Hunter asked.

Oakley blanked. She could see the face but couldn't remember the name. "It's on the tip of my tongue," she said.

Hunter smirked. "Funny, you can remember the name of a girl I went out with *once,* but you can't remember the name of your brother's girlfriend."

Oakley laughed it off, knowing that if she wasn't careful, she'd give too much away. She shouldn't remember as much as she did. She was over Hunter now. It had been nine years since the last time he broke her heart. Memory lane was a place full of land mines. If she didn't guard her heart, she would end up pining for what was always out of her reach. "Yeah ... very funny," she murmured.

"I remember sitting in the back of my truck trying to convince you about some made up constellations. I think I had you fooled that I was an expert astronomer." He laughed and it sounded like music to Oakley's ears.

She poked him, "I already knew you had no idea what you were talking about the second you started using stars from the Big Dipper to make your constellations." At the time, however, she'd liked the attention he was giving her and thought it could mean something to him—especially when he'd spent so much time with her instead of with his friends. When she thought about it later though, it was probably Hunter's way of helping Travis out so that he could spend time with his girlfriend without his annoying little sister around. Still, it had been a moment she'd treasured. "And you were sweet to let me borrow your hoodie when it started getting colder." She'd worn it for a week afterwards before she reluctantly gave it back to him.

Hunter looked at her for a long moment. "Look at you admitting that I can be sweet and thoughtful sometimes."

"I'll give credit where credit is due," she said. "I remember things accurately."

"So do I."

She gave him a half smile. "I'm sure you do." His memories were vague at best.

"You wore your favorite green shirt that night," he continued.

Green was Hunter's favorite color. Of course she wore it all the time. In fact, more often than not, she was wearing some shade of green when she would do anything with them. Most of the clothes in her closet were green. It was her favorite simply because it was his favorite. She really had been so smitten with him when she was younger. "I had a lot of green shirts. That's an easy guess."

He glanced over at her, his eyebrows drawn together. "It was the green one with the white collar and the white buttons down the front."

She sucked in a breath. "And you wore a hoodie, until you gave it to me." She had breathed in the scent of him, a mixture of his cologne and shampoo, surrounding her like she was in a perpetual hug. Hunter had been her whole world growing up.

He laughed. "I remember the exact shirt you wore. That has to be worth some points or kudos or *something*."

She smiled, not quite convinced he ever *really* noticed her, even if he could remember such a distant memory. "Fine, have ten points." She laughed at the game they used to play, awarding each other verbal points for whatever it was that deserved recognition. He gave her points all the time, and she almost always took points away from him just to get a reaction out of him. It made sense in her twitterpated teenage brain and proved she was definitely not good at flirting.

They laughed together as they reminisced about their childhood. They recalled pranks they'd pulled on each other and Christmas moments from junior high and high school.

Oakley's breath caught as she realized how many times she imagined driving like this with Hunter. No, they weren't on a date like she once romanticized, but the tension between them had lifted considerably as they talked about fun moments together. She realized how impossible it was to think of significant memories without getting her brain tangled in the crush that was Hunter.

The drive passed quickly, and they pulled into the hotel parking lot. Oakley waited in the truck while Hunter grabbed his stuff from his room, checked out, and threw his suitcase in the backseat. He hadn't brought much with him, certainly not enough to stay through the end of the project. But she didn't need to worry about that. He could stay or leave and it was all the same to her, wasn't it?

They arrived at Gregor's ten minutes before closing and hurried down the aisles. Oakley put a few things in a small basket for herself, and then went to grab her mom's short list. She pulled the boysenberry syrup from the shelf. "Does this brand work for you?"

"It's my favorite, but you already knew that." He looked at her, smiling.

"I remember lots of random things," she countered.

He blocked her path from leaving the aisle, reaching around her to grab something. He held up a small glass bottle of amaretto pecan syrup.

"Changing your mind?" she asked.

He leaned closer to her, dangerously close enough this time to smell his fresh breath along with that amazing cologne he'd chosen—a woodsy scent with a bite of mint.

She inhaled deeply, but holding her breath didn't help her notice him any less.

"Not changing my mind," he said with an air of triumph as he placed his selection into her cart. "That is *your* very favorite kind of syrup, though you'd occasionally add jam on your waffles first, or mix the boysenberry syrup with it. And you like to make your whipped cream into the shape of a flower before you eat any of it."

Oakley's insides melted like syrup as Hunter recalled her exact breakfast routine. This memory seemed more significant. Hunter and Travis bounced back and forth between their houses for all meals, especially in the summer, which meant she'd had breakfast with Hunter almost every other day. Hunter and Travis had basically lived at each other's houses, securing their own seats at each other's kitchen tables. Occasionally, Oakley had even joined them for breakfast at Hunter's house. She lived for those moments. "You really remember that?" she asked.

He nodded. "Of course I remember that. I thought it was adorable. I remember a lot of things." He pointed to the chocolate counter. "Would you like something? A strawberry cream filled chocolate or a turtle?"

She shook her head. "My mom is making your favorite pie." She was surprised when she saw disappointment cross his face and added, "Thank you for the thought though."

He nodded. "Pie will be good. Are you gonna stay for dessert when we get back to your parents' house?"

She bit the inside of her cheek to keep her smile in check. "You think I'd skip it and let you polish off the entire blackberry pie? No thanks, I'm definitely staying."

She paid for the food, unwilling to let Hunter pitch in. He opened the store door for her, and she savored the moment. He'd always been one to open doors for her, even when they were younger.

He reached for his truck's passenger-side door, then paused with his fingers on the handle. "Oakley, can we be friends?"

Oakley drew in a breath. Hunter was so close to her. "What else would we be?" Her heart tripped over the idea of them being something more, but she was beyond thinking that was possible. Especially since there had been nine years of silence since her worst holiday memory.

He ran his hands through his hair and cleared his throat. "Your parents have been very generous to let me stay at their house. I don't want them to regret that. If you and I can't get along, I'll stay here in Sunset Meadows."

"They wouldn't want that," Oakley said quietly.

"I'm sorry for what happened the last time we were together," he blurted out.

She looked into his eyes and nodded. He was sorry for kissing her … but she already knew that. The admission stung nevertheless, and she had to push it aside or years of hurt would spill out onto her face. She was sorry, but not in the way he meant. "Me too."

"You don't have to … I'm not expecting forgiveness for it."

She waved a hand to dismiss the uncomfortable moment. "Don't worry about it. It's long been forgotten."

Pain etched across his face. "Will things be okay between us?"

Us. There was that word again. She wanted to repeat her earlier sentiment from yesterday, that there never was an *us*, but the look in his Kryptonite blue eyes stopped her. An apology was one thing, but he looked like he carried a burden around, like it was important for her not to dismiss it. She could swallow her pride, swallow the hurt, swallow all the years of pain. It was like a jagged pill; she just needed a big enough glass of water. She mustered up her strength. "Like I said before, there's not a problem between us now."

Hunter nodded, though it didn't look like he believed her. "We'll be able to get along during this project, then?"

Oakley smiled and nodded. "I thought we did a very good job on the way here." Although, if she were being honest, she'd spent most of the ride reliving some of her favorite memories with Hunter, and all those wonderful moments made the sadness well up stronger.

He finally pulled open the truck door for her and helped her up. When they were back on the highway toward Golden Ridge, he turned on the radio. A beautiful rendition of *"Have Yourself a Merry Little Christmas"* filled the space between them.

"This might not be the right version, but this is one of your favorite Christmas songs," he said quietly.

She smiled. He was right. The song reminded her of her grandma. She'd given Oakley a music box that had played the simple tune. It had been years since she'd heard the rendition that she loved the most, but the song was still one of her favorites. "Good memory. I suppose that's worth ten points."

"I don't want points. I just wanted you to know that you weren't the only one paying attention." He patted her hand that rested on the console.

Her giddy teenage heart pierced through her adult sensibilities. He *had* noticed her, at least on some level. Heat ran over her skin, spreading from the spot where he'd touched her all the way to her toes. She blinked. She wasn't over Hunter at all, not by a long shot. She was in so much trouble.

CHAPTER 6

Hunter took Kyle's call early in the morning. It would have been around the time Hunter normally drove from Sunset Meadows to Golden Ridge, but he decided to leave out the detail where he was now the Larsen's guest. Hunter gave Kyle a status update on how the last week went, maybe adding in a few too many details.

"Be real with me, Hunter," Kyle said. "Is this the right project for you? Is being in Golden Ridge a smart move after everything that has happened in the past between you and Oakley?"

Hunter exhaled sharply. He'd made great strides on the actual project, but Kyle was perceptive with knowing how hard this was. "I've already pledged my money to this project. I'm not sure it would be a good idea to switch now. But working with Oakley—well, let's just say it's a work-in-progress."

"I just don't want to see you get hurt again," Kyle said. "This competition is not worth heartbreak. Kandice and I will let you switch projects if that's what you want to do."

"You remember me telling you about her?" Hunter asked.

"You talked about Oakley the way I talked about Kandice. Of course I remember her. She broke your heart on more than one occasion, if I remember right. Not that I was going to say anything during our first call about it, especially if you didn't want to share that with Kandice, but Kandice caught on to the tension. And whatever you decide will work for us. You won't be penalized if you swap projects at this point."

"I appreciate that, but I think we've come to an understanding," Hunter said. Not that it fixed the past, or the two times she'd broken his heart, but maybe there was a way to move past it. In some ways being in Golden Ridge felt exactly like the place he should be. He hoped it stayed that way.

"Well, keep me posted on that. I know you want to help out with this project, and Kandice and I support any decision you make, but just know that there is no shame in trying a different venture."

Hunter couldn't tell if it was just his competitive nature, but his resolve hardened. Whether or not he could win Oakley over was a separate matter from the pact they'd made on the yacht. "No. I'm committed. I will see this through."

"Keep up the good work, and keep us posted on your progress."

"I will. Thanks, Kyle," he said, and then hung up.

The aroma of freshly made waffles wafted up the stairs and into his room. Hunter padded down in flannel pajamas, half expecting to see Oakley already with a stack already drizzling her syrup. She'd almost always beaten him to the table when they were growing up.

But Oakley wasn't in the kitchen. Disappointment ran through him. Hunter didn't want to admit that he made a mistake staying at the Larsen's, and staying there only one night and then going back to the hotel would be very awkward. Her parents had been like a second family to him since he was little and he didn't want to hurt their feelings, but being here and expecting to see Oakley created a new kind of torture. Everything around him reminded him of her.

Last night he and Oakley had laughed and reminisced on their drive like they were old friends. It had been so nice, and healing in some ways. He hoped time would soften the blow he'd unknowingly dealt to her, but he had felt the ache on his end, too.

Sure, he could see how Oakley thought he had been a player … but he'd been secretly in love with her for years. How else was he supposed to act? She'd never thought about him in that way, and the thought stung. He wasn't sure why he'd really come back to Golden Ridge for the bet to begin with, but seeing Oakley again meant he couldn't leave, nor did he want to.

Ellen pulled two waffles from the waffle iron and set them on a large white plate. "Breakfast." She smiled as she held it out for him.

"Thank you," he said, accepting the plate of food. He took the new bottle of boysenberry syrup and drizzled it over the hot waffles. He sat at the island, on the barstool he'd basically claimed since he was a boy. Oakley often sat next to him, and the thought of seeing her again today excited him.

Ellen looked toward the kitchen door. "Did Oakley say anything about coming for breakfast this morning?"

Hunter shook his head. "She didn't mention anything to me. Why?"

Ellen pointed to the syrup that he'd added to the cart yesterday. "She's the only one who likes this kind. I assumed that meant she was coming."

"I put it in the cart," he admitted, wishing that Oakley was here too.

Ellen shrugged her shoulders. "No matter. Maybe that means she'll come by more often in the mornings." Her voice sounded hopeful.

"Is Travis coming home for the holidays?"

Ellen nodded. "He'll be here for Christmas, but not Thanksgiving. Speaking of, what are your plans for Thanksgiving? Is your family getting together?"

"I haven't firmly settled my plans for Thanksgiving. My parents are visiting with my younger brother back East, and my other brothers and sisters are at their in-laws this year. We'll all be together for a big family Christmas this year though."

"Well, you're welcome to join us for Thanksgiving, we would love to have you."

"Thanks, Mrs. Larsen. I really appreciate the invitation," Hunter said.

"Don't mention it," Ellen said. "And hopefully the timing works out for you to see Travis before you leave to spend Christmas with your family."

"I'd like that. It's been a while since I've seen him," Hunter admitted.

"That's what happens when you live across the country from

each other. You have to at least stay until he gets here. He should arrive a few days before Christmas."

"Are you sure I'm not too much of a burden?" Hunter asked.

Ellen rolled her eyes, similarly to the way Oakley did. "Hunter, if it was up to me, we would have turned that upstairs office into your bedroom ages ago. You know you're always welcome, and I don't say that lightly. We love having you here."

"Thanks," Hunter said, trying to process the compliment. "I always love being here."

He finished up his waffles and praised Ellen for the meal. "I intend to earn my keep while I'm here. Is there anything I can do for you?"

"You really don't have to do anything. It's just nice to have you here."

He glanced through the large windows behind him to the treehouse. The treehouse at his own home growing up was chopped down before he turned twelve due to disease. "Are the boards still loose up there?" he asked, motioning to the tree.

She nodded. "It's hardly been used, though Oakley will occasionally take a book up there. It just hasn't been a priority."

"I'd be happy to secure the boards," Hunter offered.

"Thanks, Hunter. That'd be wonderful."

Hunter was grateful for some way to help. "It's my pleasure. I'll work on it this afternoon."

Ellen nodded. "Oakley mentioned coming over in time for dinner. I can't wait for the three of y'all to be together, but in the meantime, I suppose two of the Three Musketeers are better than nothing." She smiled, cleaned up the batter, and put the syrups away.

Hunter nodded, holding back a grin. For the purpose of

getting to know Oakley again, he was glad that the third musketeer wasn't here.

HUNTER SWUNG THE HAMMER AND IT COLLIDED WITH THE LAST nail. The final board was secured in the treehouse. The same pictures still graced the wooden walls. The whole space was the size of a small bedroom, big enough for four sleeping bags to comfortably stretch across the floor with a little room for walking. In his mind it had always been bigger—a place where he and Travis would build their fort against the pirates, or aliens, or whatever bad guys they'd been fighting that day. He loved it when Oakley would join them—their plots always became more complicated and interesting. He lost himself in the memories as he gazed out the small window.

Almost as if thinking about her conjured her up, Oakley came out of the back door of the house, and walked toward the treehouse. His heart jumped into his throat. Her fitted green sweater was the perfect color to bring out her eyes, though he could only imagine it at this distance. He hit his head on the rafter above the window.

"Everything okay up there?" Her sing-song voice both thrilled and tormented him.

"All good. Just finishing up a few things," he said, looking around for the next board to secure to draw his attention away from her.

She poked her head through the entrance. "I heard a bang."

He pointed to the offending beam above him. "I hit my head."

Her smile widened. "Hammers are great for hitting things. Heads, not so much, but you're the expert there," she teased.

He smiled at her, trying to suppress the memory that, directly below where they both stood, she'd broken his heart when she'd refused to go to Senior Prom with him. The wound still stung, raw as the weathered treehouse wood in need of an extra coat of stain.

As a senior, he was on top of the world, unaware of the power a sophomore held over him. It never crossed his mind that she would actually reject him. He'd assumed that she would be flattered to be invited to Senior Prom, and that she'd accept, even if she didn't return his feelings. Boy, was he wrong. He blinked, casting the memories aside. "Looks like I'll have to be more careful if I don't want to get hurt again," he replied.

She touched one of the faded pictures. The plastic frame held a picture of the Three Musketeers as teens, smiling on a lazy summer day. Travis had wanted to keep it a 'boy's only' treehouse, but Hunter had been secretly glad when Ellen insisted that Oakley be included. "It's always good to be careful, especially when you're dealing with something so …"

"Close to the heart?" He guessed at her words, wondering if there was ever a chance she'd feel the same way about him as he always had about her.

Her smile faded. "I was gonna say *old*," she said, looking around the room. "So many happy memories in this place." She sighed.

"And a few not so happy memories connected to this place as well," he muttered. Oakley's rejection swam in the foreground of his mind, refusing to be pushed aside. The moment he said it, he wished he could take it back.

She moved closer to him and placed a hand on his arm. "Like your boyish games of scaring me with insects and rodents up here? I don't hold it against you."

"I only scared you with a spider *once*. I learned my lesson after that."

She laughed. "True, true. I'm terrified of them, you know. That was all Travis had to do to keep me away. He'd say there was a spider up here, and I wouldn't come."

"Wasn't I on spider patrol for you?"

"You were, and I probably didn't thank you enough at the time." She breathed in deeply, her fingers brushing along the rough, wooden walls. "They're happy memories. You always made me feel included ..." She paused.

Hunter's heart warmed at her words. At least she'd felt included from him when they were growing up. That was something.

She continued, "Even though I was just the tag along little sister."

He took a step closer to her. She'd already mentioned feeling like a tag along last night, and he hadn't known quite what to say. After all, he couldn't negate how she'd felt in the past, but he could certainly clear the air on how he viewed things. She wasn't the reason Hunter was best friends with Travis, but he'd always enjoyed her company. His eyes locked onto hers, and he braved another step closer, his hand resting next to her own on the rough wall. "Oakley, you were never a tag along." His fingers covered hers, and her eyes widened. "Not to me," he said.

She swallowed. "That's kind of you to say."

"I'm saying it because it's true, not because I'm trying to be nice."

She looked away. "You always were the charmer."

He blinked. She didn't believe him. He needed to say the words. Now was his chance to tell her how he felt about her. "Oakley, I mean it. I—"

She waved away his words, pulling her hand out from under his. "Hunter, the past is in the past. I can remember the happy moments. It's okay that I wasn't really part of your *Secret Boys' Club,* or whatever you called it. In fact, in some ways, it still feels like trespassing when I come up here." She glanced through the small treehouse window then jumped back. "Oh, I forgot. Mom wanted me to let you know that dinner was almost ready. Now that I've stalled, I'm sure it's actually on the table by now." She moved toward the doorway. "Coming?"

Heat ran through him. Her simple touch from before felt like fire on his arm. When he covered her hand with his own, his mouth went dry. He needed a moment to collect himself. "I'll be right there."

DINNER WENT BY IN A BLUR, AND AFTER HUNTER TRIED TO HELP with the dishes. Oakley waved him away trying to reject his offer, but he threw the dish towel over his shoulder and began filling the sink anyway. "It's my turn to do the dishes," he insisted.

Oakley shook her head. "No. You're a guest."

"I may be a guest, but I am also a gentleman. I'm staying

here, and I can help. Technically you're more of a guest than I am, since you have your own place in town."

She laughed then smeared soap bubbles on his cheek. "Fine. You do the dishes. I'll dry."

Ellen smiled. "Just like old times." She put a hand over her heart. "It's been too long since you've been here, Hunter. Quit being a stranger. You need to visit more often."

He glanced to Oakley, wondering how she would feel about that. Her thoughts seemed hidden under the straight face she kept as she dried each dish with interest.

"I'd like that," he said. "I've missed … being here. It's always been like home."

Ellen clapped her hands together. "That's what I like to hear!" She turned to Oakley. "Are you staying for game night tonight?"

Oakley looked at Hunter before answering. "Mom, we don't have to play games tonight. Hunter is here."

"And that's exactly why it's fixin' to be a great game night! He evens out the teams."

Hunter grinned. "As I recall, you always won, especially when we played Rummikub. How you always got the wilds, I'll never know."

"Luck," Oakley said playfully.

"Rematch?" Hunter asked.

"Trav has Rummikub," Oakley said. "You'll have to pick a different game."

They finished cleaning the kitchen, and Hunter chose a new game from the game closet. They gathered back around the kitchen table and set up Ticket to Ride.

"Oakley, are you available this weekend?" Ellen asked, playing her cards and laying her green train route.

Oakley glanced to Hunter, her cheeks reddening as she spoke. "I haven't set anything in stone yet. What's up, Mom?"

"I was just thinking that after another hard week of work on the General Store, it might be nice to get all of the Christmas decorations up."

"*Before* Thanksgiving?"

"Why not? I'm in the holiday mood already. What do you say Hunter, will you help us?"

Hunter smiled, enjoying the fact that he was included in the discussion. "My schedule is open. If it works for Oakley, it works for me."

"Nothing but Christmas movies, games, and music this weekend until all the decorations are up," Ellen said.

"Sounds like a wonderful weekend," Hunter said, especially because it meant spending more time with Oakley.

CHAPTER 7

Oakley's heart leapt out of her chest. There had been times growing up when Travis had been somewhere else, and Hunter had just come over to hang out. When Hunter said her house was like a second home to him, he meant it.

She smiled, trying to act like she was winning with the routes she'd been dealt, instead of thinking about Hunter. She couldn't help herself. He'd been so sweet to her over the last couple of days when he didn't have to be. There was no reason for him to really pay any attention to her. He could just stay at her parents' house and visit with them, and yet he seemed to care if she would be there or not.

"Yeah, it'll be fun," she said, finally agreeing. She smoothed down her hair. Hunter was making his confident face, but he kept shuffling his cards around. She knew his tells and could see he wasn't solid on his strategy. His concentration on the game worked to her advantage; he was completely unaware of the girlish grin giving away how much she looked forward to decorating with him.

The rest of the game was filled with conversation about the specific routes filling with trains and how lucky Oakley always seemed to be on game night.

Oakley suppressed the desire to gloat at the end of the game and stood up. "I'm headed home. Thanks for dinner, Mom. And thanks for the fun game, y'all. I'd better quit while I'm ahead." Okay, maybe she had to gloat just a little.

Hunter laughed. "You beat me *every* time. You always win."

Oakley grinned. "I'm just that good." It was true, she always beat Hunter in board games. His strategies were constantly written on his face. But in matters of the heart, she lost to him. Every time.

Oakley needed a different thought to walk out of the house with. "Mom, you're really serious about the Christmas decorations?"

Her mom nodded. "If we wait until Travis gets home to decorate we won't enjoy it for very long. We might as well start decking the hall."

Oakley understood. "I'll be here Friday after work. See y'all then," she said to the room in general, though she looked directly at Hunter.

"Will you be helping with the General Store this week?" Hunter asked.

"I'm volunteering throughout the week. I'll be there tomorrow around lunch time," she said casually. She wanted to ask Hunter what his exact schedule was, but it was better to be nonchalant and play it safe. She wasn't a lovesick teenager anymore, and she didn't need to act like one.

The drive to her home wasn't far. She rented a tiny house just off of Main Street after she'd graduated from college. Golden Ridge was home, and it was as good a place as any for her to set up her online business. As she walked into her house, her phone buzzed. She looked down at the notification. The text was from an unknown number.

Hi, Annie Oakley. I have a question for you.

She stared at the screen in surprise, as another text popped up.

This is Hunter, by the way.

I know who this is. She set her purse down, wondering what question was urgent enough to text her tonight instead of just asking her tomorrow when she got to the General Store.

You have my number? I had to get yours off of your parents' fridge.

Oakley curled up on her couch, pulling her knees up and resting a pillow on her lap. **I didn't have your number. You're the only one who calls me Annie Oakley. It's not my name, you know.**

Are you sure?

Did you want to see my birth certificate? I have proof.

Lol. We both know you're way too clever with document manipulation.

Oakley laughed. She'd once created a copy of her birth certificate, and put the name "Annie Oakley" on it as a funny April Fool's Joke, and Hunter bought it. She had him convinced for over a year that her actual name was Annie and that she went by her middle name. It had been amusing in a flirtatious, teenage sort of way. **I have amazing Photoshop skills.**

Among your many other talents.

You try to flatter me, but I know your tricks. What do you want? She bit her lip. Seeing him in the treehouse had brought her back to her youth. She was the irritating little sister spying on her brother and his friend, but he talked to her like she belonged there.

A bubble appeared and disappeared as she waited for Hunter to respond. Finally his text popped up. **It's not flattery if it's true.**

Always the charmer.

Except I could never charm you.

Oakley's heart rate sped up. Was he toying with her? Maybe she could detect his level of sincerity if they were face to face, but over a text it was impossible. When she'd let herself be vulnerable with him in the past, she'd only gotten hurt, and a third heartbreak from Hunter without ever dating him would be insanity. It was best to play it safe with her response. **What can I say? My superpower is the ability to resist your charm superpower.**

The entire text was a lie. She couldn't resist it, even if she pretended she could. It was good that he couldn't see her face right now. He'd be able to read her lie, just like she could read his. She flashed back. That was how the last heartbreak happened nine years ago. She had read on Hunter's face that he wasn't being honest with her and it crushed her. Recovering from the look in his Kryptonite eyes had been difficult and, even with all those years of healing, she doubted she'd be able to do it again.

That's a very specific superpower.

I have lots of superpowers. It's just one of many.

So when I said you have many talents it was just truth, not flattery.

Oakley resisted the urge to fall into the moment. **You had a question for me?**

I wanted to make sure that you're really okay if I help with Christmas this weekend.

Why wouldn't I be? She knew exactly why she wouldn't be. But what could she do? It was obvious that her mom wanted to reach back into the past and create a memory. Sure, Travis wasn't there, but her mom wanted to recreate the experience from years ago.

I guess I wouldn't blame you if you didn't want me there.

Oakley hugged the pillow tighter to her chest. They weren't really having this conversation, were they? Over text messages? **My mom wants you there.**

Say the word, and I can make an excuse. I don't want to cause you more pain than I already have.

Oakley's heart beat rapidly. It wasn't putting up the Christmas decorations with him that was the problem, it was what all of those memories did to her. Nothing had been the same since the last time they'd been together in her parents' house putting up the decorations. She blinked. **I'm not going to uninvite you.**

Oaks, I'm sorry. I wish there was a way to fix the past. If I could do it over again, I would.

That was the difference between them. He thought that the past needed fixing, and maybe it did, but not in the way he meant. If she could do it over again, she still would have kissed him. Years of crushing on him would have made that the logical choice for both her head and her heart. She just wished it had ended differently. **We're adults. Please don't make any excuses to my mom. She really wants you there.**

Do you want me there?

She took a calming breath. Of course she wanted him there. And at the same time, she didn't. What a frustratingly impossible question to ask. Finally, she settled on the only safe answer she could give without admitting that she loved him and would always prefer him to be there. **Christmas decorating isn't the same without you.**

It's my amazing wrapping skills, isn't it?

Levity and humor were his way of lightening the mood. She needed to run with that to avoid admitting how much she loved him when she was younger. And how seeing him again showed her how much those feelings hadn't disappeared. **You think using a whole roll of tape is a skill?**

Oh, for sure. Better yet, it's another superpower.

Humility is also one of your superpowers ... oh, wait.

Ha ha.

Oakley loved their banter. She had missed it. An ache settled inside her when she remembered that he'd be leaving as soon as the General Store project was done. She was going to miss him all over again. Her fingers hovered over the digital keyboard, not knowing what to say.

Another text came through from Hunter. **See you tomorrow?**

Oakley wanted to let her heart take the lead, as if it somehow mattered to him that she'd be around tomorrow. She shook her head at the ridiculous thought. He was simply ending the conversation. That was Hunter. The same irresistibly charming Hunter. **I'll be there to help around lunchtime.**

Night, Oaks.

Goodnight, Hunter.

CHAPTER 8

Oakley wanted to throw something, but the couch pillow was just out of her reach. She'd spent the whole day trying to solve her website problem, and hours of troubleshooting on the phone with her developer hadn't solved anything. She hadn't realized until this morning that her site had been down all weekend. The timing was rotten, not just because it affected people's Christmas orders, but because what she really wanted had nothing to do with fixing her website. She wanted to get to the General Store and see how things were coming along, almost convincing herself that Hunter's presence had nothing to do with it.

Oakley rubbed her neck, listening to instructions over the phone, and trying to implement the changes. Nothing was working. Her eyes glared at the laptop screen that seemed to brighten as the sunlight dimmed. The developer's technician had taken over, assuring her he'd spend the rest of the night trying to get everything working. She thanked him and hung up, wishing she had the whole day to do over again.

She took out a medium saucepan to boil water. She pulled out the noodles when her doorbell rang.

She opened the door, and her heart dropped to her toes. "Hunter? What are you doing here?"

His brow scrunched together. "Sorry, I didn't mean to interrupt your evening—"

"You're not interrupting. I was just making some dinner. Did you want to come in for a few minutes?"

He nodded and followed her inside.

She headed to the kitchen, resisting the urge to straighten the pillow she wanted to throw earlier on her way to check the boiling water.

Hunter studied her house, and she wished she could actually read his mind. His opinion had always mattered to her. He met her gaze and smiled.

She poured the noodles into the water, shoving them beneath the bubbles with a spoon. "How did work go on the General Store today?"

Hunter pulled at the sleeve of his jacket and winced. "It went well. There were a lot of people helping today, so the work went quickly. At the rate we're going, we'll be out of wood again by the end of the week."

"That's great!" Oakley said excitedly. "I'll have to coordinate with John on what he needs more of. They decided that too many supplies at a time is difficult to manage."

Hunter agreed. "There isn't room to store much more than what we have right now. We're already using all of the available space we can get on Main Street. Any more supplies would just overwhelm the area." He pulled a white envelope out from his inside coat pocket. "John had some paperwork for you but he had to leave early today. Since you said you'd be coming at lunch, I told him I'd give them to you."

"Thank you." Her fingers brushed his as she took the envelope, and her skin felt like fire where they had touched.

He turned to go, then looked over his shoulder at her with pain in his eyes. "It wasn't because of me that you didn't come today, right?"

She shook her head, stirring the noodles again. Was that what was bothering Hunter? "It wasn't because of you. Turns out my site was down all weekend. I got stuck trying to fix a few things online for my business. It was just a messy day." She pointed to her laptop and the papers strewn all around it.

"What projects are you currently designing?" Hunter asked, leaning over to look at the scattered papers.

"I have a few custom orders for Christmas due by the end of the week. Mostly presents—ornaments, coffee mugs, a journal, and a few throw pillows. There's also a company that wants a hand-lettered logo, so I'm still working on that."

He studied one of her mock-ups—a simple drawing of a snow-covered landscape. The words above it read, *"I'm Dreaming of a White Christmas."*

Hunter took one of the papers and held it up. "This is very good."

Oakley could feel her cheeks heating at his praise. "Thanks, I have fun with it." She moved to clear the papers, but he took the stack before she could, looking through several other designs.

"You were always such a great artist," Hunter continued. "You're very talented."

She lifted a half-shoulder. She couldn't disagree with him when his eyes were sincere. She swallowed and took in a shallow breath. "Would you like to stay for dinner?"

His eyes widened. "I didn't come over expecting you to feed me," he said, backing up.

She shrugged. "It's nothing fancy, just spaghetti and meatballs, but you're welcome to stay."

"Thanks," he said, his blue Kryptonite eyes working their magic. He pulled off his jacket, laid it over a chair, and pushed up his flannel sleeves. "I'm a bit of a mess."

"You can use the sink, free of charge," she said, pointing to the kitchen sink.

"Such hospitality."

She smirked. "I try." She pulled a salad from the fridge, dished up the spaghetti and toasted a few pieces of garlic bread. They sat down at the kitchen table. It was the first time Oakley could remember feeling nervous and tongue-tied at her own table, in her own house. It was Hunter's eyes. He'd always had that effect on her, even when she suppressed it. She constantly had a tingle of anticipation in her stomach around him.

"I missed you today," he admitted.

She laughed. "I already invited you to stay for dinner. Charmer."

He shook his head. "Charmer? You're still using that nickname? I have other ones, you know."

"I know. Hunny Bun was always a great one." She smiled wide, remembering the first time she'd heard the nickname.

Hunter rolled his eyes. "*That's* the one you choose? You could always go back to Arrow."

She remembered the time when she, Hunter, and Travis had

set up targets in the backyard and shot at them with their bow and arrows. One time they went out shooting, and both she and Travis took their guns, but Hunter had brought his bow and arrows. He was Arrow for a long time after that. "Yeah, that was a fun one. Or there's always *Hunny* or *Hun*." She laughed at the nickname she knew he didn't like.

He made a face. "I think I prefer charmer over Hunny or Hun, even though it doesn't describe me."

"Seriously? You were always the guy everyone wanted to go on a date with. You were always saying the right things, and being sweet and—charming."

"I think you have me confused with someone else," he said, taking a small bite.

"Are you fishing for compliments? All the girls fawned over you in high school," she said, teasing him. All of them, including her.

Hunter twisted the spaghetti tightly around his fork, swirling in a slow, deliberate pattern. He looked at her, his eyes searching hers. "Not all of the girls," he said finally, then shoved the bite into his mouth.

Oakley laughed. "Not *all* of the girls? You're back in town for less than two weeks, and already there's been a buzz about you everywhere I go. Everyone talks about you and notices you."

Hunter blinked. "They do?"

Oakley rolled her eyes. "Of course they do. I'm sure they're all wondering if you're really as on the market as you seem. Like I said, *all* the girls."

Hunter chuckled. "No. Not all. I've been turned down, so it's definitely not all."

"Please. I don't believe you. Who turned you down?"

Hunter broke the garlic bread in half. "You turned me down," he said quietly.

Oakley's fork stilled an inch from her mouth. "I hardly count," she whispered back.

His eyes snapped to hers. "Why is that? Because I'm more like a brother to you?"

"It's not that," she confessed.

"It's not?"

She shook her head, wishing he could understand without her having to explain that she'd loved him too much to let her heart get its hopes up. He hadn't actually *wanted* to take her to Senior Prom, he'd only needed someone to go with because his options with senior girls were non-existent. It was not the way she wanted to create that memory. She took a deep breath, wondering just how much to tell him. She put a hand on his arm, squeezing it gently, trying to convey some of that feeling. It was confession time.

He winced and pulled his arm away. His features were pulled tight.

"What's wrong? Are you hurt?"

He shook his head. "It's just a scratch."

"It's more than a scratch with that reaction." She grabbed for his hand. "Let me see it."

Lines formed on his forehead. "No, no, don't. It'll be fine. It's just a little scratch," he said.

"A shirt is not a Band-Aid, Hunter. Let me see."

He looked the other way but finally extended his arm toward her.

Oakley carefully pulled back the flannel shirt.

Hunter cringed and made a fist. "Really, I think you should leave it."

"I'm trying to be gentle." Oakley moved slower. Dirt and dust mingled in the dried blood on his arm. Oakley clenched her jaw, determined to be brave for both of them. "Hunter, this is really nasty. Have you looked at this?"

Hunter had his face angled away from the arm she held. "I'm trying not to," he said between labored breaths.

She added pressure to the very outside edges of the wound. "It hurts here?" she confirmed, not quite able to tell how long the actual cut was with all the dried blood surrounding it.

Hunter kept his face completely turned from both Oakley and his arm. "A little."

"And the blood?" she asked.

"Bothers me worse than the pain," he said through gritted teeth.

"It looks pretty bad. Like borderline stitches bad," she said.

He shook his head. "No. I'm not going to the hospital."

"I've got a first-aid kit in the closet. Let me see what I can do," she said, leaving him at the table while she grabbed clean towels, a bowl of water, and the first-aid kit. She remembered a time when Travis had cut his knee badly. Hunter couldn't handle the blood then either.

Hunter still had his eyes closed when she returned to the table. He looked green. She moved the food away, clearing a place for his arm to rest comfortably. She put her hand in his, loosening the fist he held tightly. She could work one-handed for a little bit.

Oakley used the cloth to clean his skin, starting at the

fringes of dried blood. All of his muscles were tense. "Are you doing okay?"

"You probably think I'm such a baby. I'm a grown man who still can't stand the sight of blood." He recoiled when she moved closer to the center of the cut.

"I've never thought that you were a baby about anything."

He faced her, keeping his gaze level with the top of her head, not looking down at his arm. "Thanks for saying that, even if it's not true."

"I still can't handle spiders," she said, hoping to keep him distracted with something else while she cleaned his blood-stained arm. She worked quickly, but carefully. "You never made fun of me for that, even though Travis tormented me with them. You got rid of them from my bedroom more than once," she recalled. "Did I ever thank you for that?"

Hunter grimaced. "How did you know I got rid of them?"

"I was playing in my closet once when Travis brought in a glass jar with a couple of spiders in it. I heard y'all talking about it. You tried to talk him out of it, but Travis left the jar in my room."

"I remember that, but I don't remember you were in the room," he acknowledged.

"I was playing with my dolls and it was 'night-time' for them so the lights were off in the closet, but I still had enough light from the bedroom windows. Then y'all went out to play or something, and a few minutes later, I heard footsteps back up the stairs. I stayed where I was, wondering if y'all were bringing another jar to add to the first, when Travis called up to you from downstairs. You said you were coming, and then you grabbed the jar. From my window, I watched you dump the spiders outside and hide the jar from Travis."

Hunter shrugged. "I felt bad for you about the spiders. I may have been your brother's best friend, but that didn't mean I always agreed with his practical jokes."

"And I loved you for it," she blurted. The words came out without effort. Her gaze locked on his and her eyes widened. Had she just said that aloud?

His eyes held hers, seeming to ask a question though he didn't verbalize it.

She stuttered, barely able to draw in a breath. She tried to laugh the moment off, but it felt forced. "Uh, so, your arm is looking better. The blood is almost cleaned off." She returned her focus to his arm pretending to study the dirt.

"Travis never knew that I can't handle blood," Hunter said.

"I never said a word about it," Oakley replied. She kept her head bent as she applied some ointment to the cut. She needed to stay focused on her task otherwise she might say something highly embarrassing again. "It doesn't look deep enough to need stitches, but you've given yourself a couple splinters. Let me see if I can dig them out."

"I'm not going to the hospital, so you're gonna get them out," he said firmly.

She narrowed her eyes. "Mr. Paxton, you'll do whatever you need to do to get over this injury. If that means the hospital, then you'll be going to the hospital. Don't worry though, I'm pretty sure I can save your arm."

Hunter chuckled. "That's a relief."

"Try relaxing a little."

Hunter's grip on her hand loosened. "I'm trying to relax," he said through his still gritted teeth. "You're gonna have to keep talking. I need something to focus on."

"Okay, well, what did you want to talk about?" she asked, not wanting to pick the topic again and possibly admitting something else she adored about him. She cleaned out three more splinters.

"Tell me about the Christmas designs you've been working on," he said, his gaze focused on the papers at the other end of the table.

"You saw the 'White Christmas' one I finished. I have lots of other ideas. I started working on a few, but they're not finished yet. I want to do something with love and Christmas, but nothing has clicked, and now my website isn't working …" She let the sentence fade as she leaned over his arm, focusing on pulling the last of the splinters out.

He winced. "What exactly happened with your site?"

She went through all the boring details of her website mess, hoping the monotony of her technical jargon would focus his mind elsewhere, as she cleaned and bandaged his arm. She took the bandage wrappers off the table and crinkled them into a tiny ball. She threw it away, not bothering to finish the saga of her website disaster. "Good as new," she declared.

Hunter stood, trying to help Oakley put away the first-aid kit, but she waved him away from it, knowing how much medical supplies bothered him. "I've got this," she said.

"You don't think I'll need stitches?" he asked, his brows drawn together.

She shook her head. "The cut wasn't too deep. It will heal."

"Not without a kiss," he said.

She stared at him, not sure what to say. She'd been down that road before, and it only led to heartache.

He must have realized how his words sounded to her, because understanding dawned on his face. He held up his arm. "I meant, you didn't kiss it better. Isn't that what you used to do?"

"Yeah, I used to do that when I was helping toddlers or babysitting." She rolled her eyes and blew him a kiss. "Better?"

He pretended to catch the kiss and put his hand over his arm. "Much better. Now it might actually heal."

She shook her head. "You think that kissing solves all problems."

He raised one shoulder in a half shrug. "It's a pretty serious injury. If I died from it, I bet you'd wish that you'd spared a kiss for it."

"I blew you a kiss," she countered. This exchange was getting more dangerous by the second. "On second thought, perhaps you should go straight to the hospital," she said straight-faced.

The color drained from him face. "You *do* think I need stitches, don't you?"

She smirked. "No, I think you need to get your head examined."

"It's functioning well enough." He carried the dinner dishes to the sink.

"If you say so," she said in a sing-song voice, loving the banter between them.

"I can prove it to you," he said.

Oakley looked up at him. What was he going to prove? She'd gotten lost in their conversation, taking a mental detour down memory lane. She wandered through times growing up when he would verbally spar with her. “Prove what?” she finally said.

“That my head is fine,” he said. "Pull up your laptop for me.”

“Why?”

“I’m fixin’ to prove to you that my head doesn’t need to be examined.”

She tilted her head at him, but she handed him the laptop after she logged in.

“Will you get into your site for me?” he asked.

“It’s down right now.”

“I meant will you log me into the back-end of it?”

She quickly pulled up the page that she’d been working on with the technician. “There’s a lot of problems with it. The tech couldn’t figure it out.”

He smiled. “That’s probably because your tech doesn’t really know what’s wrong. Give me fifteen minutes to look around and see what I can find.”

“Okay.” Oakley agreed. She washed the dishes and wiped down the table. Hunter was facing her, but his focus was only on the laptop. She forced herself to pay attention to her own tasks, since she found herself watching him more and more often. She finished wiping off the counter, and then sat down next to him. “What have you found?”

“Your site is completely unprotected and is open to several hacks and viruses,” he answered, his fingers flying across the keyboard, his eyes never leaving the screen.

Oakley watched Hunter work his magic with each keystroke. He went from one screen to the next, writing code, and enabling lots of things that Oakley didn’t really understand.

She sat motionless as his fingers typed feverishly. It was hypnotizing.

He hit a few more keystrokes, ending with a flourish. "With any luck, that should fix your problem."

"No way. Really?" She couldn't keep the giddiness out of her voice.

"Try it and see," he said, angling the laptop toward her.

She leaned closer to him and typed her web address into a fresh browser. "It's working. It's working!" She wanted to jump up and down.

"See if you can order something," he suggested.

She scrolled through her product pages. No 404 errors. It was a miracle. She clicked on the cart, loaded up one of her Christmas tote bags, and filled out all the information needed to place an order. No errors. No missing pages or broken links. She canceled the order on the confirm order page. The entire process that had been broken all day was now working. She breathed out a sigh of relief.

"You saved me." Oakley wrapped her arms around Hunter's neck and gave him a huge hug.

He cringed. "Anytime."

She realized too late that she had added pressure on his freshly bandaged arm. "I'm so sorry. I didn't mean to hurt it more."

"You just really want to send me to the hospital today, don't you?" Hunter joked.

"Of course not." In a show of goodwill, she took his arm in her hands again, moving it gently to her lips and brushed a light kiss on the top of his bandage. She could feel the strength of his muscles as he stood still under her touch. "There. All better. No hospital needed."

He tilted his head. "Thanks," he said, his voice raspy.

"Thank you … for fixing my website." She cleared her throat. "I think it would have taken me over a week to do what you did in less than thirty minutes."

"It helps that I enjoy this sort of thing. Being on the managerial side of coding is different than getting into a problem and fixing it like this," he said. He glanced around the room, then stood. "I should probably get going. I don't want your mom wondering where I am."

She almost laughed at the idea, but he wasn't wrong. "Thanks for coming by, and delivering the paperwork for the General Store. And thanks again for helping me with my website."

"And thank you for dinner and saving me a trip to the hospital."

She walked him to the door, wanting him to stay, craving more time with him, but all she could say was, "So I guess I'll see you later."

"I hope so. Will you be around the General Store this week?"

She nodded. She wanted to be around Hunter more than she'd like to admit. "Because of the site issues, I'm behind on work already, and it's only Monday. But I will be there when I can."

"If nothing else we have Christmas decorating this weekend."

She definitely wanted to see him before the Christmas decorating. "It's a weekend full of fun."

"It has always been one of my favorite times at your house."

"It won't be the same without Trav," she said, sure that he was missing his best friend.

"It will still be fun," he said, his lips curving upwards.

She nodded. "Good night, Hunter."

His gaze dropped to her lips for a fraction of a second before returning to her eyes. "Good night, Oakley."

CHAPTER 9

HUNTER - CHRISTMAS SEASON NINE YEARS AGO

Hunter let himself in through the front door of the Larsen home. Winter break of his final year in college hadn't come soon enough. The smell of sugar cookies hit him as soon as he stepped into the entryway of the house that had been a second home to him growing up.

He put four presents by the tree, making sure to hide the small velvet bag beneath the other presents.

Oakley poked her head around the corner, her eyes widening. "Hunter? You're here!"

"Merry Christmas, Annie Oakley," he called.

She ran to him, giving him a big bear hug. He held her tight, enjoying the feel of her in his arms, even if the moment was brief. He caught the scent of her hair, carrying the smell of cinnamon and sugar from the kitchen.

"It's so good to see you. I didn't expect you today," she said, finally releasing him from their embrace. "Trav mentioned you might not be coming until Christmas Eve."

"I wasn't sure of my plans," he replied. "My brothers and sisters all made it into town this year too."

"Well it's a huge surprise. I hate that we have to share you with your actual family, but I'm glad they came into town too." She smiled, a blush forming on her cheeks. She dusted her hands on her apron. "Sorry. I'm a bit of a floury mess," she apologized, smoothing her fingers down her Mrs. Claus apron.

"You're never a mess," he said, smiling at a smudge of flour on her cheek. He instinctively brushed it away with his thumb. Sparks flew through him, and he cleared his throat. "Is it sugar cookie delivery day?"

She nodded, then nudged his shoulder. "Your timing is amazing as always. Always showing up at the right time."

"I planned it that way." He laughed, following her into the kitchen. Every surface was covered with flour and dough. Some pans held baked cookies, while others were full of raw dough waiting for their turn in the oven. "Looks like you're having a party in here."

She laughed. "We were. Trav drove my friends Jill and Michelle back to their houses to pick up some of their favorite cookie cutters."

"And they left you here by yourself?"

Oakley shrugged. "I don't mind," Oakley leaned closer to him. "Besides, I think Trav is crushing on Jill. I didn't want to interrupt."

Hunter couldn't believe his good luck. He'd wanted to talk to Oakley while her brother wasn't around. There was so much he wanted to tell her. This Christmas he was going to be brave. He was finally going to tell her how he felt about her and let the chips fall where they may. He swallowed. "You didn't bring a boyfriend home for Christmas, did you?"

Oakley scoffed. "Yeah, no. I don't have time for that. School is keeping me busy enough."

"I thought dating was an important part of college."

She leaned against the counter, looking at him like she was trying to figure him out. "And you're the expert? Last I heard you weren't dating anyone."

"Well, that's because—"

"Are you here to help or to talk?" she interrupted, a playful gleam in her eye.

"Um, both?"

"Good, because I could use some help." She gave him a star and a candy cane cutter. "Push them close together. You don't get to eat the cookie dough in between."

He left a wide space and pushed them both into the dough. "Like this?" he asked, pulling the large piece of dough in between the cutters, and popping it into his mouth.

She shoved his arm playfully. "You don't follow rules very well," she said.

"I keep all the rules," Hunter countered. "It's a tradition. You create the cookie dough rules every year, and every year, I have to eat some before we start."

She smeared flour on his face. "If you want to eat dough, steal it from the mixing bowl, not when it's already rolled out."

"There's a rule I can live with," he teased, reaching around her and grabbing more rolled out dough from the table. He popped the piece into his mouth before she could stop him.

"Quit it! That's not fair," she said, her eyes dancing. She tried hard to hide her smile, but Hunter could see it.

"Open your mouth," he said.

"Why?" Oakley asked.

Hunter promptly popped a small cookie dough ball into her mouth. "There. Now you're not following the rules either."

"That's not how it works!" she cried, laughter bubbling through. "You're bending the rules."

He grinned. "Okay, I'll keep all the rules from now on," he said, placing the cookie cutters closer together. "See?"

She came over to inspect his work. "I'm not giving you a medal for following instructions, but good job. That's better."

"Better? It's perfect."

She smiled. "You're so helpful."

"Admit it, it's perfect."

She rolled her eyes. "Fine, you're perfect."

He stilled, his eyes searching hers. "*I'm* perfect?"

Heat flooded into her cheeks and she looked flustered. "I mean, your cookie cutting is perfect." She slid a metal spatula under the cut dough and placed the shapes on a cookie sheet. She averted her gaze eyes from him and instead glanced at the ceiling.

He followed her gaze. "Mistletoe? In the kitchen? Are you expecting someone?" He wiggled his eyebrows up and down, hoping she really wasn't expecting someone else.

The heat from her cheeks ran to her neck and her ears. She cleared her throat. "No. You know how Mom and Dad like to kiss in the kitchen? Trav and I thought it would be funny, so we moved it from the front hallway."

He pulled her closer to him, so they were directly below the berried plant. "I just gave my word to follow all of the

Christmas rules," he said, looking up at the mistletoe and then back into her eyes.

"*Now* you're gonna start following the rules?"

His heart stuttered, and he didn't want to let the moment pass. "It's bad luck to not kiss under the mistletoe." His gaze never left hers, searching for an indication that his feelings were reciprocated. He saw a spark in her eyes. Something was there. Could it be that she wanted to kiss him too? He didn't let himself hope for that, but she didn't pull away. That had to be a good sign, right? He had never been so unsure of anything as he was when he was around Oakley. She didn't know how she affected him, but this year it was time to tell her.

She stood on her tiptoes and gave him a peck on the cheek. "There."

Fire spread through him from where the heat from her lips lingered on his cheek. He pulled her close, his hands cradling the sides of her face. He lowered his lips to hers, not caring that she tried to pass up the opportunity with only a kiss on the cheek, and their lips connected. The kiss was sweet—an explorative dance. He let his hand move to stroke her red hair. The feel of her in his arms was his Christmas wish. His heart pounded in time to hers, speeding up like they were each running a race. Somewhere in the moment, she wrapped her hands around his neck, her fingers running through his hair.

Hunter pulled back. "I've wanted to do that for a long time," he whispered.

Her eyes widened. "You have?"

He nodded, finishing off the moment with another kiss. He held her closer, and she didn't pull away.

The oven timer went off, and they broke the kiss. Her breathing was heavy, matching his. She blinked at him, her lashes fluttering. Her mouth half-open like she wanted to say something, but she didn't.

"The timer," he said, moving toward the oven to turn off the sound.

"Right." She grabbed the holiday pot holders from the counter, pulled out two trays of cookies, and set them on top of the trivets to cool. She slid two more trays into the oven, then spun in the kitchen toward Hunter, a small smile on her kissable lips. "So … that just happened."

He gave her a half smile. "If you keep standing under the mistletoe, I'm gonna have to keep following the rules."

She swallowed. "We wouldn't want that. Would we?"

"Wouldn't we?" he asked as he pulled her close, wrapping her in a hug. Her breathing was still erratic, like his own. He needed to tell her how he felt—how he had always felt. The heart necklace he got her for Christmas was wrapped simply in the velvet drawstring bag under the tree. He hadn't been able to find the words to write a proper Christmas card, so he used a small note card from the jewelry store to jot down a few lines. Now would be just as good as Christmas morning to give it to her—probably better. He caught hold of one of her hands, entwining it with his own. He brought it up to his lips and kissed the back of her hand. "I have something—" His thoughts were interrupted as the front door opened and the chatter of Travis and Oakley's friends filled the space.

Oakley jumped back from where she'd been enfolded in Hunter's arms, immediately pulling out the next ball of dough to roll out. Their eyes met after he resumed his position cutting out candy canes and stars.

"Talk later?" he whispered.

She smiled at him, nodding.

"We've got the Santa hat and snowman cookie cutters," Michelle announced.

Travis had his arm around Jill as they entered the kitchen. "We're ready to make these cookies." Travis stopped short. "Oakley, you still have way too much dough left in the bowl. It's a good thing we're back, or this would never get done."

"I couldn't roll it all out and let the dough get dry while you were gone," Oakley said, her cheeks reddening.

Travis spotted Hunter. "No wonder you didn't get anything done. Hunter was here helping." He shook his head, laughing as they gave each other a back-slapping hug. "How are you doing, man?"

Hunter nodded. "Good. Really good." His eyes avoided Travis's when he thought about how much he enjoyed kissing Oakley. And if Travis was gonna get mad about it, it was a risk he was willing to take. What he felt for Oakley would trump their friendship if it had to. He hoped it wouldn't have to come to that. "How are you doing?"

"Can't complain," Travis said. "You remember Jill?"

Hunter nodded, saying hi to both Jill and Michelle.

The kitchen bustled with noise while the group kept cutting out cookies. Each time Hunter looked up and made eye contact with Oakley, he smiled. She blushed and smiled back.

"Travis, did you and Jill want to cut shapes out of this dough?" Oakley pointed to where she'd finished rolling out a large ball of dough on the opposite side of the island from Hunter.

"Thanks, Oakley. Where will you work?" he asked.

She looked toward the table where cooling racks held more and more cookies. Michelle was frosting some of the cooled cookies. "I'll roll out another batch where Hunter is when he finishes with his dough."

Hunter glanced at Travis and said, "It would go faster if you help me, Oakley. I'm trying to follow the rules and not leave any extra dough between the shapes."

Oakley seemed to ponder for a moment, then said, "Sure, I suppose I could help you."

Travis laughed. "You follow the rules, Hunter? That's funny."

"Hey now," Hunter said. "I'm learning." He looked at Oakley and they shared the private joke. He handed her the star cookie cutter and they worked together. He bumped his arm against hers.

"You're gonna make me mess up," Oakley whispered, laughing.

He guided her hand to the center of the sheet. "I think you should put a star right in the middle."

"Just because these cookies are little doesn't mean it will all work out if I just throw one in the middle."

Jill and Travis filled a cookie sheet with large Christmas trees and snowmen. As Jill headed to put the tray in the oven, Jill looked up and pointed. "Look, Trav ... *mistletoe*." Her voice was flirtatious.

Travis gave her a smile, taking the tray from her hand before he kissed her. "That's good mistletoe," he advertised. "You should try it out, Hunter."

Hunter looked up at Oakley, studying her wide eyes. No way would she be comfortable kissing him in front of her brother, and he definitely didn't want things to get awkward. "No thanks, I'm good." He went back to cutting out the cookies.

Travis slapped him on the back. "What? Hunter never turns down a mistletoe opportunity," Travis said to Jill.

A question pulled on Oakley's face, but she said nothing.

"Really, it's okay," Hunter said, silently willing Trav to drop it.

Travis shook his head. "Michelle, will you come and kiss Hunter, please?"

Michelle nodded, standing up from where she'd sat at the table. "I'll always give Hunter a mistletoe kiss," she said.

Travis laughed and turned to Jill again. "Hunter is the mistletoe *king*. He never lets an opportunity pass. How many did you get up to that one year? Eleven?"

Hunter's jaw tightened. In high school he'd dated a lot of girls, and so he had kissed a lot of girls. But none of them were Oakley. "I don't remember."

Travis laughed hard. "Always hard to keep track with him." Travis snapped his finger. "No, I remember now. It was twelve! One kiss for each of the Twelve Days of Christmas."

Michelle stood next to Hunter, batting her lashes.

"Sorry, Michelle, but I'm not in the mood," Hunter said, annoyed.

"How many mistletoe kisses have you had this year?" Travis probed.

Hunter wanted to punch Travis, but he ignored him instead. It had been a long time since he kissed anyone, though he'd gone on a few dates here and there this semester of college. He couldn't admit to Travis that he already shared two mistletoe kisses, especially since they were both with his sister.

Michelle shrugged, putting a hand on Hunter's arm. "Well if you change your mind later, let me know," she said with a wink, and went back to frosting the cookies.

Hunter glanced at Oakley, her face full of doubt. He tried to catch her gaze, but she kept her eyes fixed on the star she was cutting out. All he needed was five minutes alone with her to talk and explain things.

Jill ate a cookie and giggled as she sat next to Travis. "Oakley, you're much too quiet over there. You were telling us great stories before. Have you ever had a good mistletoe kiss?"

Hunter held his breath. This would be the moment of truth, and if Travis gave him a black eye for kissing his sister, well, it was okay with him. It had been worth it.

Oakley's laugh sounded strangled. She looked directly at Jill, her eyes never straying to Hunter's, though he could feel that she watched him from the corner of her eyes. "A good one? No. Never. As y'all are well aware, mistletoe kisses don't mean anything anyway."

She flicked her gaze from Jill to Hunter. The full weight of her words sank into him. He wanted to explain, and opened his mouth to say something, but she continued, "It's just a silly tradition someone made up so that kissing became a *rule* to be kept. Nothing more."

Her choice of words felt like a slap in the face, but hurt even more. *A rule*. That was directed at him. He winced. His fingers brushed against hers, and she immediately drew her hand back from his, like she'd been burned.

Michelle held up two plates. "We should start delivering. We already have several plates ready."

Travis jumped up. "I'll take the first shift."

Jill stood. "I'll go too. I'll make sure he doesn't eat all of the cookies on the way."

Michelle looked at the cookies still needing to be frosted. "I'll stay," she said.

"Me too," Hunter said, trying to catch Oakley's eye.

"Actually, why don't all y'all go?" Oakley said.

Travis looked at his sister, concern on his face. "Oakley, you don't have to stay. You love delivering."

Oakley waved her hand in the air, dismissing Travis's thought. "I also love having a clean kitchen, and right now this kitchen is suffering from a few too many cooks. I'll take my turn delivering later. Besides, I bet I can get most everything cleaned up while y'all're gone. Now that all of the cookies are cut and on trays, it will go pretty fast."

Travis nodded. "Are you sure?"

Oakley smiled widely. "Absolutely. Take all of the plates that are ready, and I'll have more once you're back."

Hunter watched Oakley carefully. She flashed her brother the kind of smile that she used to cover up pain and hurt. He had to talk to her.

Travis took a plate in each hand, and both Jill and Michelle followed.

"I'll stay and help clean up," Hunter said, as the rest of them moved toward the front door.

"No, I'm really good. I'll be faster if I'm by myself." Oakley's voice was firm.

"Come on, Hunter. You're no help in the kitchen," Travis

called. Both Jill and Michelle laughed. Their merriment sounded like tinsel, grating against his nerves. It was nothing like Oakley's rich laugh.

He looked to Oakley once more, who was watching the cookies bake through the oven door. "I'm coming," he called to the group by the door. "Just getting some cookies."

He picked up two plates from the table, then stopped next to Oakley. "We need to talk. I—"

Oakley's face was glassy. "Talk about what?"

"You know," he said, lowering his voice. "About our kiss."

She tilted her head, her bright green eyes clouded behind a mask of something. "You mean about our obligation to tradition? I already gave you my feedback on it. We followed the rule, and I'm sure we'll continue to follow the rules."

"It was an obligation?" he asked, stunned.

"Like you said, it's bad luck if we don't follow it."

"But I thought—"

"You thought wrong," she said. "Take the mistletoe away and none of it would have happened." She gestured between the two of them.

Hunter's heart was breaking. "So you don't feel anything for me?"

She straightened, her eyes blazing with fire. "Do you usually ask that question after a mistletoe kiss?"

"No, but I—"

"Then now isn't the time to start."

"Oakley—"

Michelle's high-pitched voice came through the house. "Hunter, Travis says to hurry."

"I'm just about ready," he called.

Michelle stopped when she came into the kitchen. "Wow, Hunter. Posing under the mistletoe? I knew you really wanted a kiss." She moved forward, planting her lips on his before he could do anything about it. She took the plates from him. "C'mon, we've gotta go."

Hunter followed Michelle out of the kitchen, feeling like an idiot. "Tell Trav I'll be out in a minute. I forgot something."

Michelle nodded. "Hurry."

Hunter grabbed the velvet bag from underneath the tree. He needed to make things right with Oakley before he gave it to her. He looked for a quick place to hide it. It couldn't stay under the tree, but he didn't want to take it with him right now either. The large music box on the mantle was the perfect size. He opened it up, hoping it hadn't been wound recently. When it began playing, he quickly put the velvet bag inside and shut the lid, removing the key before he could think the better of it.

"Hunter, what are you still doing here?" Oakley scolded, coming through the far entrance of the family room.

He moved his arm behind his back as casually as he could, hiding the key in his hand. "I'm … just … admiring the tree," he lied.

"They're waiting for you," she said sharply.

"But I want to stay with you."

She shook her head. "Please go." She turned swiftly and walked back into the kitchen.

He couldn't unlock the box and remove it now, it would make too much noise. She asked him to go. And she didn't feel the same about him. He glanced down at the ornate key in his hand. He couldn't risk the music box being opened. He swallowed, his heart breaking. He headed out of the front door and pocketed the key. Nothing about this evening had gone as planned. And the kiss that had completely electrified his nerves was nothing more than an obligation to the woman he loved. He forced a smile as he met the group outside. No one would guess that this was the worst moment of his life.

CHAPTER 10

On Friday night, Hunter brought down the last box of Christmas decor from the attic with Andy. It had been a long day of working on the General Store, but he'd spent the entire time anticipating putting up decorations with Oakley. It was getting late and she still hadn't shown up.

"Thanks for your help," Andy said, as Hunter stacked the last box in the front room. "It means a lot."

"We've only brought down the decorations. The fun is just getting started," Hunter said, hoping Oakley would join them soon.

"Still, I appreciate it. This usually takes me a lot longer by myself, and Ellen still insists on decorating each room to the nines. Last year she added even more decorations."

"I like how every room is decorated for Christmas," Hunter said.

Andy shook his head. "You don't have to agree with it, you know. I personally think it's too much."

"Where is Ellen?" Hunter asked.

Ellen appeared from the kitchen. "I'm right here, and I can hear every word you're saying about my decorations." She grinned at Andy.

Andy shrugged. "You know it's excessive, right?"

"If I agree with you, will you let me keep all of it?"

Andy smiled at his wife. "Of course, I just want to hear you say it."

Ellen laughed, then kissed her husband. "It's excessive, but it's Christmas. It only comes once a year, so we can make it a special celebration. Besides with Hunter here, we've got more help than we've had in years."

Andy slapped him on the back. "That's true. He's made this job much easier. Ellen, I've got a few things I need to check on. I'll be back in a little bit."

Ellen opened up the top box. "Thanks, dear."

"How can I help?" Hunter asked as he stood next to the pile of boxes.

Ellen looked around the room. "Oakley should be here in a few minutes. How about the two of you set up the Christmas decorations here in the front room and I'll start with the dining room."

Oakley came through the front door, dressed in a silvery white sweater. Her auburn hair was swept up in a loose ponytail, curls framing the sides of her face. "You started decorating without me?"

"Just barely. You and Hunter work on the front room. I've got the dining room," Ellen repeated the instructions.

Oakley nodded. Christmas music played through the ceiling speakers, and Oakley turned up the volume. "Last year's record was just an hour for this room. Want to try and beat it?"

Hunter nodded, and Oakley handed him the box with the stockings and the fireplace garlands. "Stocking duty?"

Oakley nodded. "You're so good at hanging all of them," she said.

He rolled his eyes. "I know enough about this house and its decorations to do more."

"Oh, you're not getting out of actual work," she said.

He took out the handmade stockings from the box, and began hanging them on the mantle. Each of them had a name stitched into the top and were decorated in that individual's favorite things. Andy's featured a horse with a Santa hat on it, and Ellen's had a pie in front of a Christmas tree. They were the easiest ones to place. Travis was next; his had a snowman with sports balls surrounding it. He pulled out Oakley's, a winter scene, and hung it next to Travis's. With the stockings hung, he affixed the garland and plugged in the attached strings of lights.

He stepped back to admire his work. "I'm all done."

Oakley looked up from where she sat on the floor, lining up the ornaments. She always had a system for decorating the tree, lining up the matching ornaments together, so that the tree would be balanced. She stood and walked closer to him to survey the mantle.

"You're definitely not done," she said, heading toward the box that he'd taken the garland out of.

"What are you talking about? It's perfect."

She reached into the box and pulled out a grocery bag. She opened the sack, retrieving one more stocking. "You forgot one."

She handed him the reindeer stocking with an emerald embroidered 'Hunter' along the top. He was almost surprised they still had his stocking. "You're sure?" He still wasn't certain that she was really okay with him staying for Christmas. Nine years ago he'd left early, making all kinds of excuses for not coming over for any of the Christmas Eve or Christmas Day festivities.

"Put it up. It belongs up there," she answered.

He didn't want to bring up the past, not if she was willing to forget it. The raw heartbreak her rejection had caused him seemed fresh again. He took the stocking from her, wanting to put it back in the box, and leave some of the painful memories packed away. What was he really trying to accomplish by being here with Oakley?

She must have sensed his hesitation, because she added, "Really, Hunter. It's fine. Besides you helped me with my computer issues, so it's the least I can do."

He raised an eyebrow. "If you're sure."

She took the stocking from him, hanging it next to her own. "There. Now come help me with the tree."

They fluffed the branches and hung the ribbons of the Christmas tree together. Oakley stepped back after every other ornament, taking in the full picture before finally placing the next ornament on the desired bough.

"At this rate, we'll be decorating this room all night."

She swatted his arm playfully. "The tree needs to look good from all angles."

"It always looks amazing."

She grinned and held a sparkling ornament by the string,

letting it spin in the air. "That's because I take the time to make sure every ornament is where it should be."

He hung glittery ornaments on the higher boughs, and Oakley bent low, putting more on the inside of the tree, giving the lights more ornaments to reflect off of. It made the tree richer.

When the tree was finished and the star secured on top, Oakley stepped back to admire their work. "Yes, this will do nicely."

Hunter stood beside her. "You're right, it's wonderful."

They stacked the empty boxes to store them back in the attic. Oakley opened the last box. "Here you are," she said, pulling out the intricate music box and placing it on the shelf that Hunter always pictured it on.

"You still have the music box?" he asked in surprise.

She tilted her head at him. "Why wouldn't I have it still? It's my favorite Christmas decoration."

He checked himself. "I know it's your favorite." Maybe they had a spare key to it, or maybe they just opened it up with a paper clip or something. "I thought it didn't work anymore."

She opened her mouth, then shut it again, looking at him ponderously. "I guess the last time you were here was the year it stopped working. What an odd thing to remember."

"So it doesn't work, but you still keep it on display?"

She nodded. "I don't have the key anymore. It was ... lost somehow. I always kept the key in it so I could turn it on. It was a present from my grandma." She caressed the box lovingly. "But it's still beautiful, even if it can't play anymore."

"Have you tried finding a replacement key?" he asked.

She nodded. "I took it into a jewelry store. The original

maker of these music boxes went out of business years ago, and the lock on the box was too delicate to use tools other than the original key. The jeweler was afraid of breaking the box if we tried to force it open."

Hunter made a mental note of what she said. "I wish I could help," he said.

She waved off his suggestion. "It's okay, really." But the look in her eyes suggested otherwise.

"I'm sorry—"

"Why? This isn't your fault. It must have gotten lost in the decorations or fallen out accidentally and been vacuumed up or something. Anyway, it's still one of my favorite Christmas decorations."

Hunter agreed with her, racking his brain to figure out how he could make it right. He knew exactly where the key was, but getting to it would prove difficult. Now that he was here he was in no hurry to go back to his home to retrieve the key ... but he would figure out a way. He had to.

The rest of the room came together in no time, and Ellen praised their efforts. "You're staying for games and a movie night, right, Oakley?"

"Mom, that was a tradition when we were kids. I'm sure Hunter doesn't want to—"

"I was asking *your* plans, not Hunter's." Ellen smiled at her daughter. "Are you staying or not?"

Oakley looked between her mom and Hunter. Hunter kept his face neutral, though the suspense of waiting for her to answer was excruciating.

Finally she nodded. "Yes, I'm staying."

Ellen beamed, then turned to Hunter. "And you're staying too, right, Hunter? Tradition is tradition."

"Far be it from me to break tradition," he said.

"It's settled. Now, I just need Hunter's help with one more thing before your dad gets back."

"How can I help?" he asked.

"I need help with the mistletoe. A few years ago the kids decided to put it in the kitchen, and it surprised me and my husband."

Hunter looked at Oakley, and her cheeks colored. Hunter vividly remembered the year it had moved, however, admitting that detail with Oakley present seemed precarious.

Ellen continued, "Since then, Andy and I take turns hiding it in different places. I thought of a great place, but I can't quite reach it, even with the ladder."

"I'm happy to help," Hunter said, avoiding Oakley's gaze.

After securing the mistletoe to the ceiling, Hunter climbed down a few of the steps. "What do you think?" Hunter asked Ellen and Oakley.

"It looks great from here," Ellen said.

Hunter climbed down the ladder. From the look on Oakley's face he knew she wanted to make a comment too. He raised his eyebrows, trying to coax it out of her. Ellen bustled into the kitchen, leaving them standing near the ladder that was directly under the mistletoe. "Well?" he asked finally.

"Well what?"

"What do you think?"

She arched an eyebrow. "I think you and mistletoe are a dangerous combination."

"I mean, does it look straight? It was hard to tell when I was putting it up."

Her cheeks flamed a bright red. "Just ... don't get any ideas," she said a little breathlessly.

He knew he didn't affect her. She'd made that clear enough, but surely, they could at least be better friends now, couldn't they? "Trust me, I learned my lesson," he said.

They played a round of Christmas Trivia, and then Andy took a phone call. When he came back, he spoke to Ellen in a hushed tone. They both made their apologies saying that they needed to go and help a neighbor.

"What about the movie?" Oakley asked.

"You're still welcome to watch it. We'll be back from the neighbor's in no time," Ellen said.

Oakley nodded, but when her parents left, she turned off the TV anyway. "Well, I guess we can take a rain check," she said, putting the remote back on the shelf.

"I'm still game for a movie marathon," Hunter said.

"You don't think it's childish to watch all of the Christmas movies back to back?"

Hunter grinned. "It's completely childish, but that doesn't lessen the enjoyment. Besides, it feels just like old times, especially when I'm here." He wanted to add on *'with you,'* at the end of his sentence but thought the better of it.

Oakley picked up the remote and started the movie. She turned back to the couch, where Hunter assumed sitting in the exact middle. She smiled, then picked one side of the couch, hugging a pillow in front of her.

Halfway through the movie *A Christmas Love*, Oakley turned to Hunter. "I can't believe I didn't ask earlier, but how is your arm?" Hunter pushed up the sleeve of his sweater, and she scooted closer to examine it. "It looks like it's healing well. No signs of any infection, so that's good."

He caught the scent of her vanilla shampoo, and the glow from the Christmas lights danced across her face. "Thankfully, I was spared the trip to the hospital by a beautiful redheaded nurse who took pity on me."

"First aid kits can do some amazing things," she said softly.

"I'm pretty sure it was the kiss from the best nurse ever that made it better."

She snorted and shook her head. "I'm pretty sure digging out the splinters was the key ingredient."

He winced at the memory of splinters and blood on his arm. "I owe you, Oaks."

"You don't owe me anything." Her hand stilled on his arm. "Besides, you're already here helping with the Johnson's store so much ..." Her voice trailed off. "Hunter, why are you here?"

Hunter gulped when he looked into her green eyes—eyes that were so full of intensity and fire. "I'm here to help."

She tilted her head. "But why?"

He knew that he couldn't tell her about the bet. That was off limits, but that was only partially the reason why he was still in Golden Ridge. If he were honest with himself, Oakley had always been part of the equation as to why he chose this town to find a project in. It was more than just his hometown, it almost felt like a way to rewrite some of his past mistakes with Oakley. He turned his attention back to the screen, as a Christmas miracle played out on the television. "Maybe what I need is something like that."

"Something like what?"

He swallowed. "A Christmas miracle. Or a second chance. What do you want for Christmas, Oakley?" He rushed his answer with a question, hoping that the awkwardness of the moment would pass. It only seemed to transfer to Oakley.

"What do I want for Christmas?" She repeated his question.

He nodded. "Isn't that what we always discussed when we put up the Christmas decorations or during the movies?"

"I don't ask Santa for anything anymore."

"It's a shame to miss out on some of the fun of Christmas. C'mon, you always knew what you wanted."

"Truthfully, with the decorations up before Thanksgiving, I haven't compiled my big list of wants and needs." She laughed lightheartedly. "I can always count on a new pair of Christmas pajamas from my parents, and an ornament for my own tree. What about you?"

Hunter shrugged, though he knew what he really wanted. Would he be brave enough to ask for it this year?

"I know you have something in mind." Oakley lifted an eyebrow. "It's written all over your face."

He turned to her, facing her straight on, and putting a little distance between them. The distance did nothing to help him concentrate. "How do you know?"

She looked at him as if he had grown a third eye in the middle of his forehead, then her lips parted into a smile. "You were my brother's best friend growing up. I can read just about everything from your facial expressions."

Panic filled him for a second, and he forced himself not to stare at her lips.

"You just panicked. I saw it. Tell me I'm right," she said with a triumphant smile.

He nodded. "I suppose it's unnerving hearing that others can read my facial expressions so well. Am I really that transparent?" Had she known that he liked her? That nine years ago, he was going to ask her to be something more than friends? Maybe that was why she'd dismissed him at the time, because he'd been so easy to read and she didn't reciprocate his feelings.

"Not everyone can do it. Some of your gestures are actually quite subtle," she said, her nose wrinkling just a little, like she was trying to soothe him.

"Subtle?"

"You put your hand to your chin when you think you've won a game, for example."

"So that's how you know when to play your best cards?" he asked.

She shrugged. "Maybe, or maybe I'm actually just better than you at games."

He elbowed her playfully. "I can hold my own."

"*Sure* you can. Just keep telling yourself that, and someday it might work for you."

"Fine, Annie Oakley. What else did you observe about me over the years?"

"More than you realize." Her eyes widened, and she covered her mouth like she'd revealed some big secret.

"Like what?" He scratched the back of his neck while he waited for her to respond.

"You scratch the back of your neck when you're nervous."

He immediately brought his hand down. "Maybe my neck was itchy."

"Maybe. But when your neck is itchy you scratch it and then rub it. Right now you just scratched."

"It's uncomfortable being in the hot seat like this, rethinking everything I do all the time."

She bit the inside of her cheek. "Well, like I said, I'm probably more observant than others. Call it another super power, or maybe because I spent so much time with you and Travis." She pulled the pillow that she'd been holding earlier back onto her lap, and played with the corner.

"You are amazing, Oakley. I remember details like that, but it's been impossible for me to figure out the meanings."

She cleared her throat. "Well, you didn't come all the way from Portland to figure me out. I know you have other work to do, and yet here you are still working on the Johnson's store. Don't you have a business to run?"

The words weren't accusatory, they felt like honest questions. And even without her super power picking apart his every word, he wanted to tell her the truth. "My reason for coming might be different than my reason for staying."

She studied him. "What *is* the reason?"

"I was serious when I said I wanted a second chance," Hunter said.

"A second chance?"

He took her hand. This was the moment he had wanted nine years ago, and he didn't want to blow it. "Maybe it's more of a first chance."

Oakley stared at their hands. "I don't understand what you mean."

Hunter's heart raced when he realized she hadn't pulled her hand away from his. Now was the time to tell her, no matter what had happened in the past. This was his time to figure things out. What he wanted had always been clear in his mind, but maybe this was the time to say it aloud. Was there a way to explain to her all the feelings that jumbled up inside of him every time she looked in his direction? He couldn't tell her everything right now, could he? The shock of just one revelation might be enough to move them in the right direction, but he didn't want to scare her off either. Slow was a good approach. He was still holding her hand, and she made no motion to remove it from his. Their fingers weren't fully entwined, but it was a start. "Oakley, I have a confession to make."

CHAPTER 11

Oakley had reoccurring daydreams about Hunter for years. No other guy had captured her attention like he had. She'd turned down more dates than she accepted while in college. Actually, the same had been true in high school until Hunter graduated and moved away. After he left, she figured it was time to move on, and so she went on lots of dates. But she compared every guy she met to Hunter. She really had been so smitten by him growing up.

She looked down at her hand in his. She had daydreams like this many times—sitting on a couch with him, cuddling during a movie, holding hands, maybe sharing a kiss or two. The vision played in her head on repeat for years. And here she was, her fantasy becoming a reality as she felt her hand within his. She wanted to subtly pinch herself, but there was not a way to do that without Hunter noticing.

Oakley's mind drifted to a memory from their youth when they'd played a murder mystery hand-holding game in the backyard. She'd sat next to Hunter at least half a dozen times during that game, hoping her palms didn't sweat against his as they played, each squeezing hands around the circle in turn. And there was the time he'd squeezed her hand when she was about to take her driver's license test. He had seen her in the hall, given her one of her favorite strawberry cream-filled chocolates, and wished her good luck with a light squeeze of his hand. It had been a friendly thing to do, but she saved that candy wrapper in her locker for three months. Each time she looked at it, it reminded her of the touch of his hand.

This moment was different. She was no longer the same twitterpated teenager, she was an adult. Hunter had taken her hand to convey some meaning, but he kept his hand almost ridiculously still. No moving, no caressing of her hand, no lacing his fingers through hers, just holding it.

"Oakley?"

Her name on his lips took her breath away. It pulled her out of the past to focus on Hunter's face. She knew what his Kryptonite did to her, but in that moment she didn't care. "Yes, Hunter. You have a confession?" She wanted to lighten the mood with a joke, but she couldn't do it. What would he confess? Maybe he'd been the one that took her chocolate orange from her stocking every year. She'd always found it back in her stocking once the rest of the contents had been emptied out. Was that his confession?

Hunter's brows drew together, and she watched him intently. A mixture of uncertainty crossed his face, and she squeezed his hand. When that didn't help, she waited.

He cleared his throat. "I don't know where to begin."

She swallowed. She could tell whatever it was he was about

to say had been held in for a long time. "You know you can tell me anything. I keep secrets really well."

He smiled at that. "Can you give me an example of a secret you've kept?"

She laughed lightly at the joke. "If I gave you an example, I wouldn't be a good secret keeper, would I? You'll just have to trust me."

"This isn't much of a secret, or maybe it is." He laced his fingers through hers and scooted closer to her.

Oakley was glad she was already sitting because she wouldn't have been able to keep her feet underneath her. Her hand was completely cradled in his. His subtle shift in position didn't feel subtle at all. She inhaled swiftly, suspecting she might forget how to breathe if she didn't draw in oxygen quickly.

"Look, I know the last time we were here that things went badly, and I'm sorry for that."

She waved the apology away. "You already said that, remember? It's completely forgotten." Well, not quite. There was still the matter of her broken heart, but now there was this new sensation of hand holding. Her brain couldn't dwell in the past and savor the present at the same time. She had to choose one, and right now, the soft touch of his fingers in between hers won out over her past heartbreak.

He winced. "You say it's forgotten, and I hope forgiveness came with that. But for me … it's not forgotten."

She nodded and settled against the back of the couch. He needed to get the past off his chest, therefore she would listen to him. "It's okay. You can let go of it now. Just forget it ever happened."

His jaw tightened. Anger? "That's just it, Oakley. Maybe you want to forget, but I don't. Kissing you is something I haven't forgotten, and I don't want to."

Oakley tried to remove her hand from his, but he held her. "I'm not sure what to say," she whispered, feeling the heartbreak from years ago well up. It was more painful to hear his issues with the past when they involved her. She wasn't the person to talk to about getting over it—Wait. Did he say he wanted to get over it? Or that he didn't want to forget it? The words spun in a blur around her brain as the past collided with the present.

"Oakley, I want another chance with you. I messed everything up nine years ago. I—that mistletoe kiss—it meant more to me than you realize. It was different … special."

She wanted to respond with the fact that she'd loved him for as long she could remember, but she couldn't get the words out. They were rooted too much in the past—trapped in a dream she wished over and over would come true. Now here she was, nervous and tongue-tied. It was a frustrating combination. She opened her mouth then shut it again.

Hunter continued. "I don't expect you to change your feelings about me in just one day, but, I'm here and I'd like to have a chance to change your mind."

If he only knew that her mind didn't need changing, and that she remembered every moment with him with such clarity. But that also meant that she could recall all of her feelings from nine years ago. The risk of being hurt again swirled around her, sounding the alarm. But was that risk worse than the lovesick wounds that threatened to bleed again each time she saw him and he wasn't hers? She thought she was tough, that she could be professional around him, but he was all she had wanted for as long as she could remember. She swallowed, needing to ask one question before she could respond. "Why?"

Pain ran across his face, with a myriad of other emotions. He shoved them away, and she didn't have a name for the look he gave her. It was almost like he was searching for a reason, discarding all the other thoughts that clouded his mind. Finally he answered, "Because I think we'd be great together."

"And you think that my feelings about that kiss need to change?"

"Maybe just your current feelings about me," he replied.

He didn't have a clue about her true feelings if he thought they needed to change. Questions about him asking her to Prom danced through her mind, but she pushed them away. This didn't have to do with high school, this had to do with what happened after the mistletoe. She didn't need to dig up everything and show all her wounds. Reliving them wouldn't help heal them. She adjusted her spot on the couch, leaving her hand in his, as she leaned against the back of the couch again. "And your feelings about me have changed since you kissed me nine years ago?"

"You ask questions, but you answer none of them," he said, frustration evident.

She blinked. "I'm not sure which question I'm supposed to answer."

He closed his eyes. "I'm not good at this and you know it."

"Not good at what?"

"At talking to girls I have feelings for."

She almost laughed at that. "I don't believe that at all. You charmed all the girls, and you always talked to them like it was no big deal."

He tilted his head. "Not all the girls, remember?"

It was a jab at her for the Senior Prom rejection, but there was no way he actually cared about that. She went back to what he'd just revealed. "So, you have feelings for me?"

He squeezed her hand, bringing it to his lips and kissing the back of her hand in a way that made her lips envious of the touch. "What do you think I've been trying to say?"

She hadn't been sure—her brain had been so muddled with emotions and feelings and thoughts and memories and hand-holding. All of it felt surreal. She really should have pinched herself. "It's been a difficult conversation to follow."

"Because you keep changing the subject," he murmured.

She pushed playfully against his arm. "You started it."

"And you get to finish it. Will you give me a chance?"

She bit the inside of her cheek. It wasn't quite like pinching her arm, but it was close.

He grinned.

"What?"

"You bite the inside of your cheek when you're nervous. It's one of those subtle gestures I have a super power for detecting."

Her cheeks flushed. "You don't know that."

"Yes, I do. It accentuates your dimple. So what's your answer, Annie Oakley? Will you give us a chance?"

Us. That two-letter word again with so much meaning it could fill oceans. If there was ever a moment to put in a time capsule and send to her junior high self, this was it. He was finally showing some sort of interest to her, and waiting for her to answer if she would give him a chance. She wanted to scream, laugh, and dance all at the same time. "I think that sounds nice," she answered.

He squeezed her hand again, and this time when the electrical current flowed between them, she didn't try to stop it. He brought her hand to his lips again, turned it over, and kissed her palm.

Her lips were again jealous by the contact they didn't receive, and she pressed them together to suppress the squeal that nearly escaped at the tender gesture.

He pulled her in close, wrapping his arm around her shoulders. "Will you go to dinner with me tomorrow evening?"

"You mean come for dinner at my parents' house," she corrected.

"No. As much as I love your parents, I think our first official date can just be the two of us."

"I'd like that. Where did you have in mind?"

"How about the Sunset Grille in Sunset Meadows?"

"Did you know that's one of my favorite restaurants?" she asked.

She felt his smile form against her head as she leaned closer into him. "You're not the only one who remembers things. Like you said, some things stick."

CHAPTER 12

Hunter arrived at Oakley's door right on time. He'd never been so nervous for a date in his entire life. He'd also never cared for a woman before as much as he cared for Oakley. If life had gone his way nine years ago, he'd have been married to Oakley for almost a decade by now. The thought immediately brought regret and hope. He couldn't undo the past, but he could move forward. Oakley had said yes to a date. That was a good start.

Oakley opened the door, a smile on her face. "Hi."

Her voice was music to his ears. "Hi. You look great."

She bit her cheek, then seemed to notice that he'd noticed, and stopped. "Thanks. So do you." She grabbed her purse from the small table in the entryway and practically jumped out the door.

"I told your mom we were going on a date," he announced awkwardly as he opened the truck door for her. That was definitely not the smoothest thing he could have said.

He couldn't believe how tongue-tied he felt around Oakley now that he'd officially asked her out. Shouldn't that have calmed some of his nerves?

He'd felt awkward explaining to Ellen over breakfast that he wouldn't be at dinner that night. When he said he was going to have dinner with Oakley, Ellen immediately replied that Oakley was always welcome home to have dinner with them, and he nervously admitted to her that it was an official date. Ellen didn't seem to mind at all. In fact, she gave him details about Oakley that he already knew, and told him to make sure she had a good time. He'd smiled at that and was glad the conversation wasn't as uncomfortable as he'd imagined. But explaining all of it to Oakley now felt more awkward.

Oakley only smiled. "I'm sure you made her whole day by telling her that."

He tilted his head, wondering exactly what she meant by that, but she didn't elaborate.

Hunter drove toward Sunset Meadows, and they listened to Chrismas music and made small talk about the progress on the General Store until they came into the city.

Suddenly, Oakley laughed.

"What's so funny?"

"Sorry, I'm just trying to figure out how this works exactly. Normally, a first date is the 'get-to-know-you date' with tons of questions, but I feel like I already know everything I would normally ask, and then some."

He laughed as well. "You definitely have the advantage. Usually by the end of the first date, I know enough to know that I don't need to ask for a second date."

Oakley sobered. "Is that so? I suppose you're pretty consistent with that."

Hunter shook his head. "Well, I hope this isn't the only date we have."

"I suppose you'll know soon enough."

"This isn't going quite the way I expected it to," he mumbled. And he felt like an idiot for that.

She laughed it away. "So, Mr. Charmer, why only one date? What's that all about?"

They were barely ten minutes into their first date ever. There was no way he was going to tell her the real reason—that he compared all of his dates to her. Then he'd have to explain that he'd been interested in her way before the mistletoe kiss that he'd already admitted to. Instead he settled for the true, but more vague answer. "I suppose I realized they weren't my type. No sense in going on another date when I didn't see the long-term potential." He could feel Oakley studying him, but he kept his eyes on the road.

Finally, she said, "That makes very logical sense. Still the sheer number of girls you dated—I mean at some point you kind of know your type, right?"

He shrugged.

She leaned back in her seat and faced out the front window. "What is Hunter's type?"

"That's hardly a question to ask someone on a date," Hunter said, though he wanted to admit that she, Annie Oakley, was his only type. There was so much he felt he should explain, but he just couldn't. There was no need to totally scare her off.

Oakley shrugged. "Why not ask? I mean, it's a good get-to-know-you question, and it's one that I've been baffled by for years."

"You've literally thought about that question for years?" That was an interesting tidbit.

She bit her lip. "Okay, maybe not *years*. But really, what is your type?"

"Oh you know, the typical things."

"What does that mean? Cute, smart, funny?"

He wanted to hand her a picture of herself, or maybe just a mirror. "Sure. Those things are great, but it's more than that. She's someone who makes me laugh. Someone who understands me. Someone who isn't afraid to be themselves. Someone who is creative and fun to be around. Someone who is driven to succeed." He wanted to give specific examples, but knew he couldn't. Not yet.

"Sounds like a total illusion. No one person is all of those things." She laughed. "No wonder you went on so many first dates, and so few second ones."

He wanted to disagree with her. She was all of those things, and more. But he was trying to take things slow, trying not to mess things up like he had before. "What about you, Oaks?"

"What about me?" she asked.

"What do you look for?"

She brushed at her jeans. "Oh you know. The typical things." She flashed him a grin.

"Oh no, you don't get to use my words against me. Bad form, Oaks. I'm taking away ten points for that."

"What? That's hardly worth a *full* ten point deduction. Maybe five points, but not ten." That flirtatious grin was back on her lips, driving him crazy.

"And an extra seven points off for trying to sway the points judge."

"Wait a minute—" Oakley could barely speak through her laughter.

"Nope. Answer the question, or you'll be deducted again." He laughed too.

She took a deep breath. "Okay, fine, what do I look for?" She gave another half-shrug. "I've never written it out in a list form. I know what I want, I am just not sure how to verbalize it."

"Do you need yes/no prompts for this, Oaks? It's a preference on the type of guy you like to date, not a college final."

"Fine. Give me the prompts and I will answer with a yes or no."

"Handsome?"

She smiled. "Yes."

"Tall?"

"That's a great height."

"Chivalrous?"

"Define, please."

Hunter drummed against the steering wheel as they drove. If he was making up the yes/no prompts, he should find a way to lead her toward him. It only made sense, right? This was the most unique first-date conversation he'd ever had. "Someone who opens doors for you, let's you order first, that sort of thing?"

"Oh, definitely a yes. I mean I've been way too spoiled growing up. I can't actually open my own door."

"You can't open your own doors?"

"Not when I'm on a date. I've had a couple dates who didn't pick up on that until halfway through the date."

"What happened?"

"The evening ended early, and I blocked their calls on my phone. I don't have time for that sort of thing."

"Harsh, Oaks. Harsh. Some guys need a few chances to learn."

"He had like twenty on the date, and he still couldn't get it."

"Sounds like you're breaking lots of hearts," he said, laughing.

She tilted her head. "Hardly that."

He swallowed. She had no clue how easily she could break hearts. He avoided commenting on it, and thought of another question. "Gets along with your family?"

"Of course. These questions seem too obvious."

"Rancher?"

"I don't have a preference on profession."

"Really? I kind of always thought you wanted that to be part of the package deal."

"Because I stayed in Golden Ridge? Lots of people have jobs besides ranching here."

He'd ruffled her feathers on that, and he wasn't sure why. "Would you ever live outside Golden Ridge?"

She met his eyes for the briefest of seconds before she directed her attention out the front window again. "I suppose if the right opportunity came up I'd be willing to look at it. I can work from anywhere, and most of everything I make is shipped to customers."

He was silent for a few minutes, taking in her response. She'd be willing to move, if it suited her. Would that mean she would move for him? And why did he care right now? They were not at a place in their relationship to even discuss that.

"No other questions?" she asked, sounding surprised.

He shrugged. "It's hard to ask lots of yes/no questions."

"I suppose I also like the thoughtful type, someone who knows me."

"Someone who will protect you from spiders?"

She laughed. "Yes, I will definitely need someone to protect me from those horrid things."

"I suppose they'd also need to be strong."

"Sure. Strong is good."

"And probably someone who can handle the sight of blood," he said, feeling vulnerable. Weakness at the sight of blood didn't give off a strong or protective vibe.

She reached over and squeezed his hand. "That's never been a requirement for me."

Hunter's heart soared a little, unsure why it mattered to hear her say it out loud. One thing was certain though, he was more compatible with Oakley than he'd hoped for. They were a great fit, and he just needed to show her that he was all the things she wanted—the man of her dreams.

CHAPTER 13

Oakley sat across from Hunter at the restaurant. The drive to Sunset Meadows had passed by in a blink. Giddiness had enveloped her when Hunter had said what his type was like. She could hit all the criteria without any stretch. It would almost be too easy. Could Hunter see that about her? Could he see her as more than his best friend's kid sister? Didn't being on this date mean that?

They ordered their food and Oakley enjoyed his Kryptonite eyes while they waited. The blue pools were mesmerizing. She discreetly pinched herself three times. Sure enough, she wasn't dreaming.

They chatted through the appetizers and first course, filling each other in on the last decade of their lives. Oakley told him about growing her business during college, and coming back to Golden Ridge after she graduated. Hunter told her about his family, and adventures with his nieces and nephews. He also gave her the full story of how he decided to go into coding.

They laughed through the meal, and Oakley couldn't remember a time when she'd laughed so hard or enjoyed a date so much. Wishful thinking wasn't even part of it. This was real and right in front of her.

She shook her head in wonder. "I can't believe that I'm on a date with you."

Confusion crossed his brow. "You can't?"

She bit the inside of her cheek. This had been her dream for so long and, now that it was finally happening and she was actually on a date with him, the entire thing seemed surreal. "I meant that in a good way. It's just … you were my brother's best friend growing up."

"You never really pictured going on a date with me before?"

She wasn't going to admit on their first date that the exact opposite was true. She needed to do some evasive maneuvering. "I can't imagine you ever pictured this either—being on a date with your best friend's little sister."

"It wasn't quite like this, but I imagined what a first date with you looked like," Hunter admitted.

She was taken aback. "You did? When?" But then the thought struck her like lightning and at the same time he said the words, she joined in. "Senior Prom."

He continued, "You broke my heart that day, you know."

She smiled at Hunter's dramatics. No way she'd broken his heart that day the way he'd broken hers. The memory reached with painful claws, but she left it alone. Things were different now, they were both grown up and mature. Not everything in the past needed to be rehashed. Weren't they looking forward, and not backward? He'd asked for forgiveness on the mistletoe kiss, and shouldn't she extend that forgiveness back to Senior

Prom? He didn't even know there was something to apologize for. It wasn't his fault she'd overheard him that day. No, she hadn't broken his heart. She might've bruised his ego, but she doubted his reputation had been tainted for long by the rejection of a sophomore. He went to prom with someone else, and the sophomore who ended up on his arm talked it up for weeks afterwards. "I am sorry for how that turned out."

He pushed his food around the plate with his fork. "Why didn't you want to go? I thought for sure you'd love coming to Senior Prom as a sophomore."

She'd been more than excited about the prospect of going with *him*. She didn't care at all about claiming a date to the dance as a sophomore. She shrugged. "Just because you were bored with all of the Senior girls wasn't a good enough reason for me to go, I guess."

He opened his mouth, then shut it, and nodded. He jabbed his fork at his food, and once he'd taken a bite he chewed for a long time. Finally he swallowed. "You went to Senior Prom as a Senior though?"

She nodded. "With John."

"John? The *foreman*, John?"

"Yes," she replied.

"How did that go?"

Were they really having this conversation? She blinked. She hadn't thought about her own Senior Prom since her senior year in high school, though she thought about Hunter's Senior Prom more than that. "Let's see, Senior Prom for me was eleven years ago. John took me out for a very nice dinner, kissed me before dessert, and I fell in love with him during the first song."

"Really?"

"No," she said flatly.

"What really happened?"

She shrugged. "We had a group of six couples. We ate at one of the guy's houses, took pictures by the old barn, the dessert was supposed to be a family favorite Dutch oven recipe, but ended up being a flop, and John stepped on my feet more than once. I think I had bruises on my toes for a week."

Hunter grimaced. "I guess Senior Prom didn't turn out for either of us the way we'd hoped."

"You didn't have fun with Gina?"

"The person I wanted to go with wouldn't give me the time of day, so I asked someone else, and she—"

"Told you no." Now she felt bad that she'd been the second girl to turn him down for the same dance.

"No. She told me yes, and then she spent the entire night with a group of girls. Maybe we danced once or twice—I don't remember. I went and played basketball on the outside court and ripped my tux jacket."

Oakley covered her mouth, holding in a laugh. "That's not the way Gina told it. According to her, y'all were joined at the hip the entire night. She went on and on about it for weeks."

"Did you date John after Senior Prom?" he asked her.

"We went out a few times, but decided we'd be better off as friends. It was for the best, anyway, cause he's married now and has a couple of kids. His wife is one of my really good friends. But why the sudden interest in my dating life?"

Hunter shrugged his shoulders, but his Kryptonite eyes betrayed him. "Just curious about who you liked or didn't, and what went wrong so that it didn't work out long-term."

She smiled. What was wrong with all of them was that none

of them were Hunter, but she kept that to herself. "John never made me laugh the way—well, he just couldn't make me laugh. I think he tried to, poor guy."

"Do I make you laugh?" he asked her.

Heat crept up her neck and onto her cheeks. "You've always made me laugh."

He breathed a dramatic sigh of relief. "Well, at least I have one up on John."

"You also haven't stepped on my toes while dancing."

He frowned. "To be determined still, since I've never danced with you."

She forced a smile. "I suppose that's my fault." After all, she'd been the one to turn him down. So many *'If Only'* thoughts ran through her head, but she couldn't latch onto any of them. He said she'd broken his heart, but that was the day he'd really broken hers. And then there was the matter of her pride. It wasn't going to be appeased just because her crush had asked her out. No. She wouldn't fall harder and faster than she already had. The pain would have been too much for her to bear.

"Maybe someday we can remedy that," he said. "I have a feeling I won't step on your toes as much as John did."

Oakley laughed. "Way to set the standards high. I'd rather not have any bruises on my feet."

Hunter pursed his lips. "A reasonable request. I think I can accommodate that."

"Always the charmer," she said, the word slipping out.

Hunter cleared his throat. "Any chance that helps my case? Maybe you find me charming?"

"I said, 'charmer,' not 'charming.'"

"Semantics."

"No. They're totally different."

"How is that?" he asked.

"Simple. One is a good thing, and one is not a good thing."

"Great," he said. "Then sign me up for the one that is the good thing."

Heat rose to her cheeks. "That's not how it works."

"Sure it does. You want someone who is chivalrous, and I am. And I can be charming. So there you go. It's a two birds, one stone kind of a thing."

"You can't just choose that."

"C'mon, Oaks. Let me be charming. Be a little bit charmed by me."

"Who says that I'm not?" she asked, before she could think the better of it.

A slow smile crossed his lips. "You just admitted that you *are* charmed by me. That has to be the biggest win of the night."

She shook her head and laughed. Admitting she was charmed by him now wasn't the same as admitting to being charmed by him growing up. "Bravo. Ten points to you."

Oakley and Hunter talked for a few more hours at the table, and by the time they left the restaurant, she couldn't believe how late it was. Time went by so quickly with Hunter around. Laughing and talking with him felt so natural. They'd cleared up some of the past, but mostly it was fun just to hear about what he'd accomplished in his life. He was full of surprises.

The drive back to Golden Ridge felt comfortable. Her hand slid into his as he walked her to her front door.

Daydreams of this scenario had played in her mind for years, but she pushed them aside to be completely present in the moment. She was going to savor her first non-mistletoe-obligatory kiss with Hunter.

He leaned in close and wrapped his arms around her. When he pulled back a little he pressed his lips to her forehead.

"Goodnight, Oaks," he said.

She blinked. The expected kiss didn't come. He'd chosen her *forehead*? "Night, Arrow."

Oakley watched Hunter drive down the road until he turned onto Center Street and out of her view. She knew how long it would take him to reach her parents' house. Would he get a grilling from her mom? Most likely her mom would encourage him. She sighed. So much of the last week felt surreal. She decided to text him anyway.

A kiss on the forehead is your style? That's news to me. Why was she getting so worked up about it? As far as kisses on the forehead go, it was a *good* one. Maybe she'd read too much into what going on a date with Hunter meant.

It's only our first date. You want a chivalrous gentleman. That's what I am.

Look at you. I never thought I'd be surprised by you.

I'm full of surprises. You don't know everything about me.

Giddiness spread through her. **I'm pretty sure I know all your secrets, Arrow.**

Not all of them, Oaks.

What don't I know about you?

If we're playing that game it's a secret for a secret. You made up the rules.

Oakley hesitated. Was it safer to tell Hunter about her feelings when she didn't have to stare into his eyes? Or was it better to say it in person, so she could read his expressions? **I don't have any secrets.**

Not true.

Absolutely true. I'm an open book.

I feel like we should be playing this game at Red Rock Point.

Oakley grinned. Maybe he didn't really pay attention to her growing up, but he remembered some things about her. **Just like old times!**

Want to take a drive out there tomorrow to see the stars?

Is it a date? She held her breath.

Only if you want it to be.

Can't make up your mind?

My mind is made up. Oaks, will you go on a second date with me?

He was asking her for a *second* date. That had to mean something, right? **I mean, since you're asking, sure.**

CHAPTER 14

OAKLEY - FRESHMAN YEAR OF HIGH SCHOOL

Oakley stood on the fringes of the small group surrounding the fire, feeling like a fish out of water. Sure, come Monday she'd be the coolest freshman in school for getting invited to the junior party at Red Rock Point, but she only got an invite because her mom had made Travis take her along. He'd pouted about it, since he wanted to spend time with his new girlfriend, Dana. Oakley couldn't blame him, not really. She'd shrugged it off and headed upstairs to her room when Hunter came through the front door.

"Oaks, are you coming tonight?" he asked.

She'd turned around to see the hope in those blue eyes as he looked at her. At least, she'd imagined that they were hopeful.

Travis had nudged Hunter, and Oakley caught the movement. "I'm not sure if I'm in the mood," she said, waffling at the obvious annoyance vibe her brother was sending everywhere.

"C'mon, Oaks, you know you want to hang out with the cool kids. You can ride with me," Hunter invited.

Butterflies filled her stomach and throat, almost making it difficult to speak. "I'll be right down," she answered.

In hindsight, she probably should have changed her shirt or grabbed a jacket instead of just spritzing her perfume and only grabbing her lip gloss.

Oakley moved closer to the fire for a moment, letting her hands warm up. Travis and Dana sat on the opposite side of the fire from her. She took a seat, trying to join in the conversations, but mostly she listened and just soaked everything in. She was definitely the odd one out, but that was okay. She was used to that. Natalie sat as close to Hunter as she could without sitting on his lap. It was clear Natalie liked him. What girl didn't? But Hunter's posture was fairly rigid. Maybe it was the chair he'd chosen that made him uncomfortable.

He looked up at Oakley and for the briefest moment their eyes met, but she quickly averted her gaze to watch the flames. She could have sat next to Hunter on his other side, but then she would have been sandwiched between him and her brother. She was a freshman now. She could hold her own.

Besides, she didn't want Travis to think of her as the bothersome little sister. She'd stay where she was. Couples came and went throughout the night. Away from the glare of the fire, more chairs were set up for stargazing. An hour later, someone cranked up the music, and it drowned out the crickets and other nighttime sounds. Oakley relished all of it.

A boy with dark hair sat next to her. "Are you the new transfer student in my biology class?"

Oakley laughed, and out of the corner of her eye she saw

Hunter shift to watch her. She straightened, then shook her head. "Not a transfer student."

He nodded. "I don't think you've been in any of my classes. I know I would have recognized you."

Hunter stood up and walked toward them. "She's Trav's sister, Don. Leave her alone."

Don's eyes widened, and he blinked hard. "Oh, sorry. I didn't know." Don stood up, and walked around the firepit, taking Hunter's old spot.

Don immediately began flirting with Natalie. The short blonde laughed at everything Don said.

"He was just making conversation," Oakley said, when Hunter took the spot next to her.

Hunter glared across the fire to where Don was now flirting with his date. "He was hitting on you."

"I'm a freshman now. I can take care of myself." She laughed, until she realized he was serious. "You don't need to babysit me."

"I do if you're not gonna be careful with who you talk to." Hunter's words were quiet, but they left no room for argument.

Oakley leaned forward. "He was just being nice."

"That guy is a player, Oaks."

Oakley sighed. It was nice to have Hunter looking out for her, even if the only reason he paid any attention was probably because her brother had given him the task. She leaned forward to watch the firelight, putting Hunter out of her peripheral vision.

He leaned forward. "Have you had a s'more yet?"

She shook her head.

"Want me to make you one?" he asked, his tone soft, sounding like a peace offering.

"Sure," she said, keeping her gaze on the fire.

Hunter stood. "I'll be right back," he said, and went to where the s'mores ingredients were. On the way a girl chatted with him, hitting him playfully on the shoulder. Oakley diverted her attention away from Hunter. She didn't want to see him flirt back with other girls. He was a charmer.

In the firelight she noticed a spider crawling along the ring of the fire pit. She shivered. Hunter was gone, and she wasn't going to bother her brother about a spider. She headed back to Hunter's truck and jumped into the bed. The metal was cold through her jeans, but she'd rather take her chances freezing in the truck than with the spider by the fire.

She leaned against the side of the truck and rested her head, looking up at the stars. The cloudless sky made the viewing conditions practically perfect. She picked out some of the constellations she knew, and looked for shooting stars. A chilling breeze swirled around her and she folded her arms around her middle. She should have brought a jacket. Her green striped shirt was cute, but not warm enough. She really needed to invest in a green hoodie, one that looked good with her complexion.

"Is this seat taken?" Hunter asked.

"It's your truck. You don't need to ask my permission," she replied.

He handed her the s'more he'd made for her. "Sorry it took me so long," he said.

"Thanks," she said, taking a bite of the dessert.

"I made it golden brown, just the way you like it," he said. "Want to come back and sit by the fire?"

Oakley shook her head. "I'm good out here." Besides, when she was over there, she didn't really feel like part of the group. It didn't help that Hunter's protective older brother instinct was to get rid of anyone who talked to her. Her own brother wasn't even that protective of her. Of course, that probably had something to do with his new girlfriend, Dana. Travis wasn't paying attention to anyone else.

He scooted back into the truck. "It's more comfortable if you lean against the cab," he said.

"You can go back to the group. I'm really okay by myself."

"What were you doing all by yourself?"

"Looking at stars. Isn't that the point of Red Rock Point?"

Hunter pursed his lips. "It definitely is."

"You don't have to stay here and babysit me."

Hunter scrunched his brows. "I'm not trying to babysit you … but you're freezing, Oaks. Where's your jacket?"

"I didn't bring one."

He shrugged out of his hoodie, and wrapped it around her shoulders. "I thought that's what you went back upstairs for."

She definitely should've grabbed a jacket instead of her lip gloss, but then she wouldn't have Hunter's hoodie wrapped around her. "You'll be cold without this."

He shrugged, then helped her maneuver her arms into the sleeves. "Not as cold as you. Come and sit back. You'll be more comfortable."

She followed his example, leaning her head against the window of the cab and shifted to find a comfy spot.

"Here, try this," Hunter said, extending his arm out behind her, and letting her use his arm as a pillow.

Oakley took a steadying breath and leaned into him.

He wrapped his arm around her. "Better?"

"Better," she said, barely able to get the word out.

"Which constellations were you looking for?"

Her brain felt like mush at his simple question. She was basically cuddling with her crush, how could she recall actual facts like constellations? "All of them."

He laughed. "Did you see that one?" He pointed to the sky. "Did you see the bear constellation?"

"The bear?" Oakley looked in the direction he pointed. "Where?"

He pointed to a random cluster of stars, then drew an imaginary line across part of the sky, showing her how they connected.

"That does not look like a bear," she said.

"None of them look like what they are. That's why they are called constellations."

She nudged him. "Admit it, you have no idea what you're talking about."

He grinned at her. "I don't give away secrets for nothing. It's a secret for a secret."

She smiled at the game they used to play back when the secrets were about where her candy stash was located or what her locker combination was. "You want to know my locker combination? That's a pretty big secret."

"Is it now? Pretty sure I've seen you open your locker this year. You're using the same combination you told me about when we played this game last year … so that's not a new secret."

"Looks like I'm changing my combination on Monday."

"Not if I change it first, and then refuse to tell you."

She laughed. "You would do that, wouldn't you? Pick on a *freshman* like that." She shook her head.

"I don't think of you as a freshman, so yeah, I probably would."

"You don't think of me as a freshman? What do you think of me as?" she asked.

He was quiet a long time, and she realized that his silence meant that he still thought of her as younger than a freshman. Someone who wasn't quite on the high school level with them. They still thought of her as younger than them—perpetually a middle schooler. She held up a hand. "Never mind, don't answer that." She needed to switch the subject. She pointed to the sky. "That's the big dipper. That's the north star. Start with that when you talk to Natalie about the stars."

"Natalie?"

"The cute blonde you flirted with for most of the night. She seems nice."

Hunter sighed. "She's nice enough, I guess."

"And there's the little dipper." She drew the outline of it with her finger.

"I admit it, I don't know very many constellations."

She snorted. "You don't know any. There's a difference."

He tickled her side. "Take it back, Annie Oakley. I can find the bear."

She laughed, enjoying the momentary thrill of being next to

Hunter. "You used two stars from the big dipper for your made-up constellation."

"I told you my secret. Now you tell me yours."

"I told you. I don't have secrets."

He sighed. "I shouldn't have admitted mine so soon then."

"Sorry, I just don't have any." None that she could share with Hunter.

"Who are you crushing on these days?" he asked her lightly.

Oakley's heart pounded. "What?"

"C'mon, Oaks, you're in high school now. Surely there's someone who has caught your eye."

Oakley's mouth went dry. "No one new."

He raised an eyebrow. "Someone old? Or someone older than you? C'mon, who is it? Please tell me it's not Don. That guy is a total player."

"No, thank you. Not Don."

Hunter looked around at the different groups of people hanging out near the fire. "Who then? There're lots of options here."

Oakley's heart sank. Hunter was searching the crowd for a good option for her, and wasn't including himself in the equation. He thought of her not only as his friend's kid sister, but as his own. It was apparent from his over-protectiveness. "No way I'm telling you," she said.

"Why not?" He tried tickling her again, but she grabbed his hand.

"Because you'll go all crazy about it."

"Look, if he's not a good choice for you, I'll say it. Who is it? Travis is busy with his girlfriend, so I'll step in to size him up."

She shook her head. "Yeah, that probably wouldn't go over

very well." She tried to think of someone else—anyone else that could help her escape this interrogation. Had she ever crushed on anyone else? Nope. Just Hunter. It was always Hunter.

"How about I tell you a secret I know about you?" he said, his voice dropping to a whisper.

Oakley froze, her breath catching in her throat. Could he know? How? She was always so careful and discreet. She didn't even tell her best friends at school that she liked Hunter. It was a secret between her and the locked diary underneath her mattress. Maybe it was easier this way. If he already knew, it took a whole lot of pressure off of her. "Okay."

"I know when you're thinking about your crush."

She searched his eyes, which was more difficult to do in the semi-darkness. "You do?" Was that the secret he knew about her?

"You get this look in your eyes. It doesn't matter who you're looking at, I know when you're thinking of him. Who is it, Oaks?"

She laughed lightly. "Maybe I'm just thinking of you, Hunter."

His eyebrows rose and then fell. "C'mon, Oaks, just tell me who it is already."

"You're right. I have a crush. He's here tonight," she said, her heart draining.

Hunter looked around, studying all the people in front of them.

Oakley needed to end this conversation before she said something she'd regret. "You should probably get back to Natalie. She's probably wondering if you got lost."

Hunter shook his head. "Don seems to have kept her company just fine."

Oakley felt bad that Hunter was sitting in the truck with her, his girl becoming the object of someone else's affection. "Sorry about that. Y'all seemed cute together."

"Don't be sorry. I'd rather be here with you." He squeezed her shoulder lightly, his voice changing tone. "I mean, I need to learn my constellations *obviously*."

Oakley pointed out a few more constellations while absorbing every minute with Hunter. They talked and laughed about everything and nothing, and Oakley adored every second.

Suddenly Travis's voice carried toward them. "Hey, Hunter."

Hunter immediately dropped his arm from around Oakley. "Over here, Trav."

"Hey, Dana and I are gonna get some ice cream at the creamery in Sunset Meadows before it closes. Any chance you could do me a favor and take Oakley home?"

"No problem," Hunter said.

"Thanks," Travis said in a quieter voice, though Oakley could still hear him. "And thanks for keeping her company tonight and having my back."

"Anytime," Hunter said.

Oakley wasn't sure if Travis had seen her next to Hunter. The way he whispered the last phrase made it sound like he had. Travis left, and Oakley brushed at her jeans, before standing. "Guess we should get going," Oakley said.

"We don't have to leave yet," Hunter said.

Oakley paused. "I can wait here while you go chat with your friends."

Hunter stood too, but shook his head. "There's no one else I need to chat with other than you. Would you like to go get ice cream? I'm buying." He gave her a huge grin.

Hunter always offered to pay because he was nice like that, but Oakley didn't want him to feel obligated. "And crash Trav's date? I don't think so. If it wasn't obvious before, he doesn't want me around tonight."

"We can still go have fun. Forget Trav, we'll sit at our own table. What do you say?"

Oakley knew he was just trying to make her feel better, so she smiled. "You don't have to do that. Besides, don't you want to give Natalie a ride home?"

He shrugged. "Here's a secret for you, Oaks. I'm not really into Natalic. Shc's not my type."

She laughed. "Liar. You totally like her. You're always uncomfortable around the girls you like. I saw that tonight."

"You did?"

"Rigid posture in a camp chair. You had uncomfortable written all over you."

He put a finger to his chin, tapped it, and then tapped her on the nose. "Maybe you're right. Maybe there is someone here tonight that I like."

Oakley masked her own feelings and smiled widely. "See, I knew it. You can't keep secrets from me."

He jumped down from his truck, then put his hands on Oakley's waist to help her down. She leaned forward, bumping into him, and he steadied her. "You okay, Oaks?"

Okay? She couldn't even think straight. The boy she liked had his arms wrapped around her and she was wearing his amazing-smelling hoodie. Other than that, she was fine. "Yes, great. Perfect. I'm … good." She pushed off his chest, not letting her hands linger too long.

He opened the door for her, and they left Red Rock Point. He came to a complete stop at the fork in the road, then turned toward Oakley. "Well, what's it gonna be? Ice cream or home?"

She wrapped the hoodie tightly around her, her hands drowning in the length of the sleeves. It felt like something from a movie—wearing a boyfriend's jacket and extending an impromptu date night—until reality came crashing in. Travis had asked him for a favor, and Hunter was always willing to help. Maybe he didn't want to miss out on the rest of the evening. "What do you want to do?" Oakley asked.

He shook his head. "This is your call, Oaks? I'm just the driver."

Just the driver? Like a chauffeur? "I should probably get home," she said flatly.

Hunter looked disappointed. "You sure? I'm paying."

"I really don't want Travis to think that I'm crashing his date. I'm pretty sure that's why he asked you to take me home. Besides, I'm probably too cold for ice cream."

He nodded, and turned right instead of left. "How about a hot chocolate through the drive-thru before I take you home? Since ice cream isn't gonna work."

She smiled. "Thanks, Hunter. That'd be great."

"It's the least I can do."

Hot chocolate had been a good choice. Oakley wrapped her hands around the Styrofoam cup. It was just hot enough that the taste buds on the tip of her tongue burned. She pulled back and blew through the hole in the lid, hoping some air would cool it.

They sat for a moment in the parking lot, drinking their hot chocolate in silence.

"How is Brown's English class for you this year?" he asked her.

"So far, so good. I like English."

"The assignments are more important than the tests. She doesn't tell that to everyone at the beginning, but they are weighted heavier."

"Thanks for the heads up. Trav didn't warn me about any of my teachers."

"Well, he's related to you, so maybe he never thought about it."

"You're practically related to me too … I mean I see you as much as I see him." She felt her cheeks pink. "You've given me advice on classes every year since I began middle school."

"Practically related?"

"You know, you're over at the house all the time."

"I guess I just didn't realize you thought of me as another brother."

She gulped. Not precisely a brother. Not even close. "You've always felt like a member of the family."

He drank the rest of his hot chocolate quickly and took her home. Something had changed and the moment felt different somehow. "Thanks for the ride, Hunter."

He helped her out of the truck. "Thanks for coming with me for hot chocolate. I'll take a rain check on ice cream for another time."

She shrugged. "Your favorite flavor is always stocked in our freezer. Feel free to come have some any time."

He tilted his head. "Maybe I'll do that."

Oakley walked up to the front door, then came back. She handed her hot chocolate to Hunter and started taking off his hoodie. "I almost forgot to give this back."

He shook his head and handed the cup back to her. "What kind of gentleman would I be if I let you walk up to your house without a jacket in this cold? I'll grab it from you another time."

She nodded, then hurried into the house. She kept the hoodie wrapped around her for the rest of the night. Somehow it made everything, even her being just an annoying kid sister, better. As soon as she was safe in her room, she pulled out her diary from under her mattress and wrote about her evening with Hunter. Her almost, sort of, kind of, date with him.

CHAPTER 15

Hunter turned at the small stick in the road marking Red Rock Point. A small valley separated Red Rock Point from both Golden Ridge and Sunset Meadows. The large rocks and boulders were the perfect perch for watching stars, though most of the time he'd come, camp chairs and truck beds were more comfortable.

"I used to come out here to think," Oakley said, when Hunter stopped the truck.

"Did you?" Hunter asked, wondering what she'd share.

Oakley nodded. "Yep. Just me and the stars. Crazy how you can see them even better than from the backyard. I don't think I appreciated that enough when I was younger."

"What would you think about?" Hunter helped Oakley out of the truck.

"Life, mostly."

"I thought you were fixin' to say boys."

Oakley laughed. "Ha. Boys. Shows you how much you know about me."

"Admit it, Oaks. You did think about boys. In fact, I remember being out here with you once, and you admitted you liked one of the boys in our group." He set up two chairs and they both gazed upwards.

"We must have been in the middle of our Secrets Game if I told you that much. Though, I did think of a particular boy who used to make up constellations occasionally. I suppose that memory always crosses my mind when I'm out here."

"You just admitted that I've been on your mind. I think I will take that as a compliment."

"Have you learned any *real* constellations since your junior year in high school?"

"I'll have you know I took an astronomy course in college and learned all of them."

She looked at him. "I didn't know that. You really took astronomy?"

He shrugged. "Some girl in high school told me I didn't know the stars well enough. I figured if I ever wanted to impress her …"

"You wanted to impress *me*?" Oakley's voice sounded shocked.

Hunter took her hand, running his fingers up and down her arm. "Is that so hard to believe, Oaks? I was trying to impress you back *then* with all of my constellations. I didn't realize you actually knew the official ones."

Oakley laughed, swatting at his hand playfully. "You're so full of it, Hunter."

"I'm not full of it. I learned my lesson. No more making up stuff to impress people. There's my secret. Now it's your turn."

"Okay, well, honestly, I thought it was kind of cute that you made up constellations. After that night, I remembered laying in the backyard and trying to come up with creative constellations. So, what can I say? You inspired me."

Hunter took the moment in, as she pointed out a few constellations. It was a small thing to say that he'd inspired her, but it meant a lot to him. Maybe she *had* noticed him a few times when they were growing up. Maybe he wasn't just her brother's best friend all the time. Maybe she'd thought of him as her friend, too. The idea persisted, and he had to know. "Oakley, when we were growing up, did you ever think of me as more than just your brother's friend?"

Oakley's features stiffened, but she kept her gaze on the sky. "What do you mean?"

"I mean, were you and I friends? Or did you always lump me in a category with your brother?"

Their eyes met, and she studied him for a long time. When she spoke, her words were carefully measured. "I always thought of you as more than just my brother's friend, but I was the annoying little sister. Travis wasn't usually excited to have me around." She bit her lip, a sign he recognized that meant she was embarrassed.

"I was never bothered by you hanging out with us," he said, wondering if he needed to prove himself in the past in order to find a future with Oakley.

She nodded. "You were always nice like that."

His heart sank a little. It wasn't because he was just being *nice*. The truth was, he'd liked when Oakley would hang out with them. He liked her. She had never been an inconvenience to him. In fact, in the weeks leading up to graduation, she'd completely stopped hanging out with them. Hunter wasn't quite sure what to do with himself. Everything had blown up because of Senior Prom, and he found himself missing her more and more.

"I didn't always feel nice. I felt like you didn't want to hang out with us after a while."

She cleared her throat. "Well, I was likely stuck in the 'I'm the annoying sister' mentality. It's hard always feeling like the outsider."

Hunter felt the raw pain of their past. He knew that no matter how many examples he could come up with of times when he wanted her around, she'd likely be able to find just as many times when she felt left out. "I'm sorry if I ever made you feel like an outsider," he said. "Will you forgive me?"

Oakley sucked in a breath. "The past is in the past, right? We should probably move on from it."

There was so much in the past that he didn't want to move on from though. "Probably a good idea," he said. He hoped agreeing with her would help him move on the way that she had.

She cleared her throat, then prompted, "Okay, another secret. You're up."

"What do you want to know?" he asked.

"What went wrong with your last relationship? The one the media speculated about."

"Talking about a previous relationship while we're on a date doesn't seem very smart."

Oakley shrugged. "You spill, I spill. That's how it works."

"The media spun it into a big deal because we went out three times. That's hardly a long-term relationship," he said.

"Why would they think it was?" Oakley asked, interested.

"Probably since it was the most I'd ever gone out with anyone that they could document." He shrugged.

"So … there was *no* relationship?"

"We just went to a few social functions together. The third and final time we were out in public was only because the date she wanted to bring came down with the flu. So we met at the function, smiled for a few cameras, and went our separate ways."

"And *that* was the longest relationship you've had?"

He squirmed. He couldn't tell Oakley that the reason he hadn't had a long-term relationship was because, after comparing everyone else to her, there was no point in going out a second time. "I've been busy building a company. There are a lot of late nights, which isn't super helpful for dating," he finally said, giving her an insight that was true, but not the full story.

"What happened to the charmer who was always whisking people away on dates?"

"I didn't date the same girl twice in high school," he said, trying to prove his point.

"Exactly. You were charming *all* the girls. Everyone tried their best to catch your eye."

"The things you remember," he said, shaking his head.

"It's hard to forget being swarmed by girls in the bathroom every single day who would ask me question after question about you."

"Did they really?" he asked. "You never told me that before."

"I guess that counts as one of my secrets then. Of course I

wouldn't have told you before. Your head would've never fit through the doorway if I had!"

He smiled. "Maybe. Or I would have told you which ones to give the wrong information to."

She grinned. "Which ones would you have given wrong information to?"

"All of them."

She pushed his arm. "You wouldn't have."

He nodded. "If people were just trying to get my attention, without really knowing me it would have been better to just skip those dates altogether."

"Huh. That's deep."

"I wasn't shallow in high school," he countered.

"I know that. I just thought that you wouldn't give people a chance unless they measured up to your expectations."

"I like to think I'd always give the *right* person a chance."

She smiled. "Well, regardless, several girls were nice to me because you hung out at my house so often. I think some were even jealous of that. Not that I was hanging out with you all the time or anything."

"You could have though. Your company was much better than the other girls." He wanted to explain more. He wanted to tell her everything.

She laughed. "Well, that's not saying much about them then, if you preferred your best friend's kid sister's company to all of theirs."

He looked into her eyes. "Maybe that's why I never went on many second or third dates."

"Charmer."

"Could I charm you though? Even if I couldn't before."

"Ha. You never tried before."

He took that comment in stride. Back then, Hunter couldn't be obvious about his interest in Travis's sister. It was a boundary he would not cross. Just telling Travis that he'd asked Oakley to Senior Prom felt like walking on thin ice. Travis was cool about it in the end, and it hadn't actually mattered because Oakley had turned him down. But maybe she needed to know that. "Actually, that's not true."

She tilted her head. "What's not true?"

"You said I'd never tried before. But I did try to charm you before. I asked you out to Senior Prom with your favorite chocolates. You shut me down."

"You didn't really want to go with me," she said.

Was that what she thought? "Why would I ask you if I didn't want to go with you?"

She gave a half shrug and looked away. "I was a sophomore. You'd already dated all the seniors. I guess I was a natural pick, but ..." She shrugged again.

Hunter was stunned. That was her reason for not going with him? Where did she even get that idea? He'd asked her because he wanted to go with her. He would have asked her to all the high school dances his senior year had he not been concerned that Travis would flip out about it. He wanted to tell her all of that, but he just admitted to going on dates with women that he only partially liked, or going on dates because it was a favor. It wouldn't bode well for him to lump her into that same category. "Like I said, I tried, and my charms didn't work on you."

Oakley sat next to Hunter, taking in what he'd just said. She tried with all her might to keep her thoughts straight, but her head still spun in circles when he was around. She wanted to brush off his comments, but she couldn't. She didn't *fully* believe that Hunter wanted to take her to Senior Prom, especially after what he told Travis in the treehouse, but she couldn't divulge that. She couldn't let him know how much that moment had scarred her. "Why does it matter if you can charm me?"

"It matters a lot to me, actually," he said, his eyes sincere.

Her heart raced as she racked her brain for the reason it would matter to him so much. There was only one potential answer. "Why? Because you don't want a failed attempt on your record? You want to charm me now because you couldn't before?" She couldn't let him know that she had been charmed by him for as long as she could remember. In fact, he still charmed her even when he'd broken her heart again four years later, right after he'd given her the best mistletoe kiss she'd ever received. And though she'd dated enough since college to not be a novice at the activity, no one else had ever made her stomach flutter with massive butterflies the way he had.

He took in a slow breath, like he was deep in thought and choosing his words very carefully. "Oaks, I want to date you, and I plan on charming you in the process. Is that okay with you?"

Had she heard him right? Did he really just say those words? Electric currents ran through her, sparks filling the air between them. She smiled. "I'd like that."

He exhaled loudly, like he'd been holding his breath waiting for her response. "I have another secret to share," he confessed.

"I've wanted to hear those words from you since I came back into town."

She nodded, knowing the feeling—but revealing the secret that she'd wanted to date him for years would probably scare him away. "That's a long time," she finally mustered a response.

He took her hand, his touch igniting the fire between them. "You have no idea," he said.

She smiled. She had more of an idea than he could realize.

CHAPTER 16

Oakley spent the next few days before Thanksgiving running on pure adrenaline. She worked hard on fulfilling design orders like she'd done since mid-October, but now the orders were picking up at a rapid pace with Christmas just weeks away. She also spent a few hours every day volunteering at the Johnson's General Store.

She helped Hunter and the other volunteers as they worked through the remodel. The job was coming together much faster than she'd originally anticipated. Hunter's ability to work full days on the project was huge. His consistency gave John someone to truly rely on.

In the evenings she was either with Hunter, or texting him.

Thanksgiving with Hunter had been the most fun Thanksgiving she could remember. After a full day of food, playing games, and watching Christmas movies with Hunter by her side, she was in heaven. She couldn't imagine a better holiday.

Her parents came into the family room. "I finally got a hold of Travis," her mom announced. She held up the video chat on her phone, so Oakley was seen in the small box in the corner.

Oakley was secretly grateful for the blanket over her and Hunter's entwined hands. She discreetly unlaced her fingers from his and took her mom's phone. "Hey, Trav. Happy Thanksgiving."

"Same to you, sis," he said. "How was the turkey? Dad said he didn't burn it, but ..."

Oakley laughed. "He didn't burn it, but it was pretty close. Hunter had to take over your job of watching it through the oven door."

Travis's face scrunched. "Hunter watched the turkey?"

Oakley pointed the phone toward Hunter, and Hunter waved. "Hey, Travis. It's been awhile."

Travis raised both eyebrows, surprise written on his face. "Hey, it *is* Hunter! It's been a long time. What brings you to Golden Ridge?"

Before Hunter could answer, Oakley pulled the phone back to her. "Hunter is here while we fix up the Johnson's General Store. I told you about the lightning damage to the property. Hunter came into town and offered to help on the project."

"How long are you in town for, Hunter?"

Hunter looked to Oakley, and then back to the screen. "I'm here until the project is finished. We're making progress, but I'm not sure how long I'll be here. The deadline for the project is still up in the air."

"Where are you staying?"

"Your parents offered up your old room while I've been here. I hope you don't mind."

Travis smiled. "Not at all. Just like old times."

"Yeah, like old times."

"You should stay through Christmas, even if the project gets done before," Travis said.

Oakley looked to Hunter. The thought of Hunter being here at Christmas made her shiver with delight.

"You think I should stay that long? I don't know. I don't want to wear out my welcome," Hunter said.

Ellen protested from the other side of the room. "You've never worn out your welcome."

Travis grinned. "See? You're practically one of the family. Isn't that right, Oakley?"

Oakley felt the blush settle into her cheeks before she saw it on her image on the phone. "Right," Oakley said hurriedly.

"There, it's settled," Travis said. "Now I'll be able to see you when I come into town, just like the good old days."

"Can't wait," Hunter said.

Ellen clapped her hands. "My Three Musketeers together again. It really will be Christmas."

It would be a wonderful Christmas with Hunter here, but would it be the same with the three of them together? What would her brother think about her dating Hunter? She had a few weeks to figure it out with Hunter before Travis arrived.

CHAPTER 17

The day after Thanksgiving, Christmas filled the air. Truthfully, it had felt like Christmas for much longer, thanks to the decorations around the Larsen home, but the entire town seemed to glow with the holiday spirit overnight. Main Street was a hub for window paintings, garlands, and bells jingling. Hunter wasn't exactly sure what traditions the Larsens still carried out, but he knew he wanted to participate in them all, especially with Oakley.

He hadn't seen her around the Johnson's store that morning and didn't want to wait until later in the afternoon to talk to her. On one of his breaks, he pulled out his phone and texted her. **Is the tree-lighting ceremony still a big deal?**

Her answer came almost immediately. **Are you kidding me? It's bigger. You won't want to miss it.**

Will you be my date for the evening?

A long pause followed. Finally she wrote back. **Sure. I'm happy to show you around.**

I'd rather have a date than a tour guide.

Okay, if you insist. ;)

I'll pick you up at six.

Tree-lighting doesn't start until eight.

Let's do dinner before.

"GOLDEN RIDGE CAFÉ OKAY FOR TONIGHT?" HUNTER ASKED Oakley when he picked her up for their date.

Oakley smiled. "Of course." She tilted her head. "But I get the feeling that's not where you *really* want to go."

She was always perceptive like that. He smiled. "There's not enough time to go to the restaurant I really want to take you to."

"Oh? You found a new place in Sunset Meadows?"

"I was thinking of a restaurant in Portland, actually." If Hunter was in Portland with Oakley right now, he knew exactly where he'd have taken her out for dinner before the Christmas festivities. The Red Dragon restaurant on the pier had a heated outdoor seating area with a beautiful view of the city's reflection in the water. If it hadn't been for the deadline of the Johnson's store, he'd have flown them both to Portland for the week to show her the sights and eat at his favorite restaurants. There wasn't sufficient time before the Annual Tree Lighting Ceremony to go to a different town for dinner, let alone a different state.

Oakley looked at her watch dramatically. "What's the wait time like there? Would we be back before the tree lighting?"

He laughed. "If we skipped the appetizer and dessert, we

might make it back in time, but the appetizers and desserts are all really good, so I wouldn't skip them."

They walked through the doors of the Golden Ridge Café, and everyone in the restaurant seemed to take notice of them as they were seated. Oakley didn't seem to mind the added attention, and if she didn't mind, he wouldn't either.

"What's Christmas like in Portland?" Oakley asked once they'd ordered.

He told her all about the city and filled her in on some of the adventures he'd been on during the Christmas seasons since college. Usually he got together with his family, but there were a few years that he'd taken off with his business partner or his college roommates and they'd taken ski trips to the Alps.

Oakley laughed at the stories he told, asking questions throughout. Finally she said, "That sounds a lot colder than here," Oakley said.

Hunter nodded. "I suppose you're not one for a lot of snow?"

She took a drink of her water. "I didn't say that. I've gone skiing before, I just don't live in the snow for months on end."

"I'm not living in an igloo, Oaks."

She laughed. "And you don't have penguins as neighbors? Such a shame."

He held back a laugh, trying to keep a straight face. "The polar bears are next door, the penguins are down the street and around the corner."

"My mistake."

"The weather isn't terrible in Portland. It gets colder than here, but it's not mountains of snow, like where my parents' cabin is."

Oakley grinned. "I don't mind the snow. At least it would be an adventure for part of the year. Not sure about the polar bears though."

"They're really nice once you get to know them." How did Oakley feel about traveling and being in new places? He was getting a glimpse that she was more open to the world outside of Golden Ridge.

The server brought their meals, and their conversation turned toward the flavors of the food. Chef Wayne had been there for years, and the flavors were consistent and reliable.

After laughing about inside jokes, Hunter brought the conversation back to their original discussion. "Do you travel much?"

Oakley smiled. "A little. I get to travel for work. In fact, I'll be gone for a few days next week to get some orders created and delivered for the Christmas rush."

Oakley's news surprised Hunter. She was going out of town? "How far does business take you?"

"Not very far," she admitted, naming the cities that were in the surrounding area. "But I'd like to travel more someday. There're a few places on my list."

"I'm gonna miss you when you're gone," he said.

She laughed. "No, you're not."

He nodded. "I will. You'll have to send me a postcard."

A blush stole across her cheeks. "It's only a few days. I'd be back before my postcard was even delivered."

"Fine, texting and a few pictures will have to do for a digital postcard."

"I'll send you pictures of miles of road and big skies. That's where I'll be for most of the time."

"I'll take it."

After their meal, they walked around the Main Street shops, finally stopping by the outside of the Johnson's General Store.

Oakley sighed. "I was hoping it would move a little faster than it has, but it really is coming along."

"Everyone is working really hard on it," Hunter said.

"I've noticed that." She bit her lip. "And I'm glad you decided to stay and help with it. It really means a lot to me."

He squeezed her hand. "I'm glad I decided to stay too." He loved the feel of her fingers intertwined with his as they walked hand in hand.

Hunter pulled her close as they approached the large tree at the end of Main Street. The area was purposefully darkened, and even the Town Hall lights were off in preparation for the Tree Lighting Ceremony. They each grabbed a battery-powered candle from the tables set up for the occasion and Oakley lifted two silver sleigh bells tied with red ribbon off an adjoining table.

Music played from the speakers and everyone turned on their candles as the town joined together in song. The familiar melodies of the carols called to Hunter from so many Christmases ago. He wrapped his arms around Oakley, breathing in the moment that he'd thought about for years. This felt right. Being with Oakley in Golden Ridge felt right.

After a few carols, they sang *"O Christmas Tree."* Like a choreographed dance timed precisely to the beats in the music, the candle lights were turned off one by one. The final verse of the song was sung in the dark. As the last note disappeared in the darkness, lights flooded the tree. A few people cheered and clapped but the prevailing sound from the town was the jingling of the silver bells.

The tree sparkled with light, and the ringing from the bells ushered in *"Jingle Bells"* and *"Silver Bells"* as the next two songs. At the end of the singing, everyone took their bell and hung it on the tree.

Hunter waited with Oakley while parents and young children took their turn at the Christmas tree. "I love this tradition," Hunter said, feeling a sudden magnetism toward the town, the holiday, and Oakley.

"Me too," Oakley said. "Thanks for coming with me, Hunter." She hung her bell on the highest bough she could reach, and Hunter hung his right next to hers.

"Thank you, Oaks."

CHAPTER 18

Hunter put down his hammer and wiped sweat from his brow. The Johnson's General Store was coming along nicely. He'd stayed busy over the last two days while Oakley delivered some rushed Christmas orders, and the work was almost complete.

His phone buzzed and he pulled it out of his pocket, hoping to see Oakley's face on his screen. They usually exchanged texts and talked only at night since she was focused on her deliveries, and he'd been in a loud working environment during the day. He hadn't told her that he was working around the clock to finish up the General Store. So much of the town was in Christmas prep mode now, and the number of volunteers since Oakley left had dwindled. It would take extra work to make sure this project finished before Christmas, and he was the one to do it.

The picture on the screen wasn't Oakley, but Hunter answered it anyway.

"How are things going?" Kyle asked when Hunter picked up.

"Slowly, but surely," Hunter said.

Kyle laughed.

"What's so funny?" Hunter asked.

"I can't quite tell if you're talking about your Christmas project or how things are going with Oakley."

Hunter laughed too. "I suppose the answer is the same for both of them, but things are good between us. I'm not over her like I thought I was, though."

"I could have told you that."

"Why didn't you?" Hunter asked.

"I knew you'd figure it out at some point," Kyle said.

"The crazy thing is I don't want to be over her anymore, you know? I think things might actually work this time. The timing seems to be right."

"I'm happy for you, Hunter. I really am."

"She's out of town right now," Hunter said, and then explained how he'd been working longer and harder on the job. Part of his motivation was the deadline for the Johnsons to come home, but he knew that the real driving force for him wasn't the Johnsons or even Kyle's competition. It was Oakley. He wanted to prove himself to her, and he had focused on that while she was away.

They talked for a few more minutes. Before hanging up, Kyle recapped, "We'll be making the final decision next week for the winner of the competition. We'll get your last report before we do that. Nice work on this."

"Thanks," Hunter said, realizing that it didn't matter whether or not he won Kyle's competition. The way things were going with Oakley, he already felt like a winner.

While he had his phone out, and she was on his mind, he texted Oakley. **Miss you. Can't wait to see you when you're back in town. Want to go dancing?**

He waited for a few minutes to see if she would respond, but when she didn't, he pocketed his phone and continued working. All that was left was finishing work at the Johnson's. Thankfully he had learned all the trades growing up. In some ways it was the physical world of construction that had shaped him to remodel the digital world of coding. Coding was more satisfying and less physically draining than the construction work he did growing up, yet he still found this hands-on work enjoyable. The time passed quickly when he thought of Oakley. If he worked until midnight, he could make significant progress on the store. The upstairs living quarters were almost completely done.

He secured more shelves to the walls. The project would be finished before Christmas. His heart warmed at the image of the Johnson family seeing their newly redone store and home. That was the joy of serving with the Christmas spirit.

Footsteps sounded behind him, and Hunter whirled around.

"Oakley? I didn't think you'd be back until tomorrow."

She smiled at him. "You're still here?" She looked dramatically at her watch, pointing to the time.

He shrugged. "A couple of the other volunteers are having a hard time getting their hours in, with it being so close to Christmas."

Oakley nodded. "I figured that would happen at some point. But you don't have to make up the difference all by yourself. It's not your responsibility."

"Just doing my part," he said nonchalantly.

"It's more than enough," Oakley said. She surveyed the new improvements. The flooring and the light fixtures had been finished while she was away. The paint was applied before she left, but now that it was dry, Hunter had secured the shelves to the wall.

She ran her hand along the newly installed register counter. Three cashier stations took the place where two had been before. That had been one of the few changes Mrs. Johnson had randomly told Ellen she would change. "It looks amazing." She gave him a hug, and he held her close. "It feels like a dream that you're back in my life."

"Am I back in your life?" he asked.

She blushed. "I mean, you're back in everyone's life now that you're here in Golden Ridge, helping with this project."

He brushed a curl away from her cheek, and her eyelashes fluttered at the movement. "But, Oaks, Golden Ridge is nothing to me without you. I want to be in *your* life." He knew he needed to approach their relationship gently. That seemed to be working for them since he'd come into town. He could move on from the past and the heartbreaks, and moving slowly was a safe way to continue. "Oakley—"

She cut off his sentence, drawing him to her and kissing him. The exhilarating moment caught him off guard, but he swiftly responded by wrapping her up in his arms. Their passion under the mistletoe nine years ago had been amazing at the time, but it didn't hold a candle to this kiss. Years of hoping for returned affection from Oakley surfaced, and a longing that had been buried for almost a decade poured through him. Everything else disappeared. This moment was just them. He pulled her closer, cradling her head, and running his fingers into her hair.

He withdrew his lips, giving them both a chance to inhale. Her breathing was irregular, like his own.

Her eyes widened, then she smiled. "I really like having you in my life too."

He wanted to kiss her again, but he held back. "So where do we go from here?"

"I think you mentioned something about dancing?" she responded playfully.

He held her close and they swayed to the inaudible music keeping them in time. "Dinner and dancing tomorrow night?" he whispered, when the imaginary song came to an end.

She nodded. "I'd like that."

CHAPTER 19

Oakley savored holding Hunter's hand on the way to his truck. They'd gone to a new restaurant in Sunset Meadows where they laughed and talked all through dinner as they each told stories about times when things had not gone their way. Hunter spoke about lessons he'd learned from starting his own company. Oakley told him about a few times when orders had been sent to the wrong addresses.

Hunter seemed to be taking a detour to the highway back toward Golden Ridge. "Are you up for an adventure?"

Oakley nodded. "Definitely." With him, she was always up for anything. She liked the adventurous side of Hunter who was always trying new things and exploring new places.

He turned at the next traffic light. "There's an indoor Christmas-themed ice-skating rink. What do you say, Oaks? Want to ice dance, or would you rather go regular dancing?"

"I'm game for something new," she said. "But if we're dancing on the ice, you definitely can't step on my toes."

"Deal," he said.

AFTER GETTING THEIR SKATES, OAKLEY AND HUNTER ENTERED the rink. Christmas music played while red and green spotlights covered the ice. Oakley grasped Hunter's hand tightly as she found her balance on the ice. A Christmas tree with presents graced the middle of the rink, and they joined the other couples skating around.

After the song finished, a man's voice came over the loudspeaker. "We will begin our next Christmas song game. Please use caution and beware of those around you as we play this next song."

Oakley and Hunter joined in on a skating version of red light/green light. With the entire rink covered by red and green light patterns, they skated on the green lights, and had to stop on the red when the song stopped. They stayed in for the first couple rounds, then landed on the green squares when the song stopped. They skated to the middle of the rink, using the smaller inner circles to skate until the game was over.

"That was really fun," Oakley said.

Hunter agreed.

The song ended, and they joined in for a couple's game on the next song. The Christmas song talked about mistletoe and snowy winter nights. When spotlights landed on a couple, they kissed. It was an amusing game to stop in the middle of an ice rink to share a kiss. The rest of the skaters cheered and made noise. Suddenly the light surrounded her and Hunter.

He pulled her hand, then skated backwards so he was facing her. He raised an eyebrow. "What do you say, Oaks?"

She skated closer to him. "It's all part of the fun," she said.

That was all the encouragement he seemed to need. He scooped her up into his arms, and lifted her from the ice to kiss her.

Oakley melted into his kiss, not caring about anyone around them. The light soon faded from them, she could feel it more than see it, but she didn't release from his kiss. Ice skating with him was like dancing in a cloud, pure magic.

THE ENCHANTMENT OF SKATING WITH HUNTER LAST NIGHT WAS still running through Oakley's head the entire way to her parents' house. Her mom had said that there was an urgent surprise at home, but she hadn't said what. She knew Hunter was over at the Johnson's General Store, so that ruled Hunter out of any involvement. She rounded the corner, and the house came into view. She quickly parked the car and jumped out.

"Travis! You're here early!" Oakley said, as she ran up the front steps. "We weren't expecting you until right before Christmas."

Travis gave her a hug. "I thought I'd come early and spend a little more time with you."

Oakley smiled. "That's great."

Travis tilted his head. "So how long have you and Hunter been an item?"

Oakley blanched. In her head it was years, but in reality, it had only been a few weeks. How did Travis know about it? "Did Hunter tell you we're dating?"

Travis shrugged. "He didn't need to, your face said it all."

Oakley blushed. "A few weeks."

Travis nodded. "Is that why he's in town?"

Oakley shook her head. "He didn't come to town for me. He came to help with the Johnson's General Store. That's where he is now."

"Cool."

"That's all you have to say? Cool?" Oakley asked, disbelief settling in her stomach. No way was she getting off that easy. She could feel the lecture from her brother starting. He'd tell her something about dating his best friend.

Travis shrugged. "What should I say about it?"

Oakley blinked. "I don't know, I'm just surprised you don't have anything to say."

"He's a good guy, and he was my best friend growing up."

"I know that."

"You could pick a lot of people worse than him to date."

Oakley rolled her eyes. "That's reassuring."

"I don't know what you want me to say."

"Okay. Well, if you're cool with it?"

"I'm cool with it." Travis headed off the porch toward his rental car.

"Are you staying for dinner tonight or do you have other plans?"

Travis unlocked the car with the remote. "I'll be back for dinner."

Oakley nodded and then walked inside.

CHAPTER 20

Hunter packed up his tools. He'd be back later tonight to finish up some more work, but right now he was excited to have dinner with Oakley and her parents. Ellen had been doting more than usual. He and Oakley hadn't specifically told her parents they were dating, but he was sure it hadn't escaped Ellen's notice.

He tucked his tools under a work bench, and said bye to the rest of the volunteers. He walked outside and stopped when he saw someone next to his truck.

"Travis. Hey." He walked toward his friend, the feeling of possibly being punched had him gritting his teeth to prepare for the blow.

Travis smiled, shook Hunter's hand and gave him a slap on the back. "Hunter. You sly dog, dating my sister."

Hunter coughed. "Did Oakley tell you we were dating?"

Travis raised both eyebrows. "Aren't you dating her?"

Hunter nodded. "Yes."

Travis shrugged. "You just told me."

"I guess I did," he said, feeling awkward since they hadn't really discussed their relationship. They hadn't even talked to her parents about it, and he was staying with them.

Travis grinned. "So, you like my sister?"

"I do. Does that make things awkward?"

Travis shrugged. "I don't want details about you kissing my sister. That *would* be awkward."

"So, you're not gonna punch me?" Hunter asked, with a laugh.

Travis laughed. "Not unless you give me a reason to punch you."

"Fair," Hunter said.

"Are you heading to dinner?"

"Back at your parents' place, yeah."

He nodded. "Great. Well it will be an amusing dinner time, to say the least."

"You're sure you don't mind me dating your sister?"

Travis scratched his jaw. "Would it make a difference if I minded?"

Hunter shrugged. "I plan to keep dating her, so I guess not."

"Just don't break her heart," Travis said firmly.

"I don't plan on it," he said, knowing that from his track record so far with Oakley, he didn't want heartbreak in the equation on either end.

HUNTER WAS GLAD TRAVIS HAD SHOWED UP BEFORE DINNER TO

talk to him about dating Oakley. It made dinner time more relaxed, that is, until dessert was served.

"My Three Musketeers together at last. Just like old times. Christmas has definitely come early for us," Ellen said to no one in particular.

Andy answered. "It certainly has."

Travis widened his eyes. "Not quite like old times though, Mom. Last time I checked I wasn't the odd one in the group."

Oakley blushed furiously, but didn't say anything.

"Not that I mind, of course," Travis continued. "I just never saw it coming—my sister falling for my best friend." He shook his head.

Ellen covered her mouth. "Is that true?"

Oakley swallowed, studying Hunter's face. "We're taking things slow."

"But so far so good," Hunter added.

Oakley nodded, then focused on her dessert.

Ellen clapped her hands together. "I feel like I have so much to prepare for before Christmas."

Oakley looked up. "Mom, it's the same preparation that you had before."

Ellen shook her head. "Yes, but it's not *exactly* the same."

AFTER THE DINNER CONVERSATION ENDED, HUNTER AND OAKLEY went for a walk outside.

"So, I guess the cat's out of the bag," Hunter said, gauging the moment with Oakley.

"Looks like it is. Sorry about that. Trav cornered me when I came over for dinner. I assumed he'd talked to you about it, so there was no sense in denying it."

"He pulled the same trick with me! Are you okay with it?"

Oakley nodded. "You?"

Hunter was more than okay with it. "It was bound to happen eventually."

"It's only a matter of time before the whole town knows."

"Gotta love small towns for the way stories spread," Hunter said.

Oakley bit her lip. "I know we were trying to keep it quiet until we figured out this … thing … between us, but what does this mean for telling your family? I mean, would someone from Golden Ridge talk to your mom about it?"

Hunter blew out a breath. Likely Ellen would be among the first to call his mom. He wanted something long-term with Oakley, and he wanted to be the one to tell his family. "I've been thinking about that. What would you say to coming up to Colorado for some of the holiday celebrations?"

"Christmas with your family?" Oakley asked eagerly.

"Or right after. Until New Year's? They'd love to see you, and we can tell them together."

Oakley nodded. "I'll talk to my mom about keeping the news to herself for now, and that we want to spend some of the holiday up with your family."

"You're sure you don't mind?"

"It will be great," she said.

Hunter breathed in the moment, then wrapped Oakley up in a kiss. "Thank you," he said.

She squeezed his hand, and they walked back to the house.

Hunter opened the door for her, and they stepped inside.

"You're under the mistletoe," Travis said from the stairs.

Hunter looked up at the same time Oakley did. "That wasn't there before."

Travis grinned. "You're right, it wasn't."

Hunter looked to Oakley, a mixture of so many emotions on her face, then spoke to Travis. "Thanks for the heads up, but I'm not kissing your sister in front of you."

Travis waved the suggestion away. "Obviously not. I'm headed up to my room. You two take your time."

"Trav—" Oakley started to say, but Travis interrupted her.

"Not listening, not looking. You kids have fun."

Oakley turned to Hunter, her eyebrows drawn together. "It's not that I don't like kissing you—" she began.

Hunter nodded. "Just a bad memory from before. I get it."

Oakley nodded. "I'm just not sure how to separate it."

He cradled her chin. "Maybe it's time to make a new memory. A happy one with the mistletoe, instead of what happened nine years ago."

"It's a little risky, don't you think?" she asked.

He nodded. It was more than a little risky. It was a lot risky. "But will we never have a mistletoe kiss because the last one was so painful?" If that was the case, it was better to know that now. He could avoid mistletoes if that was what she wanted. "Say the word."

She bit her lip only for a second before shaking her head.

"No?" he asked, trying to read her thoughts and answer his own question. Disappointment shot through him.

"No, it's not a no." She smiled slowly. "It would be silly to avoid a tradition just based on one moment."

Hunter didn't hesitate. He scooped her up in his arms,

letting his lips caress hers. He pulled her close, not wanting to let her go. Years of wanting to change the way their mistletoe kiss ended swam across his mind, but he ignored everything but the sensation and feeling of her. She sighed lightly when their lips parted, her long lashes fluttering open.

She smiled, then wrapped her arms around him again for another kiss. Their lips danced together slowly, tenderly.

When their kiss ended, he was speechless, having already said everything he needed to without words.

CHAPTER 21

Oakley was still reeling from her mistletoe kiss with Hunter a few days ago. Sure, they'd kissed a few other times since then, but their mistletoe kiss do-over carried so much more meaning than the others. For the first time they were both on the same page. There were only four days until Christmas, and everything was going her way. They were making huge progress on the Johnson's store, and she was dating Hunter. She was working hard on his Christmas present whenever she wasn't with him. Her order would arrive by December 23, just in time for Christmas.

Oakley spent the day pulling together as many donated Christmas decorations as she could get her hands on. The Johnson's were coming into town tomorrow, just before Christmas. Their good friends and neighbors, the Parks, had asked them to come and celebrate for at least a few days of their Christmas time. After staying with family for the last several weeks, they'd agreed to come back to Golden Ridge for the

Annual Golden Ridge Christmas Party. The Johnsons had always donated the food and decorations for the party, but this year the Parks told them that all of the planning had been taken care of. The venue for the party had changed to the newly rebuilt General Store, of course, but they didn't know that.

The store bustled with volunteers. Oakley carried another box of tinsel to the front windows. She searched for an empty space on the Christmas tree to add the decoration, but it was already bursting with ornaments and trimmings. She placed the box at the base of the tree and made her way over to Hunter.

An anonymous Christmas donation had been made to the store, stocking it almost completely with goods, and delivering furniture for their living quarters above the store. Hunter stood next to the door giving directions to the movers with the large cardboard boxes.

Oakley could not contain her excitement. "This is quite the Christmas miracle," Oakley said in wonder, gesturing to the large furniture truck outside the door.

Hunter nodded. "The town is very generous."

"You wouldn't happen to know where this last-minute donation came from, would you? We didn't have the budget to furnish the upstairs."

"Maybe someone just decided to fill a need."

"Well, I hope that the anonymous donor knows how much he is appreciated around here."

Hunter shrugged, but smiled. "I'm sure whoever it was wasn't worried about that."

"Still though. It's above and beyond anything I could have originally hoped for with this project."

"We're cutting it down to the wire though. What time did

the Parks say the Johnsons would arrive tomorrow? It feels like we don't have enough time to get everything done."

Oakley looked around the General Store. Everything was in order, and only a few decorations were left. People added Christmas decor to the shelves, and a banner welcoming the Johnsons back to town was being hung up across the store. Oakley had designed it, but everyone who volunteered or helped in some way was invited to sign it. Signatures covered the entire banner in permanent marker.

"It seems like everything is taken care of," she said in relief.

Hunter nodded. "Down here it is, but there's still the living space upstairs."

"You keep directing traffic and I'll go help upstairs," she said.

He squeezed her hand. "Thanks, Oakley."

She wanted to thank him again, wishing she could tell him just how much his donation had meant to her. Without him they may never have been able to complete such a grandiose project in such a short amount of time. Especially not like this. He'd worked longer and harder on the construction side than anyone else. He'd given up his time and his own work to come back to his hometown to help when help was needed. And in the process, they'd found something between them. She leaned forward and gave him a small peck on the lips before hurrying toward the stairs to help set up the bedrooms and arrange the furniture.

Boxes of home decor lined the family room space including comforters, pillows, and everything for putting a bedroom together. Once the movers set up the furniture, she focused on decorating. She made the beds, hung towels, and stocked the kitchen drawers. Finally, the only thing left to do was decorate the small Christmas tree that was in the family room. She positioned the ornaments that were in the last cardboard box, but the tree didn't quite look festive enough yet, even with the lights on. Suddenly she had a use for the tinsel she'd left downstairs. She bounded down the stairs, then made her way to the front of the store. Most of the volunteers were gone now, and she hadn't realized how long she'd spent getting the living quarters ready.

The box of tinsel was at the base of the tree, right where she'd left it. She stopped to admire the finished store. It seemed so full of life from all the decorations and the care put into the rebuild. This was what Christmas was about.

"What do you think, Oaks?" Hunter said from a ladder, a large snowflake dangling from his hand. Rows and rows of them hung over the aisles. "It's coming together, isn't it?"

"It really is. It's beautiful. I'm almost finished upstairs," she said.

Hunter nodded. "I'll be finished soon, too, and then we can go on our date." He smiled at her, and her heart warmed.

"I can't wait," she said, and hurried back upstairs to finish decorating.

The tree was completed in no time, and a rush of excitement filled her. Hunter had talked about their surprise date for tonight for the last week, but he hadn't given any details away that would help her guess what they'd be doing.

Hunter was still on the ladder when she came down. "I'm just finishing up the snowflakes."

"Where is everyone?" she asked.

"There are still a few volunteers in the back, finishing up the last-minute preparations. The rest are done and gone. It's been a long day."

"Can I help you with anything?" she asked.

"I'm almost done. I have a few more snowflakes to hang, and then I have a few sprigs of mistletoe to add in," he said, wiggling his eyebrows.

She laughed. "Put me to work," she said with a grin.

"There's one more box of decorations that was just delivered to your parents' house. Would you mind picking that up while I finish hanging up these snowflakes? I was gonna just bring it over tomorrow morning before the Johnsons arrive, but maybe we should just finish it up tonight?"

Oakley nodded. "Sure. What's in the box so I grab the right one?"

He smiled. "Matryoshkas, the Russian nesting dolls."

"Like the ones Mrs. Johnson used to display at Christmas every year?"

He nodded. "I'm hoping they are a close enough replica to the ones she lost. We won't know until we see them up on the shelf."

"You are something, Hunter."

"I'm just glad they arrived in time. Ebay couldn't guarantee arrival before Christmas, but I just got a notification on my phone that they were delivered less than an hour ago. Hopefully it will be a fun surprise for them."

"I'm sure it will be." She grinned, she would have kissed him right then if he hadn't been on a ladder. "Speaking of fun surprises. Where are we going for our date tonight?"

He smiled. "Oaks, the point of a surprise is that you are *surprised*."

She bit her lip. "What is the dress code for tonight? I still don't know what we're doing."

"Wear something you're comfortable eating and dancing in."

"Are we going dancing?"

He grinned. "That's part of the evening. We still have to see if I can step on your toes less times than John did, remember?"

Oakley shushed him, her eyes widening. "Don't say that so loud. People will think I really hold that against him, and I don't."

Hunter laughed. "Fair enough."

"I'll be back in a few with your Russian dolls."

"They're not for me. They're for Mrs. Johnson."

"*Charmer.*"

He smiled. "Admit it, you like that about me."

"You're right, I really do."

He smiled like he'd won the biggest prize at the carnival.

OAKLEY STUDIED THE THREE PACKAGES ADDRESSED TO HUNTER on the front porch. One was significantly larger than the others. Would that be it? He hadn't said that there were multiple packages, but maybe he didn't know.

She bit her lip, debating if she should bring all three. Since coming to Golden Ridge, he'd ordered several things online.

Travis came out the front door. "I thought you were going on a date tonight," Travis said. "What are you doing here?"

"Just picking up Hunter's packages for the store. He wanted to get the last of the decorations finished tonight."

Travis picked up the heaviest of the three boxes. "I'll help you load them."

Oakley popped the trunk open. "How do you know about my date tonight?"

"It's all Hunter's been talking about this week."

"He didn't mention what we're doing, did he?"

Travis raised an eyebrow. "Nice try, Oakley. I know he's surprising you. I'm sworn to secrecy."

"C'mon, Trav, give me one *little* hint."

Travis laughed. "You'll know soon enough. And you'll like it."

Oakley rolled her eyes. "You're no help at all. Whose side are you actually on here?"

Travis looked up toward the sky. "I'm pretty sure in this case, I don't have to pick sides."

"Fine. I guess it's good to know I'll like the surprise."

"I didn't say a word."

Oakley pulled up to the General Store and picked up the largest box. As she passed the first large window display, she admired the handiwork of the decorations. She knew the Johnsons would be so happy when they saw it the next day.

She pushed her way through the door, noting that they still needed to hang the bell so that it rang every time someone walked through the door. They chose to save that until the end so they weren't hearing it throughout construction and all the finishing touches.

Oakley headed toward the far end of the Johnson's General Store, but was stopped dead in her tracks. Hunter was kissing Gina Stowell under the mistletoe he'd just hung. Her heart pounded as she tried to maintain her grip on the box, but it was no use. The package fell to the ground, and with it her heart fell and shattered into a thousand pieces.

Hunter turned to her. "Oakley—wait—"

Oakley tried to breathe, but the wind had been knocked out of her. She left the box on the floor, not worrying about whether the contents had survived the fall, and ran back through the door. What was she supposed to do now? Her mind blanked as her entire body went numb. She was so stupid, and she hadn't seen it coming. She closed her eyes against the pain that threatened to engulf her.

She gasped for air and answers, as she stormed back to her car.

Years of emotion, love, hope, and excitement vaporized, with no trace that they ever existed. She'd misread all the signs. Misread everything. He'd practically *advertised* that he didn't have long relationships with the women he dated. And here she'd thought she was different—that she was special—and that their spending every day for weeks together meant something.

She fished out her keys, and unlocked the car. Her world, her Christmas, *everything* was gone, and there was nothing she could do about it. What was she going to do? And what was she supposed to do about the boxes in her trunk?

"Oakley, wait. It wasn't me. She caught me off guard. She surprised me and for a moment I thought it was you—" Hunter's voice rang in an unusually echoing and distant way, but maybe it was just the fury of the blood rushing through her ears that made it sound different.

"I don't want to hear it," she said. "It's *never* your fault … it's just the tradition and the rule of the mistletoe."

"Oakley, it's the truth" His eyes pleaded for understanding.

Something inside her snapped. She opened up the trunk and pulled out the other two boxes, practically shoving them into his arms. "These are also yours."

His mouth held a lazy grin, and she wanted to smack the look that she'd loved right off his face.

"Technically both of these will belong to you on Christmas."

Anger flared in the form of a bitter laugh. "Don't waste your time. We're done."

His eyes widened like she'd actually slapped him. "I … don't understand."

She shook her head. "You know, there was a time in my life when I believed everything you said. When I gave you every benefit of every doubt. And look where it's gotten me." On the wrong side of love. Every. Time. She pushed aside all the past heartbreaks because of him. Her current one would take more than all her strength to deal with.

"Oakley, I love you." His dark, blue eyes were sincere.

Oakley snorted. "Sure you do." She moved toward the driver's car door.

"Oakley, I'm sorry. She caught me off guard. You believe me, don't you, Oaks?" He said her name soft, like a caress.

She almost fell for the sincerity in his eyes, but then the sight of him kissing Gina flooded through her again, and she balled her fists at her side. What a stupid question to ask. "I thought you were different, but you're not. You just can't help being the Mistletoe King."

"Oakley, I'm not the Mistletoe King any more. I promise I'm not. If you had any idea how that entire Christmas has haunted me, you'd believe that." He adjusted the boxes he held and reached out to her with one hand, but she pulled away.

She steeled herself against the moment. There was no way to verify anything he'd said. And as for loving her—well, that was a line she couldn't fall for. "It's my own fault for loving you like I have." She held up her hand. "I don't want to see you again."

Pain etched across his face. "Oakley—"

She got in her car and reversed out of the parking stall. Adrenaline coursed through her. She'd watched him kiss another woman, and all the apologies in the world hadn't changed that. She couldn't be with someone who did that to her no matter what his excuse was. It was time to get over Hunter Paxton once and for all.

Numbness filled all of her senses, but somehow she made it into her house. Her phone buzzed in her purse, but she ignored it. She was in no mood to listen to Hunter's excuses again.

She wanted to curl up on the couch and cry when her phone rang again. She dug in her purse for the offending object. It was time to turn her device off for the rest of the night.

As she was about to power down, she saw the name on the screen. Travis. Still, her brother calling her probably meant that Hunter was close by on the other end of the line. She didn't want him tangled up in this, and she needed to let them know that.

She answered the phone, but before she could speak, Travis started into the conversation.

"Oakley? I was beginning to think you weren't there," Travis said.

"Look, Trav, I meant what I said to Hunter when I told him we were finished. I don't want to see him again, and nothing you say about it is gonna change my mind."

There was a long pause on the other end of the line. Finally, Travis said, "Are you okay?"

The concern in his voice broke the dam that had held back the tears. With the floodgates open, she slumped onto the couch, her eyes unable to focus on anything.

"Oaks?"

She sniffed, but the sob came out. "No. I'm not. I'm so stupid."

"Where are you? Are y'all already at The Pepper Ridge?"

That was where Hunter had planned their date? At the fancy country club two cities away? Her heart rate quickened for a moment at the trouble he'd gone to, to create that kind of an evening. Her head pounded. It didn't matter how much trouble it was. He'd kissed Gina. "I'm at home," she said.

"I'm coming over," Travis said.

"I'll be fine. You don't need to come over."

"Y'all just broke up?" His voice was kind. "What happened?"

She snorted. "What happened is I was stupid enough to believe that people could change. And they don't. He's still a player."

"He was never a player, Oakley."

"Don't defend him to me. I watched him for *years*, never going on more than one or two dates with everyone he dated. He's still the Mistletoe King, or whatever you used to call him."

"We were best friends, Oaks, of course I teased him about it."

"I thought things were different this time, but nope. Him kissing Gina right before our date was a pretty big sign."

"*This* time?"

He focused on the timing and not on the fact that she'd

caught Hunter kissing someone else less than an hour before her date. She sighed. "It doesn't matter. It's over."

"Oakley, come on over. Mom should be home soon, and y'all can talk and—"

"No. I can't be over there right now. Not with him there."

"How can I help you feel better?"

Oakley let the tears fall, not bothering to wipe them away any longer. Years of heartbreak and old wounds flooded her, and there was no way Travis would be able to fix any of it. "You can't. No one can. I just need some space right now."

"Y'all are—"

"Over. Done. And there's no going back this time." She bit her lip, holding in any more words that tried to escape. What was the point of telling Trav all her past woes? She'd been a lovesick teen who'd fallen for her older brother's best friend. Telling that to her brother now would only make her look pathetic. *Stupid*. She should have known better.

Travis sighed. "You know I never like seeing you sad."

She sniffed. "I know. Thanks for caring."

"I wish there was something I could do to help."

It was a sweet sentiment, but there was nothing he could do. "Just knowing you care helps," she said.

They said their goodbyes, and she hung up. She pulled a throw pillow close and buried herself in it. Cold pain sliced through her, cutting every feeling and emotion that tried to grow in her. She had thought that the pain from having her heart broken nine Christmases ago was the worst, but it didn't hold a candle to the raw intense agony of this one.

CHAPTER 22

Hunter circled Oakley's block a dozen times waiting for her to come home, and called her just as many. She didn't answer her phone or her front door. Maybe she'd gone for a drive, and he'd hoped by circling the small street he'd catch her driving into her garage. He racked his brain for the right words to say when he finally saw her in person. Gina had cornered him under the mistletoe, completely catching him off guard and kissing him. It was brief, not enjoyable, and he hadn't initiated it. Still. Oakley hadn't let him fully explain all of that.

He headed back to the outskirts and up the drive that was as familiar to him as his own house. The Larsen's house had Christmas lights shining from every window and large strings of bulbs illuminating the roofline and the mature trees.

"You're home early," Travis said from the porch swing as Hunter approached the steps.

Hunter nodded. Travis had been surprisingly cool about

him dating his sister, but now Hunter wasn't even sure what to say, or how much to say, about anything.

"Yeah, the date night didn't work out," he said, hoping to ease Travis into the conversation.

Travis's eyes widened. "She didn't like the idea of The Pepper Ridge?"

"We actually didn't get that far," he said, taking a deep breath and preparing to tell Travis how confused he was at the breakup. He'd thought things were going so well, and that the feelings he had for Oakley were mutual. But apparently they weren't strong enough to overcome Gina's decision to steal a kiss.

Travis stood up, his eyes hard. Without warning his fist came up, connecting with Hunter's face.

Hunter stumbled backwards. He caught his balance, but his face was on fire. His cheek throbbed below his right eye. Travis already knew, but he only had a piece of the story. "I know you think I deserve that, but I can explain. It's not what she thought," Hunter said, when he finally gained back his breath.

"I told you not to break her heart," Travis said, throwing another punch.

"I know how bad it looks, but she's the one who broke up with me," Hunter admitted, realizing that the words came out sounding like a pitiful excuse.

Travis shook his head, his voice sharp. "If you were looking for a fling, you picked the wrong girl, and you picked the wrong family to stay with."

"It was never a fling," Hunter said slowly, his mind reeling from the accusation.

Travis balled his fists and looked like he wanted to punch Hunter again. "Kissing Gina, of all people. Really, Hunter?"

Travis swung his arm, but Hunter blocked the blow before it connected with his other eye. "I can explain that."

Travis shook his head. "Explain? Wow, Hunter. I was hoping you were gonna deny that it happened." He swung at him again, and caught Hunter on the shoulder.

"Gina kissed me and took me completely by surprise," Hunter said between swings, as they danced around the porch together, connecting fist against face and shoulders. "I don't want to fight you."

"You can't treat my sister that way without one."

Hunter was not in the mood for a fight, but he was in the middle of it. "I told you I can explain. It's not what you think." After defending himself from three more blows, he finally threw a punch of his own. His fist connected with Travis's jaw, and he received another hit for it.

"I don't want an excuse, Hunter. She's my sister. You broke her heart." Travis landed another punch to the Hunter's face.

Blood trickled from his nose as Hunter tried to find a way to end the fight.

"Boys! What is going on?!" Ellen's sharp voice from the driveway brought Hunter back to their teenage years or younger. Her question was enough for them both to turn toward her. She surveyed them both.

Travis spoke first. "Sorry, mom."

"Sorry, mom," Hunter said. With the heat of the moment diluted, nausea at seeing the blood took over. He took a steadying breath.

"Can someone please explain this to me?" Ellen said, fire in her eyes.

Hunter was about to explain, but Travis cut him off. "Nothing. Hunter is just leaving tonight, and won't be able to stay through Christmas after all."

Hunter wanted to disagree, but what could he say?

The wrinkles on Ellen's forehead didn't disappear. "It always was hard to see you go, Hunter. But Travis, did you really need to give him two black eyes for leaving early?"

"I was just giving him something to remember this moment by," Travis said. He eyed Hunter, a challenge in his eyes warning him not to disagree. Hunter felt the weight of his friend's words.

"Travis Andrew Larsen, there are other ways to express frustration about people leaving than with your fists."

"Yes, ma'am," Travis said in a humbler tone, though when he looked at Hunter, the fire was still blazing.

"And Hunter, what is this about you leaving? I thought we had you for another week before you and Oakley left for your parents' house."

Hunter cleared his throat. "Like Travis said, a sudden change in plans."

Ellen frowned sympathetically. "Well, you'll have to come back soon. Maybe after you visit with your family you can come back this way."

"That's the trouble, mom. He's going back to his own life after the holidays. The Johnson's store is done, so his reason for coming back is gone."

Hunter wanted to disagree, but he couldn't, not without Travis likely telling the whole story to his mom. He sighed.

"Well, I hope you come back soon, whenever it is. You know you're always welcome."

Except that he wasn't right now. Not with Travis, and certainly not with Oakley. "Thanks," he said. "I've always felt like one of the family here."

"Now, let's get you boys cleaned up before those cuts get infected." She swept past them, leaving them no room for arguing.

An hour later, his bags were packed and he said his goodbyes to everyone. He gave Ellen a long hug, and blinked rapidly. The last time he'd left nine years ago, he hadn't had the closure of goodbyes, but he knew this time it was permanent.

Breaking up with Oakley was by far the worst pain of the day, over his two black eyes and split lip and seeing the blood up close. The remorse of leaving because of a breakup tore at him. Ellen eventually learning the wrong information about why they broke up stung, but it couldn't be helped. It was nothing compared to the ache he felt at losing Oakley.

Travis offered a handshake, probably because his mom had told him to be polite. Travis's grip was crushing, but they both said goodbye like they'd actually be friends the next time they saw each other.

"Have you said your goodbyes to Oakley?" Ellen asked.

"Not yet," Hunter said.

"You should. I imagine she'll want to see you. Do you have time before your red-eye?"

Hunter had his assistant book him a flight while he was packing. Travis may have started the lie about him needing to leave early, but if that was what he had to do, then he'd at least make the plans real. "I have time," he said, knowing it was in the opposite direction of the airport. His heart lurched at the idea. He needed to explain, and he didn't want to say goodbye. Not like this.

Ellen nodded her approval. "Oh, let me get one more thing," she said, and then she ran back into the house.

While she was gone, Hunter said goodbye to Andy. Andy wasn't one to show a lot of emotion or affection, but he brought Hunter into a hug. "Thank you for taking care of my daughter," he said, then smiled.

Hunter felt like a fraud, and all he could do was nod and push the lump in his throat down further. This whole moment felt unfair, but maybe there was still a chance to fix things. He could at least try. He'd go and apologize to Oakley in person, and explain everything.

Ellen came out of the house carrying four large presents. "Not all of your presents are wrapped yet, but I'll make sure Oakley brings the rest with her when she comes up to Colorado."

Hunter tried to protest, but his words were lost when Ellen started explaining the presents.

"Now this top one is for you and Oakley to open together, but it needs to be opened before the other ones," Ellen said.

"Maybe we should just leave it here and Oakley can open it for both of us," Hunter said.

"Nonsense," Ellen said. "You two can open it together right now."

Hunter's heart raced. "She's not here," he said.

Ellen smiled. "I know that, but when you go say goodbye, you can open it together."

Any possible thought of skipping Oakley's house was

dashed. He'd at least have to drop the present off. But maybe this was exactly what he needed. Things would work out. He knew it. It would be fine.

He smiled for the first time since Oakley had dumped him in front of the General Store. "I think that's a great idea," he said.

Ellen beamed. "I hope you both like it," she said, then explained the order of the other presents for him.

"I'm gonna need a bigger suitcase," he said, laughing.

"I thought you might say that." She opened the front door again and pulled out a duffle. "Here you go."

"Oh I don't want to take your—"

"You can borrow it and send it home with Oakley."

Hunter nodded, though he knew that wouldn't be possible at the moment, but maybe soon. If nothing else, it wouldn't be a hassle to mail it back when he was finished using it. "Thanks," he said.

Ellen smiled. "Only just make sure you take the cookies I packed in there out before you stack the presents inside."

Hunter gave her another hug. "You've always been so kind to me," he said.

"Have a safe flight," Ellen said. "And we'll see you soon."

Hunter swallowed. "I hope so."

Hunter took the cookies out and loaded the presents into the duffle bag. He drove around the rounded drive of the Larsen home, giving everyone a final wave. He hoped with his entire being that this wouldn't be the last time he was here. Only time would tell. In less than fifteen minutes he'd know whether or not he'd be able to repair the damage that was done today.

Hunter knocked on Oakley's front door. There was no answer. He rang the doorbell. Still nothing.

He tried calling her, and she wouldn't answer.

Finally, he took a picture of the Christmas-wrapped box with her front door in the background, and sent it to her with a text. **Your mom wants us to open this together tonight.**

He waited for a reply. He didn't want to tell her that he was leaving tonight. If they could patch things up, he could change his flight no problem. If Travis didn't want him staying at his parents' house, he'd gladly drive in from Sunset Meadows. He'd done it before, and he could do it again.

Footsteps sounded on the other side of the door. His heart leapt into his throat. "Oakley?" he said, putting his mouth close to the door.

"I meant what I said. We're over." Her voice was clear through the door.

His head pounded. He needed to tell Oakley the truth of what happened. "Oakley, she kissed me, and it came out of nowhere. She totally caught me off guard. I thought it was you at first because she covered my eyes from behind. I swear I wasn't trying to kiss anyone else."

"That's easy for the Mistletoe King to say."

"Please stop saying that. That's not who I am."

"That's the difference between us. I was stupid enough to believe that things were different this time. I won't make that same mistake again."

He knocked on the door. "Oakley, please open up. We need to talk. I've loved you for a long time. Does that count for nothing? Doesn't our history give us some kind of way to get through this?" More than anything he wanted to apologize to Oakley in person and show her his sincerity, but without her opening the door, there was no way to get that. He leaned against the doorframe. "I'm not interested in Gina."

"But you still kissed her."

"Oakley, it was a mistletoe kiss. I didn't initiate it. I'm in love with *you*." He'd always been in love with her. Frustration mounted at having to explain it through the front door instead of while she was in his arms.

"This is just history repeating itself. I'm done with living that way."

"Oakley—give me a chance to prove it."

Silence spread between them until she finally said, "My heart can't take any more heartbreak from you."

Hunter stared at her front door. All his hope that they'd make up after this misunderstanding was dashed. She didn't want more heartbreak, and that was understandable. He didn't want it either, and yet he'd risked it this time. He was all in, but it hadn't been enough. "Mine can't either."

"Please go away. I don't want to see you again. Ever."

Those eleven words packed more of a punch than Travis's fists. "That's a long time."

"Goodbye, Hunter."

"Please give us a chance, Oaks." When five minutes passed with no response, Hunter left the present on the doorstep.

The radio silence from her while he drove to the airport was brutal, but with each passing mile he focused on his new resolve. He had to grow up and get over Oakley Larsen once and for all. It was time to put her behind him. He couldn't spend the rest of his life pining for what might have been with her. He had to move on.

"I'll Be Home for Christmas" played through the speakers, and Hunter turned off the music. Oakley's favorite Christmas music wasn't going to play in his head right now. Besides, just because he was going to visit his family for Christmas didn't mean that he was going to be home for Christmas. He was leaving home for the final time. Golden Ridge, Oakley—especially Oakley. It was time to get over her. It would be his Christmas wish, and his New Year's Resolution every year until it happened. And it would happen. He would make sure of that.

CHAPTER 23

Oakley looked into the sea of smiling faces who waited eagerly with her for the Johnsons to arrive at the General Store. Practically the entire town lined both sides of the street for the event, filling the sidewalks and spilling out onto Main Street. Though the sun was above the horizon, bathing the world in light, all of Main Street was still lit with Christmas lights in the windows.

As the sound of the Johnson's old car hit their ears, the entire town began cheering and waving signs.

Oakley could see the car, but she couldn't quite make out the Johnson's expressions since the car drove slower when they noticed the crowds. They rolled down their windows and stuck their arms out, waving to everyone as they passed them by.

Oakley saw the moment Mrs. Johnson noticed the store. She stopped waving through the open window, a gasp escaping before she covered her mouth with both hands. Mr. Johnson quickly parked the car, only to be surrounded by the sea of neighbors and friends who had gathered for the event.

The crowd parted, making a pathway for Mr. and Mrs. Johnson to walk through to the front of their store. The crowd followed behind them, filling the available spaces in the store, the rest gathering on the outside.

A lump formed in Oakley's throat when she saw Mr. Johnson's eyes fill with tears. He was too overcome to speak. Mrs. Johnson had plenty of words for both of them. "Our store! Our house! It's here. This is like a dream."

Mr. Johnson spoke up. "Not a dream. A Christmas miracle." He hugged his wife.

A group close to them pointed out the mistletoe, and the sweet couple kissed. Cheers surrounded them. Then Mr. Johnson began reading the large banner, saying each name on the banner aloud. The entire process took several minutes, and he expressed his thanks to everyone.

Oakley drew in a ragged breath, blinking rapidly. Mr. Johnson had said her name right after Hunter's, like they belonged together. They'd signed the banner together. She'd spent the entire time on the project working with Hunter. He'd been so essential to this moment.

Her heart ached. She'd pictured this moment with him. She scanned the crowd, forcing herself not to notice him, but there was no sign of him anyway. Maybe he'd waved to the Johnsons from further down the street. She pushed her way back through the General Store doors and into the street. Several volunteers were at the end of the street, manning tables of donuts and juice.

Every person she passed thanked her for her service and for

her organization of this project. She smiled, and passed on the praise to everyone who had helped volunteer in some way.

Her brother and parents were part of the next group waiting their turn to go into the store to greet the Johnsons. She waved to them, but they were too far from her to ask where Hunter might be. Travis's face looked a little swollen, but when she glanced back toward Travis for a closer look, his back was already toward her.

Oakley mingled for over two hours as more people filtered in and out of the store. This should have been a moment of complete joy and excitement for her—Golden Ridge had done the seemingly impossible task of building and funding the General Store and the Johnson's house—yet the entire experience felt wrapped in sadness. Hunter was nowhere to be seen, and Oakley couldn't tell if not seeing him was contributing to her sadness or not.

She thought back to last night. He'd left the present to both of them on her front porch. She wouldn't open it, not until Christmas. She'd explain to her mom why later, but she just couldn't do it right now. Her pain felt too raw. If she didn't need to be at the Johnson's Grand Opening to help coordinate and attend, she would have taken the whole day off and stayed in bed.

Maybe there was still time for a full day of chocolate and binge watching. She needed something mindless, something where she didn't have to think and wasn't reminded of Hunter at every turn. This morning had been a rude awakening of that.

Every building down Main Street had fresh memories with Hunter. Even the few minutes she'd been inside the General

Store had her envisioning Hunter hanging up all the snowflakes that floated so delicately from the ceiling.

Oakley almost pulled out her phone to text Hunter to see where he was, but at that moment she saw the mistletoe and her resolve hardened. She couldn't call him. She wouldn't.

Mr. Johnson came up and gave her a hug. "I hear I have you to thank for this, young lady."

Oakley smiled. "Everyone helped. It wasn't just me."

Mr. Johnson shook his head. "I've heard from multiple people that without you and your boyfriend it never would have happened."

Oakley's cheeks heated at the mention of Hunter. She wanted to correct Mr. Johnson about their relationship status, but now wasn't the time. Not on the Johnson's big day. Besides, she would give the credit where it was due. "Hunter's generosity in time and funding made all the difference on this project."

Mr. Johnson nodded. "That's Hunter for you. Always thinking of other people and putting them before himself. Where is he? I want to thank him personally."

Oakley shrugged. "I'm not sure where he is," she said, though she knew he was around, he was likely just avoiding her. "I'll send him your way when I find him."

Mr. Johnson nodded. "And, Oakley, one more thing."

Oakley turned. "Yes?"

"My wife wants to thank you personally for the beautiful Matryoshkas. They are exactly like the ones she had before. You're so kind to track them down for her."

Oakley tilted her head. She definitely couldn't take credit for that one. "How does she know it was me?" she asked. Maybe they just assumed she'd made all the decisions when it came to the house and the store. The truth was that she only coordinated things and she let others have ownership in the process too.

"She found your note underneath them," Mr. Johnson smiled. "Truthfully, of anything, those dolls are the decoration that made all of this feel like home again."

Oakley smiled. "I'm glad she likes them. Hunter also helped with that."

Mr. Johnson nodded. "The two of you seem like a good match."

"You think so?" Oakley asked, almost wanting to shatter Mr. Johnson's illusionary bubble, but then thought the better of it. What would be the point? It wouldn't matter.

He nodded. "I may be old, Oakley, but I'm not blind. That boy would come into my store and wait until you showed up before he'd make his selection on treats. Some days he knew he'd work late and would miss you, so he'd always ask me to give you your favorite chocolate. Of course, he'd picked it out earlier. I remember there was a year where you had a new favorite on almost a weekly basis."

Oakley smiled, remembering that year. "All this time, I thought you just liked me more than everyone else and gave me free chocolates."

"I like you a lot, Oakley, and you reminded me of my own daughter, but I would have been out of business a long time ago if I'd have given away chocolate for free every day."

Oakley blinked. She remembered Mr. Johnson spoiling her with chocolate as early as elementary school, and it continued until well after Hunter had moved away to college. "What about when I was a junior and a senior and Hunter was off at college?"

Mr. Johnson shrugged. "Hunter paid a chocolate tab. He said he didn't want me to pay for it, and he was the one who started the tradition."

Oakley blanched. "I wouldn't have taken all the chocolate if I'd known he was paying for it."

Mr. Johnson smiled. "I always thought it was a nice gesture."

Oakley didn't have the words to combat Mr. Johnson. Whatever else Hunter Paxton was, he was always thoughtful. "He's full of surprises."

"And it looks like he finally found the way to your heart."

"Finally?" Oakley raised her eyebrows.

Mr. Johnson tilted his head. "Well, it's taken this long, hasn't it?"

Oakley nodded. Mr. Johnson seemed to think that Hunter had liked her for a long time. Could that be true? Could there have been truth to his words yesterday that he really did love her longer than just this visit back to Golden Ridge? And did that change things between them? "I'd better go … find him," she said, and said goodbye to Mr. Johnson.

She kept an eye out for Hunter for the next hour while she socialized with the town. Obviously, he was doing a very good job of avoiding her, which made total sense after their conversation last night. She sighed. She couldn't reconcile him kissing Gina at all. Each time the memory floated across her consciousness it felt like another punch in the gut, knocking the wind out of her. Eventually she'd be over at her parents' house, and then she and Hunter would discuss everything. But until then, her instincts were still on high alert, boiling mad that everything had fallen apart.

OAKLEY WENT OVER TO HER PARENTS' HOUSE FOR DINNER. Nervous energy ran through her. She'd sat next to Hunter for weeks, holding his hand at the dinner table, even when Travis was there. Would it look weird for them to not sit by each other? Probably. Still she wasn't going to cancel all the Christmas traditions she loved just because she and Hunter were no longer on the same page.

Travis opened the door, his face bruised.

"What happened to you?" Oakley asked. "You look like you got into a fight."

"Uh, it was something like that," Travis said.

Oakley took a closer look. "No seriously, what happened? You look awful."

"It was nothing," Travis murmured.

Their mom walked by. "That's what happens when you pick a fight with your best friend." She shook her head. "What got into the two of you any way, Travis?"

Travis broke his eye contact with Oakley. "Mom, it wasn't a big deal."

Her mom groaned. "He goes home early to his family with two shiners and a split lip and you don't call that a big deal? How will his family think we've treated him when he shows up?"

Travis flexed his fingers. "We took a few punches at each other. We do that sometimes."

Their mom sighed. "Never in my life have I seen you that worked up about anything. And don't think for one minute that I bought your story that the fight was about him leaving early. Next time you see him, you work it out." She glanced to Oakley and then back again to Travis. "No need to have your poor behavior ruin others' relationships in the family."

"I'll remember that," Travis said, starting to follow their mom toward the kitchen.

Oakley grabbed his arm, and he turned back around. She raised an eyebrow, but he shrugged her off. "Wait," she said.

"Spare me the lecture, Oakley. I just got one of those from mom."

Oakley pulled on his arm. "I'm not gonna lecture you. I want answers."

Travis rolled his eyes, but followed her back onto the front porch.

Oakley paced back and forth. "You and Hunter got into a fight?"

"Mom just told you that much."

"And then Hunter left? He's *gone*?" That was news to her. The fraying nerves that had kept her on edge all day fell to the ground. "I don't understand."

"Look. I admit I'm not always the best older brother, but after what he did to you … I wasn't gonna let that fly."

"So you gave him a black eye?"

Travis shook his head, then grinned. "Nope. I gave him two black eyes."

"And a split lip, I heard."

"He'll heal from it," Travis said. "I could have broken his

nose, but decided two black eyes would get his attention. He can't break your heart without consequences like that."

Oakley leaned against the porch rail. "He's done it before," she mumbled to herself, but he wouldn't do it again. Not after today. "Thanks for defending me though. It's ... sweet of you."

Travis came and stood next to her, leaning in the same position she was. "What do you mean he's done it before?"

She hadn't realized her words were audible. She shook her head, not wanting to go into how this was the third time her heart had been broken by Hunter, and now two times had revolved around mistletoe. "It really doesn't matter."

Travis studied her for a long minute, and Oakley turned her attention to the darkening horizon. "Are you referring to Senior Prom?"

"What? No." Oakley said the words a little too quickly. The reality was she'd only been thinking about nine years ago, not beyond that.

Travis scrunched his brow. "I've always wondered why you didn't go with Hunter to Senior Prom."

Oakley shrugged. "It wasn't my Senior Prom, it was his."

"Still, wouldn't it be flattering to go with someone when you were a sophomore? I'd think most sophomore girls would jump at the chance to go."

Oakley laughed. "This is the strangest conversation to have with my brother. That was high school. Besides it's not like he liked me then. He'd just run out of senior girls to date."

"I think that's what I thought at the time, too. But whether you caught onto it or not, Oakley, he really liked you then."

Oakley snorted. "No, he didn't."

Travis raised his eyebrows. "He was my best friend from the

time we were in preschool together. I'm pretty sure I would know."

Anger flared. She'd studied Hunter for as long as she could remember—had liked him and loved him for almost as long. She'd categorized his looks, his facial expressions, everything. But admitting that to her brother now would only be pathetic. She shouldn't care. She didn't care. But she would set the record straight. "I heard the two of you talking the day he asked me out. He didn't like me then."

Just like he hadn't really loved her now. She swallowed down the bitterness. She'd known since she was a sophomore and even before that his attention span for dating was small—one date, maybe two. He'd even admitted it again, but here she'd thought she was different. That she was special. That he might settle down. She'd thought she'd cried out all of her tears last night, but a fresh new wave threatened to spill.

Travis looked at her, his brows knit together. "What did you hear us talking about?"

"I hardly remember now."

"Not true. Tell me."

She shrugged. The words would sound petty, childish, and yet in light of the last twenty-four hours, they still stung. She kept her gaze on the horizon. "That he'd dated all the senior girls, and had waited until the last minute to ask me." She exhaled. "I was the backup date."

"Wow, Oakley, I had no idea."

"What do you mean you had no idea? He was talking to *you* when he said those things. You gave your permission or whatever for him to take me out, but it wasn't like it meant anything. So why would I go to a dance with someone who didn't want to go with me?" The words spilled out of her with such force that she almost had to catch her breath after the explanation.

"That's not what I meant. I meant, I had no idea that *you* liked him back when we were in high school. Wow. If that doesn't just turn the tables."

Oakley let out a laugh that sounded like a cough. "What are you talking about? *Me* liking him?"

He shook his head. "I remember that conversation in the treehouse, Oakley. I remember thinking that if he was done with dating all the senior girls that you were the *natural* choice of a sophomore to take to Senior Prom. So, yeah, I didn't think too much of it at the time, to be honest. I didn't think he actually liked you on the day he checked with me."

"See." Oakley blinked back the tears that threatened to create waterfall-like paths down her cheeks.

"Oh, I do see. But *you* don't."

"What's that supposed to mean?"

Travis leaned his head back. "You didn't see how disappointed he was when you turned him down, but I did."

She brushed off her brother's observation as something inconsequential. "He didn't know how to handle rejection. No girl had ever turned him down before."

"I thought the same, at first. Then I noticed how sad he was. It took him a ridiculous amount of time to pick someone else to go with. I pressured him into picking someone, but at that point, he'd basically said he wasn't going to the dance at all. So he asked another sophomore, and I don't think he cared much after the first two or three dances when his date decided to chat next to the refreshment table. He went out and shot hoops."

"So?"

"So he wanted to go with *you*. I watched him try and get your attention for the rest of the school year, but it's like you were completely oblivious to him. You treated him basically the same as you always had, and until right now, I took that to mean that you *didn't* return his feelings. I didn't realize that you'd liked him when he asked you out."

"I never said I liked him."

"Your reason for not going with him makes it sound like you did."

Oakley knew that the more she protested the dumber she would sound. Her brother could tell by the way he was asking such pointed questions. She'd given herself away. "Fine. I had a crush on him back then. So what?"

"So, I don't know what," Travis said. "I knew Hunter liked you during senior year, even though he never brought it up to me. It made sense since we were best friends, and I'm not gonna lie … it was hard for me to picture the two of you together in a relationship. I mean, it was always the three of us, and it was strange to think of the two of you … together."

"Well, we weren't together then. And we're not together anymore either."

Travis shook his head. "I really had no clue that you ever liked him before now. He'd tried for years to get your attention after we graduated. I thought something might happen with y'all the last time he was here."

"Why?" she asked.

Travis shrugged. "College feels like a long time ago, Oakley. It's not like I documented all of our conversations. But he always asked if you'd be home during our school breaks. If you weren't coming, he made his excuses; if you were, he would come."

"There were lots of breaks he didn't come home, even when I was in high school."

Travis scratched his chin. "I just know he asked every time. Never in a direct way, but he always wanted to know what you were up to and if you were dating anyone."

"He asked about my dating life? Did you even know when I was dating someone?"

Travis shrugged. "I made educated guesses. One time I thought he'd come when you had a boyfriend. I thought maybe he'd try and win you."

"Well, he never did."

Travis sighed. "Well, like you said, it doesn't really matter at this point, does it?"

"The last Christmas he came back—he asked about me then too?"

"He did."

"But not after that?"

Travis shook his head. "He still asked about you, but I had moved away, and it wasn't like I was coming home every Christmas either."

"Did you send him away this time? Or did he leave on his own?" She bit her lip.

"Does it matter?"

Oakley rubbed a hand over her forehead. Travis's insight on her time in high school had been revelatory, but it didn't change anything, right? "I'm ... not sure."

"I announced to mom that he was leaving last night. In some ways he didn't really have a choice. Even as best of friends that we were in the past, I'm not okay with him treating my sister that way."

"It's probably for the best," Oakley said, wishing she could unsee what she'd seen, and unfeel what she had felt for Hunter.

"I really am sorry," Travis said, giving her a side hug.

"It's not your fault."

"If it helps, I don't think he was insincere when he was trying to explain the whole thing. If he had been, I would have broken his nose without a second thought. I think he did, and probably still does, care for you."

That made it worse. So much worse. She tried to push the lump in her throat down, but when that didn't work, she talked through it. "Well, at this point, it doesn't matter either way. Even the past is all speculation."

Travis looked like he was going to object, but she stopped him. "Mom is probably trying to keep dinner warm. We shouldn't keep her waiting." She walked in the house, trying to sort through everything Travis had told her. Reframing her whole past to add in the information that Travis had provided was exhausting. Hunter had never once given her the impression that she was the object of his affections when they were younger. And even if he had, the fact was that she wouldn't date a cheater.

CHAPTER 24

Hunter turned over his phone during cards with his family, eager to see the caller, but it wasn't Oakley. Again. He needed to stop doing this to himself.

"Is it Oakley?" his sister, Kendra, asked.

Hunter shook his head. "Business. I'd better take it." He excused himself from the family game, almost grateful for the chance to escape the happiness that bubbled around him. His heart refused to absorb any of their merriment. This whole week should have been spent with Oakley. Pain still tore through him. He answered Kyle's call on the last ring.

"The Johnson's General Store made the headlines," Kyle said. "Congratulations."

Hunter stared off into the beautiful Christmas tree in his parents' living room. The scene was picture perfect, except Oakley wasn't here. "Oh, it did?"

"The paper reported it up here," Kandice said. A rustling came through the line. "I printed it, let me find it. There were a dozen stories on it in all the local papers. Here's my favorite: *'Restoring Christmas—Golden Ridge Didn't Wait for Santa to Bring a Christmas Miracle.'"*

"I didn't see the articles," Hunter admitted.

"How did you miss them? I imagine that's all the town is talking about," Kyle said.

"I'm actually already in Colorado," Hunter admitted.

"Oh, I thought you and Oakley weren't headed up to your parents' until after Christmas," Kandice said.

"That was supposed to be the case," he admitted, then headed to his dad's study before he explained what happened.

"That's rough," Kyle said.

Hunter ran a hand through his hair, and leaned against his dad's desk. "You're telling me."

"Did you stay for the Johnsons' arrival yesterday?"

"No," Hunter said. "But I'll go read the articles about it. I'm glad that it went well."

"I'll overnight our final decision for the competition to Colorado. What's your address there?" Kandice asked.

Hunter gave it to her. "Thanks for putting this on," Hunter said. "It's been a good experience."

"Even with what happened with Oakley?" Kyle asked.

"Yes," he said. "It was rewarding to help the Johnsons. Being back in Golden Ridge was exactly what I needed." Oakley was exactly what he'd needed, and now he'd lost her again—for good this time.

"Would you do anything different?" Kandice asked.

"Not for the project. It was what needed to happen. I wasn't the only one working on the store, but what I did made a difference. I'm not happy about the way it ended. It's not what I would choose … especially not with Oakley. But I'm glad I helped out the Johnsons."

"I have a question that's not related to whether or not you'll win," Kandice said.

"Sure," Hunter said.

"If you won, and I'm not saying one way or the other the results, how would you use the three million dollars to help a charity, since helping the Johnsons rebuild isn't exactly tied to a charity?"

Hunter thought about that. His project was outside the scope of a typical charity that could be easily donated to in the future. "Every year Golden Ridge does a Christmas service project. My prize money could be used to help fund that, but I think that some of the magic of what they're trying to do would be lost if I just funded it. You should see how this town really pulls together to give help where it's needed."

"So, you're saying that's *not* what you would use the money for?" Kandice asked again.

"I think it would take away some of the joy of serving. People coming together to sacrifice for neighbors is what Golden Ridge is built on. I would hate to mess with that."

"But you said that your donation helped spur others on," Kyle said.

"And it did at the time, but I'm not sure a hefty bank account to pull from would do the same thing in the future. I'd probably look at helping the city from an insurance standpoint and make sure that people are covered that way."

"Thanks for your update," Kyle said. "Like Kandice said, you'll receive the results tomorrow. The competition is officially over for you and you're finished with your obligations for the bet."

"Thanks again for putting this together."

"Are you ... I mean ... Is there anything you can do to make things work with Oakley?" Kandice asked.

Hunter sighed. "I tried, and I think it only made things worse. As much as I hate to say it, it's time for me to cut my losses with Oakley. I don't want to be stuck in the same perpetual heartbreak that I've always been in anymore."

"I'm sorry to hear that," Kandice said.

"Chin up," Kyle said. "And enjoy time with your family."

"Merry Christmas, Hunter," Kandice said.

"Merry Christmas, y'all," Hunter said, before hanging up. He blew out his breath slowly. He knew that he should probably tell his family that Oakley wouldn't be joining them the day after Christmas.

He shook his head. No. Tomorrow was Christmas Eve. He didn't want to spoil the holiday by bringing it up before all the festivities. It was better to wait. He wasn't holding out for a miracle, like the Johnsons had received, but he just couldn't deal with the reality of it right now. He'd tell them, just not tonight.

"Hunter, are you coming to take your turn?" his sister called up to him.

"I'm coming," he said. "Just a minute."

"Tell Oakley that you'll see her when she gets here," Kendra teased.

He looked at his phone and scrolled through his recent texts and calls. Nothing was from Oakley. He'd already checked in with Kyle and Kandice and coordinated with his personal assistant before she took off for her Christmas vacation so there was no reason to be tethered to his phone anymore. He wasn't expecting any messages, and the person he wanted to talk to most wouldn't be calling him anytime on this side of forever. He swiped down on his screen and touched the airplane icon. It would be better this way. Maybe he'd be able to focus more on his family without constantly checking his phone to see nothing from Oakley over and over. He walked back to the table, slid his phone into his pocket instead of leaving it on the edge of the table, and picked up his cards. He looked over his hand and at the cards in play, and placed a card in front of him, determined to enjoy the holiday time with his family, and to not think about Oakley any more. Easier said than done.

"UNCLE HUNTER, THERE'S A SURPRISE FOR YOU AT THE DOOR," HIS niece, Emily, said.

A surprise for him? Thoughts of Oakley raced around his head. "I'm coming," he said, running his hand through his hair. He should have left his beanie on from his early morning skiing with his brothers and brothers-in-law.

"And after, you promised to come build a snow fort with us," her younger brother Wyatt said.

"We'll go out and play when you're in your snow clothes," Hunter called back.

Laughter filled the Paxton house on Christmas Eve Day, and Hunter barely made it to the door without being trampled by his nieces and nephews. His thoughts about the surprise being Oakley were immediately thrown away like a snowball when he saw the older man in a postal uniform. The man held out a device, and Hunter signed the screen and accepted the very thin envelope.

"What is it?" Wyatt asked. "That doesn't look like a present."

"I never said it was a *present*, I said it was a *surprise*."

"Is it a surprise, Uncle Hunter?" Wyatt asked.

Hunter pulled out the red envelope addressed to him. "It looks like a surprise," he said.

Wyatt wrinkled his nose. "It looks like a love letter from a girl."

Hunter opened up the enclosed letter. It was from Kyle and Kandice. The results of the Billionaire Christmas Bet. "Not from a girl."

He read through the first page of the letter. Congratulations to all the candidates, and then an outline of some of the specific highlights of his own project were displayed. He flipped over the paper, and continued reading.

Congratulations, Hunter! You've won the Billionaire Christmas Bet! Your ability to make a difference in Golden Ridge has been inspiring to us. Our charity, Happy Moments, focuses on helping people create happy moments for themselves and for others, and that's what you've done this Christmas season.

The three million dollars are yours to help Golden Ridge in the future and set up the trust for your insurance coverage if that is the way you want to go. Thanks for sharing your story with us.

We can't wait to see what you do in the future with Golden Ridge.

Merry Christmas!

~ Kyle and Kandice Montgomery

CHAPTER 25

Oakley wandered into the coffee shop on Christmas Eve. Work had kept her busy until almost 5:00 p.m., when she'd sent out the last of the digital orders for last-minute Christmas shoppers. She'd debated going straight to her parents' house but ultimately realized that all the plans she'd hoped for today had included Hunter. Hopefully, the less time she was there, the less she'd pine for something she couldn't have.

Breathing became more difficult as she stood in line for her order. She should have stayed at home. Every part of Golden Ridge had memories with Hunter in them. She really was pathetic.

She ordered a steaming mug of hot chocolate and tucked herself into the corner of the shop. Her brain knew she shouldn't still have feelings for Hunter, not after what he'd done. Her heart was almost in agreement. She would stay strong. After Christmas she'd donate the present she'd created for Hunter to charity, and at some point before she was supposed to board a plane on the 26th to go visit his family, she'd tell her mom that they'd broken up.

She would wait until after Christmas. She couldn't spoil her mom's ideal Christmas this year. Her mom had raved about her and Hunter, had bought them joint gifts, and had hinted more than once about seeing small boxes under the tree. Oakley had seen no such thing, and now the thought made her stomach turn. Her mom had had such high hopes for them. Oakley had too. At least one of them would have a Christmas with happy memories. Her mom would be disillusioned the day after, but at least it wouldn't spoil the celebrations in the moment.

After resolutely setting her plans, she took a large sip of her drink. The hot chocolate burned her tongue and scalded her throat until it reached her stomach. She sputtered and reached for the napkins but the dispenser was empty.

She went to the side of the ordering counter and asked for a few napkins but froze solid when she saw Gina's face through the glass dessert case. Thankfully, Gina hadn't seen her.

Gina and her friend were laughing. "You should have seen her face," Gina said. "I mean, she looked like she'd seen a ghost."

"How did you see her if you were kissing her boyfriend under the mistletoe?" her friend asked.

Oakley's heart pounded. They were talking about *her*. She clenched her fingers at her side, wishing she could punch Gina the way Travis had punched Hunter. But that would give Gina way too much validation. She was better than that.

Gina hit her friend's arm. "Because I set him up to kiss him under the mistletoe when she came back into the store. I saw her pull up and timed it perfectly so she would see. She dropped something and ran out the door … such a klutz. It was so funny."

"I can't believe you kissed Hunter Paxton."

Gina lifted a shoulder. "He owed me one since he didn't kiss me at Senior Prom. Besides, all he talked about that night was Oakley. While he was on a date with *me*. Turnabout is fair play."

"So, are you and Hunter together now?"

Gina laughed, then ordered her cream puff. "That was not the point of the kiss, Tiffany."

"So you *wanted* to break them up?"

Gina touched the side of her nose. "She'll think twice before she invades my turf next time. I should have been the one running the Johnson's General Store rebuild, not her."

"I thought you told everyone you wouldn't accept the position this year."

Gina rolled her eyes. "I did, but I didn't want Oakley to do it instead."

"I thought she did a great job, and the Johnsons seemed really happy when they got home."

"Not the point. I could have done a better job."

"Is Hunter a good kisser at least?"

Gina pouted. "Probably, though he wasn't doing any work on his end to make it a good kiss. It was all I could do to keep his lips against mine until Oakley could see."

The cashier who'd gotten Oakley a few more napkins came back to where Oakley's back was pressed against the larger stand. "Is there anything else you need?" the woman asked.

Oakley put her index finger to her mouth and shook her head. If she was spotted by Gina now, it wouldn't be good.

Oakley peered up to see Gina and Tiffany walking to a table on the other side of the room from where she'd previously sat. She waved the cashier back over. "Any chance I can get two cream puffs without waiting in the line again?"

The cashier looked at her and nodded. "Sure, I can help you with that. Which ones did you want?"

"Whatever those two just ordered."

The woman confirmed the order and handed her a plate with the delicacies on them.

Oakley shook her head. "They aren't for me. Would you mind delivering them to their table when I leave?"

The woman nodded. "Any message to go with the cream puffs?"

"Tell them they're compliments of Oakley because she's grateful they said everything she needed to hear. Tell them they helped make this the best Christmas ever."

Oakley called Hunter on the way out of the coffee shop, but he didn't answer. She texted him before she started driving, and by the time she arrived at her parents' house she still hadn't heard from him.

Her heart sank, but at least it was intact and no longer shattered. She left him two voicemails, feeling like a broken record. She went through all of the scenarios that gave her hope that he wasn't just ignoring her. Maybe he was skiing with his family. Maybe he didn't have great reception at the cabin. And it was Christmas Eve. She would probably ignore her phone during the festivities regardless of who was calling too. There were so many reasons why he might not answer the phone right now, and she clung to all of them. He'd call back.

She walked through the door and tried to put a bright smile on her face, but her mom only had to take one look at her. "What's wrong, Oakley?"

She glanced to Travis, who shook his head. At least he hadn't spilled her secret. "Nothing, mom. I was just trying to get a hold of Hunter, that's all."

Her mom nodded, her smile wide. "Oh, I'm sure he'll be calling you in no time," she said.

Oakley nodded, holding onto that thought, but as the hours passed by and they finished a Christmas movie as a family, she still hadn't heard from him. She sent him one more text message. **Merry Christmas, Hunter.**

When they finished their Christmas Eve celebrations, she headed up to her childhood room. She plugged in her phone, hoping to see something from Hunter, but there was still radio silence. Her heart ached to redo the irrational moment where she wouldn't let him explain his kiss with Gina under the mistletoe.

Christmas dawned bright with a chill in the air. Oakley woke up determined not to let her heartbreak ruin Christmas. She raced Travis down the stairs, and after opening up their stockings, they started breakfast. It had been a tradition to bring their parents breakfast in bed on Christmas. It was the way they ensured that breakfast happened as soon as possible so they could open their Christmas presents without delay.

When they were just about finished with the breakfast tray their parents came down the stairs.

"Anxious to open presents this year?" Oakley's mom winked at her.

"Oh, I mean, it was more the tradition of it, right, Travis?"

Travis shook his head. "Mom, she woke up four hours ago and tried to drag me out of bed so we could serve breakfast at 3:00 a.m."

Oakley shoved him on the shoulder. "Don't make stuff up. That was like fifteen years ago."

"Feels like it was this morning," Travis said, yawning.

Their mom laughed. "You kids. We don't wait for breakfast anymore, you know. I'll grab the hot chocolate and let's go open some presents."

OAKLEY WAS SPOILED WITH GIFTS, AND SHE LOVED HOW HER parents and her brother raved about her gifts to them. All in all it was a beautiful morning of gift-giving except something was missing. She really felt the loss of Hunter not being there, like she hadn't felt in nine years. She glanced at her phone again.

Travis nodded to it. "You're glued to that thing this morning."

Oakley pocketed the phone. "Sorry, I was just hoping … that I would hear from Hunter."

Travis tilted his head, but didn't respond.

"Maybe he has no reception where he is," her mom suggested.

"That must be it," Travis quickly agreed.

Oakley forced a smile. Travis chiming in felt more like he was trying to convince his mom than convince her. She took the loose pieces of wrapping paper and wadded them up into a large ball before aiming and shooting it at the garbage can.

"Oh, Oakley, here is another one for you. It was tucked way back in the tree."

Oakley accepted the box. "Thanks, Mom," she said.

Her mom shook her head. "It's not from me."

She looked to her dad, and then to Travis and each of them shook their head. The tag said her name, but there was no other name written on it. Oakley's heart leapt at the possibilities of this small box and what it might contain.

She tore the paper off, and found a small velvet box.

Her mom gasped, but there was no way it contained what she was thinking. It wasn't a ring.

Oakley gingerly opened the box, and then it was her turn to gasp.

"What is it? Is it from Hunter?"

"I'm not sure who it's from," she said, though Hunter was the logical choice. Still, it made no sense why this was under the tree. He could have given this to her weeks ago. Why wait until now?

Oakley lifted up the small key that had a gold ribbon through it. Had Hunter found a jewelry store to replicate the key she'd lost all those years ago? The idea seemed out there, but then again, there she was holding a key that had been missing for nine Christmases. Anything was possible. She lifted the cardboard from the box, and found a small note, folded tightly.

"I'm returning this to you. I'm sorry I haven't before now."

She stood, reverently carrying the key to the music box on the mantle. She inserted the end, and happiness poured through her when she heard the delicate click of the latch. Before opening the box's lid, she wound it up as far as it would go. Oakley carefully opened the lid, and the small tinkling sound of *"I'll Be Home for Christmas"* thrummed into the space.

Her mom gasped. "I haven't heard that in years."

"Me either," Oakley whispered, listening to the familiar tune and letting it carry her back through many happy Christmas memories.

"You know before the key was lost, you would always wind it up and let the song play through, and no one could open gifts until the song was completely done."

"What did you hide in it the last time it was opened?" Travis asked.

Everyone knew Oakley used it as a place to hide trinkets and treasures. She'd often surprised herself when they put up the decorations, since she couldn't always remember what she'd put in it from year to year. "I don't remember at all," she said, lifting the special compartment lid inside the music box. Her fingers wrapped around the velvet bag, but she couldn't think of any memory that was associated with it. She pulled out the contents. The chain of the necklace was simple, but the heart dangling from it was outlined in diamonds. Her eyes widened. She'd never seen this before. She opened up the small faded paper.

"You've always had my heart. Merry Christmas, Annie Oakley. Here's to many more of them together. Love, Hunter"

"What is it?" Oakley's mom asked.

Oakley held up the diamond necklace.

Her dad whistled, and her mom gasped.

"Who's it from?" Travis asked.

Oakley clasped the necklace around her neck, rubbing it between her fingers. "It's from Hunter, actually."

"What a clever way for him to hide the gift—get a key to the box, and hide it there."

Oakley nodded, though the assessment wasn't quite accurate. According to the date on the card, this gift was from nine years ago, not this year. He had the key this whole time. "It was very clever of him." Based on how things ended after their first mistletoe kiss, she supposed that Hunter had kept the key for the past nine years to ensure that the necklace would remain undiscovered. He'd left it here for her, when he could have removed it at any time. But then again, all of this was orchestrated for him to be here when she opened the box, until Travis sent him away.

Oakley read the small card one more time before slipping it into her pocket. She'd always had his heart. She closed her eyes to think. Could she possibly *still* have his heart?

She needed answers, but he wasn't returning her calls. There was only one thing to do.

"I've had a change in plans," she announced. "I'm leaving for Colorado tonight."

Her parents gave her hugs, and she headed upstairs to pack. Travis followed her into her room. "Oakley, are you sure you know what you're doing? I don't want to see you get hurt again."

She appreciated her brother's concern, and told him so. She

explained about everything she'd overheard the day before in the coffee shop.

Travis winced as she told him the conversation. "Now I feel really bad for giving him the black eyes. I'm sorry."

Oakley shook her head. "Don't be. It was sweet at the time. But now that I know the truth, I only hope I'm not too late."

CHAPTER 26

Hunter trudged down the stairs at his parents' cabin, groggy and disheveled. Since arriving in Colorado, he hadn't slept well at all. His parents blamed it on him not being used to the elevation or the cold air, but he knew that wasn't the case. Today was the day he and Oakley should have arrived together. They'd have come in just after dinner, according to their original travel itineraries. He had about eight hours to figure out how to tell his family the truth—that Oakley wasn't coming today. He'd avoided having the conversation all week long, not wanting to bring it up with anyone.

He sighed. It was better to get it over with. There was no sense in waiting until this evening to tell everyone. He walked into the kitchen, and said good morning to everyone. The entire family sat at the table, like they'd been waiting for him, but their breakfasts were usually much more casual than this. His idea of telling only a few people at a time dissolved. It was better to tell everyone at the same time and get it over with. He ran his hand through his hair. "I have something to tell y'all about Oakley." He swallowed. Admitting things were over was harder than he thought. "The truth is, Oakley is—"

"We already know," Kendra said, practically bursting with excitement.

"Wait, what do you already know?"

Kendra rolled her eyes. "Why you've been so mopey the last week. You've missed her, that's to be expected."

"But now you can stop being mopey, because today is the day," his other sister, Meg, joined in.

Hunter blew out his breath. "About that … Oakley is actually not coming tonight."

"We know that," his mom said.

He wasn't sure if his mom's admission made the moment easier or harder. "You do?"

His mom smiled. "Of course, dear. She arrived an hour ago."

Oakley poked her head in from the dining room. She threw her hands open wide. "Surprise. I got here a little early." She bit her lip. "I … hope you don't mind my change in plans."

Hunter blinked. "I-I …"

"I didn't know if my messages were coming through or not, and didn't want to bother you with the hassle of coming to pick me up."

Hunter could barely recover. What was Oakley doing here? He looked around the room. "No one thought to tell me Oakley was here?"

His brother smiled. "That would have defeated the purpose of this moment."

At the prompting of his brother, Hunter hugged Oakley, and

gave her a small kiss on the cheek. His siblings all groaned, and Oakley blushed.

"Can we talk?" she asked, fingering the diamond heart necklace he'd bought her when he was still in college.

His heart rate soared. "Yes," he said. "Do you have a coat?"

She nodded, and he led her to the front door. His brain ran a million miles an hour, but he walked slowly as he led her outside and down the freshly shoveled sidewalk. When they were beyond the view of the front windows, Hunter stopped walking and turned to Oakley. He didn't dare hope that things were repaired between them. "I'm surprised to see you here," he said slowly.

She bit her lip again. "Not an unwelcome surprise, I hope."

He stepped closer to her. "Just a surprise. The way things were when I left ... I wasn't sure I'd ever see you again."

She touched his arm. "I know. I'm sorry about that. I was gun-shy."

He tilted his head. "I never thought Annie Oakley could be gun-shy. It's not in her nature."

"Hunter, I had a *major* crush on you in junior high and high school. And I basically compared everyone in college to you. I thought I was able to get over you when you broke my heart nine years ago, but I didn't, not by a long shot. So, when I saw Gina kissing you—I freaked out. I know the truth about it now, but I just—it was a moment that was really hard to handle. I watched you date *so* many girls and after a date or two, you moved on. It was easy to just assume that you hadn't changed."

"Oaks, we both were burned in the past."

"I know," she whispered.

He narrowed his eyes. "How do you know?"

She lifted a shoulder. "Travis told me."

"I never told Travis anything about you."

"He figured it out when you were so disappointed about Senior Prom."

Hunter nodded. "That was a rough one for me."

"Me too."

"Gina came out of nowhere. She surprised me. I wasn't looking for anything. I promise."

Oakley nodded. "I know. I overheard her talking with a friend in the coffee shop. She orchestrated the whole thing as some sick revenge." She rubbed the necklace between her fingers and quickly changed the subject. "I've *always* had your heart?"

Hunter nodded. "Always. Why do you think I only went out with girls once or twice? None of them were who I wanted. None of them were *you*."

"Really?"

He smiled. "Now you know my biggest secret."

She bit her lip. "I have a matching secret. I've been in love with you for just as long."

He held her close and kissed her gently. The only thing he ever needed was here in his arms and his world was right again. He savored the moment, his lips expressing his apologies for the misunderstanding between them. Their lips parted, and he stared into the green eyes he'd fallen in love with over and over throughout the years. "I guess it was good thing I took that key nine years ago."

Oakley blushed at his words. "I guess so."

"I had hoped to see your face light up when you heard *"I'll Be Home for Christmas"* again from the music box."

"It felt surreal, but I learned something." Her irresistible smile teased him.

"Oh?"

"'*I'll Be Home for Christmas*' isn't about a place, it's a promise to who you want to be with. It feels like Christmas now," she said, her cheeks blushing. "I finally feel like I'm home."

"I couldn't agree more." He cradled her face in his hands, and kissed her until snow began falling around them.

EPILOGUE

TWO YEARS LATER

Oakley couldn't see a thing through Hunter's hands across her eyes. "Are we close to the surprise?"

"Almost there," Hunter said. "Just a few more steps. No peeking, Mrs. Paxton."

Oakley giggled. "I'm not peeking."

"Hold on right there," Hunter said. "I'm gonna open the door."

Oakley felt the whoosh of the door when he moved around her.

He took her hand and led her forward.

"Can I open my eyes now?" she asked, a giddy anticipation running through her. She wondered what new surprise Hunter had in store for her.

Hunter put his arms around her, resting his hands on her belly. A sharp kick hit his hand. "He's active today," he said.

"Hey, who says it's a he? It might be a she."

"I'd be okay with a little Annie Oakley."

"And I'd be more than happy with a little Hunter. Now, can I see the surprise? This little one wants to see too."

"Well it will still be a few weeks before the baby gets to see it, but I thought I'd show you what the baby will see in the middle of the night."

"Let's hope the baby sleeps soundly and sees nothing in the middle of the night."

"Open your eyes," Hunter whispered.

Oakley did, and she saw—nothing. "Hunter, it's dark in here."

"That's the point, my darling. It's the nighttime view we are going for."

Oakley stood in the dark completely confused. Had she missed something?

"Look up."

"It's still dark," she whispered.

"Wait for it." He pushed a button on his phone, and the ceiling glowed softly.

She gasped. "You did all of this while I was taking a nap?" she asked in wonder. The entire nursery wing had stars, galaxies, and a moon shining from the ceiling.

"I had a little help with it," Hunter confessed. "It wasn't easy getting the LED wiring into each of the stars. I've been working on it a little here and there."

"And you made constellations too?" She easily found the big and little dippers, close by where the crib was arranged.

"It's not to scale."

"It's perfect. You even made the bear constellation!"

He laughed. "Without using any stars from the big or little dippers."

"Hunter!" Oakley exclaimed, then kissed him before she could finish her thought. The baby kicked harder, apparently not appreciating being squished. Oakley tilted her head, glancing again at the stars and then back into Hunter's eyes. "I love you so much."

"I love you too." He pulled her in closer and kissed her again, and the entire world faded around them.

Like the Book?

Please leave a review for The Billionaire's Second Chance Christmas on Amazon.

It's the best way you can say thank you to an author!

Thank you so much!

Read Scott's Story Next!

Read Finding Christmas with the Billionaire Now!
It's included in this Box Set!

She's trying to save her charity. He's trying to save her. Together they might find a very unexpected Christmas!

Join Chelsea's VIP Reader's Club

to stay updated with new releases, get free books, access to exclusive bonus content, and more!

Join Chelsea's VIP Reader's Club.

See all of Chelsea's books.

Books in this Series:

Troy's Story: The Billionaire's Christmas Miracle
Hunter's Story: The Billionaire's Second Chance Christmas
Scott's Story: Finding Christmas with the Billionaire

ACKNOWLEDGMENTS

I love Christmas time! The magic, the warmth, the message of the gift of Christ given to the world. All of it. Without that first gift, we would not be celebrating, and I'm grateful daily for the babe who was swaddled and laid in a manger. He gives us the reason for this beautiful time of year, and shares His love through his merciful gifts that can be accessed every day of the year, not just at Christmas. I am grateful for a Savior in my life who gives me a reason to hope and allows me to feel a heavenly peace.

My husband is always top of my list of people to thank. He is amazing on the Superman scale with those Kryptonite eyes. What would I do without you? Definitely not as much or as well. I love you. Always. Next, my children are remarkable. This year their support has been a more beautiful part of the journey. I'm grateful that they listen and read the words I write. I love cheering for them, and I'm grateful they cheer for me.

Friends and editors make my life and my books better! I'm

grateful to so many who make it possible to do what I do, and to do what I love.

Of particular note on this specific book, thanks to Tracy, who keeps me sane with deep perspective that makes my characters and me better. You're awesome. I'd much rather walk miles in Disneyland with you, but for now, I'll take early morning walks. Thanks for chatting through countless story ideas as we circle the neighborhood yet again.

Thanks to Ami. I will forever sound like a broken record, but every book seems to have your stamp of approval in many places. I am grateful for your patience with me and my characters and so grateful for your help. Thanks for keeping me in line, and for seeing beyond just the words I've written to the messages I want to share.

Thanks to Holly. Kindred spirits make navigating being an author so much easier! Thank you for the countless daily checks and reports that keep me motivated and on task. I'm grateful for so many things that you do and say, but it all boils down to gratitude for you being you!

Thanks to Stephanie. WOW! Really, wow! Your help was so needed. Thank you for helping me fine tune my ideas into beautiful prose. I'm grateful for your skill and sharp eye. Thank you for your incredible speed and agility in helping me with my book. I'm so grateful for you. Your honesty, boldness, and Texan expertise has brought characters to life in a way that gives them more depth and more power than they had before. Thank you for the laughs, the face palms, and the squeals. I needed all of them! I'm grateful for your friendship and your beautiful voice. Thank you for everything!

Thanks to my readers. I am amazed at the amount of email,

messages, texts, and comments from so many who praise my books and share their favorite parts or what resonated with them. You have no idea what a profound difference this makes. Thank you for sharing. Thank you for reading. And thank you for caring! I'm sure grateful for all of you!

All y'all're awesome! Merry Christmas!

FINDING CHRISTMAS WITH THE BILLIONAIRE

A BETTING ON CHRISTMAS ROMANCE - BOOK THREE

CHELSEA HALE

"I will honor Christmas in my heart, and try to keep it all the year. I will live in the Past, the Present, and the Future. The Spirits of All Three shall strive within me. I will not shut out the lessons they teach!"

- Charles Dickens, A Christmas Carol

PROLOGUE

HOW THE BET BEGAN - (PLEASE NOTE EACH PROLOGUE IS SIMILAR)

Scott breathed in the salty Mediterranean air from the top deck of Hunter's yacht. The last couple of days catching up with his three college roommates had been exactly what he needed to gear up for the upcoming months with his business.

"This has been a great trip," Scott said. "I'm sorry to see it over so soon. Are you sure you can't stay another week, Kyle?" Scott could use another week, or maybe two.

Kyle Montgomery only laughed. "You guys are welcome to stay, but my team won't be happy if I miss Saturday's game. We're up against the rivals. Just missing practice this week might get me in trouble."

"We can't stay without you," Hunter said. "It wouldn't be the same without all four of us."

They lounged on the top, watching the land in the distance. Europe was beautiful this time of year.

"Just like old times," Troy said.

"Old times?" Kyle repeated. "I suppose, but not really like old times. I haven't been a bachelor in a long time. I have kids now. It's not the same for me." He was the only one of the group that was married, having married his high school crush after college, the same year he signed with Dallas and started in the NFL.

"How's your charity going?" Scott asked Kyle. Kyle's work in putting together a successful charity that ran projects all over the world intrigued Scott. He'd thought about doing his own charity work and wanted his friend's advice.

"Every year it does more good in the world," Kyle said vaguely. "Happy Moments is dedicated to just that. Bringing happy moments to others. It's rewarding. It's too big for us to manage on our own any more, but Kandice and I still play an active role in it."

"I think I'd like to do that," Troy said.

"Having a charity foundation and being involved in the work are two completely separate things," Kyle said. He leaned forward, resting his elbows on his knees. "But I could help you, if you're interested in getting involved or starting your own charity."

"I'd like that," Troy said.

Scott listened to the exchange with interest. Troy had started the exact conversation Scott had been thinking through in his head. Though all the roommates had reached success in their chosen professions, Kyle seemed to take on the role of mentor among the group when it came to life outside of the work. Still, a little ribbing Troy would be fun. Scott laughed, tilting his sunglasses down. "I bet you a million you couldn't do it."

"I'll take that bet," Troy said, his eyes narrowing his gaze on Scott.

Even after graduating together, there had been lots of competitions over the years between them. Most of them were good-natured, but Scott knew that he pushed himself harder when Troy was determined to beat him.

"A million for what?" Hunter asked. "I'm in for a million."

Scott rolled his eyes. "You don't even know what the bet is."

Hunter shrugged. "It's only a million. Chump change."

"Betting for charity seems to defeat the point," Kyle said.

Troy nodded. "Fair enough. How about when I win your money goes to the charity of my choice?" Troy looked at Scott.

Scott shrugged, trying to act casual as he mentally prepared to beat Troy. Their last neck and neck competition ended with Scott losing by only a fraction of a second. He wouldn't be bested this time. "You can do whatever you want with money you win. But you're not going to win, so it's a non-issue."

"I'll win," Troy said confidently. "Just give me the stakes."

"You have to start a charity," Scott said, trying to think of something that would be impossible in a short amount of time.

"Or, we could open up the entire bet to everyone," Kyle said.

"It wouldn't be fair to include you," Scott said to Kyle. "You already own a charity."

Kyle leaned back in his chair. "I'll be the moderator then. The judge."

"What are the rules?" Troy repeated.

"How about you need to start a charity by Christmas?" Scott suggested. He could absolutely do that. His company donated to several charities, and his assistant found new charities to sponsor every year. It wouldn't be hard to whiteboard out the ideas and start one of his own. He was resourceful.

Hunter shook his head. "It's mid-October. If you want to make an impact by Christmas you need to scale it back."

"What if you have to help a charity that's already up and running?" Kyle suggested. "*That* could be done before Christmas."

Scott tilted his head. He already did that regularly so it didn't seem like much of a competition, but he'd already geared up for a victory against Troy. He wasn't about to pass up an opportunity to win at something. "How would we determine the winner then?" He gazed at the water as the sun gleamed on it, but the view gave him no answers.

Troy was quiet.

Kyle snapped his fingers. "I've got it. You need to be personally involved with helping a charity succeed. I like the deadline of Christmas, and it would be nice to pick a winner before the New Year. Entrance fee is one million dollars. The winner gets the three million dollars to donate to the charity of his choosing—most likely the one that you choose to help, but I'm open to negotiation on that point. The person who donates the most will win."

Hunter laughed. "I can donate the most. I can write a check tomorrow. Easy enough."

Kyle shook his head. "Not monetarily. I'd say you need to cap your own personal or business donations to $10,000."

Scott scoffed. "How do we determine a winner if we're only allowed to give such a small amount? We'll all just give that amount and then we'll be tied." Kyle was losing his touch on creating competitions.

"You have to make a difference in the charity. No assistants can help, and you can't just assign it to a team of people from your companies. You have to *personally* be involved with it. Help with your time." Kyle shrugged. "Be creative. You're all brilliant—you can all figure out a way to do something."

"And we only have from now until Christmas?" Scott confirmed.

Kyle nodded. "What if we make the deadline December 23rd, and the winner could be announced on December 24th."

"And you're the judge?" Troy asked.

Kyle scrunched his face. "No. I don't want to be accused of being partial to anyone. I'll have Kandice be the judge. Maybe we'll have a weekly check-in phone call and she can hear all of your progress and what you've been up to. She can be the one to make the final decision. Whatever she decides, stands."

Hunter, Scott and Troy all nodded.

"Sounds fair," Troy said. "I'm in, if everyone else is."

Scott shrugged. "Why not? My company is a well-oiled machine right now. I have some extra time. Hunter, what about you?"

Hunter sighed. "This eats into my plans to spend the next month on my yacht, but yeah, I'm in. When do we start?"

"As soon as it works for everyone," Kyle said.

"I have a few things to wrap up at work before I can take the time off," Scott said.

Kyle nodded. "How about we start in two weeks? Maybe that will give you time to research which charity to help."

"And we need to spend the full eight weeks helping the charity of our choice?"

Kyle nodded. "Eight weeks of helping. No assistants helping

you with the charity. And don't try and get past the rules. Kandice will find out."

All of them laughed. They shook hands on it and within an hour they'd wired money to Kyle for the bet.

The Billionaires' Christmas Gifts Bet was officially underway.

THE RULES

OF THE BILLIONAIRES' CHRISTMAS GIFTS BET

- *Find a charity of your choice*
- *$1,000,000 Entry fee*
- *8 weeks of helping a charity of your choice – You must be personally involved*
- *No assistants*
- *No delegation to teams at work*
- *No talking to participants about the bet*
- *$10,000 max you can donate to the project*
- *Check-in with Kandice (and Kyle)*
- ***Deadline:** December 23rd; Winner announced on December 24th.*
- ***Winner receives:** $3,000,000 to donate to the charity of their choice.*

CHAPTER 1

The scent of cooked vegetables wafted through the air as Kasey scooped a spoonful of green beans onto the plate in front of her. The green beans were a favorite side at The Soup Kitchen, which was good since this was the third time they'd served them this week. She hopped back and forth between serving the green beans and the creamed corn, trying to keep the line in front of her moving. An occasional no-show of volunteers had never bothered her much before. But lately, it had been happening more and more.

Kasey's heart rate increased as she watched a man next to the front door survey The Soup Kitchen. From his pressed clothes and tie to his combed hair and clean face, it was obvious he didn't belong. Not in this building anyway. She took a cleansing breath. She'd worked too hard as the director of the charity to let an auditor ruin everything she'd built.

A woman with a worn scarf came up to Kasey and pointed to the creamed corn she was serving. Kasey added a scoop to the woman's plate and gave the woman a smile. Edna was a regular here.

Kasey's gaze wandered back to the man, and her stomach twisted. Edna was just one of the hundreds of people that she served every day. She didn't want that to change. There had been several offers for the building. The Soup Kitchen was located in the heart of downtown Chicago, and she knew the real estate that housed the charity was considered valuable and full of potential. And yet, she was adding value to the city by providing the service that The Soup Kitchen did—serving two meals a day to any who came through the door. She'd heard the rumors of expansion in the area, but unless there was a problem passing inspections, their lease was secure.

She waved her best friend and assistant director over. Trish was one of the few people she knew she could rely on for anything.

"What's up?" Trish asked when she stood in front of Kasey during a short lull in the line. "You look panicked. Are we short food this meal? Want me to go open up a few more cans in the kitchen?"

Kasey shook her head. She'd been the director here for over two years, and had volunteered for more than double that before assuming her position. She constantly calculated the food and knew the portions were good for at least the next hour. "There's a man over there," Kasey whispered, tilting her head discreetly in his direction. She immediately felt a little foolish. It wasn't that she wasn't used to seeing handsome men, but a well-dressed man at The Soup Kitchen could only mean one thing. "I think that's the guy who wants to shut us down."

Trish picked up the large metal spoon in the creamed corn

and banged it against the side of the pan. "We aren't going anywhere. The City Council granted us an extension to continue raising the money so The Soup Kitchen could remain in operation. Besides, where would we go if this building was sold? This is the prime location to get food to people. It can't be relocated to some place farther outside of the city where it's more *'convenient.'*" She made air quotes on the last word. "The Soup Kitchen helps a lot of people *right here.*"

The line started moving again, and Kasey dropped her voice. "I know that."

A volunteer came over to Kasey. "I'm so sorry to interrupt," she said apologetically, "but the man by the door is looking for the person in charge."

Kasey nodded to the volunteer, who then hurried back to her work. She blew out a breath, and turned to Trish. "Will you take my place for a minute? I'll go settle this."

Trish nodded. "It's unfair when the enemy is so gorgeous. It'd be hard for me to stand my ground. You stay strong though. When you're finished, I'll make the rounds."

"Thanks, Trish." Kasey was grateful that her college roommate had jumped on board with her at The Soup Kitchen. Trish did some freelance work on the side, but almost always came to volunteer one shift a day in addition to her other assistant director duties. Breakfast shifts were the hardest to fill, and yet Trish worked them several mornings each week. She played a large part in keeping this charity running.

Kasey smiled and offered hellos as she passed a few of the regulars. She tried to keep her expression happy, or at least neutral, as she made her way toward the man who was going to make her life miserable. She'd been very clear at the City

Council meeting that her ability to meet with anyone would have to happen during the lunch break when no one else was in the building. The Soup Kitchen was off limits during the two meals they served—breakfast and dinner—and at close to 6:30 p.m., it was solidly in the dinner shift. Ugh. But no one seemed to respect that, and she wished she could give this guy an earful for interrupting her.

Kasey pushed her shoulders back, walking with purpose. She touted a confidence that she didn't actually feel, but needed to muster up anyway. As much as she wanted to tell him off, she couldn't. His inspection report could color the way the City Council viewed her *and* The Soup Kitchen. She needed to play nice, even if that was the last thing she wanted to do. "Hi," she said when she approached him. "I'm the person in charge here. You wanted to see me?" If he expected a tour of the building while they were in the middle of dinner he was going to be disappointed. Still, she would be kind to him, even if she was bothered.

"I'm here to learn about the charity," he said with a smile.

She forced a grin in return. A surprise inspection was something she'd been expecting for weeks. As far as auditors went, he seemed pleasant enough. Maybe he hadn't received the memo regarding the off-limits times. She gestured to the room filled with people, seated at the tables, and those still in line. "As you can see, we're right in the middle of the dinner rush, so I can't visit with you tonight. Feel free to stay and see what we do here, but lunch is the only time I can give you a tour."

The man raised an eyebrow, an amused smile on his lips. "Lunch works for me. Tomorrow?"

She cringed. The way he said the word lunch made it sound

like a leisurely enjoyable thing—at a table with a white linen table cloth and a single red rose in the center. Almost like a *date*. That had rarely been her experience with these guys. Still, his eyes seemed to capture her. She cleared her throat and cleared her mind of that ridiculous image. Obviously he'd want a working lunch. Could she get all the paperwork ready by tomorrow? Her portfolio proving that the building was worth saving and worth leaving as it stood was far from ready ... but if she worked late tonight, and early tomorrow morning, maybe it was possible. At any rate, it would be better than having to give him all of the information tonight. She needed time to finish straightening out all of her thoughts and figures, especially now that his eyes were staring into hers and jumbling everything further.

She swallowed, surprised that she could push off an inspection to a more convenient time. It would make a difference in her presentation, and she'd make it work. "I can meet with you tomorrow during lunch, but not before. Thank you for not disrupting the flow of dinner tonight. You're welcome to stay and observe if you'd like." She repeated her offer, hoping that he took it as a gesture of good will in all of this.

"What about the volunteers?" he asked, surveying the room.

She didn't want to draw more attention to the conversation they were having, especially not from those being served their meals. It was one thing to have the staff jumpy about the possibility of being shut down, and quite another to spread unnecessary panic through the group of people who relied on this charity for their meals. She lowered her voice. "I can give you all the details tomorrow, along with a tour, and answer any questions you need then, but I really need to get back to work."

He turned his head, looking around the room, before finally settling his disarming gaze back on her. He nodded. "It seems you have a very efficient organization here."

He was trying to pry, but she couldn't deal with his questions now. "And I'm happy to answer any questions you might have tomorrow."

"Lunch," he confirmed. "What time is convenient for you?"

Convenient? He was actually asking *her* that question? He was disrupting her entire world. He was going to audit her and try to shut her down, and he wanted to know when would be a good time for it? She didn't even want to have the unpleasant conversation that meeting would bring. "How about 12:30? We serve breakfast until 9:00 and then there's clean up, and it will give me time to show you around before I have to prepare for the dinner rush." That would give her the morning to get all of her ducks in a row, and she could get it all over with by 1:30 or 2:00 at the latest. It would just be ninety minutes of her life. She could handle it.

"And when is dinner?"

She kept her smile wide. "Starts at 4:30. We start preparing food two hours before, and the volunteers show up thirty minutes before."

"Volunteers come at 4:00," he concluded. "It sounds like an exciting and full day. I look forward to it."

So, he planned to observe the full dinner rush tomorrow also? Suddenly, Kasey wished she'd just let him inspect during the meal tonight. Would he show up for breakfast too? "I'll be here," she said, though except for seeing his eyes again, she wasn't looking forward to their next meeting.

He turned like he was about to head out the door, then swiveled back around. He blinked. "I don't think I gave you my name. I'm Scott."

She swallowed, taken off-guard. "Kasey."

He stuck out his hand, and before she could think the better of it, she shook it.

He smiled. "Nice to meet you, Kasey. I look forward to working with you."

She couldn't answer the same. She was not looking forward to working with him, even if his eyes were captivating. She looked forward to defending her position to the auditor about as much as she would getting a root canal during the holiday season. But she only said, "Tomorrow."

He surveyed the room once more and then left.

Kasey rolled her shoulders and headed back toward Trish.

Trish raised an eyebrow, but Kasey couldn't say anything about the exchange with Scott while there was a line of hungry people waiting for their meal.

"Everything okay?" Trish finally asked.

Kasey nodded. After all, she'd expected the auditor would come sometime before Christmas, she just hadn't expected it so soon. She was hoping she'd have through Thanksgiving to prepare. This was the time of year when The Soup Kitchen was needed the very most.

They were weeks away from hitting their financial goals to keep it open and in business for the coming year, but the uppity developers who wanted to see this building torn down were chomping at the bit to get such a valuable piece of property in the downtown area. "Up for some paperwork tonight? I have a meeting at lunch tomorrow that I need to prepare for, and it might take me until then to get everything ready."

"You know I am. Besides, I'm not going to let you have all the fun preparing that portfolio by yourself."

Kasey smiled, grateful for such a good friend. "Thanks, Trish. You're the best."

Trish smiled. "I am."

Kasey settled back into serving the vegetables, trying to let go of her fears about tomorrow. She'd do everything she could to show Scott and all the people he represented that she wasn't intimidated by them. She might have been caught off guard today, but tomorrow she'd be ready for him.

CHAPTER 2

Scott arrived at The Soup Kitchen on time. From the very quick conversation he'd had with Kasey the night before, he was excited to learn more about the charity. He knew he didn't have the corner market on helping all of the charities in the greater Chicago area, but his company donated a significant amount to several high-profile charities. He'd even donated the money for an entire wing at the local hospital. But for this Christmas bet he was supposed to find a charity that he hadn't worked with before. In some ways that made his decision harder. He could have easily donated to a cause where he already had a vested interest, but that wasn't what Kyle wanted for this bet.

He wished he had worn a suit, so he could straighten his tie, but somehow he didn't think that would impress the director here. He'd opted for slacks and a polo instead. His first job interview when he was sixteen flashed across his mind. He'd gotten all dressed up, but he knew that the suit couldn't hide his nerves. He shook the feeling away. This was a non-profit. Interviewing volunteers was part of their process, and he shouldn't worry about it. He was here to help, and he'd overheard a few of the volunteers yesterday mention that the place was understaffed. If nothing else, that information had given him confidence.

He pulled on The Soup Kitchen door, but it was locked. He knocked on the door, feeling foolish for knocking at a business like it was a residence. He was about to check if there was a back door when the door finally opened.

Kasey stood on the opposite side of the door, holding it open for him.

He'd hoped it would be Kasey who would help him. He hadn't for sure decided that this was his charity of choice, but there was something about Kasey that intrigued him. While he observed the dinner process last night, he had watched her specifically for a few minutes before their brief conversation. She'd been one really talking with the people in the line, smiling, and genuinely seeming interested in serving. He'd exited the building after talking to her, but he'd continued to watch from the outside for more than fifteen minutes after, taking everything in. From the outside, it definitely felt like a place where he'd be happy to be involved for the next eight weeks. Especially if Kasey was around. "It's good to see you again." He smiled.

She arched an eyebrow at him. "Follow me."

Had that been the wrong thing to say? He caught up to her brisk walk. "Where do we start?"

"I'll give you the tour first, and then we can go through paperwork."

He nodded. It was simple enough.

"This is the main eating area. We call it The Gathering. It's less formal than dining room or mess hall."

The Gathering. It had a nice ring to it. He'd seen the main room last night when the tables were completely full of people eating their food, and the food line was out the door. With only the two of them in the space, the room felt much bigger than it had the night before. "How many people do you serve every day?"

She tilted her head, her expression guarded. "We can get to the specific numbers when you look at the paperwork. Last night was a good representation of what we do on a typical weekday. We serve between 400 and 500 people a day. We average 200 at breakfast and 250 at dinner."

"That's an impressive amount of people, especially with being understaffed," he said, amazed at the woman in front of him. This was going to be a great opportunity.

She cleared her throat, her blue eyes widening. "Who said we are understaffed? I don't recall saying anything like that." Her tone was curt, and it was obvious he'd struck a nerve.

"A volunteer said it yesterday while I waited to talk to you."

Her gaze didn't soften. "I hope you won't hold that against us. The Soup Kitchen does a tremendous amount of good in the city, especially this time of year."

He blinked. Did she think he wouldn't want to volunteer at a place that was understaffed? Was that her concern? He needed to dispel her fears about that. He hadn't decided on his project for sure, but helping a place that was light on volunteers was not a detriment to him. In fact, in some ways it made him feel like his contribution would mean more here. "It's not a problem for me."

She nodded, her smile tight. "Let me show you around the kitchen and the offices. Then we'll start on the paperwork."

Scott followed Kasey as she showed him the kitchen in great detail. "As you can see, we are up to code on everything. We have the kitchen regularly checked by the Health Director. Each of our volunteers who cook or work in the kitchen must have a food handler's permit. Our head cook is certified to teach the course and it's held on the second and fourth Saturdays of the month. We encourage all of our volunteers to come and be certified, but if not, they are trained on their specific jobs during the orientation meeting before each shift."

He asked questions, trying to show interest in both the charity and its process. He wanted to understand exactly what he'd be expected to do here and wondered if it was possible to serve in a capacity that would help him win the bet. But with each question, Kasey seemed more hesitant to answer.

"Our staff is fairly small, but it helps us keep our expenses low. We rely heavily on local volunteers and church groups to staff meal times. Most of the paid staff is required for logistics and coordination with different groups." She led him down a narrow hallway where photos of different youth groups were displayed. Individual photos hung on the opposite wall.

"Are these volunteers?" Scott asked.

Kasey nodded. "Several groups come back on a regular basis. Once a group has come a certain amount of times, they are recognized on this wall. Individuals who volunteer over 100 times are added to The 100 Club. It's not exactly an incentive to keep them coming back, but it's the way we show our appreciation for the groups that help us and make our jobs easier."

"I think it's a great idea," he offered.

Kasey smiled, and it felt like the first genuine smile Scott had seen from her today. "Thanks," she said.

After seeing a few other offices, Kasey led him into her own office. She sat down in the chair behind the desk, then motioned for him to sit as well.

He took the seat across from her. The office was small, and he supposed their ability to save money on the administrative side of things meant they could spend more on what the charity was really about. The idea caught hold of him. Was this a place where he could *actually* make a difference? Everything here already seemed to work like a well-oiled machine. Perhaps he should keep searching for another charity to help where he could make a bigger impact. He wasn't quite sure how to tell Kasey his thoughts. "I really appreciate you showing me around. I can't believe I never knew this place was here, and I've lived in Chicago for years. It's fantastic."

She smiled, looking at him appraisingly. "You've probably never needed our services before and that's a good thing."

"The Soup Kitchen seems like a great place to volunteer."

Kasey handed him a folder with a surprising amount of papers in it.

He opened it up. "Is this the volunteer form?"

Kasey looked amused. "I doubt we'd be able to keep any volunteers if we bogged them down with this much paperwork." She pulled out a one-page sheet from her desk drawer. "This is the volunteer form." She turned it over so he could see that it had questions on both sides. "We keep them on file for one year. All of them are stored in these binders."

"Could I have one of the volunteer forms?" he asked. He wanted to have a copy, in case he was ready to fill it out by the end of their meeting.

She handed him the paper.

He glanced over the questions and the waiver on the back. "You keep everything in paper form?" he asked, surprised it wasn't all digitized.

She nodded. "We've got an intern who is digitizing it, and making it available to fill out online, but it's convenient for the groups to gather the paper copies ahead of time with signatures, and then it's their ticket in the door. After groups are established and they already have their name badges, we don't need to collect them again."

"Have you thought about having a digital interface they can sign when they show up?" he asked. "Having a screen like an iPad would be convenient." He scanned the shelves in her office. They were completely full of 3-inch binders, each holding what he'd guess were hundreds of volunteer applications. His brain started spinning about all the possibilities and the ways he could help and he got excited about the prospect. Building a database where she could keep track of all the different volunteers might be helpful and exactly what The Soup Kitchen needed.

She nodded. "It would be convenient, but it's also an added cost, and a liability."

"What do you mean?"

"Technology is expensive. Trying to maintain a digital system is also expensive. Not to mention we'd have to secure that information online. All of our extra funds go toward feeding the homeless and any who come through our doors. Spending money on extras seems superfluous."

He nodded, feeling deflated. "That makes sense," he said, though from an efficiency standpoint he didn't think so. He surveyed her office, noting that the laptop she had on her desk was a few generations older than the current models out in the store. The worn furniture was well-loved, and had obviously seen better days. Nothing about this charity was pretentious. Perhaps this was exactly where he needed to make a difference. He wanted to tell her that, but his eyes landed on a Christmas snow globe on the edge of her desk. It appeared to be the most expensive item she had in the room. "You decorate for Christmas before Thanksgiving?" he asked.

She raised an eyebrow. "We typically decorate for Christmas after the Thanksgiving holiday."

He nodded toward the snow globe.

"Oh." She picked it up lovingly, becoming instantly entranced in the small winter scene. He realized that none of the smiles he'd seen on her earlier today had been as real as this one. As if detecting she was being watched, she blinked and put the snow globe back down on her desk, but closer to her. She waved her hand in the air. "It was a gift. I keep it on my desk all year long."

"There's more to that story, isn't there?"

She peeled a small sticky note off her desk and replaced it on her folder. "Why would you say that?"

He shrugged, more intrigued than he'd originally been. "Most people wouldn't keep a Christmas decoration out all year long." He wanted to ask more about the woman and why that gift was the only decoration in her entire office—the only personal item that seemed to be around, but she spoke before he could form the words.

"We should focus on this paperwork. There's a lot I still need to explain and clarify before we can get to lunch. I don't want to keep you," she said.

"Let's go now," he said, standing. At the mention of lunch his stomach rumbled. The tour had lasted longer than he'd expected, and he really would like to take the beautiful director out for lunch. He smiled as he recalled the way she'd brought it up last night. Even then her blue eyes had held a spark. There was something in them that challenged him, but he couldn't put his finger on it.

She scrunched her brow. "Go where? I've already given you the tour."

"Lunch. You said we can discuss the charity over lunch."

"I meant over the lunch-time hour, not actually lunch. The Soup Kitchen doesn't serve lunch."

Was she purposefully being difficult? He shrugged it off. "You said we'd talk over *lunch*."

"But—" She looked around her office.

"Did you already eat?" he asked her.

"No, but—"

"Then it's settled. It's time for lunch." He tucked the thick black folder underneath his arm. "We'll discuss the rest of this paperwork over food." He wasn't sure what training manuals he needed to read to become a volunteer, but he knew if he asked her what was in the folder she might just give him a short answer, and he'd miss out on lunch with her.

"The Soup Kitchen doesn't pay for lunches out," she protested.

He nodded. "I wasn't expecting you to pay. My treat."

She looked at him skeptically. "You're going to pay for lunch?"

"Yes."

"Why?"

Her question surprised him and he almost laughed at the way she was looking at him, but decided against it. "Why? Because I'm hungry, and from the look of this folder we still have a lot to discuss." And he wasn't sad about that at all. He'd happily go through mountains of paperwork if it meant spending more time with Kasey. As long as he could find a way to make a real difference, he planned on making this the charity he would help. Lunch with Kasey was just the icing on the very amazingly decorated cake.

CHAPTER 3

Kasey tied her scarf around her neck and buttoned up her coat. Scott's insistence of lunch had her stomach in a bundle of knots. The Health Department had sent in a charmer, and that made this whole process ten times worse.

"Where would you like to go for lunch?" he asked.

"You don't have a place in mind?" she asked back. The idea of picking anything close by flustered her, but parking at this time of day would be a nightmare. She definitely didn't want to take him to any place that she frequented—not that she went out to eat very often—but occasionally she and Trish had lunch at the bakery on the corner.

"I have several places in mind, but, I don't really know your preferences."

The kind gesture warmed her for a moment, but she quickly realized it was likely her coat and scarf since they were still standing indoors. "I … don't really have a preference. Somewhere close, I guess."

"There's a bakery on the corner—"

"How about somewhere else?" she suggested quickly. "What's your favorite place to eat in Chicago?"

He scratched his chin. "My favorite restaurant is reservation only. I suppose I'll have to take you there a different time."

She almost laughed at the joke, but instead just shouldered her bag.

"There's an Indian place not too far from here," he said.

"I like Indian food. That sounds great." And it was even better because Kasey didn't normally go for Indian food, so she wouldn't know the staff there. It was a relief that the bakery would not be a spoiled cafe in her life. Just having to lunch with the auditor would be bad enough. She didn't want questions about him later. She only imagined the amount of gossip it could stir up.

"My car is just over there in the parking garage. We can grab it, and we'll be at the restaurant in no time."

"It isn't within walking distance?"

Scott tilted his head. "It's a ten-minute drive away."

She should have stuck with the bakery, a place they could easily walk to, and a place where she could conveniently leave and get back to work. She didn't want to suggest that now, after she'd so quickly dismissed the suggestion.

She rambled while they drove, explaining all the great things about the charity, trying to make sure she was giving a positive impression. She couldn't let her guard down just because he'd offered to pay for lunch. She planned on paying for hers anyway. She explained the different measures they were taking to save money, hoping that she'd say the right things in the short amount of time they had in the car. Maybe, over the course of lunch, Scott would see exactly why they should be allowed to continue their work at the location they were in. After all, they weren't too far off track to secure the funding they needed to continue another year … as long as they weren't pushed out by big business.

They arrived at the restaurant, and as soon as they walked through the doors, Kasey knew exactly why she didn't recognize the name of the restaurant. Not only had she never eaten here, but everything from the entrance to the waiting area and the decor screamed fancy and rich.

"I can't pay for this," she said anxiously. She couldn't afford it on The Soup Kitchen's dime, and definitely not on her own. She'd planned on paying for herself, even though Scott had offered, but with the pay cut she took to be able to reinvest in the charity, she would have a hard time paying the grocery bill for a month with such an extravagant lunch.

"You're not paying," he said, walking straight toward the maître d' and asking for a table for two.

"You shouldn't be paying for this either," she said. Her brain spun.

He pursed his lips. "Would you be okay with eating here if I told you my company has a tab here?"

"It does?"

He nodded. "I'm allowed to bring anyone I want here."

That made her feel slightly better, though the obvious waste and extravagance of the commissioner's office bothered her. "And we are having a business lunch," she said aloud, working through her justification.

He nodded, but a muscle in his jaw worked hard.

The maître d' looked between the two of them. "Your host is ready to seat you whenever you are ready," he prompted.

"How about it?" he asked.

She nodded slowly. Fancy lunch or not, she wasn't going to cave in her position regarding The Soup Kitchen.

The host sat them in a booth, and Kasey tried not to gasp at the outrageous prices listed on the menu. At least there were prices. She settled on something small, avoiding the price of the dish as she ordered. Scott didn't seem to notice her discomfort as he ordered something for himself.

When the waiter brought their drinks and took their menus, Scott pulled open the black folder he'd carried into the restaurant.

"So, how do the finances of the charity work?"

That was the question she dreaded the most, though she knew it was one of the first he'd ask. The surprise health inspection was merely a cover for the real investigation, and she knew she shouldn't be surprised by it. It always came down to money and profitability. She had to defend her position.

She referenced a page number for his folder. She'd spent the majority of the night going through all of the numbers. She pointed out all of the information he asked for, ready for his next question.

He looked through the rest of the portfolio. "This is very thorough information," he commended.

She warmed at his praise, grateful that her hours last night and this morning were noticed in some small way. "Thank you."

He poured over a few of the pages. "Wow, there is so much

here. Do you mind if I read over this later, or is it a requirement for me to get through it before this evening's volunteer shift?"

Kasey's brain spun. What if he was just complimenting her on her detailed work so he could soften the blow that it didn't matter how thorough she'd been—it wouldn't be enough to save The Soup Kitchen—and that the location was doomed regardless of all she tried to do? She'd spent over an hour tossing and turning last night, trying to fall asleep, but this scenario and a host of others had run through her brain on repeat. Scott had been nice to her, was good-looking, and they were out at a very pricey restaurant that his company wanted to the foot the bill for. Warning flags were shooting up all over the place. She would not let down her guard. "I want you to know that I'm not giving up on The Soup Kitchen. I'm going to fight this."

He tilted his head at her and closed the folder. "What do you mean?"

"I mean I'm not going down without a fight. The Soup Kitchen is important to me. It's important to a lot of people. We do a great service for the community. Yes, we may be understaffed. Yes, I take a pay cut so that I can give back to the charity, and yes, sometimes things don't go as planned ... but that doesn't mean that it isn't an asset to the city."

Scott opened his mouth and then shut it again. "Of course it's an asset to the city."

Was he saying that to placate her? What was his angle? She'd dreaded meeting with the auditor for days, and especially last night, yet here he was—agreeing with her. "I'm confused."

"Why? I think what you're doing is incredible." He opened the folder and took out the green volunteer sheet, filled it out and signed the back. “In fact, I think The Soup Kitchen is exactly the sort of charity I’ve been looking to get involved in.” He handed her the filled-out form.

She took it automatically, not really focusing on the form. The food came just then, and Kasey sat stunned. Had Scott just agreed to help her? Why? His chocolate eyes watched her every move. “You want to *help* The Soup Kitchen?” Was she being punked? How could Scott say he wanted to get involved when he was the messenger sent to deliver the fatal blow to The Soup Kitchen? It made no sense. She ate a bite of food, hoping to dispel some of his scrutiny.

“Of course I want to help. This all looks great.”

“I guess that’s not what I was expecting,” she said in shock.

“I’d like to come help tonight if there’s room for me.” His dark eyes sparkled. He already knew from the volunteer yesterday that they were understaffed this week.

Her nod was an automatic response that she couldn’t prevent. “We can always use the help.”

“You look surprised,” he said.

She tried to focus on the exotic flavors of the food, savoring them through the heat. “Of course I’m surprised. First, you come to inspect The Soup Kitchen all to bring it down so it can be sold, and then you decide that you want to help by volunteering. What’s your angle? I can’t follow it.”

“Inspect? I’m not here to inspect. I was here to learn about volunteering.”

Heat rose to her cheeks. “But last night you said you wanted to see the person in charge.”

He nodded. “It’s the best way to get all of the information. And, may I say, you brief your volunteers extremely well.”

"I didn't realize you were just a volunteer."

"*Just?* From what I've learned about The Soup Kitchen, no one is *just* a volunteer." His eyes danced.

Her mouth went dry. "This isn't some kind of joke, is it? You really aren't from the City Commissioner's office come to shut me down and turn The Soup Kitchen into a parking garage?" She had to vocalize her fears. She needed to read on his face that he was sincere.

He was holding in a laugh, she could tell by the crinkle on the corners of his eyes. "I'm definitely not from the commissioner's office, and I'm not trying to shut you down. Is that what you're up against?"

She nodded slowly. "I was told to expect an auditor before the end of the year. You were so out of place in your suit last night, I guess I just assumed …"

Scott's lips twitched. "I've been mistaken for a lot of things, but an auditor is a new one."

"You really want to help volunteer?"

He nodded. "If that's okay with you."

"That would be great. I suppose I can take the portfolio back then." She shook her head, smiling as some of the stress she'd held onto since yesterday melted away. "I can't believe I stayed up half the night making sure this packet was perfect for a volunteer." Her eyes widened. "I didn't mean it like that."

"No offense taken," he said. He flipped through the portfolio again. "As I said, it is very thorough. I wonder if I could read through the entire thing before I return it to you."

"Sure. Most of the information is public knowledge anyway," she stated. After all, he'd seen the overview of it already. Would it do any harm if he read through it? It was highly improbable, considering that he only wanted to volunteer.

"So, now that you know I'm not trying to shut down The Soup Kitchen, let's talk openly."

"Okay."

"Why is The Soup Kitchen in trouble? Why would the City Commissioner get involved?"

She cleared her throat. "In a word? There are a lot of very uppity developers who are vying for that particular piece of property."

"Uppity?"

"You know, the rich and wealthy—you know the type."

"People or companies?" he asked.

"Does it matter? It's all the same." She tried to keep the bitterness out of her voice, surprised that she allowed it to sink in at all. Maybe it was the way Scott had noticed the snow globe on her desk. Even though she hadn't tipped it over to free the tiny white specks in the water, just holding it stirred up a hundred memories. Or maybe she'd just been on edge all day because of the supposed audit meeting.

"Companies are not the same as people," he said slowly.

She shrugged. "They're still run by the same type of people."

"The rich?" he asked, his expression guarded.

She nodded. She didn't want to dwell on the past and the reason why the bitterness poked into this conversation. It was better to move on from it. "There are a few companies who have petitioned the City Commissioner's office for a way to take over the building. Our one-story building in the middle of downtown has a huge potential for growth and progress for the city. They can't legally push us out, but they could potentially block the funding we get for the building if there was a legitimate concern. They'd love nothing more than to condemn the building, knock it down, and build another skyscraper in its place."

Scott nodded slowly. "Is there anything that you can think of that they could condemn the building for? The kitchen looked to code from all the certificates you showed me earlier."

She smiled. He was trying to lighten the mood. "That's what the portfolio is supposed to prove. We've followed every rule and code and restriction. I can't think of a single thing that they'd be able to bring against the building."

"Then it sounds like you have nothing to worry about," he said confidently, his smile widening.

"Thanks." Kasey was captured by the assurance in his voice and the way he smiled at her. She couldn't help but smile back, and instantly a shiver coursed through her. This morning she had been so on edge about meeting with Scott when she thought he was the auditor, but now that he was a volunteer, she found herself able to enjoy his dark eyes and his swoon-worthy smile.

CHAPTER 4

After lunch, Scott dropped Kasey off at The Soup Kitchen. Part of him wanted to follow her inside and ask more questions about the charity and about how he could specifically help. She was worried about funding, and he got the very strong vibe that she wasn't the kind of person who would look for a handout. The first few pages of the portfolio outlined the way they were cutting costs and getting donations in addition to the funding that was already put in place.

He drove back down the street where they'd eaten and where his building was only two blocks away. He pulled into his reserved parking stall and took the elevator up to his office. He felt each of Kasey's words as if they'd meant to sting him personally, though she didn't know who he was. *Rich people who owned companies.* That combination of words had never bothered him before. He blew out a heavy breath. He couldn't blame her for that mindset, not really. Especially not when they seemed to be the demographic that wanted to take over the place that was obviously so dear to her. He'd seen the way she'd looked around The Soup Kitchen, and it wasn't just a job to her.

He exited the elevator and looked around the floor. Cubicles were scattered throughout the middle of the expansive floor, with windowed offices on the perimeter. Did he look around his office with the same kind of love and devotion that she'd looked around The Soup Kitchen?

His personal assistant, Nancy, looked up from her desk, her bright blue glasses perched on top of her platinum hair. "Mr. Parker, I wasn't expecting to see you back in the office today, or any other day until after Christmas."

Scott smiled. Kyle and Kandice had given Nancy and his other friends' personal assistants specific instructions regarding the bet. "I'm not asking for your help, so I'm not breaking any rules by being here."

Nancy laughed. "You're getting too defensive for someone who isn't doing anything wrong."

Scott chuckled. "I'm going to volunteer tonight at The Soup Kitchen. Have you ever heard of it?"

Nancy nodded. "On the other side of town? Yeah, I know where it is." She leaned forward and lowered her voice. "Is that the charity you've decided to help?"

"I think so. I just need to work out a few things. Could you get Kyle on the phone for me? I need to talk to him if he is available."

"Sure thing," Nancy said, picking up her desk phone. "Is there anything else I can do for you while you're here?"

"I think I'm good for right now."

"Well, feel free to email me a to-do list on a daily basis while you're out of the office. What you've given me so far will barely last me through this week."

"Thanks, Nancy."

"That's what I'm here for," Nancy said, then held the receiver to her ear. "Mr. Montgomery? I have Mr. Parker on the phone for you." She covered the receiver and mouthed, "Line one," to Scott as he walked into this office.

Scott picked up the phone. "Hi, Kyle."

"Hey, Scott. Is it reporting time already? You're fast."

"I think I found my project," he said.

"That's great. Let me get Kandice on the phone so she can hear the details too."

Scott waited, and soon Kyle was back on the phone with Kandice.

"Hi, Scott. I can't wait to hear what you have in mind," Kandice said.

Scott told them both about his meeting with Kasey the night before and this afternoon. He filled them in on the details he'd learned about how The Soup Kitchen was under review. He finished by explaining his interest in the project with helping the charity succeed, and in his plan to work as a volunteer during dinner that night.

"Sounds like you're off to a great start," Kyle said.

"I agree," Kandice chimed in. "Have you thought about how you'll use your $10,000 toward the charity?"

"Not yet. I'm still trying to figure out the best way I can make an impact on the charity."

"And serving as a volunteer is part of it?" Kyle asked.

"Actually, I don't know. I just thought it would be a good place to start." Scott drummed his fingers on the glass top desk.

He was still trying to figure all of this out and he didn't really have a plan. The only thing he was sure of was that he was intrigued by Kasey, and he very much wanted to help her. He'd just gotten so excited about the whole thing, especially the amusing part where Kasey thought he was from the City Commissioner's office, that he knew he needed to share the information with someone. Normally he would have called Troy to tell him the news, and also to see if he had already come up with an idea, but Kyle had specifically banned them from talking about their individual projects with each other. Scott wasn't sure he liked that rule at all, but he'd comply with Kyle's directives. It wasn't like Kyle had banned them from talking to each other *altogether*. They just needed to avoid information about their specific projects.

"I think it's a great idea to help that way," Kandice said.

"Thanks. I'm going to read the portfolio that Kasey let me borrow, and see if there is anything else that stands out to me that I'd be good at."

"Thanks for keeping us in the loop. Let us know if you find anything," Kyle said.

"Congrats, Scott. You're off to a really great start," Kandice added.

"Thanks, guys. I'm looking forward to this challenge."

"That's what we like to hear," Kyle said. "Call us when you have an update."

"I will," Scott said, and then he hung up.

Scott spent the next twenty minutes reading through the portfolio, and while it was very detailed, it didn't leave Scott with any ideas on how he could specifically help the charity. It made sense that the portfolio was written that way. If there was something lacking, Kasey had done a very good job at not bringing any attention to it. After all, this portfolio was intended for the auditor, and it would still go to him at some point.

Nancy knocked on his door, and then let herself into his office.

Scott looked up from his desk where he'd spread out several of the sheets from Kasey's portfolio.

"I have a few things for you to sign, if now is good for you," Nancy said.

He nodded. "Happy to." He took the stack of papers that were tabbed with arrows pointing to lines. He went through several of them.

Nancy gathered the stack when he was finished. "Thanks. I'll email you any that need your immediate attention while you're out."

"I still plan on being in the office a couple times a week," Scott replied. Sure, he'd love to spend lunch with Kasey every day, especially now that they were on the same page, and she didn't think he was trying to shut the charity down. But, he imagined that with the morning and evening hours taken up with her managing the volunteers during the meal shifts, the middle of the day was probably when she accomplished her administrative work. He wanted to help, but he didn't want to be in the way.

Nancy looked at him skeptically. "I thought Kyle said you were supposed to be at the charity full-time."

"No, that's not quite the stipulation. Yes, we're supposed to help a lot, but I'll still be connected here when things are slow at the charity."

"Okay. I will save myself the hassle of digitizing these files then, and you can just sign them when you're here."

"That sounds like a great plan."

"I come up with fairly good plans," Nancy said. "Too bad Kyle and Kandice banned all personal assistants from helping. I have lots of great ideas."

Scott's curiosity was piqued. "What kind of ideas?"

"I think what you meant to say is what kind of *hypothetical* ideas." Nancy raised her eyebrows expectantly.

"Sure. Wordsmith my sentences."

"It's part of my job," Nancy retorted. "When you were telling Kyle and Kandice about the City Commissioner's office it got me thinking."

Scott smirked. "Eavesdropping on a conversation you're not supposed to be a part of?"

Nancy waved a hand in the air. "You encourage me to listen to your phone calls. It speeds up our discussions. Besides, I can be prepared for meetings much better if I know the back story."

"Yes, but you're not supposed to help with the charity."

"Technically I'm not supposed to do any of the work, and you can't delegate things to me, but they never said anything about me listening in and making hypothetical suggestions about the politics surrounding a charity."

"Feels like a stretch," Scott speculated.

"Then don't take the advice to reach out to the City Commissioner's office to see if there is any way they'd back off. After all, your name carries a lot of weight in this city." Nancy shrugged. "Anyway, it was just a thought—a *hypothetical* thought," she corrected.

"I like it. Thanks, Nancy."

"Happy to not help anytime." Nancy laughed.

Scott pushed the papers back into a stack and tucked them back into the portfolio. "I'd better head out for my volunteering shift."

"Enjoy that. What a good experience," Nancy expressed. She always helped arrange the company service projects and, while Scott always picked which charities the company would donate to, Nancy was the one in charge of facilitating the payments and keeping good relationships between his company and the charities.

SCOTT WALKED THROUGH THE SOUP KITCHEN DOORS AT THE appointed time for the dinner volunteer shift to start. There were two dozen other people in the room, but Kasey was not among the group. They handed in their volunteer forms and were each given an assignment. When everyone had a job, the curly, brown-haired woman checking in the volunteers hushed the crowd. Scott recognized her as one of the staff that was talking to Kasey yesterday shortly after he'd arrived.

"Hello, everyone. I'm Trish. I'll be your volunteer coordinator for the evening, so if you have any questions at any time during the evening, please don't hesitate to ask. Thank you so much for coming. We are so grateful for everyone here! We really appreciate it when youth groups come and we really love having our returning volunteers. Thanks for making this a regular part of your month. You each have your assignment, but I want to go over a few safety guidelines first."

Trish continued talking about food safety, logistics of the

line moving through the room, and what to do if anyone wanted seconds. She explained a brief overview of the policies and procedures, which was similar to the guidelines printed on the back side of the volunteer form. When she finished the orientation she asked, "Are there any questions?" Trish scanned the room, and called on a youth in the front.

"Can we switch off between food assignments?"

"Yes, every half hour we rotate to a different station," Trish said. "Are there any others?" She answered a few more questions.

Scott glanced over the room, looking for any sign of Kasey. He couldn't see her at all. Disappointment settled around him. He wanted to talk to her about how he could make a difference, but there was more to it than that. He wanted to see her blue eyes again, especially since they'd seemed to sparkle ever since she cleared up the misunderstanding that he wasn't the auditor.

Trish stood in front of him. "Hi, um, Mr. ..."

"I'm Scott," he said. He was the only one still standing in the middle of the room.

"Hi, Scott. So the rest of the volunteers went this way. There's a room to put any belongings you brought with you, as well as several sinks for washing before we start. That is—actually, I'm confused. Are you here to volunteer?"

He nodded. "I was hoping to see Kasey."

"You're the auditor, auditing the way we work the volunteers?"

He held up his hands in a sign of innocence. "No, I'm not the auditor, or anything like that. I'm just someone who came to volunteer."

She smacked his shoulder playfully. "Well, how about that!

Such great news. You really are too gorgeous to be a snake or an auditor. You've basically made my whole night." Trish was practically bouncing on her toes, bubbly and excited.

He supposed that she was giving him a compliment, and that her animated personality was a helpful thing around here. "Uh, thanks," he answered. "So the first door here?" He pointed to the way she'd indicated before.

"Yep, just right around the corner. But, if you're *not* the auditor, why are you looking for Kasey?" Trish's eyes grew large and seemed to be suspicious of his every movement.

"Oh, I just assumed she would be here because she was here last night," he hedged. "And I was hoping to ask her a few more questions that I didn't ask at lunch today."

Trish put a hand over her mouth. "Wait. I thought she went out with the auditor today for lunch."

"She thought I was the auditor."

"If you wanted to ask her out, you didn't have to pretend you were the auditor."

Scott smiled. This conversation was getting strange. "I didn't pretend to be the auditor on purpose. Just a case of misunderstanding is all. And I'm here to help however I can." Which was why he wanted to see Kasey, well at least one of the reasons why he wanted to see her. He had to ask her about the portfolio.

"So you came to volunteer?" Trish asked.

"Until I can find other ways to help." Scott entered the small room as most of the volunteers were filtering out, hung his coat, and washed his hands.

Trish was waiting by the door as he exited the room. She turned off the light, locked the door, and turned to Scott to explain. "We don't guarantee that possessions brought here will stay safe, but we do lock this room during meals so that no one can access it unattended."

"That's smart," Scott said, following Trish out to The Gathering. The volunteers assembled and took their places for serving food. He waited until everyone else was situated before he asked Trish, "Are there other things I could help with around here, besides just helping at meal times?"

"There are some other projects, but we don't usually get to them." Trish tilted her head. "Are you single?"

Confusion settled around Scott. "Is that a requirement?"

Trish laughed. "Oh no, of course it's not a requirement. I was just curious. I mean this place takes a lot of time, and most people don't have a lot of time to spend hours on end here. So, are you dating someone?"

Scott smiled. "Not at the moment."

"How is it possible that a guy as handsome as you has not already been snatched up?"

Scott looked around, but none of the other volunteers seemed to pay any attention to their conversation. "I work a lot."

Trish scrunched her face. "Then how—"

"But I have a lot more free time in my schedule for the next couple months. I have very little work to do from now until the New Year," he said. He hoped that him saying he worked a lot wouldn't get back to Kasey and hurt his chances of helping with the charity.

Trish's smile spread wide. "Fair enough. Kasey is practically married to her work too. I mean, she hasn't said actual vows, but her whole life revolves around this place."

"So Kasey isn't seeing anyone?" His heart rate picked up.

"She's definitely single."

Scott lowered his voice. "I'd really like to help The Soup Kitchen in a more meaningful way."

"We've been short-staffed for a while. We just had one of our coordinators quit." Trish covered her mouth with her hand. "I probably shouldn't have told you that. Kasey doesn't want it to be public knowledge, especially when the real auditor could show up at any time."

"I'm not going to tell anyone, but I would really like to help."

Trish looked him square in the face. "You like Kasey, don't you?"

The question caught Scott off guard. "I don't really know her that well."

"But you want to get to know her better?" she probed.

"I would really like that," Scott said, still surprised by the turn this conversation took. Warmth spread through him. He really would like to get to know Kasey better.

Trish's smile looked triumphant. "I knew it."

The doors opened and for the next two hours Scott busily scooped food onto plates. There was a moment when he thought Trish might come and talk to him again, but while people continuously filtered inside, he was too busy with his job to even notice Trish or look for Kasey again.

After the shift was over, Scott let the rest of the volunteers go before him. He wasn't in a hurry to leave, and he still wanted to talk to Kasey about ideas for how to donate his $10,000. Of course, he didn't want to lead with that idea. He remembered all too well her statements at lunch about the rich and privileged. There had to be some way to change her mind about that. In the meantime, he'd focus on how to help. There had to be something they needed that he could take care of. And in the meantime, maybe he'd ask Kasey out.

Another volunteer coordinator unlocked the room where they'd kept their belongings.

"What time does the shift start in the morning?" Scott asked the older woman with the keys.

She smiled. "6:30 a.m. Breakfast is served from 7:00 until 9:00."

"Thank you," Scott said. As he was about to leave, he spotted Trish coming out of the kitchen. "Hey, Trish. No sign of Kasey tonight?"

Trish shrugged. "Sometimes she gets caught up with other duties."

"Will she be here tomorrow?"

"I think so. She's for sure on the schedule as coordinator for the breakfast shift. I may take over on the evening shift again."

He nodded. "If you see her before I do, let her know I'll be here tomorrow, and I still want to figure out how to help her. The portfolio she gave me is interesting, but it doesn't give me the details I need. I'd really like to talk with her again."

Trish glanced toward the kitchen door and back at Scott. "I'm sure she'll be able to find some time to talk to you tomorrow."

"Thank you, Trish. I really appreciate that."

"No problem. Have a good night."

CHAPTER 5

Kasey pretended to busy herself in the kitchen. It had been a hot couple of hours taking her turn cooking and preparing the food, but she'd been able to see Scott from where she was serving without him noticing her. She wiped down the kitchen counter for the fourth time, convinced it would be clean only when Trish came through the door to give her some news.

As if her thoughts could actually summon her friend, Trish walked through the kitchen doors, a grin on her face. "I think Scott is the nicest volunteer we've had all month. Now, why did you decide to avoid him through the entire evening?" asked Trish, giving her a pointed look.

Kasey went to the sink and rinsed out her dish cloth. "I'm not avoiding him. Not exactly. It was my turn in the kitchen."

"You're totally avoiding him, and you know it."

Kasey shrugged. "Maybe just a little. We spent the whole afternoon together, and he bought me lunch."

Trish's smile widened. "See, now we're getting to the good stuff. You let him buy you lunch—so it was like a *date*."

"Not a date. I let him pay because I thought he was the auditor and—"

"And he's gorgeous!" Trish exclaimed.

That wasn't what she was going to say. "No."

"No? You don't think he's gorgeous?" Trish looked at her skeptically.

"Okay, yes he's good-looking, but that's not what I was going to say."

"Good-looking? Kasey, are you blind? The man is gorgeous, not just handsome, not just hot, but like seriously *gorgeous*. Admit it."

Heat creeped onto Kasey's cheeks. She wanted to blame the stuffy kitchen, but when she thought about Trish's observation again, the heat increased. "Okay, I admit it."

"No, that's not admitting it. Say the actual words."

Kasey rolled her eyes. "We're not in college anymore, oogling guys."

"I'm not oogling. It's not a crime to notice when someone is gorgeous. It's a crime *not* to notice."

"Okay, fine. He's gorgeous. Happy?" Kasey leaned against the kitchen counter for support.

"And, lucky for you, he's also not the auditor *or* the health inspector."

"Where are you going with this, Trish?"

"The point is you need to seize more opportunities in your life."

The conversation came to a halt when Ann, The Soup Kitchen's head cook, came back in from taking the garbage out to the dumpster in the back alley. "Are you still here, Kasey? The kitchen looks great, and I'm about to lock up. Thanks for your help in the kitchen today."

"Anytime, Ann. Thank you." Kasey gave the kitchen a once over. Ann was right, everything was done. She ran her fingers along the immaculate counter. "Goodnight."

"See you in the morning," Ann said.

Kasey left the kitchen, and Trish followed close behind her.

"Don't think you're getting out of this conversation," Trish said. "We're not finished discussing this."

When they reached her office, Kasey grabbed her coat off the back of the door and pulled her purse from the drawer. "What do you mean? I seize opportunities all the time." She buttoned up her coat.

"Not when it comes to love, you don't."

Kasey scoffed at that. "Trish, noticing a hot guy is not love. Besides, he's probably not on the market."

Trish waved a hand in the air. "Actually, he *is* on the market. He's not dating anyone."

"How did you find that out?"

"I find lots of things out. He asked about you and looked for you the entire night. He wants to do more to help than just mealtime volunteering. And you know we're understaffed."

Kasey had known that from the half dozen text messages that Trish sent her during the meal, which was exactly why she'd decided it was better to stay in the kitchen. It was sweet that he came to volunteer, but twenty-four hours ago she thought he was the auditor. "That doesn't mean anything. After all, you said it yourself, he's looking for a way to help The Soup Kitchen, not to go on dates."

"Then why did you avoid him?"

Why had she? Possibly the embarrassment over thinking he was someone else—someone who'd come to shut them down? She took a steadying breath. "I don't have time for relationships, Trish. I'm here every morning and every evening, and all the time in between. How does that schedule actually work for dating? The work here is important to me, and with the possibility of the city taking this building away, I don't have time."

"He sounds like he's normally busy too, so maybe you're a perfect match. Except, he did say that he was going to be volunteering through the holidays. Who knows what would happen if you don't hide out in the kitchen for the rest of the month?" Trish teased.

"I wasn't hiding out. I was helping."

Trish laughed. "You can't fool me. He's coming back tomorrow. And if you stay in the kitchen for the whole day, I will tell him where to find you."

Kasey laughed. "You're not going to let this go, are you?"

"Not until you agree to give him a chance if he asks you out."

Kasey adored Trish, but she had it all wrong. Kasey had spent the better part of the day with Scott, showing him everything about The Soup Kitchen. She'd shared with him all the highlights, because that was what she needed to do when she thought he was the auditor. Now she knew the truth—he really was just looking for a way to volunteer. He'd signed the volunteer form without hesitation, and came to the first available shift. The Soup Kitchen had a way of drawing people in like that, all full of excitement to help in such a noble cause.

She'd seen people's enthusiasm before about volunteering,

especially during the holiday season. Today's experience with Scott followed that pattern. There was something about the change in the weather and the spirit of Thanksgiving and Christmas that motivated people to volunteer more than they normally would. It was a great thing, but those folks never lasted. The holiday busyness would inevitably kick in, and volunteers would drop out of their commitments. She couldn't hold it against them, though. Life had a way of hindering important service, and she understood that. But she also didn't hold her breath when people said they were here to help for longer than a day. She'd learned that lesson the hard way growing up.

She could be pleasantly surprised by people, but she wouldn't get her hopes up … even when the promises were something she wanted to believe in desperately. Scott was feeling the initial excitement because she'd shown him the entire process today. Of course he was going to feel the need to help. Most people that she'd given an in-depth tour to felt that way. "He's not interested in me. He's interested in helping the charity."

"But if he asks you out …"

It was a moot point, so Kasey said, "Fine, if it comes up, I will think about it."

Trish wiped her brow. "Whew, it's exhausting trying to knock some sense into you."

"And what if he's really just here to help—will you drop it?"

Trish rolled her eyes. "Sure, but what a tragic waste. He's so gorgeous."

Warmth spread through Kasey. She wasn't blind. Scott was gorgeous, but there was something more to him. There was a depth in his chocolate eyes that whispered of the possibility that he might be the kind of person who would stick around. She didn't want to hope for it, but hope bubbled up inside her anyway.

KASEY WAS A BUNDLE OF NERVES THE NEXT MORNING WHEN SHE came into work. Trish's words from last night stuck with her all morning. She fished the keys out of her purse to open The Soup Kitchen door.

"Good morning," uttered a deep voice.

She turned to see Scott standing on the sidewalk. Her pulse quickened. "Good morning, Scott. You're here early." It was thirty minutes before volunteers were expected to arrive.

"I wanted to make sure I caught you before the breakfast rush. I went through the entire packet you gave me yesterday, and I'm hoping you have some ideas for me."

She didn't want to put her trust in something that wouldn't happen. "The lifeblood of this organization is our volunteers. We're grateful for everyone who helps on a daily basis."

"Like I told Trish, I can already do that, but I want to do more."

She held the door open and let him in. It was still early, but the breakfast line would start soon. She locked the door behind them, and they made their way to her office. "Volunteering last night is already more than you've done though, isn't it?"

He nodded slowly. "I suppose it's more than I've been doing. But I feel this push to go above and beyond that."

She pasted on a smile, even though her heart sank. She'd

seen this scenario so many times. It always started as a big push for a big dream, but the energy and the excitement would burn out quickly. "Sometimes it's best to start slow."

He tilted his head. "I didn't take you for someone who refused volunteer service just because it's big and immediate."

"The Soup Kitchen needs steadiness."

"But right now it's understaffed and it's under scrutiny from the city. I could help with both of those things, if you'd let me."

"You really want to help?" Kasey tried to read the sincerity in his eyes, but her ability was stifled by how his eyes captured hers. Trish was wrong though, he was here to help the charity, not to *date* her.

"That's what I'm here for. And I'm okay with taking shifts helping during mealtimes, but I'd like to help on other projects in between."

Kasey nodded. "Two of our full-time staff just quit, and three of the college interns we hire each semester had to cut back their time due to finals coming up in a month. In addition to getting ready for the actual auditor, we're also raising money and asking for donations. The interns were making calls to businesses that have donated at Christmastime in the past."

"I can handle phone calls to businesses. What else?"

She smiled. He really was the go-getter type. Did that mean he would burn out quickly? "Let's start with that for today. I have a few other things as well, but I need to get a handle on them first before I pass them off."

"Fair enough. I have time in my schedule today."

"I can put you to work as soon as breakfast is over."

"I already told Trish that I'd volunteer this morning during breakfast," he offered.

"She mentioned that." And immediately Trish's other words about him being gorgeous and asking questions about her popped into her mind, heating her cheeks. He raised an eyebrow, as if waiting for her to say more, but she couldn't come up with anything. They'd been talking about volunteering, and now her brain was off the rails thinking about *him*.

She was saved by the bell as Trish popped her head in. "Oh, hey guys. Nice to see you again, Scott." Then Trish turned her focus. "Kasey, I was thinking that if Scott is going to help us with more than meal shifts, he should have an office. We could put him in the interns' office for now." Trish's eyes sparkled.

Kasey flushed. The interns' office was conveniently located right next to her office. The rest of the offices weren't far away, but now that it was mentioned, Kasey couldn't think of a good reason to put him anywhere else.

"Sure," Kasey said.

Trish beamed. "I reformatted one of the laptops last night so it's ready for use again. I'll leave it in the office, and make sure the phone is working in there."

"Thanks, Trish," Kasey called, as Trish hurried out the door.

"She seems nice."

"She's really nice. And she's a good friend."

"She's very friendly," Scott said.

"She's also dating someone," Kasey said, then covered her mouth. "I mean, not that you need to know … never mind."

Scott smiled. "That's good to know, but she's not my type."

Kasey resisted the urge to ask what his type was, but instead she pushed an application form toward him. "We usually have everyone who volunteers here fill out this form."

Scott frowned at it. "Does it require more personal information than yesterday's volunteer application?"

"No, just the standard stuff. It goes into a file. No one looks at it unless you're injured or something. I mean, our HR department is pretty small." She gestured around the room, then toward the locked file cabinet.

He nodded. "I'll fill it out." He took a pen from her, and made quick work of the questions. When he was finished, he handed her the paper.

Kasey immediately put it into a folder without glancing at it. It was mostly routine information, and she wouldn't need it unless she needed to get a hold of him. "That was easy enough," she said. "Now we have your information if we need to get a hold of you."

He nodded. "But what if I need to get a hold of *you*?"

She handed him a business card from her desk. "Feel free to call me anytime. I'm always here." She cringed. She'd made it sound like she *wanted* him to call her anytime. Ugh. She was going to have a talk with Trish. Their conversation about Scott was messing with her head.

"What if it's not during business hours? Is this your cell?"

She raised an eyebrow, her heart rate picked up speed. "It's my desk phone here."

He nodded. "I guess I should get started at my desk?

"Sure. The interns' office is just right next door." Ugh. That sounded dumb. Why was she sounding dumb? She got up from her desk and walked out the door, as if he needed help finding the office that was right next to hers. There was only one option. She flipped on the lights. The room held a few desks and chairs, and a small round table in the center of the room for collaborative discussions. The space was cramped when it held three or four people working at the same time, but for one person, it was fine. At least she hoped it would be fine. "That's the laptop Trish mentioned. And she will have all the information about where the interns got to on their calling list."

Scott nodded. "I'll follow up with her. Thanks, Kasey."

She swallowed. "I'm just around the corner if you need anything. Or you can call." She laughed nervously at herself. How ridiculous! "I mean, not that you need to call me when you're right next door. Well, you know."

He smiled. "I'll keep you posted," he said. "Where would I find Trish to get the calling list?"

Kasey pointed down the hallway, and he walked that way. When he was around the corner she slumped against the wall. Scott had turned her head—asking for her number like he'd cared to ask her out, and then what had she done? She'd given him a business card with her business phone number. Ugh. Trish was right. She really was out of practice with the dating stuff and, she definitely did not seize opportunities when they were in front of her. Maybe it was time to change that. She straightened up with a new resolve. The next time an opportunity came to give someone her number, she wouldn't blow it by giving out her business card.

CHAPTER 6

The first thing Scott noticed about breakfast at The Soup Kitchen was that it was just as busy as dinner the night before, but there were less volunteers. Maybe that was to be expected. After all, the volunteer hours overlapped the start of the work day. When Scott pointed that out, Trish had explained that volunteers included more than just the workforce and ranged from scouts, to college students, to stay-at-home-moms. There wasn't just one need and so there wasn't just one way to solve the need. Scott liked that. The breakfast meal was much simpler, allowing for less volunteers overall. Scott scooped out oatmeal next to a man who handed out one piece of fruit to each person.

Kasey helped in various places throughout The Gathering during the two hours breakfast was served. Scott recognized a few of the faces that came through the line. He tried hard to keep his attention on the oatmeal and the people he served, but more than a few times, he found himself searching for Kasey.

He spotted her next to the old piano where a little girl handed her a paper. Kasey bent down to the girl and gave her a hug. The little girl smiled, and Kasey took the picture and taped it above the piano where several others were hanging.

"I'd like some oatmeal, please," a man with a scruffy beard and toothless grin said.

"Of course," Scott said, handing the man a bowl.

"Thank you," he said. "God bless you."

Scott smiled, wanting to reply but the next person was already in front of him. If he wanted to carry on a quick conversation, he'd need to speak up faster in the future.

When he looked back toward the piano, both Kasey and the little girl were gone. He wouldn't have time to look for Kasey and ask her about the little girl while the line moved increasingly faster. Scott got into a rhythm of serving food and asking questions. He talked with the volunteers next to him during the short lulls between people, and soon the breakfast line waned. Most received their food and were completely done by the time they closed the door at 9:00 a.m., though a few took their food outside with them.

Scott followed the other volunteers to get the cleaning supplies, and they divided the tables to be cleaned. It only took them a few minutes. When the volunteers began filing out, Scott lingered behind.

Kasey caught up to him. "How did breakfast go?"

The words felt stuck in his throat. "It went well, I think. There wasn't a lot of food leftover, so that's a good sign, right?"

"A very good sign. Ann is pretty amazing at the food prep. She's in charge of it most days."

Scott nodded, following her back to where were. "I saw you with the little girl."

Kasey smiled. "That's Tess. She loves art. Some Saturdays we have paper and crayons out for the kids, a color pictures. Tess made one at school of The Soup Kitchen, and she brought it to me."

"That's adorable," Scott said. "Do you get to know a lot of people that come here?"

Kasey nodded. "I've been here for over four years. I know the regulars. Some are more chatty and friendlier than others. I see them more than I see most people. And some of them, like Tess, become very dear to me, almost like family." Her voice was wistful.

Scott let Kasey's words sink in. "You really care about this place, don't you?"

Her mouth hung open. "Of course I do. It's my life."

"But not your whole life?"

She shrugged. "It's what I do."

Scott spent the next four hours working hard at The Soup Kitchen. He made dozens of calls to the rest of the phone numbers on the list, but with each call he felt like he was getting the cold shoulder. No wonder the interns didn't last long. It was grueling work. He never had this kind of trouble at his own job. Rejection was never so obvious or frequent. He'd gotten used to his name and status in the community getting him a little more notoriety. Not all of the calls were outright rejections though. Some of them were very polite like, *"Don't call us, we'll call you,"* or *"Someone will get back to you on this."* He didn't count all of them out completely, and he'd left several messages … but announcing himself as "Scott, from The Soup Kitchen," didn't grant him any extra favors.

He poured through the list again, calling more numbers, and researching businesses to call from the list. He left more messages. He was nothing if not persistent. He'd keep trying to raise money.

He ended his calls with a few donations, though none of them felt especially impressive. He thought about his own $10,000 that he was allowed to put toward the charity for the bet. Would $10,000 be impressive to Kasey? Or was there a better use for his money than simply the donation lumped in with the rest of what he collected over the phone? He'd have to think on that. Kasey had made it clear from day one that she wasn't a fan of rich people who owned companies—and that prejudgment still sort of bothered him. Perhaps it was for the best that he hadn't asked her out yet. She intrigued him, and more than once when they were in the same room together he'd felt her watching him, but he wasn't sure if she'd be okay with his status. It was funny, he'd never thought his status had hurt him before ... or maybe he just hadn't noticed before, the way he noticed now with Kasey.

He turned Kasey's business card over in his hand. He hadn't thought of a reason to call her yet … well, other than to ask her out. Why was that so hard? He picked up the receiver he'd used all afternoon. He'd made phone calls and been rejected for the last several hours. He could absolutely make another phone call. But this time the possibility of being rejected felt way more personal. He hesitated before dialing the number, then held his breath.

"You've reached The Soup Kitchen. This is Kasey. How can I help you?"

"Hi, Kasey. This is Scott Parker, from the office next door."

She laughed. "Hi, Scott. How are you?"

"Good. I wasn't sure if you were in your office." He rubbed his forehead. Where else would she be at this time of day?

"How are the calls going? Do you need something else to keep you busy?"

"Calls are going fine. But that's not why I'm calling."

"How can I help?"

"You can say yes when I ask you to go out with me."

"You're asking me out?"

"That's what I'm trying to do. What do you say? Will you go out with me?"

She cleared her throat. "You know my schedule is busy …"

"You have to eat sometime. Why not with me?"

"Okay, but nothing too fancy."

He remembered her comments about the rich, and he didn't want to push her right now. Not until he'd thought of a good way to show her that rich didn't equal uncaring. "You can pick the place."

"I'd like that."

Scott breathed a sigh of relief. "Are you working the dinner shift tonight?" he asked. He knew that Kasey relied on Trish and a couple other staff members so she wasn't needed to run things every night, but would tonight be too soon?

"Patty is handling the volunteer coordination today, so I technically have the night off. But I have some work I need to catch up on like donations for this weekend. Tomorrow is better."

He smiled. She technically had evenings off half the week, yet she'd been here every single day working or helping volunteers. Her compassion and the way she helped others was admirable. "Tomorrow it is."

A few hours later he knocked on her door and entered when he heard her say to come in.

"You're still here," she said, surprised.

"I figured if you were staying late, I could work late, too. I doubt I'll get any further on calling businesses after hours though. Is there anything I can help you with?"

She thought for a moment, then gave him a new project coordinating the fundraisers for the month, focusing on gathering donations for Thanksgiving.

He looked at the large whiteboard calendar across the hall. Thanksgiving was a big event, but Christmas was even more detailed. Different service projects were written in different marker colors. How much of that had already been planned? Maybe some of those projects could use his $10,000 donation. Thanksgiving Day weekend had a lot of activities. He made a mental note to ask her about it later, after he really sank his teeth into the project she'd just given him. He went back to his office and got to work.

An hour later there was a knock at his door. He looked up, his pulse speeding when he saw Kasey standing in his doorway. "I'm going to call it a night," she said. "You about ready?"

He nodded, shutting down the computer and locking his files in his drawer. "I'm ready," he said. He turned off the light and followed her out of his office.

She went back into her office, and lifted a heavy box of files.

"Here, let me help," he said, taking the box from her.

"Thanks," she said, grabbing a second box.

"What are all these?" he asked.

"More work. I might do a little tonight, but tomorrow Patty is taking the morning shift, so I'll work from home in the morning before coming in. Some of this stuff just needs a little more thinking room, you know? It's easier if I spread all the papers out on my kitchen table and just look over it for a few hours."

"Oh, I get that," he said as they walked out through The Gathering. The room was completely silent since everyone else had left for the night.

They made small talk while he helped her carry the boxes to the parking garage. After he loaded them into her car, he moved to open the driver's side door for her and his fingers brushed against hers. The touch had his mind spinning in a hundred different directions, but the thing that stuck out the most was the fact that he didn't get her actual number earlier. Now would be a good time to remedy that, especially if he was going to go into his own office tomorrow and she was working at home.

She smiled at him, lowering herself into the seat. "Thanks for all your help today, and for helping me with the files."

"I'm happy to help with anything you need." He went to ask for her number but the words felt stuck in his throat. They were going out to dinner tomorrow … maybe he should just leave it until then. "So, I'll see you tomorrow then," he said.

She scrunched her brow. "I'm working from home in the morning …"

"Right, I mean for our dinner plans, remember?"

She nodded, inserting her key into the ignition. "Oh, yeah. Dinner—that'll be great."

"We'll leave from The Soup Kitchen? Or I can come pick you up?" Why was this so difficult? It shouldn't be this hard. He'd already asked her out, but if she wasn't going to be in the office in the morning, and he only had her work phone number, he wouldn't be able to coordinate with her tomorrow.

"I'll be here in the afternoon for sure. There's so much to do, and I can't bring all my files home."

"You could if they were digital," he said automatically.

"Touché. Maybe that's why we haven't converted everything over digitally then," she said.

The statement gave Scott pause, but he laughed it off. Maybe there were businesses that did better when ease of access to information was restricted. Kasey put in such long hours that she practically lived at the office. He could only imagine that the additional time she spent on work at home would increase if she was able to have more than just two banker's boxes full of files to go through at a time. "Since you'll be gone in the morning, is it okay with you if I head into my office to work for a few hours? I'll make the rest of the calls from there. I shouldn't be there too long."

"Sure, it's okay with me. Thanks for working through the call list. Trish and I divided all the calls up between us and the interns and a few other staff. I know it seems like a lot, but it was a lot more originally. I still have some calls to make too. I try to spread out the calls over a few weeks. It's hard when there's too much rejection all at once, and I have my other responsibilities too. Sorry, I'm rambling. Thanks again for helping."

He was going to sound like a broken record if he focused on her praise. He was happy to help, but he'd already said that multiple times. "I'll see you tomorrow afternoon. Goodnight, Kasey," he said. He closed her door and waved goodbye to her then headed toward the stairs to the next level where his car was parked. He was almost to the stairs, when he heard his name.

He turned around, and Kasey was out of her car and coming his way. His heart leapt for a brief moment. Maybe she didn't want to wait until tomorrow afternoon to talk with him either. The thought rooted him where he was. If she said the word, he'd go to a late dinner with her tonight, or even just coffee. They didn't even have to order anything, he just wanted to spend time with her outside of the charity. Maybe that meant he wasn't focusing on the bet like he should, but there was no harm in being attracted to the person you were helping, was there?

She smiled wide, her lips perfectly framing her teeth. "I'm glad I caught you," she said, when she was only a few feet away from him.

He wanted to wrap her up in an embrace and explore what it would be like to kiss her lips. The thought had him returning the smile, anticipation running through him. It was ridiculous. They hadn't even been out on a date yet, though they'd shared a meal and spent time together at The Soup Kitchen. "I'm happy to be caught by you." He said the words, immediately wishing he could take them back. He didn't want to come on too strong. Besides, he was helping the charity and that was his priority, wasn't it? He cleared his throat. His mind spun with all the reasons she'd come after him, but he couldn't settle on any with real clarity.

She didn't seem to notice his hesitation and completed the final few steps, standing directly in front of him. "I have a favor to ask you."

A favor? What did that mean? "How can I help?" he asked.

"My car won't start. Is yours close enough that you can give me a jump?"

That had not been what he was thinking about, but the idea of helping her and spending a little more time with her tonight excited him. "I'm a level up. I'll drive down and give you a jump."

"Thank you," she said, her arms wrapping around him in an unexpected hug. "Car trouble during the holidays is hard."

He held her for a moment, breathing in the scent of her almond shampoo. She was opening up to him. He squeezed her, hoping to give her some reassurance. "We'll have it jumped in no time," he said confidently. He ran up the stairs, surprised that she followed him up. They reached his car and he unlocked the door with a single touch on the passenger side door, then opened it to her.

Her eyes widened, but she didn't say anything until they started driving down to her car. "This is *your* car?"

He pursed his lips, forgetting he drove a different car when they'd gone out for Indian food. It wasn't a fancy sports car, though he did have a few of them at his house that was miles outside of the city. The Italian car was imported, but it was versatile for the city and more of a business car. He knew what she was asking with the unspoken question between them. The vehicle wasn't in his own name, it was in his company's name. "Company car," he said finally.

She ran her fingers on the leather door handle. "Looks like a very generous company."

He nodded, pulling his car so it was nose to nose against hers. "I like to think it's a generous company."

She hopped out of his car before he could grab her door, and he wished he'd been fast enough to open it for her. She unlocked her own car door and popped the trunk.

Scott was thankful he'd learned how to jump a car growing up. He pulled out the cables, connecting their two batteries. Once he was situated he said, "Okay, turn your car on."

Nothing happened.

"It didn't work," Kasey confirmed.

"Try again," Scott said.

"I've done nothing but try," Kasey said.

He turned off his car, took off the cables, reattached them, looking for anything else that he could troubleshoot, as he set up the entire system again. "Let's try one more time."

She turned the key but the engine wouldn't turn over. Scott took everything down, shutting the hoods when he was finished. "It could be your alternator," he said.

She nodded, rubbing her forehead. She checked her watch and blew out a breath. "Okay, so if I just take a few of the files in my bag I can make the train home and—"

"Kasey, you don't have to take the train. I'll take you home."

She bit her lip. "I live forty minutes outside the city. I don't want to inconvenience you." Her eyes wandered to the sign about cars left overnight and how they'd be towed at the owner's expense. "On second thought, maybe I should just stay here tonight. I really don't want my car impounded on top of not starting."

Scott's heart went out to Kasey. In the short time since he'd met her, he knew there was a connection between them. He really wanted to help her, and that included helping her outside The Soup Kitchen. The words she spoke about her bias against the wealthy from their first lunch together rang in his ears, but he pushed them aside. He could prove to her that wealthy people helped those in need and didn't just look after their own self-interests. "I have an idea," he said. "Let me make a few quick phone calls. I'll be right back. Don't leave for the train just yet."

Kasey had a puzzled look on her face, but she nodded.

He jumped into his car. He didn't want Kasey to hear the phone call he was going to make to his personal assistant. Yes, he needed to pull some strings, and she could quickly help him get the car towed to a safer location for the evening. Kasey could have the car looked at tomorrow, but until then, at least her car wouldn't be impounded.

Nancy's yawn was loud when she answered the phone. "Mr. Parker? Is everything alright?"

Scott glanced at his watch. "I'm sorry to wake you," he said. "And you can call me Scott, you know."

Nancy laughed. "I wasn't quite asleep, and old habits die hard, Mr. Parker. What can I help you with?"

"I ran into a little trouble, and I need your help. You know I'm working on the charity—"

"I am under strict orders from the Montgomerys not to help you with that," she said, her voice distressed.

"It doesn't have anything to do with the bet," Scott assured her, and then he explained about Kasey's car, and the dilemma of leaving the car at the parking garage.

"Okay, Mr. ... I mean, Scott, wow. So you really like The Soup Kitchen's director, then?"

Scott ran a hand through his hair. He wasn't going to unload all of his feelings on his personal assistant, but he needed her help with Kasey's car. "More than I should admit," he finally said.

"I'll help," Nancy said. "I'll have a tow truck there in ten minutes. I can't promise it will get fixed tonight. They're off the clock."

"I'll give her a ride home, we don't need it fixed tonight, just moved to some place secure."

"Which parking garage are you in?"

Scott gave her the rest of the details. "Thanks for your help with this, Nancy," he said. "You really are the best."

"No problem. Find out which auto shop she'd prefer and I'll make sure it's transferred there in the morning."

"Thanks, Nancy," he said again.

They hung up, and Scott stepped out of his car.

"I have good news," Scott said to Kasey when she looked up at him. "Your car will be safe. A tow truck will be here in a few minutes. Which auto shop would you like it delivered to?"

Kasey's eyes widened. "I just need to find the cheapest place. Normally I'd take it to the one close to my apartment, but it's going to be expensive to tow it there."

"Don't worry about the cost. The tow truck will take it wherever you'd like," Scott said.

Kasey bit her lip but nodded. "Thanks for your help," she said.

Scott smiled. "You're welcome. Let's get the boxes out of your car and into mine so they don't get towed away."

"Maybe we can just put them back in my office and I'll come in to work in the morning."

Scott shook his head. "Don't change your plans. I'm taking you home. You don't need to take the train."

"Don't you live in the city? That's completely out of your way."

He stepped closer to her, taking her hands in his. "I don't mind. Besides, by the time the tow truck gets here, it will be a race for you to get to the train station on time. And then what will you do?"

"It's only a mile from my house. I can walk."

He looked at the dress shoes she wore. "You're not equipped to walk a mile in those shoes. Stop being so stubborn."

Pain etched across her face. "You're sure you don't mind?"

He shook his head. "I don't mind at all."

The tow truck arrived, hooked up Kasey's car, and asked for specifics on where to take it.

"It's a little out of town," Scott said, raising his eyebrows toward Kasey for the street address of the shop.

Kasey shook her head and pulled out a business card. She scribbled something on the back of the card before handing it over to the driver. "Actually, would you take it to the nearest shop around here? I'll be at my office tomorrow afternoon, and will be able to pick it up then. Here is my cell so you can let me know where you drop it off," she said as she handed him the card.

The man nodded and then left.

Kasey turned and walked back toward Scott. "You're sure you don't mind taking me all the way home?"

"I don't mind at all." Scott opened the door for her, helping her into his car.

"Then what is that look you're giving me?" She raised her eyebrows.

Scott smiled. It was time to admit what was on his mind. "You know, it's funny. I've wondered all day how I could get your cell number, and now I know all I had to do was be the person towing your car to get it."

CHAPTER 7

Kascy's heart bounced around like a small silver sphere in a pinball machine. It seemed to hit her throat and her stomach repeatedly when she heard Scott's words. She leaned back into the seat, settling into a more comfortable ride than the one where he drove to lunch as the auditor.

Tonight's experience with her car not starting brought back Christmas memories that she'd rather not think about. She tamped down the emotion and the feeling that came with it. It wasn't the same as when she was fourteen, but the flashbacks had settled around her anyway. She swallowed, grateful that Scott had helped her to her car with the boxes and that he had still been in the parking garage. It had made the moment bearable. He'd taken care of everything. Why hadn't she thought to call for a tow? She didn't have the capacity to think straight when it came to car trouble in the winter. Just thinking of the imagery froze her. But Scott had been here. He'd helped her, and her heart continued to bounce around.

They pulled out of the garage and into the busy Chicago traffic which never seemed to die down no matter what time of the day or night it was. Scott's gaze was focused on the road, but somehow she felt that he was watching her.

She gripped the arm rest, as if that would somehow stop her heart from ricocheting. It didn't. She broke the silence. "So you want my number?"

He glanced over at her, then looked immediately back at the road, merging with the traffic in the direction she'd given him. "Is that a surprise? I did ask you out for dinner tomorrow night."

"It does feel a little surprising."

"I should probably get it now though, if for no other reason than I can check on you in the morning and make sure you have a ride back into work."

She rolled her eyes. "I can take the train."

He nodded. "I know you can, but I'd still like it."

Her fingers shook as she pulled a card out from her bag. Flipping it over, she wrote her name on the back with her number on it. She looked at the card, trying not to analyze her handwriting in a car while her hands were shaky at the request. Had she really scribbled a heart off the end of her 'Y'? What was wrong with her? It wasn't like she could just start over with a new card. How dumb would that look? Trish was going to have a field day with all of this.

Kasey handed the card to Scott before she could overthink it.

"Thanks," he said.

They pulled onto the freeway, the traffic becoming a standstill. Scott rubbed his forehead. "Oh, right. I completely forgot that there's a home basketball game tonight. This might take longer than I thought."

"Hm. Maybe the train wasn't such a terrible idea after all," she joked.

He laughed. "Between the stress of your car, and two boxes full of files, I'm pretty sure this was the better option."

She laughed. "I agree."

They inched forward and more cars joined behind them. It was slow going for a while. Scott turned on the radio and jazz music quickly drowned out the honking cars around them.

"I saw on the calendar that there are a lot of projects planned around Thanksgiving," Scott said.

Work. The topic had turned to work. She guessed that made sense, and she didn't want to overthink it. Work was definitely a more comfortable topic. "Yes, it gets really busy from now until New Year's. There's so much going on. We always have more volunteers this time of year. So many people want to help because they get into the spirit of the season, and wanting to do something outside of their normal routines. At The Soup Kitchen we've found that it's important to take advantage of the short time that we have with those volunteers and keep them really busy, so we have to add more activities. There isn't a need for us to have 75 volunteers serving one meal."

Scott nodded, but was silent for a minute. "You see a pattern in the way people volunteer throughout the year?"

"It makes sense that people want to help around Christmastime. The plight of the homeless and the less fortunate is more obvious to others in the winter months. The poor are always there though, not just during Thanksgiving and Christmas."

"I guess that means that you won't need as much help right now, with so many people signing up for volunteering?" he asked.

"This year it's a little more challenging than most because we've lost so many staff members. It's great to have help from volunteers, and we want to provide opportunities for others to serve … but managing the projects becomes a bigger task because we don't have the resources on our staff that we normally have. That's why we're grateful that you showed up when you did." She kept her eyes staring at the taillights in front of them, not wanting to make eye contact with Scott right now.

"Tell me about the Thanksgiving traditions at The Soup Kitchen," he said.

"Thanksgiving Day is a bit of a celebration itself. Ann makes an amazing turkey soup, and we have a lot more fixings on the side than usual. We can't go over the top, but we try and make it special. A local bakery donates pies, and it ends up being a lot of fun. The Soup Kitchen is open for a few extra hours that day. A volunteer will play the piano and occasionally some of the volunteers will sing Christmas carols or provide other activities for the children there. We also have a coat drive during the week leading up to the holiday. After the charity closes to the public on Thanksgiving Day, we spend the entire evening decorating The Gathering for Christmas. It looks like a winter wonderland when we're finished. On Black Friday the children of the volunteers are allowed to come early for craft time, and they make ornaments. They can choose to hang them on our tree here, or take them home to their own trees. If they come back again after Christmas, they can take their ornament home."

"That sounds very nice," he replied. "And you do this every year?"

The memory of the last several years of Thanksgivings and Christmases swelled inside of her. Her throat felt thick and her voice shook. "Every year since I started at The Soup Kitchen."

"Where did you grow up?" Scott asked.

"Ohio," she said quickly. "What about you?"

"California," he said. "And you don't go home for Thanksgiving?"

She knew that this wasn't a loaded question, not really, but it felt like one. "The Soup Kitchen is my home during the holidays. I can go home any time of the year, but November and December are the months when I'm needed the most here."

"That makes sense. Does your family still live in Ohio?"

"Yes. My two younger brothers live just a few miles from my mom. Yours still in Cali?" She quickly diverted the conversation back to him.

"They are. In the same house I grew up in," he answered. "My sisters and brothers are spread out a little more, but most of them are still in California."

"That must be fun to go back to your childhood home when you visit," she said longingly. She didn't know what that was like. The last several years of her childhood wasn't a childhood at all. She swallowed the lump in her throat. She was always more sensitive about this around the holidays, but she didn't need to be. She had moved on, and she didn't need to dwell on it further.

"It really is. I love the way I can always count on things to be in the same place. Even the decorations are familiar, you know?"

No, she didn't know, but she smiled and nodded like she did. "Are you going home for the holidays?"

A line creased on his forehead, and she watched him carefully as they slowly crawled through the traffic. "I'm actually not sure of my plans this year. I planned on it originally, but after hearing you talk about the holiday traditions at The Soup Kitchen, I think I'd really like to be around for the Christmas decorating." He glanced toward her. "Would you be okay with that?"

He wanted to skip family time in favor of spending time with her? Okay, probably not exactly *her*, but for the good of The Soup Kitchen. Still, she would be there, and he was asking her permission. It sounded as if he really cared for her opinion on the subject.

"You'd skip Thanksgiving with your family for The Soup Kitchen?"

He glanced over at her. "I want to help, and you're short-staffed. I'd really like to be part of this."

"That's really kind of you to offer, but—"

"No buts about it. I want to stay here and help you." His words were determined.

The gaze in his eyes was so sincere, that Kasey couldn't turn him down, and she realized that she didn't want to either. "Thanks, Scott. That means a lot."

He let go of the breath he was holding. "For a second I thought you were going to turn me down. I'm glad you're not."

She bit her lip. "It's hard to get my expectations and hopes up, especially this time of year." She swallowed, her mind wading through her past. She closed her eyes briefly against the pain she felt there.

"You mean expectations of volunteers not showing up? I'm not one of those people," he reassured.

She nodded, wanting to believe him. "Something like that," she pretended.

"So what do you do for work?" she asked, wanting the subject to be as far away from her past and her family as possible. There was a reason she didn't go home for the holidays, and almost none of them had to do with working at The Soup Kitchen.

"Most days it feels like I'm a firefighter putting out the fires around me. Sometimes I'm not even sure what I'm supposed to be doing. I work in online advertising and merchandising."

"I hear you on the firefighter part. I feel like that's definitely part of my weekly job description, too."

"Did you always know you wanted to work for a non-profit?" Scott asked.

Kasey drew in a breath. "I always knew I wanted to focus on helping people. I was in a service club in college that volunteered here every month. I made The 100 Club my second year in college. After that, they asked if I would like to intern here. My major wasn't really related to it—I was in communications—but at the time, I felt a strong pull to serve here, and I've never looked back. I've been the director for two years now, and before that I held other positions, some paid and some just volunteering."

Telling him why The Soup Kitchen was such a big part of her life crossed her mind, but she shoved the thought as far away as she could. She'd made a promise to herself that when she came to Chicago she was going to leave her past solidly in Ohio. That hadn't been hard to do, until she met Scott. His questions stirred up old memories. She swallowed. Maybe it wasn't Scott. Maybe it was just the holidays. They always seemed to affect her a little, but she'd done a very good job of keeping her emotions in check every year. This time would be no different.

Before he could ask her any more follow-up questions, she asked, "What about you? Have you always wanted to be a … firefighter?" They both laughed at the joke.

"Actually, when I was a little boy, I wanted to be a real firefighter. It felt like there were always fires in California, and I guess I wanted to show that I could do something about it, you know?" His tone was wistful, as if he wished for that life now.

"How come you didn't become a *real* firefighter then?" she asked.

The traffic was moving faster now, and he kept his eyes on the road. "I kind of did. I went to college in Colorado and became a volunteer firefighter there."

Kasey hung on his every word. "And did you discover that you didn't like it as much as you thought you would?"

The crease formed on his forehead again. "Just the opposite, actually. I really, really liked it. More than I thought I would."

The energy in his voice was contagious and she wanted to know more. "What did you like about it?"

"I loved *everything*. The rush of adrenaline, the fire engine, working as a team with others, helping people. Especially helping people. There's something about saving a person's life and helping them when it matters most. I mean, yeah, you feel like a hero, but that part of it wears off. It's very hard work, but it was so rewarding."

Kasey was stunned by Scott's passion and the intensity that he spoke about something he truly loved. "I know how you feel, at least about the service part of it. It's how I feel about The Soup Kitchen. But if you loved it so much, how come you didn't stick with it?" Pain creased his brow. She'd probably overstepped her boundaries with the question. After all, she wasn't offering up her past for dissection, but here she was quickly hacking into his. A feeling of guilt suddenly consumed her. She'd done her best to dodge all of his personal questions, responding with vague and short answers, and turning the conversation as quickly as possible back to him. She was asking him about his past to avoid having to explain any more about herself. She shook her head. "I'm sorry. You don't have to answer that. I didn't mean to pry." She spoke the words softer, barely above a whisper. Why had she probed the way she did?

Scott took her hand, squeezing it gently. "It's okay," he said, his voice calm and reassuring. "I brought it up, and I will tell you. I'm at peace with the decision, though it wasn't what I wanted at the time."

She waited for him, as he seemed to search for the right words. She squeezed his hand back, hoping to give him the focus he needed to share the rest of the story, but all it did was zing right back at her. She wanted to remove her hand from his, but she couldn't right now when he was about to open up to her. So she let the electricity between them run its course, circulating through her as she kept the rest of her body completely still. If she thought she could convince herself that she was not fazed by her hand enveloped in his, she needed to try harder, because there was no doubt that she was affected by him.

"I couldn't meet the physical requirements. I trained hard and worked hard. The week I spent volunteering was one of the best weeks I've ever had, but I have sports-induced asthma. Most of the time I manage it well. I don't really notice it, and even when I took up running with my roommates, I felt like it was under control. I didn't want my limitation to define me, so I pushed the limits on it." He blew out a breath. "In the end, it wasn't enough. I was fine during drills, but even with a mask on, I couldn't handle the smoke. I'd be fine in the moment—I think mostly the adrenaline overpowered it—but afterwards, the asthma attacks were too much."

She squeezed his hand again. "I'm sorry, Scott."

He shook his head. "It's okay. I talked with the chief about it. I knew I could push through a few times, but my concern for the safety of the people I was rescuing ultimately made the decision easier. I wanted to help people, but I couldn't trust that the asthma attack would wait until I was out of the burning buildings. People were counting on me. The rest of the firefighters who risked their lives also watched out for each other. I couldn't be the person they always had to worry about … and I couldn't give the job what I needed to if I couldn't be reliable."

"That's brave of you to realize that," she said finally. "So, now you rescue people in other ways?"

He shrugged. "Like I said, most of what I do at work is about putting out business fires. I'm not really saving anyone's life with that."

"You saved *me* today," she said. "I'd still be stranded in the parking garage without you."

"I'm sure you probably would have taken the train." His mouth lifted into a half smile.

She shook her head, not wanting to let him dismiss the gratitude for what he'd done for her. "But then my car would have been impounded."

"Still, it's not quite the same thing," he countered.

She nodded. "Maybe not to you, but it was still a rescue to me."

CHAPTER 8

Scott's heart swelled at Kasey's words. Is that how she saw the small act of service? He was more than happy to help her out of the bind, and giving her a ride meant that he was able to spend more time with her. He enjoyed getting to know her better, though he had to admit, he felt like he'd shared way more than she did. Her questions kept him talking, and he realized he wanted to know more about the woman next to him.

They talked for the rest of the drive. When he exited the freeway, Kasey gave him directions to her apartment. The well-lit group of red brick buildings sported a Colonial look with pillars, dark gables, and a black wrought iron fence. The first floor housed small eateries, a nail salon and a few other shops. A low hedge surrounded the entire complex, giving the area a manicured look. "This is a really nice place," he admired.

"Thanks," she said. "It's home."

He pulled into a visitor parking stall outside. He put the car in park, and when she reached for the door handle herself, he stopped her. "Wait," he said, a little too loudly.

Her eyes flew open wider as she turned back to face him. "What's wrong?"

"My sisters would kill me if they found out that I wasn't opening doors for women."

Kasey's lips twitched. He shouldn't have noticed the movement, but he did. "Your sisters?"

He nodded, holding up a finger, as if that would stop her from moving out of the car on her own. "My mom raised me to be a gentleman, don't get me wrong, but it was my sisters who enforced it."

"I can open my own doors. I've been doing it most of my life," she said, suddenly a wistful tone in her voice. What was that about?

"Well, I can't face my sisters if I let you … so, help a guy out?"

Her breath caught. "I guess I'll have to. Your sisters sound amazing."

"They are. I think you'd like them." He held her gaze for an extra heartbeat, then hurried out his door to open hers. He held out his hand, and she took it. The cool air between them crackled with energy. He pulled back, not wanting to linger on the moment of just holding her hand, when he'd done that for much of the drive here. He opened up the trunk and lifted out one of the boxes. "Where to?"

"Oh, you really don't have to help me. I can come back down."

He shook his head, leaning closer to her ear. "I don't think you realize the fear my sisters have instilled in me. Blame them for me being helpful, but I'm going to carry at least one of these boxes for you."

She laughed. "When your sisters come into town, I definitely want to meet them." She met his gaze then blinked and grabbed the other file box from the trunk. She nodded toward the stairs closest to them. "It's this way. I'm on the top floor." She led the way up the six flights of stairs. "There's no elevator," she said apologetically.

The fact surprised him, but he found the silver lining. "What a great workout!"

"Yeah, exactly. At least the stairs are covered. The apartment building is old, but I love the view from the top floor, so it's worth it."

"It's always nice to have a great view," he said, thinking of his own place in the city. Height was something he preferred.

She stopped in front of a dark green door. "This is me," she said. "You can just leave it here."

He raised an eyebrow at her. She was trying to get rid of him again, and he wasn't going to let that happen. "I can take it to its final destination. Just let me know where to put it." He helped her balance the box she carried while she fished her keys from her purse.

She turned on the light and held the door open, taking the box back from him. "These boxes can go in the office. It's the first door on the left."

Scott stepped inside, angling himself through the doorway so he wouldn't bump into her. He took in the minimalist decor as he headed to the office. He placed the box on her desk, noting how impersonal her office was at home. There were a few more things than at The Soup Kitchen, but not many.

There was a photo of her with her family when she was younger. She was with her parents and two brothers with a lake and mountains in the background. Everyone was smiling. Another frame next to it held her in a cap and gown. Her brothers and mom were also in that picture. He straightened when he heard her approach behind him.

"Thanks," she said. "I suppose in here is better than the kitchen, though I may still spread all my files out on the table there." She laughed. "I do my best thinking when files are spread out and I can make sense of all of them at the same time."

He nodded. "It's good when you know your process to work most efficiently."

She glanced around the room. "I guess I know my process. I know that when I have too many things in my office, I get distracted. I focus better in a simplistic environment." She bit her lip.

"I can see that," he noted. "So you must really like the lake then?"

Her brow wrinkled. "Why would you say that?"

"There's a picture of you at the lake with your family."

"Oh, right. Yeah, the lake picture." She glanced toward it, a crease between her eyebrows. "Yeah. I guess I like the lake. I have fond memories of it anyway."

"Did you go a lot as a kid?" He was always on the water growing up, but it was usually the ocean.

She nodded slowly. "When I was young, we went just about every year. What about you? Did you spend time at the beach when you were growing up? Or did you live inland too far?"

"We lived pretty close to the beach. I mean, not on the actual beach, but we weren't far from it. I surfed a lot growing up."

She smiled, leading him out of her office. "Do you still enjoy surfing?"

"When I get the chance. My family and I love the beach and the ocean."

"If I grew up in California, I'm sure I'd feel the same way," she said. "Thanks again for helping me with the boxes, and for the ride home."

"Anytime," he said.

She raised an eyebrow at him, as if she was challenging his sincerity.

"I mean it," he emphasized. "Anytime you need a ride, I'm happy to give you one." He glanced around the apartment, taking in the simple furnishings. The style seemed to fit Kasey's easy-going personality. "Would you like me to come get you tomorrow?"

She shook her head. "Trish doesn't live too far from here. If I need a ride, I'll ask her."

He nodded. "Goodnight."

"Night," she said, opening the front door for him. Then she eyed him. "I am allowed to open my own front door, right? Or would your sisters disapprove?"

He laughed. "Since you own the place, I guess you can open it."

He squeezed her hand. "Let me know when you decide where you want to go for dinner tomorrow."

She blushed. "Right, my choice. I'll let you know."

Scott headed out of her apartment and down the stairs toward his car. Before he drove away, he pulled out Kasey's business card and punched the number into his phone. He texted her. **In case you end up needing a ride tomorrow, my cell is the easiest way to get a hold of me.**

Thanks, Scott. I appreciate the offer. Goodnight.

That was probably code for her repeating that she wouldn't need a ride, but he wanted her to have his number just in case. He said goodnight once more over text, then connected his phone to the car and headed back to the city. He hoped the time in the car would help him clarify his thoughts surrounding Kasey.

"EXPLAIN TO ME WHY YOU'RE HERE AGAIN?" NANCY ASKED FROM the doorway of Scott's office.

Scott smiled, looking up from his desk. It was still early, but he found he could catch a lot of people before their first meeting if he started pinging them early. "Because I want to make a difference, and Scott from The Soup Kitchen doesn't have the persuasion that Scott Parker from Talk Tech has."

She tapped the side of her temple. "Let me guess, you've raised millions now from your work line?"

"Not millions, but definitely more than I was getting before. Plus, I can get through the assistant guard much better if I'm being myself. I can actually have a conversation with a CEO rather than pretend I'm an intern. I'm making progress."

Nancy smiled. "You must be since I have three people on hold waiting to talk to you. Would you like me to take messages?"

Scott nodded. "I'll take one now, and I will call the other two back."

Nancy nodded. "One of them is your mom."

"I left her a message earlier this morning." He knew he was calling too early because of the time difference, but he'd left a message to call him back. "Go ahead and send her through."

Nancy nodded and headed out the door to her desk.

Scott picked up the phone and pushed the blinking red button. "Hi, Mom."

"Scott! You said it was urgent, I'm calling you back. Is everything okay?"

"Everything is good here, I didn't mean to worry you."

"When you call me first thing in the morning and tell me to call you back before lunch, it sounds urgent."

"It is urgent, sort of. I have to cancel Thanksgiving with the family. I'm sorry. I want to be there, but—"

"You won't be coming to Hawai'i at all?" Her voice sounded shocked. "But you love Hawai'i ... and the surfing is good this time of year."

He blew out a breath. He knew that this would be harder than he'd originally thought. "I know, and trust me, I want to come ... but I'm helping with an important service project right now. I'm working with The Soup Kitchen. Thanksgiving through Christmas is such a busy time for them, and I want to help."

His mom was quiet for a moment, and then finally said, "What's her name?"

"Who's name?"

"The woman involved in this service project."

He cleared his throat. "The director of The Soup Kitchen is Kasey."

"And you like her?"

"Mom, it's a little too early to tell on that sort of thing."

"It's not too early to tell if you are rearranging your holiday plans to spend time with her. Admit it, you like her."

Scott thought for a moment. There was *so much* he liked about her. He loved laughing with her and the time he spent with her taking her home the night before had given him new insight into her. "I don't know her very well yet."

"I see, but you want to get to know her better."

"That's about right …" he said, knowing he wouldn't be able to deny it to his mom. She'd see right through him.

"I'll let everyone know you won't be with us at Thanksgiving."

"Thanks, Mom. Sorry for the change."

"It's not a problem, Scott, though we will miss you. Now the question is, will we meet this Kasey at Christmas time?"

Scott's mouth went dry. Their first official date was tonight. He'd only known her a few days, but Kasey had said that she stayed in Chicago for all of the holidays and never traveled during the busiest time of their year. "I haven't solidified my plans yet. I guess we'll see how it goes."

"Keep me posted," his mom said, then said goodbye and hung up.

Scott glanced at his watch. Kasey should be up by now. He pulled out his phone to send her a quick text. **Good morning. Can I give you a ride into work?**

Her answer came a few minutes later. **Thanks for the offer. I'll grab a ride in from Trish. She lives pretty close to me.**

He figured she wouldn't take his offer, but he'd see her this afternoon, and they were still going out to dinner tonight. **Okay, let me know if you need anything.**

Thanks.

Scott spent the next hour on the phone, talking with different businesses and CEOs, along with several friends. The donations grew higher with each phone call. Calling from his office was the right move. He also hoped the sizable donations would have a positive impact on Kasey's opinions about rich people.

He called Kyle and Kandice and gave them an update. He didn't have much to report, other than he was finally making traction with donations, and that he was sticking with his choice of helping The Soup Kitchen. As he finished up the call, another came through.

"This is Scott Parker," he said into the receiver.

"Scott, it's James. How are you doing?" James's voice was upbeat. As the owner of Chicago's premier basketball arena, and other large real estate developments, he was on top of Scott's hopeful donors list. Scott also loved to frequent his upscale Italian restaurant, *Il Cibo Dei Sogni*.

"I'm good. Thanks for calling me back."

"No problem. My assistant said it was top priority today. You need tickets to a game?" he asked, laughing.

Taking Kasey to a game sounded like fun, but he wasn't sure how she would take it. It was strange how much he cared. Normally women he'd been interested in and dated couldn't wait to spend his money, yet Kasey had asked that tonight's dinner not be too fancy. Of course, she also didn't know how much money Scott really had either. "Actually, I was hoping you could help me with something else, a charitable project I'm working on." He explained the details of the non-profit's goal to keep the building they were in, despite some conglomerates trying to petition against it on the City Council.

"Sure, I can help with that," James said. "Let me talk with Emery and get back to you. I turned all of my charitable donations over to my wife, and since then she's done wonders with it."

"Thanks," Scott said.

"No problem. I'll fill her in on the conversation, and she'll get back to you later today."

"I appreciate it."

"And keep me posted when you want to go to a game. I'll have VIP tickets with your name on them."

"You're always great like that," Scott said.

James laughed. "You've helped me out of more than one scrape before. I'm always happy to return favors."

"Helping with the charity is my priority at the moment, but I'll let you know if I can get a night off to see a game."

"Sounds like you're working hard at this," James said.

"Kasey works harder at it, I'm just trying to pull my weight."

"I might've guessed there was a girlfriend involved!" James laughed. "You can't leave crucial details like that out, man."

She wasn't his girlfriend yet, but he hoped maybe soon. "No, Kasey is the director of The Soup Kitchen."

James called his bluff, "I'm not buying it. Maybe she's not your girlfriend, but I think this is still a matter of the heart, am I right? I'll make sure to let Emery know that little tidbit. I'm sure it will make a difference on the contribution."

Scott didn't want to correct him if it meant a larger

contribution for The Soup Kitchen. "Thanks, James. You guys are the best."

He hung up with his friend, anticipation filling him at James's assumption that Kasey was his girlfriend. His heart thudded. The idea of it becoming a future possibility kept his energy high over the next hour as he made more phone calls, and coordinated with Nancy on work.

SCOTT ARRIVED AT THE SOUP KITCHEN WITH DONATION PLEDGES totaling over $100,000, and that didn't even include the personal money he was allowed to contribute for the bet. He couldn't wait to tell Kasey the good news.

He passed Kasey's office on the way to his own. The door was closed and the lights were off. He sighed, wishing she'd already come in. Texting her about his success with donations wouldn't help him see her face light up at the good news. He could be patient. He pulled out a few files and got to work on plans for the Thanksgiving donations.

Trish walked by. "Hey, Scott. How are you doing?"

"Great," Scott said, wanting to mention his good news to Trish as well, but not before he told Kasey. "Is Kasey back by you? She wasn't in her office …"

Trish scrunched her brow. "I haven't seen her today."

"She didn't get a ride with you into work?"

Trish shook her head. "I got a ride in with Mateo, but did she need a ride in?"

Scott shrugged. "I offered to pick her up and she said she'd get a ride in with you."

Trish's eyes widened. "You offered to pick her up at her place? I thought you lived in the city."

He lifted an eyebrow.

She waved a hand in the air. "I'm in charge of the new hire paperwork. I may have remembered that you lived downtown. Why did you offer?"

"She had car trouble last night. I'm guessing it was either the alternator or a dead battery since we weren't able to jump it, and I gave her a ride home."

Trish's face brightened. "You are seriously the nicest guy. If I wasn't already committed to Mateo through Christmas, you could definitely be my new boyfriend."

"Uh, thanks?"

Trish smiled. "So, you gave Kasey a ride home and now she's not here." She hurried toward the door. "I'm going to text her and make sure everything is okay. She takes the train in sometimes, even though it's not super close to where she lives."

A few minutes later, Trish came back. "I just heard back from Kasey. She is on her way in."

"Thanks for letting me know, Trish." He smiled, grateful that she was safe.

Trish smiled brighter. "You're so cute to worry about her." She shook her head. "Seriously, it's so sweet."

A few minutes later, Scott heard the door to The Soup Kitchen open. He peeked out of his office, confirming it was Kasey. He didn't want to wait a single minute to tell Kasey the good news. A gust of air roamed in through the open door, and Trish squeaked, running to her friend. Scott went back to his desk. He'd wait until Trish was done talking to Kasey before he gave her the good news.

CHAPTER 9

Kasey was greeted by Trish almost as soon as she walked through The Soup Kitchen's doors. "You've got some explaining to do," Trish said, giving her a big hug. "I want to hear *everything*."

"What are you talking about?" Kasey asked.

Trish rolled her eyes dramatically. "Don't play dumb. You're grinning from ear to ear."

"So? I smile all the time," Kasey deflected.

Trish lifted her eyebrows, showing her disbelief. "Usually when you arrive to work, you're totally stressed … but right now you can't stop smiling."

"I can too." Kasey tried to pull her lips together tightly, but the grin felt even wider than before.

"Oh, you've got it *bad*. Scott said you were supposed to call me for a ride this morning, and you never did. So … I need some details. Why didn't you call me last night?"

Understanding dawned. Trish wanted to know about her

car trouble. "He rescued me last night … but trust me, I would have called you if I needed you to give me a ride. Scott was helping me carry file boxes to my car and then it didn't start. We tried to jump the car, and when that didn't work he arranged for the car to be towed. Then he offered to give me a ride home, and I didn't think about asking you to come get me. He was already there."

"Yeah, that's all back story that I don't really care about," Trish said, following Kasey into her office. "I mean, of course I'm sorry you had car troubles, but I want the details about you and Scott."

Kasey's cheeks heated. Minus the hug she'd given him when she'd been overcome with gratitude, and holding his hand for a few minutes while they drove to her house, there wasn't anything to tell. "There's nothing to tell," Kasey lied by omission.

Trish shook her head. "You need to give me details. I suppose I could always go and get more information from Scott. He's just next door."

Trish looked like she was about to go through the door.

Kasey ran around her and closed the office door. "Scott is already here?" Kasey whispered loudly.

Trish nodded. "How else do you think I found out about him giving you a ride home? Now spill."

Kasey rubbed her forehead, keeping her voice low and gesturing to Trish to do the same. "Trish, these walls are paper thin. You can't just say things so loudly, especially when he's right next door."

"Ah, so you *do* care what he thinks. Now we're getting somewhere," Trish said. She pulled Kasey into a chair and leaned forward, waiting for more information. "I want *all* the details," she said, raising her eyebrows. "I really will go ask Scott."

Kasey rolled her eyes. "There's not much to tell."

"Humor me. He seems really nice."

"Didn't you tell me to stay strong because he was the enemy, even if he was handsome?"

"That was when he was the auditor. He's not the *enemy* anymore. So, spill."

"There's not much more to say," she replied. "I didn't think it was noteworthy or I would have called you last night. He gave me a ride home, opened the doors for me—"

"He opened doors for you? This is getting serious." Trish smiled.

Kasey shook her head. "He blamed his sisters. It was actually pretty cute."

"Finally, you're talking some sense about him."

Kasey felt the heat rise in her face. "It was fun talking with him on the way home. I had a great time, which is saying something considering I was stressed about my car."

A soft knock sounded at her office door. "Come in," she said.

Scott popped his head in. "Hey, Kasey."

"Hi," she said, smiling at the way he said her name.

"When you get a minute, I have a few things I want to talk to you about."

"Okay." She cleared her throat, hoping to keep her cheeks from blushing. "Let me just get settled."

"Great," he said, then closed her door.

"Oh. You *definitely* have some more explaining to do," Trish whispered.

"I'll tell you when there's actually something to say, but really, that's about it. He *was* really sweet." She grinned again. "And maybe I hugged him when I was relieved that he could help me."

"Do you need a ride home tonight?" Trish asked.

Kasey shook her head. "We're going out for dinner. I'm not sure what time we'll be done."

"My advice for the evening … don't let him drop you off at the train station. Let him take you home. He was asking about you this morning and seemed concerned about you when I told him that I hadn't given you a ride in."

Kasey nodded. "I assume my car will be fixed by tonight. I guess I should figure that out before the day gets away from me."

Trish squealed. "Okay, you owe me *all* the details after your date. I can't wait to hear how it goes. I need to get back to work, but, I think Scott wanted to talk to you about something personal."

"Why do you think that?" Kasey asked.

"Because he was asking where you were earlier, and he had this look in his eyes, like he really wanted to talk to you."

"You always think people want to talk when they have a look in their eyes, maybe he was just looking at you."

"I know what I'm talking about." Trish ignored her deflection. "If it would have been work-related, he would have asked *me* the question."

Kasey bit her lip. The fact that she'd thought about him all last night and this morning was on her mind. Maybe it meant something, and the idea sent tingles up and down her arms. The Soup Kitchen usually consumed all of her brain power, and to have that replaced with Scott was still a new concept. "It's been so long since I've been interested in anyone," Kasey finally said.

Trish nodded. "That's because you focus most of your time and energy into The Soup Kitchen." Trish held up a hand when Kasey started to protest. "I'm not judging your methods. The last few guys that came around weren't really worth your attention anyway. But it's not a conflict of interest to have other attentions outside of work time."

"It's not a conflict of interest to like an intern?" Kasey held in a laugh.

Trish rolled her eyes. "It's a non-profit, not Wall Street. He's not trying to climb the corporate ladder here. Besides, he's basically only here through the holidays to lend a hand. I'm not really counting him as an intern."

"He's only here through the holidays," Kasey repeated, the words coming out slow and sad. "Doesn't that bother you?"

Trish shook her head. "No. We take help when help arrives, and you know as well as I do, that we are grateful for any help we can get. We were in a bind losing so much of our staff over the last month. He's basically an answer to prayer. It's fine if his help is only for the short-term."

"But after the holidays he'll leave, so relying on him—"

"Sure, it has an expiration date, but look at the turnover we usually have with all the volunteers or the school groups or the interns. Not everyone comes and stays like we have."

The gentle reminder stung just a little. Kasey wasn't sorry for the decision she'd made to stay, but she did feel the loss when groups or staff left for the final time. It felt like the only constant in her environment was change. When would it be more stable? "And you're taking care of his compensation?"

"That's what I've been trying to tell you. He's here to *volunteer*, not to earn a paycheck."

Warmth spread through Kasey. "I don't see how that's possible. He's putting in solid hours."

"He obviously has another job, and when the rush of the holidays is over, we're going to be glad we accepted as much help as possible during this crazy time."

"So, what should I do?" Kasey asked, more to herself than to Trish.

Trish supplied an answer anyway. "You should enjoy going out to eat with him and let yourself have some fun for once during the holidays."

Kasey's throat constricted. The holidays were a time of work, and a time of grief. Reminders of her painful past were triggered by the twinkling lights and holiday cheer. Her words felt strangled across her vocal chords. "You know why this time of year is hard for me."

Trish nodded, putting a hand on Kasey's arm. "Kasey, I'm not discounting that. But, allowing yourself to have a fun date night is okay."

"Even if he leaves after Christmas?"

Trish raised an eyebrow. "A date isn't a life-time commitment. It's one evening of your life. Before you spiral down the road of when he's going to leave and why it's not going to work out, just press pause. You don't have to know everything about the future in order to enjoy the moment *now*. Sometimes a date is just a date. And it's only dinner, right? That's pretty much as low key as you can get."

"How do you figure that?"

"It's a staple meal of the day. You're going to eat it whether you eat with someone else or not. So, it's really not putting you out to have dinner with someone. Also, you can skip the food here tonight, though I know how you love those canned carrots." Trish made a face. Carrots were served often and even though Ann did a good job preparing them, they were one of the things Kasey struggled to enjoy.

"You think I should enjoy the date and let what happens, happen?"

"I'm not sure how many times I can roll my eyes in this conversation without you worrying over whether I've done permanent damage to my optic nerves. Yes! That's what I'm saying."

Kasey smiled. The conversation had helped her work through several of her insecurities. "Thanks, Trish. I needed this."

"Always happy to talk some sense into you." Trish hugged her. "Also, don't mess this up. Sure, he's only here for a couple months, but there's no need to make it awkward."

"Okay, so I won't—"

"Don't grill him about his plans. Don't pry into everything right now. It's dinner. Keep it light."

Kasey laughed. "Fine. I can do that."

"He's waiting to talk to you, remember? Go find out what he wants. I'm guessing it's not about work. You've stalled long enough talking with me." Trish winked.

Kasey looked around her office. There wasn't anything that needed her immediate attention. Tingles spread through her middle. "I guess I have."

"Then get in there, and then come tell me everything the two of you talk about."

Kasey rolled her eyes. "You don't get to dissect my love life the way you do with yours."

Trish raised her eyebrows. "Love life? See, we're already moving in the right direction. Now go!"

Scott's office door was slightly ajar, so Kasey knocked quickly before entering.

Scott looked up from his desk, his smile bright and disarming.

Kasey smiled back. She'd follow Trish's advice and enjoy the here and now instead of worrying about the eventual end of his time at The Soup Kitchen. He'd only started, and there was plenty of time to get to know him. She didn't need to rush or stress. But after last night, her head was still spinning about him. The kind way he'd brought up her boxes, opened her doors, and how he was just there for her. It was still a little too early to think that any of those things meant something, except to prove that he was a nice and helpful guy. Her cheeks heated when she thought of the hug she gave him. It was a hug, after all. She was standing there, not saying anything, and his smile widened, knocking some sense into her. "You wanted to see me?" She realized after the words came out how they sounded. Was that too flirty? They were his words.

He smiled, melting her again. "I did. I've done a lot of thinking this morning."

Me too. She hadn't stopped thinking about him. She cleared her throat and a smile spread across her lips without her permission. Trish was right, she could explore the idea of going out with someone. It was okay. "What were you thinking about?"

"Well before I tell you what I was thinking about, I want to tell you my news. I've been so excited to tell you, so I haven't told anyone else yet."

"News?" Her mind raced around that word, searching for what it could mean, and the zillion ways it could be negative. It didn't take long for her brain to latch onto one of them.

He pulled out a folder, motioning for her to come see the papers. "Now, it's not finished yet, but this morning I took time to make a lot of phone calls and I had a lot of success." He smiled triumphantly.

She tilted her head. "Weren't you at your other job this morning?" When did he have time to make phone calls?

He nodded slowly. "I did, but as it turns out, all of my projects are pretty well delegated and there was almost nothing for me to do."

Was that a good sign or did that mean he was slacking? Or did it mean he could focus on The Soup Kitchen more? She wasn't following what he was trying to say. "That's nice that everything is delegated."

He smiled wide. "It just means more time that I can help here at The Soup Kitchen."

"I-We really appreciate your help here. The holidays are always such a busy time." She couldn't keep from smiling. "So you made some phone calls?"

He nodded. "This is what I've come up with so far. I'm still waiting to hear back from several places, but I was too excited about the number to wait until I heard back from more."

She looked down at the pledged donations. The blue writing on the paper was meticulous, almost looking like a font. The total at the bottom of the page had her blinking. "Is that decimal in the right place?" she asked, stunned.

"It is. It's exciting, right?"

Her jaw hung open for a moment. "Wow. I don't know what to say. $75,000 is more than double what we raised last year. That's huge. Wow. The things we could do with that amount would be incredible."

"I'm not finished with the calls. I still have a lot more to do. I just wanted to let you know I'm working hard for The Soup Kitchen." He smiled at her.

"Well, The Soup Kitchen is very grateful for your efforts," she said. Who was she kidding? She was grateful for his efforts, and still a little in shock. Could he know what this meant for her? To have someone jump in and help without expecting compensation? It was almost too good to be true. "How did you manage to get such a large amount? We've never been able to achieve that, let alone in just a few days of making phone calls."

"I decided to branch out," he said.

She tilted her head. "What does that mean?"

"I think the approach of the interns is a little … well, dated, for lack of a better word."

She was reminded of their first meeting, how she'd thought he was the auditor, and now hearing the intern's approach—the one she'd come up with as an intern—was *dated*, felt like a blow. "You don't like our system?"

He held his hands up in a sign of surrender. "I don't mean to offend you, or the system. I'm sure it's worked great for a long time, but I think there could be a few changes made."

Kasey focused on keeping her face interested in what he was saying, not showing her annoyance at his words. "Like what?"

"For one, the list of the donors is small."

"It's based off the previous year's donations. We always contact them."

"I understand that, but there's a huge section of the entire city that you're missing. Hundreds of corporations and big-name companies that would love to give to their local community charity."

Kasey closed her eyes briefly, taking a cleansing breath. There was a reason why she'd excluded those companies. They were run by the rich—the ones that never cared about her, her family, or places like The Soup Kitchen.

When she opened her eyes, he was watching her intently. She looked away, not able to hold his penetrating gaze with those eyes that seemed to read her soul. Could he see the pain there? The hurt? She swallowed. She hoped not.

He sat back in his chair, and when she glanced back at him, some of the light had gone out from his eyes. "You've avoided calling them on purpose. It's not a shock to you that your list is an incomplete one of all the Chicago businesses."

"It would be impossible to contact every single business individually at this time of year," Kasey said, feeling defensive of the choice she made years ago.

Scott nodded. "I agree with that."

He agreed with her? "You do?"

"Of course. You're having interns and staff and volunteers make dozens of calls a day. There's no way to reach everyone. I've been leaving messages with people, hoping they'll call back. It's grueling work."

"So you can see why the list is small."

"I can see why you spend time contacting the businesses that have already donated," he said slowly. "But that doesn't answer why the most successful companies in Chicago aren't included on any list. Expanding your reach is going to open up a bigger pool to draw from."

"That's how you were able to get so much so fast? You didn't use our list?"

"I did use the list, but it wasn't getting me very far. So I made calls to companies I know are big into donations and tax-deductions this time of year, and asked for donations. This total only represents a few of the companies I called. I expect there will be more."

She crossed her arms. "I don't like getting money from people who are worried about their tax-deductions."

"I'm confused," Scott said. "All the companies that give donations will claim them as a tax-deduction."

"Yes, but it's the motive behind those big corporations. Only looking after themselves while they pretend to care for the poor and those in need." The charity during past Christmases ran across her mind. The pain. The humiliation. She shuddered, but she couldn't dispel the images or the words about being nothing more than a tax-deduction on a submitted form. That was the problem. Companies contributed just to look good to others, and bragged about their donations like they would a sale or a merger. It felt so cold and empty. The inside of her was hollow.

Scott blinked. "I don't think judging people's motivations for giving is very charitable."

"It's not charitable if people give with an ulterior motive."

"That's an awfully big accusation to lay at the feet of businesses you don't know," he said slowly, then he shook his head. "I thought you'd be excited about the amount of money I helped raise."

"I am happy," she said, forcing a smile. "The money will do a lot of good."

"But you don't like my methods," Scott confirmed.

"I just think that there's nothing wrong with doing things the way they've always been done."

"If that's the thought process then you'll always get the results you've always had."

"We're not a big corporation," she said.

"But does that mean that you're going to ignore people's generosity?"

She huffed out a breath, trying to wrap her head around the moment. She wasn't mad at Scott, not really. She was just frustrated that he'd gone behind her back to get donations from people that really didn't care at all about The Soup Kitchen. She looked at the list. None of the companies listed were ones that sent volunteers. None of them were connected with the charity. "They're just looking for a place to put their tax-deduction dollars. When have any of them come to help and volunteer here? Never."

"And they never will if they aren't given a chance," Scott said. "People might surprise you, if you let them."

"In my experience people disappoint you, especially when you put your trust into hoping they'll show up."

Scott looked down at his paper. "I really thought it would make you happy to have such a big donation with more on the way. I wasn't trying to ..." Disappointment crept into his voice. "Do you want me to call them back?"

She shook her head. "No, don't call them back."

CHAPTER 10

Scott slumped back in his chair when Kasey left his office. He hadn't felt this defeated since his first attempt at a merger, back when he was green and didn't know how to negotiate the way he wanted to. At the time he'd felt raw, numb, and completely raked over the coals. He hadn't expected his work rounding up huge donations for The Soup Kitchen would create those same feelings. He took a steadying breath. What had he expected? That Kasey would be overjoyed at his work? That she'd give him another hug, or even a kiss? He shook his head. He was a fool. He'd thought that this would make her happy, but he'd obviously struck a large nerve. Now he didn't know how to get out of this situation.

Kyle and Kandice both made it clear that this competition was more about giving of yourself, not just about the monetary value of the donations. He knew that, but it still didn't stop him from pushing hard to get donations. And yes, it had helped that he'd called from his company's office, and been 'Scott the CEO' instead of 'Scott the Intern' when he'd talked to his network of friends and colleagues. He had hope that once a relationship was formed between his friends and The Soup Kitchen, that the donations he'd asked for this year would become a regular part of their tax-deductions for future years. Why was that such a bad thing? He needed to figure out a way to fix this with Kasey, but he had no clue what the real problem was. She had mentioned her dislike of rich people before, but did that really mean she would snub their gifts and their donations?

He walked around his small space, realizing the inconvenience of not having room to pace like he did at his own office. He usually walked around the furniture as he tried to focus on the solution to whatever his problem was. Even though his office here was cramped, he mentally put the problem in the middle of the round table at the center of the room and walked carefully around it, staring directly at the center. He focused his mind to think, and to see the problem differently from each different angle as he moved around the room.

"What are you doing?" Trish asked, poking her head through his office door.

He smiled. "Trying to solve a problem. Pacing usually helps me think."

"Kind of a small office for pacing. You could always use The Gathering if you need more walking space."

"Actually, maybe you can help me figure part of it out."

Trish raised her eyes. "I'd be happy to help. What's going on?"

Instead of launching into Kasey's reaction, he decided to get Trish's response to what he'd done. If Trish acted the same way

Kasey did, then he'd know that it was his method that had really rocked the boat. "I want to show you what I've worked on this morning," he said. He handed her the piece of paper and watched her expressions closely.

Trish spent more time reading each item, her eyes following the dotted lines and growing wide each time they landed on the company's associated donation. She turned the paper around, pointing to the total. "Are you kidding? This is like the biggest win for The Soup Kitchen ever! How did you do this?"

"You're not bugged about it?" Scott checked.

Trish's brow wrinkled. "Why would I be bothered by it? I don't know all the numbers off the top of my head, but this is way more than we usually expect in a whole year, and you've accomplished this in just a couple of days."

Scott smiled at her praise, then explained Kasey's reaction to the news and the money.

Trish nodded like she understood, and Scott hoped that she would explain. Trish pursed her lips together. "Kasey isn't big on change. I mean, she's comfortable with how things have been. Change is hard for her."

"What should I do?"

Trish shrugged. "Beats me. She'll probably be over it in a few days, once she's had time to really process it."

"Any chance she won't hate me on our dinner date tonight?" he asked anxiously.

Trish laughed. "She doesn't hate you. She's been praising you up to the skies. I think if she got to know some of these companies better, maybe she wouldn't be so fearful of them, you know?"

He picked up on Trish's words. If there was a way to

introduce some of the companies to Kasey—a way to help her feel comfortable with their motives of wanting to help and be generous, even if they did get a tax-deduction—maybe that would help. He wasn't trying to push her too much, but he knew the charity would benefit from these companies. Resolve filled him. "I want to fix this."

"And that's why you'll probably get through to her. I wouldn't worry about it too much, and I wouldn't cancel your date."

He nodded. "Thanks, Trish. I appreciate it."

"No problem. Let me know if I can help you out again." She made her way to the door.

"One more thing?" he asked.

She turned. "Name it."

"Are there any spots left to volunteer tonight?"

Trish's eyes widened. "Who are you thinking about?"

"I need spots for me and Kasey, and probably a few others. I'll let you know on the exact number soon."

"We can always use a few more volunteers," she said. "We aren't full on our schedule until the first week of December, but even then, we'll put anyone that shows up to work."

"Good to know. Thanks, Trish," Scott said, the wheels spinning. He only had a couple hours, but hopefully it would only take a few phone calls to set everything in motion.

CHAPTER 11

Kasey was determined to not let the tense moment between her and Scott get in the way of their dinner. It would be okay. She buttoned up her coat before knocking on his office door. "I'm ready when you are," she said, hoping the brightness in her voice didn't sound too forced.

Scott looked up from his screen and stood when she came into the room. "Hey, I actually thought maybe we should stick around for the volunteering tonight, and then we can grab a quick bite after. What do you think?"

Apparently, the earlier moment was going to keep her from their date after all. "Volunteering, sure." She forced the corners of her mouth to push against her cheeks. "I always like helping. Trish is in charge tonight."

He nodded. "I thought we could volunteer together. It might be nice."

Was this the way he was trying to show that things were

okay between them or that things were not okay? "I guess we should let Trish know that we are planning on staying," she said.

Scott nodded. "I told her to save us a couple places, I hope you don't mind. I didn't want to suggest the idea unless I knew we were needed today. There were a couple of spots that weren't filled, so I said we could help before leaving for dinner."

"Sounds good," Kasey said. She was going to give Trish an earful later. She unbuttoned her coat. "I'll go hang this up."

"Let's join the orientation meeting, too."

She raised her eyebrows. She normally didn't attend as a volunteer.

He cleared his throat. "I'd rather not stand out when we're volunteering. We're here just like everyone else today."

She smiled. "I suppose that makes sense."

In the orientation meeting, Kasey noticed several dark suits among the group. Auditors? Health department officials? She squirmed. "I wasn't expecting a surprise visit from the health department today, so I guess it's a good thing we decided to stay," she whispered, hoping her admission would calm her. It didn't.

He put a reassuring arm around her, and the touch warmed her, making her insides do a cartwheel. "Actually they aren't from the health department, and it's not a surprise inspection. I want to introduce you to a few people."

Once Trish was done giving the orientation lecture and asking for questions, Scott led Kasey over to the four men in suits who she'd noticed earlier. All of them shook Scott's hand and then extended their hands to Kasey. Kasey took each one in turn, as Scott introduced her to them.

"Happy to be here to volunteer," James said. "Scott says what you do here is very important, and I'm sad to say I didn't know about The Soup Kitchen until today. We've pledged our donation, and we'll look at allocating resources from our company to create volunteer groups to send here as part of our service days."

Kasey wanted to focus on the part about the allocating resources—it made it sound like such an impersonal way to talk about serving—but she stopped herself. Scott had introduced James as the CEO of DiverTech Investments. That was one of the companies on Scott's list. And here he was, at the end of his work day, coming to volunteer at The Soup Kitchen? The thoughts swam around her, and she could barely grasp onto what it all meant.

"My wife, Emery, loves this sort of thing. She's out of town visiting her sister right now, but when she gets back in town we'll both be back here. Thanks for this opportunity," James said. "It's important to us to make a difference in the city that we love. Chicago has been our home for a long time."

The other three introduced themselves, with similar thoughts and similar expressions of gratitude for Scott bringing this place to their attention.

Kasey was amazed by all of it, but didn't have time to do more than smile and thank each of them for their generous donations.

"I'll show you where you can hang up those suit coats and ties," Trish said, leading the men toward a room back by the offices. They came out a few minutes later with their sleeves rolled up and aprons on. Trish assigned places to everyone.

Scott was next to Kasey, but then Trish positioned herself between them.

Kasey leaned closer to Trish as she served the rolls. "How is it that four CEOs all showed up tonight?"

"Our *intern* is apparently really resourceful," Trish said, as she served a spoonful of peas.

"That's not what I mean."

"You may not like the way he's doing his job, but are you really going to hold that against him? He's trying to help."

Kasey took a deep breath, handing out another roll, and smiling to the woman in front of her. As soon as there was a lull in the line, she turned to Trish again. "He canceled our date night."

"No, he postponed it so you could see who he was able to get to volunteer tonight."

"He did that?"

"*Obviously*," Trish whispered. "Now, are you going to hold his methods over his head, or are you going to let The Soup Kitchen thrive with some new help in it?"

Kasey lowered her voice until it was barely audible to her own ears. "These are the kinds of people working *against us* so they can have the land for a skyscraper."

"That's not fair! You don't know that for sure. Not everyone is like that, and I think Scott was brave in trying to show you that today. Don't tell me you're going to be annoyed that people came to volunteer."

"Scott asked them to come," she said, feeling her argument grow weaker.

"And youth groups are asking youth to come too; service groups are the same way. Not everyone who comes here has a happy attitude about serving when they arrive; but everyone who gives it an honest chance can find something about the volunteering that touches them. Give them a chance."

"You're right." She could do this. Suddenly it became so clear. "Will you tell him thank you from me?"

Trish looked at Kasey like she had asked her to eat a frog. "Nope. I'm not going to be in the middle of this." She stepped back, moved Kasey over, and took over the roll station, passing the large spoon to Kasey for dishing out the peas. "Now you can tell him yourself."

Kasey bumped into Scott's shoulder as she was moved into place by Trish. "Sorry," she mumbled.

"No worries. Is everything alright?" he asked. "I noticed you talking with Trish."

Had he heard their conversation? "Everything is good," she said. "Trish is good at talking sense into people."

Scott smiled. "I'd have to agree with that."

"Thank you," she said finally. "It was really awesome that you got those donations, and that it brought new volunteers."

He nodded. "I care about The Soup Kitchen. And I care about you too, Kasey."

Heat rose to her neck and cheeks. She wanted to blame the steaming green vegetables in front of her, but she knew that it was more than that. "Thanks, Scott."

A man stood in front of her, pointing to the peas, and Kasey realized the line was backing up because of her. She put the peas on the man's plate.

Scott leaned down, whispering in her ear. "Looks like I'm too distracting for you to do your job."

She chuckled. "That's it, Scott. I'm not going to be distracted by you again during this volunteer shift."

"I don't believe it," he said.

"Well, watch me, I'll do it."

"Oh, I'll be watching you."

Heat flooded her cheeks again, and she grinned, then refocused on the people in front of her. Scott was a charmer, and she was definitely enchanted by him.

KASEY SAID GOODNIGHT TO THE OTHER VOLUNTEERS AND TO TRISH, then went to her office to grab her coat. She came out in time to see Scott shaking hands with the four men who'd come at his request. Curiosity niggled at her. What was his story? How did he know these men? Her heart had been softened as she'd watched each of them serve with smiles throughout the entire evening. Maybe she'd been too hasty to lump them with her past experiences. The idea stuck with her as she joined Scott saying goodbye to James.

James reached his hand out to Kasey. "Thanks for letting us come on such short notice. It was a treat to be here. Scott speaks highly of the way you run The Soup Kitchen, and I'll have my assistant schedule us for another volunteer shift soon. And next time we'll bring different representatives from each of our departments."

"Thank you," Kasey said. "That's very kind of you." She caught her breath, feeling like this was a big step to say her next words. "And, truly, thank you so much for your very generous donation. It will greatly benefit The Soup Kitchen." Tears pricked her eyes, but she forced the unwanted moisture back. She'd done it. She'd thanked James for his contribution regardless of her preconception of what she thought he was like.

James smiled. "I was just telling Scott here that we need to all get together, especially when Emery gets back into town."

Kasey's eyebrows shot up. What was he talking about? Double dating with the billionaire? "Um—"

Scott cleared his throat. He seemed to sense her confusion, and gave James a look before saying, "They want to pick your brain about how they can help more here."

James tilted his head. "That too," he said. "Whatever makes the most sense. Scott says you stay pretty busy throughout the holidays."

"We do." It was all she could make her mouth say.

James nodded, shook their hands again, and then left.

She glanced at him in wonder, hoping she could convey her gratitude. "You really asked four CEOs to come volunteer tonight?"

"Technically one of them is a COO, but yes, I did." He cleared his throat, looking around. "Are you mad?"

She shook her head. "Why did you do it? And how did you get them to come?"

Scott opened his mouth, and then closed it. Finally he said, "I thought maybe it would be a good opportunity for you to meet them while they volunteered, and then maybe you'd be able to accept their donations easier. And as far as how I got them to come, it was simple. I picked up the phone, called their assistants, and invited them to come and have the most unique dinner experience they'd had all week. I'm sure it intrigued all of them."

"Thank you for this. And also, you're brilliant."

He smiled. "Winning your approval is hard."

She pursed her lips. "I know."

His lips twitched. "I know it's a bit later than we were originally thinking for dinner. Where would you like to go?"

"How about the cafe on the corner?"

He tilted his head. "I thought you didn't like the corner bakery."

"I never said that," she said.

"I distinctly remember you not wanting to go there when we had lunch together."

She nodded. "That was when I thought you were the auditor. I didn't want to be bombarded with questions about you at a place that I frequent on a weekly basis."

He raised an eyebrow. "And now that I'm not the auditor?"

"I'm not as concerned about it."

"I'll take that as a win."

KASEY AND SCOTT SAT DOWN AT A TABLE AFTER ORDERING THEIR food. The restaurant was busy with conversation, laughter, and the smell of freshly baked bread.

The food came out quickly, and they began eating, and chatting about the flavors of the food, and the best way to eat a bread bowl. They discussed the plans to prepare for the Thanksgiving celebrations at The Soup Kitchen. Kasey went into detail about all the different aspects of donations, more than she ever had before.

"It all sounds wonderful," he admired. "I'm really excited to see all of it come together. Aside from phone calls, which I will run by you in the future, what else can I do to help?"

"You don't need to run the calls by me," she said, smiling. "Really, I'm okay with it. I was making assumptions about people's motives and the reality is, I shouldn't care about that. Not all volunteers come with a good attitude," she said parroting Trish's wisdom from earlier. "But that doesn't mean that we should be less grateful for their help. I think you were right to point out the old way of doing the calling. Please feel free to revamp the system and make it run the way you think it should."

Scott nodded. "Thanks, Kasey. I hope you know that I really only had The Soup Kitchen's best interest in mind. And I just knew that those guys would be on board with donating their time and money if they came and actually saw this place in action."

Kasey tilted her head. "How could you know that?"

He shrugged his shoulders, but the gesture looked uncomfortable. "I just had a hunch that it would work. I plan on extending more invitations to corporate executives to get them involved."

She nodded. "Like Trish always says, we can always use more volunteers."

"How else can I help for Thanksgiving? I'm really excited about the whole weekend and seeing how it comes together."

"I thought you would spend Thanksgiving with your family in California?"

He shook his head. "That was the other thing I wanted to tell you earlier. I talked with my mom today and let her know that I'd be staying to help you … er … I mean The Soup Kitchen for Thanksgiving weekend. They're going to Hawai'i, and it's totally fine. I won't be missed too much. I'll do a video chat with them at some point during the day."

"They're going to Hawai'i, and you're going to skip that?"

He looked directly into her eyes. "I believe in what you're doing, and you and Trish have talked up Thanksgiving weekend so much that I have to see it and experience it myself."

She bit her lip. Had anyone ever chosen her over something that big before? Of course, he was really doing it for The Soup Kitchen, wasn't he? But still, the electric zing seared straight to her heart. "That's very generous of you."

"I told you, I'm here to help, so put me to work."

They talked for the rest of the meal about her plans for various projects. Kasey gave him the options of different things that he could help with, now that she knew he'd be in town for the holidays. She tried to remember another holiday season that she looked forward to as much, but she couldn't remember a single one.

CHAPTER 12

Scott hung up on a call in his office at The Soup Kitchen. He'd had his personal work line forwarded to cell phone for the last week while he'd been helping with Thanksgiving Day preparations. Since their dinner date last week, helping Kasey each day at the charity made their relationship better and better. They'd eaten lunch together almost every day and he loved spending time with her. A couple times Trish had joined them, but mostly it was just the two of them.

He'd invited more people to volunteer, and they'd all shown up. Kasey had been impressed by the display, and he was grateful for that. He wanted to help change her mind about executives, and from the warm way that she'd responded to all of them, he could feel it working. He'd raised even more money and was pleased with the generosity of the people he knew.

When they'd arrived to volunteer, he'd made it clear that he didn't want people talking about his work or his job, and wanted the focus to be on Kasey and the charity too. So far, it had all gone according to plan. He didn't like keeping who he really was, that he was a *billionaire,* from Kasey, but he wanted to make sure she'd accept him before he told her about his true connections with all of the volunteers and donors.

Today he was going to help Kasey shop for winter coats and hats for part of the Thanksgiving Day weekend. Another charity worked with toy donations and would bring several boxes of toys for the kids during a joint effort at Christmas time. He was excited to see that tradition as well.

Kyle called him before he left his office, and Scott gave him the report of how he'd helped and about the donations he'd acquired. Kyle seemed pleased with the efforts. "So, you're spending your $10,000 on the coats?" he asked.

"I'm not sure yet," Scott said, rubbing his forehead. "I want my donation to be meaningful for Kasey, and I'm still trying to figure out what that entails. If I lump it in with the rest of the donations, would it be good enough? For some reason that feels lacking to me. I want to make it something really important, you know? And we already have the donations allocated for the coats today."

"So you like Kasey?" Kandice observed.

"More than a little bit," Scott admitted.

"I'm sure you'll think of the right thing," Kyle said. "Keep up the good work. We're cheering for you."

"Thanks, guys," Scott said, before hanging up. He headed out of his office and was on his way to Kasey's when Trish came sprinting down the hall.

"Oh good," Trish said. "You're both here. This will make

things easier." She grabbed Scott's arm, practically dragging him into the office.

Kasey's brow wrinkled. "What's wrong, Trish?"

Trish put a hand to her chest, trying to catch her breath. In between gasps of air, she asked, "What are you guys doing tonight?"

Kasey looked at him, then back to Trish. "My plans are flexible, Trish. What do you need?"

"What about you, Scott?"

His plans were the same as Kasey's, but if she was going to be flexible on them, he could be too. "I'm flexible, too. How can we help?"

Trish stopped huffing and smiled widely. "That's so good, because I absolutely need help from both of you."

Kasey tilted her head. "We're here for you. What's up?"

"Tonight is couple's paint night. Mateo is going to teach it, and I really don't want to be there alone. He said I could bring friends, so I thought of you two. Please say you'll come. It will be super awkward if I'm there by myself."

Kasey pursed her lips, but before she could say anything, Scott jumped in. "Of course we'll be there. Happy to help. Right, Kasey?"

Kasey nodded. "Sure, Trish. But you do realize that this is art, right? I'm not really an artist."

Trish rolled her eyes. "Trust me, Mateo is the best teacher there is at the studio. You'll do great."

Kasey laughed. "He's your boyfriend. You're way too biased."

"That's probably true. But seriously, he breaks down the steps, tells you what brushes to use, and how much paint to mix. It's practically a paint by number," she said desperately.

Kasey sighed dramatically. "Okay. We'll come to paint night with you. Should we ride together?"

"Oh, no. Just meet me there. I'll give you the address."

"I'm working the volunteer shift tonight, so I might be late," Kasey said.

Trish grinned. "I already asked Patty to cover for you. She said she owed you one anyway, so you're free for the whole evening."

Kasey smiled. "Thanks, Trish. I guess I have no excuses left."

Trish gave them both hugs and then left the room skipping. "Don't be late," she called down from the hall.

Kasey covered her mouth then looked to Scott, her eyes widening. "So, couple's paint night?"

He shrugged. "There are worse ways to spend an evening. It could be really fun."

"I mean, sure. But it's art, and I'm not really an artist."

"Well, let's go enjoy it anyway to support Trish."

Kasey smiled. "She's not really going to need our support, you know?"

Scott looked at her. "I'll take any excuse I can get to spend time with you," he said warmly.

She nodded. "I like being with you, too," she said with a smile. "So should we go get the coats?"

Scott nodded. "Lead the way."

Scott spent the next three hours combing the department store with Kasey for coats on sale. Though they had more than enough donations to cover the expense, Scott noticed Kasey's price-sensitive attitude as she shopped for the coats. She was frugal and smart with the money that was entrusted to The Soup Kitchen.

They picked out coats in all sizes. There were colorful coats for children, and a variety of dark coats for men and women. After the fourth trip back to the different sections of the store, Scott finally asked, "How will we be getting all of these coats back to The Soup Kitchen?"

Kasey smiled. "We're going to have them delivered. It's much easier that way, and we won't be limited by the amount we can carry or stuff in a car. Also we won't have to store them. They'll arrive on the Friday after Thanksgiving."

Scott beamed. "I bet it feels like Christmas when they all get new coats."

Kasey nodded, her expression neutral as she told the facts. "A lot of Christmas Spirit is felt for sure. It's probably an expected tradition now, but the first year we transformed The Gathering overnight with Christmas decorations, it was magical." They walked passed the children's section, grabbing a few pairs of boots in different sizes.

Scott grabbed purple boots. "Now all we need is the purple coat that's on display."

"Why purple?" Kasey asked.

"I think Tess would like them, and they'd go well with the coat if we can find a size that fits her."

Kasey nodded. "Tess loves colors."

Scott walked closer to Kasey, feeling the sparks between them as he interlaced her fingers between his, as they wandered back for the purple coat. "I like this idea a lot."

She looked down at their entwined fingers. "Me too."

CHAPTER 13

Kascy's mind felt like mush through the entire coat shopping experience. Scott held her hand through most of it. Originally, she thought it was to keep them together amid the other shoppers, but each time they gathered more coats, his hand found hers again.

Over the last week they'd grown closer together. Scott had kept her posted on the donations and each day the numbers exceeded the previous ones. Part of her thought that maybe Scott was just good with people. She'd seen the way he talked with the volunteers he brought in, as well as the staff and patrons. She remembered how he'd helped with her car, and so many other little examples like that that showed he was a people person. Her heart thrummed at the notion that the reason he tried so hard to make The Soup Kitchen successful was because of her.

He drove them to the couple's paint night, and they talked and held hands as they walked from the parking garage a block away. Kasey's heart skipped a beat at his touch, but she kept her walking speed in time with his. There was no way this hand-holding could be explained away as not wanting to lose someone, like in a department store.

The art studio was bright with large windows, and a sleek black sign. Scott opened the door for her, just like he had since they met. She was getting more used to it now and waited for him, instead of rushing in. The whole process had her feeling like royalty, or some important dignitary.

Trish rushed to both of them when they arrived and put one arm around each of them, pulling them into a hug. "Oh, thank you guys so much for coming! This is going to be a fun night!"

"Anything for you, Trish. But you owe me," Kasey said. "Where are you sitting?" She surveyed the room. Rows of tables with two chairs each faced the side wall, where the instructor would teach from a raised stage. Two easels, each holding a white canvas, were on every table along with water jars, paint palettes and an assortment of brushes.

On the wall behind the chairs was a banquet table with beverages and finger foods spread over the entire red and green tartan table cloth.

Trish tilted her head. "Oh, right. So, funny thing. Mateo wants me to help him demonstrate at the front, so I'm going to be up with him, but I saved you both a great seat, right in the center. It's really the best way to absorb the entire night."

"What's the theme?" Scott asked.

Trish's gaze darted between Scott and Kasey. "Christmas, mostly."

"Sounds like a good time to paint a holiday scene."

Trish's smile widened. "That's the spirit, Scott! Let me show you to your seats."

The rest of the class began assembling. Some people picked up the finger foods and mingled, while others took their seats and studied the brushes. They joined the line and both grabbed a small plate of food and a drink before taking their seats again.

Mateo stood at the front of the studio classroom. His dark hair was styled back, and his olive skin was tanned. "Welcome, my friends. We are so glad you are here today. I see both regular studio painters as well as some new faces. Welcome to each of you." His soothing Spanish accent sang across the crowd. Trish had mentioned that Mateo had spent his growing up years overseas, but now Kasey couldn't remember where exactly he was from.

Mateo continued. "Grab some food and take your seats. We are in for a great treat tonight. As you know, Couple's Paint Night is one of my favorite paint nights each week. Today we will be painting a scene that will extend from one corner of your painting, all the way to your partner's painting." He used a brush in the air, creating swoops and swirls as he said the words. "Now, my lovely *bella* Trisha is going to help me paint. You decide where you would like to start. Each picture will look like a reflection of the other, with two exceptions. You'll both sign your names however you choose, they do not have to mirror each other, and if you wish to hang your pictures separately and not together, then feel free to make your moon in the sky however you like. Trisha and I will paint our moons so that they connect as a perfect picture. The other thing I suggest, is one person paint the clump of trees and one person paint the snowman, but again it's up to you. We will start all together, but partway through the class, we will go into the details of each separate picture."

Kasey leaned over to Scott. "This sounds more complicated than Trish made it sound."

"You'll do great. It's just paint." He grinned at her, waving a brush in the air. "Which side do you want?"

Kasey almost choked on her laugh. "You really want to paint this as a couple's scene?"

He raised an eyebrow, and whispered, "Don't you? Besides, see that couple over there? I think we can totally take them in a paint ball fight."

Kasey snorted. "You're going to get us in trouble."

"You can't get in trouble in paint class."

Trish shot them a look.

Kasey pulled on Scott's hand. "We better be good. Trish is giving us the evil eye."

"No, that's to the couple behind us who are only eating and not paying attention."

"And now, I will show you which colors to start with," Mateo's voice interrupted their conversation.

Kasey and Scott squeezed the paint out onto their plastic trays, and started mixing the blue with different amounts of white and black in the different palette wells for the variation on the winter scene.

Scott leaned over to her again, and Kasey breathed in the spicy scent of his cologne. "What would you rather paint? The Christmas tree or the snowman?"

Kasey looked up at the finished examples at the front of the room. She knew which one she needed to paint. "The snowman looks much easier. I'll do that one," she answered.

"As long as you make the snowman with a hat," he teased.

"There's no hat in their example," she countered.

Scott swirled his paintbrush in the air, mimicking Mateo's earlier swirls. "It's art … you can do it however you want."

She laughed and pushed the paint palette toward him. "Painting time," she said, making her first strokes of the dark blue sky at the top of the canvas.

Over the next hour, the room progressively became livelier as more people started painting, eating, talking, and laughing.

Kasey couldn't remember when she'd had so much fun in an art class. Usually her work was disastrous, and her scenes were hardly recognizable; but today, something seemed to click for her. She followed the strokes and used the proper brushes. Scott seemed like a natural with the paintbrush in his hand, easily creating the scene on his canvas.

Mateo walked around giving encouragement and admiring everyone's progress. He stopped next to Kasey. "No, no, no. My friend. This is not the way to do it."

Kasey looked at her painting. She knew there were flaws, but she was following pretty exact. "What do you mean?" she asked. "It looks like the example—sort of."

Mateo waved his clean brush in the air. "The painting is fine. It's easy to mimic the colors and you're doing a great job there. It's your grip that is most distasteful."

Kasey's eyes widened, trying not to laugh when she saw Scott start to mock Mateo with his own large swirls with his paint brush behind his back.

Mateo didn't seem to notice, and pushed Kasey's right shoulder down. "There should be no tension when you are painting, or your strokes will be not good." He rattled something off quietly to himself in Spanish. "Good, now loosen the grip on your paint brush. You are painting, not hammering your brush into the canvas. Now, try it like this." He looped his brush through the air. "Don't tense. Don't move your shoulder. Yes, that's better. Sort of better. You will work on it, and it will become more natural."

He moved next to Scott. "Your form is good. Nice and loose. Help your girlfriend to not strangle her brush."

Scott nodded, and Mateo moved away to the next table to offer more advice to the couple painting there.

"Teacher's pet," Kasey said, twirling her brush toward Scott.

"Hey now, watch that paint brush, you need to stay loose in your shoulder." He laughed at the joke.

"You're actually really good at this," Kasey complimented.

"Thanks, Kasey. I took my fair share of art classes when I was a kid. I don't make time for it now, but I guess it's kind of like riding a bike—once you learn how, it just comes back." He stroked his paintbrush against his canvas, then dragged it away when he realized his mistake. He'd dipped the brush into red instead of green as he painted the Christmas tree.

Kasey laughed. "You're right. Just like riding a bike."

He waved his brush in the air at her, but she blocked his flourish with her own paintbrush. The collision dripped paint splatters on both of them, and a few stray red and white splotches on their canvases.

Kasey nudged him. "Teacher's pet is going to get in trouble."

"Teacher's pet doesn't care," Scott said, filling his brush with a little more paint and waving it toward Kasey.

Kasey laughed. "You wouldn't dare." Her eyes widened.

"Wouldn't I?" His cold brush touched her cheek.

"You're in so much trouble," Kasey threatened.

Mateo cut her off when he took his place at the front of the room again. "You're all doing well. And the important thing to remember is the more you paint, the better you will become. Now let's go back to the hills in the background. We will make them more distinctive under the moonlight you are about to create. Remember to push your easels closer together to make sure you have lined up your hills and your moon properly."

Mateo gave more instructions, and in the middle of his description about shadows and background, Kasey reached over to Scott. She moved as if she was going to borrow some of his paint, and she left a stroke of white paint on his hand instead. She held in her grin and went back to focusing hard on what Mateo was saying, keeping her hand next to her easel.

"You're not getting away with that," Scott said quietly, giving her a similar paint smudge on her wrist.

There was a break about twenty minutes later, and Kasey stood up to stretch. Trying to find clever ways to mess with Scott's paints or adding paint to his almost covered hand was hard work. She was equally covered. Thankfully, most of it seemed to be on her hands or on her apron. She didn't notice any on her clothes.

When Mateo started walking around the room, Trish came over to both of them. "What are you guys *doing*?" Her whisper felt more like a pleading.

"Um, painting," Scott replied, at the same time Kasey said, "Keeping my strokes loose."

Trish rolled her eyes. "You're both a mess! I don't want him seeing you like this. Go clean up in the back room before he gets around to you." She surveyed their paintings. "Also, nice job to both of you. So far they're looking good. I was wondering how much paint was actually getting on the canvases, but it looks like you can flirt, paint, and get messy all at the same time. That's a lot of multi-tasking. Now, go clean up."

Scott stood, holding his hand out to Kasey. She took it, and they hurried back to the backroom with their glass jars for fresh water and to clean up. The free-standing wall at the back of the studio divided the studio from the cleaning stations. The counters were splattered with paint in an artistic way. Five sinks lined the wall with cabinets above and below them. Kasey and Scott each stood in front of their own sink and washed off the paint.

Kasey washed the paint off her hands, holding in her laughter as she thought about their paint fight. She glanced over at Scott who was washing up at the next sink over. He looked like he was trying hard to keep his composure too. The class was on the other side of the wall, so Kasey held her laugh in tighter. It made her grin more. Once the paint was scrubbed off her hands and wrists, she pulled down the lever on the paper towel dispenser, then ripped it off. She folded the towel into a square, soaked it under the faucet, squeezed it out, and started dabbing at the paint splotches on her cheeks and her chin.

"Here, let me help," Scott said, taking the paper towel from her.

Her grin widened. "You're the one who made the mess! I'm just supposed to trust that you'll actually clean it all off?"

He laughed quietly. "Well, for starters, I can see where the paint smudges are, and there's no mirror around."

"Fair point."

He wiped at her cheek with such gentleness that Kasey wouldn't have noticed the movement except that the paper towel was wet. She stilled under his touch.

His eyes never moved from hers as he wiped off the paint.

She swallowed. "For someone who said they could see the paint, you're not focusing on it."

"Oh, I'm definitely focusing," he said. He glanced at her cheek. "It's all off."

She rubbed at the spot where his fingers had been and immediately missed his touch.

He stepped closer, handing her the paper towel. "Will you return the favor?" he asked, pointing to his cheek.

She nodded, her finger shaky as she gently washed off the white, blue, and gray paint from his cheek. "There," she said, when she'd finished the job.

He took her hand, keeping his gaze on her, and brought her fingers to his lips. He kissed the tips of each of her fingers. Her lips had never been so jealous of her hand before. Her eyes closed as she enjoyed the sensation of him kissing her fingers.

"Kasey," Scott whispered her name.

She opened her eyes and Scott's gorgeous face came into focus. "Hm?" She blinked. He was still holding her hand, and she was completely swept away in the moment. Her brain worked overtime to fill in the blanks and translate what the kisses he'd placed on her fingers would feel like on her lips. She tried to regain her hand, but he held onto it tightly, the intensity in his eyes matching her racing heart.

He slowly bent down and cradled her face in his free hand. He pulled her chin closer to him and gently pressed his lips against hers. The kiss was sweet and pure, full of mutual adoration. Their lips parted briefly and then he released her hand and wrapped her up in his arms, drinking her lips in fully this time.

She savored the moment as sparks sizzled around them. She returned the embrace, wrapping her arms around his neck, and tangling her fingers in his hair. His cologne filled her senses as their kiss intensified and they were completely lost in each other. Finally, their lips separated, and he softly touched his forehead to hers, keeping her in his arms. Her eyelids fluttered open, wishing she could stay there for a little longer.

"We should probably get back to painting," he said quietly.

She nodded. "Do we have to?" she whispered back.

He ran his hand down the length of her arm, sending electricity completely through her. He held her hand, bringing her fingers again to his lips, and kissing them one by one. Her knees felt like they'd go weak.

"I agree with Mateo," he whispered as they walked back out to their seats. "Couple's Paint Night is definitely my favorite night of this week."

Kasey smiled. She couldn't agree more.

CHAPTER 14

Thanksgiving Day at The Soup Kitchen buzzed with energy. Several families were there to volunteer during the breakfast shift. Scott helped in the kitchen, along with some of the other staff members. He brought out pots of oatmeal and replenished other food items when they ran low. The kitchen door was constantly revolving with staff going in and out. Today was a big day, but tomorrow would be even bigger with the transformation of The Gathering into a winter wonderland.

Kasey headed toward the door with a tray of assorted pastries—a special treat for holidays.

Scott held the door open for her. "Good morning," he said.

"Morning." She grinned at him with her kissable lips. "Thanks." She hurried passed him, bumping his arm with her elbow.

Scott couldn't stop thinking about their kiss. Something had obviously changed between them. He'd hung his painting in his office at The Soup Kitchen. The sloppy work on the Christmas tree affirmed just how much he hadn't focused on finishing the painting, especially after he'd just kissed Kasey for the first time.

The rest of the day proceeded with even more volunteers spending their holiday serving, and Scott was touched by their selflessness and generosity.

Kasey was in her element helping the volunteers, answering questions, and bringing food back and forth throughout the day. The Soup Kitchen wasn't closed for very many hours usually, and tomorrow it would be open for the entire day, which made for a much busier time. Scott was glad he'd made the choice to stay for the holiday.

As the final patron left after dinner, a new wave of college-aged volunteers arrived.

"Now the real work begins," Trish said. She directed the volunteers to a back room.

"Every Thanksgiving we see if we can beat our decorating time from the year before. Some years it works. Last year we set everything up in four hours," Kasey said.

He could see the determination in her eyes. "I bet we can do it," he said confidently. "Put me to work."

Kasey laughed. "We do get to help, but the service club from the University is part of The 100 Club. They're the ones who are in charge of the specifics this year, so we'll take our cues from them." She winked at him. "You don't mind taking directions from others, do you?"

"I'm game," he said.

A dozen college students emerged from the back carrying boxes. They all had on matching shirts and name tags. A guy with a nametag that read Cooper started giving instructions regarding the window decorations, and then moved on to the placement of the trees.

When most of the volunteers started working, Cooper walked over to where Scott stood with Kasey and Trish. Cooper extended his hand to Kasey. "Thanks for letting us come tonight. This is such a great thing. We'll be here all day tomorrow too. This really gets us in the mood for Christmas, you know? We have two weeks of service planned before we start The Dickens' Festival, and this just kicks everything off."

"What are you doing for The Dickens' Festival?" Scott asked.

Cooper smiled. "All of us are actors in the festival this year. As part of our contract, we use a couple weeks to get into the spirit of the season through service. Our motto is, *'Service - we don't just perform, we act.'* Each section of the festival has its own service goals, and we try to work as a team as much as possible."

"I've never been to The Dickens' Festival before," Trish replied.

"Me either," Kasey added.

Cooper looked to Scott, like he was expecting the same answer. "I've been before. I really enjoyed it," Scott complimented.

Cooper grinned. "It's a week of immersing yourself in Christmas. As actors, all of us will be in period costumes the entire time, even when we're not on the stage. A lot of the vendors and shopkeepers will also be in costume. You'll find unique Christmas decorations and presents, and then there are the theatre productions and different readings of Christmas stories, of course."

"The best one will be The Christmas Carol," a volunteer

named Carol said, from where she stood hanging up snowflakes near the front windows.

Everyone else laughed.

Cooper chuckled. "Obviously, we are a very biased group," Cooper said. "I'm playing Ebenezer Scrooge in The Christmas Carol. We all have parts in the musical … and we'd love to have you come and see it. Of course, this isn't meant to be a sales pitch. We are here to help."

"When is The Dickens' Festival?" Trish asked. "It sounds exactly like something I'd love to go to with Mateo."

"We start two weeks from tomorrow," Cooper said. "And it goes for a solid week."

Trish sighed. "Shoot! I'm leaving next week. I'm sad I won't be able to see it. I'm going to meet Mateo's family in Spain." She turned to Kasey. "That's still okay, right? I know December is a busy time around here." She bit her lip. "I'll be back the day before New Year's Eve though. Mateo says he wants to be here for the New Year."

Kasey turned to her friend. "It's totally fine. I want you to meet his family. It will be an awesome adventure."

"And you're really going to be okay here through the holidays?"

Scott put his arm around Kasey. "I've got it, Trish. This place will run as smoothly as ever."

Trish smiled brightly. "Perfect."

"Thanks," Kasey whispered to Scott. "I really don't want her thinking she has to miss her trip."

"Of course she shouldn't do that. We've got this covered, right? You and me?"

Kasey nodded. "I'm so grateful for your help."

Cooper helped steady the Christmas tree base, while others straightened the branches. "What about the two of you?"

Kasey and Scott moved to help with the second Christmas tree. "What about what?" Scott asked.

"Are you in town for The Dickens' Festival?" Cooper asked.

Scott smiled, and they both nodded. "We are."

"Then you should come," Cooper insisted.

Scott looked to Kasey, and there was a question on her face. "What do you say? Want to come with me to The Dickens' Festival?"

"It sounds like a lot of fun. Count me in," Kasey answered.

"The shows are in the afternoon and the evening, but there are literally enough booths and events to fill a whole weekend, so give yourselves plenty of time," Cooper said.

"Sounds like a great date," Scott replied.

Kasey nodded. "I'm looking forward to it."

The group worked fast. Lights were strung on the trees and around the windows. Large snowflakes were hung from the ceiling. A small reading corner, complete with Christmas books and a few small stools, was assembled in front of a cozy fireplace backdrop. Cotton snow decorated the top of the piano.

"This is incredible. You've got decorations *everywhere*!" Scott said in awe.

"There's no such thing as too many decorations," Kasey said with a smile.

A lively debate began about proper Christmas decorating etiquette. The group compared whether Christmas decorations should go up before or after Thanksgiving, and it was amusing to listen to them argue their points.

"When do you put up your decorations?" Scott asked Kasey.

Kasey spread out the white snow fabric as a tree skirt. She cleared her throat, before looking at Scott. "The Soup Kitchen tends to be the last decorating I do for the holidays."

He nodded. "Makes sense that you would already put up your own decorations since you're so busy here during the holidays."

She hesitated. "Right, something like that. What about you? When do you put up your decorations?"

"Growing up it was always set for the day after Thanksgiving. So, I guess that's what I'm used to."

Their last preparations took longer than expected. Everyone sorted coats from the coat drive, along with the ones that Scott and Kasey bought, by size. Each pile was then covered with a sheet. It made the mounds appear like snow hills on the back wall.

When everything was finished, one of the performers sat down at the piano. "Could we practice the number we want to sing tomorrow?" she asked.

Kasey smiled. "Of course. We'd love to hear it." She moved and stood closer to Scott.

He put his arm around her, pulling her close, as the group began singing in beautiful four-part harmonies. The carol filled the space, and Christmas spirit filled the air. Now that Kasey was by his side, Scott's life felt exactly perfect.

CHAPTER 15

Friday was busy at The Soup Kitchen. Kasey helped with the crafts, while several other staff members and volunteers helped with food and distributing the coats. The Dickens' Festival volunteers came for the breakfast shift and helped with small groups of children and teenagers. They did little skits with them, and sang with them around the piano.

Kasey turned back to the craft table, waiting for people to join her table. A few did, and she helped them make popsicle ornaments and paper snowflakes. Cards were also on the table with pens and crayons.

Tess came over to her. "I want to make one," she said, pointing to the ornaments.

"I can show you how," Kasey said. She helped Tess lay out the different pieces, making it easy for her to follow the steps.

Volunteers took turns playing the piano, and people joined in singing or listening all around her. Kasey swallowed down the lump in her throat. She wouldn't cry today. She couldn't. These emotions seemed to bubble to the surface every year—it wasn't a surprise. Yet the pain from all those years ago still pulled her down into the despair that had filled the Christmas when she was fourteen. Memories swelled, and her eyes filled with tears.

"Does this look good?" Tess asked, large eyes looking at her.

Kasey blew out a slow breath, focusing on Tess. "It looks beautiful."

Tess tilted her head. "Are you sad?"

Kasey smiled, forcing the tears down. "A little," she admitted.

Tess gave her a hug. "It will be okay. Today is a happy day! The decorations make everything look like Christmas is already here." She grinned widely.

Kasey swiped at her eyes. She had to remember that it was her job to provide a wonderful Christmas to those around her. That's what she'd always done since she was fourteen. Her feelings about Christmas didn't matter as they were not universally shared by those around her, and that was okay. No one knew the ache and the pain of Christmas that weighed on her shoulders. As memories filled her mind, she resisted the anguish and pushed them away. Her job wasn't to wallow. Her job was to provide Christmas for everyone who walked through The Soup Kitchen's doors from now until December 25th. And she'd do it well. As the misery threatened to consume her insides, she would just have to work harder to pretend that everything was okay. She hugged Tess again. "I'm feeling much better now," she told the girl.

Tess smiled. "That's good. Christmas is a happy time." Tess

looked around the room. "Will you help me hang my ornament on the tree?"

Kasey nodded. "I'd love to." She didn't have to love it for herself, but she could give Tess the gift of helping her, since that's what she was here to do. That's what Christmas was about for her, it was all about making sure everyone else enjoyed it. Times were hard for so many here, and she wouldn't bring her haunted memories of Christmas into this place. She helped Tess hang her ornament, and then brought the girl over to the coats.

Kasey held up a few that were Tess's size. "Which one do you like?"

Tess's eyes widened. "I can choose?"

Kasey nodded, her heart swelling. "You can choose."

Tess leaned closer to Kasey, her voice a whisper. "I really like the purple one."

Kasey handed her the coat, and she tried it on. It was a little big, but that was probably okay.

"It fits!" Tess said excitedly.

"It sure does. You want to know a secret?"

Tess nodded.

Kasey pointed toward Scott. "The man over there … his name is Scott. When we were at the store, he picked this coat out especially for you."

"Just for me? How did he know?"

Kasey shrugged.

Tess's eyes lit up. "I know. He probably asked Santa. I've always wanted a purple coat."

Kasey blinked back the tears at Tess's Christmas miracle. "You know what else Scott found for you?"

Tess shook her head, but her eyes were bright with anticipation.

Kasey went over to the table, and reached beneath the tablecloth. "He found you some matching boots. I hope they fit."

Tess clapped her hands, then gave Kasey a tight hug. "Thank you, Miss Kasey."

Kasey helped her try on the boots, grateful that they were a good size for Tess with maybe a little bit of growing room for the winter.

"I want to go and show Scott," she said, jumping up from where she'd sat.

Kasey helped a few more people find coats, gave out a few new pairs of boots, and generally tried to keep everything running smoothly. Tess had given her spirits a boost, reminding her that everyone else in this room needed Christmas more than she did. She could proceed with making sure that everything was perfect for everyone else. It was all she could do since the thought of letting Christmas be happy for her only made the loss and the sorrow deepen. She was grateful The Soup Kitchen could provide these joyful moments for people and families, but deep inside she shielded her heart away from the emotion and the pain that came with it. She'd anxiously count down the days until the Christmas season was over.

Trish came up to her. "Hey, are you okay?"

Kasey's face smoothed as she smiled a little wider. "I'm fine. Did you see how cute Tess was in her new coat? I love that we can help people like that."

Trish nodded. "You're sure you're okay?"

"Yep. I'm great. Just getting through the holidays as usual. This is always such a busy weekend."

"It's definitely busy, and, unfortunately, it just got busier. Do you have a minute to talk privately?" Trish asked in a quieter voice.

Kasey looked around The Gathering. Noise and laughter were heard above the piano playing. This room did not hold any privacy. She nodded. "Let's go talk in my office." They made their way to Kasey's office, and she shut the door behind them. "What's going on?"

Trish bit her lip. "Mateo had some commitments he couldn't get out of, and he said he'd let me know if he could come and help today. So I went back to my office a few minutes ago, just to see if he called."

Dread filled Kasey. This wasn't the first time a boyfriend had disappointed Trish. She didn't want to think the worst of Mateo, especially since he and Trish made such a cute couple, but most of her boyfriends didn't come around to volunteer. But if they were going to break up, it would be better to do it before she went to Spain to meet his family. "Is everything okay between the two of you?" Kasey asked.

Trish waved a hand in the air. "Of course. Mateo is working hard this weekend to finish up a large Christmas mural before we leave. I don't blame him for having to work through the holiday this week, especially since we'll be gone for three weeks during a very busy time of year. It'll all work out."

Kasey blinked. "Oh. Sorry, you looked like you had bad news for a minute. I thought you guys had broken up."

Trish laughed. "No, we're good. I'm meeting his family soon, remember? Things with us are definitely solid. But I do have some news, and I'm not sure if it's bad or not. Maybe it could be really good."

"Spill it, Trish."

"So I was back by my desk and noticed that your phone line was ringing, and then it forwarded to me, instead of leaving a message on your machine. Well, I picked it up. It was the Health Department. They wanted to send someone over today, but wouldn't if they couldn't get inside, so they wanted to know if we were open."

Kasey put a hand to her head. "An inspection *today*?"

Trish shrugged. "Technically, we've known they could show up at any time. By saying we were open today, at least we have a little bit of a heads up." Trish bit her lip. "But I'm sorry. If I hadn't answered the phone, maybe they would've come next week instead."

Kasey huffed out a breath. "It's not your fault, I just don't have my head wrapped around an inspection today. Did they give you a time frame for when they would arrive?"

"Sort of. They were on their way to another inspection across town, which is why they called to see if we were here before braving the traffic. Also they are bringing the auditor from the City Commissioner's office with them. I guess it was a two bird, one stone kind of thing." Trish winced. "Maybe I should have started with that information."

"I can work with that. I just need to find my portfolios." She opened and shut a couple of drawers before beginning a frantic search. "Ugh. Where are they?" Then it came to her. "Oh, no. I took them home with me. I was going to work on polishing them a little more, but then didn't get around to it, and I never brought them back." She hadn't been able to focus since the night that Scott took her home.

"Can we reprint them? I can help you collate or hole punch or whatever you need."

Kasey shook her head. "I don't have digital files of everything. It would take me hours to compile what I've already done."

"Okay, well we can give them the tour, and then explain that we can give them the portfolios next week. Easy enough," Trish said confidently.

Kasey thought about Trish's proposed solution before she shook her head. "No. I need to go home and get them." She pulled out her purse and grabbed her coat. "It will look unprofessional if they show up and I have to make excuses about why I'm not prepared with the paperwork … especially when I've had weeks to get it together. That would hurt The Soup Kitchen more than it would help it."

"Okay. What can I do to help?"

Kasey buttoned up her coat and shouldered her purse. "I'm going to slip out the back door. I don't want people thinking that being here isn't my top priority. I'll be fast. Just keep things running like normal."

"What if they show up and ask for you?" Trish asked.

"Stall. I won't be long. I just have to grab the portfolios and I'll be back. You can have the inspector and auditor join in with the celebration. Maybe have them make an ornament or join in singing or reading with the kids. I don't know, but you'll think of something brilliant. If they arrive soon, you can give them the very long tour of everything, and I'll be back as soon as I can."

"Okay, drive safe. I'll stall … or have them join in with the volunteers. Which I guess is also stalling." She laughed at the joke.

"You're a lifesaver," Kasey said. She rushed out the door and down the back hall. With any luck, she'd grab the portfolios and be back before anyone realized she'd been gone. And the inspector would have no clue how much stress he'd caused her by coming today, of all days.

CHAPTER 16

"Trish, have you seen Kasey?" Scott asked. He'd watched her all day helping people find their new coats, involving others in the songs, and just enjoying the Christmas season, but hadn't seen her for the last few minutes. Tess had been so cute when she'd come to show him her new purple coat and boots, and he wanted to tell Kasey all about his conversation with Tess.

Trish shook her head. "She's not here. She had to leave, and she didn't want to worry anyone. She got the phone call saying that the Health Department would be here this afternoon with the auditor, and then she panicked because the portfolio she had prepared for them was at her house. You know how she is with her paper copies. Some of that information wasn't stored electronically, and so she didn't have copies of everything she needed."

Scott rubbed his forehead. Of course they chose this weekend, chock-full of festivities, to show up and add stress to the already chaotic time. "No, she gave me both copies. They're in my office."

Trish bit her lip. "I'll call her and save her the drive. She'll tear her whole apartment apart looking for them until she knows." She pulled out her phone and held it to her ear.

Scott went to his office to retrieve the portfolios when he heard Kasey's ringtone. Maybe she hadn't left yet. He went into her office but she wasn't there, and her phone buzzed on the desk. He exited Kasey's office and found Trish down the hallway.

"Kasey isn't answering," Trish said.

"Her phone is on her desk," he said. "Maybe she hasn't left yet."

Trish shook her head. "I watched her walk out the door. She couldn't find you, so she said to say she'd be back in a couple hours, right before they arrive."

"I'll see if I can go catch her. If nothing else, it will save her from looking for the portfolios for a long time."

Trish nodded. "Good plan. I'll stay here and manage the rest of the volunteers. I'm used to this weekend rush."

Scott took Kasey's phone and grabbed his coat. With any luck he wouldn't be too far behind her.

SCOTT ARRIVED AT KASEY'S APARTMENT AND KNOCKED ON THE door. Kasey answered the door, stunned. "Scott, what are you doing here?" She ushered him in. "I'm just trying to find my portfolio."

He held out her phone to her. "You forgot your phone," he said.

She smiled. "Thanks, but you didn't have to bring it to me, I would have been right back."

He knew that, sort of. "Yes, but Trish thought you might be scouring your apartment for the portfolios, and I have both of them back in my office."

She smacked her forehead. "Oh my goodness! I forgot I gave them to you. Well, Trish was right. I would have gone crazy looking for them here."

Scott took in her apartment, like he had the first time he'd come here. It looked exactly the same. There were no Christmas decorations, not a tree or a wreath, or *anything*.

She tilted her head. "I guess we can leave now. I feel so dumb for making you drive all the way here."

"We tried calling. I thought it would be helpful for you to know."

She nodded and gave him a hug and a kiss. "You really are so thoughtful, driving all this way."

"It wasn't a big deal," he said, his heart pounding loudly in his ears.

"It's a big deal to me," she replied.

She locked up her apartment, and they walked down the stairs together. "Thank you so much for taking the time to come out here. You probably saved me an hour of looking and stressing over the portfolio."

"No problem," he said and opened her car door for her. He helped her in, but before he shut the door, he asked, "How come you don't have your Christmas decorations up?"

Her face flushed. "Oh, I didn't get to it this year."

"You said last night that The Soup Kitchen was the last thing you needed to decorate for the season." Did that mean that she wasn't planning on putting them up at all?

She cleared her throat. "I did say that, didn't I? It's a busy time of year, and my focus is really only on The Soup Kitchen," she said, giving him a half smile.

"That makes sense." He returned her smile, then closed her door. He sort of understood where she was coming from, but not really. Was he reading too much into this? She was always taking care of people, and she made decorating for Christmas such a huge deal. That's why there had been a huge crew of volunteers just to come and help set up. This morning was all about helping the kids decorate the tree. He'd watched the way she helped little Tess and others make their ornaments and proudly display them. She'd spent a long time making sure the tree skirt looked exactly right. Maybe she just didn't have the time to decorate her house by herself. An idea started forming in his mind, and he couldn't shake the thought. He was going to do it for her. She helped so many people, and it was time to focus on helping the person who helped everyone else … but he was going to need some help.

Scott found Trish, while Kasey worked with the auditor and the health inspector. "Trish, did you already put up your Christmas decorations?"

Trish nodded. "Of course! Since I'm leaving for Spain for most of the month, I wanted to enjoy them for as long as I could."

"I need your help with something. I want to surprise Kasey."

Trish's eyebrows scrunched. "With what?"

"I want to surprise her with dinner at her house," he said, cautiously testing the waters.

Trish's eyes widened and her face broke into a smile. "I love it. A romantic evening. That's so great. Do you cook?"

"A little. I can do BBQ and seafood."

"Seriously, you are so sweet. What a catch." She laughed. "Don't worry, I know you're taken. How can I help?"

"I need a few hours in her apartment. The prep work takes time, and it's best if it's hot when served."

Trish nodded. "What about tomorrow? I'll go pick her up for a girls' afternoon out, and make sure the door is unlocked when we leave." She bit her lip. "You can wait off in the bushes or something and then go in once we've left. I don't want to leave her unlocked door unattended."

"Name the time, and I'm there."

Trish smiled. "This is going to be so much fun. I'm giddy and the dinner isn't even for me!"

"You and Mateo could come if you wanted to," Scott offered.

"No way. We're definitely not crashing this date night, but I want to hear all about it afterward." She stuck out her hand like they were closing a business deal and they shook on it.

"Deal," he agreed slyly.

"What's going on here?" Kasey asked, smiling.

Trish beamed, taking Kasey's arm. "Scott and I have agreed that I get your entire afternoon tomorrow, before your date night in the evening."

"Is that so? Are we going on a date?" She raised her eyebrows playfully.

"Of course I was going to ask you first," he said. "It's going to be a surprise."

She nodded slowly. "Okay."

"And I figured it was a good chance for us to spend time together before I leave," Trish interjected.

"Sounds like fun. What are we going to do, Trish?" Kasey asked.

"Oh, that's going to be a surprise too," Trish said, laughing. "Don't worry. You'll like it, and it will be fun."

"Okay, I trust you ... *both* of you."

"How was the meeting with the auditor and the inspector?" Scott asked.

Kasey bounced on her toes at the question. "They were really impressed. The improvements and upgrades we made this summer were a smart move. They checked everything, and I wasn't feeling panicked about any of it."

"We passed?" Trish asked hopefully.

"I'm not sure yet," Kasey said. "They're going to write up their full report sometime next week. But none of it seemed bad. They made lots of notes, and reviewed the portfolio. It was stressful to have it be today, when so much is already going on, but it's finally over with, and I don't have to think about it until they give me the write-up next week."

Scott wrapped her up in a hug. "I knew you could do it. This is huge."

"I think practicing the entire thing when I thought you were the auditor helped calm my nerves about it."

"I'm glad I could be helpful," he said.

She leaned up and placed a swift kiss on his lips, and he wished he could pull her in for a longer one.

Trish cleared her throat. "Okay, okay. There is still a room full of people around you. Don't get me wrong, I like PDA as much as the next person, but it's weird standing next to the two of you right now. I guess that's my cue to leave." She winked at them and then went over to the reading corner where a few kids were gathered.

"So, you really arranged for me to have some girl time with Trish?" she asked Scott.

He nodded. "Something like that, but don't ask me for any details. Trish is taking care of the surprise." Hopefully that would divert her mind away from the surprise date night afterwards too.

She smiled. "Thanks. It's been a while since Trish and I have gone and done something together outside of work. Mateo has definitely lasted longer than most of her boyfriends, which is great in so many ways, but it means I'm either the third wheel or I see her at work."

When the volunteer orientation started before the dinner shift, Scott pulled out his phone. He texted his assistant, Nancy. **I need your help.**

Her reply came almost immediately. **Do I have to break my word to Kyle to help you?**

It's not regarding the bet. It's for another project.

Then I'm in. What do you need?

Christmas decorations for an apartment. I want to surprise someone with them. I need everything delivered tomorrow afternoon.

Sure thing. I need the delivery address and a budget. Also, is there a color scheme you'd like to match?

Scott ran his fingers through his hair. He didn't want to

mess this up, but he really didn't know what kind of decorations would match what Kasey already had. He blew out a breath. Was he jumping the gun on this? Maybe she was planning on putting her decorations up later in the month. But, she had said that she was done with her decorating after The Soup Kitchen. **Nancy, you have a classy style. Pick out whatever you'd like.**

Oh, so the decorations are for me, then? Don't tell me a budget then, because I already know exactly what to get. JK. Who are they really for?

Someone I work with at The Soup Kitchen.

The one you went to the paint night with?

She's the one.

Oh, is she? :)

Not like the one, the one. Just the decorations are for her.

And you need them by tomorrow?

Tomorrow, yes.

Consider it done.

Thanks, Nancy. You're the best.

That's what I'm here for.

THE NEXT DAY SCOTT STAYED DOWN THE STREET FROM KASEY'S apartment, waiting for Trish's car to pull out of the parking lot. Trish had told him exactly where to park to wait. The delivery truck was behind him, waiting for his signal to move forward. So far everything was working out perfectly.

"Delivery up six flights of stairs?" Nancy asked. "And no elevator?"

Scott shrugged. "She likes the view and the exercise."

"Makes sense that you're having it all delivered then," Nancy said, putting a large department store bag on the kitchen table. "These ones are a little more fragile, but I thought they'd be nice on the tree. Everything else should be labeled or self-explanatory."

"Thank you, Nancy. You've been a huge help this weekend."

"No problem. It's fun to shop for Christmas decorations." She looked around the apartment. "Are you sure you won't need any help?"

"I have five hours before she'll be back. Trish promised to take Kasey to lunch before they go to a movie and maybe shopping. I'm hoping that gives me enough time."

Nancy pursed her lips. "If you say so. It does feel a bit ambitious, but if everything isn't done, she could always help with the rest."

Scott shook his head. That defeated the whole point of the surprise. "No. She already said she didn't have time to decorate. She focuses so much on her job and making a perfect Christmas there that I don't want her to have to lift a finger. I just want her to be able to enjoy it."

Nancy nodded. "Then let me help you put up the tree at least. You're going to have a hard time getting all the decorations done *and* cooking the dinner." She moved toward the largest box and unpacked the Christmas tree.

"I'm not going to cook everything before she gets here." He put a few things in the fridge and then joined Nancy in putting up the Christmas tree. The artificial tree immediately lost some of its fake pine needles.

"Smart to show off your cooking skills," Nancy said. "You really like her, don't you?"

"I really do," he said, pulling down on the tree branches to try and shape them.

"I wasn't sure if she wanted a real tree, so I opted for a fake. Hopefully that's okay."

"It was a great choice," Scott said. The pre-lit tree went up relatively fast, then Nancy helped him with the ornaments, expertly placing the colored balls around the tree. Most of the ornaments were gold or silver interspersed between the red and green ornaments. It gave just the right feel for not knowing exactly what Kasey's preferences would be—Christmassy without going overboard on cheesy. Even with Nancy's help the tree took over an hour to decorate. "I think you bought every ornament in the store," Scott teased, when he saw another box full of ornaments.

"You asked me to design it the way I would, so I did. It's a good thing I'm still here helping you, or you would have skipped all of the best ornaments," she said, walking over to the kitchen table and retrieving the bag. She pulled out several clear glass domes with winter scenes inside of them.

"She will love those," Scott said, hanging one on the tree. He stood back and looked for a good place to hang another one. They reminded him of the snow globe that sat on her desk at work.

Nancy set out festive placemats, dinnerware, and napkins. She left one plastic box for Scott to store all his dishes from dinner in, and she had all the other boxes and garbage taken away.

"Thanks for all your help, Nancy," Scott said sincerely as

Nancy headed out. "I'm so lucky to have you as my personal assistant."

"Yes, you are," she joked back. "Everything looks wonderful. She's going to love it. Good luck with dinner." Nancy turned to head back down the stairs.

Scott finished up with the final details—a garland on the mantle, a centerpiece for the table, and a small Nativity for the coffee table.

His phone buzzed with a text from Trish. **Leaving from shopping. Headed to Kasey's house. Be there in less than ten minutes.**

Scott threw the noodles into the boiling water and started working on the shrimp. With any luck, he'd be almost ready for their dinner by the time she got home. He couldn't wait to see her and surprise her. His heart thumped loudly. He hadn't cared this much about impressing someone in a long time.

CHAPTER 17

Kasey unlocked her apartment door, confusion setting in as the savory aromas of dinner hit her senses. Trish hinted that she wanted to hear about Scott's surprise, but Kasey assumed it had to do with wherever they were going for dinner. She hadn't expected dinner to come to her. Her heart rate picked up, and she pushed the door open.

Christmas decorations assaulted her from every direction. Every surface was covered with something cheery, and a tree now stood next to her fireplace, crammed with decorations like it was straight out of a designer magazine.

Scott came out of the kitchen, stirring something in the frying pan he held. "Surprise!" he cheered. "I wanted to surprise you with dinner here."

"You've certainly surprised me ... *and* you've been busy decorating too," she replied. She put on the biggest smile she could muster but it was almost too much to take in. She forced herself to take calming, slow breaths. "It smells really good."

He seemed to try and gauge her reaction. "I'm making a Thai chicken and shrimp."

She nodded. "That sounds delicious."

"It's almost ready. What do you think of the decorations? I wasn't quite sure of your style."

"Where did all of this stuff come from?"

Scott shrugged. "Various stores. A ... coworker ... of mine helped me with it." He plated the shrimp, serving them on a bed of noodles.

"Wow, you certainly went to a lot of trouble." She tried to keep her smile in place, but she could feel it slipping. Maybe it would help her to know why Scott had chosen to surprise her by decorating her apartment. "What inspired the decorating with dinner?"

"You don't like it," he said matter-of-factly.

Tears threatened to spill down her cheeks, but she swallowed them back. "I didn't say that."

"You've been working so hard, and you said you were finished decorating for the season, and then yesterday when I stopped by there were no decorations. I figured you've been working so hard that you probably didn't have the time or energy to decorate your own place ... but the way you looked at all the decorations at The Soup Kitchen made me realize how much you love them."

She nodded slowly. It really was her own fault for playing the part. She swallowed, then gave Scott a hug. "This really is so nice. Thanks."

She went to the sink and washed her hands. She could get through this, right? It was only decorations. In her apartment. She could handle it.

They sat down at her table. "I feel like I'm in a restaurant with such fancy plates. You really went all out."

He smiled. "I figured it was a good use of a Saturday."

They started eating, and an ornament caught her eye from behind the centerpiece. "What's this?" she asked.

Scott held up the enclosed dome ornament. A small truck was inside with a large Christmas tree hanging out of the back of it. "I thought you'd want to hang at least one ornament on the tree. It kind of reminds me of your snow globe." He dug into his plate of food.

A flood washed over her, and she couldn't contain her tears any longer. She swallowed her food and reached for the festive napkin, blotting at her eyes. She'd get through this; she always did. But it was much harder when everything was decorated, creating the illusion of joy and merriment. For Kasey, all it did was bring back the pain, the ache, and the longing.

Scott dropped his fork. "Kasey, what's wrong?"

She shook her head, wishing she could force the tears aside. If she tried to stop them now, it would only make it worse. "I have a confession to make. I don't like Christmas," she said abruptly. "Excuse me, I need a minute." She left a bewildered Scott at her dining room table, and bolted for her bathroom, locking the door. She grabbed a clean washcloth, ran it under cold water, and blotted at her eyes. Ugh. What a way to start a date night. She rubbed at the mascara under her eyes. She would be a hot mess if she didn't do some damage control. A few cleansing breaths helped. She grabbed a tissue, blew her nose, then pocketed a few more. She had no doubt that she was going to need them. After another moment to collect herself, she washed her hands and dabbed once more at her eyes. She hoped they wouldn't end up a red, puffy mess before the end of the night.

It was time to open up to Scott and tell him exactly what her problem was with this time of year. She grabbed one more tissue, just in case.

CHAPTER 18

Of all the responses Scott thought he'd receive from Kasey, this was not it. Her confession about not liking Christmas confused him. She seemed so into the decorating and the celebrating when she was at The Soup Kitchen. He glanced around the room, now stuffed to the brim with overbearing Christmas decorations and lights. Offending her with such things hadn't been his intention.

He heard the door down the hall click and open, and his eyes fell on hers when she emerged from the hallway. Lingering redness around her eyes was the only sign that she'd cried, but his heart ached that he'd been the cause of it. "I'm sorry," he said softly. "I didn't know you didn't like Christmas." His mind raced to the ideas he'd planned for them during Christmas—The Dickens' Festival, ice skating, looking at lights, Christmas concerts. She hadn't said anything to oppose the date night ideas when he'd brought them up. Now he needed to rethink all of it.

She shook her head. "It's not your fault." She looked around the room, tears beginning to form. "It really is so beautiful." She drew in a shaky breath.

"We can get rid of it. It doesn't have to stay."

She looked at him. "It's not the decorations. And it's not really Christmas that I hate. It's the memories that it stirs up every single year."

More tears sprang into her eyes, and he wanted to wipe them away, but instead he reached for her hand. He hoped it would give her some comfort and that she would continue to explain what the memories meant. He remained silent, waiting to see if she would.

She looked down at her plate, most of it eaten. "This was a really delicious dinner," she said, abruptly changing the subject.

He swallowed, not sure how much he expected in their new relationship. She didn't have to tell him all about her past, but he wanted to know everything about her, even the painful parts. "I'm glad you liked it. Want any more?"

She shook her head. "I don't think I can eat another bite."

He nodded and picked up both of their plates, carrying them into the kitchen. Her words felt like a dismissal. He braced himself, not wanting her to clean up after the meal, or leave her with the task of getting rid of all the Christmas decorations herself. He'd call Nancy on the way out and let her know he'd need those boxes back as fast as she could get them here. He didn't want her feeling obligated to keep all of it around—not when she hated Christmas memories.

He rinsed the plates and exited the kitchen. He would clear everything from the table, and then he'd leave to go get the boxes. Simple enough.

She stood when he came back in to remove the rest of the dishes. She grabbed her goblet and motioned toward the living room. He followed her, but instead of heading to the front door, she sat on the couch. "Want to sit and talk?"

He opened his mouth, but the words felt stuck. "You're not kicking me out after I bombarded your apartment with all this?" He held his hands out, gesturing to the entire room.

She gave him a small smile that seemed to fall as soon as it was formed. "You didn't know. I guess I should tell you the story."

He shook his head. "You don't have to tell me anything you don't want to."

She nodded. "I know. That's why I want to tell you." She gestured toward the couch, and he took a seat close to her.

His hand found hers, and he longed to kiss away the tears that streamed down her cheeks. He'd seen more than his share of tears from his sisters, and he'd never known what to do for them. It was different with Kasey. A desire to protect her swelled inside of him. "I'm here for you," he said.

"I didn't always hate the Christmas season," she began. "I don't even think I knew it was happening at first. It wasn't like I meant to hate it, or to let it remind me. But each year it became worse. Over the last few years, I have learned to tolerate it. Painting a winter scene at the couples' paint night was close to my breaking point. Trish knew I wouldn't have gone if the scene had been too Christmassy."

"That was the reason you wanted the snowman side?" he asked.

She gave him a sad smile, but tried to laugh. "That, and the Christmas tree side looked really hard."

He glanced over at the tree. Only a few hours ago he'd expected her to love it, especially because ... He bit his lips. "I thought you'd love the tie in of those ornaments. They looked so much like your snow globe." He shook his head. "It's very confusing that someone who keeps a Christmas snow globe on their desk all year long doesn't like Christmas. I thought the opposite was true. Especially with the way you helped decorate everything at The Soup Kitchen. You said there was no such thing as too many decorations."

She nodded. "You're right. It *is* confusing. I didn't mean for it to be. I pretend to love it because not liking Christmas when you work at a place like The Soup Kitchen feels wrong, you know?"

"I guess I can see that," he said slowly.

"I don't need to be the Grinch around everyone else. The Soup Kitchen is a place where all sorts of memories are made, and everyone is coming from a place that looks different from mine. My goal is to provide what Christmas could be to everyone, even if it's not like that for me."

"You said you didn't always hate Christmas. Was there a time when you liked it?" he asked.

She nodded. "I'm pretty sure I enjoyed thirteen beautiful Christmases without a second thought. We decorated the tree as a family, hung stockings, built snowmen, and skated on the lake when it would freeze." She looked toward the tree, like she was looking back in her mind at those moments. "I can't remember them being anything but wonderful."

"What happened after that?" He squeezed her hand, and her grip tightened.

"The Christmas season started out like any other. We'd

planned a whole Saturday to decorate together as a family. The live tree stood in a stand next to the windows. My brothers and I woke up early and brought out all the boxes of decorations. My brothers were younger than me, only five and seven, so it took a while with their help. At breakfast, Dad said he'd have to postpone our plans until the afternoon. He'd been working a lot of overtime as things got busier for him, and he was called in to work on Saturday. That was becoming more of a regular occurrence, but I was a stubborn teenager and didn't take the news well, especially since I'd gotten up early and had all the decorations ready for a full day of fun as a family."

She leaned against him, and he put an arm around her. He stroked her arm, but didn't want to break the fragile silence.

"I was so stupid, so mad. I didn't want to wait for him to come back from work. He wasn't supposed to go in. His boss was a workaholic who expected that from everyone, and I hated that his boss could just call him up and he'd have to go to work. Dad said that I didn't understand and explained that sometimes emergencies come up, but he promised that he'd only be gone a few hours and then we'd decorate the tree." Her shoulders shook against him, and she covered her eyes with a hand. "He promised, and he never broke a promise." Her last word broke on a sob.

He reached to the tissue box on the side table and pulled one out, handing it to her.

She blew her nose and wiped at her eyes. "Thanks," she said.

"What happened?"

"We didn't decorate the tree. He went to work, and at dinner my mom got a call. My dad had been in a severe car accident.

We rushed to the hospital through the terrible winter storm, but he was already gone by the time we got there."

Scott's heart went out to the girl she'd been in that moment. The pain, the loss, everything. He ached for her and her family. He brushed a hair off her cheek, tucking it behind her ear.

"The storm was so bad, we stayed in the hospital waiting room for most of the night. Everything was hazy for a couple of weeks. Between the grief and the weather and the funeral, everything just blurred past me. My mom got sick, and mostly stayed in her room. A neighbor came over to watch us, though I didn't need a babysitter. She helped with meals, I think. Or maybe cleaning. It was the neighbor who suggested that we should decorate the tree so it would look Christmassy when my mom was feeling better. I didn't want to because it didn't feel the same without my dad, but my brothers loved the idea. The Christmas boxes were stacked up in front of one of the couches, and as time passed they just blended into the furniture. I hadn't really seen them or thought about them."

Kasey reached for another tissue. "My brothers started decorating with my neighbor, and I sat on the couch and pouted. This was not how Christmas was supposed to be. I wasn't supposed to be decorating the tree with a neighbor. We were supposed to do it as family. With dad. Partway through the decorating, she came and sat next to me and told me she knew what I was going through—but she didn't. She hadn't ever lost her dad before Christmas. She had no idea what I was going through. She said that even though things were different that my brothers still needed me to be their big sister, and that I should help them decorate. She said that it was selfish for me to pout when everyone in the family had lost someone, not just me … that it was my duty to find a way to make Christmas happy for them."

Scott swallowed. The words from the neighbor felt so genuine, so loving, and so misguided. "What did you do?"

She gave him a sad smile. "I did my duty. I pushed away my grief. And every year I made sure Christmas was the best for them. For my mom. For everyone. I got a part-time job after school. I paid for things for my brothers. My mom was in a legal battle with my dad's company for four years—and it was only finally resolved around the time I graduated high school. My dad had praised his boss, and had defended him to me. But for all the work my dad put in, the boss still withheld his Christmas bonus that year, because he didn't work to the end of the year. But he was dead. He couldn't work. It wasn't prorated."

"The company did nothing?"

"They sent flowers to the funeral, I think. Maybe a company Christmas card. He was a rich boss whose priorities were clear—making money for his company, at the expense of others."

And there it was. The real reason she didn't like rich people. He swallowed down that secret. He wasn't her dad's boss, and self-reflection told him he never would be. "That's not okay," he said, not knowing what else to really say.

"Eventually it was fine, I guess. I got good at making every holiday, not just Christmas, an over the top celebration for my brothers. My neighbor was right. They were young and they needed some happy memories. My mom grieved for a long time. So I kind of felt like the mom and the big sister until I graduated and moved to college. After that, going home for the holidays felt even more painful. I went a couple of times, but now my job demands a lot, especially during the holidays. And there are other people who want and need to be with their families at Christmas. So, my working makes it possible for them to have a happy Christmas. And I can create a happy Christmas for the people here. It's my duty to make sure of it."

Others were allowed to be happy at Christmas, but not her. She'd taken the misguided neighbor's advice to heart and done her duty. He winced at the realization. Christmas was always for others. "You never put up your own Christmas decorations, do you?"

"Christmas is a time to focus on others. I'll put up the decorations for others. I'll sing carols for others. We make Christmas amazing at The Soup Kitchen—"

"For others," he finished.

She nodded. "It's just me in this apartment. I don't have to pretend here. I don't have to be forced into the obligation of the season here."

It was her breathing space—until he'd brought in the smothering reminders. Still, there was one piece that didn't seem to fit. "Why have the snow globe then?"

Her laugh felt bitter. "That's part of the story. Sadly, Dad's boss didn't even have the courtesy to have Dad's desk cleaned out after he passed away. His boss said it was because he didn't want to burden us with more stuff in the middle of our grief, but after the way he treated our family with my mom just trying to obtain the last of my dad's income, I knew that wasn't true." She shook her head. "A coworker brought Dad's stuff over to our house sometime after the New Year. Four wrapped presents were among all of the office supplies. Dad was really good at hiding Christmas presents. I never guessed in all my years of searching around the house that he'd used to hide them at work. The snow globe was the last present I ever got from him. And he didn't even get to see me open it. At that point, all of our Christmas decorations were down, and I put it on my desk in my room. Each Christmas after that I thought about putting it away with the Christmas decorations to be brought out every year, but by then it seemed like a permanent fixture on my desk."

The room felt heavy. The weight of Kasey's past Christmases felt like it was bearing down on all the decorations. "We can take them down. You don't have to keep them."

Kasey let out a deep sigh, leaning into him more than before. "Thanks for understanding," she said. "But I'm not sure if that's the right answer now that they're up. I don't usually tell the full story of what happened."

He could see why she didn't. "Does Trish know?"

"Of course. She knows all about it. She pulled it out of me the first semester we met. Trish is the type that's always determined to figure out the answers to everything. Except in this case, once she knew my story, she couldn't come up with an answer to solve it." She took a long, slow breath. "Thanks for listening."

"Thanks for telling me. I wish I could make things better. It feels like I made things worse, bringing all of the decorations here," he said apologetically.

"You didn't know. It was sweet, Scott. Really, the place looks beautiful." She briefly kissed him on the cheek. "And who knows, maybe this year will be the year to let it stay up." She eyed the tree warily.

He nodded, not quite convinced, but okay with accepting whatever she decided to do.

Kasey blew out a breath. "Wow. That was heavy. Sheesh. Sorry to dump all that on you."

"I'm glad you told me. And truly, I'm not going to be offended if you take all of this down. I'm happy to help you take it all down, if you want," he said.

She hesitated. "I'm not sure what I want yet." She bit her lip. "I might need to process everything for a few days."

"Whatever you need," he said. She'd been through a lot, and she seemed to relive the memories over and over each year. He couldn't expect her to love Christmas the way he did, and he wished he could think of something to help her. He'd originally hoped to bring her joy from the decorations, and that had backfired in a way, but he left the decision of what she wanted to do with them up to her. The way she spoke of her dad's boss still felt like an open wound against the rich in general. Would she compare him to her dad's former boss? He hoped not, but until he knew for sure, he'd keep his wealth a secret a little longer. He had to figure out a way to show her that everyone wasn't like her dad's boss—that he was different.

CHAPTER 19

Kasey walked into work Monday morning with a splitting headache. Crying did that to her. It had been a rough couple days of pain and pressure, and it hadn't helped that she'd really looked at the Christmas tree in her apartment—her Christmas tree. The decorations weren't sentimental. They weren't filled with reminders from previous Christmases of hanging ornaments on the tree. They were new to her. And for the most part it looked like the kind of tree that would be on a cover of a magazine, not one that would actually be put in a home. Except for the globe ornaments. She teared up and, as she surveyed each of them, the dam behind her eyelids finally broke. They'd reminded her so much of her dad.

She'd thought about taking down the tree then, giving it to charity, or bringing it to work, but as she reached to take down the first ornament, she wept again at the sight of the globes. After going through an entire tissue box since Scott left her apartment on Saturday night, she decided that it would be too emotional for her to take the tree down herself. She hadn't ever felt that at The Soup Kitchen. Volunteers always surrounded her, and it was easier to stay void of feeling, void of emotion. She'd grasped onto that hollow feeling on and off since she was fourteen. The empty space had made it easier to put on a bright smile for her brothers and her mom, as she shouldered the burden of dragging the Christmas tree out to the curb.

She had an obligation to be strong. She'd had to get through the moments even with a broken heart and a grieving soul. Everyone else seemed to pass through the holidays without any inclination of her true feelings. She swallowed the pain like a scalding drink of hot chocolate. It burned her tongue and her throat, but she'd done her duty to put the right face forward. She couldn't take those moments back, and she didn't want to. Focusing on everyone else had helped her from sinking into the same despair that so often captured her mom. And she had done it for her brothers. The voice of her neighbor rang in her ears like loud Church bells each Christmas, refusing to be silenced. She'd do the duty required of her. Her brothers could have the Christmases she'd never again have, because she'd focused on them.

Kasey put a hand to her head as she saw the Christmas decorations hanging all around The Soup Kitchen. She took a deep breath and walked to her office. She was not going to cry at work. She was not going to make a scene. She was going to carry on as she always did, because she was a professional. She pulled out a bottle of pain reliever from her desk drawer and took a drink to swallow two pills. It was going to be a long day.

Two hours later, Trish rushed into Kasey's office. "You owe me details," Trish said, panting loudly.

"Details?" Kasey asked.

Trish rolled her eyes. "Come on, your surprise date with Scott. He cooked for you, right?"

"Ah, so you are the one who let him into my apartment?" she guessed. "I was wondering how he got in."

She squealed. "He literally came in right after we left. Said his cooking prep took a long time, and he wanted it to be perfect." Trish shrugged. "So, is he a good cook? I expected a phone call at some point over the weekend at least!"

Kasey had been a mess of tears all weekend. Of course, Trish would have understood if she would have called sobbing. "You were with Mateo this weekend. Besides, I know you guys have a lot to do before you leave, and we'd just spent most of Saturday together."

Trish tilted her head. "Can he cook?"

Kasey smiled. "Best shrimp and noodles I've ever had."

Trish squealed. "Seriously, I'm just so happy for you. He is the cutest."

Kasey raised an eyebrow. "I thought Mateo was the cutest."

Trish waved a hand in the air. "Obviously, he's the best and the cutest and the everything-est. I meant out of everyone else. So, it was good? Then what did you do? He said he had big plans, but he literally wouldn't even give me a tiny itty-bitty clue even though I told him I'd swear to secrecy."

Kasey tried to keep her smile in place, but she could feel it slipping. At least the medicine had kicked in, dulling the pounding in her head.

Trish frowned. "Are you okay? Oh my goodness, what's

wrong? You *never* cry. Did he break your heart? Never mind about being cute … I'll give him a piece of my mind."

Kasey shook her head. "No, he didn't break my heart."

"Then what happened? Why are you crying?" Trish came over to her friend and wrapped her in a hug.

"He decorated my apartment," Kasey said, choking the words out, forcing her tears to stop falling. She grabbed a tissue and dabbed at her eyes.

Trish tilted her head up. "Nope. I'm still confused. What does that mean? He took down your pictures and put up his own?"

"He decorated it with *Christmas* decorations."

"Wow. I did not see that coming. No wonder he wanted extra time to make food. He was decorating. Well, that's sweet, right? Kind of?"

"It was really sweet. But of course I lost it. I told him all about my dad and Christmas."

Trish nodded, her eyes compassionate and understanding. "You know what? I think that's good."

Kasey blinked. "You do?"

"Yes, I do. Now, the question is, did you take the decorations down?"

Kasey shook her head. "Scott left it up to me to decide what to do with it. After pouring out the whole story, I couldn't just take it down. Besides, you should see it. It really is amazing. Like picture-worthy-tree amazing."

"Does that mean you're going to keep them up?" Trish asked, her voice hopeful.

"I-I haven't quite decided yet. I mean, it's so in my face when I'm at my house."

"Well, I think it's good that you told him."

"Why?" Kasey asked. Normally she could follow Trish's train of thought, but today, she felt like the train had already pulled out of the station, and she was still trying to pay for a ticket.

"Because this is the first time you've opened up about it to a guy, right?"

"Yeah, I guess." Kasey eyed the snow globe.

"So, it had to happen at some time, right? I mean, Kasey, this is kind of a big deal. If someone doesn't understand the things you have against Christmas, well, that's not going to build the foundation for a long-term relationship, right?"

"Scott and I are hardly in the long-term relationship category," Kasey said briskly. "I mean, we just started dating."

Trish shrugged. "What do I know? I usually have a new boyfriend for each calendar month, but when it comes down to it, the relationships that last are going to be the ones that are built on trust and on sharing and on being vulnerable and having those vulnerabilities treated gently."

"Wow, that's deep." Kasey replied. "Is that the way you feel about Mateo?"

Trish smiled. "It's the way I feel about all of my boyfriends."

Kasey pursed her lips. "Then how do you know that Mateo is the right one for you?"

Trish laughed. "That's a really good question. I mean, he's taking me to meet his family, so maybe that's the key. I guess we'll find out."

"So, I should be more open in general?" Kasey asked, trying to make sense of what Trish was not saying.

"No. I'm saying that I'm open with people more than you are. But that's the point. You're rarely open to anyone, but you were open with Scott. That should mean something to you. Maybe it means that you're ready to be open with everyone, or maybe it just means that you found someone that you can truly be yourself around, and that it's okay to let people in."

"So you think—"

"What I think doesn't really matter, Kasey. It's what *you* think about it. I know there's more to the story than you've told me ... I just know there is."

Kasey nodded absently.

"But I'm not going to be the friend that pries that out of you. I'm the friend that lets you keep what you want to keep private, and share what you want to share openly. Maybe Scott knows the whole story, and maybe he doesn't, but you get to choose that. Do you want to be with someone who knows all the things about you, even the hard stuff, or someone that you have to hide things from all the time?"

"I wasn't trying to hide things from him," Kasey said. She was just so used to hiding this from everyone that she didn't feel like she was trying to hide it specifically from him.

"I know that. I know there's a whole lot under the surface of that topic. But maybe this weekend was a new leaf being turned over."

"Maybe," Kasey wondered aloud. "The tree really is beautiful."

"You tried to take it down?"

"Until I started sobbing."

"Maybe that's one reason to leave the tree up then."

Kasey drew in a steadying breath. "Maybe you're right."

"I'm always right," she teased. "Now, the real reason I came in here was to give this to you. It just arrived by postal courier. Urgent delivery." Trish held up an envelope.

Kasey's eyes widened. "And you waited to tell me this?"

Trish shrugged. "I figure if it's opened today, it's soon enough. Besides, I needed the specifics about your date with Scott."

Kasey smiled, but shook her head. "I pretty much cried all over his shoulder while I told him the story," she said.

"You cried in front of him? Wow ... do you see the vulnerability scale? It's huge for you right now. This is seriously a good thing. A huge break through."

"Thanks, I think." She took the envelope from Trish and ripped open the top.

"Wait," Trish said. "We need to get Scott."

"No, we don't," Kasey said, feeling her cheeks flush.

"We just got a huge notice. It's going to be good news, and we should let him come celebrate with us."

"What if it's bad news?"

Trish shrugged. "He's already heard some of your real-life bad news, and he sounds like he was really sweet. Why not share this moment with people you care about?" She opened Kasey's office door, disappeared around the corner and then came back, Scott on her heels.

"What does it say?" Scott asked with raised eyebrows.

"Not sure yet." Kasey pulled the paper out of the torn top of the envelope. She scanned the justified form letter. Everything felt sterile—the greeting, the opening paragraph, the compliments. Buried in the second paragraph she found the meat of the problems.

"You're not reading out loud. Is it good or not? No more keeping us in suspense," Trish complained.

"Mostly good, I think. Hard to know. Lots of legalese."

"What's not good?" Trish asked.

"*'We regret to inform you that the commercial stove and ovens you are using, while still within an acceptable age range, have been recalled and must be replaced. For you to receive your permit, you must send a written response no later than seventy-two hours from the arrival of this letter, informing the Health Department of your acknowledgement of this problem, and the immediate actions you will take to solve it. This, and all other issues stated in this letter, must be resolved no later than seven days from your dated letter. Failure to comply will result in immediate termination of any and all permit(s) and license(s) previously granted to the establishment of The Soup Kitchen.'*"

"That's not the worst thing," Trish said. "It could have been a lot worse."

Kasey blew out a breath. "There's also a concern with some of the plumbing, though it looks like that one is only a few rusted pipes in the bathroom."

"Where do we go for a new commercial appliance?" Scott asked.

"We can order them online, but they won't be here within a week," Kasey replied.

"Maybe we can rush order them. Plus we have three days to respond to the letter, and another seven after that to be in compliance." Scott sounded hopeful.

"True," Kasey said. "That could work. New commercial appliances are expensive though."

"You've raised plenty of money," Scott said. "You can definitely use that."

Kasey shook her head. "We'll have to check with the specific forms you sent the businesses. Some of those forms promise earmarking for specific things. We have to honor how the money was donated."

Scott smiled. "I know of at least one donation that will be able to be used. I'm sure there will be more."

Kasey looked thoughtfully. "They will cost thousands of dollars apiece."

"We have it," Scott said. "We can go shopping today."

Trish smiled. "Oh, Scott, that will be so helpful if you could join Kasey. I'm going to be busy with a few things I have to get done before my trip."

"What things?" Kasey asked.

Trish practically glared at Kasey. "You know ... *things* ... which can only be done at my desk. I'm totally swamped today, so thanks for going with her. Also, thanks for filling in for me while I'm gone. I really appreciate it!" Trish waved her hand and headed toward the door.

"No problem, Trish. I'm happy to be here every day while you're gone." He looked at Kasey as he said the words. Trish smiled at them both and left the office.

"So, is there a store we can go to, or do we just shop online for it?" Scott asked.

"There's a company we can go through online. It's really more about specific measurements and making sure they'll fit in the space more than anything. And we'll want to get Ann's opinions on which ones she likes the best, since that's her area of expertise."

Scott nodded. "How are you doing?"

She smiled, grateful he asked the question. "This weekend took a crazy turn, didn't it?" She practically cringed at the memory of crying all over his shoulder.

"A little unexpected maybe, but not crazy. And I've been doing some thinking," he said.

"You have?" Nerves sounded through her voice. She hadn't meant to cry all over him, to pour out her past. She was fine when she was around lots of people. They made it easier to keep her smile in place through the season.

"I don't want anything to trigger you, and I want you to have a real choice."

"Okay," she said. He wasn't really making sense. Was he referring to taking down the Christmas tree again?

"I just don't want you to feel pressure to go to The Dickens' Festival, if that's something you really don't want to go to."

She swallowed the lump forming in her throat. It was the first time someone other than Trish had cared to ask her about Christmas activities in that way. "I do want to go to The Dickens' Festival. We promised the volunteers, and I want to support them."

He looked like he didn't quite believe her. "Are you sure?"

She nodded. "I want to go. It will be fine."

"Just fine?" he asked.

"I'm excited to go and watch the volunteers that helped during Thanksgiving at The Soup Kitchen. It will be okay. I promise I'm not going to go all crazy and cry on your shoulder while we're there."

"No harm done if you do. This shoulder likes being cried on." She pushed him playfully and he wrapped her up in a hug.

"I mean it," he said. "If it's too much just say the word and we'll go do something entirely non-Christmas related."

Kasey took in his words. His concern for her was evident. He was giving her a real choice. "Thanks." She savored his hug, then said, "I guess we should find ourselves a new range and oven."

He nodded, letting her go. "We'll help Ann find the perfect replacement."

CHAPTER 20

Scott filled in more at The Soup Kitchen after Trish left on her trip. He came in early every day, not leaving until Kasey left in the evening. They'd gotten into a groove of helping with the volunteers, and somehow, he always ended up handing out the food right next to Kasey on the line.

He'd reported to Kyle and Kandice again, filling them in on all of the details. It had been exciting to tell them what he finally decided to spend his money on. The immediate need for a range and oven had helped his decision.

Scott brought an empty tray into the kitchen, grabbed the filled tray of rolls, and headed back to The Gathering. Kasey came close as he moved through the doorway, and he stepped back to hold the door for her as she switched dishes.

"Thanks," she said. "We make a great team."

He smiled at her. "Agreed."

She lingered in the doorway, almost close enough to kiss, but before he seized the opportunity, another volunteer came between them. Kasey went through the doorway, and Scott continued holding the door as the other volunteer grabbed more food and went back through. Finally, he headed back to his station.

The breakfast time flew by as they worked together.

"I'm excited to go to The Dickens' Festival today. Patty is taking over the entire evening shift tonight," she said, as she served the food.

"I'm looking forward to the Festival too." The fact that she'd brought it up several times had to be a good sign. He took it to mean that she was okay with doing the Christmas activity, and he decided not to ask her again if she really wanted to go. She'd made her decision.

After serving breakfast and cleaning up, the volunteers grabbed their personal belongings, and Scott grabbed his coat from his office. He knocked on her open office door and said, "I'll drive, unless you want to walk down by the river."

"Walking sounds like fun," Kasey said.

THE DICKENS' FESTIVAL COVERED THE ENTIRE FLOOR OF THE convention center. A village was set up to represent London, with street names for the aisles hanging from replica gas lamps that lit up each street. Booths and food stands were intermingled with shops. A food court with tables and chairs was set up in an indoor park, surrounded by a forest of fir trees and fake snow.

Each booth gave a different demonstration or lesson about London life in the 1800's. They stopped next to the display of the blacksmith and the haberdashery. Actors mingled among the crowd dressed in Victorian finery. They stayed in character, tipping hats and speaking in accents, along with many of the shopkeepers.

After learning the finer points of 19th century welding, how to properly care for your carriage, and how to pick the proper height for your top hat, they came to a photo booth. The backdrop was a snowy London scene. The man in charge tipped his hand offering a greeting to both Scott and Kasey. "Are you ready to have your portrait painted in the most fantastically rapid way? Step right up and grab a costume, and your portrait will be available before you can say *watery tea.*" He gestured to the taped X on the floor.

"What do you say?" Scott whispered. He was keenly aware of her and the bombarding effect that Christmas had on her. He didn't want to push her toward any particular choice.

She smiled at him and grabbed a gray top hat from the hat stand, placing it on his head. "I think it sounds like jolly good fun. Imagine getting an instant portrait of yourself. It's practically magic." She attempted an English accent that sounded mostly correct, but then she laughed. "Okay, yeah, I really don't know how to do an accent." She grabbed a decorated hat, shawl, and a satin purse for her ensemble.

He cleared his throat and tried his best version of an English accent. "That hat looks beautiful on you." He laughed. "I'm afraid I'm in the same boat with the accent."

She put a hand to her mouth and whispered loudly. "The accent was fine, but I'm pretty sure it's a bonnet for a lady, not a hat."

"Touché." He grabbed a cape from the pile of costumes and

swung it around his shoulders. Then he grabbed a pair of gloves and a walking stick. He put his arm around her, and she leaned into him as they smiled for the camera. The man took a few pictures of them, then they waited for the machine to develop them. Two identical pictures came out, in a film strip style. At the bottom of their four pictures was The Dickens' Festival logo along with the words, *Remembering Christmas like it's 1843.*

"I want to see the pictures too," Kasey said, after taking off her costume accessories.

Scott blinked, then handed one to her. "Right, sorry. 1843 was apparently a great year."

Kasey laughed. "The fashion is a little off from the looks of it though. Next time we'll have to be more authentic."

Next time? Scott caught on to those words, rolling them around in his mind. Spending more time with her like this, more Christmases like this, would be magical. He held her hand, savoring the sensation as they continued down the street. "Next time? You'd do this again?"

Kasey's cheeks blushed. "It's been fun so far."

He'd take that as a win, especially since he knew that she didn't like Christmas. "That's good to know," he said.

They came to an ornament shop, and Scott paused. "Mind if we look around for a few minutes?"

Kasey tilted her head at him. "Sure."

He looked around trying to find the perfect ornament but nothing caught his eye. They moved on to the next shop and then the next.

"Well, if it isn't two of my favorite people," a familiar voice said to them. The guy was dressed in an elaborate costume with a lot of stage makeup on, but it was hard to tell exactly who he was.

"Cooper! It's good to see you. You look great!" Kasey said.

The name jogged Scott's memory. Cooper was one of the actor volunteers who'd given them the tickets to The Dickens' Festival. "Thanks again for the tickets," Scott said.

Cooper nodded. "No problem. It's actually nice to know that I will have some friends in the audience on opening night. I always get a little jittery. Are you guys coming to the matinee or the evening show today?"

Scott looked to Kasey. He didn't have a preference, so he waited for her to answer.

Kasey smiled. "Which one would you prefer?"

"Come to the evening show. It will be better. It gives us a show to warm up," Cooper said.

"Sounds like a plan," Scott replied. "We'll be there."

Cooper patted them both on their shoulders. "It's so good to see you guys. I'd better make my way over to the carolers. We're each taking turns singing in the town square." He lowered his voice. "It's the small stage near the trees by the food court."

"We'll make sure to catch the singing too," Scott said.

Cooper nodded. "I'm glad I ran into you. Look for me after the evening show. I'll be around with the rest of the cast outside the theatre."

"Should we go for lunch and enjoy the music?" Kasey suggested.

Scott nodded. "Let's do that. I want to see the ornament shops on the way over there, if that's okay."

Kasey nodded. "Sure. What is it you're looking for?"

Scott shook his head. "That's the tough part. I won't know it until I see it." They stepped toward the next ornament tree in a small booth. This one was covered with handmade wooden ornaments.

Kasey pulled one off the tree. "Does this one work?" It was a wooden disc with the words *Happy Christmas from 1843* burned into it.

He smiled. "It's nice, but it's not quite right."

"Okay, tell me what you're looking for and I'll help you search."

"It's a tradition in my family to buy everyone an ornament for Christmas. When I was younger, my parents used to give all of us different ornaments from either a vacation we went on, or from something significant that year. We still follow the tradition now, but we buy one for everyone. I've gotten all of mine done already except one of my sisters has been really hard to buy for this year. I still haven't found her one yet."

"What do you usually get her?" Kasey asked.

"It's different each year. She's not usually a hard person to buy for, I just haven't seen anything that looks like something for her."

"That's a cool tradition," Kasey said, looking at the rest of the ornaments.

"Nothing here is working though. I'm sure it will come to me eventually." They made their way over to the food court, got some food, and found a table close to the front.

The carolers sang a collection of old and new Christmas carols, and Kasey and Scott talked , ate, and enjoyed the music. Scott couldn't imagine enjoying this moment with anyone else.

CHAPTER 21

Music filled the theatre as The Christmas Carol began. The actors immediately pulled her into the world of Charles Dickens as the London scene unfolded on the stage. Knowing the story and seeing it were two very different things. As the Ghost of Christmas Past took Scrooge on a journey through his early years, Kasey's mind swam. A mixture of emotions came through the stage including happy moments with his family, followed by sadness when his mother passed away. Though Kasey was aware of the ways that Christmas triggered her, the play brought her back to what life was like when her dad died. Her heart ached for Scrooge as he watched his young self deal with the acute loss.

Work, schooling, and making a name for himself filled the young Scrooge's memory on the stage. The Ghost of Christmas Past stood with Scrooge off to the side and out of the way of the scene playing before him. With each new scene Scrooge explained the rationale for his choices—why he'd worked so hard, why he'd pushed so many out of his life. Scrooge moved to where his younger self took center stage, walking around him and Belle as they sat on a bench discussing their engagement.

Scrooge motioned to the Ghost. "Belle was the love of my life. Why did I not focus on her more?"

Kasey's heart broke for old Scrooge as he tried to tell his younger self to pay attention to what was in right front of him. In his advanced years, he realized his dream of making more money to ensure he didn't end up in the poor house wasn't worth losing her.

"These are the things that have been," the Ghost of Christmas Past repeated. "They are what they are, they are what they are."

"Help me change them," Scrooge pleaded. "I want to redo these moments."

"You cannot change the past. These are the things that have been. They are what they are," the Ghost repeated a final time as the Ghost's voice disappeared in the darkness.

Suddenly, Scrooge was in the middle of his bed, tangled in the sheets, repeating the words the Ghost had spoken.

At that moment, the Ghost of Christmas Present came onto the stage with boisterous appeal. The loud laughter, happy music, and tap dancers seemed to make the scene into a party, but Kasey could not focus on it. She looked over at Scott and squeezed his hand in hers. He squeezed back, but his gaze was focused on the stage. Kasey stared forward, but her mind raced through the last few scenes showing the past, and Scrooge grappling with the reality that things in the past were not things he could change.

She took a steadying breath, realizing for the first time how much she wanted Scrooge to be able to change his past, but that wasn't possible. Pain tore through her as she remembered all the Christmases where she felt completely empty inside, all while trying to fill everyone else with holiday cheer. The past was so painful for her, but wanting to change it wasn't an answer, and trying to forget it only made the memories push back harder. And here she felt the pain of Scrooge's loss, his heartbreak, and his realization that his past was not what he wanted it to be.

The Ghost of Christmas Present continued on with his merrymaking, and Scrooge followed to all the current situations that he had chosen to stay away from: his nephew's family, his clerk's life, and the general population of London that he ignored.

At each new location, the Ghost of Christmas Present pointed out the good things about each place, and then repeated the fallacy that Scrooge himself believed about these moments. His nephew was a reminder of losing his sister, he didn't see his clerk for who he was, and London as a whole was too poor to be within his notice. As Kasey watched the change in Scrooge, she silently cheered at his success. These small examples helped him make a connection toward moving forward and healing.

When the ominous Ghost of Christmas Future came onto the stage, he only silently pointed at what Scrooge was to see, and would not talk through the entire scene. The future Scrooge had created for himself was cold, dark, and threatening, as a tombstone etched with his name came into view on the stage. The despair in Scrooge's voice came through as he pleaded with the final ghost to let him have a chance to make a difference, to live. The pleas became frantic. "Men's courses will foreshadow certain ends, to which, if persevered in, they must lead," said Scrooge. "But if the courses be departed from, the ends will change. Say it is thus with what you show me!" The Ghost did not respond and the scene changed, leaving Scrooge almost magically back in his own bed.

Scrooge's pleas became more fervent, as he faced the audience in his monologue of what the night had taught him. "I will honor Christmas in my heart, and try to keep it all the year. I will live in the Past, the Present, and the Future. The Spirits of all Three shall strive within me. I will not shut out the lessons that they teach." He continued with his lines, finding out that Christmas was still ahead of him, and that he hadn't missed it like he'd thought. He ran through the streets, trying to do as much good as he could, but the words he'd spoken stayed with Kasey.

Throughout the production she'd gone through a rollercoaster of emotions—she'd felt some of them coming, but some of the emotions had surprised her. She wanted to see herself in the character of Scrooge. The past was painful, which made the present unbearable, and the future was more of the same on an intensified level. It was the path she was always on —the same path Scrooge had been on before his awakening with the three Ghosts. Could she need the same awakening? Could Christmas be found in the future in a happy way, even if the past had been bleak and the present had mostly been avoided? Hope bubbled up inside her as Scrooge gave to the poor, bought the prize turkey, and spread goodwill to the Cratchit family.

Tears slipped down her cheek as she felt for the first time that she could let the past live in the past. Yes, it had brought her to the present, but that didn't mean that she had to stay in the grief and the pain every time a Christmas song came on or every time a Christmas tree was decorated in a store. Christmas had been hard for a long time, but that didn't mean it had to stay that way forever. She could let the present and the future take on their own time and their own emotions, without the past dragging it down forever. Scrooge did it. His life drastically changed, even if he couldn't go back and change the past.

"Are you okay?" Scott whispered softly.

She wiped away a tear and nodded, whispering back, "I will be." She could honor the past, without being buried by it. Her heart soared at the realization. Snow began falling on the stage, and a light jingling of sleigh bells started. The cast on the stage joined hands and sang a Christmas carol, followed by *"We Wish You a Merry Christmas."* They weren't idle words to her, something that she could just pass on feeling. A stage full of people were wishing *her* a Merry Christmas—not a sad Christmas, not a bleak and hopeless Christmas, but a *Merry* Christmas. And she could decide what to do with it. She could choose to let it be merry, changing the present and therefore the future, or she could choose to ignore it and live the way she always had.

A sudden desire to join in the singing filled her. Forgetting the past wouldn't happen, but being at peace with the past was something she could work on, something that seemed to already be working on her.

The song ended, and Scrooge took the center stage. A woman stepped forward, gestured to Scrooge, and said, "And it was always said of him, that he knew how to keep Christmas well, if any man alive possessed the knowledge. May that be truly said of us, and all of us!"

Tiny Tim ran to Scrooge, and he picked him up, hoisting him on his shoulder. Then Tiny Tim said with a very loud voice, "God bless us, every one!"

Every one. It included every person. She wasn't excluded from that blessing. Christmas could be for her too. The feeling swept through her and she stood as the curtain fell, clapping loudly until the curtain rose and each character took their turn bowing.

Scott stood next to her, also clapping. He leaned toward her and whispered, "Best Christmas Carol production I've ever seen."

"It was really good. I-I learned a lot," Kasey admitted.

He nodded. "Me too. What did you learn from it?"

Kasey bit her lip. "You first," she said as they walked toward the exit of the theatre.

"It's funny how you hear certain things, and you think they're bad things, and they're really not."

"What do you mean?"

They headed toward the area where Cooper said the actors would come out. On the way there they looked at another booth with ornaments. "I mean, as a society we say, *'Don't be a Scrooge.'* When we say that, it implies that Scrooge was stingy, but did you see him at the end? That wasn't him at all. It was inspiring to see all the good that one rich man could do in the world, when he put his mind to it."

Kasey nodded and pulled off one of the ornaments depicting

Scrooge. "So this would be your ornament because you want to be like Scrooge?"

Scott nodded. "Exactly. I guess I never realized how important it is to acknowledge the Scrooge we refer to should be the one after the Ghosts come to visit him, the *changed* Scrooge, and not the miser before he had his change of heart. I think it might be my new mantra."

Kasey laughed and handed him the ornament. "I like that a lot. Be the Scrooge after the haunting night of ghosts."

"Thanks," he said, looking at the ornament for a long moment, and nodding. "That's what I want to do. I want to be a 'changed Scrooge'." He put the ornament back on the tree.

"You don't want the ornament?" she asked him. "I thought all of your ornaments were supposed to be symbolic."

Scott nodded. "Yes, but I never buy my own ornaments. It's always something we do for others."

Kasey looked back at the small Scrooge figurine, an idea forming in her head. "Ah, that makes sense," she said.

"What did you get out of the Christmas Carol?" he asked. "You were emotional in a few parts."

She nodded. It was too soon to tell exactly what this moment meant to her, but she wanted to tell Scott about it. "I really came to understand some things about myself, and my own journey. I saw myself through the whole musical, wishing that the past could be fixed. But I realized, just like the Ghost of Christmas Past said, that the past are things that have been. Those moments are what they are. Wishing they were different doesn't mean that they will be different."

Scott's eyes held warmth. "That's a very brave realization."

She nodded, feeling her eyes fill with tears again. "And I also realized that all that matters now is how I can change the present to frame my future. Scrooge changed completely in one night. I don't think I can do that, but I know I want to change. I want to see what's around me and what's in my future differently." Being with Scott had helped her realize just how much differently the future could look.

He squeezed her hand, then pulled her in for a hug as they waited for the cast members to emerge. They talked with Cooper and a few of the other actors. Kasey was overwhelmed with emotion again as she talked to Cooper about his performance as Scrooge. Cooper answered their questions, and when he was finished, she was a mess of tears again. But these tears were different, they felt more cleansing and healing somehow, like she was on the right track. She dabbed at her eyes, then excused herself to go to the restroom and wash her face, and possibly apply a fresh layer of mascara. Crying had been a therapeutic release, but now it was time to calm down the puffy eyes and soothe some of the redness away.

CHAPTER 22

Scott stared at an ornament depicting the three Ghosts. Scrooge stood underneath them and the gold letters on the base of the ornament read, *"I will live in the Past, the Present, and the Future. The Spirits of all Three shall strive within me."* After looking at dozens of ornaments all day long with Kasey, he'd finally settled on the ornament that would fit her. At least, he hoped that was the case. He'd watched how emotionally moved she was by the entire musical. He couldn't blame her. He'd been moved by it too.

Toward the top of the tree, a glittery star with a Victorian pattern on it caught his eye. He pulled it down. It was exactly the kind of thing that his sister would love. He placed the star and the three Ghosts ornament on the small counter and paid for them. The man in a cravat, waistcoat, and top hat in front of him wrapped the ornaments in bubble wrap and then in brown paper.

"Did you find something for your sister?" Kasey's voice came from behind him.

Scott turned to face her and smiled, grateful she'd asked a question he could answer honestly. "I did. It looked like this." He pulled down a glittery star from the tree fashioned exactly like the one he bought. "She loves stars and when I saw this one I knew it was the right one for her."

She hoisted her purse higher on her shoulder. "What a great tradition to be able to share." She surveyed the tree, and he hoped she wouldn't notice or buy the one that he'd just purchased for her. Her gaze stopped momentarily on a part of the tree, and she admired several of them.

He held his breath, hoping to leave the store before she made a purchase. She looked around for a few minutes longer, complimented the booth owner, and then they left.

"I think this has been the best day I've had during the Christmas season, in I can't remember how long," Kasey said, laughing as they walked out of the Dicken's Festival. The walk along the river to get back to The Soup Kitchen wasn't far, but the humidity bit into them. Kasey wrapped her coat tighter around her.

"Since you were fourteen?" Scott guessed. He squeezed her gloved hand in his own.

She let out a breath, but the expression on her face was light. "Easily that long, but this year feels different somehow. The Christmas Carol really touched me, and I-I liked what you said about wanting to be a 'changed Scrooge'. It feels like a good thing to strive for."

Festive Christmas lights along the river lit the dark water, making it look like a dark pudding with sprinkles on top of it.

For a moment Scott thought about walking in London along the Thames with Kasey, not just pretending at the Dicken's Festival. The idea had his heart soaring. "I think you're already being a 'changed Scrooge', Kasey. The work that you do touches a lot of people. I admire that about you. You're giving and kind and put people first. It's admirable." It was just one of the many things that he'd admired about her since he met her.

"What about you? You're already more like Scrooge than you know, too."

"Am I? Which Scrooge—the one at the beginning or the one at the end?" Her words from their first lunch together about her bias against rich people swirled doubt around him. He'd put the pieces together when she'd told him the story about her dad and his boss, and he couldn't help but think that maybe she'd still hold his wealth against him. He didn't want to be like the Scrooge at the beginning of the musical, but his insecurities about not doing more and not doing enough sunk into him. Even in the bet with his buddies he was trying to prove himself that he wasn't just a suit, but he often felt like an imposter trying to put on a show, like the actors on the stage.

"The 'changed Scrooge,' of course! Look at how you've helped The Soup Kitchen over the last several weeks. The donations we've received because of your dedication have been astronomical, and way beyond what we'd expected. You've really helped and connected with people. I've watched you take this whole Christmas project on for us, during a time where you must be busy fighting fires at your own job."

He laughed at her reference—fighting fires was all he told her about what he did at work when he hadn't wanted to reveal his real position. Now, he wanted to tell her about it. No, his company didn't do the kind of things she did every day at her job, but he was trying to make a difference—trying to be involved. After watching Kasey and how she worked, and after the message of The Christmas Carol resonated with him, he realized what he wanted to do and the person he wanted to become. "I feel like I'm so far behind with what I want to do and how I want to help." He admitted the vulnerability aloud, feeling the weight of the realization. He wasn't sure if he'd win the bet through the efforts he'd put into the charity, but it was more than that. Was he worthy of Kasey? She saw goodness and sacrificed, and he wasn't equal to it.

"I guess that's the beauty of The Christmas Carol, isn't it? The woman at the end talked about Scrooge as someone who kept Christmas well and was the best at doing it, but that had to come through change. It wasn't the reality on his first Christmas—the one that's in the musical. It was about all the other Christmases after. It's kind of a freeing thought for me. This can be the year to move forward toward that, but it comes from reconciling with the past and wanting to be present in the here and now." She grinned. "Will you help me with something?" she asked.

"Anything."

"I want to create new memories this year. Christmas memories. Everything I used to avoid at Christmas, I want to participate in."

Scott's mind spun, thinking of all the things they could do that he'd love to experience with her. "Like ice skating?"

She nodded. "And Christmas stores."

"You've really avoided them?"

"Of course I have. Unless I have to go in them for work, or

to buy something for others, I don't go. And I want to listen to Christmas songs—really listen to them on purpose." A laugh bubbled up from her. "I don't even know what else there is, but I want to do that too!"

"My sisters love popping popcorn and watching Christmas movies. They'll dedicate a whole weekend to Christmas movies, and watch them all day long."

"There's enough Christmas movies to actually do that?"

He laughed. "And then some. They love it."

"And I want to decorate gingerbread cookies."

"What about a gingerbread house?"

"I'm literally going to need to do a Pinterest search on how to make the cookies, I think a whole house is too advanced for me this year."

"You could do it," Scott encouraged.

She laughed, the beautiful sound capturing him. "I'm so excited! I feel like I've won something huge!"

He smiled. "You have won something huge," he said. "You've won a future of new possibilities for Christmases to come."

Tears glistened on her lashes, and he wanted to erase each one of them. She blinked rapidly, and the shimmering vanished. "Thank you for that. It feels like the future is a big present. It's pretty amazing."

Scott took the leap. "It looks amazing, and I want to see it with you."

She lifted her eyebrows. "See what with me?"

"The future." He squeezed her hand.

"I'd like that a lot, too," she said, pulling on his coat and kissing him.

Scott walked Kasey to her car, and Kasey rummaged in her purse. “I don’t have my keys.” She looked up at him, then focused on her purse again.

“Do you think you lost them at the Dicken’s Festival?”

She rubbed a hand over her forehead. “I can’t remember seeing them at all today. But I should have them since I locked The Soup Kitchen when we left earlier.”

Scott shook his head. “I locked the door with my key, remember?”

“Oh, good. That probably means I didn’t lose them, they’re just probably at my desk, since we walked to the Dicken’s Festival.”

Scott pulled out his key from his coat pocket, waving it in the air. “Luckily for you, I still have *my* key.”

She laughed. “It is a good thing, because my backup is usually Trish … and it’s kind of a long commute from Spain.”

They headed down the stairs and out onto the street. Scott unlocked the door, and held it open for her, grateful that he was able to spend a few extra minutes with her.

“That’s weird,” she said.

“What?” Scott asked.

“The light isn’t working,” she replied as she flipped the switch on and off.

Scott let go of the door he’d been holding and moved toward the light switch, bumping into her. “Sorry,” he said.

“It’s okay. I’d make some joke about turning on the light, but it’s obviously not working.”

Scott pulled out his phone and turned his flashlight on. The small beam did little to illuminate The Gathering. "Where is the breaker box?"

"At the end of the hall," Kasey said, fishing out her own phone and turning on her flashlight as well.

"I'll go look at it while you get your keys," he said, holding her hand as they made their way toward her office.

Kasey held on tighter to Scott's arm. "Whoa. This floor is slippery."

"We have been out in the weather," he said. "Shoes get slick."

"Good point," she said, regaining her balance.

"Be right back," Scott said, leaving her at her office door and continuing down the long corridor until he found the breaker box. The panel was old and looked like it was in need of some care. He wedged it open, the metal grating and squeaking as he pushed it to the side. The labels for each of the switches was unintelligible. He went to a few of the surrounding offices, turning the light switches to the on position, unsure how he would determine the right breaker for the front hallway. The office lights did not turn on. Some of the switches looked like they hadn't been used for a long time. He started flipping switches, looking down the hallway to see if it made a difference, but he couldn't tell. The lights were on down the street, so the problem looked like a local one. He started at the top and flipped switches hoping that the offices would respond with illumination. Still, nothing happened. He'd almost finished flipping the first of the five columns of panels, when he heard a crash, followed by a loud cry, then another crash.

"Kasey? Are you okay?" He ran toward her office, feeling his feet slip underneath him. Someone had left the floors very wet after mopping. He found Kasey on the floor in her office and moved his flashlight so it wasn't shining directly in her eyes. He looked down at the floor and saw that it was covered with quite a bit blood.

"No! My leg is stuck and hurts and my hand is cut." Her words were labored as she said them.

He helped her get her foot free from where it was wedged between the desk and the toppled chair, then helped her up. She held one hand close to her. The gash through the middle of her palm was sizable.

She crumpled toward him. "I can't put weight on it."

He helped her into the chair. "What happened to your hand?"

She looked unfocused toward the floor. "My snow globe slid off my desk. I tried to catch it, but didn't reach it until it had smashed."

"We need to get you to the hospital," he said.

Her eyes widened and her face drained of color. "I can't. I hate hospitals. I—"

Rushing water broke from the ceiling, pouring through a hole. "What's happening?" Scott asked alarmingly.

She looked up. "I've always had a small leak above my desk."

"We need to get out of here now!" Scott pulled her up but she couldn't stand. He cradled her in his arms, carrying her out the door.

"My snow globe," Kasey said, her voice faint, her body feeling more limp in his arms.

He held onto her tighter, wishing he could make eye contact with her in the dark. "Kasey, you're going into shock. I need you to sing the ABC's for me."

"The ABC's is such a funny name. How come they made A first?"

He set her down on a small chair in The Gathering. He took the scarf she had around her neck and made a quick bandage around her hand. He was sure there were medical supplies at The Soup Kitchen somewhere, but finding them in the dark wasn't ideal. Even though Kasey would know exactly where they were, she was in no state to give actual answers.

He propped her leg up on a stool, being as gentle as he could with it. "Ouch, ouch. That does not feel good at all. My leg feels like it's on fire." She whimpered in between her breathing.

"Sing the ABC's, Kasey. You know that song. A, B, C, D, ..." Scott started the song for her, hoping it would help her brain focus on it. He pulled out his phone and called 911. He kept his voice calm, knowing that whatever Kasey remembered from this moment, he did not want to show how panicked he felt. Sometime during his call, she started singing the ABC's. She stopped on different letters to make commentary about them.

"Help is on the way," he said, when he'd finished his call. "You're going to be fine."

"My boot is tight," she said, a bead of sweat dripping down the sides of her temples, her eyes unfocused.

He touched it tenderly, and she cried out in pain. "It's likely swelling," he said. He knew removing the boot could do more damage, and didn't want to cause her more alarm. She needed attention for it immediately, but it would be better to wait until the ambulance arrived.

Scott saw the flashing lights outside of the windows. "Help is here," he whispered. "I'm going to let them in." He opened the door, and a group rushed in as Scott explained the situation. He took her hand as she was laid on the stretcher.

"Scott, I don't want to go to the hospital." Her breathing was uneven.

"I know. I'm going to be right behind you though. I'll be at the hospital with you. It's going to be okay." He gave instructions on which hospital and they loaded her into the ambulance. He went back into her office, the floor now covered with more water. He grabbed her purse from the round table, only splashed with water, and looked around the floor for her snow globe. It was on its side, the dome of it mostly gone with huge shards of glass poking straight up from the base. He was grateful that the injury on her hand wasn't worse than what it was. He surveyed the scene, trying to make sense of how she'd fallen, and hoped that it was only a sprain that made it impossible to bear weight on her leg.

As he drove to the hospital only a few minutes behind the ambulance, he called the owner of the building about the leak. Scott left it in his hands so he could focus on Kasey and how to help her. A text came through from Kyle, and his car read it to him. He'd sent Kyle a text earlier when he'd been by himself for a few minutes at The Dickens' Festival. He gave the voice command to respond, and instead of just sending an email, his phone dialed Kyle.

"How are things going? You said you had some big news earlier?" Kyle asked.

The big news had been sharing how much this project had brought him closer to Kasey. Now was not the time to focus on that. "They just took a turn for the worse," Scott said.

"You and everyone else," Kyle muttered.

"What was that?" Scott asked, not sure he'd heard right over the road noise.

"Nothing. What's going on?"

He gave a shortened version of what happened during the day and then Kasey's accident, and the water all over the floor. As he told Kyle about the power being off and the leak from the ceiling, he wondered if that was what had caused Kasey to fall … and if that was the case if there would be lawsuit about it. He gave his report of helping this week, but then said, "I'm going to be honest, Kyle. I'm not sure what's happening with Kasey. My mind isn't on the charity right now."

"Fair enough. I won't keep you. But, call me later when you find out how bad it is, okay? Kandice and I will send prayers Kasey's way."

"Thanks, Kyle," Scott said. "That means a lot. I'll let you know what happens."

"You're doing a good job," Kyle said.

"Thanks," Scott said then hung up. He shouldn't have left her in her office alone while he'd gone to try and fix the power issue. He should have been with her, and then maybe this wouldn't have happened.

At the hospital, Scott paced up and down the S. Parker wing. Sitting, waiting, and watching the same late-night broadcasts on the flat screen TVs only made him more anxious. Even as a donor to the wing, he didn't have privileges to observe the surgery. He found out from the head nurse that Kasey had been fairly unstable in the ambulance, and needed sedation. "That's because she doesn't like hospitals," he murmured, glancing to the white floor, wishing he'd just rode in the ambulance with her. He looked back at the nurse. "I want to see her as soon as I can. I promised I'd be with her in the hospital."

She nodded, her eyes sympathetic. "We'll let you know as soon as she is out of surgery."

"Surgery? Is her foot broken then?"

The nurse shook her head. "It's not broken, but it's a bad sprain. She still won't be able to put much pressure on it, though. Her hand was what needed plastics and a lot of stitches. It was very badly cut. There were lots of little glass shards in her palm."

He nodded, his stomach churning. "Will she be discharged when she's finished?"

The nurse shrugged. "Those are questions for the doctor." She tapped at her clipboard. "Kasey wasn't fully aware of anything when she arrived. This is the paperwork we will need filled out before she's discharged."

"I will fill out as much as I can," he said, feeling like he had a purpose. He held her purse, not wanting to go through it, but just so that she'd have it in case she needed it. He found her wallet without disturbing the rest of the purse's contents and took most of the information needed from her driver's license. He left the medical history blank, and looked through the cards she had in her wallet when he came to the questions about insurance. He couldn't find a card. That was strange. He flipped through them again. Still nothing.

Scott called Patty, and asked her to help with coordinating the shifts for the next few days, promising that he'd be in when he could. He explained the abbreviated version of what had happened, focusing mostly on the power outage and the flooding of Kasey's office, and how that would affect The Soup Kitchen. Patty said she'd coordinate with the owner of the building and would follow-up with him regarding the disaster cleanup. On a whim, he asked, "Patty, does the charity provide health insurance to their employees?"

"They do, but not everyone takes advantage of it," Patty said.

"Thanks," he said before hanging up.

Scott thought through what Patty had said. He wondered if Kasey had insurance or not, but either way he knew what he was going to do. Kyle wouldn't be able to hold this against him, because helping Kasey wasn't part of the bet. An ambulance ride was expensive, but he knew that it got her the help she needed faster than if he'd driven her to the hospital himself. He didn't regret the choice for getting her the help, and he knew that regardless of her current insurance situation, he'd pay for this. It was the least he could do.

He handed the clipboard back to the nurse, then explained his plan. She took him to billing where he signed all the paperwork to pay for all of the expenses associated with Kasey's care.

Scott sent Trish a text message. He didn't want to disturb her in the middle of the night, but she'd likely see the text message in a few hours, and Scott felt certain Kasey would want Trish to know what had happened.

He wanted to solve something. Do something. He paced around the room again, hating how helpless he felt when the woman he'd fallen for was in pain.

CHAPTER 23

Kasey felt the pain even before could force her eyes open. It coursed through her with dull and sharp forces, and moved through her body with such speed that she couldn't pinpoint it. She tried moving her hands, only to find that they were strapped down. Panic rose above the pain, and she forced her eyes open, willing them to focus.

A blurry white form moved in the corner. "Oh good, you're awake." The voice was kind and cheerful.

"Where am I?"

"In the Parker recovery wing at Jefferson hospital," the nurse said.

"I can't move my hands," she said, panic forcing its way to the surface.

"You're okay. Your right hand was badly injured, and you were trying to take the bandages off, so we had to restrain your left hand. I can untie your hand for you, if you'd like."

"Yes, please," she said.

The nurse undid loops on the side of the bed, and she moved her left hand with no problem, but pain tore through her again as she tried to move her right hand. In a sling, wrapped in several layers, it was hard to tell how it looked or what was wrong with it.

"How is your pain?"

Kasey winced. "I can definitely feel it." She moved her hand and fiery flames shot through her wrist and arm.

"I'll add something to your IV to help with that," she said. "The best thing you can do is stay on top of the pain. You'll heal faster. You were out much longer than we'd planned."

Kasey's eyes adjusted, noticing the morning light glowing from behind the closed shades over the window. She took a steadying breath and looked down at her foot, in a large boot that extended all the way to her knee. "Is it broken?"

The nurse shook her head. "Just badly sprained. It looks like you took a bad fall, but they were able to pop your ankle back in place with no trouble. The doctor will come in and give you instructions when you're ready," the nurse said.

"Thank you, um, what was your name?"

The woman beamed. "I'm Emily."

"Thanks, Emily. I need to see the doctor, and then I need to see the billing department." Dread filled her. Hospitals were already a triggering place for her. She remembered very little of the ambulance ride, except for trying to get out of the ambulance while the sirens were on. But she knew that ambulances were expensive, and she had all these procedures done, and it looked like she was going to have to stay in the hospital for a while. How was she going to afford all this? It all felt overwhelmingly heavy.

"I'll get you the doctor, but you won't need billing," Emily said.

"I will need billing. I need to talk about a payment plan." Insurance was so minimal that she had to hit a sizable out of pocket before it would kick in at all. There was no point in running this claim through insurance when it was so close to the end of the year.

Emily took Kasey's vitals and smiled. "Your bill has already been taken care of by the donor of the wing."

"What? I don't even know the donor of this wing, or any of the wings in the hospital." Confusion settled in around her, and her brain felt fuzzy.

Emily tilted her head. "You're teasing me. That's probably a good sign in your recovery. Mr. Scott Parker, *the tech billionaire,* has been waiting to see you all night. He's wearing a rut in the waiting room floor. I'll let him know you're awake and ready for visitors. I'll send breakfast up so you have some strength before I send the doctor in." She exited the room before Kasey could respond.

Kasey tried to make sense of Emily's statement, but with her brain as fuzzy as it was, she wasn't even sure she'd heard Emily right. Maybe she was in the middle of a dream. Scott wasn't a *billionaire*—he would have told her that.

A few moments later, a knock came at the door. Emily had sent breakfast up much quicker than she'd expected. "Come in," she called.

Scott entered the room, not the breakfast tray. He smiled, approaching slowly. "How are you feeling?"

How was she feeling? Confused. Unsure. The pain seemed to be lifting though. Whatever the nurse had given her seemed to be working its magic, and the pain mostly felt like pushing into marshmallow fluff. It was there, but it was hard to identify as a shape or a feeling. "I'm not sure what the nurse just gave me. I'm feeling kind of disoriented. I think these meds are making me delirious." She wanted to shake her head to clear the confusion, but she couldn't clear it.

"What do you mean?"

"I could have sworn she just said you were the donor of this hospital wing. That can't be right."

His eyes widened for a brief moment, but then he nodded. "Actually, you heard right. I am the donor of this wing."

"What? I'm ... still so confused. She said that you paid for my medical bills?"

"That's true. I couldn't find an insurance card in your wallet." He held up her purse and placed it on the table closer to her bed.

"It's a high-deductible plan and it covers almost nothing until I hit the deductible. Everything is basically out of pocket for me."

"I figured as much," he said softly. "So I took care of it."

Anger and frustration rose. "I can take care of myself."

He put his hands in the air, holding them up in a gesture of surrender. "I know that. I wasn't trying to overstep. I just didn't want you to worry about it. And I felt responsible."

"How did you feel responsible? I'm the one that fell."

"I made the decision to call the ambulance," he said. "It was too dark to tell just how badly you were injured. And you must have hit your head too, because you were kind of out of it, so I did what I thought was best."

"She also said you were a billionaire," Kasey said, watching his expression closely.

Color touched his cheeks. He nodded. "Also true."

She let out a big breath, the effort feeling exhausting. Her thoughts ran in so many directions, and she knew she couldn't run after them. "Why didn't you tell me?" Hurt built up inside her. They'd been close. They'd talked about their future together only yesterday. Emptiness filled her.

"I've wanted to," he said. "But I wasn't sure how you'd take it."

"I feel like that's kind of a big deal … that I didn't know. You've been helping us with our small project, and all this time there was no real need for it. Is that why you refused The Soup Kitchen salary?"

"I wanted to volunteer, to feel the magic of Christmas on a level that was different from how I normally do things. And then I met you, and I didn't want the money to change your opinion of me."

Kasey leaned back against her pillows, unsure why sadness wrapped around her so tightly. "You didn't trust me with knowing." They weren't as close as she'd thought.

"No, Kasey, that's not it." Scott's eyes were wide. "The reason why—"

A knock came at the door. Kasey looked for the expected breakfast, but it was a man in a large white coat and dark-rimmed spectacles. Still not breakfast. "Hi, Kasey. I'm Dr. Linwood. I'm here to go over your recovery plan and answer any other questions you might have before you are discharged."

Scott retreated toward the door, but Dr. Linwood motioned for Scott to take a seat by Kasey. "It helps if we have someone else here who will remember all the information. We're going over a lot, and while it is all written out, it's nice to have another person knowing what to expect for recovery."

Scott looked to Kasey with an unspoken question on his face, and Kasey wasn't sure how to answer. She only shrugged, and he took a seat in the chair on the opposite side of the bed from Dr. Linwood, near the window.

Kasey couldn't see both Scott and Dr. Linwood at the same time, so she turned her head to focus solely on Dr. Linwood. She tried with all her mental capacity to remember everything that he was saying. He talked about managing the pain, as well as elevating her leg while it was still swollen, and went into detail on her hand. "The plastic surgeon did a great job on your hand. It was a lot of work to remove the glass, so there may be some extra tenderness in it. Expect bruising. We'll want to check on the stitches in your hand in a week to make sure everything is healing properly. Avoid stairs, and although it's a mild sprain, I'd stay off of your foot as much as you can. We'll give you a special brace you can wear once the swelling goes down, but for right now, the boot offers more protection while it's swollen. We'll check it at your follow-up appointment next week, and go from there."

"I walk upstairs every day. It's how I get to my apartment."

Dr. Linwood smiled. "It's good to be active, but until it's completely healed, I don't recommend the stairs. Take the elevator."

Kasey squeezed her eyes shut. "You don't understand. My apartment doesn't have an elevator."

"Well that does pose a problem," Dr. Linwood said. "I recommend staying with friends or family while you recover.

Stairs are one of the worst things for your condition, especially where your hand will not be able to grasp the handrails while it heals."

Kasey felt Scott's hand on her shoulder. "We'll figure this out, Kasey. You have a lot of options."

Kasey could feel the exhaustion of the last several hours catching up with her, even though she'd been able to get a few hours of sleep. She nodded, trying to pay attention to the rest of what Dr. Linwood was saying, but it was almost impossible to concentrate.

She caught a few words and heard a few phrases here and there, but mostly her head swam with all the questions of how this was really going to work. She wasn't allowed to drive until she was completely healed. She couldn't do stairs. Everything felt overwhelming. Scott said she had lots of options, but she couldn't see any. She was supposed to keep her foot elevated for the next week while the swelling went down, which basically meant she would be confined to a bed or a couch. She thought about hopping up and down her stairs on one leg, using her good hand to grasp the handrail, and then had to admit that Dr. Linwood was right. There was no way she'd be able to be at her house.

Dr. Linwood left her with a stack of papers stapled together, but the look of the fine print was too hard to concentrate on. She closed her eyes as he left.

"What am I going to do?" Kasey whispered, trying to think logically about everything.

A knock came at the door, then opened. "Here's your breakfast," a short woman said, bringing in a tray and setting it on the small table next to Kasey's bed. She swung the table so that it extended over Kasey's lap for easy access to the food.

Kasey looked at the pancakes, fruit, and juice and tried to smile. "Thanks," she said, wondering if she'd even have an appetite for it.

She picked up her fork, trying to cut the sides of the pancake with only one hand. The table wobbled, and she put the fork down. "This is going to be harder than I thought."

"I can help," Scott said, cutting the pancakes and the fruit into small enough pieces that Kasey could manage to stab them with the fork without rocking the bed table.

Kasey still wanted to be upset at Scott for keeping a major part of his identity a secret from her, but she was grateful he was helping her to eat. She hadn't realized how hungry she was until the smell of the food hit her senses. "Thank you," she said, her emotions softening.

He nodded, pulling up the chair he'd been sitting in, positioning it closer to her bed. "We should discuss what we're going to do about your recovery."

She swallowed her bite of pancake. "Thanks, but you don't have to worry about it. I'll figure something out."

"Kasey, I'm here to help you, remember? I still want to explore what our future looks like *together*."

"I'm not sure I can think about that right now. I just can't."

Scott nodded. "I understand. Let's table that discussion for now. But, regardless, I'm here to help you. You can't go to your apartment. What other options are there? What about Trish?"

Kasey shook her head. "Trish has stairs too. Not as many, but even if she were in town it wouldn't work."

"I imagine you don't want to stay in the hospital," Scott said, looking around the room.

"The less time I spend at a hospital, the better. It's already felt too long, and I haven't been awake for much of it."

"And your family?"

"They're two states away. I don't want to recover away from the important things in my life. How will I go in to work?"

Scott looked at her doubtfully. "You are going to have to take some time off from work," he said carefully.

"Yes, but when I start feeling a little better, I want to be there." She leaned back on the pillows, trying to think of actual solutions. "I could stay at a hotel."

"Wouldn't it be better to stay at a friend's place, where they could help you?"

She nodded. "But it's Christmas time. I don't want to impose on anyone, especially not when so many people have family coming into town. I think a hotel is the best option." Though she hated the idea of spending so much money every day, it was the best idea she could come up with. It would be fine. Positive thinking would have her healing fast, and before she knew it, she would be back on both feet again, literally.

"You'll still need someone to help you, Kasey. You couldn't even cut your pancakes yourself. And the doctor made it clear that—"

Kasey bit her lip. "I won't eat pancakes for the next week then. I didn't break my ankle, it's a mild sprain. Once I get used to doing things with my left hand, I'll be fine."

"My place in the city is very large. You can stay in the guest room while you recover."

"No, I don't want to take your charity." And being under the same roof felt really awkward under the circumstances.

As if reading her mind, he said, "I have another place I can stay while you're using the suite."

Kasey didn't want to be a burden and didn't want to displace him from his regular home and routine. Besides, she only had to rest. Scott was right, she wasn't going to be going into work for at least a week, so she wouldn't be going up and down the stairs every day. "I'm going to my apartment. It's where everything is, and I can recover there. I won't be leaving to go to work."

Scott looked at her doubtfully. "I don't think this is a good idea."

She bristled. "I can make the decision myself."

He blew out a breath. "At least let me help you. The doctor won't let you leave without help. I'll drive you there, and help you up to your apartment."

She nodded, her eyelids feeling heavy.

"I'll go get the nurse for the final discharge paperwork."

Scott drove her to her house, and she mostly kept her eyes closed. He helped her out of the car, but she focused on not leaning into him as she made her way to the stairs. Six flights. She only had to do it once. She glanced up at the enormity of them, her senses starting to come together. Maybe this was too difficult. She hopped up the first two steps, wincing at the pain.

"Yeah, this isn't going to work for me," Scott said. "Come here."

"I can do this," she said, trying to convince herself.

"I know you can. But you don't have to do it alone. I'm going to carry you up."

Her protests died before they could even form as he lifted her into his arms, and carried her up the six flights of stairs. The gesture was sweet, but the earlier revelation of him not trusting her crept up again. He put her down in front of her door, and she used him to maintain her balance as she fished her keys from her purse.

"Kasey, I want to talk about—"

She shook her head. "I need some time to think."

"I can come by tomorrow and check on you," he offered.

"More charity? So I can be your newest tax deduction? No thanks. You've done enough." Anger bit through her words. This whole situation wasn't working for her anymore. If he'd just been honest from the beginning, maybe she wouldn't have questioned his motives, but this just felt like he was trying to overcompensate. She pushed on the door, frustrated that even opening it felt difficult.

"That's not fair. How could you think that of me? Don't you know me at all?"

"Apparently not." She shut the door behind her, her heart breaking and smashing like the snow globe she'd tried to save, only to be sliced open instead. If only she could take medicine to numb the pain of a broken heart.

CHAPTER 24

Two days after Scott had taken Kasey to her apartment, he arrived at his penthouse. It had been another long day of working at The Soup Kitchen. It wasn't the same there without Kasey, and he worked hard in spite of his emotions regarding her, though the work didn't distract him as much as he'd hoped it would. The place felt full of memories of him and Kasey, laughing and having fun, but that wasn't how things were at the moment. Things between them still felt rocky since he hadn't heard from her at all. He really wanted to check on her and see how she was. Every day since dropping her off, he'd thought about texting her or calling her at least a dozen times, but each time he pulled out his phone, her words about not knowing him stung like frostbite on rosy cheeks. He'd give her the space she asked for, even if it was painful for him.

He swallowed the lump in his throat. He wished she'd taken him up on his offer to have her recover at his place, even if that meant he'd live out of a suitcase in a hotel. He wasn't offering out of pity, but because he cared about her. Sure, she could be in her apartment for a week or two, have groceries delivered and not need to leave. But what if there was a fire or some other emergency? Those kinds of thoughts always crossed his mind. In an actual emergency, she'd be stranded, and he hated that she'd talked him into such a dangerous situation. She wasn't just another tax-deduction, and the way she'd thrown out the accusation felt like a slap in his face.

He'd spent a frustrating morning yesterday with the owner of the building that The Soup Kitchen leased. The owner wasn't at all surprised or sympathetic toward the flooding, or Kasey's accident because of the slippery floors. He pushed blame back, presumed that the renter's insurance would be responsible for paying for everything, and would not entertain the idea of taking proactive measures to fix up the dilapidated building.

Today, as the disaster team came in to fix what had happened, they'd found signs of tampering, and also signs of possible future problems in the old plumbing throughout the building. Scott's annoyance at the owner's negligence grew. The owner didn't want to put more money into the building, saying that it was a money pit as it was. As he dug further, Scott discovered the owner's signature on several forms that detailed items that should have been inspected and weren't in compliance. This posed a huge threat to The Soup Kitchen as a whole, but he didn't want to bring up his concerns until he had solid proof that it was purposefully done.

Either way, something had to be done. The owner had offhandedly mentioned on the way out that he'd like to see the land put to better use, and that a parking garage would make him a much larger profit than the grant that paid the lease of the building for the non-profit.

He reported in to Kyle and Kandice, trying to keep his spirits up as he told them about his work at The Soup Kitchen. They expressed their concern for Kasey when he told them about the accident, and then he told them about the breakup. It was rough to talk about, but at least he could verbalize the words. That would help him move forward, right?

He called up his personal assistant, Nancy. He needed answers before the Health Department came for their final inspection.

"How is Kasey doing?" Nancy asked when she picked up.

He'd been asked that by all the staff at The Soup Kitchen, and several of the regular patrons. It had been hard to dodge the question there. Mostly he'd replied with, 'You know Kasey. She'll be back on her feet in no time.' That had satisfied everyone who asked, but Nancy didn't know Kasey, so it wasn't a line he could really use. "I wish I knew."

"Things still rough between the two of you?"

"She asked for some time to think through things," he admitted. Of course, that had been before she slammed the door in his face, so he wasn't quite sure. He just didn't want to reach out and be rejected again.

"Anything I can do to help?" Nancy asked.

"Not with her, unfortunately, but I have a different task for you."

"Name it," Nancy said.

"Will you look a few things up for me? I want to see if there is any connection with the owner of The Soup Kitchen building and the push to get the land rezoned for different structures, like a parking garage."

Nancy lowered her voice. "Scott, you know the deal. I'm not supposed to help with—"

"I'm not asking you to work on the charity side of things, only to see what you can find out. I have a hunch that the pipe bursting and the surprise inspections are connected, and I'd like to see if I can make that case."

"I'll look into it. What is your intention with all of this?"

"I think I might buy the property and get it fixed up."

"That goes way beyond your donation," she protested.

"This isn't about the competition, Nancy." It hadn't been for a long time. He paused, needing Nancy to understand. "The Soup Kitchen is Kasey's life. If I can save it from being turned into a parking lot, like the owner wants to do because of all the repairs required, then that's what I'm going to do."

"You really like her, don't you?" Nancy asked.

"I love her," Scott said, without hesitation. He realized that he needed to tell Kasey.

"I'll look into this, and get back to you when I know something. Hopefully it won't take too long, even though it's the holidays."

"If you can work your magic, do it. If it needs to wait a few days, I understand."

CHAPTER 25

Kasey tried to sleep, but she'd tossed and turned for over an hour, which was hard to do with a boot on. It had been the same routine for the last three nights since she'd gotten home from the hospital. Maybe it was inevitable since she'd slept most of the day again and wasn't really tired, and she was also really uncomfortable. She'd left Trish an urgent message when she'd first arrived home, but she still hadn't heard anything back.

She turned on the light, propped her pillows up behind her the best she could with one hand, and tried to get comfortable. She took a book off of her nightstand, but the medication made it hard to focus on the words, and more restlessness set in. This week would be the slowest of her life. She grabbed the remote and turned on her on-demand streaming service, in the mood for a documentary or a lifestyle piece about service in foreign countries. Those always grabbed her interest. As she scrolled through the titles, multiple Christmas movies were advertised. She snort laughed at the idea of watching a movie about Christmas. It was more than a little funny to her. The medication really must be playing with her mind.

She paused as she remembered the conversation she'd had with Scott after The Dickens' Festival. He'd mentioned that his sisters loved Christmas movies, and they made plans to watch them together every year. She thought about her experience during the musical, and how much she'd connected with the ghosts and the lessons they taught. She held the remote up, almost willing herself to switch off the advertisement, and then stopped herself. Watching a Christmas movie with Scott, with the way things were between them, was definitely out. But she still wanted to create new Christmas traditions. And it wasn't about anyone else. It was about her. She didn't want to come to love Christmas through someone else or for someone else. She wanted to know what Christmas meant for her individually.

She pushed play on the movie. Christmas spirit filled the screen and she tried to give it an honest chance as the holiday romance played out for an hour and a half. As the credits began to roll, she turned off the TV, settled against the pillows, and closed her eyes. For ten minutes she tried to sleep, but sleep had fled from her eyes. She turned the TV back on and loaded the next Christmas movie. Emotions spilled across her face as the second show took an unexpected turn in the middle of it. She pulled a tissue from the box on her nightstand to wipe her eyes and blow her nose. The story was sadder than the first one, but ended happily. She started a third one, not daring to look at the hour as the movie started. This one pulled at her heart strings again, and happy tears fell as the couple destined to get together made progress in that direction. Partway through the third movie, her phone buzzed. She glanced at the screen, grabbing it and sliding the button to answer the phone.

"Hi, Trish," Kasey said.

"Kasey? Why can't I see you on the screen?"

Kasey moved the phone away from her ear. "Sorry. I didn't realize it was a video chat."

Trish moved her face closer to the screen. "I'm sorry for calling in the middle of the night, but I just saw your message, and thought I'd leave you a video message of the beautiful landscape. Reception has been spotty for me over here. Kasey, what's wrong? You've been crying. Are you okay?"

Tears welled up in Kasey's eyes as she glanced at the TV screen. She had paused on an image that showed the couple together, but not yet realizing their differences. "I'm fine, but they're not right now." Kasey flipped the screen around showing Trish the paused image.

Trish smiled. "Ah, that's a classic. I watch it every year."

"How have you never told me about these before? They're like a magic box of Christmas emotions." Kasey wiped her eyes, trying to keep herself composed.

Trish raised her eyebrows. "Um, let's see, for starters, you don't like Christmas or anything about Christmas. You don't like Christmas decorations, or Christmas traditions, and that's what all of those movies are about. So, I'm confused why you're confused that I never talk to you about my Christmas movie addiction."

"Well, things have changed. And I've changed. And I am loving these movies."

"Okay, I'm so glad you're loving them, but you need to

understand that if you watch them all night long you're going to wake up in the morning with a pounding headache from crying. And the insides of your eyelids are going to be so salty they'll literally make your eyes feel like they've been wind-burned. Take my advice: Super cold towel on your eyes for at least ten minutes, and hydrate. Otherwise the hangover is real."

Kasey grinned. "Sounds like you have a few movies you need to recommend to me."

"Are you serious?" Trish squealed. "This is like a Christmas miracle. Who are you and what have you done with my best friend, Kasey the Grinch?"

Kasey smiled. "I'm still the Grinch, I'm just the Grinch after the moment on the mountain where his feet were frozen in the snow. My outlook on Christmas might be changing … but slowly, of course."

"Slowly, huh? Well, this is huge. I'll text you the names of my favorite Christmas movies. I have them categorized in a list on my phone."

Kasey laughed. "You really have them categorized on your phone?"

"Of course." Trish looked at her like she was stupid.

"Why?" Kasey asked.

"So that when my friends ask for my favorite movies I can bombard them with my top twenty-five without having to think of them each time. I have a rating system and it's complex. I can't be expected to remember the order of all of them off the top of my head."

Kasey laughed. "Fair point. So far, the two that I've finished made my list. This third one is on its way to rounding out my top three favorites list."

Trish looked off the screen for a minute, and then came back. "Okay, sorry, we're going to be at some ruins for most of the day, and I wanted to catch you while I had reception. Sorry, I just got so distracted by your sudden change over Christmas and watching Christmas romances, that I basically forgot the whole reason why I was calling. But we're almost to where we are going, and so I have to hurry."

"Okay, what's on your mind?"

"Scott told me what happened. How come you didn't tell me everything?"

"I told you to call me." Kasey gave a weak smile. "I didn't want you to worry about me from an ocean away."

"We were out of reception for a couple days. I didn't even realize it. It's been amazing here." Trish waved a hand in the air. "Anyway, I'm glad you're not seriously hurt, but that's not what I was talking about. I asked Scott for details, because you know, I'm the best friend and all … but really, I would have preferred to hear the story from you, how he carried you out of your office like a hero." Trish wiggled her eyebrows.

Kasey blushed. "He would have done that for anyone," she said. "Besides, I hardly remember it."

"You must have been more out of it than he let on, because that is something memorable."

"We were dating, and I thought things were going well—"

"See, that's a step in the right direction," Trish said confidently.

"But he's not who I thought he was." She tried to condense her thoughts down to the main point. "He's only at The Soup Kitchen for a tax-deduction. And I fall into that category."

Trish narrowed her eyes. "Are we really talking about the same person?"

Kasey nodded.

"You guys broke up?"

"I guess we did. I was mad. Then he got mad because I was mad. It all kind of happened so fast."

Trish opened her mouth and then closed it. "Kasey, I'm really sorry. I thought things were going so well. He left the cutest message about you on my phone, and I got it right before I called you."

"He probably left that message before I called him out for not being honest with me."

"Are you glad it's over?" she asked softly.

Tears pricked Kasey's eyes, and she blamed the TV screen for her sudden wave of emotion. "Of course I'm glad. I don't want to be with someone who isn't honest, and who hides who he really is." But inside she desperately tried to believe the words she was saying—the pain was still raw.

"You know that you can't pull that past me. I can see you're hurting from this."

"I'll get over it."

Trish bit her lip. "As someone who has had a lot of experience in the break-up department, just know that sometimes there are things that are worth working through."

"This one isn't."

"Kasey, I don't even think you know yet. Don't make a decision yet either way. You've just had surgery, and you've been through a lot. Plus, you're watching Christmas movies, and I can tell that you're enjoying them."

"The Christmas movies are pretty great."

"See what I'm saying? The Kasey from two weeks ago would have never said that. I don't know all the details of what happened between the two of you, but I've seen the way he looks at you, and the way he treats you. He genuinely cares for you."

"What if that isn't enough?"

Trish sighed. "I've had my share of heartbreak. Some of the time it could have been avoided because some of the relationships should have ended way before they did. I guess my point is we all do stupid things or say stupid things to the people we love. That's not an excuse for bad or abusive behavior, and I'm not okay with that kind of thing, but we're all human. We make mistakes. We make choices, and sometimes they're not the best ones. Hopefully we can apologize and give and receive forgiveness when it's in a relationship that we want to keep. It's okay that we're not perfect in everything we do. We can change and be better."

"You think I should give him another chance?"

"I'm not saying that. I don't know what exactly happened, or why. But even if I knew those circumstances, it's not about what *I* think you should do. This is your relationship, and I see it from an outsider's perspective."

"You think we made a cute couple though."

Trish nodded. "I really do. But again, I know enough about relationships to know that looks can be deceiving. Maybe things looked good between the two of you and they weren't ever good. I'd never advise people to stay in a relationship solely based on what others think. This is your life. You get to choose what makes you happy and what doesn't. Maybe that means you don't watch Christmas movies for years, finally discover them, and find out you like them. Or maybe you watch them and realize that they weren't for you all along."

"I still don't know what to do. You're my best friend, you're supposed to tell me what to do."

Trish smiled. "I gave you my advice—washcloth on your eyes, and hydrate, remember? Everything else will work itself out. Maybe you'll find out that you're okay with moving on from Scott. Or maybe you'll find that the time apart isn't what you want. Time will help with some of that. It's okay that you don't have the answer right now. Sometimes answers just take time."

Kasey felt the wisdom of Trish's sage words. "Thanks, Trish."

"That's what I'm here for—or I guess that's what I'm on the video chat for. If I were there in person, I'd join you and watch all the Christmas movies and eat all the chocolate."

"Thanks. Maybe we can do that when you get back from Spain."

Trish grinned. "I'd love it. Keep me posted on what you decide to do."

"I'll let you know," she promised, still not sure what she'd do, or if there was anything to do. But realizing that she didn't have to make that decision right now helped lift her spirits. Trish was always helpful that way.

"Okay, well we're here at the ruins, so I'll let you go and get back to your movie … or sleep, like most normal people do during this time of the night."

"Thanks, Trish. It's good to see you."

"You too. Feel better, Kasey." Trish moved her face closer to the screen and whispered, "And if something happens between the two of you, you better tell me all about it *before* I get home."

Kasey nodded. "I will." She ended the video chat and finished the end of the movie, before finally being tired enough to sleep.

THE NEXT MORNING A PACKAGE ARRIVED FOR HER WITH NO return address. She opened the box and found a gingerbread kit inside. Kasey couldn't be sure if the online box had been ordered from Trish or Scott or someone else who knew she was home for the week. The idea of decorating a gingerbread house by herself filled her with a mixed bag of emotions. On one hand, doing it by herself felt a little sad, but then again, she was doing it for her and for no one else. The idea of creating Christmas traditions without others' expectations interfering with her feelings was freeing.

She took the box to the kitchen table, sat down, and propped her foot up on a cushioned chair as she unpackaged the contents. Everything she needed was included in the box. After watching all those Christmas movies last night, she almost felt like she'd had a tutorial on how to make a gingerbread house stand up with the proper amount of frosting, but this house was already made. She only had to decorate it. How hard could it be?

She put a Christmas movie on in the background, and angled her body to see the TV as she began organizing the candies in rows by type and color. She pulled her hand out of her sling at one point to use it to brace against while putting the frosting tips on, but quickly put it back when the pain started flaring up. She paid only half attention to the movie, as she placed candies in red and green around the miniature structure. The process took longer than expected using only one hand, but as she stood back to admire her creation, she had to admit that she liked decorating gingerbread houses.

CHAPTER 26

Over the last week, Kasey had had her fair share of time to think. She thought in great detail about the conversations she and Scott had had at the hospital and when he'd dropped her off at her house. A week of reliving every moment of those painful words she'd spoken came back to her. And now, with the heat of the moment removed from her, she had to admit that maybe she wasn't seeing things clearly in that moment.

Maybe the pain of the events surrounding her dad's death really prejudiced her against the wealthy. She didn't need to keep that thought any more. She reminisced about all the good Scott had done at The Soup Kitchen, and about the way he served and cared for others, and she saw the world in a much different light. She couldn't generalize any longer about his wealth status. Scott had helped her with her car, and he'd decorated her apartment. He'd seen the needs of others, and he'd filled them. He'd thought about the individual children at

The Soup Kitchen, and had picked out coats and boots for them specifically. In every instance that she could think about, he'd focused on truly helping others.

Maybe Trish was right, maybe his motivation for all of this had been wrapped up with her. But even if it was, he'd been the one to show how much he cared. He'd done that with the donation list, and the actors, and the way he picked out ornaments for his family. He wasn't looking for something in a general way. He'd been specific. He'd paid for her hospital bills, and she realized they probably weren't even a drop in the bucket to him. He had money, but it was the way he used it to make others feel important and valued and special, that melted her. She was grateful, and more than that, she was smitten. She needed to have a conversation with Scott, and she didn't want it to be over text message.

It had been nine days since her surgery and she was going stir crazy. It was time to get out of the house. She'd had groceries delivered, and she'd received regular updates from Patty every couple of days about The Soup Kitchen, but it wasn't enough. Patty had mentioned how many hours Scott was at The Soup Kitchen working, and she wanted to see him for herself.

The swelling was down on her ankle, and with a brace she carefully managed the stairs. Not yet willing to risk driving, though Scott had driven her car home the day he'd dropped her off, and not feeling up to walking to the train station, she took a cab into the city. After her post-op at the hospital to monitor her healing, she took another cab to The Soup Kitchen. The bright red door felt cheery on the overcast day. Just breathing in the fresh air felt nice.

She was met in the middle of the day by a crowd of people. She'd mentioned to Patty briefly that she would try and stop by for a few minutes after her doctor appointment. Cheers and shouts came from the staff, and they held a banner up for her with Get Well Wishes written all over it. Patty's eyes were shining as she embraced Kasey. "Glad you were able to stop by and say hi." She pointed to the banner with written notes and colorful drawings. "Everyone who came through the door over the past week signed this for you. I was going to bring it by your house if you didn't stop by today."

Kasey smiled widely. "This is seriously so nice. Thank you, everyone." She inspected the notes up close, reading a few of them. "Patty, is Scott here today?"

Patty shook her head. "I haven't seen him today, though he's been here every day except today. He's even been here for all of the meals."

Kasey nodded. If he'd been here for all of the meals, maybe he'd be here to volunteer tonight. She hoped so. She needed to see him and talk through some things with him. And she had a small peace offering for him, tucked into her purse. "Maybe he'll show up tonight then."

Patty continued talking. "It's been busy around here. I promised I wouldn't bog you down with all of the news while you were still recovering, but there's so much that's happened."

"Patty, I want to know all the news." Maybe it would distract her from not seeing Scott yet.

Patty nodded. "I figured you would, but shouldn't you rest your leg?"

"The doctor says it's healing nice, but yeah, I should probably prop it up while we talk."

"I'll gather the staff. There's been such a buzz since yesterday. Oh, and also, your laptop was ruined, and most of the documents in your office."

Kasey nodded, taking the news in stride. "I figured as much. I guess it's my own fault for not digitizing things sooner."

Ten minutes later, Kasey settled into the small conference room with the staff still on duty over the holidays. They filled her in on the progress of the repair, how much the kids had missed her and asked for her, and the state of everything since she'd been out.

"The owner has been helping all week," Patty said. "It's been amazing to see how much he cares about this place."

"I'm glad that he's stepped up after all these years." Kasey stared at Patty. "I guess that's the great thing about this time of year … people *change*." Her mind went immediately to Scott. Over the last week, she'd thought through Trish's words about her situation. She couldn't firm up a clear answer in her head, but she knew what she needed to do. She had to talk to him about why he did what he did. Maybe that would give her clarity on the situation. Her heart still ached for him, as much as she tried to push it away, and she knew that she wanted another chance with him if he gave any glimmer of a reason that she could accept.

Patty shook her head. "Scott is the one who's been doing all of the heavy lifting."

Kasey's heart softened just a little at Patty's words. "He's always been so helpful here," she admitted.

"Speaking of …" Patty turned to the door, and Kasey followed her gaze.

Scott looked decidedly uncomfortable standing in the doorway.

She smiled, suddenly feeling shy. "Hi. I've just been hearing about all the work you've done around here. Thank you. The Soup Kitchen is so grateful." She wanted to say more, but not in a room full of people listening to their conversation.

He nodded, his brows furrowed. "The Soup Kitchen does a lot of good. I didn't know you were going to be here."

Her heart sunk. "Oh. I hadn't planned on it, but then I came in for my doctor appointment." Her face heated. "I didn't know you'd be here either." Her heart jumped and bounced at the sight of him. She wasn't over him. Not by a long shot.

He cleared his throat, then looked around the room. "I apologize, I didn't mean to interrupt your meeting. I can't stay. I just came to drop these off." He held up a black portfolio, not unlike the one she'd lent to him weeks ago. "And I wanted to wish … The Soup Kitchen, a very Merry Christmas."

The rest of the room began chatting at once, thanking Scott for all of his hard work, but she kept her gaze locked on his. He handed her the portfolio, shook a few hands out the door, and left.

Kasey's cheeks flamed with heat. "Where were we on the progress of everything?" she asked the question to the room.

Patty only looked out the door. "He's going to be a much better owner."

Kasey blanched. "What do you mean?"

Patty's eyes widened. "I mean, that's what he's here for, isn't it?" Patty smacked her hand on the desk. "Don't tell me you didn't know? I figured he told you, since you guys are so close. I've known for a few days now."

Kasey opened the folder. It was a new lease on the building, from the new owner, Scott Parker. "I'm not sure I understand."

"He found some shady stuff on the owner and threatened to take him to court, as well as several councilmen, over the deal. They'd worked to try and get the building condemned for months, and had hoped the pipe breaking would do the trick. Once he showed the proof he had, they were willing to negotiate a deal."

Kasey had heard enough. She stood, and clunked her way to the door, hoping to catch up with him. "Scott," she called his name through the building, but there was no reply. She pondered this new revelation, and the way her heart had fluttered for the brief moment when they'd made eye contact.

She bit her lip. She needed to talk to him in person, but first she had to find him.

CHAPTER 27

Scott paced around his kitchen. Seeing Kasey today had felt like a dream. He'd been in shock when she smiled at him. Or had he just imagined that she smiled? He'd planned to stay for volunteering for the dinner shift that evening, but with Kasey there, he knew he couldn't stay or go back to The Soup Kitchen. He couldn't think straight. At least Kasey had seemed in good spirits. He hadn't asked after her recovery per se, but she looked good. He blew out a breath, wishing he'd been allowed to at least help her in some way over the last week and a half.

His cell phone buzzed and he picked it up—momentarily convinced it would be Kasey, like he had so many times this week—but it wasn't.

"Hi, Nancy."

"Hi, Scott. Just thought I'd check in to see if there is anything else you need from me before I head home."

"I can't think of anything." Truthfully, he hadn't been able to concentrate on much of anything, especially not work. Doing manual labor at The Soup Kitchen had been a welcome reprieve from thinking too much, except when he was working through the details of the corruption with the owner. But he'd basically checked out for most of the last week from his regular work

"Are you volunteering tonight?" she asked.

"Not tonight. I think I'm just going to stay at home and relax."

There was a pause. "Well, good for you, Scott. You deserve a break."

"Thanks, I think." He didn't want a break though. He wanted to see Kasey, but he didn't want to invade The Soup Kitchen with their unresolved issues, not when he'd already seen her there today. Hopefully they'd work things out to the point where he wouldn't have to avoid showing up at his new building for fear of offending her, but for right now, he felt like it was the best course of action.

"I mean it, you've been working so hard, especially on your extra project."

"The competition is coming to an end though," he said, more to himself than to Nancy.

"True, but now that you've bought the building, I doubt you'll be less involved."

He sighed. "Maybe it was a mistake to buy the building."

"I don't think it was. I think it shows where your heart is."

"Service?"

Nancy laughed. "I meant with Kasey, but sure … call it whatever you want."

"I saw her today while I was dropping off the lease paperwork."

Another pause. "Oh? And how did that go?"

He blew out another breath. "I'm pretty sure I screwed it up again."

"I have a feeling you didn't blow it ..." Her voice trailed off.

"Why do you say that?"

Nancy laughed lightly. "Oh, no reason. Just trying to make you feel better. Anyway, enjoy your night in. I'll check in with you tomorrow."

"Thanks, Nancy."

Scott ate a quick dinner and was finishing washing the dishes when the doorbell rang. That was odd. Usually he buzzed people up. The only one who had access to do that remotely was Nancy, though he supposed it could be a delivery. Often the doormen would sign and bring up packages. He froze as he looked at his door camera on his phone, did a double take, then hurried to the door to open it.

It wasn't a trick of the camera. Kasey stood on his doorstep. He swallowed, emotion thick in his chest, and invited her in.

She nodded hesitantly, but stepped into the room with a step clunk against the floor.

"I'm surprised to see you here," he finally said.

She nodded. "It took me awhile to track you down."

It dawned on him that she hadn't known where he lived. He'd never brought her here.

She filled in the mystery. "Nancy, your assistant, gave me directions here ... since you weren't coming in to The Soup Kitchen for volunteering." Color touched her cheek.

Suddenly his recent phone call with Nancy made much

more sense, and he nodded. Depending on how this went, Nancy would either get an earful or a bigger bonus. Time would tell. "What are you doing here?"

"You left so quickly this afternoon, and I felt like maybe we should talk … in person."

"Sure," he said, leading her into the living room. She sat in a chair and propped her leg up on the ottoman. Then he took a seat in a chair next to hers angling his body so he could face her.

"You've got a very nice place," she said, looking around.

"Thanks."

"I'm pretty sure that, if I hadn't found out that you were rich at the hospital, your penthouse might have raised a few suspicions."

He nodded.

"About our conversation in the hospital," Kasey began.

"I'm really sorry that I didn't ask your opinion before I paid for your hospital bill," he said, rushing the words together. "And I'm sorry I wasn't completely honest about what I did for a living or how much I made."

She tilted her head, as if trying to read him. "Why didn't you tell me?"

He blew out a breath. "I'm not going to make any excuses. There were a few times when I *wanted* to just tell you, but it was a risk, and one that I didn't want to take. We had a good thing going between us, but it was you and the version of me that used the intern desk. I didn't want my money or my job to get in the way of that, because you'd made comments about rich people." He shrugged, the reasoning sounding stupid to his own ears. "I just didn't want you to only see me in that category without getting to know me first."

She nodded. "I've thought about that," she said. "And I can shoulder some of that blame. I can see that I made it difficult for you to want to trust me with that. But looking forward into the future, into *our* future, I would hope that we could be open and honest about things, even if it's hard."

He nodded, his heart thundering when she talked about her future—their future—*together*. "I can absolutely do that."

"Me too," she said. "And I came to the realization that the way I viewed the world and the people in it was flawed."

"How so?"

She drummed her left hand against her leg. "For most of my life, it was easy to think that everyone who was rich was like my dad's boss. It was a convenient scapegoat when things didn't go my way. It was easier to push those feelings onto others. But now I see how wrong that was. The only thing that you had in common with my dad's boss, was that you had employees underneath you. That's it. The wealth was comparable maybe, but I started looking at the differences in how you treated people versus my fourteen-year-old perspective on what I understood about my dad's boss. I want to believe that I've grown up since then, but sometimes I get sucked back into that mentality. But hey, Scrooge changed, which means there is hope for everyone, even me."

"There's always hope to change," he said.

"It's kind of beautiful to find all of these things at Christmas time. Each new thought like this feels like a present I want to open and keep opening."

"So where do we go from here?"

"I'd like to give us another chance, if you do."

He nodded, his heart pounding. "Thanks for giving me another chance."

She gave a saucy smile. "It was only a matter of time. I'm just glad that it didn't take a haunted night of apparitions to get me there."

"What did it take?" he asked, curiosity forming.

"A week's worth of Christmas movies and a gingerbread house from an anonymous source." She eyed him.

He laughed. "I don't know anything about the Christmas movies, but I may have had something to do with the gingerbread house."

"Thank you for that. I loved starting new traditions and really thinking about Christmas in a fresh way. I'm glad I was able to come to that conclusion by myself over the past week, but then I realized something else."

"Oh?"

"Wanting to do Christmas traditions *with* someone else, isn't the same thing as doing the traditions *for* someone else. And now that I realize that, I know that I want to create those traditions with *you*."

He reached over, grabbing her left hand and stroked the back of it with his thumb, before bringing her hand to his lips and kissing it. "I couldn't agree more, though we'll probably have to take a rain check on ice skating together this year."

SCOTT SPENT CHRISTMAS EVE WITH KASEY. SHE USED HER

scooter to prop her leg up behind her and was mostly able to get around without help.

After a day full of Christmas Eve celebrations and new traditions, he pulled out a gift from under the tree. "It's tradition in my family to give a present on Christmas Eve." He pulled out the wrapped box that held her ornament inside. Elation filled him. He'd never looked forward to giving an ornament gift as much as he had this time.

Her eyes widened. "Oh. Gifts on Christmas Eve, not Christmas Day?"

He shrugged. "It's just one, sometimes we open more, but usually just one."

She smiled. "Okay, just a minute then. I'll be right back."

She took her scooter and made her way out of the room with ease, and came back a few minutes later with her purse hanging from her scooter handles. Once she was seated on the couch she pulled a small gift out of the purse, and handed it to Scott. "I've been wracking my brain for something to get you," she said. "My foot kind of got in the way of some of my shopping plans."

"I'm sure I'll love it," he said. He pulled out a small box wrapped in red and green striped paper. Inside the box was bubble wrap, and he pulled at the mound, finding the seam, and ripping along it gently. A card fell out.

Scott,

This was the one that reminded me of you.

Love you, Kasey

He pulled out the ornament of Scrooge smiling, his hat waving in the air. On the bottom in gold pen was a small message: *"Be like Scrooge."* He clutched the ornament tightly.

She'd grasped onto his tradition and had found him the perfect ornament, and he was beyond grateful. "Thank you for this. I really do love it. And I love you."

She smiled. "I love you too."

He scooted closer to her and kissed her, pouring in his emotion.

He hung the ornament on the tree. "I had a different present in mind for you first," he said, picking up a smaller present from underneath the tree, "but this is the one you need to open."

She took the small box and opened it, revealing the ghosts' ornament he'd bought for her. She smiled wide. "This is perfect. It really is my favorite new thing about Christmas."

He smiled. "More than the Christmas movies?" He bumped his shoulder playfully against hers.

"Okay, it might be a tie." She laughed. "Will you help me put it on the tree?"

He shook his head. "I can't."

She raised her eyebrows. "What do you mean you can't?"

"I mean, it's tradition. Everyone hangs their own ornaments on the tree."

She used her scooter and moved next to the tree, hanging hers close to where Scott had put his new ornament. "They go together, I think," she said when she'd moved back to see the tree.

"A perfect match," he said. He pulled out another gift, grateful that it arrived in time. "I have one more thing for you," he said.

"You really didn't have to get me anything," she said.

"It's technically not a new gift." He handed her the box. "But I thought you'd want it for Christmas."

She tilted her head with wonder, but accepted the box, which was much heavier and bigger than the last one.

He held his breath as she opened it.

She gasped, pulling out the snow globe. "Where did you find this? It looks exactly like the one I had." She turned it upside down, and her face lit up as she watched the snow fall down on top of the winter scene.

"It actually *is* the same one. I found a glass manufacturer who was able to make a new dome for it."

Her eyes brimmed with tears. "This is the best gift you could ever give me. Thank you."

He smiled. "I sure hope I can give you something in the future that's equal. I plan to spoil you for as long as I can."

"Is that so?"

He nodded. "Definitely."

The doorbell rang, and though he wanted to ignore it, he went to answer the unannounced guest. A doorman gave him an expedited envelope. He turned it over, not expecting anything.

"Who was it?" Kasey asked, when he entered the room again.

"Delivery, but I wasn't expecting anything." He ripped open the envelope and pulled out a red envelope with his name on it. He lifted the red envelope and pulled out the single sheet of paper. Skimming through the contents, he looked up and smiled at Kasey. "I can't believe it. I won."

"What did you win?" she asked.

"It's a long story, but the short of it is, The Soup Kitchen has three million dollars at its disposal."

"Really?"

He nodded. "Really."

He sat next to her, and she embraced him tightly. "You really are amazing, Scott. Thanks for helping me find Christmas."

"I'm just happy I found you," he said. He let the red envelope drop to the floor as he kissed her, running his hands through her hair, and enjoying the moment in the present, with the hope of a very happy future.

EPILOGUE

CHRISTMAS - 2 YEARS LATER

"Are you sure this is going to work?" Kasey asked Scott.

Scott nodded. "I've handled more complicated construction projects than this before. Trust me."

Kasey laughed quietly. It was true. Scott had had his share of construction projects, especially when they'd decided to add a few extra floors to The Soup Kitchen. They'd decided to expand their services to providing temporary housing. "It sounds so easy, but I'm really not sure how to do that with one hand."

"Hold the top of the roof, and I'll secure it with the frosting. It's teamwork." He put a thick layer of frosting on the bottom, while she held it steady. When he approached the corners she carefully twisted the house to reveal the next unfrosted side.

"I think we're great at teamwork," she said, glancing down at their three-week old baby boy in her arms. They'd named him George Scott, after her dad.

"I agree, Mrs. Parker," he said, leaning over the table and kissing her.

Once the base was secure, Kasey pulled out the rest of the candy decorations and sprinkles. George started fussing, and she bounced him lightly. Scott prepared a bottle for him, and handed the bottle to Kasey. "Thanks," she said, soothing George with it. She looked at her husband, with both of her hands occupied. "So, it looks like I'm the designer and you're the construction crew."

Scott laughed. "That sounds about right, Mrs. Gingerbread House Designer. The construction crew is awaiting your orders."

She nodded toward the white tube of frosting. "Let's do the roof in white."

The gingerbread house came together over the next half hour. Scott took a mint from the bag and popped it in his mouth.

"Hey, no eating on the job. We've got a lot more supplies to place on this overloaded house."

Scott stole a red gumdrop. "The construction crew is tired, and maybe if they eat some of the supplies, we have less to find a place for."

Kasey shook her head playfully as she continued to hold George. "You're incorrigible."

"Yeah, but our house is looking very delicious. You can't blame me too much."

She stole a few candies from the stack. "You're right. It is pretty good." She looked down at her son. "What do you think, George? Do you like your very first gingerbread house? We let you stay up late to finish it with us, but just know that won't always be the case." She waited for an answer, but George only cooed. She smiled triumphantly. "Great news. He loves it. It's a success!"

"George looks awake enough to open his ornament. What do you say, my love? One more Christmas tradition before we put the baby to bed?"

Kasey nodded. "Don't tell him what it is, Scott. His presents are a surprise."

Scott smirked. "He'll have to learn that ornaments on Christmas Eve aren't a surprise, they're a tradition." He held his hands out, and Kasey put George in his arms, then grabbed out the three ornaments.

They helped George open his present—a shiny dome shaped ornament with a winter scene inside that read, "Baby's First Christmas."

"George, it's tradition that everyone has to hang their own ornaments on the tree," Scott said.

Kasey laughed. "He's not going to be able to do that this year."

"I know, but we can still set the expectation." He stood, bringing George closer to the tree. "I suppose we'll help you out this year. Do you have a favorite branch to hang it on?"

"I think he likes the one right in the middle."

Scott nodded, and they moved George's little hand close to theirs as they hung his first ornament together. Then Kasey and Scott took turns holding George and opening their own Christmas presents. Kasey's mouth twitched as she opened her ornament—a matching one to George's, except the words said, "Mommy's First Christmas." Her eyes filled with tears. "It's perfect," she said. "I love it." And she hung it next to George's ornament.

"I saw it and I thought of you. I picked it out before we bought the one for George," Scott said.

"I love this tradition where the actual ornaments are a surprise," she said, trying to hold in her laughter. Scott had no idea how well they matched up. He opened his box and started laughing at the identical ornament with the words, "Daddy's First Christmas."

He hung it on the tree next to the other two ornaments. "Look at that. A perfect match."

He wrapped Kasey and George in a hug and kissed Kasey next to the Christmas tree, until George started to fuss. "We are a perfect match, and this is the perfect Christmas," he said.

"Every year with you is my perfect Christmas," she whispered, before kissing him again.

Like the Book?

Please leave a review for Finding Christmas with the Billionaire on Amazon.

It's the best way you can say thank you to an author!

Thank you so much!

Read Troy's Story Next!

Read The Billionaire's Christmas Miracle Now!

Included in this book!

A grieving niece trying to save a Christmas tradition, a billionaire determined to win a bet, and the Christmas Tree Festival that will reveal secrets that are meant to be kept hidden. It will take more than a Christmas miracle for these two to both get what they want for Christmas.

Join Chelsea's VIP Reader's Club

to stay updated with new releases, get free books, access to exclusive bonus content, and more!

Join Chelsea's VIP Reader's Club.

See all of Chelsea's books.

Books in this Series:

Troy's Story: The Billionaire's Christmas Miracle
Hunter's Story: The Billionaire's Second Chance Christmas
Scott's Story: Finding Christmas with the Billionaire

ACKNOWLEDGMENTS

I love Christmas time! The magic, the warmth, the message of the gift of Christ given to the world. All of it. Without that first gift, we would not be celebrating, and I'm grateful daily for the babe who was swaddled and laid in a manger. He gives us the reason for this beautiful time of year, and shares His love through his merciful gifts that can be accessed every day of the year, not just at Christmas. I am grateful for a Savior in my life who gives me a reason to hope and allows me to feel a heavenly peace.

My husband is always top of my list of people to thank. I love you. Always. Next, my children are remarkable. This year their support has been a more beautiful part of the journey. I'm grateful that they listen and read the words I write. I love cheering for them, and I'm grateful they cheer for me.

Friends and editors make my life and my books better! I'm grateful to so many who make it possible to do what I do, and to do what I love.

Of particular note on this specific book, thanks to Tracy, who keeps me sane with deep perspective that makes my characters and me better. You're awesome. I'd much rather walk miles in Disneyland with you, but for now, I'll take early morning walks. Thanks for chatting through countless story ideas as we circle the neighborhood yet again.

Thanks to Ami. I will forever sound like a broken record, but every book seems to have your stamp of approval in many places. I am grateful for your patience with me and my characters and so grateful for your help. Thanks for keeping me in line, and for seeing beyond just the words I've written to the messages I want to share.

Thanks to Holly. Kindred spirits make navigating being an author so much easier! Thank you for the countless daily checks and reports that keep me motivated and on task. I'm grateful for so many things that you do and say, but it all boils down to gratitude for you being you!

Thanks to Stephanie. WOW! Really, wow! Your help was so needed. Thank you for helping me fine tune my ideas into beautiful prose. I'm grateful for your skill and sharp eye. Thank you for your incredible speed and agility in helping me with my book. I'm so grateful for you. Thank you for the laughs, the face palms, and the squeals. I needed all of them! I'm grateful for your friendship and your beautiful voice. Thank you for everything!

Thanks to my readers. I am amazed at the amount of email, messages, texts, and comments from so many who praise my books and share their favorite parts or what resonated with them. You have no idea what a profound difference this makes.

Thank you for sharing. Thank you for reading. And thank you for caring! I'm sure grateful for all of you!

Merry Christmas!

LEAVE A REVIEW FOR THIS BOX SET

Like this Box Set?

Please leave a review for A Betting on Christmas Romance Collection on Amazon.

Thank you so much! It's so great to hear when you like my work! It definitely keeps me going.

ABOUT THE AUTHOR

Chelsea Hale is the author of the #1 bestselling Sundaes for Breakfast Romance Series, the #1 bestselling A Falling for You Clean Billionaire Romance Series, the #1 bestselling Betting on Christmas Romance Series and others. She writes sweet, swoony, and flirty romances with sigh-worthy kisses and witty banter.

Chelsea is passionate about writing, reading, Broadway musicals, singing, and capturing life through a 50 mm lens. She loves to travel and gains inspiration for her books wherever she goes.

In her mind, caramel improves every dessert, movies are better with romance, popcorn always benefits from more salt, and cookies are better raw.

She is married to her Prince Charming. They have four children and live near the Rocky Mountains, where they are living their happily ever after every day.

If you liked this book, please take a few minutes to leave a review for it on Amazon. Authors (Chelsea included!) really appreciate this, and it helps draw more readers to books they might like. *Thanks!*

Chelsea loves to connect with her readers! You can do that in several ways.

When you join her newsletter Reader's Club - *http://smarturl.it/ChelseaVIPClub* - you'll also receive a free book, exclusive content, and news about her releases and sales!

Connect with Chelsea:

Website: www.chelseahale.com

Facebook: Author Chelsea Hale

Twitter: @chelseamhale

Instagram: Author Chelsea Hale

You can also find her on Amazon, Bookbub, and Goodreads!

Made in the USA
Coppell, TX
26 November 2022